PRAISE FOR ANNA SALTER's MICHAEL STONE THRILLERS

FAULT LINES

"A fast-paced novel with lots of little twists and turns and surprises. A quick, fun, very hard to put down read."

—*The Pilot* (Southern Pines, NC)

"Salter, a forensic psychologist experienced in the ways of sex offenders, writes with chilling authority."

—*The New York Times Book Review*

"Offer[s] a more realistic side to forensic psychology than many recent thrillers."

—*Publishers Weekly*

SHINY WATER

"The best first novel I have ever read. Anna Salter takes us into the disturbing world of forensic psychologist Michael Stone with just the right amount of wit and humanity. Don't miss this memorable debut."

—Anne Perry

"Forget about your demolition experts and your air-traffic controllers; Michael Stone, the stressed out heroine of Anna Salter's jolting debut mystery, *Shiny Water*, has the real job from hell. A forensic psychologist at a Vermont hospital, Michael carries a caseload that would make the angels weep. . . . [An] interestingly abrasive protagonist, whose own testy personality gives her a sharp perspective on her difficult patients and a dangerous edge when she testifies on their behalf in court . . . [where] a misapplication of justice . . . turns Michael into a tiger for the truth. . . . [Salter] handles this touchy material with integrity, tugging on our hearts even as she ties our nerves in knots."

—*The New York Times Book Review*

"A terrific tale with plenty of twists and turns and an almost lethal twist of the tail."

—*The Toronto Star*

"Forensic psychologist Salter has graced her protagonist with a compelling and likable voice in the tradition of Patricia Cornwell."

—*Library Journal*

"Salter weaves a tight, compelling chain of consequence."

—*Ms.* magazine

"A tough, quirky narrator carries this engrossing debut. . . . [Salter's] skillful pacing, a gift for sketching minor characters and a clear passion

BOOKS BY ANNA SALTER

Shiny Water

Fault Lines

Published by POCKET BOOKS

FAULT LINES

ANNA SALTER

POCKET STAR BOOKS
New York   London   Toronto   Sydney   Tokyo   Singapore

This book is a work of fiction. Names, characters, places and incidents are products of the author's imagination or are used fictitiously. Any resemblance to actual events or locales or persons, living or dead, is entirely coincidental.

 A Pocket Star book published by
POCKET BOOKS, a division of Simon & Schuster Inc.
1230 Avenue of the Americas, New York, NY 10020

Copyright © 1998 by Dr. Anna Salter

Originally published in hardcover in 1998 by Pocket Books

ISBN: 0-671-00313-5

First Pocket Books paperback printing March 1999

10 9 8 7 6 5 4 3 2 1

POCKET STAR BOOKS and colophon are registered trademarks of Simon & Schuster Inc.

Cover design by Tony Greco

Printed in the U.S.A.

For my father,
Theodore Salter, M.D.
1917–1993
He had the gift of healing.

ACKNOWLEDGMENTS

I would first of all like to thank Sandi Gelles-Cole, who edits all my books privately, and who makes an enormous difference in their quality. Sandi has a lot of Michael Stone in her.

I would also like to thank Helen Rees, my wonderful agent, who is warm, humane, and exceedingly competent—a rare combination.

Likewise, I would like to thank Linda Marrow, my editor at Pocket Books, for her vision and her support.

I would like to thank Lt. H. John Wojnaroski III of the Michigan State Police, Polygraph Section, for the use of one of his many superb interrogation techniques.

My appreciation too goes to my colleagues at the Midwest Center for Psychotherapy and Sex Therapy: Dan Brakarsh, Kristi Baker, Harvey Dym, Carol Endicott, Jane James, Pat Patterson, and Lloyd Sinclair. These folks are my professional family.

ACKNOWLEDGMENTS

I would like to thank my long-term mentor and friend, Regina Yando, Ph.D., for her suggestions, her support, and her love.

I would like to thank Minna Alanko for her superb care of my children and for her friendship. Knowing my children are well looked after gives me the ease of mind I need to write.

How can I teach her
some way of being human
that won't destroy her?

I would like to tell her, Love
is enough, I would like to say,
Find shelter in another skin.

I would like to say, Dance
and be happy. Instead I will say
in my crone's voice, Be
ruthless when you have to, tell
the truth when you can, . . .

—MARGARET ATWOOD

FAULT LINES

1

He's dead. He's dead." The woman on the other end of the phone was sobbing. I tried to shake the sleep off. I looked at the number the emergency service had given me—Clarrington. If the call came from Clarrington, chances were she was standing over him with a gun. Clarrington was a small, industrial town twenty miles from the thriving university community where I worked. Mills were closing in Clarrington; people were more or less constantly being put out of work, and maybe because of that—or maybe because of some esoteric reason I knew nothing about—Clarrington was, I thought, the center of violence in the known universe. Clarrington was like that square mile in Mexico where all the monarch butterflies go, only every antisocial, drug- or alcohol-addicted, violent person in the world seemed to pass through Clarrington.

"Where is he? Is he there?" I wasn't sure what to say. Nothing in my training as a forensic psychologist specializing in child abuse and domestic violence cases covered some of the things I ran into in the real world when I worked emergency for the Department of Psychiatry at Jefferson University Hospital. I was pretty sure "How do you feel about that?" wouldn't cover it, at least not until I figured out if she needed an ambulance.

The sobbing woman ignored me. "He's dead," she repeated. She was crying so hard I could hardly hear her. "I read about it in the paper." I slumped down in the bed. This was another ball game, entirely. I glanced at the clock. Three A.M. Grief time, maybe, for my unknown caller. Still, if she cared that much, odd she had to read about it in the paper.

"I'm sorry to hear that," I said. I wasn't sure what she wanted me to say.

"I didn't know," she said, "I didn't know he was alive."

Wait a minute. Someone she didn't know was alive is dead, and she read about it in the paper. Why is she upset if she already thought he was dead? I sat up straight again and rubbed my eyes. Was I dealing with someone who wasn't playing with a full deck?

"If I'd only known he was alive . . . if I'd only known. . . ." I waited for the list of regrets: the call never made, the apology never delivered, the

2

amends only planned. "If I'd only known," she wailed, "I'd have killed him myself."

I was stumped. Ah, Clarrington. We all have regrets when someone dies, but being deprived of the chance to murder him? I opened my mouth to say something, I'm not sure what, but my unknown caller hung up. It's just as well. I'm sure there was nothing in my training to cover this.

I glanced at the black emergency book on the table beside me. It was passed back and forth from emergency worker to emergency worker. It included all of the chronic callers—the dependent and the hysterical and the entitled folk, not to mention the truly crazy—that made up the vast bulk of calls on emergency. Without a name I couldn't check to see if my unknown caller made a habit of scaring emergency workers. Certainly, her call didn't fit the pattern of any active emergency caller I had been briefed on. It was a strange fact that almost none of the calls that came in on emergency were true emergencies; mostly they were chronic callers who somehow figured out that a voice on the end of the phone pushed back the night.

I had too much adrenaline from the call to go back to sleep. I got up and walked downstairs and crossed the living room of the tiny A-frame and walked out onto the deck. There was just enough moon to see the small stream glistening below. I glanced at the darkness where I knew the trees began, beyond the stream.

I had retreated to the country a few years ago, to a tiny A-frame with no room for guests. The small deck, the stream below, the hot tub tucked around the bend of the L-shaped deck had all brought something I was looking for. But in my line of work I meet violent folk from time to time, and after I had moved, one had stalked me, gotten into my remote cabin, and eventually tried to kill me. Now there were times when I wouldn't go onto the deck at night without my .38 revolver tucked in my pocket.

On impulse I walked back into the house and picked up the phone to call my office answering machine. At least I think that was the impulse. Maybe I just wanted an excuse to get off the deck, where I felt exposed. I was like a drug addict these days, always thinking up excuses when I didn't want to face the real reason I was doing things. It was more than a little silly to be calling my machine. I checked it before I went to bed, and all my clients had the emergency number for anything urgent enough to be calling at night— but to my surprise there was a message that had come in at two A.M.

"Dr. Stone, this is Camille." Camille was a new client coming in today for the first time. "I wondered if it would be okay if I brought my seizure dog to the session today. She's licensed so she's supposed to be able to go anywhere, grocery stores and things like that. Please let me know because I don't think I can come without her." The voice was tiny and had something in it I couldn't identify: not anxiety, not depression, something odd.

A seizure dog. What the heck is a seizure dog? If people can't do anything about someone having a seizure, what's a dog supposed to do? And why is Camille up at two A.M. worrying about this? She was upset enough to be up and calling me, but too polite to call the emergency number I had given her when she made the appointment. That meant the question was important to her and not just an excuse to make contact.

Was she depressed? People who couldn't sleep in the middle of the night were almost always depressed. But maybe I'd be depressed too if I had seizures so often I couldn't go for a fifty-minute therapy session without my seizure dog.

I was still thinking about it on the way into my office the next morning. The drive was fifteen minutes of green, leafy, postcard New England stuff—three quarters of the year. Whoever put together New England decided that it was only fair—given that New England has green, rolling hills dotted with old farmhouses, given that New England has small, winding back roads that meander next to small, curious streams, given that New England has possibly the fewest

McDonald's of any place in the nation and, Vermont at least, has people with enough sense to ban highway billboards—given all those gifts, it seemed only fair that New England miss out on something. New England has no spring.

I am a Southerner, born and bred. And while the South has many things that keep me out of it—Mama for one—you have to take your hat off to the South when it comes to spring. Spring starts in February in the South, and the whole world explodes. There is more color in Chapel Hill in February than there is in the entire state of Vermont in May. And the light. In a North Carolina spring there is light—glorious, endless light—light when you wake up and light when you go to bed. But who could go to bed? I remember sitting on my grandmother's porch on the swing in the evening—everybody sat on their porch in the evening—watching the azaleas sway in the breeze off the water.

I glanced at the brown landscape. It was May and the leaves were clearly waiting for mud season to end before they made an appearance. Mud season is the time when the snow melts leaving enough mud that casual visitors assume some sort of flood has gone through. It is also New England's substitute for spring. It looked less like spring and more like a setting for a horror flick.

By 9 A.M. I was sitting in my private practice office waiting for Camille. I had called at eight to let her know I had no problem with her dog. I heard the door to the small waiting room in the old Victorian house open and walked out to meet Camille. A rottweiler roughly the size of my couch walked in, sat down calmly, and looked at me in a decidedly unfriendly way. She had that I've-got-the-distance-to-your-throat-measured look that attack dogs have. She was definitely a working dog. This is a seizure dog? This dog could cause seizures.

I moved forward to shake hands with the woman on the other end of the leash and saw the dog's muscles bunch. Camille was my height but much rounder. She was pale and looked out-of-shape. Her coloring was all wrong, but I was so focused on the dog it took me a moment to realize why. It was the mismatch. Her skin was fair and her eyebrows were blond, but her hair was dark brown, almost black. Very few natural blondes dye their hair an unflattering shade of dark brown, but she had. She had bright eyes, and somehow the body she was living in, her whole appearance, didn't seem to go with those eyes. She was also shaking noticeably, but if she had seizures, maybe she had cerebral palsy too. The shaking didn't explain the dog. You don't need an attack rottweiler just to help with seizures. I know you're supposed to call them protection dogs these days, but somehow when I looked at this one, the term "attack dog" just kept coming to mind.

Camille shook hands with me limply. "I don't know if I can stay," she said as soon as we were seated. "I'm not feeling very well." She was sitting across from me, but she kept glancing at the windows over her shoulder.

"Is there anything that would make you more comfortable?" I asked. She looked extremely uncomfortable.

"Not really," she said, and silence filled the room.

I waited a few moments and then asked, "Where would you like to start?" This was clearly not someone I could just fire questions at. Probably the dog was trained to bite anyone who fired questions at her.

"I . . ." Her voice trailed off, and she looked down. She seemed to be fighting back tears and trying to steady herself.

"Take your time. Say what you can." I considered the options while I waited. Paranoid? No, paranoids are more concerned with what was in the room than what is outside. Paranoids scan the room and inevitably fasten on the couple of videotapes on my bookshelves. Then they look around for a camera. Paranoids keep glancing at the notes I'm writing until I hand them over for inspection.

If not paranoid, what? Battered spouse. Possibly. Battered spouses are often in pretty bad shape, and they are sometimes afraid their husbands will find out they are seeing a therapist. An estranged spouse might be stalking her. But there was something in her level of fear that I had never seen before, not even in a battered spouse. I didn't think it was battering.

"I can't talk about it." She was crying. "But I need to know if I'm ever going to get better. It's been five years. I don't think I'm going to get better. I can't go outside, and I haven't been alone without Keeter since then. And sometimes I think he's in the house, and I know he's not because Keeter is just sitting there, but it really seems like he's there." She paused and cried for a few minutes.

"I didn't used to be like this," she said. "I was never like this. I was a nurse," she said as though that identity was now light-years away, which it probably was.

Rape? A violent, stranger attack? Maybe. I had seen some people in pretty bad shape from that, but never this bad. Something had shattered her whole sense of identity. She was hiding in the dark hair and the overweight body—which I'd be willing to bet she didn't have before—hiding in the house and behind the rottweiler, but what besides rape would make someone hide like that?

"Most people get better eventually from almost any kind of trauma," I said. I didn't say how much better. Some don't get a whole lot better, but it probably wouldn't help her to hear that right now. "I don't know what happened, and I know you can't tell me right now. But when I learn a little more about what you've been through, maybe I can give you a better idea of time." This woman needed whatever reassurance she could get, even if it was just a vague, most-people type.

"When I talk about it, it makes it worse."

"I'm sure that's true. It kicks off the flashbacks, right?" She nodded. "Tell me about Keeter," I said. She looked up, surprised. She looked at Keeter and then at me. "She won't hurt you," she said. "She's very well trained."

"She looks very well trained," I said. She had to be because it was only her training that was controlling her; this lady sure wasn't emotionally strong enough to control an attack dog right now. "I didn't ask because I was worried," I said gently, which I think was true—although I did know a dog trainer once who was attacked by a rottweiler while she was sitting behind a desk signing its owner up for a class. The rottweiler had gone over the desk straight for her throat without any warning. I glanced at Keeter again.

"I asked because you can probably talk about her without kicking off your flashbacks since she wasn't part of whatever happened to you. You got her, afterward, right? So she's related to what happened, but she wasn't there, and maybe I could learn a little bit about your symptoms without triggering anything if you talk about Keeter and your relationship with Keeter."

She looked at me thoughtfully. I was glad to see she could pull out of herself for a moment. It was a good sign, small, but good. "I've been to counselors before. They always want to talk about what happened."

"But you can't, or you start to fall apart, right?"

"Yeah, but then they just let me talk about anything."

"We'll go at this sideways," I said. "We won't hit it directly at first, and we won't go away from it entirely either. We'll get as close as we can without tearing things up for you. Okay?"

She nodded and sighed, looking ever so very slightly relieved. "I do know a little bit about this problem," I said gently. She was lost and frightened, and she needed to know the person she was asking for directions had a clue which way to go. Otherwise, the anxiety about being lost would make the problem worse.

"What's a seizure dog?"

"Well, she's trained to press a button on the phone, which dials a number for medical help, and also, she takes me home if I'm out somewhere and get confused. I've had seizures all my life, but I didn't get a dog until a few years ago. My first dog was a little terrier, and she was wonderful, but I didn't feel safe afterward. I wanted a dog who could protect me too, and I know Keeter can, it's just . . . I just don't feel safe anymore, even with Keeter."

"So Keeter's a protection dog who's also trained to deal with seizures?" She nodded. It must have been something, trying to train Keeter to let help in instead of keeping people away if Camille was hurt. The two jobs didn't seem all that compatible, and I wondered which way Keeter would go in a pinch.

Camille's shaking had stopped, and I realized it was more likely anxiety than cerebral palsy. This woman was a train wreck, but what kind of train had hit her and how was she ever going to tell me?

"I was never like this," she said. "I was a nurse," she said again. "I was an ICN nurse." She looked up, and I saw her face fill up. That is part of what happens with trauma: People end up grieving their own lost lives. Camille couldn't get used to not being who she had been.

And who she had been was probably a whole lot different than who she was now. The Intensive Care Nursery is one place where nurses never get stuck putting patients in and out of examining rooms. Half the preemies are critically ill at any given moment, and codes are as common as visitors. ICN nurses have a ton of responsibility and do some procedures restricted elsewhere only to doctors.

"Tell me about being a nurse."

12

Her hands stopped twisting the shredded Kleenex in her lap, and she sighed. "I had a rotating shift. I could have had an escort to the car. I mean, I was on the night shift, and I got out around midnight, and some of the other nurses would call for security to escort them to the parking lot. But I was just never afraid, and security would take twenty minutes, half an hour to come. I just didn't want to sit there. So I always walked down." She stopped abruptly, and when she spoke again all the fluency was gone, and she sounded almost aphasic.

"I just never . . . I didn't expect . . . I *know* I locked the car . . . It was still locked when . . . I still don't know . . . mummy, oh, mummy." Her face had paled, and her eyes were scanning like she was watching something. Keeter stood up, looked at Camille then looked at me. Keeter had a hell of a job. How was she supposed to know whom to attack? I was just sitting there, but Camille was clearly reacting like someone was coming after her with a knife.

Keeter distracted me, and I didn't redirect Camille quickly enough. By the time I opened my mouth to get her back to safer ground she had stood up and was turning to the door. "I have to go," she said.

"Wait," I said urgently. "Don't go yet. Let's pull this together." This was no way for her to leave. I take seriously the idea that therapy shouldn't

13

make people worse. I like to think people leave my office in at least as good shape as they came in. If Camille left now, she would have a dreadful day of flashbacks and fears.

She paused and turned back toward me.

"I want you to imagine a safe place. Sit down for a moment," I said quietly.

She stood a few minutes longer, and I said nothing, just waited. You can't just order trauma victims around; they have to make their own decisions. Finally, she perched hesitantly on the edge of the seat. I guess you'd call that sitting.

I opened my mouth to ask her to shut her eyes and then realized what a stupid idea that was and said instead, "Just imagine any place you'd feel safe—a garden, a fortress, a boat, anything. It doesn't have to be a real place. It can be anything you can imagine." If she could do it, it would bring down her autonomic arousal. Her heart would quit pounding, her palms would quit sweating, the racing thoughts would slow. It would distract her from the threatening imagery and decrease the chances she'd spend the day having flashbacks of whatever had happened to her.

She looked in the distance for a moment and then at the floor. "There isn't any place that's safe," she said. "There isn't any place he couldn't be."

"Then imagine a place where you would feel a little *less* afraid, however improbable a place. A cloud, sitting at the right of God, surrounded by tanks, whatever." I waited for her to think it through.

"A grave," she said, finally. "Maybe there." I hoped against hope she'd laugh ruefully, but she didn't. Instead, for the first time a fleeting look of peace passed over her face at the thought. I felt my heart drop. When a grave is the only place people feel safe, sooner or later they try to get there.

After she left, I thought it over. It sounded like rape, but it didn't sound like rape. Something more had happened, not that rape wasn't bad enough, but I had always been impressed with people's ability to recover from some pretty terrible traumas. Most women who are raped regain their ability to function more quickly than this lady had. Someone had been waiting in the parking lot that night, and something had happened— something worse than rape—but what?

I was still musing when the phone rang. Carlotta, my longtime best friend despite the fact that she had wasted a six-foot frame on modeling, for God's sake, instead of basketball, was on the line. She was a lawyer now—at least she had come to her senses and gotten a real job. Funny how you can tell if something is good news or bad just by the sound of the voice. I didn't like it when Carlotta's voice sounded like it did now. Once she had given me some very bad news, indeed, and ever since then, I cringed when I heard that sound in her voice.

15

"What's up?" I said.

She sighed. "Have you seen the papers?"

"No," I said. "What's in them?"

"Why don't you go get one? I'll meet you for lunch. You'll probably be able to talk by then," she said.

I glanced at my watch. It was 10:30. "No," I said evenly. "You're scaring the shit out of me, and I don't want the anxiety of racing around looking for a paper not knowing. What happened?"

There was a pause. "I'm sorry," she said. "Nobody's died." I realized I had been holding my breath as I let it out. "It's just that Willy's out."

"Willy's out? Willy's out? Willy is not out. What? How the hell could he get out?"

Carlotta started to speak, but I kept going. "How could Willy get out? Have you been in a maximum security prison recently? Those things are fortresses. He could not have gotten out. This is a joke, Carlotta. Just the sort of trick that son-of-a-bitch would play. He likes to give me a heart attack."

There was another pause, and I realized this was just what Carlotta had been trying to avoid. I was screaming at her as if she had personally smuggled Willy out of prison. I shut up. After a moment Carlotta spoke.

"He didn't escape, Michael. He won on appeal. The court remanded the case back for a new trial and released him in the meantime."

"What? On what basis?"

"Suggestibility. The court ruled that some of the social worker interviews of the abused children were leading and suggestive."

"I don't believe this." My decibel level was rising again, but what sane person's wouldn't have?

"There's more. I don't think the case will see court again, but look, I don't have time to get into it; I've got a hearing. Go get a paper, and I'll see you at Sweet Tomatoes at noon." Carlotta hung up. How could she leave me hanging like that? Why wouldn't it go back to court?

Carlotta had joined the county prosecutor's staff this year, which meant, even though Willy's case hadn't been in our county, Carlotta could probably get the prosecutors on the case to talk to her. I wondered if she had called them already and that's how she knew it wasn't going back to court.

Alex B. Willy was out of prison. I had never known Alex B. Willy out of prison, and I didn't care to now. When I met him three years ago, he was starting a thirty-year sentence for child molestation. That was long by today's anemic sentencing standards for child molestation, but it had come to light in the sentencing phase of the trial that Willy had had quite a string of victims.

He had turned out to be swimming up to his ears in narcissism, and he had delighted in telling me about all the offenses he hadn't been caught for. As bad as his known track record was, the truth was worse: Willy was not a simple, manipulative, get-the-children-to-trust-him-and-then-molest-them-pillar-of-the-community-dime-a-dozen child molester. Willy was a sexual sadist. What turned him on was hurting people, children, to be specific.

I made it to the corner and stared at the machine holding the *Upper Valley Times* as though it were a mortal enemy. God damn that son-of-a-bitch. No sane person would have put him on the street. I finally came up with the quarters I needed and jerked the paper out. I couldn't wait to get back to the office, so I just stood there and went through the paper until I found it.

MINISTER WINS APPEAL.

APPLETON, NH—The New Hampshire Supreme Court ruled today that Alex B. Willy was entitled to a new trial on charges of first degree sexual assault against a minor. In a case that many felt was marked by overzealous prosecution and naive faith in the credibility of children's testimony, the court ruled that Mr. Willy's accusers, a six-year-old boy and a seven-year-old boy, had been subjected to leading and suggestive questioning by county social workers during their investigation. The Supreme Court

18

held that the lower Court had erred in permitting the children's testimony without first holding a "taint" hearing to determine whether the children's recollections had been too influenced by suggestive interviewing to be reliable.

The ruling stated that a new trial cannot occur until such a hearing takes place. Prosecutors must prove in the "taint" hearing that the children's recollections are reliable and were not unduly influenced by suggestive questioning. If they fail to do so, the state is barred from seeking a new trial.

Mr. Willy stated that, "I'm just grateful for the chance to prove my innocence, and I am confident that a new trial will do just that. Hopefully, this dreadful ordeal will soon be over. I hold no malice in my heart toward anyone. I know the adults involved meant well, and the children, of course, were just children and as such were easily swayed by those around them."

Classic Willy. I could feel the pull of the words even in print. He sounded exactly like an innocent man, and the average person reading that statement wouldn't even question his innocence for a second. In fact, Willy sounded like a *kind*, innocent man who wasn't even angry about the horrible things his accusers had put him through.

Willy had a gift. Dealing with Willy was like dealing with an emotional chameleon. He knew, as though he had radar, just what kind of emotional tone people wanted to hear, and he could produce it unfailingly. I had studied Willy for countless hours, but I still didn't know how he did it. Something in me couldn't grasp it.

Slowly, I walked back to the office. Just to reassure myself of my own sanity, I opened the drawer with my Willy-tapes in it. With his permission I had audiotaped some of my interviews with him—getting a sadist to really talk was such a rare thing I had decided to tape so I could go back over them. I could learn a lot from Willy although what he had to teach was pretty depressing.

I thumbed through the cassettes until I found the one I was looking for: the label read "Ways to Con Adults." Willy had signed permission for me to tape his interviews with the written stipulation that I could never share the tapes with anyone else. Just like Willy to tantalize me with something and then make sure I couldn't use it.

I pulled out my tape recorder and popped the tape in. I had left the tape set at the section it seemed to me was the most important. "It's very simple, Dr. Michael," Willy was saying. "Simply find out what people need. What do they need? Do they need money? I'll loan it. Do they need a listening ear? I'll be there. Do they need reassurance? I'll supply it. People are full of needs." He had laughed.

"The only difficult part is figuring out what they need *most*. What do they need badly enough that they will sell their firstborn, so to speak. What do they need badly enough that they will ignore what is right in front of their eyes? I have molested kids in the backseat of a car with their parents in the front seat."

I had been floored by that and hadn't spoken for a moment. Willy had laughed again. "Indeed, I have. I'd simply pull a blanket over a sleepy child and fondle them with their parents in the front seat. They'd wake up, of course, and that trapped look they'd give their parents was *so* satisfying. They knew they wouldn't be believed. Somehow they knew. And they were right. Their parents wouldn't have believed them if they had reported me on the spot.

"There are subtleties, of course, which I can't expect you to grasp. You are really such a *limited* student." Which, I thought every time I heard the tape, was true.

"Like what?"

"What they need. What they hunger for. Ultimately, it's never anything concrete. Oh, sometimes it starts with money, a loan to get them out of debt or something, but it always turns out that the money represents something else—importance or support or something—something that turns out to be much more addictive than money.

"The highest level"—and I could still remember Willy's eyes starting to shine—"is to supply something crucial that the person is not even aware of needing, something completely unseen that they become totally dependent on my providing. Then you can take chances, which of course intensifies the excitement."

"Like what?"

"Oh, you can make the abuse of their child a little more obvious and a little more obvious until they have to work not to see it."

"And what is it that people need badly enough, even unconsciously, to tolerate your molesting their child? Friendship? Self-worth? What is it you supply, Mr. Willy, that is worth so much?"

"Well, Dr. Michael, no good cook shares *all* the ingredients. Really, you don't expect me to do all the work for you, do you?"

And what was it that Willy had supplied *me* with, that kept me coming back to see him? Willy didn't want to talk about that, but then again, neither did I.

I popped the tape, picked up the newspaper, and stared glumly at the article. A taint hearing. The case was over. There wasn't any way to prove something didn't exist. It was like trying to prove a white elephant *wasn't* in the room. Some misguided fool had asked a leading question somewhere along the way, and after that, anything the children said would be considered tainted.

Never mind that the children disclosed abuse *before* the interview with the county social worker—otherwise, there wouldn't have been an interview. Never mind how many symptoms the children had—and Willy had described to me their deterioration in gloating detail.

The bottom line was simple: One thing people surely needed was to believe they could tell who was safe and who wasn't, and a whole lot of people had trusted Willy. He looked good; he talked good; he was a popular minister in his community who had regularly visited the sick and the elderly. A lot of people had been devoted to him. If there was *any* way to explain away the accusations against him, people would take it. And now they had one.

2

By noon, Sweet Tomatoes was in high gear. Non-traditional pasta dishes are their specialty, and nobody can cook pasta like Sweet Tomatoes. The area is too small for the restaurant to have any serious competition, but it would have held its own anywhere. I have tenure at Sweet Tomatoes.

I was led to the last table by the window, and waved to Harvey, one of the owners, as I sat down. He came over and joined me. "Got a minute?" he said.

"Probably more than a minute," I answered. "I'm waiting for Carlotta to get out of a hearing." Prosecutors don't control when hearings end so Carlotta might or might not show up in the fore-seeable future. Harvey sat down, and I resisted the temptation just to close my eyes and listen. He had that kind of deep, snuggle-up, male voice you can't hear without thinking about climbing into bed. He was a teddy bear of a man, a big guy carrying a little extra weight around his middle. You could easily overlook the extra weight. That voice would sound very good about an inch from your ear. But I swore off married men. I did.

"Still making the world safe from child abuse?" he asked.

"Nah, I switched. I testify for the perps now. More money in it."

Harvey looked taken aback. "Just kidding," I said. "I almost got in trouble in court with my sick sense of humor, though. A prosecutor asked me why I was charging so much less than the defense expert, and I almost said, 'Costs more when you sell your soul,' but I didn't."

Harvey laughed. "Why not?"

"Too risky," I answered. "I've already had one judge recluse the jury in the *middle* of my testimony and say to the prosecutor, 'Your witness has come perilously close to calling the defense a flim-flam.' "

"You can't call the defense a flim-flam?"

"Nope. Not even when it is. You're supposed to be respectful. What's up with you?"

"Nothing really. We're going to Italy again. Testing new wines for the restaurant."

"Tough life," I said.

"I wanted to ask you something, about a neighbor of mine. . . ."

"Shoot," I replied. I hated this. People always

want me to diagnose their spouses, their children, even their cats. But you have to listen. At least you do if you want the last table by the window.

"I have this neighbor with this vicious-looking dog, and I'm a little worried. . . ." My ears perked up. Could it be? Small areas are like that: You run into all kinds of crossovers—once my dentist turned out to be the battering husband of a new client. But even in small areas, I reminded myself, there is more than one neighbor with a vicious-looking dog.

I didn't get to explore it because at that moment Carlotta walked in. Heads turned discreetly. No one actually stares at anybody in New England. Charles Bronson could—and did—walk down the street in the town where he had a vacation home without a single fan drooling on him. But people do notice interesting folks, and Carlotta had been six feet tall and interesting-looking since she was twelve.

Harvey saw her too and stood up. "Never mind," he said. "I'll catch you later."

"Give me a call," I said with, I hoped, nothing in my voice but ordinary friendliness. Sexy men always pull me off center.

Carlotta may have just rushed out of the hearing, but no one in the restaurant would have known. She walked unhurriedly to the table and sat down. She was dressed very simply in black crepe pants, a black matte blouse, and a black blazer. Around her neck she wore a handmade Native American beaded necklace. It was exquisite, and the simple black surrounding it set it off like a frame. If Calvin Klein had walked in, he would have put Carlotta on a runway just as she was. Well, actually, he had, once upon a time.

Carlotta looked worried. "Case go okay?" I asked when she sat down.

"Fine," she said, looking at me carefully. I realized I was the reason she was worried, and it hit me that Carlotta had probably chosen Sweet Tomatoes over my office because she knew I wouldn't yell there. Jesus. I've become someone other people have to manage. Maybe I ought to tone down my temper a bit.

"I'm all right," I said. "I don't like it. I think it's bullshit. I think it's worse than bullshit; I think it's criminal. I think every single judge that voted to put him on the street should be shot, but what can I say, every day somebody gets off who shouldn't."

There was a pause. What was bothering Carlotta? I was calm. Neither of us could do anything about Willy. "Well, what are you going to do?" she asked.

"Do? As in do what? There isn't a whole lot I can do."

"Michael, I don't want to remind you of anything you're trying to deny." Great. Now Carlotta's a psychologist? "But Alex Willy is a very dangerous man."

27

"So?"

"So, if I understand this right, he has told you things that no one else knows about him."

"So?"

"So, maybe I'm missing something, but isn't that likely to worry him?"

"Maybe," I admitted. "But how much harm can I do him? Obviously I can't put it in the paper. What's he got to worry about?"

"Is he going to quit molesting children?" Carlotta asked me directly.

"No, he isn't."

"What are the chances he'll get caught again?" she pressed.

"Eventually it's likely," I said. "But probably not soon. Willy controls kids with a combination of getting the kids to fear him and the parents to trust him, and the things he does to the kids are so extreme. The kind of abuse he inflicts doesn't sound plausible to most parents."

"So why is he going to get caught again?"

"He's too active," I answered. "He just molests too many kids, and he loves to take chances. He'll push the envelope until eventually he's caught."

"And when he is, what about you?"

"Carlotta, what do you mean what about me? What about me nothing."

"Are you or are you not a threat to Willy?" Carlotta said as though she were cross-examining a hostile witness, which she was, sort of. "Given how much you know, wouldn't you be a *very* effective witness for the prosecution?"

"You forget, counselor. Everything Willy has told me is considered 'hearsay' by the courts, and it is not admissible."

"There are twenty-four exceptions to hearsay. I won't bore you with the details, but the bottom line is I've gone over this carefully and checked it out with my boss—without any names, of course," she added hastily, "and I think the stuff he's told you would be admissible."

"Jesus." Willy wouldn't like that. And he would surely check it out. Willy counted on the fact that any abused child who reported him would not have any corroboration of what he was saying. And regardless of what happened to the current case, there would surely be abused children reporting him in the future.

"Patient/doctor confidentiality?" Carlotta asked. "What about that?"

"I don't think so," I had to answer. "He was never a client of mine. I never provided any services."

We were both quiet for a moment. "Michael, anything he's confided in you might even be admissible if he's ever tried again for the *current* offense."

"He won't be."

"True."

Silence fell. This conversation was not going

anywhere I wanted to go. I picked up my menu and got very involved in the choices.

"Michael, you're going to have to deal with this."

I put the menu down. From her artful makeup to her tastefully streaked hair, Carlotta looked like a woman whose chief concern in life was not breaking a nail. Not exactly. I knew Carlotta well enough to know once she got her teeth in something, there wasn't going to be any way to ignore it.

"Deal with what, Carlotta? Look. He's not really interested in adults sexually, so he wouldn't go after me just as a straight victim. And remember he's been away from kids for years now, and he's built up a lot of fantasies. He's going to set himself up somewhere and start ingratiating himself in the community.

"I don't think he'll want to take a detour to come after me just to keep me quiet. He can solve his problem with me by moving as far away as possible. I'll never know if he gets caught for something new. And the old case isn't going back to trial. You know that."

We sat in silence again. I went back to the menu, although not very hopefully. "Is it likely?" Carlotta asked. "Would he just move away? And could *you* live with it if he did? Knowing that he would still be out there molesting kids?"

"No" to everything, I thought. In my heart of

heart I knew Willy was too thorough to leave loose ends. And part of it was he'd know that even if he left me alone, I wouldn't leave him alone.

"Sure," I lied. "Why not? Look, do you know how many people there are out there molesting kids? I can't make myself crazy with it. I do what I can do." And, I thought, Carlotta was right. I needed to *do* something about Alex B. Willy.

But there was no way I'd tell Carlotta that. She would hover and scold and act like a mother hen. Worse, she'd tell Adam, the town's full-time police chief and my part-time lover, who would get protective and make me crazy with it, and then I'd lose the relationship with him and the friendship with Carlotta, and it would all be because I had told Carlotta the truth. So, really, I was just protecting my relationships with both of them by lying, through my teeth, to Carlotta.

Mama wouldn't have done it. Mama likes to let the chips fall where they may. Sometimes Mama throws the chips. But I wasn't Mama. Definitely, I wasn't Mama.

"Ummmm," Carlotta said, and I saw the indecision in her eyes. She should know better than to believe me. And then a chill went up my spine. I was selling Carlotta safety. She wanted to believe I was safe so she didn't have to worry about me, and she'd go against her own best judgment to believe it. Maybe, I had learned something from Willy after all.

3

I am not good at waiting, and I am not a procrastinator. I'm the kind that speeds up at intersections. When I jump horses cross-country I sometimes—well, frequently to be honest—have horses taking jumps too fast and too strung out, but I rarely have a horse balk. We are going over that jump if it kills us. It's a genetic thing, the price of being related to Mama.

I could have asked Carlotta to use her connections in the prosecutor's office to find out where Willy had gone once he was released. She was a Vermont prosecutor, and Willy's case was in New Hampshire, but one prosecutor would talk to another regardless. But looking at her, I didn't think it was a good idea. There wouldn't be any way I could ask her without tipping her off.

We got off Willy, finally, and onto the backlash against victims of child sexual abuse and "taint"

32

hearings and legal issues and the way the media gobbles up any perp's version of events regardless of how bizarre, but underneath it all I kept thinking about Willy. Carlotta had kicked off something. I had been so furious that some fool judge had released him that I hadn't yet thought about where his release put me. By the time lunch was over I was facing the fact that if Willy didn't go after me, I'd have to find a way to go after him. I couldn't just walk away knowing he was going to sadistically abuse eighteen million kids.

I walked back to my office thinking about the problems that come when you start on a life of deception. If I was going after Willy it would have been safer to have somebody know exactly where I was and what I was doing at all times, but it wasn't worth the hassle.

This was Carlotta's fault, I rationalized. If she weren't being so controlling I could have told her. I *would* have told her if I had trusted her to stay out of it and not blab to Adam. I, of course, would stay completely out of it when dealing with a friend who was doing something stupid beyond belief. Right.

In my defense, it had always felt better to be in the driver's seat than the passenger's seat. Willy would look me up even if I didn't look him up, and I couldn't see just sitting around waiting to be surprised. Neither of us had counted on his getting out of prison when he waxed eloquent about his various techniques for entrapping children—after all, he'd been in his sixties and starting a thirty-year prison sentence.

But the real problem—which was so formidable I didn't even want to think about it—was what the hell was I supposed to do once I found him? I couldn't just shoot him—despite my unfortunate, politically incorrect fondness for guns and the fact that I had a fair amount of expertise with them. I couldn't imagine shooting anyone in cold blood.

I wasn't going to talk him out of anything. I could see it now: "Willy, did you know molesting kids was *wrong?*"

"Gee," he'd say, "I never thought of that. I'll quit right away."

Threatening him would just put me in more jeopardy. The more Willy was sure I would try to harm him, the more he'd go after me.

Could I warn people in his community? Put it in the newspaper? Without a doubt no one would believe me. Willy was too glib and too charming.

I'd end up with a major lawsuit against me for slander plus get labeled as a crazy whose word was worthless. People have a way of ignoring evidence if they really like someone. A few months before, a teacher at a private school had been caught with mega-amounts of child porn. His colleagues had claimed it didn't mean he was a pedophile. Right. Like people who own two hundred cookbooks don't cook.

I had to smile thinking about Willy's defense. I would say truthfully that I had visited Willy in prison to learn about sadistic offenders. Willy would no doubt use the visits against me. He would portray me as a paranoid who had been harassing him for years and was now making up stories about him.

But if he did sue me, the audiotapes might be admissible under the rules of discovery. I brightened a little thinking I had one option, even though professional self-immolation would not be my first choice.

I walked back to my private practice office a few blocks from Sweet Tomatoes. My private practice was in a house I had once shared with Carlotta. I was only there one day a week. I spent the rest of my time in the Department of Psychiatry at Jefferson Medical School, where I taught, supervised residents, sat on stupid committees, and endlessly annoyed the chairman, who thought tact was an art form and that I knew less about it than anyone he had ever met.

That wasn't exactly true. I knew about tact. I just thought it was a character flaw. So what if he had had a few dozen complaints about me over the years. Nobody ever complained that what I had said was actually *wrong*. They just seemed to think I didn't need to say it exactly that way at exactly that time, if at all. Details.

I had a half hour before my next client, and I

started to pick up the phone to track down Willy. The absence of a plan was definitely a problem, but why worry about it now. First I had to find him. But the phone rang before I could pick it up.

"This is Dr. Stone," I said.

"Michael," the voice on the other end said simply.

My heart rate went up a notch, which annoyed me exceedingly. I could never seem to control the effect Adam had on me. "Good afternoon, Chief Bowman. Caught any crooks today?"

"Half a dozen before sunrise," Adam replied. He paused. "I'd like to come over this evening," he said. Adam could be more direct than I was.

"Why?" I said, suddenly suspicious. "Did Carlotta call you?"

"What's with the third degree?" Adam asked. "Why would Carlotta call me?"

I had blown it. Now he'd call her if she didn't call him.

"Nothing," I said. "Really, it's nothing. She's just on the rampage about me, as usual. I thought you were coming over to lecture me—which I would not have liked," I added sternly just in case he did call her.

"No," he said slowly, "that wasn't exactly what I had in mind."

Adam could say fewer words and get a bigger reaction from me than anyone I had ever known. I found my mouth was dry.

36

"Sounds fine," I said trying and miserably failing at keeping my voice even. "Dinner?"

"Sure," Adam said, and we got off on the when and where stuff, which allowed me to get my heart rate a tad short of tachycardia.

There was nothing I could do about the estrogen vote. I liked living alone. I didn't want a steady boyfriend. But every time Adam came around, the estrogen just started swimming in my ears.

Once Adam and I had gone to Hawaii. Well, actually I had gone, and he met me there. I wasn't even sure he was coming, and I had been walking on the beach when I realized the barefoot guy in shorts walking toward me was Adam.

The whole time we spent there had been a world apart. Like ghosts of the Aaragone, we never spoke of home. We never talked about his job or mine or sex offenders or my prickliness about independence or anything to do with the real world. I had worn long cotton dresses on the beach at night with nothing underneath, and the wind had whipped my dress around and lifted my skirts. I had felt like Marilyn Monroe standing on that grating, and I have never felt like Marilyn Monroe before or since. I could still remember the feeling of the wind on my bare thighs and bottom. I could remember the feel of other things too. Sitting in my office a million miles from Hawaii, it still made me smile.

On the way back to the mainland we had both been glum. The real world was rushing toward us with every mile, and we both knew it wouldn't be the same. It hadn't been.

I picked up Chinese on the way home. The best thing about being in my forties was making my peace with who I was and who I wasn't, and I wasn't Julia Child.

I was, however, happy to see Adam when he walked in. It was still light out, and mercifully, mud season seemed to be warming up so we agreed to dinner on the deck. I was busy unpacking cartons and didn't notice how still Adam was.

"I've been thinking," he said, finally. "How would you feel about moving in with me for a while?"

"Why?" I asked. "What's wrong with the way things are now?" I am never very smart when estrogen is roaring in my ears. I should have seen what was coming, but I didn't.

"The commute's too long from my house to yours," he said lightly.

"Fifteen minutes? Boy, you've been living in the country too long. Fifteen minutes would buy you a block in Boston at rush hour."

Adam didn't say anything, so I went on, "Look, why spoil a good thing? I am not the easiest person to live with." Actually I am impossible to live with.

Adam persisted. "Then why not move back into

town with Carlotta? You and she got along when you were living there before."

I knew, then, where this was going. He had called Carlotta. "I can't move in with Carlotta," I said sitting down to face him. "If there is any risk, and I'm not saying there is, I don't want to put her in the middle of it. You know Carlotta. She doesn't know zip about self-defense. She used to hate it when I had guns in the house."

"You can't stay here now, not with Willy out. You're a quarter mile from the nearest neighbor."

"Why not?" As if I didn't know.

"Michael, have you ever been to the scene of a homicide?"

"No," I said. "What's that got to do with anything?"

"Because I'm not sure you realize what you're getting into."

"I'm not getting into anything."

"Buy that and I've got a bridge to sell you."

"Adam, there's no point to this."

"Look, I do not want to find your bruised and broken body with needles under your fingernails."

"Cut it out, Adam. Isn't that a little baroque?" It was kind of a weak comeback, but I didn't seem to have anything convincing to say. Adam was way ahead of me. He had a full head of steam about this, and I was still flapping around on a beach in Hawaii. So much for letting your guard down.

"Not if you have found bodies like that before." Well, he hadn't, at least not in Vermont. Well, actually, maybe he had. Like most of the country, Vermont had had at least one serial killer, I remembered. He had operated for a couple of years a while back, leaving a body every six months. All right, so that kind of thing could happen here.

"He will kill you," Adam said quietly.

"You could at least say 'could.' "

"He will kill you," Adam said a little more strongly, "and then I will kill him."

"Come on, Adam. For Christ's sake. You will not. You're a cop, a good cop. You don't go around killing people."

"I will kill him," Adam said again, firmly. "But it will do no good because you will be just as dead. And then I will miss you," he said gently, "every day for the rest of my life."

I froze. He was repeating back to me something I had said to him about my daughter who had died of SIDS a few years back. Jordan was absolutely my Achilles' heel. I had had no warning he was going to raise her, and her death rose from whatever pool of misery I kept it trapped in and flooded through every pore. Suddenly I had the metallic taste in my mouth I had had for weeks after she died—grief has effects no one can seem to explain. I got very cold and knew if I wasn't lucky I would start shaking soon from

40

the cold. I looked up. Surely, the reference had been inadvertent. Surely, he had not meant to invoke Jordan. I saw in his eyes that he had, and I stood up.

My voice was dead calm, but to say it had ice in it was to say the Arctic Circle had a couple of cubes. It also had a sound in it a rattler makes when you step on it. "Don't you ever, ever in your lifetime or mine use Jordan against me again. Not for any reason. Not to save my life. Not to save the lives of all the starving children in the known universe. Not one time. Not ever."

I was dizzy and cold. I went over and picked up my car keys and my coat. Adam had gone stock-still. Wisely, he didn't speak. "Be out of here by the time I get back," I said. I knew he would. He had not heard that tone in my voice before. But then again, neither had I.

It took enormous effort, but I made myself stop at the door on the way out. I put one hand on the frame to steady myself and turned back. "I can't do it your way. I can't hide behind your coattails and live in your shadow. I can't run home to big daddy when the going gets rough. I know exactly how dangerous Willy is, far more than you do, and yes, he probably will kill me if I'm stupid or careless enough to give him the chance. But if I run and hide, I'll lose who I am anyway, and it isn't worth it, so stay out of it. I'll make it or I won't. All you will do is destroy what's between

41

us." Adam didn't speak again, and I waited for a moment, then left.

I drove around for a while, but it was difficult remembering where I was. Jordan was back in full force. Grief and depression are not even on the same planet. Depression is like a slow-onset paralysis. After a while it's too much effort to lift your arm, to get out of bed. Grief is more like being beaten up. It's a spasm. You feel like curling up in a ball to ward off the blows.

Finally, I realized the car was near Marv's house, and I headed over. I was coming up enough to realize I wasn't competent to drive. I needed to get off the road, and I wasn't ready to go home. I'd be damned before I went to Carlotta's.

Marv had a condominium in town. It wasn't fair to say he lived alone, although there weren't any other people living there. He lived with his paintings and his sculptures—folk art he had collected from all over the world. It was a soothing place, even for me, who knew diddly-squat about art. Marv was a very good psychiatrist and a bad witness in court. He was the person that I called when I needed a consult on a case if he didn't have to testify. I didn't need a consult tonight. Maybe I just needed to sit around the paintings for a while. Was that because I got something from the art, I wondered, or from the fact he loved them so?

I knocked on the door and heard the padding of Marv's slippers as he came to it. Marv's purple slippers. He always wore them at home, and they were ugly beyond belief. Marv opened the door. He was wearing his usual mismatched thrown-together colors. He was short and partly bald with a potbelly. I was never troubled by the estrogen vote around Marv, and tonight that seemed nothing but comforting.

He looked startled and began to speak. He checked himself and looked more closely. He had told me once he had counseled a cross-dressing client who had determined not to go to any therapist who didn't realize he was male. The guy had interviewed six previous therapists before he found Marv. Marv spotted him immediately by the size of his wrists. I couldn't have hidden what shape I was in from Marv if I tried.

"I was wondering . . . ," I started in lamely.

"Wondering, nothing," Marv said, putting his arm around me. "Come on in."

"Have a seat," he said pointing to the couch. "Let me stoke up the fire a bit and put on some hot tea." I didn't even drink hot tea, but I knew he was right. "Now," he said, when he finished with the fire, thinking out loud. "Before the tea, a blanket—how about an afghan from Albania?"

It was the first thing all night that had made me smile. Somehow you just knew Marv wouldn't come out with an army surplus blanket. I must be getting punchy. I had an image of some natural disaster—a hurricane maybe—and Marv running around putting Albanian and Russian and Spanish afghans around the survivors.

Marv fetched the blanket and the tea and just sat down on the couch and drank his tea quietly staring into the fire. He didn't say anything at all.

"You can go on with whatever you were doing," I said. "I just want to hang out for a while."

"I'm fine," he said. "Am I bothering you?"

"No," I said honestly. "On the contrary."

That was it. He never asked a question. I never volunteered anything. I shook for a while, despite the fire and the blanket and the tea, and then slowly I drifted off. I knew what would happen. It happened every time. I'd wake up thinking she was alive for a second and then realize she wasn't. I hated that fall more than anything in the whole world, but there wasn't anything I could do about it. Marv's was a better place than most to ride it out.

Circle of life bullshit. Death was an ugly business. The New Age philosophers chirping that everything happened for a reason made me want to vomit. Jordan's death had pretty much eviscerated me just like a child's death eviscerated every parent I had ever met who had lost one. It didn't make us wise or deep and appreciative of life; it made us hurt.

Adam didn't have a clue what I was really

afraid of. It wasn't that Willy would torture me to death. That was flat-out horrible, even though I wasn't all that afraid of dying—people who had lost children never were. But what I was really afraid of was that Willy would know enough to use Jordan against me somehow. But irony of irony, it was Adam who did that. Serves you right, I said to myself as I drifted off. Serves you right for letting the son-of-a-bitch get under your skin.

4

When I awoke there was a fresh fire burning in the fireplace and a small coffeemaker set up on the end table beside the couch. All I had to do to get fresh coffee was to flip a switch. There was a cup with milk in it next to the coffeemaker and a single crocus in a small vase next to the cup. It was still early. What time did Marv get up to do all this?

I looked at the crocus. I'd have bitten off Marv's head if he'd told me that things would get better or the darkest day was just before dawn or any other such drivel. He hadn't said anything. He just left a crocus—the first flower in the spring and the only one that will stick its head up through the snow. Hard to argue with a crocus, even for me.

I thought about it. I was more on the Carlotta and Adam side of things than I cared to admit. If

I had a friend who was on some kind of stupid collision course, I'd have ranted and raved, cajoled and persuaded, probably with less art than either of them. I wouldn't have handled things the way Marv did last night. Yet what could anybody have done for me that was better? I thought guiltily of my battered women clients. Maybe I ought to argue less and put out a few more crocuses.

Of course, I wouldn't have been stupid enough to use a dead child against anyone. The day after, I still felt emotionally stiff and sore—as though I'd taken a bad beating, which I guess I had.

I had woken with my worst nightmare, as I knew I would: a comfortable sense that Jordan was in the next room and I just needed to get up and check on her because she was sleeping so late. Then the crash—all of which happened, as usual, while I was still in a twilight state. By the time I was fully awake I was pretty much through it.

I got up and padded into the kitchen looking for Marv. He was gone, but there was a note on the table. "I'm off to the jail to do a consult. Suicide attempt last night. Stay as long as you like. The place is yours. Love."

If Marv ever came to my door, not a single question, I admonished myself. Not one. But would anyone come to my door who didn't want a single question? The whole thing was a little uneasy-making. I was like a surgeon whose answer to every problem had been to cut it out. Only now I was the patient, and I had developed something that couldn't be cut out.

The only person who could help turned out not to be a surgeon at all, but a chronic disease doc who knew how to manage the kind of things that didn't kill you and didn't go away. I had learned something from Marv, but I doubted I could use it. Surgeons make bad chronic disease docs and vice versa.

I went out to the car to get my travel bag. I had a habit of traveling impulsively, and a packed bag, as always, was in the car. I don't own a lot. I make a point of never owning more than two hundred and fifty things total in my life, but one thing I never skimped on was the travel bag. It had everything I need in it to stay a weekend or even six.

What do you really need to travel: two pairs of shorts, three T-shirts, one bathing suit, two pairs of long pants (one of which you wear), two shirts with collars, one dress, one sweater—if you needed a coat you shouldn't go there—five pairs of underwear, and two bras. A few toiletries, and that was it. Everything was wrinkle-free, everything went together, and everything washed out in the sink and dried before morning. What else do you have to have? I was never trapped as long as I had my travel bag and a credit card, which I also kept in the bag.

I retrieved my toothbrush from the bag and the only dress: a generic stretch-velvet, long-sleeved, black turtleneck that came down to mid-calf. It was modest enough to wear in the Vatican or the Middle East, shiny enough to wear to a symphony, and plain enough to wear in the daytime. I don't believe in single-purpose items.

I had no sooner arrived at the Department of Psychiatry, where Marv and I both worked, when Judy, Marv's secretary, sought me out. "Do you know where Marv is?" she said.

"Actually," I said, "I do. He's at the jail. Someone made a suicide attempt last night."

"Oh, dear," she said.

"Why, what's wrong?"

"There's a woman here who thinks she has an appointment to be screened for his new group." Marv was starting a new interpersonal therapy group, and like most therapists, he screened people in individual interviews first. Otherwise, someone could join who was far too ill for a group and who might attempt suicide the first time someone confronted her. Or he could end up with a stalker in the group who would immediately pick up on the most submissive female and make her life hell. Groups worked when the people in them were reasonably well-functioning.

Even in a single screening interview a therapist could weed out the folks who were wildly inappropriate.

"So? Can't you reschedule her?"

"I could. I guess I will. I just don't think she'll come back. She seems pretty nervous."

Clearly, I owed Marv, and while Marv's ability to calm down a nervous client was probably far better than mine, it was probably better for her to see me than be rebuffed and told to come back later. "Okay, I'll screen her for him," I said.

"I put her in his office," Judy said. "Ginger's in the waiting room again, and she freaks new clients."

I almost changed my mind. I didn't want to see Ginger. Ginger wasn't my client anymore, and my plan was never to see Ginger again in my lifetime. Unfortunately, Marv's office was down the hall on the other side of the waiting room, and if I saw his new client, I would have to cross the waiting room and go past Ginger. I started to tell Judy that hell would freeze before I voluntarily walked into a room with Ginger, but I stopped.

What cowardice. After all, I was the reason Marv had to deal with Ginger in the first place. She had walked into my office a couple of years ago saying she didn't have any huge problems, she just wanted a little help with some issues on the job. This is called telling the big lie. She had immediately locked into a symbiotic, fused, hang-on-me thing that had nearly suffocated me.

Ginger was relentless. She came to my office when I was seeing other patients just to be near me. She called my answering machine to hear my voice. She showed up hours early for her appointment and slept in the waiting room. She refused to leave after her appointment. She called every day and demanded callbacks. If I couldn't or didn't get back to her she threatened suicide. If I went away, she tried it and then blamed it on me for abandoning her.

If it had gone on, I think I would have ended up on the inpatient unit myself—committed, no doubt, for killing her. Finally, when I found myself dreading to go to work every single day, I had transferred her to Marv. I had consulted him regularly on the case already, and both of us had hoped it would be different with a male therapist. It hadn't been, but I hadn't offered to take her back.

Ginger was sitting in the waiting room, dressed entirely in black. She was in her thirties, but her face was so angular and lined she looked older. She was small with dark hair cut severely short, and she was curled up in a fetal position on the couch. There was no peace in Ginger, and everything about her reflected it.

What she lacked was an ability to self-soothe. She felt at peace only when she was around whoever she was attached to at the moment. Outside that person's presence she fell into the abyss. Marv was better than anyone I knew at teaching people to self-soothe, but it looked like he wasn't getting too far with Ginger.

I don't believe in diagnosing people by what colors they wear, but in Ginger's case you could always tell what her mood was by what she had on. When she felt neglected by her therapist—which was frequently—she always wore black.

Ginger looked up when I came in, and I stopped. I had to. "How are you, Ginger?" I asked.

"Well, things aren't going too well right now."

"I'm sorry to hear that. Are you waiting for Marv? I don't think he'll be in for a while. He had an emergency. What time is your appointment?"

"Oh. I don't have an appointment until one. I just thought I'd come a little early. Do you have time to see me? You know, I really think I did better seeing a woman therapist." Whoever Ginger's therapist was at the time, he or she was always failing her, and whoever her last therapist was, that person always walked on water.

There was a major unempathic part of me that wanted to scream, "NOT ON YOUR LIFE. NOT UNTIL THE BULLS TRADE MICHAEL JORDAN. NOT UNTIL THE CELTICS OFFER ME A SPOT. NOT UNTIL THERE'S PEACE IN

THE MIDDLE EAST. NOT UNTIL THE FALSE-MEMORY HIRED GUNS TELL THE TRUTH IN COURT. THEN I'LL SEE YOU—THAT IS, IF I'VE HAD A LOBOTOMY IN THE INTERIM." I had paused too long, and Ginger looked up hopefully. Maybe she could even see two therapists at once.

"I don't, Ginger," I responded calmly. "And I don't really think it would help you to go back and forth between therapists, anyway. Why don't you talk things over with Marv and see what he thinks? I have to go, but I hope things get better for you."

And all of the screaming in my head aside, I truly did hope she'd get better, but it didn't seem likely. Ginger had no clue how to feel good without sucking the breath out of somebody else's life, and I doubted she'd ever figure it out. And worse, almost, she had no idea how hostile her leechlike behavior was. She just felt entitled.

I felt like a criminal escaping the scene of a crime, which was a big part of the problem. No matter what you did with Ginger, you never escaped the guilt trip she soaked you with.

I closed the door to Marv's office and tried to put Ginger behind me. The woman Judy brought in didn't look like the type who usually showed up for interpersonal growth groups. She had a tiny, sharp chin—far too small for her face—and it spoke not just to malnutrition in her childhood but to generations of her ancestors never having enough. Her shoulders were thin and hunched over. When she smiled nervously at me I could see several missing teeth and several darkly stained ones. She was wearing the kind of cheap polyester that mimicked the latest style but was so poorly made it seemed more mockery than mimicry. Far better, I thought, would be an honest pair of jeans and a workshirt.

It was simple: She was poor, and the teeth and the chin said she and her kin had been poor for eons. I couldn't tell how old she was: Poverty ages people so badly they are always younger than they look. I'd have said mid-fifties, so probably she was in her early forties.

My lawyer Daddy had come from people who had a little money, but my intrepid Mama had come from people who made their living from the sea. Some of them had been as poor as church mice all their lives. I had been too young to remember any of them clearly, but I had heard stories that made the Depression sound pretty watered-down in comparison. When you live off the sea, and the sea doesn't produce, and there are no societal safety nets, and your neighbors are in as bad shape as you are, you just go hungry, and some of them had.

Dresses had been made from the feedbags for the animals, which wasn't as bad as it sounds. Actually they looked a lot better than the polyester in front of me. The feedbags came in soft floral print cotton, and I had vague memories of those small floral print dresses on elderly ladies sitting on porch swings. Somewhere in my genes I knew poverty, even though I'd never seen it in my lifetime, and the woman in front of me felt like some kind of relative.

"Hello, I'm Michael Stone," I said and extended my hand. She stood up and held out her hand awkwardly, but when she took mine she surprised me with the firmness of her grasp.

"I'm Katy," she said.

"I know you're here to see Dr. Gleason, but he got called out on emergency, and I thought maybe I could help. Have a seat. You're here about his group?"

"Well, I think so," she said sitting down on the far end of the couch. "Although sometimes I have to work nights, and I don't think I can get off, so I don't know if I can do it, but I thought I'd come and ask about it, anyways. The kids are gone now, and I think maybe it's time I got out some. I haven't gotten out much for a while— well, quite a while really, but now they're all grown up and gone. The last one moved in with her boyfriend the day she turned eighteen last Tuesday, and I thought I just got to get out and do something more than just go to work and come home and sit in front of the television." She was nervous and running on, which wasn't surprising if she had gotten out as little as she said.

I started to say something, but she went on. "I just was never one of those mothers who run around all the time. I don't know why some folks have kids. They never stay home with them. Even my sister—I love her the best—but she's out at Bingo five nights a week, and her youngest isn't any more 'n ten."

"What made you choose this particular group?" I asked. I wanted to ask her about her goals for joining the group, but I didn't know how to phrase it in a way that wouldn't sound pretentious or threatening.

"Well, my friend saw the ad, but it didn't say nothing about how much it cost so that's another thing."

"It's a sliding scale," I said. Actually, I didn't have a clue what Marv was charging, but I knew he was a softer touch than I was. "It's whatever you can afford."

"Not very much right now, I'll tell you that, although I might be able to get more work in the summer. Lots of people take time off in the summer, and they're short on some of the shifts."

"What about the group interested you?" I persisted. It was hard to see her in a process, obsessing-over-your-navel, interpersonal growth group.

"I just haven't done much social," she said, "so

when Tanya said it was a social group, I thought, well, what have I got to lose? I haven't met any decent men, and I figured a dating thing like this was a lot better place to look than going to a bar. I just don't hold with bars. I've seen too much drinking and carrying on."

Uh-oh, her friend had thought "interpersonal" had something to do with dating, which wasn't a bad guess but made this awkward. "Well, it's not really a dating kind of thing. It's a group for talking about problems. And mostly, these groups are made up of women. A few men might come, but they're likely to be married. It's not really set up for dating."

"It isn't? . . . Oh."

"No, although I can see where the ad might make it look that way, but it's really for talking about problems."

"I've had my share of those, I tell you, but I thought it was a group to meet people."

"No," I said. "What kind of problems have you had?" I don't know what made me ask. I could have just let her go. Maybe I asked out of curiosity because of her handshake. Maybe I just didn't want to go back into the waiting room. Maybe it was because people sometimes lose their nerve at the last minute when they come to see a counselor and pretend they came to the wrong place.

I was a little more rabid than most about that since the day a woman came to my office and asked if it was the social security office. I said "no" and gave her directions. Three days later she attempted suicide. I saw her right after that, and only then did I begin to learn about her fears of poverty.

"Well," she said. "I seen hard times, though not as hard as some. My husband was a drinker. I didn't mind that so much, and he used to hit me too, but I could take that, and then one night he tore my little Billy up, and he weren't no more 'n five. I tell you he could do anything he wanted to me, but he hadn't never hit one of my children before, and I said right then and there that he wouldn't never hit one again.

"I tried to stop him when he started in on Billy a'course, but he was a big man, and when he set his mind to beating something, he beat it. He went out drinking, and I cleaned Billy up as best I could. He kept asking me what he done wrong, and I told him nothing, but a little child don't understand.

"I waited up for him. I knew he'd be liquored up when he came back, and sure enough, along about five o'clock he came in drunker than a skunk, and I hid behind the stairs. When he started up, I just stepped out and hit him as hard as I could right in the face with one of those big iron frying pans. I hit him square in the face, and he stumbled out and never came back no more."

"Never?" I was mesmerized. She had come for something more than the group, but I wasn't sure what. Maybe just to tell someone her story.

"Never. We did all right, although it was a hard time that first winter. We got ourselves a house for five hundred dollars." I must have looked surprised because she quickly added, "well a chicken coop, really, but me and the kids fixed it up. And we dug ourselves a well, got it down to close to twenty feet. It was hard going, but the kids helped me. I took in ironing, made twenty-five dollars every other week.

"But that first winter the day came when I didn't have any money, and the kids were hungry, and there wasn't a thing in the house to feed 'em. I heard he was up at his mother's, and I hadn't asked him for a cent since he left, so I went up to ask him for ten dollars for some food money for the kids.

"I saw him on the porch, and I walked in the screen door and came up behind him, but afore I got there he turned around and saw me. Right away, he says to me, he says, 'I'll tell you one thing. Don't you never ask me for no money cause I don't pay for no dead horses.' I turned on my heel and I left, and I never asked him for a thing.

"We got through that winter, the Lord only knows how, and then the next thing I knowed he was up in Newport jail. We hadn't heard nothing from him for the whole three years, and then he started in writing me, asking me to bring the kids up, telling me how hard it was to be away from his family, telling me how much he missed us."

"What'd you do?" I was afraid to ask. I'd heard this story before, and I waited for the ending I was used to.

"I wrote him back," she said. "I told him, I said, 'Let me just tell you one thing. I don't pay for no dead horses.' "

I was stunned. After she left I sat there for a while. This woman had a "mind of winter," as Wallace Stevens would say. She saw the "nothing that was not there and the nothing that was." What did she have that the others didn't—all the people I had seen who would have been up to Newport jail telling the kids to "be nice, now, Daddy's sorry." Come lie to me and be my love.

What was it people needed badly enough to buy the tears in his eyes when in their heart of hearts they knew better? Company, sometimes? Money? Sex? And these were folks who hadn't run out of money and out of food in the New England winter with small kids. What did this woman have that the others didn't? What did this woman have that Ginger didn't, who couldn't be alone for two seconds without clutching at someone?

Was there anything I wanted badly enough to go up to Newport jail? I certainly hoped not. Then again, I'd never tried to dig a twenty-foot well with kids to take care of and winter on the way.

My hat was off to her. Maybe it was true, as Marge Piercy wrote, that "Nothing is won by endurance/But endurance." But sometimes that is a lot.

5

I was still thinking about her when Melissa, my secretary, came in. "FedEx," she said. "I signed for you." I threw it on the desk hardly glancing at it. FedEx was routine: Lawyers never seemed to use the snailmail anymore. My mind was on Katy, and it wasn't until I swung around that I noticed the return address:

Wilbee Cingu
Never-Never Land Enterprises
64 Martin Luther King Blvd.
Cross Roads Junction, NH

I looked again. Wilbee Cingu. I didn't know any Wilbee Cingu, and there were law firms that *should* be called Never-Never Land Enterprises but weren't.

I looked more closely. Wil-bee-c-ing-u. Uh-oh. I didn't have to worry about finding Willy. He had already found me. Fear pushed its way up in my throat, and I took a deep breath and tried to calm down. Willy had gotten the jump on me, and I hated it as much as I thought I would. I didn't mind walking down a dark alley to meet him— well, I did, actually, but there was nothing I could do about it—but I could not tolerate sitting in one while Willy walked toward me.

I had a friend who twenty years back had been the first female police officer in her state. She once had to climb a dark stairwell by herself in an apartment building with a man waiting at the top with an ax. Nobody knew how she did it. I did. She was the one doing the climbing.

I hesitated a second. A letter bomb was feasible. Willy could do it. On the other hand, he wouldn't be there to see the results, so it wouldn't be all that enjoyable for him. If he sent a letter bomb, my diagnosis of sexual sadist was wrong. I almost smiled. I didn't usually have to have *that* kind of faith in the diagnoses I made.

I opened the letter. "Free at last," Willy quoted. "Free at last." I'll bet Martin Luther King didn't have Willy in mind when he said that.

"By now," Willy wrote, "you must be wondering what your role in Never-Never Land will be. After all, 'reality is the product of the most august imagination.' Show me yours and I'll show you mine." It was signed,

partytime@postoffice.worldnet.att.net.

I stared at the letter for a long time. It wasn't a very long communication, but it said a lot. I knew what was in Willy's imagination—fairly horrific ways of torturing people—and if Willy was planning on bringing them to reality, then somebody was in for a bad time.

I didn't really want to see Willy's imagination brought to life, up close and personal. The only people who saw Willy's imagination brought to reality were the victims. If he was planning on personally showing me "his," then I was the one who was in for a bad time.

So he'd managed to tell me that, yes, he was up to his old tricks and, guess what, he had plans for me. Worse, he said it without anything he could be prosecuted for. It was a threat that didn't look like a threat, even if I could tie it to Willy, which I doubt very much that anyone could. Willy wouldn't be on any of the main networks with their billing records. Willy would have software that would access the Internet directly, and he could dial up from any phone in the world.

At least I didn't have to feel bad about not taking it to Adam. What could he do about it?

What could *I* do about this was a bigger problem. I tried to think. Jesus, he hadn't been out ten minutes before he got in touch. Had he been planning this?

All right then, what role did Willy have in mind for me in Never-Never Land? I had no doubts that Willy saw himself as Peter Pan and no doubts too about what his plans were for the "lost boys" he'd inevitably pick up. But what about the females—given that he was talking about my role—where did I fit? There were only two female roles in *Peter Pan*—Tinker Bell and Wendy—and nothing terrible happened to either of them.

Well, there was also the Indian Princess. As I remember, her role had something to do with being tied at the stake in a cave while the water rose. That would be a reasonably unappealing prospect.

One thing was clear: Willy was inviting me to communicate with him via e-mail, and he didn't have the address.

I didn't really want to play games with him, and if I corresponded with him, he'd have my e-mail address and one more way to worm his way into my privacy. But if I didn't, I wouldn't have any clues at all about what was coming next.

What a hand to play by myself. Didn't I know anybody I could talk to about this who wouldn't just advise me to move to Afghanistan? No, I did not. Not even Marv.

The phone rang. I jumped and then took a moment to steady myself before I picked it up.

One letter from Willy and I was already spooked. "It's the ED," Melissa said. "The on-call doc wants to talk to you."

"Who is it?" I asked.

"She didn't say," Melissa answered.

"Put her on," I said. In my heart of hearts the ED was still the ER to me, but it was true that the "emergency room" had been a lot more than a room for a long time now: a small city was more like it. "Emergency Department" really was more accurate but still bothered us old-timers. An ER by any other name was still an ER.

"Michael, this is Suzanne. I'm in the ED, and we have a patient of yours down here, a woman named Camille Robbins."

Fortunately, Suzanne Stenson was one of the sharpest psychiatric residents Jefferson had ever produced. This was fortunate because dealing with a crazy patient wasn't half as bad as dealing with a crazy psychiatrist.

"What brought her in?"

"Who is more like it. You know Harvey, runs Sweet Tomatoes? He found her hiding in the shrubs this morning outside her house. Her damn dog wouldn't let him near her, and he was getting ready to call the police when she seemed to come out of it and called the dog off. It looks like she was having some kind of flashback.

"Harvey drove her in. She was disoriented and confused and in and out of flashbacks."

Oh, Lord. I just hoped Harvey knew something about dogs. I had the feeling he didn't, or he'd have called the police the first time that rottweiler looked at him.

"Michael, the problem here is the dog came with her. I hate to say this, but the staff down here are more worried about the dog than your client. Nobody here wants to get within two feet of him, which is a big problem since your client is clutching his lead like it's a lifeline. She says he's a seizure dog. Is that true?"

"It's a 'she,' " I said, "although I'm not surprised you didn't get close enough to look. Her name is Keeter. As far as I know she is a seizure dog, which means that she can go anywhere. She's also an attack dog so be careful."

"Look, if people here were being any more careful they'd shoot her."

"Why don't I come down and see Camille."

"Why don't you."

"By the way, she just told you I was her therapist or she asked to see me?"

"She asked to see you." Good. That meant we had at least some connection, however new and fragile. Suzanne went on, "One more thing, Michael. She needs to be admitted, but we can't admit that dog."

"Legally, you have to. She's a service dog."

"Legally we do, so we're not going to recommend admission for Camille because of it.

Nobody thinks she would part with her, and we just can't put that dog on the ward. Risk management would go nuts, the other patients would go nuts, and I am well and truly worried the dog would go nuts. Just so you know, it's not an option."

Great. I had a woman so confused she was hiding in the shrubs having flashbacks, and hospitalization was out. But I couldn't really argue with it. I wouldn't put Keeter on the ward, either. What if Camille did lose control of her and she ate five or six patients? On the other hand, what was I supposed to tell Camille if she wanted to be admitted?

Probably the truth—which meant I'd have to take the flak for it later. If the higher-ups wouldn't admit Camille because they had no way to manage the dog, they'd never be willing to tell Camille that. That would be admitting she *needed* hospitalization and they didn't provide it—too much liability if something happened to her later. The administration would want the resident to tell Camille hospitalization wasn't needed.

Medicine has always had an ambivalent relationship with truth. It has been frequently harder to get medicine to admit the truth than to find it—witness that whole long history of lying to dying people about what was going to happen to them—as if they weren't going to find out, anyway. The good part was the hierarchy already thought of me as a "loose cannon," so I didn't have a lot to lose, reputation-wise—if you could call that a good part.

I put Willy's letter in the drawer. Unfortunately, the damn thing might be evidence for a future crime, and besides, I wanted to be able to reread it and think about it. There must be some way to figure out more about what Willy had in mind.

I headed down to the ED. Fred Flintstone had designed the elevators, so I took the stairs like most of the rest of the staff. I walked in the ED and headed for the nurses' station. "I'm looking for Dr. Stenson," I said. I was wearing my hospital ID pin with "Dr. M. Stone" on it, so the nurse, whom I didn't know, merely glanced up before directing me to a room down the hall. The movies didn't always get it wrong. It wouldn't be hard to impersonate a doctor. Great. Willy was already turning me into a complete paranoid. Already, I was thinking about how easy it would be for him to get access to the places I hung out.

I found Suzanne in the doctors' room writing notes in the chart. The doctors' room had a counter running around the room at sitting height, and docs were scattered around the room writing or making calls. Generally physicians wrote notes every time they saw a patient. This sounded good and it was good except it resulted in charts so thick that, after a while, nobody bothered to read the whole thing. Every once in a while, of course, that caused some sort of Big Problem.

Suzanne was an exception. She read the charts from cover to cover, no matter how many times the patient had been admitted. Suzanne kept reading for a moment before she looked up.

When she did, I saw the familiar circles under her eyes that told me she had been up all night. Medicine works its residents dangerously hard, putting them on twenty-four- or even thirty-six-hour shifts routinely. There are only a few states that outlaw it, and unfortunately, Vermont isn't one of them.

Of course, this is terrible for the patients, who get lousy care, and awful for the residents, who come to hate their lives. There is, too, the minor problem that it is bad for their training since nobody can think when they are that tired.

Despite all the excuses the hierarchy makes, it is done solely for one reason: money. Hiring people to work all those shifts would cost a ton of money. Residents are cheap, and basically, they have no rights.

Suzanne was slim—who had time to eat?—with shoulder-length dark hair and bright eyes. I don't know why psychology spends so much energy trying to develop IQ tests. You can make a pretty good guess at how bright people are by their eyes. Anyone who looked at Suzanne's and didn't know she was very, very bright indeed, needed an IQ test themselves.

"So," I said to Suzanne. "Always glad to have a patient of mine brighten your day. I know how bored you get sitting around with nothing to do."

"Actually," she said, "we don't see that many of your patients down here. I thought you were losing your touch, but, shucks, I found out you had only seen her once. I guess we can't expect even you to fix people in one visit."

"I don't know why not," I replied. "Managed care does. So, what do you have?" I knew Suzanne didn't have a whole lot of time.

"Not much," she said. "What happened to this woman? She can't seem to tell us, and all we've got is she was crouched in the bushes hiding, going in and out of flashbacks."

"What's she saying during the flashbacks?"

Suzanne sighed. "Not much. She just goes into a panic state and curls up in a fetal position. Then we all start looking at the dog and hoping she doesn't think we're the problem."

"Meds?" I said.

"Enough Haldol to drop an elephant—assuming she didn't give it to the dog."

"You hope she gave it to the dog."

"A thought . . . ," she replied. "The question here," she went on, "is what do we do with her?

We've done all the polypharmacy we can. We can't admit her. Does she have any relatives or friends who would look after her?"

"Not that I know of," I replied.

"So," she said, leaning back in the chair and crossing her arms, "what do you want us to do with her?"

"Fix her," I said. "What else?"

I headed out to see Camille. I would have preferred to read the chart first, but Suzanne still needed it.

On the way down the hall I fretted. Despite the fashionable view found in any pulp newspaper, good therapists don't tend to make patients worse. I had thought Camille was stabilized when she left my office, so why was she here? If she wasn't a regular visitor here, if this wasn't something she did every day, I'd have to face the fact that the therapy session had caused her to decompensate: It was a little tough believing in coincidence.

And if therapy was the problem, it meant I had a bigger one. If Camille couldn't talk *at all* about what happened without falling apart, no matter how long we spent putting things back together, or how indirectly we approached it, how were we supposed to get anywhere? She had to cross *some* open ground to get to any kind of shelter. What was I supposed to do if she couldn't do it?

Worse, I had a bad feeling Camille wasn't the only one who was facing open ground. This morning Willy had just been a vague possibility, a maybe-he'll-show-up-maybe-he-won't shadow in my mind. Now, he was setting up obstacle courses on my front lawn and sending me a written invitation.

6

The largest of the ED rooms looked like a miniature gymnasium broken into small areas by curtains. Groups of people were scattered through the room in the small areas; each group was separated from the other only by the curtains, partly drawn in some places, totally in others. The curtains didn't do much for the patients. True, nobody could see your mangled body as you lay there having it poked and prodded, but each patient could hear everybody else's business. It didn't help to be lying there with your broken elbow listening to a child crying on one side as they stitched up his face and an elderly woman sobbing on the other as they coded her husband for a heart attack.

But the ED, like the operating room, is one of the places where the patients' physical needs take precedence over their emotional ones. "Guest relations"—as the policies are called that try to humanize hospitals—tread lightly in the ED. You have to keep someone alive before you can worry about his or her feelings. A big room with everybody together meant staff could get back and forth from one patient to another quickly if they needed to.

I walked around the room and then realized, what a surprise, they hadn't been willing to put the dog in the common room. I headed back to the nurses' station and asked for Camille. I was directed to a small treatment room with the door shut. I knocked lightly and then poked my head in and asked, "Can I come in?"

Camille was sitting across from the door facing it with her back to the wall. At first she looked blank, and I realized she didn't recognize me right away. She looked spacey and disoriented and slowed down. I wondered how agitated she would be without the Haldol, which would likely control the flashbacks but was a major tranquilizer and antipsychotic and probably made her feel awful. Nobody who'd had it ever seemed to want to take it again no matter how crazy they felt.

I slowly opened the door and walked in. Camille's face focused and brightened. I could have been her best friend. It was the same kind of thing that happens when you run into someone you barely know a few thousand miles from home. Relationships are always relative.

I moved slowly. People with Posttraumatic Stress Disorder are edgy, and there isn't enough Haldol in the world to fix that. I sat down as far from Camille as I could get, which wasn't far enough. I knew anybody within ten feet of her would seem like an intrusion right now.

Keeter had lifted her head when I walked in. She was lying between Camille and the door. I didn't know much about the etiquette for dealing with guard dogs, but people always like it when you acknowledge them so I figured Keeter would too. I started to speak to Keeter and realized I shouldn't do anything to imply she was the dominant figure here, so I spoke to Camille first.

"Hi," I said softly. "I hear you've had a rough time." She didn't say anything, just put her head in her hands and started crying, or maybe she just continued crying. Her face was red and puffy and streaked with tears already.

"Good afternoon, Keeter," I said evenly. "Keeping a good eye on things, I hope." Keeter did not respond at all. She looked like she was thinking, "Ha, oldest trick in the book."

"He's back," Camille said. "I knew he would be."

"He's back?" I echoed. This was going to be tricky. If I asked her too much I'd throw her into another full flashback, and she'd go away completely. But sooner or later I needed to know whatever she could tell me about whatever had happened. How much was it safe to ask?

Camille nodded and didn't say anything.

"The same guy?" I said, to prompt her.

She nodded again.

"You saw him?" I asked. It occurred to me that I needed to confirm the extent of the flashbacks. I was just assuming I knew what her flashbacks were like, but there are all kinds of flashbacks: emotional flashbacks, somatic flashbacks . . . a full-blown sight-and-sound-hallucination being the most extreme.

She shook her head sideways.

"You didn't see him?" That was a little odd. I had pegged Camille for full-blown-there-he-is flashbacks.

She shook her head again. "It was dark. He must have been there the whole time." She paused to cry some more. "I was in bed."

"Camille, you know about flashbacks, right? You know he wasn't really there, that this was a flashback?"

She looked directly at me, and for a moment her gaze was so focused and intense it surprised me. "It wasn't a flashback," she said firmly.

There was a pause. I wasn't sure what to say. Camille just kept looking at me.

"You mean you think he was really there?"

"He was there. He was really there."

There was another pause. If she believed the guy was really back, her level of panic must be incredible. Flashbacks were bad enough, but at least with flashbacks she knew the perp wasn't really there to drag her off and start the whole thing again.

"Camille," I said softly. "How could he be back? Wasn't Keeter with you? Do you think Keeter would let someone like that get close to you? Weren't you home with Keeter?"

"He was there," she said insistently. And then she looked down again. "I never thought Keeter could stop him. Nobody can stop him."

There was another pause while I tried to regroup. This woman had probably had thousands of flashbacks. What had made this one so different? What made her think he was really there? Before I could speak, Camille went on. Her voice had dropped to the point it was hard to hear her. "He said it would be worse this time, much worse."

What did this guy do to her, anyway? It must be rape, but Jesus, what kind of rape? There were some grim possibilities: rapes with objects, rapes while the person was being strangled. I had one client who was raped next to the grave the perp made her dig for herself.

"How could it be worse?" I asked. It is amazing how well you can carry on a conversation when you have no idea what the other person is talking about. Maybe it helps not to know; you lead less and listen better.

Camille didn't answer. I'm sure she didn't

know. She had ceased paying any attention to the tears, and they were running freely down her face. Her nose was running too, and she was only sniffling to stop it. If she got any more panicky she wouldn't pay attention to that either. There is a level of panic where the social niceties—even hygiene—disappear.

I spied a Kleenex box on the table and reached over to give one to her. She ignored my outstretched hand as though it weren't there and started compulsively rubbing her wrists. A chill ran up my spine; I knew what that meant.

I didn't know how far I could go, but I kept on. I couldn't ask her how long it lasted, she wouldn't have any idea, so I started at the other end. "Where did they find you?" I asked.

"Nobody found me," she said. "I prayed to God over and over, but He didn't help. Nobody helped."

I tried again. "When it was over . . ."

Camille interrupted, and it was the first time I'd seen even a flash of anger. "It wasn't over," she said. "It's never been over."

I was silent for a moment trying to figure out how to ask. "Where did you go?" I asked. "When you got away?"

"I never got . . . oh . . . ," she said as she realized what I was trying to ask. "To a kennel," she said, finally. "I crawled over the fence and hid with the dogs. I was too scared to go to a house and I . . . I didn't have any clothes. I thought I'd be safe with the dogs." She paused. "No, I didn't," she said, flatly. "I didn't think I'd be safe anywhere." I was starting to put things together—but there were still about a million things I didn't know.

"Did he let you go?" I asked. It didn't sound like the kind of situation that would have been easy to get out of.

"I had a seizure," she said, flatly. "I hadn't had one for years. I don't remember much. When I came to he was saying I wasn't worth killing. I guess I wasn't, but sometimes I think it would have been better if he had. At least I wouldn't have to go through it again."

Her voice had a kind of resignation in it that gave me the creeps. This woman really thought her tormentor was back and had no belief whatsoever that she or anybody on earth could stop him from doing it again—whatever it was. Worse, the son-of-a-bitch had annihilated her self-esteem to the point she thought she wasn't even worth killing.

By now her nose was starting to drip, but she was paying no attention. Reflexively, I started to try to hand her a Kleenex again but realized the one I had was all balled up. I tossed it and picked up the Kleenex box to pull out another. I heard a sharp intake of breath from Camille. Surprised, I looked up.

Her pupils were dilated wide open, and then they contracted to pinpoints. She was sitting rigidly, grasping the arms of the chair on both sides. Her knuckles were white. Her face started to get the kind of unfocused look that said I wasn't in the room anymore.

"Camille," I said urgently. "Look at the chair; look at Keeter. What do you see?" She was losing contact with her surroundings, and sometimes you can keep people grounded in the present by getting them to focus on what's around them. If she could look at Keeter or the room or anything around her, it might help her stay in the here and now.

It didn't even slow her down. Her eyes never even flickered toward Keeter. Instead, she slowly raised her hands and touched her cheeks. "Dear God, not my nose. Just my nose, leave my nose. I won't be able to breathe." Her voice was getting sharp, and her breath was coming in panicky gasps. "Don't cover my eyes," she said. "I can't see . . . I can't see," she said, her voice rising.

"What?" I said. "What's on your face?"

She turned her face toward me as a blind person might, her eyes showing no recognition at all. "Can't you see?" she said. Then I lost her entirely. She quietly slipped off the chair and curled up in a fetal position, covered her head with her hands, and started rocking back and forth. Silence filled the room only to be broken by Camille making some sort of slight sound. If I had leaned forward, I could have caught it, maybe. I didn't. I knew what it was.

Keeter hardly reacted to any of this. She just looked dead tired, as well she might be. Her owner had been acting like this for probably the last twenty-four hours.

I looked down at the Kleenex box in my hand, trying to understand what had just happened. It just looked like an ordinary Kleenex box. I started to put it down and froze. There, on the table, sitting behind the Kleenex box until I picked it up, was the problem. I flashed back to my office. "Mummy," she had said, and I had thought she had been calling for her mother. Boy, the things people tell me that I just don't hear.

It was a simple thing sitting there on the table. You'd find it in anybody's house, in every hospital. Most people thought of it as a reassuring thing to have around. It was nothing really, just a large, ordinary roll of adhesive tape.

7

Suzanne had the big problem, of course. Once Camille showed up at the ED, she was Suzanne's responsibility, and Suzanne couldn't exactly put her on the street in the shape she was in. She could leave her in a treatment room for hours and hours—I'd seen that happen—but it was going to be more than a few hours before Camille came back to earth.

We called Harvey—neither of us thought a neighbor was likely to know much about Camille's friends or relatives—but neither of us knew anybody else to call. There wasn't anybody else we could think of who even knew Camille, and Camille was now too out of it to answer any more questions.

The call to Harvey yielded zip. Camille had hardly spoken to him or his wife, and Harvey could not remember ever seeing anybody go in or out of Camille's house except her. Dog or no, somehow Camille had to be admitted, at least temporarily.

There was a huge fight with the powers that be. I took as much of the flak as I could—Suzanne was a shoo-in for chief resident next year if she didn't alienate the entire hierarchy first, which this little episode might. In the end we came up with a compromise. Camille was going into a twenty-four-hour bed. Some psychiatric beds were reserved for short-term crisis patients, and those beds were only available for twenty-four hours at a time.

Keeter got special attention. She was not to leave Camille's room the entire time except to be walked outside. I wondered who was supposed to walk her, but decided against asking. At the end of twenty-four hours, if Camille wasn't able to leave the hospital and go home, she was to be committed to the state hospital. Let them deal with the dog, seemed to be the administrative point of view.

Suzanne and I just looked at each other. Neither of us mentioned to the "risk-management" person we were dealing with that Camille would never meet the criteria for commitment. These days to be committed you had to be actively homicidal or suicidal—and that meant have the gun in your hand and your finger on the trigger—plus be mentally ill. Camille was certainly ill enough but not planning on killing anybody, although both Suzanne and I were both considering it at this point.

Suzanne and I had a different plan. We thought the dog was more committable than Camille. Maybe if she wasn't better after twenty-four hours, we'd just commit the dog and Camille could go along.

It had taken us the entire day, and all we had bought Camille was twenty-four hours in a safe place to put herself back together. Neither of us was surprised. It was always tougher dealing with the hierarchy than the patients.

"Keeter," I said sternly when I left, "keep your cool. Do not cause any trouble. No snacking. Not one little obsessive-compulsive disorder. Not a single major depression."

As I left I passed the resident coming in to take over for Suzanne, who, mercifully, would finally get to go home and sleep. "Watch out for the anti-social in 102," I said as I passed him in the hall. "Mean as a junkyard dog."

I stepped outside in the cool spring darkness and glanced at my watch. Eight o'clock. It wouldn't be light this late until June. I particularly hate winter, where you go to work in the dark and come home in the dark. There was a reason God said, "Let there be light." If I was God, it would be the first thing I'd say too.

I went back upstairs to my office and retrieved

Willy's note before I left. I put it on the seat of the car and just looked at it a moment before starting the car. Surely, I wasn't thinking of answering it tonight. I was too tired from all the fighting over Camille, too zonked from watching her deteriorate in such a painful way. I wasn't in shape for it.

I drove home with the note still sitting on the seat. When I did respond to Willy—which wouldn't be tonight—the big issue would be what to say.

Dealing with Willy wasn't exactly like dealing with anybody else I knew. The closest thing maybe was an antisocial personality disorder—a bully, in short. There were rules for dealing with bullies. You never cowered and you never blustered. And most of all, you never got into a power struggle. Antisocials would cut off their noses to spite their faces, they would go to jail, they would literally die—or worse, kill you— before they'd lose a power struggle. So, instead, you gave them choices. If you do this, this will happen. If you do that, that will happen. Up to you; not my choice.

"That's fine," I had said to one who had announced he was going to tear up my office. "Sure, if you choose to, you can tear up my office. No problem. Now, here's the deal. If you tear it up, you go to jail. If you don't tear it up, you don't go to jail. Up to you. If you want to go to jail, you can go to jail. If you don't want to go to jail, then we can sit down and talk about why you're so upset. But you need to understand this: Either way—whether you go to jail tonight or you don't, I am not going to jail." He had sat down.

It wouldn't work with Willy. I knew in my soul it wouldn't, but what would? Nothing. So you took your best shot.

This time I didn't hesitate to get out of the car in the dark. Willy wouldn't be waiting. This much I knew about him: He loved foreplay. He wanted to talk, so he'd give me time to answer. I walked from the car to the house feeling safe for the first time since before I had been attacked. I dropped my stuff in the living room and walked out onto the deck.

The outside lights lit up the small stream below. I hadn't been out on the deck much recently, and I had almost forgotten how the stream looked at night. Water always looks different at night. It comes alive like some nocturnal animal that sleeps during the day. Look at water long enough at night and you would swear the light was coming up from below, braided through the gurgling stream like phosphorus. I'd seen that too. Dipped my oars in real phosphorus, leaving arcs of light as it dripped off the circling oars.

Somewhere, a thousand miles or so straight south, most of my people were probably sitting out on the water tonight, just like I was. One way

or another, most of them live on the water—on
the ocean or an inlet or at the least a river. In my
family, my little stream wasn't a very big deal in
the water department, but I couldn't imagine living without it. I went back in, got some ice tea,
came out, and sat down. I felt the day start to slip
from my shoulders.

I sat quietly and let the water from the stream
mesmerize me. Water is pretty much all my family has in common. I have all kinds of relatives:
bright ones and dumb ones, nice ones and mean
ones. I have a Mama that makes barracudas look
cuddly, and once upon a time I had a Daddy
who'd rather drink than fight. But every single
one of us has salt water in our veins.

I'm the black sheep. Not my cousin Mary
Lou, who turned into a total drunk and was
picked up by the police passed out in the street
outside Hardee's. Mary Lou found God and
straightened herself out, and my family decided
Mary Lou was a testimony to the healing powers of the Lord. Not my nephew Buddy, who
spent a couple of years in a military stockade
for something or other—I didn't even want to
know what. That was just considered youthful
hijinks.

But a good Southern girl like me going up to
live in a place that froze a body to death all winter and where, everybody knew, the people were
as cold as the weather? I laughed out loud, think-

ing if Willy did kill me, nobody in my family would be surprised. What do you expect if you're going to live up North among strangers?

How would Mama deal with Willy? Mama wouldn't see the problem. "Shoot him on sight," she'd say, as if that settled it.

"It's not that simple, Mama. It's all going to be shadow and sleight of hand. By the time I see him it'll be too late." I don't know why I carry on conversations with Mama as much as I do: I couldn't live within seven states of her.

On impulse I walked inside the tiny A-frame and started to pick up the phone. For the first time I noticed the message light flashing and hit the button to play it.

Marv's voice came on, tinged with anxiety. "Michael," he said. "Thank you for seeing my client. I gather from your notes the group was not what she was looking for.

"I'm actually calling because I read in the paper that Willy got out. I am terribly sorry. I'm wondering if this is likely to be a problem for you? I'd be happy to consult with you any time about him. And . . . well . . . I hope other matters are going better."

I hadn't told him why I'd landed on his couch, but I knew Marv was well aware the only kind of thing that could put me in that kind of shape was Jordan. "Let me know if I can help. And please come back whenever you like."

He was an amazingly benign man, and maybe I would wind up on his couch again. I picked up the phone. From the benign to the . . . , but that was the problem with Mama, I never even knew what to call her. I brought the phone back outside and sat down again. I looked at it for a moment and then sighed. Might as well. I dialed and waited. If Mama was there she'd pick it up immediately. Mama didn't dillydally around.

"Hello," the voice said. Mama never identifies herself, no matter whose phone she answers. She just expects everybody knows who she is.

"Mama, this is Michael."

"Michael, well land sakes, girl. It's been many a moon since I heard from you."

"Phone works both ways, Mama." How did I do this? I could get in a fight with Mama within *seconds* of being on the phone with her.

"Well, we been busy planting the garden. You know how much work that is. There hasn't been time to breathe." Mama wasn't one to let things go. I tried to think if I had ever in my life heard Mama take even *part* of the responsibility for anything going wrong. Probably not. This was going nowhere, as usual.

"Mama, tell me about attack dogs." Mama did know her dogs.

"Attack dogs. Girl? They don't call them 'attack dogs' anymore. Doesn't look good in court. You know how people sue over every little thing these days. Goddamn lawyers are ruining the country."

I had the feeling getting eaten by an attack dog didn't meet my definition of a little thing, but I let it go. Too, Daddy had been a lawyer, but I let that go also. "Right, protection dogs. That's not what I'm asking. I want to know how a female protection dog would likely act if she had an owner who couldn't control her. Is she going to get mean? What's she likely to do?"

"Well, that owner shouldn't have her. That's ridiculous."

"I don't run the world, Mama. There's nothing I can do about the fact that somebody has a protection dog who shouldn't. I just want to know how the dog is likely to act."

"Is she mean? Some of them are just naturally mean and some aren't."

"I don't know. She looks mean to me, but I can't tell."

There was a pause. "One thing's for sure, she'll take over."

"What do you mean? Turn on her owner?"

"Not necessarily. But she'll start making decisions on her own. A good dog won't just protect a person. They'll protect their territory. Your girl will pick out her territory, and before long you won't see any more mail. The UPS man won't come around either. Lord, there was one over on Harker's Island, he attacked the UPS *truck* when it was coming down the driveway."

91

"Would she let a stranger get into her owner's bedroom while the owner was there?"

"Michael, you ask the stupidest questions," Mama said with a snort. And to think I wondered where my lack of tact comes from.

I didn't say anything. It seemed clear there hadn't been anybody in Camille's room last night. I hadn't really thought so, but she had been so oddly sure. "Sounds like you got somebody with some trouble," Mama volunteered.

"The world is full of trouble," I said.

"Ain't it the truth?" she said. It was a rare moment when Mama and I agreed. I almost felt uncomfortable.

I said good-bye, hung up, and wandered back inside. I opened the fridge looking for some more ice tea and saw cartons of Chinese food. Christ, Adam. I had almost forgotten about him; last night seemed a zillion miles away. I got up and walked around. No sign he had ever been there: no note, nothing. Maybe he'd come to the end of it. No question someone could get a little tired of my stuff. I couldn't tell how I felt about that; maybe the comment about Jordan was still too raw.

I got the ice tea and, on impulse, sat down at the computer as I was walking by. I'd just compose the note tonight. I wouldn't send it. I'd just play around with it. I opened up my e-mail program and stared at the screen. What exactly was my plan? I sat there a while before I wrote.

I'll be interested in what you choose, Mr. Willy. Sure, you can start the same old routines again, but aren't they a little "been there, done that" by now? Of course, you will eventually get caught, but a lot of people actually seem to like prison. Maybe you're one of them.

I don't think you have a choice, anyway. I personally do not believe you could control your appetites if you tried. You're not really their master; you're more like their slave. Either way, I'm not involved. I don't have a role, Mr. Willy, except maybe the Greek chorus, or else Cassandra predicting doom.

If Willy had an Achilles' heel it was his narcissism. He wouldn't like the notion that he couldn't control his appetites. In Willy's mind he wasn't a slave to anything. No sense in not trying to turn that narcissistic grandiosity against him.

My hand hovered over the "Send" button. It would be smarter to wait. Let twenty-four hours pass at least. Make Willy wait. Responding too soon might be read as a sign of anxiety. Besides, I wouldn't feel safe once I sent it.

I pressed it anyway. The story came to mind of the scorpion who bit the horse carrying him to safety across a stream. When the horse had asked why, the scorpion had said, "Because it's my nature." I had my nature as surely as Willy had his, and it was my nature to serve and volley, not to sit back at the baseline and wait for the ball.

I don't know what got me so nervous about the whole thing afterward. I just kept seeing the "Send" button in my mind, although this time it was labeled "Start," instead.

8

It was Saturday, but I didn't wake up feeling any better. I had that pregame edginess I'd had in high school before a big game. Winning was a big deal at the time, although even then I had had enough perspective to know Lombardi had gone off the deep end when he said winning was the only thing. Winning wasn't the *only* thing when you're playing a game. But actually, when you're dealing with a sexual sadist who wants to maim and murder you, maybe it is.

I ought to be circling the wagon trains and handing out rifles, but it was hard to circle a single wagon. I needed to be rallying the troops, but I didn't. It wasn't that people didn't want to help. It was just that I didn't exactly know how to take their help without feeling diminished somehow.

I put the coffee cup down on the table next to the bed and stood up. My whole train of thought was depressing. I hated running into my own limitations, and I seemed to do it all the time. I could do this; I couldn't do that. I had more knots in my psyche than any sailor knew.

I needed to expand my horizons—at least get back some lost territory—and today was as good a day as any. Ridiculous to think I couldn't go play ball in a gym alone. I had done it my whole life. Just because someone strangled me in a gym. It wasn't the gym's fault.

But why did he have to do it in a gym? Why contaminate my favorite place in the whole world? Why not a beauty parlor or the Miss America pageant or a meeting? Any meeting. Why not the Chairman of Psychiatry's office? I could live without any of those places easily.

Well, in all fairness to my attacker, probably because it would have been hard to find me in any of those other places. I'd never been to the Miss America meat market in my whole life, and I didn't hang around beauty parlors. In Psychiatry, my hatred of meetings was legendary. Not to mention that I went to the Chairman's office only when I had to, usually about some dumb meeting or other I'd missed.

I went to the closet to get my precious high-top basketball shoes and started to bend over to pick them up. But as I did so, I could suddenly feel a forearm pressing into my throat. I straightened up and tried to catch my breath. Jesus Christ.

Was this going to plague me for the rest of my life? I had Posttraumatic Stress Disorder, and I hated it.

Having PTSD meant every time something *reminded* me of being strangled, I had the same feelings and the same physical sensations I had when I *was* being strangled. It also meant reminders would kick off intrusive memories and sometimes even nightmares. Camille had the same thing, only worse. She actually heard the perp's voice. My PTSD wasn't quite that bad. But it was miserable enough.

I bent over to get the shoes again, but the memory of my assaulter's face close to mine came up so vividly I shuddered involuntarily and stood up again. I backed away from the shoes and just stared at them.

I can do this. I can make myself do this. It crossed my mind that it might be more sensible to go to the gym with someone else the first time. But as John Belushi would have said, "Nah." I didn't want to. I could just see myself: "Adam, I'm scared to go to the gym alone. Will you come hold my hand?" Unbelievable. Impossible.

I started to reach for the shoes and then stopped. The memory of being strangled was so strong I was short of breath. I sat down on the bed and thought about it. Damn it, I could make myself take those shoes and go to the gym, and some day I'd have to. But it was clear whenever I did, I'd pay a price: I'd kick up the memory again big time.

People with PTSD avoid things that remind them of the trauma for a reason. I knew that. If I went to the gym, the price I would pay would be intrusive memories and a constant feeling of being suffocated. Not to mention nightmares. I could do it. But maybe I'd better get rid of Willy first.

Between the perp in my head and the one on the street, Willy was the bigger threat, I figured. Don't get crazy because you can't stand to be controlled. Being strangled will be sitting in your head whenever you get around to it. But how many wars can you fight at once on how many fronts? If you use up your resources tackling that, you'll have less to deal with Willy.

Hell of a thing. Every fiber in me wanted to grab the b-ball shoes and say, "Fuck you, you SOB. Do your worst." But I didn't. I was going to have to live with this for a while; that's all there was to it. If I didn't, I'd end up with two assaulters in my head, assuming I still had one.

I have a surgeon's mentality—a knife-happy surgeon. Cut it out! Get rid of it! That is my favorite thing to do with problems. I couldn't believe I was consciously, deliberately making a decision to live with something—worse, something akin to a leech on my psyche. But it was true that if I didn't live with it I might die with it.

And death was the kind of problem you just didn't want to get into.

Next to my b-ball shoes were my riding boots. Why not? I was so frustrated I felt like punching something. Why not go tackle a few fixed cross-country jumps? I sighed again and reached for the boots.

I hopped in my car, which was clean and Spartan. I can't believe people spend money on cars. All cars do the same thing. They go from here to there. My idea of a car is something with four wheels and a seat. Well, okay, a motor that starts in the winter and doesn't break down. Whatever car I've had, it is always Basic Car. Small. Cheap. No frills.

Not like the Porsche a friend had when I was a student. He lived upstairs from me, and he was out two or three times a night when the alarm went off. Thieves are drawn to Porsches like mosquitoes to blood. Forget it. I never had a car I had to lock because I never had a car anybody wanted to steal.

I picked up the Interstate and headed out to the old Braxton Farm. There was a trendy riding academy closer in, where all the students and the professors' children rode, but it never crossed my mind to go there. The academy barn always looked freshly painted. Once, I went by there and they had flower boxes on the barn windows. Too precious for me. I had found an old farm in the country that trained serious event horses and that was often looking for riders to exercise them.

The sign on the gate simply said "Braxton's Farm." Braxton had been gone a century. Joe Higgins had the place now, but Braxton's Farm it was and Braxton's Farm it would stay. I pulled up next to the weathered barn and surveyed the scene. The exterior of the barn looked like it always did: gray and battered. The fences all needed a new coat of paint. Joe never got around to details like that. But the place was neat and clean and looked like it was designed to be more comfortable for horses than for humans.

Mud season was beginning to relent. The outdoor ring looked ridable, if barely. That was disappointing. I was planning on using that as an argument for going cross-country since the cross-country course was on a hill and dried out sooner in the spring. Joe thought me a little too gung-ho for the cross-country course and often restricted me to the ring. Worse, since he'd built the indoor ring, I didn't even get outside half the time.

I found him saddling up a young chestnut mare I didn't recognize. Joe was a trim, good-looking man in his sixties with graying hair wearing a flannel workshirt with riding pants and boots. I'd never seen him in anything else. He looked a lot like the barn: weathered but solid with no frills.

"Good," he said, looking up. "I was just thinking about you. I'm taking this new mare on the cross-country course for the first time, and I was wishing somebody was here to take Freight Train with us."

Had I died and gone to heaven or what? I didn't even have to argue with him. "Delighted," I said. "What's going on with Freight Train?" Freight Train was a very capable, reliable jumper, and I didn't usually get to ride problem-free horses.

"His new rider is what's wrong with Freight Train. I wish to God parents would quit buying horses their kids can't handle. Freight Train's going to hell in a handbasket. He's jumping all strung out, and he's going to kill that kid if I don't get him under control."

It seemed odd to be taking a horse on the cross-country course to get him under control. Usually, that kind of work was done in the ring, where horses were much less pumped up than in the open air galloping free. But I didn't say a thing. I sure as hell wasn't going to talk Joe out of it.

"Control, Michael. I want this horse under control. I should work him in the ring, but I don't have time. The kid's parents are insisting on a novice event next weekend, and right now, in the mood he's in, Freight Train will eat that kid alive on a cross-country course." Joe stopped saddling and looked over the horse's back at me. "We are taking these jumps slow and easy, Michael, or we are coming back to the barn. Half the time you're worse than Freight Train."

"Hey, I just got here. Don't take it out on me." I was miffed. Joe and I had a running argument about whether I jumped too fast or not. It was a bum rap. Just because I couldn't see lollygagging around in front of a jump. I always jumped in control, or at least I tried to.

I went in the tack room to get Freight Train's gear. The tack was shiny with leather oil, and the smell of leather oil was sweet in the air. Each horse's halter and bridle were hung neatly on a hook and labeled. The saddles were on racks across the room.

I got Freight Train's halter and bridle and picked out a jumping saddle—a big jumping saddle—that would likely fit him. I dropped his tack off near the cross-ties where I would saddle him and went off to fetch him with his halter and a lead line. All the stalls had wooden signs with the horses' names on them, and I wandered around until I found him. I could have asked Joe, but I didn't feel like it. He was too crabby today, and I was still miffed.

The top half of Freight Train's stable door was open, and I looked in to make sure it was really him in his stall. The horse inside was too big to be anybody else, and I opened the bottom half of the stable door and stood for a moment just admiring him as the sun slanted in across his stall.

He was a big bay thoroughbred at seventeen hands. He had thick, tough legs unlike most thoroughbreds, whose spindly legs are their downfall. The sunlight made stripes across his shiny, brown coat and it looked almost red where the light hit it. Freight Train turned to look at me with his big, curious eyes. Even munching his hay, his eyes had that deep thoroughbred light in them.

Ah, thoroughbreds. They have heart like no other horse. Who else will literally run themselves to death for you if you aren't careful? Who else will look at a cross-country jump and start salivating? They go when they shouldn't go, couldn't go, would damage themselves by going. You might have to put on the brakes a lot, but you never have to pedal.

All right, they have their flaws—high-strung natures, spindly legs—and more than a few have lousy personalities, just plain cranky. A lot of thoroughbreds would as soon bite you as look at you, and if you haven't been kicked by a thoroughbred or dumped by one, it means you don't ride them. But in the end there are thoroughbreds and then there are a lot of other animals.

"Freight Train, dear heart," I said, slipping on his halter, "care to go for a spin? Perhaps a turn around the cross-country course." Freight Train's ears perked up. Of course he didn't recognize the words, but he could hear the excitement in my voice.

I led him out of the stall to the cross-ties. Freight Train allowed himself to be led quietly. I hooked him up and went to get the cleaning supplies.

By the time I got back from the tack room, Joe had his mare saddled and was in the indoor ring warming her up, so I had the aisle between the stalls all to myself. The barn was silent except for horses munching hay and the occasional snort or wall-kick.

Something started to ease inside of me. There are only a few holy places in the world. High on my list are an empty gym with no one there but me, and a clean barn with well-cared-for, contented horses munching their hay.

I brushed Freight Train's dusty coat in short, easy strokes working backward from his neck to his haunches: Horses are always dusty and need to be groomed daily. Freight Train's coat was shiny, a tribute to his diet and the frequent brushing. He seemed to like the stroking and stood quietly. I probably brushed him longer than I needed to—Joe would be yelling at me soon to get going—but the rhythm of the quiet brushing in the nearly silent, sunlit barn was balm to my agitated soul. What was it Will Rogers said? Something about the outside of a horse being good for the inside of a man? Make that "person," and he got it right.

I picked up the hoof pick out of the box of cleaning supplies and lifted each of the big guy's feet in turn. I cleaned out all the muck on the bottom of each hoof and carefully traced the grooves with the hoof pick. I inspected his feet carefully and then felt all four legs from the knee down. I couldn't feel any heat or swelling in any of them. On a cross-country course, a lame horse who couldn't jump properly could kill you, so it wasn't just altruism that made me check carefully to see if Freight Train was fit.

But he was. He felt like a million bucks, and he looked like a million bucks, so I put the saddle on and was just finishing putting on the bridle when Joe brought his horse in from the indoor ring.

"Going to take all day?" he said. Whatever had gone on in the inner ring hadn't lightened his mood any.

"Oh, you know me," I said, "just trying to avoid the cross-country course. One more sec."

Joe snorted, and I ran to get my helmet and riding gloves. When I came back he and his mare had already started off. I scrambled onto Freight Train's back and headed after him. It was a bit of a feat getting up there, given how big Freight Train was and the fact that no one was around to give me a leg up, but I never had the patience to go find the mounting stand.

Freight Train perked up a bit as we left the barn, but didn't get antsy until we passed the outdoor ring and the cutoff for the trail rides. When there wasn't any other place we could be going except the cross-country course, his whole mood changed. He was like a kid who couldn't contain himself. He wanted to go, and I wouldn't let him, so he started dancing in place. He got so many steps out of every yard he looked like a parade horse. Freight Train pulled his head in and arched his neck so my pulling on the bit didn't do any good: His neck was as far back as it would go.

I laughed out loud and reached down to pat his neck. "Easy, big guy," I said. "We'll get there." I continued to hold the reins in one hand and pat his neck to calm him down as we made our way down the road. I don't know why I love this so much. Maybe because around people I always seem to be the one with the throttle wide open. Thoroughbreds are so antsy, around them I feel like mellowness itself. Or maybe I love being around them simply because I know so well how they feel.

We rounded a curve, and the hill with the cross-country jumps on it came into view. Freight Train got serious about moving along and gave up his dancing in place for some serious pulling on the bit. I took the reins in each hand and squeezed and released, squeezed and released. It wouldn't do any good to pull steadily. Freight Train would just brace against the pressure or get the bit in his teeth, which meant real trouble.

As the first jump came in sight I let Freight Train canter, and we started circling in slow circles a long way from it. Without saying anything, it was clear between Joe and me that he would wait for me to do whatever I needed to do to get Freight Train under control. The new mare would follow Freight Train over the jumps.

Freight Train wasn't happy about circling, but he tolerated it until he reached the part of the circle where he was facing the first jump. Then he tried to leap forward and take off, but I was relentless. I made him circle again by holding tight the rein away from the jump and loosening the other. Freight Train's head was pointing toward the circle, but for the whole first quarter of it his body tried to gallop sideways to get to the jump.

We circled this way a few times, then the next time around I switched circles so he was heading into a circle on the other side and making a figure eight. Poor Freight Train was so intent on getting to the jump he didn't see the new circle coming up and didn't switch leads when I pulled him to the other side.

That put him galloping with his outside foot leading on the new circle, and he damn near fell on his nose. He stumbled, corrected himself, and switched leads. The message I'd sent was clear: Pay attention to me, Freight Train, or you're going to fall on your head.

We did a few more figure eights, and then I headed for the first jump.

It was a particularly tough one: a platform only two feet or so high but a good five feet deep. It had no wings, and it was only ten feet wide, which meant it was very easy and tempting for a horse to run out on either side. The jump looked like a simple upright until you were right up on it, which just increased the chances a horse would try to go around.

The issue for Freight Train wasn't that it was a platform—he knew this course—it was whether his strides would be right coming into it.

No matter how good a horse is at jumping, he still has to take off the right distance from a jump. It has to be far enough away that he won't hit it going up and close enough that he can clear the whole thing coming down. Ideally he would gallop with even strides to the jump and magically find himself exactly the right distance from the jump to take off.

That wouldn't happen by accident, not even with an experienced jumper like Freight Train. It was my job to lengthen or shorten his strides from farther away so that by three strides out he would be coming in perfectly.

If he came in wrong, he'd either have to leave out a stride and jump long—not easy when the jump is five feet deep—or he'd have to take an itsy-bitsy stride and "chip" it—also not easy when you're moving at thoroughbred speed. A couple of thousand pounds has a lot of momentum when it's moving right along.

Either way, the price of screwing up was that he could land on top of the jump or fail to clear it in the first place. This would be a really big problem with a cross-country jump because they are rigid and fixed. The jump we were facing was made out of logs nailed together, and they were just about thick enough, say, to hold up the World Trade Center. Come to think of it: It is strange that I love this so.

Freight Train didn't want to listen to me. The sun was shining, and the jump was just sitting there, and by God, he was a thoroughbred, which meant he was born and bred to move at intoxicating speeds. But the whole point of the stupid circling was to establish who was the boss of this operation, and he reluctantly slowed in response to my constant hassling.

I measured the distance from the jump to where I thought the third stride out would be. I decided Freight Train wasn't coming in right so I shortened his stride even more. He responded reluctantly, but he responded.

As we got closer to the jump my own adrenaline started to soar, and I could taste the bitter edge of fear in my mouth. Putting your life on the line will always get your attention. Unless you're a loony, it'll scare the bejesus out of you. "Take your best shot, fate," I thought as I always did, "and then leave me alone till the next time"—a strange mantra but one that always comes to mind.

By three strides from the jump Freight Train was coming in right. I eased up slightly on the reins and got ready to jump. By this point Freight Train could figure out for himself what he needed to do, and he kept his stride even as we approached.

He took his last stride and soared into the air. He jumped big as horses usually do when faced with rigid, wide jumps. I stood up in the stirrups and threw myself forward so I could release the reins up his neck. He needed to be able to stretch out in the air as much as he liked without hitting the bit. Novice riders always hold on to the reins to balance themselves, and it's a wonder some horses don't just stomp them to death once they finally get off.

Freight Train had a hang time that Michael Jordan would envy, and it seemed like I was flying forever. The exhilaration hit me like, well, a freight train, and by the time I landed I had enough endorphins for major heart surgery without anesthetics. I was in the zone. I could hear birds chirping with a singular clarity and see every leaf on the nearby trees stand out distinctly. Everything had a color and vividness that nothing but jumping or drugs can produce.

I looked back as we cantered up the hill, and

Joe had gotten his mare over the jump, although barely. She looked spooked and shaken, and Joe looked determined. To a new horse a cross-country jump is a formidable thing.

I laughed out loud as we cantered. All those snide male comments about women and horses miss the mark. All that junk about that "big thing between their legs." We don't confuse horses with men; we aren't making love to horses when we ride—we are the horse. It is like becoming a centaur and suddenly acquiring four powerful legs. Freight Train and I for this moment in time were a unit, a finely oiled machine, and we were leaping like gazelles over every obstacle in our path. Jesus, life was sweet.

The second jump was a far simpler one: an upright made of logs with wings that went out at an angle and almost guided the horse to the jump. We were doing fine on the approach, when Freight Train suddenly veered to the left. Surprised—the jump ahead was nothing compared to the last one—I tried to recover my balance and press with my left leg to straighten him out. But Freight Train kept moving at an angle and looking at the trees. I glanced over—what was spooking him—and caught a glimpse of something yellow.

Yellow. What's yellow? Deer aren't yellow. But I didn't have time to think about it. Freight Train was still coming in at an angle, and we were almost on top of the jump. He chipped it. Lucky it was a small one.

I looked back. There was no way to warn Joe about whatever it was that was in the trees. But his mare was so nervous about the jumps she didn't seem to be paying attention to anything else, anyway.

I made a long, slow curve to the right toward a stand of trees. To get to the third jump we had to canter down a lane through the trees, and it was close to my favorite part of the course.

Freight Train and I were alone in the tunnel of trees—Joe and his mare were still pretty far behind—and I could hear birds on both sides. The trees were so close and so vivid I felt like I could reach out and touch them. It gave me time to think about the yellow something I saw— thought I saw—in the trees. I came up blank. It certainly wasn't hunting season, and the course wasn't close to any hiking trails.

Whatever it was, it was gone. Freight Train seemed fine. My head was thoroughly in the zone by now so everything seemed in slow motion. The sound of Freight Train's hoofs drumming on the hard-packed dirt sounded like some kind of old, lost sound vaguely remembered, almost like a heartbeat.

As we approached the end of the trees, fear broke through my endorphin-soaked brain. The next jump was a killer, loosely speaking. It started with a sharp turn to the right so that we'd be going downhill. It was fairly scary to canter downhill without jumping, but the jump itself made it worse. It was a drop jump. This meant you leaped over something on one side expecting to land at the same level you took off, only to find the ground was several feet lower on the other side. The jump hid the drop so an unsuspecting horse wouldn't see—until it was too late—that the small two-foot solid jump in front of him hid a three-foot drop straight down on the other side.

There was also the problem that we had done a U-turn and were coming back to the same bunch of trees that had spooked Freight Train—although this time from the other side.

I could feel Freight Train tense as we got closer to the end of the tunnel, and I took the time to put the reins in one hand and pat his neck. This time I was standing in the saddle and leaning forward. He wasn't going too fast now, and the point was just to keep him moving over the jump.

I saw the jump ahead and squeezed my legs slightly. Freight Train's strides weren't coming in right, and this time I thought I'd lengthen to pick up a little speed; going downhill makes horses cautious, and they tend to slow. This jump was such a horse-stopper that I just wanted to get Freight Train over it. I didn't much care about the form.

The jump was close after the tunnel of trees, and the three-stride-from-the-jump mark came up quickly. Freight Train still seemed a little off to me, so I squeezed even more to lengthen his last three strides. We weren't going over this pretty, but I'd be damned if we weren't going over it.

Suddenly, from the stand of trees on our right, something white broke from cover and ran right in front of Freight Train. I saw the blur in my peripheral vision and thought "uh-oh," but the whole thing happened too fast to do anything.

Freight Train immediately shied to the left, away from the intruder and, unfortunately, the jump: horses instinctively protect their legs by not stepping on strange things. I was already standing up in the stirrups and leaning forward, and there was no time to get back. Freight Train went left, but I went straight. I flew through the air toward the jump. The world seemed to flip, and I hit the jump hard with my back and bounced over it, landing the three feet down on the other side.

If I'd had any presence of mind, I'd have been worried that Joe wouldn't see Freight Train was loose and would take the jump and land right on top of me. But I was too stunned to worry about anything: I tried to remember what happened, but couldn't. I just lay there. It didn't even cross my mind to get up.

I heard the sound of feet running—Freight Train had gone back down the tunnel of trees, and Joe had seen him and pulled up. Then Joe was next to me saying, "Are you all right?"

I didn't answer for a minute. For some reason I hate that question. People always ask it when you get hurt before you even know if you are all right or not. You're supposed to say, "Yes, I'm fine," even if you aren't, so they can quit worrying. I couldn't seem to find enough breath to say anything, and Joe said again, "Are you all right?"

When I didn't answer he said, "Michael, can you move your legs?" That freaked me, and I said, "Of course I can move my legs," and then tried to move them. They did move, which was very reassuring. I sat up, and then it came to me.

"It wasn't Freight Train's fault," I said to Joe. "Something ran across the course right in front of him." Which was very weird, come to think of it. I had never heard of an animal running toward danger. I got a little more oriented and sat up, asking, "Is Freight Train all right?" The world started whirling when I sat up, and I leaned back on my hands and closed my eyes to stop the spinning.

"He's fine," Joe said.

"Well, go and check him," I said testily with my eyes still shut.

"To hell with Freight Train," Joe said.

"He's a forty-thousand-dollar horse, Joe. Go and check him. I'm all right."

Joe grumbled, but he went off, and I was glad for the moment alone to collect myself. I got up slowly and tried to brush the dirt off my back. I found I had to move very slowly to keep the world from spinning, and I walked over to the jump and leaned against it with my eyes shut again. Joe came back with both horses in tow, and I straightened up. "He's fine," he said.

I looked at the horses. Both had grass coming out from their bits where they had used their freedom to graze on the new grass just starting. Both looked totally unperturbed at my predicament. Horses are not big in the empathy department.

I tried moving again. The world had gotten reasonably stable. I walked over to Freight Train and started to get on.

"Are you all right?" Joe said.

"Of course I'm all right," I responded tersely. "You asked me that already."

"Well, you're getting on the wrong horse," Joe said. "It's the only reason I ask."

I looked at the horse I was getting on, and it was Joe's mare. I stepped back with whatever dignity I could summon—which wasn't much—and moved over to the other horse. Maybe I was in worse shape than I thought.

"We're going home, Michael," Joe said.

"You know Freight Train has to go over the jump," I responded. Joe knew you should never let a horse get away with not taking a jump for any reason. No matter what the reason for balking—except maybe sudden death—the horse went

over the jump it refused before you went home. Joe knew that.

"Fine," Joe said. "I'll take him over."

"Joe," I said slowly, "I need to go over the jump too."

I could hear him sigh, but he didn't say anything. "Give me your crop," I said. He gave me the crop and a leg up on Freight Train. I held the crop down my leg where Freight Train couldn't see it. Ordinarily, it would be the last thing I'd need with Freight Train, but this time might be different.

We turned and trotted up the hill. I was not going to try to make the sharp turn from the tunnel in the trees again—no point in making this harder than it already was. I wiggled various parts of my body as I went, trying to figure out if everything worked. Everything seemed to, but I did not feel well and this was going to be a major deal getting over this jump. What the hell was it? A goddamn psycho rabbit? What would cause a rabbit to run in front of a galloping thoroughbred?

Joe got on his mare and positioned himself to the left of the jump to discourage Freight Train from shying the same way he had before. Ordinarily I would have told him I didn't need the help, but this time I kept my mouth shut.

We trotted to begin with, the trees on our right and the jump straight ahead. One thing was for sure: I could throw away the left rein. Freight Train wouldn't shy toward the trees where the intruder had come from. Why had I thought that? It wasn't an intruder; it was just a stupid rabbit. If Freight Train went anywhere it would be to the left, like he had before.

We started cantering halfway down the hill, and I could feel Freight Train's body tense as we got closer. This time I was sitting as far back in the saddle as I could get in case he did balk. I saw him cut his eye toward the trees, looking, no doubt, for another rabbit. I was holding the right rein so tightly he couldn't possibly move his head to the left, but his hindquarters started drifting. Freight Train wasn't even thinking about the jump ahead. He was expecting trouble from the trees.

I had the crop in my left hand, but Freight Train didn't know it. I took the reins in my right hand and cracked him sharply on his left hindquarters. Surprised, he shot forward—the trees forgotten for the moment.

The jump was right in front of him, and he wasn't ready. I hit him again, more sharply this time, and he took off, awkwardly and late, but he did take off.

He wasn't exactly balanced, and I didn't feel like I was flying—more like falling. He stumbled when he landed on the other side and almost went down on his nose. I fell forward on his neck when he stumbled.

Freight Train caught himself, and so did I, and neither of us went down, although it was close. We were over. I pulled him up, more relieved than I wanted to admit, and Joe came trotting up, probably more relieved than he wanted to admit.

I considered whether I could get through the rest of the course. I just hated to call it quits, but I felt like shit. Freight Train would do fine, but could I get through it? Luckily I didn't have to make the decision. "We're going home," Joe said, and started off on his mare before I had a chance to argue. To be truthful, I didn't really want to.

I followed behind, and we walked back to the barn. Neither of us said anything. When somebody got hurt, Joe always got angry—from worry, I think, but it wasn't pleasant to deal with. I'd given him enough flak about it over the years that he'd learned—at least around me—to keep it to himself. For my part, the vertigo kept coming and going, and I was working at just staying on the horse.

I started to unsaddle Freight Train at the barn, but Joe took the saddle out of my hands. "Go home, Michael," he said tersely. "You look like shit."

I didn't even think of arguing. I just headed for the car. I looked back and saw Joe watching. He was probably wondering if I'd get in the wrong car. For Christ's sakes, I was moving under my own steam. How bad could it be?

I got in the car and headed for the highway, but once out of sight of Joe I turned onto a logging road that went up by the cross-country jumps. There was something I had to do, and tomorrow would be too late. I drove as far as I could, then got out and walked up the hill. I headed for the thicket of trees that had spooked Freight Train. It seemed to take a long time to get up the hill. You don't realize how much ground you cover on a horse.

I pulled aside some bushes and headed into the bramble, looking at the ground the whole time. It took me a few minutes, but I found what I was looking for—sort of. Surprised, I knelt down and touched the ground with my fingers.

There in the soft, wet dirt was a footprint. But it wasn't a large male who had stood in the thicket. There was the imprint of the ball of somebody's foot—small, about the size of mine—but where the heel should be there was only a small, deep hole. A woman had stood in the thicket, a woman who hadn't expected to be there and who was no doubt cursing her shoes as she stood. It just couldn't be Willy, not unless he had crammed his feet into a small woman's spike heels, which, come to think of it, I wouldn't put past him.

I stood up, completely mystified, and thought about it. Willy was famous for attracting female admirers. I had even run into one leaving once

when I went in to see him. Had he conned someone into keeping an eye on me? It couldn't be a
casual hiker. Nobody wore spike heels on a hike.

I put my hand on my back while I thought. It
was beginning to hurt like a son-of-a-bitch, and
when I put my hand on it, I felt a knot right in the
middle of my spine. I put my fist next to it and
compared them. The knot stood out roughly as
far as my fist.

I swallowed hard. I'd played b-ball too long to
be upset by the average sprain or broken nose,
but the memory of Christopher Reeve could send
me into near hysteria. With a knot like that, the
ED was calling my name.

9

I was relieved to see it was Jack who finally walked into my cubicle in the ED. Ordinarily I avoided him. Jack and I had spent some time together, back before I got religion, or my version of it, anyway, and quit going out with married men.

Right now I didn't feel like avoiding him. He was a very good doc, and he'd take good care of me, and at this moment that seemed like a big deal. Jack wouldn't miss a cracked vertebra, say, the kind where you go to sleep feeling fine and wake up after it severs your spinal cord.

My head felt like someone was hitting it with a hammer, and I smiled bleakly when he walked in. "So," he said. "Up to your usual quiet life, I see."

"There was this rabbit with a pocket watch," I replied. "Kept saying he was late. Fool ran right in front of my horse."

Jack took my face in his hands and lifted it. I closed my eyes for a second against the pain. Any movement was starting to make my head feel like an anvil had been dropped on it. "Headache?" Jack said.

"More or less," I replied.

He looked back and forth from one eye to the other. "Are they all right?" I said, trying to sound casual. I knew pupils of different sizes were not a good sign.

"More or less," he said. "Any nausea or sleepiness?"

"None," I said. "Just good old-fashioned pain."

"So what else is wrong with you?" he asked.

"This." I got up off the examining table and turned around. I lifted my shirt up to show Jack my back.

"Impressive," he said. "We'll need to get a look at that." He put his hand on my back and ran it over the bump. Even in the pain I was aware of how gentle his fingers felt. That man did have nice hands. I sighed inwardly. The estrogen vote was coming in again. If I ever became a multiple personality, it would be a running battle between the quasi-reasonable part of me and my estrogen-steeped, who-gives-a-shit brain stem.

"Have you seen this?" he asked.

"No," I replied. "I just felt it."

"Take a look." He turned and got a mirror and held it over my shoulder where I could turn my head and get a look at it. My entire back was discoloring from one side to the other. The knot in the center looked as bad as it felt.

"Oh, boy," I said.

"Lady," he said, "whatever you're trying to prove, you've already proved it." I laughed. Jack was quoting something a guy who played in the pick-up basketball games had said to me one time.

"Could be I should stick with the less dangerous sports." It just slipped out, and immediately I wanted to hit the "undo" button and take it back.

Jack didn't respond. Things between us had gone beyond that kind of flippancy. Worse, it was a kind of painful reminder of the difference in how he saw the affair and how I did.

He sat down and filled out the paperwork for the X-ray. It seemed to take him a long time. Finally, he handed it to me. "If you ever want to put something on the line beside your tush," he said, "call me. Otherwise, I've got a rowing machine."

It hurt, but I deserved it. I took it without reply.

I got through the wait for the X-ray and the wait for the radiologist to interpret it and the wait for Jack to come back and tell me it was fine. I'd banged myself to hell and back, but I hadn't actually broken anything. I had a concussion—even I had figured that out—but it looked like I hadn't fractured my skull or done anything permanent to my precious little brain cells. This was good—I was very attached to those little cells.

By the time I got home, my head hurt so badly, I had to put it on the steering wheel and wait for a lull before I could get out of the car. By then I was nauseated, but I was pretty sure it was from the pain.

I locked the door behind me and more or less glided up to the loft. It hurt less if I walked very smoothly. I lay down carefully on the bed and didn't move. I had only taken Advil at the hospital, but I found that I was drifting off in some spacey, exhausted way.

The phone rang, and I didn't even think about answering it. The machine was turned up, and I could hear Marv's voice. "Michael," he said, "I need to check in with you. Something came up in a session that you should know about." His voice sounded somewhat urgent, but I didn't care—not in the slightest. I didn't care what anybody said in any session. I didn't much care about anything. I was too damn tired and in too much pain.

Time passed. A whole day and night of it, and I only got off the bed when I had to. I tried to brush my teeth, but it jarred my head too much. I woke up every time I turned over in the night because turning my head would start it throbbing again.

Marv had called again, and it sounded like whatever it was, was important to him, but it still wasn't to me. My whole world had been reduced to a focus on keeping my head as still as possible.

Besides, if I spoke to Marv, he'd know immediately how hurt I was: There was zero chance I could fool him. Then he'd tell people, and they'd come out and scurry around. I'd have to deal with them, and I just didn't have the energy. The only call I answered was from Jack; I was afraid he'd come out to check on me if I didn't.

There was a little voice inside that said, "Call Marv. His voice doesn't sound right," but I ignored it. Chicken Little could have come to my door, and I would have said, "So, the sky is falling? I know that already. It fell on my head."

10

I just didn't do well with the head thing. I called in sick to work Monday and Tuesday—a flu bug, I said—and it wasn't until late Tuesday that I could even walk around without gritting my teeth. Finally, I got well enough to remember there was an outside world and noticed the machines that kept me in touch with it.

I might as well tackle the phone. I was halfway through listening to the messages when it rang. Impulsively, I picked it up and said "hello."

I felt a jolt when I heard Adam's voice. "Michael," he said. I was supposed to say something back, but I couldn't remember what—besides I realized I was holding my breath. When I didn't speak, Adam went on, "Look, I don't want to bug you; I only have a couple of things I want to say."

It didn't sound like Adam. He didn't sound all that warm—worried maybe, but not warm—and his speech sounded rehearsed. "First, I am sorry I brought up Jordan."

"Now isn't the time to talk about it," I responded. Oh, Jesus, if he triggered Jordan again I would surely lose it.

"I know that. I figured that out," he added dryly. "The second thing is—the only thing I want—is for you to promise me you'll call me if Willy contacts you."

I didn't say anything. I was not, I was absolutely not ready to discuss Willy with Adam. I didn't want Adam anywhere near me right now. He stirred up too much stuff, and I needed a clear head to deal with Willy.

I sighed but didn't say anything. I hated to lie to Adam, and his request sounded so sincere and so . . . reasonable.

"Michael, has he contacted you already?" Adam said sharply.

"I'm thinking, Adam. Don't read too much into it. I have to think about whether I can make a promise like that." I hadn't lied yet.

"If I have a problem," I said, "you'll be the first to know."

There was a pause.

"That isn't good enough," Adam said.

He was taking away all my wiggle room. "All right," I said, giving up. "I promise." Why do some people force you to lie?

"Okay," he said, sounding relieved, and I got a

full body flush of guilt; the man trusted me. "We can talk about other things later," he added, and he was gone.

After he hung up I just sat there. If it was possible to make my relationship with Adam worse, I had just done it. But what are you supposed to do when somebody has a gun to your head? This wasn't my fault. People should not pressure their friends into lying to them.

But when I thought about it I realized there were all kinds of things I could have said. Like "no," for starters. Why didn't I just say, "No, I'm not promising anything, Adam, but I'll keep your request in mind." The more I thought about it, the stranger it seemed that I had agreed. Adam always had an unsettling effect on me. I couldn't think straight when he was around. Not to mention that I could hardly think at all with this hammer banging on my head.

But it was bigger than that. There was a reason I lived alone. Relationships are like magnets for me: They pull me off course. Expectations, demands—I have that female thing that hates disappointing people. After a while, in every relationship, I start feeling less "me." Pretty soon, I'm so watered down I can't stand myself, and then I get out.

I decided to put it aside—after all, Adam had *invited* me to lie to him; he had practically *insisted* I lie to him—and I walked over to the computer. Willy was still out there, and I needed to quit obsessing over Adam and figure out what he was up to. I had thrown down a gauntlet to Willy, sort of, and it was going to be interesting to see how he responded.

I checked on my e-mail, and yes, there was a message from "partytime." I stared at it for a moment before I opened it. Just seeing mail from Willy gave me a bad case of the dreads. I finally double-clicked on "partytime," and Willy's letter popped up on my screen.

Well, well, my good doctor. I should prove to you I can control my appetites—a little reverse psychology, perhaps? Next you'll be proscribing the symptom! But no, I can't see you in the Milan school. My dear, you must think I am an oppositional adolescent to be bought off so easily. Oh, Michael, you do amuse me.

So he knew a little something about psychology. Big deal. A lot of people know about the Milan group and their focus on proscribing the symptom. If someone was truly oppositional they'd quit having the symptom just to win the power struggle.

But interestingly, I hadn't been proscribing the symptom. I had just been playing to his narcissism, which, for all his smarts, he still didn't see.

Still, all in all it was a disappointing communication. Perhaps you are simply less clever than I thought. Or then again, stress has a way of eating into your soul like acid, doesn't it? You start wondering when and how and . . . what.

You need solace! Distraction from the inevitable. There's still time—some anyway. Get yourself a dog, a rottweiler, maybe, and keep her. Perhaps some flowers—Camellias say. Have a little Kiwi fruit or quiche Lorraine.

I froze. For a moment I couldn't breathe. I read it again and again. I got up and walked around the room and sat down and read the last paragraph again. I got up and walked again, still reading it and telling myself it couldn't mean what I thought it meant. I could be wrong; I had to be wrong.

But what were the probabilities? I had a client named Camille, one named Kiwi, and one named Lorraine. He'd even capitalized the names, for God's sake. Get a rottweiler and "keep her." Keep her. Keeter.

I needed an outside person to read this and tell me I was crazy. I got as far as the phone and stopped. Anybody I knew who looked at this would tell me to spend the next two years in New Zealand.

But how could Willy know who my clients

ANNA SALTER

were? How could he possibly know? Had he broken into my files? Had he followed people who
went in and out of my office? How could he
know? Was he tapping my phone? Had I spoken
to them on the phone? He couldn't have gotten
into my computer files. I didn't keep my clients'
names on my computer.

I read the message again. It had to be what I
thought it was. It made no sense otherwise.
Quiche Lorraine and Kiwi fruit? He just couldn't
pull those out of a hat.

So he was here. Close enough to watch my
office. But how would he know their names? Was
he following them and then checking out who
lived at that address? But even if he did? He
might somehow find out their names from where
they lived, but how did he get Keeter's name? I
kept going over and over it like a broken record.
Had he broken into my office? Had he read my
files? But if he was following people, he knew
where I lived, too.

I was going in circles. I got up and got a glass
of ice tea to settle my nerves and sat down to
think. Ice tea is mother's milk to Southerners, and
somehow, under stress, I always like to touch
something from the South. I looked at the ice and
twirled it in the glass while I tried to clear my
mind. "In ghostlier demarcations," Wallace
Stevens had written, "keener sounds." Well,
things were pretty ghostly, and I was hearing

132

something all right, but what? "In ghostlier demarcations, muddy but insistent noises." Stevens had never written that.

I remembered something from long ago. I had gone sailing with some friends in college. We'd been on a twenty-four-foot Erickson, a little Clorox bottle of a boat, when the motor went out and, worse, the fog rolled in. I had been assigned the job of navigating, and I had gone below with the charts while others steered and kept a lookout—as best they could—for other boats. The fog had been so thick you couldn't see three feet ahead, and the little boat didn't have radar.

Nobody had really gotten freaked out until the ferries started coming. We'd hear the sound of their motors grow louder and louder, but nobody could see a thing. Then when the motors were so loud that we were all just waiting to be run over, the sound would slowly start fading. The damn things were passing us so close we could practically touch them, and we still couldn't see them.

"In ghostlier demarcations, the sound of ferries." That was closer to the truth. I could hear Willy in the fog, but I couldn't see anything. It was a lot like the ferries, with one difference: Willy wasn't in the fog. You might say he had radar of a sort, but the ferries used it to avoid us, and Willy would use it to circle me and circle me, getting closer all the time. More like a hammerhead shark than a ferry.

That wasn't really news. No matter what I told anybody, I knew Willy would be on my doorstep—or more likely outside my window—from the moment I heard he was getting out of jail. But I never thought he'd drag my clients into it.

I thought of Lucas, the mass murderer. When he was five years old, his mother asked him if he loved the family mule. He said he did, and she shot it in front of him. She knew she could hurt him most by hurting things he loved.

I had no children. I lived alone. I wasn't somebody you could easily threaten with things like that. But the sanctity of my therapy office was important to me, and the people I took care of were important to me. What made me think Willy wouldn't figure that out?

There were a couple of things I had to do. I got dressed and pulled the fanny pack I kept my magnum in from a drawer. I put on the fanny pack and then checked the gun to be sure it was loaded. Without children in the house, I could keep my gun loaded, and I did.

I threw a couple of speed loaders in the pack, grabbed my car keys, and headed for the car. I was moving too fast, and my head started hurting again. I slowed down—Jesus, I hated slowing down when I was trying to get somewhere—and slowly glided my head to the car.

I never noticed the ride in. It was one of those deals where my mind was so preoccupied, my brain stem took over the wheel. I got to my private practice office in Carlotta's house and sat outside. The lights were on in her part of the house, and I had no choice whatsoever. Carlotta had been my best friend since college—which I hoped to God Willy did not know—and I had to go talk to her about this.

I thought of about eighteen ways I could approach this without telling her the truth, and none of them worked. I gave up and got out of the car. Between my prickly sense of privacy and Carlotta's safety, my privacy was going to have to take it on the ear.

I went around to the back door, which opened on the kitchen. I knocked as I opened it with my key. Carlotta was standing in the kitchen in her favorite white satin pj's, mixing her nightly protein drink. Carlotta's way of living is a little different from mine. My favorite night wear is a T-shirt. She turned around as I came in and said, "Greetings, Dr. Michael. Want a milk shake?"

"No, thanks," I said and sat down at the kitchen table. I ran my fingers absentmindedly over the top of the table. It was an extraordinary object: a thick piece of solid redwood in a free-form style supported by a handmade pottery base. At the sound of my voice, Carlotta turned around again to look at me briefly, then went back to making her drink. "What the hell happened to you?"

"Fell off a horse," I said. Carlotta turned around again and looked at me. "Nothing serious," I said. "Jack was at the ED."

I didn't say anything more, and shortly Carlotta finished futzing with the blender and sat down. She didn't say anything either, just drank her drink and waited. I suppose it was obvious I wasn't there just to visit. Finally, I got going.

"How are things with Hank?" I asked. Hank Holden was a judge Carlotta had been seeing.

"Fine," she said.

I took a deep breath. There was no way I could fool Carlotta, so I might as well cut to the chase. "Why don't you go stay with him for a while?"

"Michael . . ."

"I'm not going to get into it, Carlotta. I'm just not. But I'm telling you, go stay with Hank."

"So he's here."

I shrugged.

"You're wearing your fanny pack."

I shrugged again. I got up and poured myself some milk shake just to be doing something.

"You haven't told Adam about this."

I sat back down.

Carlotta's face—which was ordinarily composed—looked like a kaleidoscope of emotions. Anger had passed through it and fear and some other things that went by too quick to identify.

"Michael, you are a goddamn fool."

"True," I said. Hard to argue with that.

"Why me?" she said.

"There's nothing specific about you," I said.

"Then I'll stay. It's you he's after."

"I wouldn't do that," I replied.

"Why not?"

"He knows some things he shouldn't know," I said carefully, looking down at the table. "It may be he got into the office."

I heard Carlotta's sharp intake of breath but didn't look up. It really wasn't a comfortable thought. Carlotta quit arguing.

"Hank's out of town until tomorrow."

"I'll stay tonight."

"Is that going to help or hurt?"

"Good question, but I have a gun and you don't. You need to think about a gun course," I said firmly. This was an old argument; Carlotta hated guns.

"If I quit hanging around you," she replied, "I wouldn't need one."

Which was probably true.

"Adam doesn't know," Carlotta said flatly.

I didn't reply. It wasn't a question.

"You know I'll call him," she said.

"It'll just cause an argument," I replied. "I, uh . . . I promised him I'd tell him if Willy showed up."

I knew I didn't have a prayer.

"That was dumb," was all she said.

Carlotta stormed off to bed. She hadn't said a whole lot, but she was as pissed as I could remember her being. Who could blame her? I had brought a maniac into her life who might even have gotten into her house, no doubt while she was sleeping. Now she had to move out without knowing when she could come back, and on top of that she had to worry about me.

Plus, when she thought about it, she would figure out I had more or less lied to her at lunch when I reassured her that Willy would take off for the hinterland and not come after me. Then she'd get doubly pissed.

And worse, what could I say? I don't know why I hate for people to worry about me so much. I just do.

So, as close as I could figure it, I was now in trouble with just about everybody I knew. I hadn't returned Marv's phone call when he told me it was urgent. I'd lied to Carlotta and Adam; one of them knew it and the other was about to.

It could be I wasn't easy to be friends with. It could be I was pretty exasperating to be friends with.

On the other hand, it could be people didn't know how to be friends with me without trying to control me. And that was on top of my not knowing how to be friends with them without feeling controlled.

It could be all of it was true.

A fault line. Willy couldn't know it, but he had hit a fault line. He had just applied a little stress, and the earth was splitting right where the fault line was. So maybe I should get a little proactive and try to keep it from splitting all the way through. Maybe I should call Marv and try to keep at least one relationship intact.

But I knew I wouldn't pick up the phone. I just didn't want to call Marv—who knew why? I didn't even know if it was because of this fault line, or a different one altogether. How many fault lines are there in my crazy psyche? How many high school football players are there in the state of Texas?

11

I woke up in the middle of a bad dream. I was driving through New York City, and halfway across I realized I had lost something. Something had just slipped away, and whatever it was, it changed everything. There was no longer any point to getting to wherever I was going, and, for some reason, it was clear there was no point to going back and looking for it. Something was gone that mattered enormously, and I woke up hungover with the loss.

I was so preoccupied with the dream, it took me a moment to realize something was different. Then it hit me: My head didn't hurt. For the first time since I hit the jump, my head wasn't the center of my universe. I slipped out of bed, testing my new pain-free state, and almost jumped with glee when nothing dreadful happened.

I didn't jump, however. Instead, I walked gingerly to the kitchen, moving only slightly more confidently as I went along. The memory of the headache was still with me, and I didn't want to start it up again. Carlotta had made coffee for me, so I guessed she wasn't terminally pissed. I poured the coffee and climbed back into bed.

Whew. What was that dream all about? I couldn't believe it was about my friendships and the pressure this thing with Willy was putting on them. Everything looked better without a headache, and I began to think that maybe I had overreacted.

Carlotta and I had hung out together through marriages and divorces. I tolerated her obsession with all things feminine. She had tolerated my bitching about it for two decades.

Women take their friendships seriously, and someday Carlotta and I were going to end up in an old-age commune sitting on a green porch with white rockers, talking about our old lovers. Women live with the fact that we will likely outlive any partners for a decade or more, so you can't make long, long-range plans with a partner.

No, it would be the friendships that lasted in the end. Carlotta and I would be rocking back and forth, trading outrageous stories—some of which would be true—smoking something and drinking brandy until we were giddy. Might as well develop a few bad habits when it was too late to matter. The problem was, if I didn't get Willy off my case and get busy, I was going to be weak in the story department.

So what was that dream all about? Jordan? How many months till the anniversary of her death? Five. Early for the anniversary reaction to start kicking in. I hoped the anniversary reaction wasn't kicking in. It was a pretty miserable business.

If not Jordan, Adam? I couldn't be getting that attached. I hoped I wasn't getting that attached. What was I losing? What was slipping away?

I gave up on it and got dressed. Carlotta was gone, and I was running late. I didn't have a meeting at Psychiatry until ten, but I had something I had to do first. I went into my private practice office and unlocked the filing cabinet. There sure weren't any signs that Willy had gotten in. How the hell could he have gotten into a locked cabinet in a locked house with dead bolts? Who knew?

I pulled out all my files on clients and put them on the couch. Even though I was only there part-time, I'd been doing therapy for a while, and there were still a lot of files. I went off to the basement and came back with some book boxes and put all the files in boxes and took them out to the car. I wasn't sure this would work, but it needed to.

I drove over to my bank and walked in. There were several women sitting at desks in the lobby. I picked the one with the least set hairdo as the best bet. Set hairdos are always a bad sign. She was free, so I went over and sat down. "I'd like a safety deposit box," I said. "Actually, I'd like a bunch of them."

"Fine," she said pleasantly. "How many would you like?"

"Uh, quite a few," I said.

"Quite a few?"

"Well, how big are they?" I hadn't brought the file boxes in yet. I didn't want to freak her. "I mean, what is your largest size?"

"Well," she said, sitting back and looking at me with a puzzled expression. "They're all twenty-four inches deep. The largest size is, ten inches high by fifteen inches wide."

I made a quick calculation. This would take a lot of boxes. "Just a minute," I said. "Why don't I bring in the stuff."

It took me several trips to bring in the files, and by then I had her full attention. "The large-size boxes cost $100 a year," she said tentatively. "Usually people use these just for . . . are you sure . . . ?"

She'd been trained not to ask so she didn't, but I answered her anyway. "Securities," I said folding my hands on the desk and looking straight at her. "My great-aunt died."

She looked at me for a long moment. Either I was one of the richer folk she had ever met, or I was a lying drug-runner storing my dope—I'd actually heard from dope dealers in my practice that they stored their dope in safety deposit boxes. I could almost see her thinking, "Could be either."

"Let me see how many we have available," she said and went off, glancing over her shoulder at my file boxes as she disappeared.

Why is nothing ever easy? I had to go to three branches to find enough safety deposit boxes, and by then I was considerably poorer and had missed another meeting in Psychiatry. Still I felt so relieved I almost felt light-headed. If this would shut down the flow of information to Willy, it was well and truly worth it. Besides, it was diagnostic. Any new info that Willy got after this point couldn't come from the files—well, any new information after I did one more thing—but first I had to go to Psychiatry.

I practically sneaked into the Psychiatry Department. I didn't want to run into anybody who was at the meeting I'd missed. How was I to explain where I'd been? "Well, actually, I think a sadist may have broken into my office and read my files, so I put them all in safety deposit boxes." Pa . . . ra . . . noia, they'd be chirping.

I could have put my private practice files in my Psychiatry office, but if Willy could break into my other office, surely he could break into Psychiatry. The department was housed in a building right across the street from the hospital, connected by tunnels, and the hospital was open twenty-four hours a day. In any event, my Psychiatry files were not going to be a problem. They were all housed in Records in the main hospital, and nobody could find them over there. Hell, I couldn't even get them half the time.

I thought I had successfully slipped in unnoticed—my secretary, Melissa, had not been at her desk when I went by—but I hadn't been in my office ten minutes when I heard a knock on the door. I turned around to see Toby, the Chair of Psychiatry, standing in the doorway. Whoa, the meeting hadn't been that important.

"Got a minute?" he said.

"Sure," I said with an attempt—a poor attempt—at enthusiasm.

Toby walked in and sat down on the couch. We had never gotten along. Toby had told me once I wasn't a team player, and I had thought it was a compliment. That miscommunication was the first of many. Toby thought I was a loose cannon who went her own way and did whatever she did without considering how it impacted the department. He told me once that I didn't care at all about the *financial* goals of the department, and his voice couldn't have been more outraged if I had mugged a little old lady on the street. I knew he thought I cared even less about *his* opinion than I did the financial goals of the department. How could he believe such things?

But Toby didn't know everything. He told me once I saw him as just a bureaucrat. I didn't see him as just a bureaucrat. I saw him as a complete pompous asshole who ought to be shot first when the revolution came. It comforted me to know I had *some* social skills after all.

I braced myself for a diatribe, but Toby was unusually subdued. I couldn't stand waiting. "I missed the curriculum meeting because I had an emergency with a client," I said. It was the only excuse Psychiatry wouldn't challenge. This lying business just got easier as you went along, and I was beginning to really get into the swing of it.

"That's not important," Toby said. "We'll send you the minutes."

Excuse me? What did he say? I was stunned into silence. It was a reasonable response. What was wrong with Toby? Was he sick?

"I wondered . . . you see people in your private practice?" I only did consults, teaching, and stupid committee-sitting in my role at Jefferson.

"Sure," I said, wary now. Oh, Jesus, don't let it be any relative of his.

He sighed. "My neighbor called. Their daughter goes to Jefferson U. It seems there was an . . . incident. Lucy was at a fraternity party, and she'd been drinking—quite a bit. She had sex with this boy at the party—willingly, she says. But she woke up, and she was being raped by several young men—three, I think, including her date." Toby looked away. Both of us knew if it hadn't been his neighbor, he would have likely said it was her own fault for getting drunk. He was not the most sensitive person I knew when it came to victims; unless it was a client of his. Toby did better by his own clients than he did by just about anybody else.

He went on. "She kept passing out and was too sick to do much to stop them, but she did keep saying 'no.' She's quite distressed." Toby looked acutely uncomfortable. I realized it couldn't have been easy for him to come to me, and I wasn't sure why he had. There were lots of good therapists in the department who saw victims in therapy.

"You want me to see her?" I asked.

"No, no," he said. "She already has a therapist. It's just that . . . the young man . . . well, he doesn't deny those men had sex with her. He says she consented."

"Not terribly likely," I said, "unless Lucy acts out a whole lot."

"Not at all," he replied firmly. "I've known Lucy all her life. She's very levelheaded. The thing is— her parents are distraught. Lucy wants the university to do something, and the young man is claiming that Lucy egged them on and invited it. Her parents are afraid what it will do to her reputation—and, I suppose, theirs. And Lucy is adamant that something has to be done."

"The police?" I said.

"Nobody's called them," he said. "Even Lucy doesn't want that kind of publicity."

I sighed. The police are much better at handling rape cases than universities are. But I knew, too, how few victims are willing to involve them.

"Toby, exactly what does Lucy want out of this? She isn't involving the police. Has she actually filed a formal complaint with the university?"

"She has," Toby said. "But, as you can imagine, the discipline committee has two conflicting tales in front of them. Lucy simply doesn't have any proof. I doubt they'll do much."

"What about the other guys?"

"Thus far, the young man won't name them, and Lucy doesn't know who they are."

"Even if the discipline committee agrees with her, what does she think they can do? The university isn't going to send anybody to jail. What does she think can happen?"

"She wants to know who they are, and she wants them gone—all of them—expelled. She says she doesn't want to walk around campus wondering if this guy or that one raped her. And"—he raised his eyebrows wryly—"she wants them to say they're sorry."

Pleeeease. People can be so naive about offenders. Did Lucy really think it would mean a damn thing if they could be coerced into apologizing? It is like asking a mugger to say "sorry."

"How can I help?" I had to admit my war with Toby seemed pretty minor compared to this. This whole thing could go very badly if it wasn't handled well, and Lucy, if she had already been traumatized, could get retraumatized pretty easily. Not to mention that if her family disagreed with what she wanted to do, there was the potential for a split that might never heal.

"The young man has agreed to go to a counselor for an evaluation, but I'm afraid—well—according to your last Grand Rounds, anyway—since most therapists are not trained in detecting deception, they often end up colluding with offenders—at least that was the implication." Implication, my foot. That was what I said, and I was merely stating the obvious.

Toby went on. "I'm referring to the research you presented on mental health practitioners and the fact that they are no better than the average citizen in detecting deception—which I gathered from your stats was not exceptional." Exceptional? The average person is no better than chance at detecting deception, and mental health is right in there with them.

"I thought . . . I just thought . . . you deal with offenders—I thought you might . . ." He took a deep breath and finally got to the point. "Would you take a look at this and maybe interview this young man and see what you think? See if there's anything you can do to prevent this from blowing up and hurting Lucy?"

Good grief. First of all it was a shock that Toby had actually listened to my last Grand Rounds. That alone was unbelievable. And he had learned something? I was incredulous, and then I realized how much it must have cost him to admit it. This pompous asshole was genuinely fond of Lucy and her family, and he wanted help for them badly enough to come with his hat in his hand to the one person in the department he personally disliked the most.

My opinion of Toby rose a notch. I had always taken him to be a hard-core narcissist, but narcissists never put anybody's needs above their own. Maybe Toby wasn't a total, dyed-in-the-wool, card-carrying narcissist like I had thought. Maybe he was only 99 percent narcissist, but he had a functioning 1 percent he could pull out of a hat when he needed to. It was something, anyway.

"I will," I said. "But you have to understand this. I will interview him, and I will use some of the new stuff I was talking about that detects deception. But—and it's a big 'but'—you have to know, Toby, I'll call it the way I see it. If I conclude he's telling the truth, I'll back him. And, even if I don't think he's telling the truth, the best I may be able to do is recommend a polygraph. Offenders don't usually confess without one."

"I have no doubt," he said dryly, standing up,

"that you will call it the way you see it. I have a lot of faith in Lucy, or I wouldn't be here."

I was still worried about Toby's expectations. "I don't work wonders, Toby," I said. "Just so you know, if he's lying, I may be able to figure it out, but he's not likely to change his story. And in the end my knowing he's lying isn't going to help a whole lot."

"Oh, just give it your best shot," he said with a wry smile, and I would have sworn there was a twinkle in his eye.

12

There was one more thing that had to be done, and the easiest way to do it was to call Adam. Not a chance. It might be the easiest way to deal with it, but I wasn't calling him. I had to know somebody else who could help.

I couldn't just open the yellow pages and look for a private eye. Some investigators are very skilled and others are a rip-off, but there wasn't any way to tell the difference from an ad. I wasn't even sure there were any in the Upper Valley who were any good. Rural New England just doesn't have a big need for private eyes. Everybody already knows who is having an affair and with whom. Finding out that kind of thing is what keeps most private eyes in business.

My problem wasn't whether my spouse was having an affair. My problem was whether Willy was bugging my office, and the grapevine couldn't help me very much with that. Damn it, if I were in the city, there were probably places that specialized in sweeping your office for bugs.

But of course. Danny. I didn't know him well, but I had been involved in a situation where the FBI was brought in. Danny was a senior special agent in the local branch, and he had been called in. When I worked with him he said he was retiring in a few months, and he thought he'd do a little private work after that. I opened the yellow pages and found him. He had a small ad that said nothing about the incredible credentials he had for that kind of work.

Danny was tall and lean and wore wire-rimmed glasses. He looked like an accountant—which actually he was, by training at least—but he was also somebody who had twice rescued U.S. hostages in South America. He was good on a negotiation team—he could talk to anybody and you couldn't help but like him—but he was always thinking a whole lot more than he seemed to be.

Both times in South America, Danny had got information on the phone with the kidnappers that was used to track them down and storm their hideouts. And he was also one of the people kicking down the door. All this I knew from Adam, who had a buddy in the FBI. It wasn't like Danny told you a whole lot about his work.

I had liked him, and we'd had lunch a few

times, but it was a little weird. He could be funny and likable, but he always managed to sit with his back to the door, and if you looked carefully, you'd see that he was always scanning the crowd—even when he laughed.

I'd thought about what it would be like to be in bed with him—my fantasy life is, shall we say, a rich and varied one—but I concluded he'd have to have the side of the bed farthest from the door, and he'd be constantly scanning the room even when he . . . laughed.

But a case was another matter. I dialed his number and waited. I smiled thinking he knew who I was before he answered the phone. What were the chances that Danny had the kind of Caller ID that gave you the person's name as well as their number? Oh, about 100 percent. I was gratified that his voice was warm when he answered.

"Hello, this is Danny Barns," he said.

"Danny," I began, "this is Michael Stone." He would never admit he had known who it was, and I wouldn't put him on guard by mentioning it.

"Doc," he said. "How are you?"

Private eye work was pretty boring, he said, but he did a little consulting on the side, and that was interesting. He didn't say to whom, and I didn't ask, but I had a feeling he was still tied up with the old agency in one way or the other, and it was probably very interesting. We went on like that for a few minutes, and then I got on with it.

"I want to hire you," I said. I was prepared to tell him the truth. I didn't think there was any other way to get him to take it seriously. "Somebody may be bugging my therapy sessions. It's somebody I know, and he's sent me a teasing message that sounds like he knows who my clients are. I don't know how he'd know, and I want to be sure he isn't bugging me."

"What phone are you calling from?"

I laughed. Adam had told me once how many people who thought they were being bugged called about it on the same phone they thought was bugged. "I'm calling from a different office."

"How do you know he bugged you? Could he have gotten into your records?" Danny asked.

"Maybe," I answered. "They're in the same office—this is all in my private practice—but I've got dead bolts, and there's no indication of a break-in. Anyway, I've put all the records in safety deposit boxes, just to be sure."

I was struck by how focused and intent he was. His voice was all business with none of the warm, fuzzy overtones I'd seen him use when he wanted to. This was a whole different side of Danny than the public one I'd seen before, closer to the bone, I thought.

"How much does he know?"

"Beats me," I said. "All he's done thus far is drop their names."

"That doesn't sound too bad," Danny responded, sounding less interested. "Could be he's just watching your office and following people."

"Maybe," I said. "But he's not someone who'd be satisfied with a cheap thrill. He's a planner. Likes long, drawn-out, meticulously scripted stuff. If names were all he had, he wouldn't have dropped them just like that. Whatever he's up to, this is only the opening volley."

There was a pause on the phone.

"What kind of 'scripted stuff'?" Danny asked finally.

"Uh, well, he's a sadist. Card-carrying. Not a nice man. And he's more or less told me some things he wishes he hadn't." And right now, I thought, I wished he hadn't either.

"Well, is it 'more' or 'less'?"

"Actually it's 'more.' A whole lot more than he'd like me to know now that he's been suddenly released from a lengthy and just incarceration by a group of judicial assholes I hope he moves next door to."

"How does today sound?" Danny offered. It looked like I had gotten his attention back, which was probably not a good sign. It was like being a "great case" in medicine. Anything that interests the doctors is bad news for the patients.

"Sounds good," I replied. "If you've got the time." He said he'd make the time, and we agreed to meet at my office first thing after lunch.

It turned out it was a big deal sweeping for bugs. Microphones are about the size of the tip of a pencil these days, and they can be anywhere. If someone gets access, he can put them in a wall socket, in the receiver of the phone, almost anywhere. Those two places are most common, Danny said, because bugs need power, and the only way not to have to keep coming back to change the batteries is to hook them directly into a power source.

Bugs can also be on any frequency. Great, so we had something that was practically microscopic in size and it could be on any frequency. But technology works both ways. Danny went all over the room with his bug detector, a small device that went up and down the frequencies. Nothing, nothing, and more nothing. Danny did it thoroughly. But nothing.

"It could be turned off," he said. "You can turn them on and off remotely. He could be just turning them on for the therapy sessions. How cautious is he?"

"I wouldn't say cautious," I said. "He's pretty egotistical, and he likes to brag. On the other hand, he's not exactly a fool, and he's telling me he's bugging me so he has to expect I'll look for it. This could be a problem if he's just turning it on for therapy sessions. I can't exactly ask a client to have a seat while I sweep for bugs."

"Sure you can," Danny said, "if you ask the

157

right client. You're about to have a new client. What kind of problem would he have that would interest your perp so he'd stay tuned?"

"Pedophilia," I replied without hesitating. "If he heard a pedophile in here, he'd stay tuned."

We made a plan. Danny would call and leave a message on my private practice phone asking for an emergency appointment. He'd identify himself as John, no last name, and ask if he could come in as soon as possible. He was having some thoughts, again, about children, and . . . well, he needed to talk to someone quick. I'd call back and set up an appointment at nine A.M. on Friday. My usual nine A.M. was Kiwi, someone Willy had mentioned. If he was bugging, he was bugging her. I'd cancel Kiwi and put in "John" instead, who'd show up right on time with a small device in his briefcase.

13

Alexander Hammil, Lucy's alleged tormentor, wasted no time in calling me. He sounded unbearably preppy over the phone, but I reminded myself preppies are obnoxious by nature, but that doesn't mean they are all rapists. I told him my terms, and he still wanted to see me, which meant he was either an arrogant little twerp or he was telling the truth.

I told him I would send him a letter outlining what we had talked about. Never, I knew, *never* trust what someone says on the phone in a situation like this. He'd have to sign my letter and bring it to the appointment with him before I'd see him. He seemed impatient with all of this and wanted to know if he could pick up the letter to speed things up. Sure, I said. I'd have it ready tomorrow and I'd see him in my private practice office on Friday.

I hung up the phone and sat down at my computer to write. I knew I could screw up myself and the situation royally if I didn't set things up properly:

Dear Mr. Hammil:

I am responding to your phone call requesting an appointment regarding the matter before the university's discipline committee. I am writing the conditions under which I will see you in order that there be no possibility that we might misunderstand each other. As you know, Lucy MacDonald has filed a complaint with the university saying that you and several other men had intercourse with her without her consent. She claims she was incapacitated from alcohol ingestion and passed out repeatedly. She states that she did tell you and the other men "no" and that you ignored her protests. You have asked me to evaluate you in terms of the charges against you.

I have explained that standard psychological tests will not determine whether or not a specific event happened and that there is no psychological profile of a rapist. I have agreed only to interview you but have been clear with all parties in this case that the greatest probability from this assessment is that I will be able to make no firm determination of any sort.

Ordinarily, a psychological assessment is confidential. However, in this case I have explained that I will only evaluate you if the results are available to both sides of the dispute. This is so whether I conclude that there is a possibility you committed the offense as alleged or whether I agree with your description of events or whether I can make no determination. You have agreed to sign a release of information prior to my evaluating you consenting to these terms.

I have explained to you that you should consult a lawyer prior to agreeing to this, and you have informed me that you have already consulted a lawyer and he has indicated his willingness for you to pursue this evaluation. Please be sure that your lawyer sees this letter and is fully informed of all conditions attached to this evaluation.

If this is agreeable to you, please sign this letter and the attached release of information and return both at or before your appointment time.

I gave the letter to Melissa for Mr. Hammil to pick up and called up Lucy. There wasn't anything I could really tell her until Hammil signed the letter—not even that he had an appointment—but I told her I had agreed to look into the matter. She sounded so relieved that I wondered what Toby had said about me. I asked her for a written statement of exactly what happened to her from the time she left her dorm until the time she got home. I told her I needed it by Friday with a signed release to share it with Mr. Hammil.

Lucy agreed readily. Probably doing something felt a whole lot better than doing nothing.

By Friday, my ducks were in a row. At nine A.M., "John" arrived right on schedule. At his request I pulled down the shades and only then did he take his bug detector out. "John" started wandering around the room scanning it with his bug detector, all the time talking about his preference for children, how long he'd been out of jail, and how much he didn't want to go back.

I was amazed. Danny couldn't have been any more convincing if he was sitting down and concentrating on what he was doing. I was the one who was having trouble concentrating. I was hearing one thing while at the same time Danny was wandering all over the room, climbing on chairs to check the ceiling, crawling on his hands and knees to check the floor, without ever missing a beat.

"Nothing," he finally said, after a full hour of crawling and climbing and checking and rechecking. "At least nothing that's turned on now."

"Good," I said, relieved. "So, it's wait-and-see time. Maybe it was just the records."

He turned to go and then stopped with his hand on the doorknob and turned back to me. Clients do that all the time. "Doorknob comments," we call them. They are invariably the most important part of the session. "You're in over your head," he said flatly. It didn't sound like he meant to be hurtful. It just sounded like a factual assessment of the situation.

I just shrugged. What could I say?

"There are other ways to play it," he said.

I shrugged again.

He paused a moment longer as though waiting for me to say something, but I didn't. I just didn't feel like trying to explain myself. Besides, I wasn't sure I could.

"All right," he said, "you want some advice?"

"Sure," I said. For some reason, advice from Danny didn't seem as threatening as Carlotta or Adam.

"Don't stay on the defensive. Don't sit around waiting for him to find you. He'll have everything on his side: the time, the place, the circumstances. If you're going to play this by yourself, at least find out where he is and go after him."

"Right. And what do I do when I find him?"

"Don't hesitate."

I didn't respond. I knew what he meant. Adam had once told me that a surprising number of women who have guns and know how to use them still get raped or murdered. They don't pull the trigger, he said. They hesitate too long. It sounded like Danny thought I might be one of them.

He handed me a card with a number on it. "You can always reach me with that," he said. It didn't look like the number in the phone book. Probably a mobile phone, I thought. Maybe a number not everybody has.

Then he handed me the bug-sweeping device. "Sweep before every session," he said. "Maybe he had a cold today. Maybe he took the day off. It doesn't mean he won't be back."

He left, and I sat thinking for a moment. I felt better but wasn't sure why. I hardly knew Danny. He had so many layers of onion skin, I wasn't sure if there was a real Danny under all of them. If there was, you'd never know it if you'd found it.

But that meant I could listen to his advice without feeling bad if I didn't take it, and he could give it without being that upset if I didn't take it. If I got myself killed, Danny would work that crime scene just like any other. Probably it was not a sign of major mental health that Danny was the only person I could even imagine talking to about this. To hell with it. Alexander Hammil was waiting.

I pulled up the shades—the room looked serious with the shades drawn, and I did not want

Mr. Hammil on guard—and walked out to greet him. He had arrived right on schedule, and I went out to the waiting room to find a tastefully dressed, good-looking young man sitting confidently on the couch.

He stood up when I walked in. Oh dear, this was going to be one of those "yes, ma'am, no, ma'am" things. "Hello," I said reaching out my hand. He shook it with exactly the right degree of firmness. "I'm Dr. Stone. I'm glad you came in, and hopefully we can clear this whole thing up today.

"I am running a little late, and I thought to expedite matters I would have you fill in a brief questionnaire for me. It just gives your version of what happened. I'm afraid it looks a bit long, but there's only one question on most of the pages, and it really would help, if you don't mind." I handed him a questionnaire and a pen and said quickly, before he had a chance to protest, "Would you like some coffee? Tea?"

He said "no," and I turned to go before he had a chance to think things over. I glanced back and saw him shrug and sit down. Well and good. The interview had begun.

The questionnaire was a simple one. It asked him to explain what he did on the day of the alleged rape from the time he got up until the time he went to bed. It asked him his opinion of how these charges came about. It asked him why

I should believe him, and it asked him if he was lying. I left the door of my office partly open so that I could walk by and see how he was doing.

He wrote furiously for twenty minutes, and then he put his pen down. I came out a couple of minutes later and collected the questionnaire. I offered him coffee again, and this time he accepted. I told him I needed a few minutes to look over the questionnaire.

I read through the questionnaire. All I wanted to know was whether he said he didn't do it. Over 90 percent of people lie by omission rather than commission. Unless you ask them a direct question, like "Did you do it?"—unless you force them to lie—the vast majority of people evade the question. For some reason it turns out to be hard to say, "I" (first person) "didn't" (past tense) "do that" (thing he was charged with).

I went to the last page first. It asked why I should believe him and whether he had been truthful in his statement. "Why should I lie?" he had written. "I was raised to tell the truth. It's not the sort of thing I would do." Uh-oh. There wasn't anyplace where he said he didn't do it.

I started from the first page of the questionnaire and read forward. There wasn't a single place where he denied it, if you read carefully. I read his description of the day. There were indications of missing time, changes in verb tenses, out of sequence information, and changes in pro-

166

nouns—all of the sort that were consistent with deception. We had a problem. He was a lying little twerp after all. But knowing it was different from proving it. For that I needed his help.

I walked out again and smiled. "Your questionnaire is very helpful," I said, "and it clears up a lot of things. I wonder if there is one more thing I could ask you to do. Here is Ms. MacDonald's story of what happened. Could you just take this red pen and cross through everything that she says that you don't agree with. Then on every line that you cross through, I want you to write a number and initial it. Then I want you to put that number on this clean sheet of paper and write what really happened."

I went through it a couple of times to make sure he had it. He was plenty bright, but he wasn't expecting this, and his mind was on other things—mainly impressing me—so it took him a couple of rounds to get it.

"If you'll just do this, I'm fairly confident we can clear this whole thing up today." He agreed. It sounded good to him, and he sat down to work with relish. When he had finished, I came back and asked him if he was sure he had crossed out everything that wasn't true.

"I think so," he said.

"Oh, no," I replied. "I don't want you to *think* so. I want you to be sure. Absolutely sure. I want to give you all the time you need to be *sure* you have crossed out everything you don't agree with. So take a few more minutes and go over it."

I turned to go, and he looked perplexed and sat back down. In a few minutes he knocked gently on the partly opened door. "I'm done," he said.

"Great," I said, standing up from my desk and walking over. "You're sure you've crossed everything out you don't agree with?"

"As far as I can tell," he said.

"Well," I said. "I don't want you to have any doubts. Sit back down and go over it again. Don't come back until you are really *sure* you have crossed everything out that isn't true and have written in *exactly* what really happened."

He was pissed off, but he sat back down. For this to work he had to be *committed* to what he had written, and I was prepared to go on indefinitely until he made that commitment.

This time when he came back he was ready for me. "I'm finished," he said. "I've gone over everything," he added quickly.

"You're sure," I said. "You've crossed out everything?"

"I'm sure," he replied. He did not want to sit down and go over this again.

"Come on in," I said and opened the door. I looked over the statement as he sat down. He had followed instructions carefully, and there were red lines on a number of places on Lucy's statement. Each one had his initials next to it and a number. I took the extra sheets of paper he had given me and went back and forth going from the numbers he had put on Lucy's statement to what he said really happened on the other pages. Finally, I shook my head.

"I'm not sure you and Ms. MacDonald mean the same things by some of your terms," I said. "Just so I'm sure. What do you mean by 'assault'?"

"Assault?" he said, surprised.

"Assault. I don't mean that you need to come up with a dictionary definition, but just roughly, say, what do you mean by the term."

"Well, I'd say assault involves inflicting some sort of violence on someone."

"Against their will?"

"Well, sure. Most people wouldn't agree to violence being inflicted on them," he said sarcastically and then caught himself.

"And what about 'passed out'?"

"Unconscious," he said.

"Would you write those down?" I said sweetly, handing him back the piece of paper where he'd written what really happened.

He paused for a minute to think it over, but couldn't see what the problem would be, so he wrote them down. "Would you sign them?" I asked.

"Why should I sign it?" he replied.

I rolled my eyes heavenward for him to see. "I've got material from you and Ms. MacDonald, and I want to be clear what's what, plus this whole thing is very emotional, and I don't want Ms. MacDonald, or even you later, to claim I made anything up. It's standard procedure. Is there something wrong with the definitions that you don't want to sign them? If there is, just change them."

He looked at them again and then signed them.

I picked up the statements again—Lucy's version and his rewrites—and looked back and forth from one to the other. I shook my head, perplexed, but kept reading. Silence filled the room. He started shifting in his seat. I just kept reading and let the anxiety build.

Finally, he couldn't stand it. "Is anything wrong?" he asked.

"I think so," I answered, but didn't elaborate. I went back to comparing the statements point by point.

He waited a few more minutes and then said, "What's wrong?"

I waited another long moment before I answered.

"Well, you and Ms. MacDonald agree on what happened. I wasn't expecting that."

"We agree? We don't agree. She says we raped her. I never said that."

"But," I said, holding the statements for him to see, "in Ms. MacDonald's statement she used the word 'assault' three times and 'passed out' five, and you didn't put a red line through any of them. You crossed out other things, but you never once crossed out those words." He looked quickly at Lucy's statement, and then he blanched. "I . . . I . . ."

"Well," I said while he sputtered, "here's what I think. I know there's a whole lot of truth in what you said. A whole lot. Well, let me put it this way." I took a piece of paper and drew a horizontal line with 0 on one end and 100 on the other. "I know you're not down here," I said, pointing at the zero. "I'd be willing to bet that you aren't anywhere close to here," I said still pointing at the zero.

"But I know, too, you haven't told me everything," I said, pointing at the 100. "Where would you say you are?" I asked, holding out the pen for him. "Just put a line at what percentage of the real story you've shared."

It was hard, at that point, to put the line at 100 percent because, for one thing, if he did he was admitting that Lucy had been correct in her use of the words "assault" and "passed out." He put a line at 95 or so, but that, too, was actually a confession of sorts.

"You know," I said looking at the mark, "I think I know what the problem is. I can understand your objecting to being called a 'rapist' just because you got drunk and things got a little out of hand. After all, a sex offender is somebody who jumps out of bushes.

"But the thing I don't understand is why you don't really tell your side of the story. If I don't miss my guess, you were almost as drunk as she was. I'd be willing to bet that, if she was incapacitated by alcohol, so were you. She can't really use alcohol as an excuse for her behavior and not yours—if you were really as drunk as I think you were.

"Maybe I'm wrong, but I don't think you really thought she meant it when she said 'no.' Hell, it was probably so weak, you might have thought she was just playing. Not to mention that you couldn't really control those other guys anyway."

He looked shell-shocked, and he was sitting completely still. The breeze from the window was ruffling his hair. Without that he'd have looked like a statue. "Is that true?" I asked. "Were you drunk too?" Then I realized my rhythm was off. I should have had him saying "yes" all along and getting used to answering the questions. Shit, a little thing like that could make the difference in his fessing up and not.

"So you were drunk?"

"Everybody was drunk," he said. "Roger just kept pouring vodka in the punch, and by the end it was about 100 proof. And you're right," he said rallying. "I was as drunk as she was." I had given him only one way out of the blind alley, and he had decided to take it.

"Had you just met her or did you know her?"

"I had just met her."

"So she was a pretty easy lady, because you had just met her and she had already hopped into bed with you," I said shaking my head. "I can see why you didn't take her 'no' seriously. You must have thought she was just fooling around. Was that it, or did you think she really wanted you to stop?"

"No, no," he said quickly. "I assumed . . . I just thought . . . well, I mean she was coming on to everybody downstairs, I was just the one who took her up on it." He was getting bolder now and moving into the new version I had offered him. "She was fucking my brains out, and I just thought, hell, she'd probably take on anybody. Besides, it's not like I invited them in."

"They came in on their own?"

"Sure," he said, "we were getting it on, and they just walked in and . . . and . . ." He lapsed into silence.

"At that point, what could you do?" I said helpfully. "There were three of them, and you were drunk to the max. If she couldn't do anything to stop them because of the alcohol, you probably couldn't either."

"I couldn't. Heck, I didn't really know what was going on, I was so drunk."

"What I don't get," I said, "is why you're taking all the heat by yourself. If all of this is true, why is it your word alone? Why don't you have these guys backing you up? Then it would be four to one instead of just your word against hers.

"You can do what you want to, but I'll tell you what I think. I think you'd better not walk out of here leaving a lie. Because once the committee knows you are lying about part of it, they're going to think you're lying about all of it.

"I think the real story is important. I think you need to tell them how drunk you were and why you didn't believe her 'no' was any more than playing games. I think you need to tell them that this wasn't any kind of plan and you didn't invite those guys in, they just walked in.

"Now, it's up to you; but if I were you, I'd tell the committee who the other guys were and get them to back up your story. Because if you don't, the committee is going to wonder why not. The only reason to hide them is to protect them if they're guilty. Otherwise, you'd want them backing you up.

"But you do what you want. I'm going to give you the pen and paper and the chance to set it straight. To be honest, with her that drunk, I don't really want to write a report that says you are lying. It makes it seem like it was all your fault.

"But read my lips on this one, Alexander—this is a one-shot deal. When you walk out of here, the evaluation is over and I write up whatever I have. Don't come back later and tell me you didn't get a chance to give your side of the story, because this is your chance right now. Here's the pen. Here's the paper. Take it or leave it. I'll write up a report that says you're lying if that's what you want me to do."

I handed him the pen and stood up quickly. "Let me get you some more coffee," I said and walked out before he had a chance to reply.

14

The moment Alexander Hammil left, I xeroxed his confession and left the office with it. If he had the sense God gave a mosquito, he would rethink his visit with me and head straight for his lawyer's office. His lawyer would pick up the phone to rescind Hammil's release before Hammil finished his first sentence.

I drove straight to my tiny A-frame—the one with the unlisted phone number—and sat down at the computer. It didn't take long to do the evaluation, given that he had confessed. He had rationalized and minimized to the max, of course, but he had admitted that the other men had walked in uninvited and Lucy had repeatedly said "no." He admitted, too, that he knew she was in and out of consciousness and too incapacitated to do anything except say "no." And, miracles of miracles, he had named his fellow rapists.

That didn't leave a whole lot for me to add. I gave him points for fessing up, but added that rationalization and minimization were typical of sex offenders and were strong predictors for relapse. If Hammil thought there was nothing wrong with doing it this time, he wouldn't think there was anything wrong with doing it the next time.

I called up Tom Gaines, Lucy's lawyer. The only thing I had told him before the eval was to be available on Friday morning. Tom hadn't asked any questions, but I was pretty sure he'd be there. His secretary answered on the first ring and put me through.

"Miss Michael," Tom said when he got on the phone. "How is my sweet little Southern flower doing this morning?"

"I can't believe you get away with that stuff up here," I replied, but I said it jokingly. I'm a sucker for a man with a Southern accent. I had accused Tom before of taking lessons to keep his accent pure. He played his Southernness to the hilt, and it lulled a lot of people into not taking him seriously, which was a big mistake.

"Actually, I'm quite well. And I think you will be too. It appears your client has been telling the truth."

"Now, Miss Michael, you know all my clients tell the truth," Tom said sardonically. "But this one for sure," he added.

"Well, it seems Mr. Hammil has had a change of heart and fessed up. I'm faxing you my eval, which includes a full written and signed confession."

"Wonders never cease," Tom said. "And you had nothing to do with this, I'm sure," he added.

"Nothing to speak of," I replied. "He just walked into my office and decided to tell the truth. But in case there is any charge of arm-twisting, I'm also faxing you the release he signed in advance, which suggests he consult a lawyer, etc. This release ought to be good for about another fifteen minutes, so I'll send this report just as soon as we hang up."

"Just so you know," Tom said. "I am never going to let any accused client of mine get within two hundred yards of you, so don't even ask."

"Why not?" I replied. "If they're all telling the truth."

I hung up the phone and faxed the report. When it went through I breathed a sigh of relief. I hated getting stuck with info I couldn't use. It made me completely crazy to see a case go down the tubes when I had information that would turn it around but couldn't use it because someone had rescinded a release. Without a valid release, nothing left my office no matter what. Idly I checked my e-mail. I wasn't expecting anything, but since I was sitting in front of the computer, why not?

There was a message from "partytime." So Willy had something to say. What was it this time?

I double-clicked on his message.

> Bravo! I am pleased to see my faith in you was justified. Exceedingly deft handling of that poor schlemiel. My Lord, these amateurs are so naive it's almost refreshing. Putty in your hands: truly an impressive display of your skills—and your own capacity for deception, which was surprisingly impressive.

What was he talking about? It could not possibly be Hammil. He hadn't left my office more than an hour ago, and I had just finished sweeping for bugs when he came in. For a moment I was confused.

> It does make me wonder, though. You are quite a manipulative little bitch, aren't you? And, perhaps, not as naive as you pretend? "Tell me, Mr. Willy. Teach me, Mr. Willy." A little bit of a Columbo routine, perhaps? What is it they say? "Payback's a bitch."

Shock was running through me. There wasn't anybody else Willy could be talking about except Hammil. But how could he have heard that conversation with Hammil? We had swept for bugs minutes before he came in. How could he possibly have known to turn the bug off for "John" and not for Hammil? Could he have some kind of device that Danny's bug sweeper couldn't pick up? Was that possible? I couldn't believe that. Danny would have the latest, most up-to-date gizmo.

I looked at the second paragraph. The tone of Willy's communications was changing. He was calling me names, devaluing me, making excuses for going after me. He was working himself up. Which meant, of course, that he was moving in. Willy was tired of foreplay and heading for the main event, whatever that was.

I read and reread the message. It felt like a locomotive was picking up speed and heading straight for me, and I was like some kind of small animal mesmerized by the light and standing stock-still on the track. Worse, I was a *confused* small animal, obsessing over how Willy was getting his information instead of getting off the track. But there wasn't any way off the track. And how *was* Willy getting the information?

It wasn't the records. So much for the safety deposit boxes. If it was a bug it was one an FBI agent couldn't find—which, knowing Danny, didn't seem possible. But it had to be a bug. He had to be turning it off and on, but how would he get the info to tell him when? Nothing made any sense. And he was escalating too fast for me to catch up.

The phone rang, and I jumped. I stared at it for a moment before I answered it. I picked it up, and for a panicky moment I held my breath, expecting it to be Willy on the other end. It was Marv, instead, and I let out my breath in relief. Jesus, I was spooked. "Michael," he said with annoyance in his normally warm voice. "I've been trying to reach you."

"I know, Marv," I said trying to pull myself back into the present. "I'm sorry. I've just been tied up with some weird stuff."

There were lots of people I would have bit my tongue off rather than say "sorry" to, but Marv somehow wasn't one of them. He was so benign I never felt defensive around him. Not that I'd tell him I had fallen off a horse, of course. That was going too far.

His tone changed instantly. "Weird stuff?" was all he said. Marv could get people to say more by saying less than anyone I knew, but I wasn't in the mood to fall for it.

"It doesn't matter," I said, still staring at the computer screen. "What's up?"

"I need to consult you on Ginger." Guilt flooded me immediately. The albatross I had handed over to Marv to get her off my neck was pulling on his. Maybe that's why I hadn't wanted to call him. Somehow I just knew from the few minutes I spent talking with her in Marv's waiting room that Ginger was doing her millstone routine.

"I'm happy to talk about her," I said with forced enthusiasm, "but, Marv, tell me right up front: Are you going to ask me to take her back?" That, of course, was the real reason I hadn't called. I transferred her to Marv in hopes that the dynamics would be different with a male. They obviously hadn't been, so Marv would be justified in saying he couldn't be of any further help.

"Your taking her back isn't the answer," Marv said gently. "But I have to come up with some kind of plan, and worse, I made a serious mistake with her, and I need to discuss it with you."

I sat up straight. Marv made a *serious* mistake. I was so surprised I didn't speak for a moment. All therapists make minor mistakes all the time, but Marv was handling Ginger as cautiously as he knew how, and he was the best therapist I knew. What kind of *serious* mistake could he have possibly made? Oh, Lord, don't tell me he crossed some kind of boundary with her or let her cross some kind of boundary with him.

Shit, if I hadn't been so self-absorbed and focused on my headache and on Willy, I'd have called him back immediately. Great, he needed help from me within days of my camping on his couch, and I hadn't even returned the phone call.

"Are you free now?" I said evenly. No sense in beating my breast on the phone with Marv. Why didn't I just go and give him the help he was asking for?

"Yes," he said, relieved. "Right now would be fine."

He said it quietly, but somehow the way he said "right now" made me think it was all the more urgent. "I'll be right there," I said and hung up the phone. I grabbed my fanny pack and strapped it on. Willy's latest communication had left me no doubt that I'd be carrying it for a while. I picked up my car keys and started for the door. But fate just wasn't cooperating. As badly as I wanted to go see Marv, I never made it.

15

I almost did. I was almost out the door when the phone rang. I started to keep going, but then I thought it might be Marv. Maybe he wanted me to bring something with me. Maybe he was calling to tell me Ginger was camped outside his office door again and we should meet somewhere else. That turned me around. I picked up the phone, but it was Melissa, my secretary.

"Michael, I called the other office, but you weren't there. I'm sorry to bother you at home."

"No problem. What's up?"

"You had a very strange call from someone named Harvey, and I thought you might want to know about it. He said his neighbor was acting very peculiarly, and he needed to talk to you right away. I said I'd try to reach you. Do you want his number?"

I took it. Harvey was Camille's neighbor, and I

184

thought guiltily that I hadn't yet called Camille to reschedule our appointment. She had gotten out of the hospital over the weekend, but I had been trying to keep my head from falling apart on Monday and had canceled our appointment. I should have called by now to reschedule, but I had gotten caught up dealing with Lucy's rapist. The biggest problem with being a therapist is all the balls you have to keep up in the air.

I called Harvey. "Michael," he said, sounding very relieved, "I don't know what to do about Camille." Harvey knew she was my client, since we had gotten permission from Camille to call him when she was in the hospital.

"What do you mean?" I said. "What's going on?"

"I haven't seen her very much since she got out of the hospital. I've been trying to keep an eye on her, but she hasn't been out all that much, not even to walk the dog." Harvey was the kind of neighbor everybody should have. He had been aghast when we called him from the hospital and he realized Camille was that ill and had no friends or relatives around.

But Camille hadn't grown up in the Upper Valley. She had only moved here a few years ago, after the attack, and she had been a recluse ever since. How do you make friends when you never leave the house and never talk to anyone? The only people she had talked to had been a couple of therapists whom she had seen before me—neither of whom had lasted very long. Both therapists had wanted Camille to talk about the assault, and Camille had left therapy because she couldn't do that without falling apart.

As for relatives—Camille didn't have any to speak of. She had told me her mother died a few years ago, and she hadn't seen her father since her parents' divorce when she was twelve. There weren't any siblings, and if there were extended family, she didn't know about them.

She survived on disability—which, in her case, was well deserved. She truly couldn't work, and through no fault of her own. But if someone didn't work and didn't go out socially, they could live a hell of a long time in a place without knowing anybody.

I thought briefly of Camille's former life. There had been plenty of friends in Boston, but she had left all of them behind. She was fearful that if anybody knew where she had gone, somehow the perp would find out. It didn't make sense, but then trauma makes the fear center in your head the size of a watermelon, and that doesn't leave a whole lot of room for logic.

Harvey went on. "Then a little while ago, she started screaming, just screaming. Michael, it was chilling. I started to call the police, but then it stopped, and I wasn't sure I should. I didn't want to freak her. So I went over.

"The whole place was quiet. I knocked, but

nobody came to the door. It was so silent it gave me the creeps. I thought all dogs barked when they heard something. I just got back, and I wasn't sure what to do, so I decided to call you first. Should I call the police . . . or the hospital . . . or somebody?"

I considered it. What could the police do? There would likely be a confrontation with Keeter. If Camille was in a major flashback and couldn't call her off, Keeter wouldn't be likely to let strange men anywhere near Camille.

This would not be a good thing. The police would have to do something to Keeter to get to Camille, hopefully temporary but maybe permanent. Keeter was Camille's only sense of safety. If anything happened to Keeter, Camille would be in even worse shape than she was now. And, even if the police only did something temporary to Keeter, it would confirm Camille's greatest fears that Keeter could be gotten around.

Calling the hospital wasn't even an option. They had zippo for outreach. Harvey could call the community mental center. They had outreach, but they didn't know Camille. And they didn't know Keeter. Actually, the problem was more that Keeter didn't know them, any more than she knew the police.

"No," I said. "I'll check on her. Give me the address, and I'll swing by." I put the words out there and then immediately wanted to swallow them. I hate going to clients' houses. It seems like a kind of boundary crossing to me. It always has an impact on the relationship. It makes it more social and less professional.

But what could the police or mental health guys do if they came? Even if they didn't shoot Keeter, no doubt they'd haul Camille off to an inpatient unit, which would lead to her sitting around an emergency room for seven hours or so while people fought about what to do with her. If Camille could stay at home, she should. But I had no doubt she was exhibiting a level of craziness that would keep the police, particularly, from seeing it that way. If they came, they'd surely take her in.

"Michael," Harvey said. "Why isn't there somebody looking after her? Did the hospital just release her with nobody?"

"Oh, Harvey," I said. "You've missed about fifteen years of so-called progress. You know all those people eating out of trash cans and sleeping in dumpsters in every city? A whole lot of them are mentally ill. This society has taken the "enlightened" position that the mentally ill can look after themselves. Hospitals literally put people on the streets who have no money, no place to sleep, and who are hearing voices.

"It's supposed to be about 'least restrictive environments,' but it's about money and what it costs to feed and house them." I had hated community care for the mentally ill since it first came in. Mostly, it meant no care at all.

"But this is the Upper Valley!" Harvey's voice had outrage in it. I knew from the waitresses at Sweet Tomatoes that Harvey was a gentle soul who paid staff fairly and treated them well.

"Makes no difference," I said. "We don't have as many mentally ill as cities do, but hospital mental health units are pretty much revolving doors everywhere. Managed care won't pay for extended stays, and anyway, these guys rarely have any kind of insurance. People go through those revolving doors here like everywhere else."

Harvey was silent, probably speechless. If he thought this was bad, I should tell him about all the abused children I'd seen returned to violent, even sadistic parents under the rubric of "family preservation." "Child annihilation" was more like it.

I hung up and thought about what I had just agreed to. I just hated to go to clients' houses, but what could it hurt? I'd just assess the situation on my way to see Marv. I couldn't do a lot for Camille but see that she was safe and not suicidal. But then again, that wasn't small potatoes. I called Marv to tell him I had to make a stop on the way and walked out.

Camille's house was a small two-story colonial with a fenced-in yard a few blocks from the main street of town. All the towns in the Upper Valley are small enough that there is no such thing as a town house, but Camille had gotten as close to Main Street as she could. I had expected to find something like that. The remoteness and isolation of the country wouldn't appeal to her right now.

Thank God for the fenced-in yard. It wouldn't necessarily keep Keeter in—the fence wasn't that tall—but it would keep kids from wandering into her territory.

I walked around to the back of the house before I knocked just to see the whole setup. There was a park behind the houses on that block, a good place to take Keeter to play. No doubt that had made the house more appealing, since that tiny yard wouldn't do much for a dog that big. Not that Camille would have been letting her run much lately. She probably had poor Keeter's collar glued to her wrist.

Harvey had been leaving for work, so I didn't stop by. Restaurant owners, or Harvey anyway, didn't seem to fly into work at eight o'clock like the rest of us. He was always wandering in just in time to get ready for the lunch crowd. His wife taught school, so I knew she wouldn't be there either. I walked up to Camille's house and knocked on the door.

No answer. No bark.

I tried the bell.

No answer. Where was Keeter?

I couldn't just leave Camille like that, knowing she was inside. What if she had hanged herself, it suddenly occurred to me. Jesus, I should have thought of that earlier. I was going to beat myself up forever for not letting Harvey call the police if something terrible had happened to Camille.

But then again, maybe she was just afraid of who might be at the door.

"Camille," I called out. "It's Michael. I need to talk to you."

There was silence.

"Camille, answer the door. I really have to know you're all right."

Still silence.

I started to threaten calling the police—I didn't really have a choice if she wouldn't let me in—when I heard, "Michael?" The voice was faint, but it was there. At least she hadn't hanged herself. It was something. "Is it really you?"

"It's really me, Camille. Please open the door."

I heard the sound of footsteps. Camille hadn't been far, and the door opened up just the length of the chain inside. Camille peered out. "Are you alone?"

I wanted to say, "No, I brought a serial killer with me," but thought better of it. I have that weird sense of humor that kicks in at tense times, but I try to keep a leash on it. Not everybody appreciates it, and I was pretty sure Camille wouldn't.

"Of course," I said. "I'm alone." She still seemed to hesitate, but then she closed the door and took off the chain. She opened it slowly, and I stepped in.

The first thing I noticed was Keeter in a crouch about ten feet from the door. She was so tense her muscles were bunching. She looked like an ad for a weight-lifting magazine for dogs. "Meet Ms. Canine Olympia. Tell us, Ms. Keeter, how do you maintain that rippled look?"

"People," she'd say. "Breakfast of champions."

I had to admit the crouch looked like the kind dogs spring from, and the only thing that looked remotely like a target was me.

But Keeter knew me, I reminded myself. She should, anyway. I took a deep breath and started to approach her to say "hello," thinking once Keeter recognized me she'd go off red alert.

"Michael," Camille said sharply. "I wouldn't do that."

I stopped. "Why not?" I asked.

"She's a guard dog. I mean really. She used to protect a service station at night after it was closed. She's trained to let someone get *in* the door and then attack. She's really bad about her territory. Just don't move toward her. When she's in that frame of mind she feels trapped if you move toward her."

I backed up. On second thought maybe I wouldn't say hello. "Why doesn't she bark?" I asked.

"Training," Camille answered. "She was trained

to stay quiet and ambush an intruder." I halfway turned back to Camille. I couldn't bring myself to fully turn my back on that coiled spring on the floor, but the more important thing was Camille and the fact that she was making sense.

I noticed for the first time that she was clutching a bottle of pills. "What are the pills?" I asked tensely. Maybe my suicidal fantasies weren't so off after all.

"Haldol," she said. "I thought he was here, and I just lost it. I heard him. I finally got it together enough to take Haldol. I took double," she said sheepishly.

No wonder she was making sense. "Do you remember screaming?" I asked.

"No," she said and paused. "I heard some screaming, but I didn't realize it was me. Was it me?"

"It was you," I said. "Your neighbor Harvey called me. He was afraid you needed help, and nobody came to the door when he knocked."

I kept checking in on Keeter out of the corner of my eye as I talked. She looked like she was relaxing somewhat. Her muscles didn't have that tightly clenched, one-more-inch-and-you're-mine look.

"Oh," she said. "I heard someone at the door, but I just thought it was him coming back." I knew who "him" was by now: the sweet soul who had kidnapped her, taped her face and head, no doubt raped her, but also probably tortured her. I didn't know the details, but I knew they were bad enough to have almost destroyed the woman in front of me.

"No," I said, "it was just Harvey. What happened?"

"He was back again," she said. "The only way I can cope with it is by eating these," she said holding up the Haldol. "Sometimes I just wish he'd kill me and get it over with."

"Let's sit down," I said, "and talk for a minute." Camille sighed and then let me into the living room. Keeter looked better, but I took a wide berth around her just in case. Some friend she was. Enter the wrong door and you're morning snack.

"Camille," I said after we were seated, "do you really believe it was him and not a flashback?"

"I don't know," she said. "It didn't seem like a flashback. The flashbacks have always been to things that really happened. I mean, I'd wake up and see him duct-taping my face—I could feel it—or that he was . . . he was . . ."

"Stop," I said. "Better not to think about it. It's been a bad morning, and you could trigger another whatever-you-want-to-call-it. But what do you mean? How is this different from the other ones?"

"These are never about what he's *done*," she said thoughtfully. "He just keeps threatening what he's *going* to do."

194

"It isn't a replay of things that happened before?"

"No," she said. Keeter had come in and lain down at her feet. I guess she had finally decided I wasn't there to rob the gas station or mug Camille. Camille scratched her head. Keeter laid her head on Camille's feet and turned her belly up. It was a side of Keeter I hadn't seen. It was a side of Camille I hadn't seen either. She was thinking a whole lot more clearly than she usually was after a flashback. Maybe she needed to double her meds.

She was also a better psychologist than me. She was right. A flashback was *always* a repeat of the past. Always. That was the point of a flashback. The brain regurgitated images of the trauma. It didn't make up new possibilities. And Camille had told me about this before. The voice had said it would be worse next time, but I hadn't thought about how *unlike* a flashback that statement was.

"And there's another thing," Camille went on. "He's just *talking*. I can't see him."

"What do you mean you can't see him?"

"In all the other flashbacks I saw him. I saw it happening all over again, over and over. This is just a voice out of the dark. He gets in. I don't know how, but he gets in." She sighed hopelessly. "I don't expect you to believe me."

But I was starting to wonder. Flashbacks aren't

195

auditory. They may have voices in them, but they are mostly visual. Unless she was having a psychotic break. Psychotic hallucinations are usually auditory. There is no reason you can't have a psychotic break on top of PTSD. Except she was too old. Most psychotic breaks occur when people are younger than Camille. Not to mention that if this trauma was going to trigger psychosis, why hadn't the attack itself triggered it? Why now?

It occurred to me for the first time that her attacker might really be back. What if the same kind of thing was happening to her that was happening to me? What if she was being stalked by a sadist? I hadn't even thought about it because Camille had terrible PTSD and a long history of flashbacks. I just thought it was more of the same.

But a good percentage of sadists do come back. They call their victims or watch them. The only good data on this came from FBI studies of interviews with caught sadistic rapists and even serial killers—serial killers don't kill everybody they attack, particularly before they get into a killing pattern.

In the interviews they described frequently coming back after the rape. They'd stand outside their victims' houses and watch them or call them on the phone just to hear their voices. It's kind of a reverse form of PTSD. The perps get emotional flashbacks too, but they *want* to relive the memories. The reliving brings an aftertaste of the violent high all over again.

Too, some of them actually attack the same woman twice. The number of women who have been attacked more than once by the same stranger is larger than most people know.

I hadn't considered it partly because I was dealing with Willy, and it seemed too bizarre to have both of us stalked by a sadist at the same time. Yet two rare cancers might be unlikely for an internist to run across in the same week, but how unlikely is it for a specialist? And what was my specialty? Trauma.

But even if the perp really was back, how was he getting into her house? Why wasn't Keeter going bananas?

"Tell me about Keeter," I said. "How did you get her?"

"I met a guy who owned this string of protection dogs," she said. "He had a route. He dropped them off at service stations and department stores and stuff at night and then picked them up in the morning. I tried to get a dog through a regular trainer, but they wouldn't sell me one because they didn't think I could handle him."

Good thinking, I thought, but I didn't comment. Reputable dealers try not to sell dogs to people who are going to let them eat small children. And Camille had surely been in the kind of shape that would have told any vaguely responsible person she couldn't handle an attack dog. "So how did you meet this guy?"

"By accident," she said. "I told a guy I knew at a local service station that I was looking for a protection dog. I used to take my car there, and we were just talking one day while I had some work done on the car. I was getting ready to leave. I just couldn't stay in Boston anymore after the . . . Well, I kept thinking he knew where I lived and he'd come back. I hardly told anybody I was going. I was afraid he'd find out somehow."

"He," I knew, was always the perp. She never called him anything else. He was on her mind so much she always thought I knew whom she was talking about when she said "he."

"I had to have the car fixed. I didn't tell Chris what happened, but he probably figured something. I always took my car there so I knew him before, and afterward, I was a lot . . . different." Her eyes started filling up. There was always the ongoing grief for who she had been.

"You know," she said as the tears started, "I've lived alone since I was sixteen. I never had a problem. My mother was depressed all the time, and she drank. I could never get her to stop even though I tried all the time. I couldn't bring anybody home because Mom would be staggering around in her nightgown, and finally I just left. I put myself through school, and I did everything by myself. I told the other nurses it was ridicu-

lous to need an escort to the parking lot. I just
didn't know . . . I never . . ."

Camille cried for a few minutes, and we were
both silent. I had never met the woman she was
describing, although something about Camille
had always shone through the jumble of fear and
anxiety that surrounded her. There was some core
of all that she used to be still there, but it was
very far away.

"Chris introduced you to the trainer?" I said
softly. A part of me wanted to keep talking about
her life before the cyclone, and today she could.
But my anxiety about the perp being back was
growing, and if he really was back, she might not
have a life to talk about if I didn't find out more
about how he was getting into her house.

"Chris called him and called me back to say I
should talk to him. He thought he'd sell me a dog
if I really wanted one. He said he wasn't a regular
dealer, just a guy who had some dogs he rented
out to service stations and places like that."

It didn't surprise me that it had been that easy
to get a dog. While dealers are attuned to ethical
issues around guard dogs, there is a whole
netherworld out there of macho types who own
guard dogs or breed a few and who think everybody should have one. Some are survivalists or
military wannabees or whatever.

"Did Chris use the guy's dogs in his service station at night?"

"Sure," she said. "That's how he knew him."

"Did Chris know Keeter?"

"I don't know," she said. "Why?"

I ignored the question. "Why was the trainer willing to give up a dog?" I asked. "He didn't usually sell them, did he? I mean, you said he wasn't a regular dealer?"

"No, I don't think so, but, well, Keeter wasn't behaving too well. Wait a minute. Chris did know her, because I remember him telling me I should think twice about getting her. He said she wasn't too stable. I forgot all about that. But the other guy said she just needed somebody with her. He said there was a difference in being alone all night in an empty building and being with an owner all the time."

"What was she doing that was so bad?"

"I don't know for sure," she said. "I think she was maybe a little too aggressive or something. I think Chris said she gave the clerk a hard time when he tried to open the store in the morning. Chris said he didn't have any trouble with her, but he couldn't be there every day. I don't care what she did," she said defiantly. "I had to have a dog, and nobody else would sell me one."

"Was she already trained as a seizure dog?" I said doubtfully.

"No, I took her in for training right after I got her. There was a training center in Manchester. Actually," she said sheepishly, "she didn't do that well. She didn't really graduate, but I needed a guard dog more than a seizure dog, so I kept her. I just tell people she's a seizure dog," she said looking down, "so they'll let her come with me. Otherwise, there're a lot of places that won't let her in, but she didn't really get her papers.

"She might do the right thing, I mean if I had a seizure, but she might not. The guy said she was unreliable."

I looked at Keeter again. Great. She was an unreliable guard dog who'd had a little training in seizures and was unreliable there too. What the hell would she do in an emergency? Who knew?

So where did all that leave us? The guy who sold her the dog was out as the perp. She hadn't met him before the attack, and it would be too much of a coincidence for her to meet him afterward. But Chris wasn't out. Chris was somebody whom Keeter knew and who could walk into a building that Keeter was guarding without her taking his throat out. That had been their relationship. Keeter guarded the gas station until Chris got there.

And the fact that Chris knew Camille before the attack fit. A lot of attackers know their victims casually. That's how they target them. Camille wouldn't have recognized him. She had told me the perp had been wearing a ski mask, and somebody wouldn't recognize their grandmother if she were wearing one of those things.

But wouldn't Camille have recognized Chris's voice if she knew him? Maybe, maybe not. People who are abducted are so frightened they hardly recognize their own voices, and Camille had only known him slightly.

If Chris were the perp, what a stroke of luck he had. Camille comes in, and he gets to gloat over how horrible she looks. Then she tells him she wants a guard dog, and he puts her on to one who knows him and who won't react if he walks in on her turf.

But I didn't know Chris was the one. For one thing, he had warned her against Keeter. Still, whoever it was, one thing was for sure: Keeter wasn't perp-proof. There were people who could get into the house without her raising a fuss—her trainer and Chris, for starters. Not to mention that everybody who knew Keeter had rated her as unreliable.

"Did Chris know where you were going?" I asked.

She thought a minute. "I don't think he knew exactly. I told him I was going to New England. No, wait, I remember him saying he used to live in Vermont, and we started talking about it, so I think I did tell him the general area. Why do you ask?"

Uh-oh. I needed to talk to Adam right away. This might not be a job for a therapist after all. If there was a perp outside her head and not inside it, it was strictly a job for the police. I had zero expertise in catching perps.

But that, of course, was what Adam had been telling me all along about Willy. Willy was surely outside my head as well as inside it. But this was different, I reasoned. It made sense for me to turn Camille's case over to Adam and not mine. Unfortunately, the voice in my head failed me when I tried to think why.

Well, shit, just face it. This was different because it wasn't me. This was about Camille. And she didn't sleep with Adam, and she didn't have a crazy, prickly, porcupine thing about her boundaries, and most of all, maybe, she wasn't Mama's child.

There was that other thing too. I knew I couldn't tolerate Adam's rescuing me twice. I'd resent hell out of him for it. Mama's child. Unfortunately, I was truly Mama's child.

I got some paper from Camille and wrote out a couple of permission forms. Camille had had a so-so experience with the Boston police after the attack. One officer had been pretty sensitive to her confused state, and the other had pushed her to give all the details. When she couldn't—she dissociated when she tried to talk about it—he had been impatient with her and finally left.

Some progress has been made in twenty years of feminists harping about the way rape victims are treated. Cops no longer routinely hook victims up to lie detector tests, and some places even have women cops do much of the interviewing. But the truth is, there are far more rapes than women cops available to interview victims, and old attitudes still die hard. Camille's experience with the police had been better than that of most rape victims in a big city environment.

And, in all fairness, Camille would have been impossible to interview. She was found nude, in a dog kennel. She was dissociative and couldn't talk about what happened without losing it and becoming completely incoherent. Cops are oriented toward catching perps, and Camille wouldn't have been any help at all. They would have had a nasty crime on their hands with an eyewitness who was useless to them. I could see a cop getting frustrated with that.

I told Camille what I had in mind and she agreed. She still saw the police as a help, and she didn't mind my bringing Adam in or contacting the two police who had investigated the attack before. But she never would have called them on her own. The perp loomed too large in her mind. She didn't think anybody could stop him.

I left uneasily. If Camille was in danger, I didn't like to leave her there, not even with Keeter, since Keeter wasn't proving to be too helpful on this one. But even if Keeter did know Chris, I reminded myself, and Chris was the perp, that didn't mean she would let him *attack* Camille.

Camille was her owner now, and Chris had never been. She had been trained to let Chris into a building she was guarding, but she had never been trained to let him attack her handler.

And all training aside, there was the business of Keeter's genes. A rottweiler had protect-your-owner written into its DNA.

For once I used the car phone. I have a prejudice against car phones, but I had finally bought one when Adam threatened to give me one if I didn't. I had explained my prejudice to him—buy a car phone, and the next step is a phone in the shower, and soon there is *no* time you aren't connected to the world. I didn't like being connected to it as much as I was, and I surely wasn't looking for more—but he hadn't been impressed.

He just said he had a prejudice too, a thing about friends of his who routinely confronted sex offenders riding around alone without car phones, not thinking for one second about whom they were dealing with. What was I going to do, he had asked, if I were followed and run off the road—look for a pay phone?

I didn't like using it, but I wanted to be able to say enough alarming stuff to the dispatcher that she would track Adam down if he wasn't there, and I didn't want to do that in front of Camille. But I was in luck. He was there and free, and she put me through to him. I told him I had a client with a problem that might be outside her head rather than inside, and I needed to talk to him about it. He said to come on in.

He was writing something when I walked through the open door of his office. "Hi," I said softly.

He looked up and smiled. "Come on in," he said and pulled up a chair for me. The smile didn't go away when he sat back down, and for a moment I remembered how I loved to touch the smile creases in the corners of his eyes with my fingertips. I knew all the planes and creases of his face by touch.

For a moment there was silence, and the atmosphere started to pick up a charge. I remembered Hawaii and the feel of the sand on my bare back. I remembered my loft and the moon shining through the skylight across his bare chest. I remembered his fingers sliding between . . . I looked at him. I saw the look in his eye and knew he was remembering something too, whatever it was.

"Don't start," I said.

Adam didn't speak.

"I'm here on business," I said.

Adam still didn't speak.

"Look, if you're going to—" But Adam interrupted.

"Michael," he said, "I haven't said anything."

"Oh," I said. "That's right. . . . Never mind."

How could this man discombobulate me like

that? I shouldn't let myself get in the same room with him.

"Just projection," I said, sighing. "I'm talking to myself."

"Keep talking," he said.

"Never mind," I replied.

I started to tell him about Camille. Adam didn't seem to be paying that much attention—whether he admitted it or not, he had a look in his eyes I knew pretty well—until I started talking about why I was no longer sure she was having flashbacks. A lot of cops would have dismissed what I said—I had zero for hard evidence—but Adam wasn't a lot of cops.

He got very focused, and wherever he had been, he wasn't anymore. I told him about Chris, and he got even more interested. He knew as well as I did that sadists could and did return. If there was a way to get around Keeter, then what Camille was saying wasn't all that improbable.

"How sure are you?" he said, finally.

"That they're not flashbacks? I don't know. They just don't sound like flashbacks. How do you have a flashback to something that never happened? I guess I'd have to say pretty sure."

"How do you know she isn't making it up?"

"The whole thing? From the beginning? As in Munescheusen? Oh, I'd stake a lot on that. You can't fake the way she was in the hospital. Pupils dilated, shallow, rapid breathing, skin color changes. She was in a full-blown panic attack."

"Crazy?"

"Crazy? As in paranoid? And has panic attacks because she believes what she says?" Actually, I hadn't even thought about it, but it didn't sound right.

"I don't know. The content of her delusions isn't right. I don't know why, but paranoids all have the same kinds of delusions: People are broadcasting through their teeth; aliens have planted a transmitter in their skulls. This isn't anything like any paranoid delusion I've ever seen."

"Yeah, but they do have a thing about people going after them."

"True," I had to admit. "I guess I can't rule it out completely, but I don't buy it. I'd have to think about why." I paused while I tried to figure out why I was so sure it wasn't paranoia.

"Paranoids have this suspicious way about them," I said finally. "They check your office. They decide you're one of *them*. They keep looking for hidden recorders. I don't get any of that from Camille.

"But it's all the more reason to check with the original cops on the case. I can't say it's impossible. But I'd say if the original incident happened like she said, there's not a lot of reason to think she's making this one up." I knew that was where

Adam would start anyway. He'd want to get the original crime reports and find out how far the Boston cops had gotten on solving the case.

"Now, Michael, don't get upset. False Memory Syndrome?"

I rolled my eyes. "Adam, we've gone through this. The false memory zealots have zero—and I do mean zero—evidence there is any such thing. And there is a whole lot of evidence—as in tons—that there isn't. But even if you were a dyed-in-the-wool false memory crazy, you wouldn't apply it to this case. This is out-of-family-stranger attack. Not exactly the kind of case that's a candidate for the false memory bullshit.

"Besides, I really don't think the issue is going to be the original attack. I have a feeling Boston will confirm that she was found just like she said. I think the issue is going to be whether that attack did something to her so profound that this guy is back only in her head. Even by the backlash's reckoning, that wouldn't be a false memory issue."

"I'll check it out," he said, "and call you."

I gave him what I had. Bit by bit, I had gotten little pieces of what happened from Camille. She knew the exact date that she had been abducted, and, of course, she knew the name of the hospital where she had worked. She wasn't as sure where she had been found. Everything immediately after the attack was hazy, but she remembered one of the detectives' names very clearly. She had dissociated by focusing on his name badge when he was hassling her.

I left reluctantly; I just felt like hanging around. A part of me wanted to say, "So your lover is a porcupine. So?" Maybe I wanted to say, "All right, so you *could* find a less prickly lover. But could they hit the jumper from the corner?" Maybe most of all I wanted to just say, "Dinner?" But I didn't say any of it. I just said, "See ya." I figured he knew what I meant. No sense in bela-boring things.

On the way out I thought about it. Once in a while I used to pick up those books that said things like "Men are from Mars; Women are from Venus." They always made me feel like I was from Pluto. I didn't seem to fit.

Things were fine up until fifth grade. Then all the other girls started sitting on the rocks at recess and combing their hair. Boring, boring, and more boring. I couldn't cope with the rocks, so I played tight end on the football team. Needless to say, there weren't a lot of other girls playing.

I knew what I was doing. I was rationalizing the fact that it would kill me to sit down and talk to Adam about our relationship. Some part of me knew I should, but I just didn't want to. And Adam was only slightly better than I was at that sort of thing. Although, come to think of it, when a hard-nosed police chief was better than I was at talking about feelings, it could be I was pretty far out there. Well, somebody had to hold down one end of a continuum. Otherwise the normal curve wouldn't work.

I glanced at my watch. I was running a little late for Marv. As in hours late. It was getting on in the afternoon, and late afternoon is prime time for therapists to see clients. Adults work and kids go to school, so the late afternoon hours are usually the busiest.

Marvin was booked, his secretary told me when I arrived. That didn't surprise me, but the note on my desk did. "I'm seeing clients till eight. Please don't come over to the house afterward or any time during the weekend. I don't really want to talk on the phone about this either. I think it best to wait until Monday and talk to you at work. Could we meet early Monday? Name a time and I'll reschedule whatever I have to. Give the message to Rochelle."

Don't come over to the house? Name a time and he will reschedule? Reschedule a client for the sake of a meeting? That just didn't happen. Don't call. Something pretty serious was going on, but I couldn't think of any scenario that would have Marv telling me not to come by the house to talk about it. Did he have a lover I didn't know about who didn't want company? Domestic problems?

But Marv didn't have a lover except for his

211

paintings—I was pretty sure of that—and try as I might, I couldn't think of a single painting that would object to my dropping by.

And Lord, it could not be, no, it could not be somehow that Ginger was staying at his house. Even if Marv had a psychotic break, he wouldn't permit such a thing . . . I hoped. I reminded myself of the numerous times I'd been in cases where people were astonished at some of the things their friends or family members had done. Nobel prizewinners and rock stars molested kids. Presidents of universities made obscene phone calls. And every one of those people had other people who loved them and absolutely could not believe they would do such a thing.

Almost 10 percent of male therapists get sexually involved with clients. It isn't like it is even that uncommon. But not Marv. If Marv had made a mistake anywhere near that serious, I was going to set records for astonishment.

But if it wasn't that, then what? Why didn't Marv want me over to his house? The world was making less and less sense every goddamn day.

16

As long as I was at Psychiatry I might as well tie up some loose ends. I called Toby and caught him between power lunches. His secretary put me through right away. Amazing how accessible he was when you were doing him a favor. "Toby," I said. "This is Michael. I can't tell you any of the details because I don't have permission, but things worked out pretty well in that case you referred me. You might want to give Lucy a call."

"I'm very glad to hear that," he said, and his voice sounded genuinely relieved. "I'm very appreciative of your help."

"Happy to," I said, and I meant it. Toby was rarely on the side of the angels, but when he was, I didn't mind hanging out with him.

And I wasn't sorry to have Toby owing me. In the world of faculty politics, people pay their debts. In fact, Toby did almost nothing but. He generally paid more attention to whom he owed and who owed him than whatever issue was under consideration.

No doubt I'd be in trouble again, and no doubt there would be a time I needed support from Toby, and almost always when that happened, I was on the low end of the power continuum and not somebody Toby would get a lot of points out of supporting. I didn't mind at all having a chit from Toby in my pocket.

I stayed and worked for a while, and it was dusk when I finally strapped on my fanny pack and walked out to the car. My head was full of lying fraternity rapists and eavesdropping sadistic ministers, and most of all my head was full of worry about Marv and Camille.

What was it Stevens wrote, "We must endure our thoughts all night until the bright obvious . . ." Stevens, master of the midway zap. In the beginning, he was talking about a snowstorm, and by the end you realized the snowstorm was inside his head and not outside. Maybe someday all of this was going to turn into the "bright obvious," but right now a snowstorm was an understatement. It was more like swimming in mud.

Dusk settled in all around me as I drove home. I hate dusk—for the same reason I hate snowstorms—inside or out. I can't see. I can see more at night once my eyes acclimate than I can when everything is betwixt and between.

There is, I admit, the occasional splashy sunset at dusk. But it is only occasionally that dusk has a little glory to it. Nine-tenths of the time it is just a messy transition. Now, if day just went whap, like a light shutting off, and there you were, in the sparkling night sky, that would be a transition. But every single goddamn day, you have to put up with this lingering, slow, death-of-the-light business. Thank goodness, by the time I got home the day had finished falling apart and night was blooming.

I walked out onto the deck with my solace glass of ice tea just as the full moon slipped from behind some clouds. Looking up I remembered being five years old and riding home in a car with the moon following us all the way. I remember how amazed I was: Everywhere we went, there it was—no matter how fast we went the moon always seemed to keep up.

I used to talk to the moon, sitting at the window of my bedroom. I didn't understand that the half moon and the full moon were the same thing, and I waited and waited until the full moon came back.

When it did, I wouldn't throw my usual fit about going to bed: I couldn't wait till Mama closed the door and I could drag a chair over to the window. I talked, and the moon listened. Mama wasn't exactly the listening type, and if she did listen, she was likely to say something warm like, "Don't talk foolishness, girl," or she would just snort. Mama had a snort that said "bullshit" better than "bullshit" said it. The moon never said anything like that.

I remembered sneaking out and swimming under that moon when I was older. I always have liked being outside at night—most of all when the moon was shining like it was tonight. I looked at the stream below the deck: In the moonlight it had a vibrancy that hurt your eyes it was so intense, nothing like the ordinary stream it became during the day.

But then the moon gives everything a kind of grace. What doesn't look good under a full moon? Old cars look good. Junkyards look good. Shopping malls look good.

I had the feeling, suddenly, of being watched, and at first I thought it was the moon. I shook my head and smiled, thinking how easy it was to slip back into that five-year-old person—but I stopped my head in mid shake.

The feeling of being watched wasn't benign. It wasn't a feeling of being looked after or watched over: It was something different. I looked up at the moon one last time, and then I looked at the trees across the stream.

I'd chalk it up to paranoia if, oddly enough, I hadn't seen the research. The research said people could tell when somebody was staring at them although nobody knew how. Besides, if it was paranoia, I reasoned, it wouldn't have happened in the middle of my basking in the full moon, which was one time I hadn't been worrying about Willy at all. Likely, the opposite was true. If I was being watched, it probably had taken a while for it to get through my moon-soaked brain.

I sipped my ice tea and thought about it. I didn't have my fanny pack on the deck, and it was probably not a very good idea to be out here like some kind of sitting duck. What was going on? Was this the night Willy was making his move, or was he here just to scout the terrain?

Thinking about it, I felt the bitter taste of fear in my mouth, and then I got mad. Seriously mad. I just couldn't live my life sitting around waiting for someone to torture and murder me. Willy hadn't laid a finger on me, and already he had stolen just about everything I cared about. I couldn't even sit on my goddamn deck in the moonlight without worrying about him.

I got up abruptly and walked back into the house and picked up my fanny pack where I had dropped it. Goddamn it. This was totally and completely ridiculous. Who knew these woods better than me? Willy? I don't think so. Who was used to being in the woods at night? Willy or me? Ten to one Willy wasn't sneaking out of the house at fifteen to swim under the full moon, although, come to think of it, he probably was sneaking out of the house to play Peeping Tom at that age.

What the hell. You place your bets. If Willy and I were going to duke it out, I probably had more advantage in my own woods at night than I'd get anywhere else.

I ran up to the loft and stared at my clothes hanging in my closet. I didn't exactly have a lot. A limit of 250 things in my life total somewhat limited my wardrobe. Surprise, surprise, I didn't have an official night-creeping outfit. Everything had to be black—I knew that from all the rapists I had interviewed—so what could I put together?

I didn't have any black sweatpants. My two pairs of blue jeans were blue. But I did have one pair of black dress pants. I grabbed them, pulled off my clothes, and put them on. I looked for shoes. I could wear the one pair of flat black pumps I used for work, but they would be awful in the woods. I sighed as I saw my black, high-top basketball shoes. I'd never worn them off the court before, but I guessed I could make an exception. At least, I wouldn't be on concrete.

I found a black turtleneck in the drawer and pulled it on and then a black sweater over it. I rummaged around until I found a navy blue knit cap. It wasn't black, but it was close. I strapped on my fanny pack. I looked pretty funny with my basketball shoes and my dress pants. As if I cared. This goddamn thing was going to be over tonight one way or the other.

I strapped the fanny pack on my hip and ran down the stairs from the loft and headed for the back door. Just before I reached it, I screeched to a halt. Nobody who had ever seen *Silence of the Lambs* could even think about a perp at night without wondering if he had night goggles.

What if he did? Did he know what I was thinking when I looked up at the woods, got up abruptly, and went back inside? Which door was he watching, the deck door or the back door? Even without night goggles, he could see me come out of the door in the moonlight if he was watching it. How smart was Willy? Smart. But he couldn't watch both at once, so which door would he watch?

I paced around the room thinking and saw I hadn't locked the deck door in my haste. Absent-mindedly, I locked it. I was going to have to place my bets. Which door would he be watching? There just wasn't any way to know, and I could be in big trouble if Willy saw me coming out of the house and ambushed me.

I turned from the deck door—goddamn it, I didn't want to make a random choice, but I wasn't staying inside—and my eyes fell on the wood box. The wood box. I had one of those wood boxes that's cut right through the wall of the house. To load it with firewood, you had to go outside, remove a two-foot insulated plug from the side of the house, and load the wood. It was set up so you never had to drag wood inside the house.

I threw the top of the wood box open and started pulling firewood out, throwing it in all directions on my precious hardwood floor. The plug was only two feet or so wide. Good thing I was skinny. I could fit through two feet, at least on the diagonal. I got the last of the wood out and stood up. I looked around. What had I forgotten? The lights. I walked over and turned off the living room lights. I should have done it before, but the wood box was off to the side, hidden by a sofa from the huge A-frame window that fronted the deck. Nobody could have seen me unload the wood box, but now I was about to open it. I didn't want the light to shine through the open wood box door and give me away.

The wood box wasn't big enough for me to get in completely, so I leaned in as far as I could and brushed off the wood dust from the plug. This was the tricky part. The plug couldn't be pulled inside; it would only go out. The only way to get it out was to push it out on the ground, and I didn't want to make a lot of noise. If I didn't alert Willy by making noise, he really couldn't see me slipping out of the side of the house no matter which door he was watching.

I pushed on the plug gently, and nothing happened. I pushed again and got nowhere. Finally, I started hitting it with my fist with short jabs until it started moving outward. The plug was insulated, and my fist didn't make any real noise on the insulation.

I got lucky. One side of the plug opened up first, and I was able to reach my hand around it and grab the edge before the whole thing fell. I eased the plug out the rest of the way and at least broke its fall to the ground.

I stuck my head out and just waited. It would take two or three minutes for my eyes to acclimate, and there was no point in going anywhere until they did. Soon the darkness in front of me turned into trees and a woodpile, and I put my arms over my head and started to wiggle out. I wiggled out as quickly as I could and quietly replaced the plug. It wouldn't be good if Willy found it and went in while I was out.

I crouched down for a moment to get oriented. The opening was near the woodpile, and the woodpile was high enough to provide cover, so I was okay where I was for a few minutes. I was beginning to regret the full moon. The night was too bright. Anybody could see anybody in this light, and I had several feet of clear moonlit ground to cross before I could get to the shadow of the trees.

I could hear my heart beating while I waited, but it wasn't exactly fear, it was more like exhilaration. I have always felt invisible in the woods at night, although God knows that is a myth. Every woods animal within forty miles knew there was a human about, but *people* didn't expect anybody to be in the woods at night, certainly not without a flashlight. If you wanted to hide, the woods at night were the place.

Something was bothering me, nagging at me, but I was getting a taste of the exhilaration I had on the cross-country course, and I ignored it. I'd think about it later. First, I had to get to the cover of the trees. I crouched and duck-walked along the edge of the house, looking for the place where the distance to the trees was the shortest. I found the closest place and got ready. I knew I'd be faster standing up but a lot more visible, so I took a deep breath and wiggled across the moonlit ground on my belly.

I made it to the edge of the trees, then stood up and ran some distance through the trees before I crouched down and listened. Nobody shot me; nobody even shot at me. In fact, I didn't hear anything unnatural. Nothing big and awkward was moving in the woods. The crickets were still holding forth. I was surprised they hadn't piped down. I could hear an owl in the distance screeching— nature was having its nightly orgy of death and destruction.

A whole lot of me didn't want to go looking for Willy, gun or not. A whole lot of me just wanted to melt into the shadows and feel that nobody and nothing could find me. I was tired of being alert, of waiting for trouble, of having the rhythm of my life dictated by a goddamn predator. I did not like feeling like a goldfish in a fishbowl with a cat's face pressed up against the side. I could climb a tree right now, right up to the top like I did when I was fifteen, and the moon would blaze down on me like grace. Nobody would find me there.

But if I did, Willy would still be there when I got down—if not tonight, then tomorrow night or the next or the next. I started to move through the trees. I just couldn't live like that. I'd parallel the road and go down far enough that when I turned back, I'd come up behind him, no matter where he was watching the house from. There was a small hill across the stream from the house. Willy would be somewhere on that hill, looking down, if he hadn't left by now.

Then I stopped. I knew what was bothering me. Funny thing to think about at this late stage, but exactly what was I going to do when I got there? Was I actually planning on shooting him? In cold blood? In the back? Or was I planning on letting him shoot at me first? In which case what I would do might be a moot point.

But what if he didn't have a gun or didn't pull one? Was I going to march him down to my house and call the police? The very thought of Willy inside my house made me completely crazy. Also, what would they have him on? Trespassing.

Big deal. He'd be out in two days and more clever the next time.

I started moving again and thought of all the things Willy had done to children and would do to children in the future, and the thought of him dead had a lot of appeal. I didn't mind him dead. I didn't have a problem with his being dead. But the truth was I didn't even like to shoot silhouettes of people. So I was not going to be happy shooting at a real person. Much less if he didn't try to shoot at me.

There was also the small matter that I would go to jail for it. The law does frown on shooting people who are not armed. But that wasn't the main thing. The main thing was that I couldn't even imagine shooting anybody in cold blood, not even Willy.

This was the problem with me and Willy since he got out. He knew exactly what he wanted to do with me—whatever it was, and I truly didn't want to find out—but I didn't have a clue what to do with him.

But something had to happen tonight because I could not and would not keep living like this. I was going onto that hill with Willy, and I'd figure out what to do then.

I went straight out from the side of the house until I was far enough away that I knew I had to be behind Willy. At least he couldn't see the house if he was this far out, so unless he was leaving, I was going to come up behind him. It was also a good place to cross the stream. There were enough rocks that I didn't have to get wet and a lot of overhanging trees providing shade.

I crossed the stream on the rocks, feeling a little exposed. Shadow or not, I was still more visible crossing the stream than I was in the forest. But again nobody shot me and nobody grabbed me on the other side, and that was now my definition of success.

But once I got over, the questions came back: How smart was Willy? Smart. How smart? Smart enough to lure me into the woods? Smart enough to know I'd come after him if he stood there night after night staring at me until I figured it out? What would he have done if I hadn't? Lit a cigarette to get my attention? Turned on a flashlight?

The thought of Camille came back, blind with tape wrapped all around her head, while some aberrant asshole did God knows what to the rest of her. I shuddered, and my stomach started to turn. Was I really sneaking up on Willy? Or was he sneaking up on me? I looked down. Any step could be onto a trap.

I took a deep breath and tried to push the fear out of my mind. I wasn't sure anymore I should be out here, but I was still committed. I couldn't go back and huddle in the house waiting for him. I went forward more slowly than before, looking carefully at every step.

Thank God for New England forests. They are sparse enough that you can walk off the path and not have to bushwhack, at least at this time of year. The buds were just starting, and mostly the forest was filled with bare bushes. They were widely enough spaced that the lack of a trail wasn't a big problem. Things fill out some in the summer, and I would have made a whole lot more noise than I did now. Thank God it wasn't a Southern forest. I'd have sounded like a bear crashing through the woods if I ventured off a trail.

I took a deep breath. The whole thing of Willy having the nerve to hang around my woods just seemed so incredible. The forest had been my haven, and I was incensed that it was being used by a predator. But tell that to a mouse or a rabbit or just about any other creature in the forest. Life is a lottery in the forest. The damn screech owl in the distance had a taste for brains. You'd find rabbits in the forest where he had chewed off the heads so he could take the brains back and enjoy them at his leisure.

Oh, I knew what the politically correct thing was. The owl was killing to live and Willy was killing for the fun of it, and that was supposed to be some huge difference, but I don't really know how much difference it made to the rabbit. This moonlight-soaked haven of mine was more violent than any inner city.

And now I was part of it, more so than at any

time in my life. I'd always been a visitor before. Tonight I was locked into that predator/prey thing like everybody else around me. Except for one thing—the rabbit didn't usually try to sneak up on the owl. Probably that was because she wouldn't know what to do once she got there, which was exactly my problem.

I wondered if animals romanticize the city as much as people romanticize the forest. I almost laughed as I thought of the rabbits lecturing their children on the moral superiority of the city: "At least humans don't usually *eat* somebody when they kill them, not like here."

I was getting giddy. Fear of a trap and the exhilaration of being invisible were mixing in my brain, and there were enough chemicals up there to make a junkie happy. Ahead of me was the ridge, and as I saw it, my heart started to beat double-time.

I stepped behind a tree for cover, crouched down, and stuck my head out to survey the scene. From where I was I didn't see anybody on the ridge, but I was still pretty far down the hill. I'd have to zigzag back and forth going up to the top of the ridge to make sure I covered the width of it. If Willy was waiting for me, he still had to spot me, goggles or not. I got ready to move and thought, "All right, fate, take your best shot, and then leave me alone till the next time." That crazy mantra always came back.

I had a fleeting thought of how stupid what I'd done would seem to most people. I had voluntarily chosen to be alone, at night, in the woods with a sadistic sex offender who was stalking me and most likely planning on killing me. Worse, a very bright sex offender who might well be counting the steps between me and the next snare.

Thinking about it, a wave of gut-wrenching, throw-up-time, blind panic started swelling in me. I grabbed the tree and held on. "Don't be stupid," I told myself. "This is still your arena more than his. You're only guessing that he's expecting you."

But what if Willy wasn't expecting me. Even then would he be likely just to stand there with no cover? Wasn't Willy the kind who'd set a few snares just in case? I remembered belatedly that Willy had been a scout leader among his many covers for child molestation. Had he been one of those woodsy-type scoutmasters?

I waited, and the panic started easing like the tide going out. My thinking didn't have a whole lot to do with it. It was just the way panic worked. It came in waves and, just like waves, receded.

"Goddamn it," I thought. I never had those until I was attacked. I sincerely hoped I didn't get one at some point when I needed to function in some important way, like, say, when I had a gun in my hand and Willy in front of it.

I hadn't pulled my gun yet. I don't believe a gun

is some kind of magic talisman that protects you just by buying one, so I had gotten some serious training. The training said never pull a gun until you're ready to use it. I hadn't even located Willy yet. I started moving up the hill zigzag, running in a half-crouch from one tree to the next. The forest had grown quiet: By now the entire population was aware of a collision about to happen. Was Willy smart enough to listen?

I saw nothing till I got right on top of the ridge. I was moving in a crouching duck walk across the ridge when I spotted him. Even in the moonlight, there were so many shapes in the forest that I don't know if I would have spotted him if he hadn't moved. It was a slight movement, maybe shifting from one foot to the other, but it was enough.

I hit the ground. Willy was halfway down the hill and still pretty far away from me. All I could really see was a shape. He was standing in the shadow of a large tree, and I couldn't be sure which way he was looking. Had he heard me and turned around? Was he looking my way or at the house? I waited, but Willy didn't move again. I pulled open the Velcro opening to my fanny pack. It made a noise that in my mind sounded about as loud as thunder, but Willy still didn't move.

I got the gun out and started wiggling closer. If this was a trap, the only place he could be sure I would be was right here. The closer I got to him, the more likely it was I'd hit a snare of some kind.

Alarm bells were starting to go off in my head, but I put it down to the weirdness of the situation and my fear. I had to face the fact that I couldn't just shoot him, and any other scenario was pretty scary.

It was too hard to plan. I didn't have a plan. When people take their guns out, anything can happen; I just had to trust my instincts. It didn't even seem that important if he shot me—at least the goddamn thing would be over. It wasn't being shot that scared me anyway; it was being caught. My mind was racing. It seemed like I had fifty thoughts for every wiggle forward.

Willy moved again, another slight movement, and I stopped and held my breath. I was getting closer, and I was going to have to do something when I got there. I couldn't just watch him all night. I wondered suddenly what Adam would think of this. Not much. Well, fuck Adam. Adam didn't have an answer to this except to hide under his bed. I don't think so.

I realized Adam would be the only one who could figure this out. Both doors locked. Me, no doubt, dead in the woods in some very unpleasant way. Firewood on the floor. Adam would look at it, start futzing with the plug. I could see him shaking his head as he searched for footprints by the side of the house. No one else would even think somebody might do something this stupid. Adam would.

Willy crouched down, and I dropped my head to the ground. Had he heard something? Seen something? I was still fifty feet away. Too far. I waited. Several light-years passed. Willy didn't move again, and I started wiggling forward slowly: bush to bush, tree to tree, zigzagging toward Willy.

I made myself keep going. I knew the temptation would be to stop too soon, and I needed to get closer to have a clean shot if I needed one, but it was hard to keep going—a little like asking myself to crawl within striking range of a rattlesnake. And each foot forward made it more likely I'd hit a trap. Finally I was maybe twenty feet from Willy, and nothing bad had happened. I was close enough to call out and close enough I hoped to nail him if I needed to. I stayed prone on the ground, pulled the gun, and slowly extended both arms in front of me.

I fixed my gunsight on Willy, but I put my trigger finger on the trigger guard instead of the trigger. Training. Gun courses. Don't put your finger on the trigger until you're ready to shoot. I hesitated. It would take too long to move my finger if I needed to shoot. Basic rule. Don't put your finger on the trigger. Don't do it. I didn't.

My breathing was short and rapid. Goddamn it. It's hard to aim if you can't get your breathing under control. You were supposed to squeeze the trigger between breaths. What was I thinking about? I wasn't going to squeeze the trigger. Or maybe I was.

Suddenly Willy stood up, and my finger convulsed on the trigger guard. Had it been the trigger, I'd have shot. I started to move my finger to the trigger, then stopped. Something was wrong. Time stopped. It took my brain a moment or two to process the scene in front of me, but slowly it began to sink in. What was wrong with this picture?

It wasn't Willy. The silhouette was wrong. It just wasn't Willy. It couldn't be Willy. Even with a coat, even from the back, it wasn't Willy. Worse, the figure was small.

Jesus Christ. I put the gun on the ground and closed my eyes for a moment. The only thing I really feared about guns was that I'd shoot a four-teen-year-old some night who was breaking into my house to steal a stereo. Jesus Christ. I picked up the gun again and put it in the fanny pack. My hands were shaking. Tears were starting down my face. Jesus Christ. I didn't even know who was there, but it sure as hell wasn't Willy. And I didn't have a reason in the world to want anyone else dead.

I could have called out to the figure, but whoever it was might have a gun and might shoot in panic. I didn't want to start anything when I didn't know what was going on. I'd think about this later. I'd figure it out later. Right now I just wanted out of this.

I started crawling backward, away from the unaware figure now shifting restlessly, from one foot to the other, still watching the house. My God. I'd almost killed somebody, and I didn't even know who it was. I'd damn near shot somebody, and it would have been totally the wrong person. Willy would have loved that. Maybe that was the trap all along.

I was far enough away now. I got up and headed back the way I came. Who the hell was that? The tears kept falling.

But there was something else. Something about the way that figure moved was familiar. Had Willy enlisted someone I knew to help him? What revenge that would be—to con me into shooting some poor innocent kid, some kid I knew. How smart was Willy? Smart? How smart was I? Maybe the answer was "not very."

233

17

The figure on the ridge haunted me all weekend. I had dreams in which I pulled the trigger and then walked up afterward to find I'd shot a kid. As I got closer, the child always turned into Jordan. I woke up cold and disoriented with the metallic taste of grief in my mouth that I always got when Jordan was back.

The dreams didn't exactly surprise me. Probably I *had* damn near shot a kid—your basic horrifying possibility. And, too, anything that had to do with a hurt or dying child always brought up Jordan.

Besides, I knew some part of me thought I killed Jordan by going back to work. She died of SIDS at the day care, the first day I went back, and even though I knew infants died of SIDS with medical people standing over them, I had some crazy belief that it wouldn't have happened if I'd been there.

All this was on top of the bizarre business with Marv. It was miserable not being able to call him or stop by his house—I would have loved a little distraction—but his request was so odd I didn't even think about ignoring it.

Something very weird was going on. Surely there were reasonable explanations. Surely there were, like . . . like . . . well, who knows, maybe Willy was living there.

Right.

By eight o'clock Monday morning I was in my office. Actually, I was in my office quite a bit earlier, and by eight I was pacing. Whatever it was with Marv, I'd rather know than hang around wondering.

Ordinarily, he was late for everything except clients. But he wasn't late today. He was exactly on time, which I thought a very bad sign. I looked him over. His clothes were the same rumpled odd assortment of discordant colors as always. This was good. If he'd come in color-coordinated, I'd have panicked.

But his face was different. His face looked like a basset hound. Marv always had a bit of basset hound about him, but today he'd have won best of show.

I wanted to scream at him, "SO WHAT IS IT? CUT TO THE CHASE. WHY CAN'T I GO TO YOUR HOUSE? WHO'S THERE?" But I didn't. Marv's face told me he was miserable, and I started thinking about what he'd done for me when I came over the night I was so freaked out.

"What's up?" I said as casually as possible. There was enough anxiety in my voice to make any psychiatrist reach for his prescription pad, but Marv didn't seem to notice.

He sat down heavily in the chair facing my desk. "Michael," he said slowly. "I need to talk to you about something."

NO SHIT, SHERLOCK. COME ON. COME ON. GET IT OUT. I didn't say it. I just said, "Okay."

He ran his hand over his balding head and said, "I made a mistake, a therapeutic mistake, and I'm afraid it was a serious one."

I KNOW. YOU SAID THAT ALREADY. IT'S NOT GOING TO MATTER, MARV, BECAUSE WE'LL BOTH BE DEAD OF OLD AGE BY THE TIME YOU GET IT OUT. WE'LL BE FOSSILIZED. I didn't say that either. I just said, "So tell me."

"It's about Ginger." Oh, Jesus Christ. Maybe I didn't want Marv to tell me after all. I started to open my mouth, then shut it again. Marv had called me. I hadn't called him. He wanted something from me—maybe I should find out what it was before I chickened out.

"Okay," I finally got out.

Marv sighed and shifted in his seat. "She developed a very intense transference. I'm sure you're well aware of what that is like." He glanced up at me, and I immediately felt guilty for sending her to him. What a thing to do to a friend. "But at first it seemed quite stable, and nothing beyond what you had described.

"She would drive by my house frequently at night and on the weekends, just for reassurance I still existed, that sort of thing. She'd drive by in the middle of the night, too, when she couldn't sleep.

"I didn't know any of this at the time. I didn't find it out until . . . well, let me get to the point."

The shouting in my head had stopped once Marv finally got going, but for the life of me I couldn't see where this was headed.

"Unfortunately, she drove by early on the night you came to see me, and she saw your car. Of course, she knew your car because she used to do the same thing to you."

"She did what to me? She drove by my house?" Marv nodded. I automatically put my hand to my mouth. I didn't know that. I knew she drove by the office, and I knew she called my answering machine for reassurance, but I never thought about her going to my house.

"But how did she know where it was?" Surely, he was wrong.

"She followed you. She really is quite clever. The first night she followed you part of the way, then turned off. The next night she was waiting where she turned off previously, and she followed you for another section and turned off. Eventually, she got all the way to your house, and I doubt *anyone* would have realized they were being followed.

"I didn't know any of this, Michael," he said, anticipating my reaction. "Not until right before I called. I pressed immediately until she told me the whole story. I would have told you—the information release she signed when you transferred her is still valid—but I didn't know. In any case, when she saw your car at my house, she immediately got jealous—I'm not sure of whom, since she's attached to both of us—and she came back in the middle of the night to reassure herself that your car wasn't still there. But of course, it was."

"Oh . . ." It was pretty obvious what conclusion Ginger would have drawn.

"Then the next day she saw you in my office. If you remember, you were seeing a client for me. Of course, no one told Ginger anything about why I wasn't there—her appointment was much later that day, and I was back by then.

"Predictably, Ginger decided that we were having an affair. She took the office business as proof. You could go into my office when I wasn't there, and she couldn't. You saw a client in my office, but you wouldn't see her. She saw both of us as leaving her out. I'm afraid what happened fits quite well with the analytic model of the Oedipal complex: She felt totally abandoned."

For once I didn't roll my eyes. Whatever you called it, I could well believe that Ginger felt abandoned if she thought Marv and I were having an affair.

"So what happened?"

"She decompensated."

"How bad?"

"Quite badly, I'm afraid. She became self-mutilating. She cut her vagina to punish herself for being so worthless and unlovable."

And to punish Marv, I thought, and me.

"She was really in a very difficult state. And that's where I made the mistake."

"Like what?" I said softly. I still didn't get it. What had Marv done that was so bad?

"She was decompensating on the basis of something that didn't exist. That was the irony. We weren't having an affair, so I broke my rule on nondisclosure. I told her we weren't."

He fell silent. What he'd done wasn't wise. It was never wise to share personal information with a client. It changed the relationship, and it turned things into more of a social exchange. But I could see why Marv did it. And on the surface, it didn't seem so terrible.

But then I got it. I knew how things had gone wrong.

"What *did* you tell her?" I said evenly. He would never have been able to stop at just telling her we weren't having an affair. Ginger would have insisted on knowing why I was at his house all night if we weren't.

"I didn't tell her anything about your personal life," he said quickly. This was good, because if he had put the knowledge of Jordan and what she meant to me in Ginger's hands, it would have driven a stake into the heart of my friendship with Marv.

"So what then?" I said. "What did you tell her?"

Marv took a deep breath. "I couldn't lie to a client. I really couldn't. It would have totally destroyed the relationship. And I couldn't tell her the whole truth. Worse, once I had told her something, I felt as though I couldn't leave it dangling. So I told her about Willy."

"Say again?"

"I told her you had a dangerous client who had just been released from prison and that you were quite concerned about it. I told her you had some concern for your safety and that's why you were staying at my house that night."

"Oh, my God, Marv. I can't believe you did that. What'd she say?"

"It's not what she said," Marv replied. "It's what she *did* that's the issue. With hindsight," he said miserably, "it was quite predictable. I'm afraid I gave her a perfect excuse for stalking you. She's been 'taking care' of you ever since."

"Jesus Christ," I said. "Jesus Christ." Ginger was small—no more than five-two and small-boned.

"It was a grievous error, Michael. I am truly sorry."

"Boy, was it." We both fell silent while I tried to put the pieces together. The world was starting to make sense again, but I didn't like the picture I was seeing.

"Have you seen anything of her?" Marv asked. "Have you noticed anything?"

"Yes and no," I said. "I noticed something, but I had no clue it was Ginger. I almost killed her. She was on the ridge behind my house in the middle of the night—at least I'm betting it was her—and I was lying no more than fifty feet away with a gun in my hands. I thought she was Willy." Marv blinked rapidly and swallowed.

"And a few days before that she almost killed me," I said. "She spooked a rabbit—again, I'm assuming it was her. Is she still wearing those spike heels even when she's got on jeans?" Marv nodded. "Then she was the one. She spooked a rabbit, who spooked my horse, and I ended up wearing the jump." Marv's face started losing color.

"We have to get her out of this, Marv. And I mean instantly. Willy's closing in, and I have to know what's him and what's not. I can't hesitate worrying about whether it's Ginger. Besides, if Willy's hanging around, he knows she's there too, and he could easily leave her as a present on my front doorstep."

Marv looked like he would faint. "He'd do it," I said firmly. "He'd make a joke about it. That's his style. He'd say something about doing me a favor or too many cooks spoiling the broth. But she's right between the two of us, and that is definitely the wrong place to be."

"Willy's 'closing in,' " he said weakly.

"Forget it," I said. "I'm getting good help on it."

Marv looked relieved. Bob Dylan was a genius: "All I suggest is a man hears what he wants to hear." Willy's way was amazingly easy. Just tell people what they want to hear, and they buy it every time.

"So," I went on, "what do we do about Ginger? If we tell her she's in danger, she'll never leave. She'll stay to 'protect' me. You can't tell her you lied to her. It'll ruin her faith in therapists, and I doubt she would live right now without one. You can't even keep her as a client. You've screwed up the relationship by giving her info she shouldn't have. Besides, she's crossing boundaries big time."

I was trying to be gentle, but it wasn't coming out that way. I was getting more pissed the more I thought about it. If he wanted to self-disclose, why did he disclose about me? Why not tell her something about himself?

The analytic people would have a field day with this. So Marv wasn't pissed at me for transferring Ginger? Ha! He'd given her right back. Or maybe he was so pissed at her, he was unconsciously trying to get her killed. Or maybe both. When people didn't know they were angry, they did terrible things.

That was the one advantage of being angry all the time and knowing it. I kept an eye on my anger like some sort of boa constrictor in the garden. I tried to keep it focused where it mattered—on people like Willy. But poor Marv had thought he was a gentle soul. And he was—as much as anybody is.

Whatever his motivation for nearly getting both Ginger and me killed, I didn't want to touch it. Marv was a very smart man, and he'd probably go back into analysis over this. He'd be obsessing over his navel for decades, which, God knows, was punishment enough.

We talked till noon. We tried this out and that out and the other out. We canceled a series of clients and appointments, and we refused to take phone calls. The secretaries began to worry about what horrendous crisis was in the air now.

I told him nothing more about Willy. I felt sorry for Marv for what he'd done, but I couldn't change the fact that I no longer trusted him. Under pressure, he'd betrayed me, and that fact stuck in my mind—and I'd bet in his, too. Sure, it could have been worse—he could have told her about Jordan. But somehow that seemed like poor consolation. How close *had* he come to telling Ginger about her? Would he leave her out the next time? I knew the answer rationally, but I no longer knew it in my heart.

Finally, we realized the answer to Ginger was in front of us all the time. It only took four hours for us to see it. At least, maybe it was the answer. It was a good shot, the only one we could think of. But it relied on putting unbelievable pressure on Ginger, and Marv didn't like it. He wanted to cry "mea culpa" and apologize to her on his knees. I told him he could wallow on his own time. Taking responsibility for his stupidity would be the worst thing he could do to Ginger right now.

In the end, he agreed. He couldn't think of another option. He called Ginger to set up a meeting, and I went off to find Toby and cash in my chit. Great. The only time Toby had owed me in a decade, and it was going to last less than a week. I had no doubts Toby would go for it. He'd love not to owe me, and besides, Toby's blind spot was his narcissism just as Marv's was his anger. If I fed that enough, he'd buy just about anything.

As for my motivation . . . Sure, this one fed the boa a little bit, but at least I knew it.

18

I had to go past Melissa's desk on my way to Toby's office, and she flagged me down. "Michael," Melissa said with relief in her voice, "you're back. Chief Bowman has called twice. He wants you to call him back right away." My life was back to Zeno's paradox. I could only get halfway to wherever I was trying to go.

I almost decided to ignore the call. Getting halfway was costing me. After all, if I hadn't gotten sidetracked on Friday when I was heading in to see Marv, I wouldn't have nearly shot Ginger.

On the other hand, maybe my mistake was in not returning urgent phone calls. This was an urgent phone call, and I was about not to return it.

I sighed. I didn't mind paying my dues and learning my lessons in life. It was just that it wasn't always easy to figure out which lesson you were supposed to learn.

I looked at the relief on Melissa's face and decided to call Adam back. She took it personally when someone was upset because they couldn't reach one of us. Easy for me to say I'll call him later, but she'd be the one on the phone when Adam called back annoyed. Melissa's sole failing was that she was a sponge for stress.

I went to my office and called Adam. He was all business when he came on the line, and I knew from the tone of his voice he had something. "I called Boston and got lucky," he said. "I reached the detective who handled Camille Robbins's case. He's a supervisor now, but he remembers that case clearly.

"There's no question the original incident was genuine. She was a nurse who worked at Mass General. She was abducted from the parking lot and found the next day in a dog kennel in Concord. She had scaled a fence to get in. The owner found her when he came out to see why all the dogs were barking.

"She was nude and had cigarette burns on her breasts and labia. She'd been tortured extensively. She still had duct tape on most of her face. She had torn off just enough to see.

"Not surprisingly, she wasn't in very good shape to talk about it. In fact, she curled up in a fetal position when they tried. The only thing they ever really got out of her was that she had gotten in her car to go home. Her car was found a few days later at a rest area on I-93.

"They never got any more out of her. She was hospitalized at MacClean's, and they went out a couple of times to talk to her, but she went into flashbacks whenever she tried. They tried to follow up after she was released, but she disappeared, and nobody knew where she'd gone. They called the hospital, the neighbors . . . nobody knew where she was."

Nobody, I thought, except Chris.

"The detective was pretty happy to hear from me. They still want to talk to her."

"Why?" I said, surprised. "Are they still working the case?" It was an awful case, but it was five years ago, and Boston cops are pretty busy.

"It's not so much her case they worried about," Adam said slowly. "It's the two murders they had within a year and a half after that with the same MO."

I tried to get my breathing restarted. Clearly, Camille's attacker had been sadistic, but my worst fear was that he was more than that: a full-blown serial killer. "The first was about eight months later," Adam went on. "A woman was found handcuffed spread-eagled to trees in the woods near Bolton. She had duct tape all over her head and cigarette burns all over her body. Death was by suffocation."

"From the duct tape?" I asked. "Can duct tape do that?"

"Sure," Adam said. "He just finally sealed the

nose off after he'd had his fun. Raped, of course. Objects forced up the anus."

"There was another?" I said weakly. Jesus, if this guy was back, Camille was in some serious trouble.

"Same MO," Adam said. "Same cause of death. And then nothing. That's been maybe three and a half years. Nothing's happened since then. They thought either he'd moved on or he was incarcerated for something else, but they sure would like to find him. If he's back, they're thinking he'll start up again."

And maybe Camille was scheduled to be the first this time just like she was last time. "Did they talk to Chris?" I asked.

"Nope. They didn't know anything about him. Camille wasn't coherent, and I doubt she would have mentioned a guy she knew slightly who worked at a local gas station. She wouldn't have had any reason to.

"There's another thing, Michael. They brought Quantico in on this." Which was smart. The FBI profilers at the Behavioral Sciences Unit were very good at profiling offenders. "They pegged the guy as a white male between twenty-five and thirty-one, a local who knew her. He would have finished high school but probably not gone beyond it. He'd have a late model car and work in a trade."

How did they do that? How? I understood

where they got the white male from. Ninety-nine percent of serial killers are white males, and killers tend to attack their own race, so since Camille was Caucasian the odds were overwhelming he was a white male. I even knew where they got the age from. Killers tend to attack people within a few years of their age. Camille was probably twenty-eight or so at the time, so they added three on each side. But where did the car come from?

When you asked Quantico questions like that, they just said they did the profiles based on info from interviews with caught killers. But their chief honcho had once looked at a murder scene and said that the killer had a stutter—which it turned out he had. How did he get that out of his interviews with previous killers? I'd be willing to bet he had never interviewed a serial killer in his life who stuttered.

"This is looking very grim," I said.

"I'd say so," Adam said. "As far as they know, she's the only person who's survived an attack. It may be the killer is thinking what they are—if she gets better she may remember something. Or it may be he just has a compulsion to finish the job. They were pretty excited to hear about Chris. He fits their profile, and he knew where she went."

"So what now?"

"Well," he said, "on this end I have an officer watching the house from the park behind it, but

I'd like to talk to Camille. I need you with me," he went on. "I don't expect she'd take well to a strange man knocking on her door."

No, I thought, she wouldn't, and neither would Keeter.

"Can we meet at your office?" Adam asked. "I don't want to go to her house in case our perp is watching it somehow."

"No," I said quickly. Too quickly. Adam was silent, and I tried to think of a reason fast. I couldn't. "Uh, that'll be fine," I said. It killed me to put Adam in a situation where there was even a remote chance Willy might be listening in. But the truth was, if Willy was listening in, what did it matter if it were Adam or a client? It wasn't any better to have Willy listening in on clients.

"I have an appointment with her later today. I'll talk to her then about it. Okay? I'd rather talk to her in person than call her. You're sure you can keep her safe?"

"Sure. I've got somebody practically sitting on her doorstep."

"Who?"

"Jonathan." This was good. Jonathan was an ex–Boston cop who used to work organized crime. He had had a whole lot more experience with violence than most of the local officers.

"Jesus Christ, Adam. It sure is a dicey world out there."

"Take it to heart, sweetheart," Adam replied.

"You skirt around the edges of it all the time."

I hung up the phone and just looked at it for a minute. Adam was right. I got over my head more often than I knew. Probably the main difference was this time I knew it.

I turned back toward Toby's office. My head was spinning. One thing at a time. Camille was all right for now, and I still had to get Ginger out of the middle of this thing with Willy. If Ginger ran into Willy, she'd look like Camille did after the abduction. Come to think of it, so would I.

I stopped in the hall. I was upset by what Adam had told me. Camille's perp was an active serial killer who had hung around the area and had every reason in the world to want Camille dead. She was, after all, the only living witness. But I didn't want to convey any upset to Toby. What I was trying to do with him was not all that easy to pull off. I wanted Toby to take exactly the kind of case he screened out.

Toby's caseload—not that he had much of one—was full of the walking wounded. He took celebrity cases, cases referred by other chairmen. He took cases where children of wealthy donors worried about which medical school they'd get into. He took cases where surgeons were tired of medicine and considering a career change. He did not take indigent women who cut their vaginas and would come in on emergency three times a week and make his life hell with one crisis after another. It had been a long time since Toby got up in the middle of the night.

All of which was a terrible shame. Because for all Toby's faults, he was actually a gifted therapist. Clients didn't seem to threaten him in the same way that colleagues outside therapy did, and he lost that narcissistic, need-to-be-a-big-guy edge he carried elsewhere. Without it, he was surprisingly astute and compassionate.

I had heard Toby present cases and had seen clients whom he had treated in a previous counseling. They were clearly the better for the time with him. It angered me all the more that Toby had a gift and wasted it on people so functional they would get better talking to a rock.

I waited a minute and tried to get myself together, then walked up to Toby's secretary. She looked surprised to see me; I was not a frequent visitor to Toby's office—as in, usually I had to be dragged there.

"What's Toby's schedule like today?" I asked. "I need to see him about a client who's in crisis."

She looked at her schedule book. The door to Toby's office was partly ajar, not enough for a visitor to see Toby's desk but enough that Toby could hear whoever was at his secretary's desk. I heard his desk chair scrape on the floor, and then he said, "Michael, come on in."

It occurred to me that maybe Toby wasn't as busy as I thought. Maybe he sat there eating bon-

bons while the rest of us ran around like little worker bees. It made me feel better for what I was about to do.

Toby opened the door wide, but his smile was even wider. It made me realize just how unhappy he usually was to see me. I had never gotten a smile anywhere near that wattage out of Toby before.

"I spoke to Lucy," he said as he ushered me to a seat. "She is terribly relieved at that young man's confession. She says it's made all the difference."

"Tell her to forget the apology bit," I said. "It won't mean a damn thing."

"Oh, I don't think she's still considering that," Toby said, laughing. "The confession was enough. That and the fact that it looks like he's going to be thrown out of school. I wouldn't worry about her asking for an apology."

"Good." And it was good. Fake apologies just muddy the water. They put pressure on the victim to say, "That's all right," as though the guy had accidentally stepped on her toe instead of brutally raping her.

"What can I do for you?" he said, and for once I think he meant it.

"Actually," I said, "I need help on a case."

Toby looked surprised and immediately a little pleased. If he could help me out on a case, he wouldn't owe me. And that meant he wouldn't end up in the embarrassing position of having to back me some day when the press was down his throat about me—as had happened before.

"I screwed up a case," I said bluntly. "You know, Toby, I am not that big a fan of analytic theory, but I think there are times when those of us who have moved away from it miss the boat."

Toby nodded vigorously and started to say something, but I started up again quickly. I didn't want Toby to get off on a diatribe about how analytic theory had been maligned.

"I had a case where I was focusing mainly on the abuse issues," I went on. "And I ignored an increasingly symbiotic transference reaction that eventually reached psychotic proportions."

I hadn't talked that way in a long time, and I just hoped I could remember the language. It was like trying to speak Greek that you learned in high school. Marv would have done a better job on the lingo, but he wasn't manipulative enough to pull this off.

"That's very unfortunate," Toby replied gravely.

"Yes," I agreed. "I became a complete part object, and the client lost all reality testing. Her superego only functioned in a sadistic way, and her ego functioning—never strong at the best of times—became overwhelmed with id impulses." I realized I couldn't remember which particular analytic school Toby belonged to. Was he part of the ego-analytic folks? If so, I'd better cool it on the id. The id was out of favor with those guys.

I looked up. Toby was still nodding, and he had leaned back in his chair and put his fingertips together. Whatever school he was, I must be close enough.

"The client—Ginger—began to cross boundaries. Essentially she stalked me—although I didn't know the full extent of it at the time. I did know she was crossing boundaries enough that I transferred her to Marv in hopes that she might find more stability with a father figure rather than a mother figure." Toby raised his eyebrows. It was unusual to transfer a client.

"But I did not confront her about the boundary crossing—which I now think was an error." This was actually the only thing I'd said thus far that was wholly true. "She transferred readily to Marv—after all, I was only a part object to her—but it turned out the sex of the therapist was insignificant."

Toby gave a slight smile as if to say, "Obviously, dummy," although he wouldn't have phrased it that way. He would have taken ten minutes to say it, but it would have come down to the same thing.

"The client—Ginger—simply put Marv and me together as mother and father figures and is now crossing boundaries with both of us. She has us allied in her mind and feels abandoned and rejected by our so-called alliance."

Toby sighed as if to say, "Amateurs should not

mess with these difficult cases." It was okay by me if he said it, except I didn't want to spend the time for him to get it out, so I kept going.

"I really think she needs a more experienced therapist than either of us. I think she needs someone who will set the strictest possible limits on any boundary crossing, and, of course, that's something analytic therapists have always excelled at."

I'd say. Analytic therapists are known for crossing the street to avoid saying "hello" to a client. Fortunately, Toby wasn't *that* orthodox.

Not everything I said was a lie. Analytic jargon aside, Toby was what Ginger needed. She'd exploit any sort of interpersonal exchange, and Toby wouldn't give her anything to hang on to. And whatever else I thought about Toby, he wouldn't tolerate any boundary crossing.

Too, he had the best access of anyone in the building to hospitalization—which Ginger needed periodically. No matter how crowded the inpatient unit was, amazingly, there was always room for the chairman's clients.

"Well," Toby said. "Of course, if I could be of any help . . ."

"I'm sure you could," I said. "Would you consider taking her?"

"Of course," Toby said, as though there had never been a question. Right. As though every day of the week you could get the chairman to take a

FAULT LINES

case from hell—particularly when it was a case
where someone might actually kill him- or herself:
There were potential lawsuits when people killed
themselves.

"It's a very difficult case," I said. "She's periodically suicidal."

"I'm happy to help." Well, what could he say
after agreeing? What? She's suicidal? I've changed
my mind. On the other hand, now he couldn't say
he hadn't been warned.

I left quickly, and on the way out I made an
appointment for Ginger with his secretary for the
next day. I wanted to get out of there and nail this
down before Toby came to his senses.

So why did Toby take a case that ordinarily
wouldn't get past the secretary? He did it because
I told him what a big, important guy he was and
how much wiser he was than the rest of us lowly
mortals. Give me a boa in the backyard anytime
over this narcissistic stuff. It makes people
blinder than a bat.

On the way out I thought about it. Toby
would buy a dead horse any day. Not because he
couldn't stand being alone or he needed anything concrete. He'd buy it because narcissists
don't exist without a mirror around. It's not
because they love themselves so much. It's
because the only time they can see themselves,
the only time they feel they have a self, is when
they see themselves in the mirror of somebody

257

else's regard. They are whatever the mirror says they are. They have the least sense of self of anybody on the planet.

Toby had paid dearly for that look in the mirror I gave him today. The sad irony of it was, to him it would be worth it.

19

As I passed Melissa's desk, she said, "Carlotta called. She wants you to call her back. She's at work."

I sat down at my desk and immediately dialed her number. Thank God for women friends. The friendship with Carlotta had always been a haven. I got a small knot in my stomach every time I called Adam: Both of my x chromosomes would start chirping, and I could hardly think with all that dithering about. Talking to Toby was like talking to somebody who saw me as . . . well, a part object . . . somebody who existed only to meet his narcissistic needs. Then there was Marv's betrayal, which just made me appreciate Carlotta all the more today.

Whatever it was, Carlotta and I had differences that made yin and yang look like clones, but who cared? I was at my most warm and fuzzy when she came on the phone.

"Michael," she said dryly. "You are a pain in the butt."

"Excuse me? This is what I get for dropping everything to call you back right away?"

"You have cost me more fucking sleep this week."

"Like what? The thing with Willy?" Ginger was still in my mind, and for a moment I was confused about what Carlotta knew and what she didn't.

"Of course, the thing with Willy. What else? There's something else?"

"I'm being chased by the entire Russian navy," I said solemnly.

"This could be true," she said. "Listen, I haven't told Adam yet. That's what I've been obsessing over. I spent the entire week trying to figure out whether to tell Adam that Willy's here—up close and personal enough for you to throw me out of my house."

"Uh-oh," I said. I had completely forgotten she had threatened to tell him. Threatened, hell. Promised was more like it.

"So?" I said. There wasn't any point in arguing. She had decided something.

"I kept thinking you were probably right. It wouldn't do any good, and it would just cause friction between you and Adam. He can't protect you if you won't let him. Besides a fight with Adam would just make it less likely you would call him if you need him."

"Exactly," I said.

"But I decided to tell him."

"What?" I said. "After all this? You were right the first time."

"Yes and no," she said. "I finally decided—it's not that it will do you a damn bit of good if you're determined to get yourself killed—it's that I am not going to have an answer when we're both looking down at your dead body, and he says, 'You knew he was here? And you didn't call me?'

"I am just not going to live the rest of my life wondering if it would have made a difference. So, I'm having dinner with him tomorrow night to talk about it. You want to come?"

"I do not think so." As in how many wild horses would it take? I was pissed, but there was nothing I could do about it. I was not going to control Carlotta. "Look, Carlotta. Do what you need to do. I don't think it's going to help, but, you know, what can I say? In the end, you're going to do what you want to do."

"And so," she said, "are you."

Marv came in and told me he had set up a meeting with Ginger for later in the afternoon. We were planning on seeing her together to present a united front. I had insisted. I was afraid Marv would do the apology thing on his knees if I wasn't there.

I would have just enough time to see Camille at my private practice office and get back. Usually I didn't see private clients when I was at Psychiatry. But sometimes clients were in too much crisis to wait a week between appointments, and for those folks, I sometimes chased back and forth.

As I approached my private practice office, I realized what a mess I was in. How could I go into that office and talk to Camille knowing that Willy might be listening to every word? How could I *not* tell that woman that somebody had some way of listening in?

On the other hand, the thought of telling her a second sadist was running loose, this one listening to her therapy sessions, would put her into orbit. If she wasn't paranoid now, she'd be then. It would shatter any sense of safety and destroy our relationship. What was I supposed to do?

And if this was true for Camille, it was true for all my clients. I had had a full day last Friday, and the fact was, I'd known that Willy *could* be bugging me the whole time. But, I reasoned, I had checked. I had swept the room for bugs between every single client.

That didn't help last time, a little voice inside me said. You swept before the lying little twerp rapist, and Willy had still bugged him.

I swallowed hard. For the first time in my life, somebody could bring me up on ethics charges and be right.

It could be argued—maybe it would be—that I should have closed my practice immediately the moment I had a hint someone might be bugging me. Not a bad argument. But what was I supposed to do with all the folks I saw? I didn't have a caseload of surgeons considering career changes. I had a caseload of traumatized people. Camille was in worse shape than the rest, but nobody on my caseload could be classified as a functional person who would get better talking to a rock.

I could see it now. "Roberta, I know your father tyrannized your life as a child, made you fill in fifteen-minute time sheets for weeks when he was away on business trips, and sexually abused you for eight years, but I need to tell you that a powerful, malevolent male could be listening to your every word. You think you're safe? Not even here.

"Yes, Kiwi, I know your husband is beating the shit out of you, but somebody might be listening to this conversation who is far worse than he is. Somebody might be listening who likes to torture women and children. Would you like to hear some of the things he has described doing to them?"

So I couldn't tell them. But I could have said I was sick and closed my practice down. Or something. The more I thought about it the more I realized I should have done something and now had to do something. But first I had to see Camille. There wasn't anything I could do about the problem this second.

I swept the office again for bugs. It was probably stupid. I had never caught anything with Danny's little bug-sweeping device. But it was the only thing I could do to feel safer, so I did it. I was just finishing when Keeter and Camille showed up, I mean Camille and Keeter. Somehow Keeter always got my attention first. She curled up in her usual spot, on the floor between me and Camille. I couldn't help remembering how she had looked crouched to jump when I walked into Camille's house. Remind me not to crowd this dog. I wrenched my attention away from Keeter and looked at Camille.

I was always surprised at how bad she looked. This morning her hands were shaking and her eyes had a hollow look. I had seen that look before. It meant people were living someplace where nobody should even visit.

I thought briefly of Auschwitz and the descriptions I had read of the blank look that people got as they became more depleted and felt more hopeless. Other inmates learned to recognize that look. It usually meant the person was going to just quit eating and die.

And yet. Although Camille had long ago lost all her emotional fat reserves and had been using up muscle and bone, there was still something left. It wouldn't last forever. Nobody in the known universe was even close to invincible. If something didn't change, sooner or later, the flashbacks or the perp or whatever it was would grind her to a pulp. But she was a marathoner, and somehow I didn't think she was completely beaten yet.

"How are you?" I said gently.

"I'm okay," she said, "I think. Did you talk to the police?"

"I did," I said, "and Chief Bowman wants very much to help you. He called the Boston police to find out more about what happened. Camille, did you ever hear anything more about this guy or any other attacks on anybody else after you left Boston?"

"No," she said. "I never spoke to them again."

"You never read the newspapers or anything?"

"No," she said. "The newspapers are too upsetting."

I noticed she didn't ask me why I asked. She didn't want to know.

"You need to know that Chief Bowman has a very tough, experienced cop watching your house right now. He used to work organized crime in Boston, and I don't think even if the perp is back he can get past this guy."

"He can get past anybody," she said forlornly.

"We don't know that," I said. "Last time he picked on you, he picked on an unarmed woman. He didn't pick on anybody with a guard dog and a cop standing watch."

Camille didn't say anything, but I could tell she

wasn't reassured. In her mind, he was larger than life.

"I know this is hard on you," I said, "but I need to know some things about the guy who attacked you. Do you think you can talk about him?"

I hated doing this. It wasn't supposed to be my job to play junior cop. I was supposed to be a therapist. And yet, there were times when I had to use a little common sense. If there was a serial killer after Camille, she wasn't going to be around for therapy if he wasn't caught. And it was going to be a whole lot harder for her to talk to Adam than to me.

"Maybe I could talk a little," she said. "I took extra Haldol this morning."

"You never saw his face, right?" She nodded. "Did he remind you of anybody you knew? Did he sound or move like somebody you knew?"

"No," she said. "He was a stranger."

"How tall was he?"

Camille's hands were shaking worse, and she started twisting a Kleenex, but she kept going. "Small," she said so faintly I almost couldn't hear her. "Not much taller than me."

"How big?"

"Thin . . . wiry . . . and very strong."

"Camille." She had started to drift away when she said "strong."

"Camille, how old was he? And then I promise I won't ask any more questions about him."

Camille focused on the Kleenex she was twisting. "Young," she said. "I don't know how old. . . . His voice was young."

"That's all," I said. "No more questions about him."

That was all I could ask anyway. I couldn't really ask her any questions about whether he reminded her of Chris. I couldn't take the chance she was suggestible and would put the two of them together just because I said it. I couldn't even ask her in the same *session* to describe Chris. I'd have to leave that for another time and ask her to describe several people so she wouldn't know what I was driving at.

But for the first time we had some kind of description of the perp, and the cops in Boston could match that against Chris or anybody else they had in mind. I'd tell Adam about it, and when he met with her maybe he could get a few more details.

Camille agreed to meet with him, but I didn't want to do it today. She could only talk about this a little at a time. We'd done all we could on it today, and Adam would get more information if we waited until tomorrow. It also gave me another excuse to check in with her.

I walked her out after the session and watched her leave. I just had a bad feeling about this. It had changed everything when I realized there might really be someone out there who was still after her. I was still shaken up from Adam's description of what this guy had done to the next two women he got ahold of. Would I have realized he was back sooner if that son-of-a-bitch Willy hadn't been on my tail? Yes, I would have.

That was the problem with people like Willy. They could affect you without laying on a finger. I had started worrying and fretting and orienting everything around Willy from the moment he showed up. In the meantime I couldn't see what was right in front of me. Camille had to ask me how it could be a flashback if it was about the future and not the past. Duh. The poor lady was in the fight of her life, and the only help she had was from an unethical therapist with—currently—the IQ of a gerbil.

20

When Ginger walked in the next morning, Marv and I were sitting quietly on opposite sides of the room. I had suggested we sit on the couch together and hold hands, but Marv didn't appreciate my sense of humor.

Ginger looked tense, and well she might. Marv had only told her on the phone that we needed to talk to her together and that it was important. He hadn't said what about, but Ginger knew it couldn't be good.

She sat down warily and looked from one of us to the other. I began, as Marv and I had agreed. "I want to thank you for coming in and being willing to see us together. Ordinarily we wouldn't meet with you together—if I were the client, I'd feel outnumbered—but this time we thought it was important that you talk with both of us."

Ginger was too anxious to wait. "Why?" she

said quickly, although it was pretty obvious that was exactly what I was planning on telling her.

"Give me a second, Ginger. I need to go back first. When I transferred you, I told you the truth. I told you that I thought a male therapist might be able to help you more than I could. Partly that had to do with the fact that you lost your boundaries with me and were miserable when I wasn't around, and we talked about that part.

"But we didn't talk about the fact that you crossed my boundaries and intruded on my private life. That alone was enough to terminate the therapy. In a way, it already had." Ginger looked surprised. She glanced at Marv for reassurance, but he didn't respond.

"What I'm trying to say is that for a therapist to do a good job, she has to keep her own thoughts and feelings out of the therapy as much as possible. When you become a player in the therapist's private life, she—or he—loses objectivity. The therapist starts responding to you from her or his point of view, rather than simply focusing on yours.

"And I have to tell you honestly, Ginger, having someone over and over again intrude on time that's supposed to be private kicks up a lot of bad feelings in the therapist. All that has to be put aside to be neutral and objective and supportive. If the intrusions go on long enough, the day comes when the therapist just has too many bad feelings to keep them out of the therapy. I lost faith that I could help you, not *only* because you had lost your boundaries with me, but because you were stepping on mine.

"I should have told you all that. I didn't because you were going through such a hard time that it seemed like it would just be another rejection. But by not telling you, in a way, I set you up to lose Marv too. Because you started doing the same thing with him that you did with me.

"Do you understand what I mean?"

"Sure," Ginger said angrily. "You're telling me Marv's kicking me out too."

"Not exactly," I said. "It's true that you've crossed too many boundaries with Marv to keep seeing him, and it's true you've been stalking me again . . ." I used the term deliberately, and Ginger exploded.

"I did not stalk you. I was helping you. Marv told me about that guy."

"Ginger, what guy? There's always a guy getting out of jail. I've worked with six trillion offenders. There's always somebody mad at me. It's not your job to take care of me. All you can do by stalking me is lose your own supports."

"I was just trying to help." Ginger started crying.

"I'm sorry, Ginger, but it doesn't help. It doesn't help to have somebody on a cross-country jumping course scaring my horse. It doesn't help to

271

have somebody standing in the woods staring at my house."

Ginger started crying harder and lay down on her side on the couch. She pulled up her knees and started rocking.

"I'm sorry, Ginger, but I'm not going to do you any favors if I set you up to do this again."

Marv held his hand up to stop me. "Ginger," he said softly, "how are you feeling right now?"

"I feel like shit," Ginger said. "I feel like total shit. This has happened to me all my life. No matter what I do, I'm always wrong. I've never been able to do anything right. I should just die."

I gave Marv a look. The look said, "Don't get her going or she will lock into that for the next ten light-years." It was true. Ginger was winding up. When she felt desperate, she got manipulative as hell. And she had that strange business where if she could make us feel bad, she felt good. It was as if depressed affect was some kind of ball that got passed back and forth. Ginger wouldn't have to feel her own emotions if she could just give them to us.

I wasn't biting. Transferring her feelings and glomming on to us wasn't going to help Ginger. And it was going to make me want to throttle her.

"Ginger," I said. "You're still assuming we're going to throw you out."

"You are," she said. "I know you are."

"Actually," I said, "we're not. We are transferring you, but it is to the most experienced therapist in the department."

Ginger paused but didn't speak. She was still lying on her side.

"It's true," I said. "We both feel you need someone with more experience than both of us. So sit up, if you can, because you need to hear about this and make a decision about whether you want to try it."

"Who is it?" Ginger said. Then she sat up slowly.

"The Chairman of Psychiatry," I said. "Dr. Toby Cantwell. He's been in the field longer than either Marv or me, and he's, well, he's something special. Wouldn't you agree, Marv?"

I shouldn't have said it. I could tell by the look on Marv's face that he thought I was being flippant. The truth was, I wanted to say something positive about Toby, but I was so conflicted about him, everything I thought of was double-edged. Which was stupid, because Ginger would only see the therapeutic side of Toby, which I didn't have any concerns about.

Marv turned to Ginger. "He really has had more experience than anyone else in the department. He can't fix things *for* you, Ginger, any more than we can, but if anybody can help, I suspect he can."

Ginger said, "He'll probably just kick me out too," and slumped back in her seat.

"He might," I said. "And that's why we're having this meeting. Ginger, you really need to understand this. Dr. Cantwell isn't going to tolerate your crossing his boundaries any more than Marv and I will. And he won't tolerate your crossing ours either. So here's the deal.

"Tomorrow, at four o'clock, you have your first meeting with Dr. Cantwell. Hopefully, it will go well, and it will be the beginning of some healing for you.

"But remember this, if you cross anybody's boundaries—if you hide in my woods, if you start doing drive-bys at Marv's, if you start calling Dr. Cantwell's house—then the next Tuesday at four o'clock, someone else will sit in his office. And I won't take you back and neither will Marv."

The room fell silent. It was a harsh thing to say. It was really an ugly thing to say. Ginger was completely still. She was genuinely afraid of loss, and I had just deliberately threatened her with it. Maybe it wasn't ethical. All I knew was that being threatened with loss wasn't nearly the tragedy in Ginger's life that running into Willy would be. And hiding in my woods was the easiest way to run into Willy.

I wouldn't talk about other things after that. I kept coming back to the decision she had to make. If she wanted to see Toby, she could not stalk *any* of us. If she couldn't do that, she'd have to go elsewhere for therapy.

It would work, I thought. For a while. But it wouldn't last. Ginger would behave herself for a few weeks or months, and then she'd start up again. What I had done was just buy a little time. But I had a feeling this would all be over by the time Ginger started in again. Either I'd find Willy before then, or he'd find me.

21

The phone rang around eleven. I was already in bed and not inclined to answer it, but when I heard Adam's voice on the answering machine I changed my mind. Adam said Camille was freaking out—screaming again—and Jonathan was absolutely positive no one else was in the house. He didn't tell me how Jonathan knew for sure no one had been hiding in there before he got there, but my guess was he had taken a look around while Camille was in therapy.

In any case, Jonathan insisted no one had entered since he got there, and—however he knew—he was sure no one was in there already—so there was no way around the conclusion that this time, anyway, whatever was going on was in Camille's head.

I agreed to drive in. I didn't really want to, and I didn't usually do that kind of thing. If I came in every time Camille got upset, I might as well pull up a camper on her lawn, but I could hardly say no. Small town police forces don't have enough people to do a twenty-four-hour stakeout, and I knew what a drain it was on Adam's resources to do this. So when he asked for help, I just said, "On my way."

But why? I wondered on the way in. Adam had seen lots of people upset and freaking out. Why was he dragging me in? I picked up the car phone and called him. I was getting used to the damn car phone. Worse, I was getting dependent on it, which, of course, was the problem with owning. You don't really own anything; things own you.

He picked it up on the first ring. "Adam," I said, "I'm on my way in, and I don't want you to misunderstand this. I don't mind going in, but I am curious why you thought it was important for me to see her tonight."

He didn't hesitate. "Somebody has to check out the screaming. Jonathan was concerned enough that he called me at home. He says it sounds completely out-of-control, and, already, the station is getting calls from the neighbors.

"Jonathan thinks nobody else could have gotten in there, but the whole thing is bothering him enough that he wants to go in and check it out, anyway. I think he's concerned she's going to hang herself, or maybe that damn dog we ran into last time is going to shoot her while Jonathan's standing outside twiddling his thumbs.

"I told him to hold off. You know a strange man can't just show up at her door, and there's no point in my going: She's never even met me. You're the only one she knows."

"Not a problem," I said. I couldn't argue with his thinking. One of Adam's strengths was that he thought things through under pressure. He didn't just rush in like some people I knew. "I'll go see what's going on."

Ten to one Camille was just horribly upset. In suicide assessment you always have to figure out the difference in "perturbation" and "lethality." Some of the people who are the most upset aren't always serious about dying, and some of the people who are serious about dying are deadly calm. But Jonathan didn't know Camille well enough to read her. And if they didn't check it out and something happened, everybody involved would be traumatized. Not to mention that Camille might be dead.

I pulled into her driveway and rolled down the window. I couldn't hear anything. The yelling had stopped. That doesn't mean anything, I reminded myself. It stopped last time too, and Camille was sitting in the house popping Haldol and still insisting she heard the perp. But silence is creepier than noise, and I found my heartbeat quickening. There was always the chance someone like Camille would hang herself or something, and the thought that I could be the one to find her unnerved the hell out of me.

I got out of the car and stared at the house. The lights were on, and there was no sign anything was wrong. Keeter wasn't barking. But that didn't mean anything. She had been trained to stay silent and ambush an intruder. Remind me, I thought one more time, not to crowd this dog.

I looked toward the park. No sign of Jonathan. Well, he was out there somewhere, but it looked like I wasn't going to get a welcoming committee.

I walked up to the doorway and knocked, but I didn't wait for a reply. "Camille," I said. "It's Michael. Are you all right?" How many times was I going to walk up to her silent house after a report of screaming? But even if it was a thousand, I'd bet each and every time I'd still be afraid something really bad had happened to her.

"Michael," a faint voice answered very close to the door. I let my breath out. Whatever was going on, she was definitely alive.

"Could you open the door, Camille?" I asked. "It really is me, and I'm alone."

Camille opened the door a crack and peered out. Then she closed it and pulled the chain off. She opened it wide, and I walked in. I immediately looked for Keeter. There she was, crouched on the floor, ready to spring. She didn't look that much friendlier than last time.

"Uh, do you think you could do something about Keeter?" I asked. Camille glanced at her and then made a hand signal. Keeter reluctantly got up and walked over to her, but she kept her eye on me the whole time.

"He was here," Camille whispered. She looked like she was barely able to hold it together. Her pupils were dilated, and her eyes were open so wide I could almost see the whites all the way around. Uh-oh. It was beginning to look like paranoia after all. The only times I had ever seen the whites all around the eyes were in paranoids.

"Camille," I said. "Let's sit down and talk about it."

She took me to the living room, and I sat down, but Camille didn't. She was so agitated she couldn't. She rocked back and forth from one foot to the other. She looked like she might start pacing.

"How do you know he was here?" I asked.

"I heard him." She was still whispering. "He said he was coming for me soon. He said I'd die this time. He said . . . he . . ."

"Whoa, Camille, I know you thought he was here, but it couldn't have been real. There's a police officer outside named Jonathan, and he's been here all afternoon. He says no one could have gotten in. Do you want to talk to him?"

"No," she said quickly. "He's outside?" She went to the window and looked through the blinds. I had the bad feeling she was getting Jonathan and her attacker confused.

"Camille," I said. "The *police* are outside. The perp isn't."

"I know," she said turning around and looking all around the room. "He's here." Even though I knew he wasn't, the hair started to stand up on the back of my neck.

"Your mind is playing tricks on you," I said firmly. "He can't be here."

"He never comes out when you're here," she said. "He always waits. Will you stay? Please?"

"I can only stay for a while," I said. Oh, Jesus, what were the ethics of this? I was not only at a client's house involved in her private life, I couldn't get out.

"Please, Michael. Please don't leave me alone with him. Please don't." She had turned to face me, and her voice slid into pleading as she spoke.

It was painful to hear her beg, but the fear was so strong I doubt she even noticed she was begging. What, I wondered again, were the ethics of staying? On the other hand, what were the ethics of leaving?

"I would be all right," she said, "if you stayed— just for tonight. I could maybe even sleep. . . . I can't sleep here alone. . . ." Her voice trailed off.

What were my options? I could hospitalize her. I had no doubt they'd admit her in her present state, but where would that lead? Nowhere. She'd end up owing a ton of money to the hospital. We'd have another six-hour fight over Keeter, and Camille would be out tomorrow.

She had no friends or family I could call. It was too late to find a private duty nurse. There were no volunteer organizations I could think of to call, plus I wouldn't put a volunteer in with someone who might be paranoid. Paranoids are not too stable.

On the other hand, staying at a client's house is so unethical they hadn't bothered to put it in the code of ethics. It is one of those "duh" items. But what choice did I have? She wouldn't make it through the night alone in this state. And she wasn't Ginger. I didn't think she'd start manipulating around this.

"All right. I'll stay tonight," I said carefully. "I will sleep on the couch and leave early in the morning. And tomorrow we will make arrangements for a private nurse to stay with you— agreed?" Camille nodded vigorously. But then if I'd said, "I'll stay if you'll jump out of a ten-story window tomorrow," she'd also have agreed.

"Camille, you really need to understand this. I will not do this again."

"I know," she said. "I won't ask." And I believed her.

I sighed. I did not want to be there. I wanted to be home. I needed some time away from the world each and every day. Not to mention that I was acutely uncomfortable spending the night in a client's house. But there was no point in bitching, I was stuck.

I called Adam to tell him. He was apologetic for putting me in that position. I had my own apologies to make. It was beginning to look like the perp was in Camille's head after all.

I went out to the car and took off my fanny pack and locked it in the trunk. I'd been carrying it nonstop lately, but I wasn't going to go to sleep in Camille's house and leave a loaded gun lying around. The risks of a loaded gun around Camille outweighed the benefits. I didn't even want to think how I'd feel if she killed herself with my gun. Not to mention that if she got ahold of it in the night and had a major flashback, she could just as easily decide I was the perp and shoot me.

I got my travel bag and went back in. I found my toothbrush and my nightshirt, but decided I'd sleep in my clothes. It was bad enough to be in a client's house; I was not going to run around in my pj's. I spread out the blankets Camille provided on the couch.

My one fear was that Camille was so wired she would stay awake all night and keep me up. Once the nervous system goes on red alert like hers had, it doesn't usually settle down very fast. But after Camille knew I was staying, she started losing steam.

Her energy drained quickly, and she soon lost

all of her agitation. Once she let go of the fear-energy, there didn't seem to be anything else holding her up. I told her firmly to go to bed—and take Keeter with her. I'd be in the living room on the couch, and I promised not to go anywhere.

Camille insisted on leaving the door open to her room, which I wasn't too happy about. I had fantasies of waking up and finding I was nose to nose with a snarling rottweiler. It would have been nice if the couch had had a top bunk.

It didn't take long before I was drifting off. I wondered sleepily if Adam had called off Jonathan. If this one was in Camille's head, probably the other ones were too. Everything seemed turned upside down lately. I was trying to protect myself from Willy, but I had almost shot a client instead, and I'd yet to see Willy, who was hovering out there somewhere in Never-Never Land. I was sleeping at a client's house; try to explain that to Ginger who—dear God—I hoped wouldn't drive by. Marv and I had punched holes the size of golf balls in our friendship. How easy would it be to repair that? In the meantime, the only way I could get near Adam was to bring him a police problem. I didn't want Adam *in* his police uniform; I wanted him *out* of it.

I could start with the top buttons. One at a time. As the buttons opened I could run my fingers through the soft, curly hair on his chest. Somewhere around that taut stomach I'd run out of hair—briefly. As I kept going lower his breathing would change. I loved the way it deepened as his . . . interest . . . grew. I was smiling as I drifted off.

I was dreaming that I was facing ethics charges in the World Court in the Hague. The prosecutor was walking toward me when suddenly, he turned into Willy. He got very close to me and started whispering, almost hissing, in my face.

I woke in the dark, disoriented and confused with my heart rate doing 80 miles an hour. It took me a minute to realize where I was. It took me another minute to get the dream out of my head. I could still hear him whispering and another sound too, a sort of whimpering.

I couldn't get the whispering to stop. Jesus, what a dream. I sat up and looked around. And then I stopped breathing. I was wide awake, and I could still hear a man whispering, almost hissing. The whimpering was Camille.

I hit the deck and crawled around behind the couch while I tried to figure things out. I was wide awake now, but still confused. At first I couldn't even tell where the voice was coming from—and I couldn't begin to figure out how he had gotten in, with Keeter on the inside and Jonathan on the outside. Maybe Jonathan had left after I called Adam.

I tried to remember where I'd put my fanny pack and realized I had left it in the car. Great. I'd been carrying my gun to the bathroom lately, but I hadn't brought it into Camille's house.

Where was the goddamn phone? I had used it once. I remembered it was cordless. So where had I put it? I couldn't remember. The room was dark now, and nothing looked familiar. Oh, shit. I had handed the phone back to Camille. I didn't have a clue where it was, and I couldn't see Jack shit.

I could yell. If Jonathan was still outside, he'd hear me. But if the perp was in here, Jonathan probably wasn't out there. And what a chance to take. If Jonathan wasn't outside, calling him might turn out badly. Jesus, the perp had probably walked right by me while I was asleep. Had he seen me? Did he know I was here? If not, where did he think that car came from?

Keeter, you bitch. Go after the bastard. She must know him. That has to be it. I stopped and listened again. I could try to make it to the car and get the car phone, but I didn't even remember if it would work without the car being turned on, and I'd have to leave Camille alone.

First, I had to find out where he was. I started crawling toward Camille's room. The sound was coming from in there. I crawled forward expecting any minute to find a gun the size of a cannon pointed at my head, but the voice just kept going. What was he saying? I was close enough to hear, and I dropped down to listen.

"Ah, your clitoris—what a juicy little morsel. I'll give you a choice. A lighted cigarette? A scalpel? That might be best for you. Once I cut it off, it won't hurt anymore. Except, of course, for the gaping wound. Maybe pliers. But I'd like to save those for your nipples. You'll have to choose which instrument. If you don't choose, I'll just cut off your fingers, one joint at a time, until you change your mind."

Oh, boy. Verbal torture. Camille started to wail. The perp's voice didn't change at all. But that was what had always struck me about sadists. They talk about torture like everybody else talks about going to the grocery store. Sadists all have that strange flat lack of feeling in their voices.

The sound from Camille was rising, and it began to drown out the perp. Soon she'd be screaming incoherently. Who could blame her? A big part of me wanted to scream too and head for the front door. Maybe I should. If I could get to a phone in time, Adam might just catch the son-of-a-bitch.

I was almost at the door to Camille's room. I crawled to the wall next to it and looked around the corner into her room. I wanted to see where he was first. My eyes had adapted to the dark, and I looked around. I could see Camille sitting up in bed with her hands on her cheeks. Even in the dark I could see she was shaking. I could see Keeter lying beside the bed, but I couldn't see the perp. Where was he hiding? The room wasn't that big.

I paused trying to figure out which way to go. I took a deep breath and started crawling slowly forward. I could barely hear him talking under Camille's wailing. I crawled forward, inches at a time, and looked all around the room. I could hear him, but I couldn't see him. I inched toward the closet, but stopped when I realized the voice wasn't coming from there.

Finally, I got it. I really got it. I stood up and walked over to the lights and flipped them on. Camille didn't even notice. Keeter did, and she looked at me like maybe she'd finally found the source of the problem. I walked back into the living room and turned on the lights there. There wasn't anybody in either room, but the voice just kept going.

I found the phone and called Adam at home. He answered immediately. "Adam," I said. "I'm at Camille's. Can you hear me?"

"Barely," he said. Camille was sobbing and screaming. She was in a full-blown flashback and was begging the perp not to hurt her anymore.

"I think you'd better get over here," I said. "I've figured out the problem. There's no perp here, but there is a voice. There is definitely a voice."

"On my way," he said.

I walked back into Camille's room. I wasn't going to look for the tape recorder. Everything was evidence now, and I knew enough to keep my mitts off. "Camille," I said, "it's Michael." I walked around the side of the bed farthest from Keeter and held out my hand. "Come on, we're leaving." It would have been easier if I could have shut the goddamn recording off.

"Camille," I said, again. "It's Michael, we're leaving." She turned toward me. "Don't let him hurt me, please," she whimpered. "I won't," I said. In the distance I could hear the sirens starting.

"We're leaving. Let's go."

"But . . . he . . ."

"You're not tied," I said loudly to drown out that incessant voice. "You don't have any tape on. It's over. Let's go. We're going over to Harvey's house." I held out my hand again.

This time Camille slowly took it. She was half in this world and half in another. Keeter came around my side of the bed and looked at me suspiciously. No wonder she wasn't any help. What's a dog supposed to do with a tape recorder?

Camille got up slowly, and I put my arm around her and walked her out of the room. Tears were running down her cheeks, and I could feel her shoulders heave with convulsive sobs, but she had stopped screaming. The whole thing reminded me of somebody Adam had walked out of a gym not so long ago—me.

The voice got fainter as we moved through the living room. I opened the front door in time to see the red lights coming down the street. Adam lived a little farther out, and the police cars had beaten him in. Harvey came out of his house, and I asked him to take Camille to his house, I'd be right back. I walked back into Camille's house just as the police cars were pulling up. I just wanted to hear that voice one time without anybody screaming. I thought I knew it somehow. I walked into the bedroom and listened.

Son-of-a-bitch, I thought, when I realized who it was. Son-of-a-bitch.

22

By the next day, it was all over. The police found the tape recorder that the son-of-a-bitch had hidden in the bed. It was not a simple business: It was attached to a device that caused it to start randomly and rewind automatically when the tape was over. Since Camille was the only one there, she was the only one who ever heard it.

It was a custom job, not the kind of thing you could go out to Radio Shack and buy. It took a clever fellow to set it up for random play, but that was hardly a surprise. Willy was always a clever fellow.

Adam put out an APB on Willy on the strength of my recognizing his voice. But since he could easily have hit the road by now—leaving me to wonder and Camille to suffer—we all knew it might take a while to track him down, if ever.

Camille was staying at Harvey and his wife's

house for a few days. She hadn't wanted to go back home alone, and Harvey and Lenore had gallantly offered her a place. I suspected they would shortly regret their kindness or impulsiveness. It is more than a little difficult to deal with someone suffering from PTSD, and Harvey didn't much like dogs.

In the meantime the police were going to continue quietly watching Camille's house. Willy's equipment was there. Maybe he'd come back to check it or remove it or whatever.

I had gone home shortly after Adam arrived. He knew about Willy getting out of prison, and he knew all about Camille, so there was nothing I *had* to tell him that night. I did have a whole lot more to tell him—Willy and the e-mail and the bugging of my office and all that. But it would be better, I thought, to tell him in the privacy of his office in the morning.

I didn't relish the exchange—I had promised to tell Adam if Willy contacted me, and I hadn't done it—but I was too damn tired to get into it in the middle of the night. Tomorrow, I decided. I would tell him tomorrow. That would still be in time to head off Carlotta and in plenty of time for whatever help it would give in catching Willy.

But when morning came, I hung around for a while. I would tell him; I had to. But first I needed a little time to recharge my own batteries.

I made some coffee and headed for the deck. It

was a crisp spring morning, and I put on the bathrobe Carlotta had given me for Christmas. It was made from Turkish terry cloth and was luxuriously thick and soft. It wasn't the sort of thing I would ever have bought for myself: mostly I sleep in T-shirts and avoid single-purpose items like the plague.

But Carlotta had known me better than I knew myself. It was a licking-your-wounds robe, and I frequently had wounds to lick. It was the thing to wear when you missed the big shot at the buzzer, when you lost the case you should have won, or when a kid you fought for went back to an abusing parent—although there wasn't enough terry cloth in the world to help that. It was what I instinctively reached for today, when I had to face the fact that coming to see me had made Camille worse.

Camille had come into my life with active PTSD from running into one of nature's little aberrations: a full-blown, card-carrying, soul-dead sadist. She had been in awful shape, but not nearly as bad as she was now. If she hadn't met me, Willy would never have stalked her and harassed her and she would never have had the many flashbacks he had caused. She had deteriorated to the max, and that wouldn't have happened without his help. And the problem was, he would never have crossed her threshold if she hadn't crossed mine.

If I tried to tell Carlotta or Adam how miserable I felt about bringing Camille a gift like Willy—not that I was going to—all I'd get back was that it wasn't my fault. As if that helped. People are dolts, myself included.

For years, I hadn't understood why rape victims kept insisting it was their fault. If they hadn't been walking down the street at seven o'clock at night, if they hadn't worn a skirt above the knee, if they hadn't been wearing high heels, it never would have happened.

I finally got it. What would I rather believe—that I had some control and could keep it from happening again by changing a hemline? Or that it could happen anytime, anyplace, no matter what I did? Helplessness is never a plus.

And I also felt helpless. I *was* helpless in this case. I had never intended to let Willy loose on Camille. I hadn't even realized it was a possibility. And that just made everything worse. If they didn't catch Willy, he would inflict a sense of helplessness on me I'd have trouble living with. He could come back and do something—something new and nasty—to anyone I knew, anyone I cared about, anyone I treated.

I really did have to talk to Adam. Maybe he could figure out some clue from Willy's e-mail, about how he got access to my office. If there was anything at all in Willy's behavior that would help catch him, I needed to be sure Adam had it. If

Adam didn't catch Willy, sooner or later Willy would strip away any sense of efficacy I had. And I didn't even want to think about the amount of destruction he'd leave in his wake.

I got up reluctantly. There was something soothing in the robe and the stream and the sunlight, and the rest of the day wasn't going to measure up. I'd have to call Adam from the office and arrange a time to talk about this. Necessary but painful. There was the small issue of betraying his trust by lying to him. But first, Camille was coming in, and I had to get there in time to sweep the room for bugs before she came.

I drove in preoccupied with the strange way things work. Hemingway was no fool. Nobody is an island no matter how much they want to be. What would it take? I had moved to an isolated house in the country, given up on any kind of normal social life, thrown away most of my possessions, and I was still a sitting duck.

I knew what it took. You had to not give a shit about any other human being if you wanted to be invulnerable to the kind of thing Willy had pulled. Son-of-a-bitch had just set the price higher than I could pay.

I got out of the car and reluctantly took off the fanny pack. As long as Willy was out there I still wanted to wear it nonstop, but I had a few rules about guns. I never took one into my office because I saw children there. Children and guns are a bad combination. I had counseled adults who had dead children because they had hidden their guns in one locked drawer and their bullets in a different one and their kids still got into them. I put the fanny pack in the trunk and closed it, feeling nude and vulnerable without it.

I walked in, took the bug detector out of the drawer, and scanned the room with renewed vigor. The last thing I wanted to do at this point was to tip Willy off that we knew what he was up to. But again I found nothing, nothing, and more nothing.

I looked at the scanner. There was one possibility I hadn't even thought about. What if the damn thing was broken?

Oh, Jesus, what a mess that would be. I sat down and tried to think. There were other possibilities. I hadn't heard from Willy since the e-mail about that lying little twerp. For all I knew, he could be a thousand miles away. He'd scared the bejesus out of me and left his little device with Camille. No doubt he had hung around to savor her deterioration for a while, but for how long? I really didn't have any way of knowing if he was even still around. Playing a few minutes at a time, a few times a day, his recorder would run for weeks without needing new batteries.

The scanner could be working fine. Willy could just be gone.

That, of course, was the worst-case scenario I

had been mulling over all morning. He could be running blitzkrieg campaigns, wreaking havoc and then disappearing. If he stayed away for months or years until everything died down, he could resurface safely and start all over again. If he kept doing that, he could make me miserable for years and years without getting caught. Or worse, he could lull me into thinking all he was going to do was harass me.

As I remembered, Alexander the Great did something like that with some elephants once upon a time. He had marched up and down the river at random times in the night until the enemy quit even getting up to see the parade. Then one night he crossed the river.

I stared at the phone. I should call Adam. I had left myself enough time to go by and talk to Adam. This was harder than I thought. Maybe betraying Adam's trust was kind of a big deal to me, and I had well and truly done that. Who said you couldn't develop new skills in your forties. First, lying, now procrastination. Pretty soon I'd be into passive aggression—which had always eluded me before.

The phone rang, and I jumped. If it was anybody but Adam I was going to be relieved.

"Michael, do you have time to see us today?"

"Lorraine?" Lorraine was a single mom with three small boys. She tended only to call in a crisis, and then she needed to be seen that second.

In between, there was no point in setting appointments: She canceled and failed to show and left messages that everything was fine.

In Lorraine's world, problems were ignored until they couldn't be. I'd made my peace with the fact that I wasn't going to change her disorganized and sometimes abusive parenting style, but maybe I could keep the situation as stable as possible—at least I could try to keep her from killing any of her offspring.

As if reading my mind, Lorraine added, "So help me, God, I'm going to kill the little bastard this time."

"How about right now?" I said looking at my watch. Camille wasn't due for an hour, and Lorraine didn't live far.

"The sooner the better," she said and hung up.

Thank you, Lorraine. It was a short reprieve, but maybe it would give me time to figure out why I was so upset about fessing up to Adam. And it was a situation where I would have postponed talking to him even if I had wanted to.

To my surprise, Lorraine showed up with her eldest, six-year-old Daniel, in tow. Usually it was Damion, her two-year-old, or Donald, her three-year-old, who had fought or broken something or disappeared or whatever. Lorraine was one of those moms who thought it was cute to start all her children's names with the same letter.

"He's a goddamn pervert," she said, completely

ignoring Daniel, who looked more dejected than I had ever seen him. He had reluctantly followed his mother into the waiting room and stood by the door as if ready to bolt.

"Whoa," I said. "Let's let Daniel sit here in the waiting room and play for a minute while we talk." This was not a mother I wanted to see *with* the child. Lorraine's idea of talking to her child was to heap emotional abuse on his head. "But one thing I know," I said looking at Daniel. "Daniel is not a pervert."

Daniel looked slightly relieved. Jesus, the self-fulfilling prophecies people lay on their children. I gathered up some Play-Doh and Magic Markers and paper and set Daniel up in the waiting room. I smiled at him. "Your mama is upset," I said, "and she says things that aren't true when she's upset. I know you're not a pervert"—whatever Daniel thought that was. "Let me talk with her for a few minutes, and we'll figure things out." I walked back into my office and closed the door calmly. Lorraine was sitting on the couch, looking so angry she was one step short of one of her fits-of-screaming-rage attacks.

"Goddamn it, Michael," she said. "Every time I try to do something nice for them, they spoil it. They've broken every fucking toy they own. So why do I bother? Don't think my son-of-a-bitching father ever bought a goddamn thing for me. But do they appreciate a thing I do? I was so pleased he hadn't broken this one. What a joke!"

She reached into a bag and brought out something that looked like a miniature radar dish attached to a handle that looked like a joystick. There were wires hanging down and earphones. She threw it on the couch.

"Slow down," I said sitting down very slowly. I move slowly and I talk slowly when people are upset. People respond to body English more than they know. The temptation is almost overwhelming to match their agitated tempo, but that just makes things worse. "I don't have a clue what you're talking about, but one thing I know for sure, if you keep calling Daniel a pervert, sooner or later he's going to believe you."

"So it's my fault if he turns into a pervert?" she said. "Why is everything always my fault?" Lorraine sounded like a petulant eight-year-old, which in some ways she was.

"Lorraine, calm down," I said gently. "All I'm saying is your children listen to you more than you know. Tell the truth. Somewhere in your soul, don't you still believe you're what your father said you were?"

"What's that got to do with it?" she said.

"Everything," I said. "Do you want Daniel to carry around the idea he's a pervert? No matter what he's done, he's still six years old, for Christ's sake."

"He's a six-year-old pervert," she said. "You

know, they suck me in every time. I should have known. Do you know why he hadn't broken this toy? Do you know why? Because he'd discovered he could peep on the neighbors with it, that's why."

"Peep on the neighbors?" I said, surprised. It was certainly a new behavior for Daniel, as far as I knew.

"Yes, peep on the neighbors. You know how our houses are so close—well, you don't, but if my neighbor sneezes I get a cold. Anyway, Daniel's window is just a few feet from our neighbor's bedroom window."

"And he was peeping on him?"

"Yes, he was. I came in to check on him. To tell you the truth, he was too quiet. Usually, he's calling me every two seconds. He wants water. He wants a story. He has to go to the bathroom. He's scared. He acts just like a big baby. But the last few nights, he's gone to bed just like that. No water, no nothing.

"The first couple of nights I was so tired, I was just grateful. I mean, Damion and Donald were still up every two seconds, so it wasn't like I got to sit down. Then I began to wonder. Daniel hadn't seemed sick, but I started thinking maybe he was. I went in to check on him, and there he was, sitting at the window in the dark, peeping on the neighbors."

"Lorraine, let me ask you some questions,

okay? To try and sort out what's going on. Have you ever caught Daniel doing anything sexual?"

"Sure. He used to put his bottle on his you-know-what and rock on it when he went to sleep."

"When he was a toddler, right?"

"Well, he hasn't had one since then."

"Most kids play with themselves."

"Not mine."

"You've got to trust me a little bit, Lorraine. There's a big difference in kids doing things you don't like and being a pervert. Does Daniel play with himself around other children or in school or anything like that?"

"Oh, no. I'd have beat the shit out of him if he'd done anything like that."

"Has he done anything sexual with other kids that you know about?"

"My God, no."

"Has anything happened, anything at all, to make you concerned about Daniel and sex?"

"You mean before this?"

"Yes."

"No, but this is bad enough."

"Actually, to be honest with you—and I say this knowing you'll find it hard to believe—it isn't."

"It isn't? This isn't bad enough? What are you talking about? If the neighbors had caught him, he could have been arrested."

"Not at six, he couldn't. Lorraine, kids are curious about sex. You may not like it, but it's true.

302

Weren't you? Don't you remember being curious about sex as a kid?"

"Me? I knew more than I ever wanted to know about sex by the time I was six, thanks to my son-of-a-bitching father."

"Well, Daniel doesn't—thanks to the fact that he's had better parenting than you did. He's just curious."

"Well, he shouldn't have been doing it." Some of the wind had gone out of Lorraine's sails, but in her mind she couldn't back down.

"True enough. But normal kids do a lot of things they shouldn't do. It doesn't make them perverts. Look, it's good news. Right? What, you want to be raising a pervert? Or you'd rather be raising a normal kid who gets into stuff he shouldn't?"

There was silence. I probably didn't entirely persuade her, but on the other hand at least she calmed down. Later, she even looked a little sheepish when she faced Daniel in the waiting room. Lorraine called her children every name in the book when she was upset, but when she calmed down, she was usually sorry. There were even times she apologized, which wasn't nearly as good as not doing it in the first place.

I didn't get that much time with Daniel; I spent most of my time calming Lorraine down and getting her to see that, maybe, she was a bit sensitive about sex, and, just maybe, it had more to do

303

with her father than Daniel. All I could really do for Daniel was to reassure him. By the time they left, they were in better shape than when they came, but it wouldn't last.

As Lorraine opened the door to leave, Camille came in with Keeter. Lorraine and Daniel backed up and gave Keeter a wide berth. I had to smile. Ordinarily Daniel was overly friendly with animals, but this was one time his mother didn't have to tell him not to pet a strange dog. Daniel had better sense than his mother gave him credit for.

I wasn't sure what to expect with Camille. We hadn't had much chance to talk last night. Was she relieved to know that it was Willy and not the kidnapper who was after her, or would it frighten her all the more that there were *two* sadists out there? It didn't help, of course, that Willy hadn't been caught.

Camille came in and started to sit down. Daniel's toy was still on the couch, and she handed it to me before she sat down. I put it on the floor beside me. It was probably all right that they left it. I didn't think Daniel was going to get to play with it for a while, and it would just remind Lorraine of his "pervertedness."

Keeter took up her usual stance, lying between me and Camille, although she did look bored, which I took as a positive comment on our relationship.

FAULT LINES

"How do you feel?" I asked, looking closely at Camille. She didn't really look any better: same dark circles under her eyes, same fearful glancing at the windows. I realized I was holding my breath while I waited for her answer.

"I don't know," she said, slowly. "I guess I'm relieved you believe me. Nothing else has really changed. I knew he was out there."

"You mean Willy?" I asked.

"Yes," she said. "I never had a name before. I think that helps a little."

I paused a minute. What was wrong with this picture? "Camille, I'm confused," I admitted. "Are you talking about Willy or the guy who kidnapped you?"

Now Camille looked confused. "What do you mean? It's the same. Didn't you know that?"

I most certainly did not know that, and there was something very wrong with that idea. Why did she think they were the same person? I glanced down as I thought and noticed the toy on the floor. Hell of a thing. How did he peep with that thing, anyway? Was it infrared? Then I froze. Was I seeing what I thought I was?

I reached over and picked it up slowly. There was the radar-looking dish with the joystick. And there were wires. I followed them to a set of earphones and put them on. I turned the dish around and pointed it at Keeter. I clicked the joystick, and suddenly the sound of Keeter licking

305

her paw filled my earphones. I stood up slowly and did it again. Keeter had stopped licking her paw and looked up at me curiously. In the earphones, her breathing sounded like the ocean's roar. Daniel hadn't been peeping; he had been eavesdropping.

Camille was staring at me, but it didn't seem important. I walked around behind my chair and tried the toy again. Nothing. "Line-of-sight," I said out loud. "Son-of-a-bitch."

No wonder. No wonder I couldn't find a bug. I headed straight for the windows and looked up. There was nothing facing the side window, but the front windows were across the street from a church, and there was one window that looked straight down, line-of-sight, on my window.

I pointed the toy up to the window and squeezed the button. Nothing. Maybe nobody was up there now. Or maybe I just had a toy version of this thing, and the range wasn't that far. But if there was a toy version of this thing, there was a real version of this thing. "Son-of-a-bitch," was all I could say. I had wondered about Willy planting a tape and just leaving it. It wasn't like Willy not to stay around for the suffering. Well, he had.

I headed for the door. "I've got to go," I managed to say, and then I caught myself at the door and stopped. I suddenly had the feeling of hands around my throat so distinctly I could hardly breathe. The last time I had run off on my own, it had turned out badly. Who says I can't learn? All it takes is strangling me.

I turned around. I needed to get my fanny pack—but I realized I couldn't. The fanny pack was in the car trunk. If I went outside and took it out of the car trunk, Willy could see me. The goddamn car was sitting in the driveway in full sight of the church. Getting a fanny pack out of a car trunk in the middle of a therapy session would tip off somebody a lot dumber than Willy.

I took a deep breath: I'd just have to push through this. I turned around—I needed to tell Camille something to explain my crazy behavior—when I caught sight of the window. I walked over and pulled the shades down. Line-of-sight. All I had needed to do was pull the shades down. Willy had never teased me about Danny because the shades had been down and he hadn't been able to listen in. He never knew he'd been there.

I picked up the cordless phone and handed it to Camille. "I'm sorry, Camille," I said. "I really have to go, but I'll be back. If I'm not back, if you hear anything, call 911." Camille looked totally appalled. She just looked at me. I waited, but she didn't speak. I turned and headed for the door.

She found her voice. "Wait," she said. "He's out there, isn't he?"

"Yes," I said.

"You're going looking for him," she said with pure disbelief in her voice.

"Yes."

There was silence, and I started to move again when Camille spoke. "Take Keeter," she said. "Don't go alone." I turned, and she was holding out the lead. Her chin and her hand were both quivering, but still she held it out. Jesus, the courage that took.

I looked at Keeter. She looked like a big comfort right now. I crossed the room and took the lead. Keeter stood up and looked at Camille and looked at me. Would she go with me?

"Keeter," I said forcefully, "I don't have time to screw around, so let's go." I started to move, but Keeter didn't. She just stood there looking at Camille. Camille made a hand signal, and Keeter turned and trotted after me, looking excited. The leash fell slack as she automatically heeled. Clearly, something was up, and Keeter seemed to like it more than just sitting around.

I ran from the waiting room into the living part of Carlotta's house and out the back door. Keeter trotted beside me quietly. I crossed several backyards and then took a chance and crossed the street half a block down from my office. I walked through backyards all the way and came up to the back door of the church across the street from my office. Keeter was still heeling even though I hadn't asked her to. She seemed focused and intent, but she had a look that said lunch was about to be served.

The back door of the church was unlocked, and I just walked in. The building was silent. Weekdays, probably there weren't a lot of people around. I crossed the main chapel to the front of the church and found the stairs going up. I went up to the second floor and walked into what looked like the minister's office. I was glad he wasn't there. It was easier not having to explain, and besides, I didn't want anybody to know someone had been spying on my clients.

I looked out the window in his office, but the shrubs that partially covered my office windows blocked the view. Why didn't I think to notice how far up that window was? I headed back for the stairs and went up to the third floor.

Then I found it: a large room overlooking my office with nothing in it but some cardboard storage boxes. The light in the room was dim, the blind on the one window was pulled most of the way down, and the lights were off. I walked over to the window and knelt down to see under the blind. I didn't touch anything. This was a crime scene, and I didn't want to contaminate evidence.

But even peeping under the blind I could tell it was a perfect line-of-sight bead on my office window. And it looked like you could hang out here forever and no one was likely to know.

The room was empty. So maybe Willy knew the police were after him and he had fled. Whatever. But this was it. The son-of-a-bitch had sat in this

ANNA SALTER

empty, dark room and listened in on God knows
how many therapy sessions. And all my sweeping
for bugs had done exactly nothing because there
had never been a bug to sweep for in the first
place. What was he going to do, harass all my
clients, or did he just pick Camille because she
was the most vulnerable? Jesus, what had I done
to my clients by keeping my practice open? Had
he recorded them?

I walked around the room looking for signs of
Willy and trying to sort things out. Wendy and the
lost boys. I was wrong. He hadn't been taunting
me with kids he was going to molest. Wendy took
care of her siblings and the lost boys. Peter Pan
had showed up to lead everybody off to fantasyland. No doubt, he had cast me as Wendy, taking
care of my grown-up charges, while he saw himself as Peter Pan, trying to lure them away—
although his idea of fantasyland was a little different from Peter Pan's.

I had dropped the lead to let Keeter look
around. She was sniffing around the boxes, and I
noticed the hair on the back of her neck was
standing up. She was smelling something and
seemed to recognize it. Probably she recognized
Willy's smell from Camille's bedroom. He had to
get in there sometime to plant the tape recorder.
His smell would have still been there when Keeter
got back, and she wouldn't have liked it: an
intruder in her space.

310

Keeter walked behind some boxes stacked in front of the window, and I lost sight of her. No doubt that was where Willy had sat or knelt or something, since it was directly in front of the window.

I decided to join her to see if I could find evidence someone had been there—the dust on the windowsill might be disturbed—when I heard sounds on the stairs. Oh, my God. Let it be the minister. But I knew it wasn't. I knew instantly it was Willy. He was just late, that was all, but he was coming to listen in.

There was time. I could hide. But I couldn't. I couldn't stand crouching down waiting to be caught. I just stood there: What else could I do?

Willy's shadow preceded him, which didn't help my nerves any. He came around the corner with something that looked like a large camera bag slung over his shoulder. He looked startled when he saw me, and then he grinned. He put both his arms on the sides of the door, pretty much filling the door frame.

Neither of us spoke for a moment in the dim light. Funny, I didn't realize he was so big. I knew he was portly, but I thought he was medium-sized. Belatedly I realized that an average male was still taller than me at five-seven. And being a wide-body counts when there is only one door.

"Well, well, well," he said. "Clever girl. I do underrate you at times. You must grant it was quite an aesthetic little number. A rather elegant way to get to you, don't you think? I set myself a challenge: What kind of havoc could I wreak without laying a finger on anyone?"

Willy dropped his arms from the door frame and patted his portly belly. It was an oddly incongruous gesture: it seemed so normal. His tone—his gestures—he could have been discussing the weather, only he wasn't.

"I see you came alone. How nice. I was just thinking of you and how we might continue our little tête-à-tête in a more intimate way. To be honest, I was tiring of all these silly technological toys. Too esoteric. Too . . . bloodless, shall we say. How thoughtful of you to solve my little dilemma."

"Give it up, Willy," I said firmly. "The police know all about you. We found your tape recording. They're waiting for you now at Camille's." My voice sounded better than I expected. Not great, but at least I didn't squeak.

"Beside the point," Willy answered. "Given we're not there." If he hadn't known they were looking for him, he covered it well.

"Fortunately," he went on, "my motto is 'Be prepared,' a hangover from my days as a scout leader." He opened the bag over his shoulder, his eyes never leaving me. He carefully took out what looked like a larger version of the toy radar dish and put it aside on the top of a box. He reached back into the bag.

"Did you know you can torture someone in complete silence? Oh, yes. It's just a little more complicated. You have to be careful with the gags and all that. Not that it's as satisfying as actually hearing the moaning. I personally prefer the way the moaning deepens as the pain grows. But one does what one can." He sighed, then he reached into the bag and pulled out a small .45 with a silencer.

Involuntarily, I took a step backward. Oh, shit. I should have made my move immediately. Great, the first time in my life I hesitate and think about something, and it is exactly the wrong thing to do. I should have run into him as he was coming around the corner. Willy may have underrated me a little, but I sure as hell had underrated him a lot.

He reached back into the bag. Slowly, he pulled things out: a large bowie knife, precut lengths of rope, a gag, duct tape, and then some things that seemed even worse—a lighter, a scalpel, a pair of pliers, and some instrument-looking things I didn't recognize. He did it all so carefully it was almost hypnotic, pulling each one out and laying it precisely, just so, on a cardboard box he used as a table. He spaced them carefully, evenly apart from each other. I'd heard of torture kits, read about them, but I had never seen one and certainly never dreamed one would be used on me.

Strange what goes through your mind at bad

times. I thought of Faulkner's story of the man who asked for a last drink of water before being executed and kept pretending to drink long after the water was gone. Some part of me wanted Willy to keep pulling things out of his bag forever, no matter how grotesque, because push wouldn't come to shove until he stopped. He pulled out handcuffs, which hit me harder than anything—I can't stand to be confined—and then he stopped.

"Willy," I said, with whatever dignity I could summon. "Don't be ridiculous. All I have to do is scream."

"I wouldn't do that," Willy said. "Because then I will be forced to put a bullet through your throat, which I can do before you finish even one. I'll be out of here long before anybody figures out where the sound came from. But you will not be out of here. You will be lying on the floor gargling and gasping for air for quite some time, dying very slowly."

Oh, shit. But wait a minute. Where was Keeter? I had forgotten all about her in the hypnosis of the torture kit. Where the hell was Keeter? I had a goddamn maniac attack dog somewhere behind me, behind the boxes where Willy couldn't see her, and she hadn't made a peep. They were supposed to growl or bark or something. They were supposed to attack people who threatened you with guns. What was she doing, cowering with her paws over her head?

There was no way I could turn around and look over the boxes without tipping off Willy. And whether Keeter could help or not, I didn't want to give her away; Willy would just put a bullet in her brain if he saw her. I covered my face with my hands for a second as though trying to collect myself and glanced as far behind me on each side as I could see.

There in the dim light on the side of the boxes on my left was Keeter. She had crept up silently on her belly without making a sound. Of course, that was how she had been trained.

Keeter was waiting, just like she always did, for the perp to enter the building and close the door. I'd as soon she didn't wait. I didn't know when Willy was going to close the door. I didn't know if Willy was going to close the door. Actually it was fine with me if she attacked right now.

It occurred to me a little late I should have asked Camille what the signal was for "attack." It was like bringing a gun without knowing how to get the safety off. I'd have to rely on Keeter's judgment because I couldn't tell her anything.

"Willy," I said, just to keep him focused on me. "What is the point of all this? Do you really think you can torture someone in a church building on a main street with no one knowing?"

"I know I can," he replied calmly.

"It's not going to happen, Willy. You can shoot

me or not shoot me, but you're not going to hand-cuff me, period."

Willy laughed. "I don't think you understand, Michael. You are living the last pain-free seconds of your life. When I get tired of the anticipation I will simply put a bullet in each of your kneecaps. You will go down instantly, and while you are writhing in pain I will indeed handcuff you. The rest simply depends on my imagination. But I will be in complete and utter control."

Even from where I stood, even in the dim light, I could see that his eyes were starting to shine. "Oh, yes," he said. "That's never happened to you, has it? No one has ever had absolute and total control of you, able to do anything they choose, make you suffer, even take your life away.

"I doubt you appreciate the high that comes with controlling someone like that. It's better than crack, better than cocaine. Well, from the doer's point of view, of course."

The image was so gruesome I tried to block it out of my mind. What was Keeter up to? I tried to think. If she couldn't respond to me, I needed to respond to her. What was she waiting for? I put my hand on my forehead as though upset by Willy's plan—which I was—and glanced at Keeter. She was absolutely still and crouched. She looked like a spring compressed to the max. Her eyes never left Willy's face. Keeter, old girl, he's not going to close the door until he shoots me, so get on with it.

I measured the distance with my eye. He was too far away from her. He wasn't crowding her. That was the other thing that would make her go, if he crowded her.

There must be something that would draw him closer—something that would make Willy take a chance. What could I sell him that he'd want to buy enough to come closer without kneecapping me first? He already had everything he wanted: the setting, the control, the victim.

I held out my wrists handcuff distance apart. "I don't think you can do it, Willy," I said. "Shoot someone that you know from a distance maybe. But up close and personal? Put the handcuffs on my wrists and hurt me? You and I have talked for years. We've been friends of a sort. You wouldn't be human if you could ignore all that."

Willy practically sputtered. "My dear child. Surely you don't believe what you're saying. You can't be some airheaded Pollyanna who thinks I'm just a kindhearted, misunderstood soul?"

"I'm willing to bet my life on it, Willy. If you're right, you don't have to bother with kneecapping me: I'm willing to let you cuff me. But if you're wrong and you can't do it, then you go out and face the music for what you've done playing games with Camille. Deal?"

Willy hesitated. If good-hearted folk frequently don't know what to make of people who are bitter-hearted evil, then vice versa is also true. Willy wouldn't know whether to believe me or not. But he wanted to. He wanted to because betraying a trust was more exciting to him than winning a fight. Willy would get an erection just thinking about the look in my eyes when I realized he was going to do exactly what he said.

I glanced down again quickly. Keeter hadn't moved a muscle. She looked like she would wait in that crouched position forever. I looked up and saw the handcuffs flying toward me. "You put them on," he said.

I caught them and threw them back. "Not on your life. Easy to stand over there and give orders. No, you have to come close enough to see the look in my eyes. That's what you're avoiding, isn't it, Willy?"

Willy was salivating by now. He hesitated a moment longer and then moved forward slowly. "No tricks," he said.

"Well, you've got the gun and the knife and you outweigh me by about a hundred pounds. I'm not sure what more you want. But if it makes you feel better . . ." I slowly lifted my hands in the air. I was hoping that might mean something to Keeter. I wished I knew something about how she was trained.

Willy paused and then kept moving forward slowly. He was focusing intently on me, looking, no doubt, for a kick or a hidden weapon. I shut up. I didn't want to confuse Keeter with friendly sounding conversation. Willy was eight feet away, maybe seven—how far was Keeter's territory? When was he too close?

He stopped again. Willy had decided he had come close enough. And goddamn it, Keeter hadn't. What was the distance between where he was and where she felt crowded? Was I going to get shot over a couple of feet? Why was he so goddamn leery of me, anyway; I have an honest face.

I held out my hands again. Willy was way too far to reach them. "You can't do it, Willy, so let's just go. Deep down, I've always had faith in you. I've always known there was something decent in you despite all the rotten stuff you've done. Maybe it was no accident you chose a church to listen from."

Willy couldn't help himself. The thought of destroying the trusting look I held up to him was too much. He took one more step, and I saw a blur move to my left, a completely soundless blur, moving through the air toward Willy, heading for throat-height. For a second I saw the stunned look on Willy's face, and then I heard the gun go off. In the next instant Willy was down with Keeter on top of him.

This time I didn't hesitate. I flew through the door and down the stairs. I hit the front of the church door on the run and tore across the street without looking. I burst into my office and grabbed the keys for the trunk. Camille was sitting at the desk with the phone in her hand. She was shaking, but she was still functioning. "Dial 911," was all I said, and turned to leave.

"Where's Keeter?" Camille called after me. I looked down, and there was blood on my shirt. It had to be Keeter's.

"I'll be back," I said, and headed out the door. I threw open the trunk and grabbed my fanny pack. I didn't even put it on. I just started running across the street and pulled the gun out on the way.

I got back upstairs before the sirens started. Willy was still down. Keeter had missed his throat but had caught his shoulder blade. From the looks of it she had crushed the bone and then bit him a few more times for luck before she got too weak.

Willy was sweating and crying, and his shoulder was bleeding pretty freely. Keeter had him pinned under her. She was bleeding too—how badly was hard to say without moving her. Her eyes were shut, and her body wasn't moving. Willy was in too much pain to try to get her off— she weighed easily over a hundred pounds. "Keeter?" I said, but she gave no response.

"Get her off," Willy said. Beads of sweat were popping out on his forehead, and he looked like he might be going into shock, which, oddly enough, didn't bother me in the slightest. I was just sorry she missed his throat. I didn't bother to answer him, but headed back down the stairs, this time to get Camille. She was probably the only person who could do anything for Keeter.

I didn't even think about doing anything for Willy except calling the police. I personally wasn't in the mood to help Willy at all. On the contrary, I thought after we got Keeter off his chest, we ought to drive a stake through his heart.

23

The sirens came closer as I took off my blouse. I didn't care about standing around in my underwear; Keeter was bleeding badly. Camille and I tried to bind up her side as best we could to try and stop it. Then we tried to push her off Willy, but it wasn't easy. Camille said she weighed almost one twenty, and there was so much blood on the floor that Camille and I were slipping around in it. We worked as gently as we could.

Keeter was semiconscious but determined not to let Willy up, so mostly she wasn't cooperating. Whenever she was awake enough to recognize Camille, she'd listen to her and let us move her a little. We finally got her off Willy just as we heard footsteps on the stairs. Moments later Adam burst around the corner with two officers. He took a glance at Willy and asked, "Have you called an ambulance?"

"No," I said. Actually, I hadn't even thought of it. He pulled out his walkie-talkie and spoke into it, then knelt down beside Willy. Willy's eyes were closed, and his color didn't look good. Adam pulled back his eyelids to look at his eyes, then took his pulse. Willy's breathing was rapid and shallow, and I'd be willing to bet his pulse was fluttering. "He's in shock," he said and pulled off his jacket and covered him up with it. Then he started trying to bind up the wound.

In the distance we heard sirens again. "Go downstairs," he said to one of the officers who just seemed to be standing around, "and direct the ambulance."

It was very odd seeing somebody in as much trouble as Willy was and having no impulse to help him. It was worse than that; I was hoping he'd die. I'd felt the same way about Ted Bundy. I thought he had forfeited his right to be among us, and, for my money, so had Willy.

I found myself resenting Adam trying to save him, but I kept my mouth shut. People who've been exposed to torture kits aren't objective; they aren't even rational. And Adam wouldn't stop doing his job no matter what I said.

We had done all we could for Keeter. Now we needed to get her to a vet. I looked up at the one officer who was still standing around. "We need some help," I said. "We need to get her to a vet."

"You," Adam said firmly, "are not going any-where. Officer Barrett will help your friend get the dog to the vet."

I started to argue, but then stopped. Camille was functioning better than I'd ever seen her. Maybe it was a good thing for her to go deal with the vet on her own. "Call on the way," was all I said. "Let them know what they've got com-ing in."

Luckily Officer Barrett looked like he was one of those weight-lifting-type cops. He picked up Keeter easily and headed off with Camille.

The ambulance crew arrived a few minutes later, and after a period of scrambling and IVs and shots, Willy was put on a stretcher and the medics took off rushing down the stairs, leaving Adam and I standing around in the dim room. We were both covered with blood from our knees down from kneeling in the stuff.

Adam said to the one officer left, "Secure this scene and call for the state crime lab to come out. I'm going to take Dr. Stone's statement." He was not exactly warm. He was more like totally and completely pissed off, and my guess was, at me.

"Can we go to my office?" I said. I just wanted to get out of there and away from all memories of how close I'd come to losing my kneecaps and God knows what else.

"No," Adam said formally, "I want to keep an eye on things here. But," he added, seeming to relent slightly, "we can go to another room."

We found another room to talk in, and as the blood dried on our pants, I came clean with the story of Willy. It wasn't a pretty story. All Adam had asked of me was that I tell him if Willy contacted me, and I had not only not done that, I had bald-faced lied to him. Even last night I hadn't told him the whole story.

The more I talked about Willy and what he'd been up to, the more Adam's jaw set and the more his lips got thin and tight. He didn't say anything though. He just wrote down what I said and asked some questions, but he had a layer of ice around him that would have sunk the *Titanic*. I hadn't been very hopeful for my relationship with Adam before. I was pretty sure I knew where it stood now.

I started to tell him I was planning on coming clean that afternoon, but I didn't. It just sounded too weak. Too little, too late.

Besides, the truth was I didn't really know why involving Adam had been so hard for me. Disjointed images came to mind: swimming alone at night at fifteen on the inland waterway, where running into snakes wasn't even all that uncommon. Driving cars at 120 miles an hour at sixteen and waiting on every curve to see whether fate took a shot or not. I always seemed to have to walk up right to the edge of something, and I could never take anybody with me.

The only honest thing I *could* have said to Adam was, "I don't know what this is all about, Adam, but it's old."

I didn't say it. I just kept plowing through the story. I finally got through all of it, but I was getting very cold and very tired. The adrenaline was long gone, and I felt like I'd been dropped off a cliff. Adam finally seemed to notice I wasn't doing well, and he stood up. "That's it for now," he said. "There're going to be some problems with this, but now isn't the time to talk about them."

I didn't know what he meant, but I was too tired to care. It was still morning, but I felt like it was midnight and I'd crossed the Sahara before dawn.

I started to get up when he said, "Give me a minute. I'll be right back." He went away, and when he returned he said, "Carlotta's on her way over. I'd like you to wait here until she comes." He didn't sound quite as stiff as before.

I started to protest. I get a knee-jerk reaction when people tell me what to do, but then I realized it didn't sound so bad. I was beat. "Okay," I said, and Adam raised his eyebrows. I think he realized, then, just how wiped I was.

He looked at me a minute longer, and I had the feeling maybe some part of him wanted to put his arms around me. Maybe some part of me wanted to put my arms around him. But he didn't and I didn't. I was feeling like a shit for lying to him, and I didn't even know why I did it.

And Adam? I don't know what he was feeling. He just shook his head and said, "Jesus, Michael, you're a work of art," and then he was gone. I guess that meant he was still mad.

24

I was out of it the rest of the day, and that night I slept for twelve million years. I stayed at Carlotta's and had some of the worst nightmares of my life—all to do with pliers and scalpels and handcuffs. Nonetheless I kept sleeping, and when I woke up, it was eleven o'clock the next day and Carlotta was there with coffee. "Don't you work, anymore?" I said. I had gotten some of my testiness back overnight.

"You're better," she said, relieved. "Adam said you were cooperative, so I knew you were in trouble."

"Bitch, bitch, bitch," I said. "Shut up and eat your porridge." It was a revisionist version of the three bears, and Carlotta knew the joke. She laughed.

"Adam called. He wants you to stop by the station at your earliest convenience."

"Why?" I said cynically. "Has some fool set bail

for Willy?" I sat bolt upright. "How is Keeter? Is she all right?"

"Adam said she was."

I slumped down, relieved. "That is one smart dog," I said, "and one tough dog. I suppose Willy's alive too?"

"I'm afraid so," Carlotta said. "I'm not going to ask you about it now," she went on. "I think Adam's going to put you through enough, but someday I'd like to know what utter and complete stupidity you've been involved in."

"Deal," I replied, just relieved not to be on the hot seat again.

I finally made it down to see Adam, although I didn't rush. It was mid-afternoon before I started out, and he had called again. I didn't want to see Adam. I hate to see people who are right to be mad at me. How can you get righteously indignant with a friend to whom you lied through your teeth?

On the other hand, what was I supposed to do about it—grovel? Probably, he was expecting an apology. Well, fuck that. It wouldn't do any good, anyway. If it happened again, I'd probably play it the same way, and Adam knew that. I muttered all the way to the station and walked in like a sullen adolescent. I was in the wrong and resentful as hell that I was feeling guilty.

Adam looked less furious than the day before and more resigned. "Well," he said without preamble after he had shut the door to his office, "what do you want him charged with?"

"What do I want him charged with? Try kidnapping and attempted murder."

"I can do that," he said slowly, "but you have to realize the implications."

"What implications?"

"You're going to have to bring out what Willy was doing in that room and what you were doing there. I don't know how comfortable you're going to be with putting in the paper that Willy has been listening in on your therapy sessions."

I was silent. I hadn't thought about that. I'd made up my mind last night I was going to have to tell all my clients a sadistic sex offender might have listened in on their therapy sessions and just might know their most intimate secrets, but it hadn't occurred to me that it would also get put in the newspaper. "Did you get a search warrant for his house?" I asked.

"Yep," he said.

"Was he taping?"

"Yep," he said.

"How many are there?"

"I don't know whether there are multiple sessions on the tapes, but there are a dozen or more tapes. He was working as a janitor at the church, and he had plenty of access."

"Oh, Jesus," I said. "Will they get admitted into evidence?"

"I would think so," Adam said. "The prosecution would certainly want them—they're proof positive why he was there—and the search was legal: *i*'s dotted and *t*'s crossed. Even if you talked them out of it, the defense would probably try to get them admitted. Anything that would embarrass local folk would put pressure on the prosecution to settle the case. I'm assuming there're some things on the tapes you don't want made public?"

"You might say that," I said. I had affairs and alcohol problems and people who hated their spouses and people who were in love with their friends' husbands. I had spouses of batterers who were making secret plans to leave them, and I had people who were gay and their own spouses didn't know it.

"I don't think my clients would want their business made public," I said slowly. "Not to mention that there is a big question about whether it was ethical for me to keep my practice open once I even had a hint somebody might be listening in on the sessions. If those tapes are admitted into evidence, I have a feeling I'll be looking at lawsuits and ethics charges."

"Uh-huh," Adam said, and I realized he had thought of this already.

"So what am I supposed to do? Let Willy walk? What about the stuff with Camille?"

"Criminal threatening, breaking and entering," Adam said. "That's the worst we can throw at

331

him. It won't keep him in very long. Although there is one thing. . . ."

"What?" I said. Why is nothing ever simple?

"Camille said last night that he was the one who kidnapped her before."

"You sound skeptical," I said, not mentioning that I was too.

"I am," he said. "It's too much of a coincidence. I'm willing to buy—well, he obviously tried to play on her fears for who knows what sick reasons—but for somebody he kidnapped years ago when he didn't even live in her part of the country to end up as your client—I'm having trouble with it, although it's true he wasn't in prison then, so I suppose it's possible."

I had a whole lot of trouble with it, and I had even more reason. Camille had described her kidnapper to me. Like Willy, he had been into rape and torture, but the physical description she'd given me hadn't fit Willy at all. She had described him as young and slight—which Willy hadn't been for decades.

"I talked to the police again who handled her case in Boston," Adam went on. "She refused to have an internal exam at the time, so they couldn't get evidence for DNA testing. But they did get DNA testing on the murder they had later. I'm sending Willy's DNA in for testing, but I'd be willing to bet there isn't going to be a match.

"There's a thing called suggestibility, Michael.

Now don't get upset. You know it and I know it. I know you think it's misused about 90 percent of the time in child sexual abuse cases, but on the other hand—a woman as posttraumatic as Camille Robbins with Willy's voice being piped into her bedroom night after night describing rape and torture and claiming he's the kidnapper. I have to ask: What are the chances she's gotten the two confused?"

Pretty good, I thought, but I didn't say so.

"On the other hand, Michael, I've got a case that's hard to ignore. We've got his tapes from her house. There's no issue of a search warrant. It was Camille's house, and she gave permission. We've got other similar tapes in our perfectly legal search of his premises. He's clearly been emotionally torturing her, and she swears up and down that he's the same man who kidnapped and tortured her before. He says so himself on the tapes.

"The only evidence Willy could have to the contrary would have come from her therapy sessions. That's the first time she was ever able to talk about the abduction.

"The problem for Willy is that even if Camille said anything on tape that exonerated him, he'll never be able to use it. The tapes were illegally obtained, and I seriously doubt that his attorneys would even try to have evidence admitted of additional crimes the jury wouldn't know about—assuming you don't charge him with anything.

"So I'm asking you. I'm not asking *what* she said in the therapy sessions. I'm just asking you, how stable is this woman? How suggestible? Do you have any reason from your sessions to doubt Camille Robbins when she says that Alex B. Willy is the man who kidnapped and tortured her?"

I looked up at Adam's face and studied it for a moment. In for a penny, in for a pound, I thought. "None at all," I said. "Coincidences happen."

Adam looked thoughtfully at me for a long moment. "Michael . . . ," he started, and then lapsed into silence. His face was full of indecision.

I held up my sweet, lying little face for his scrutiny. "If she says he's the one," I said calmly, "that's good enough for me, and I know her better than you do." I fell silent, too, but look all he wanted, Adam wasn't going to find any indecision in my face, not a single, solitary fair-is-fair-he-didn't-do-it-so-put-him-on-the-streets subatomic particle.

25

Nothing happened right away. Willy was too injured even to be arraigned. But he got better, and a few weeks later they arraigned him, and he found out what he was facing.

I suppose I was expecting the call. I didn't have to go, but I decided to. Partly I needed to face Willy again for my own reasons, maybe to be sure I could. But there was some kind of closure that I needed, too, although I couldn't really say why.

I went down to the visiting room of the county jail and for once was glad for the glass wall separating us. I might be ready to face Willy, but I wasn't ready to be in a room alone with him, at least not without Keeter. Willy's neck and shoulder were bandaged, and he had lost weight, but he was definitely alive, unfortunately, which I was still sorry for. I guess I'm not the forgiving type. I got it honestly. Mama always said, "When you've got your foot on a rattlesnake's neck is not the time to get religion."

I sat down, folded my arms, and said nothing at all. This was Willy's show, and maybe I came most of all to see how he would play it.

"Good morning, Dr. Stone," Willy said. "I trust you have recovered from my little games. I'm sure you are aware I would never have really . . ."

"Don't insult me, Mr. Willy," I said.

"Surely you don't think . . . ," Willy started.

I stood up to go. "Well, now," he said hastily, "do sit down. We'll just move on. We may differ on whether I was really serious or not, but that isn't the issue," he added quickly. "Ah . . . there seems to be some kind of misunderstanding."

"Really?" I said.

"I believe you know what I'm talking about," Willy said. "I admit to playing a few games with Ms. Robbins's head, but it should be obvious to any moron that I wasn't the one who raped and tortured her."

"Tell it to the judge," I said. "You'll get your day in court."

"I don't think it's going to get that far," Willy said. "Not if you're who you say you are."

"Oh?"

"Well, this is where we get to find out, Dr. Stone, if you're any different than I am." Willy shifted in his seat and warmed to the topic. Clearly, he had rehearsed what he was going to say. "Oh, I know you don't have my particular aesthetic interests, but in regard to the larger issues—truth and justice and those ideals you profess to believe in—well, do you or don't you?

"Because if you do, you can't let an innocent man go to prison for something he didn't do. And you know that Camille's description of her assailant didn't match me until I started playing my little games with her—and I was just playing games with her."

"Mr. Willy," I replied calmly, "you set yourself up, not I. You tortured that poor woman until she couldn't separate you and the other perp. Who am I to get between you and the fate you set up so carefully for yourself?"

"You can't be serious," Willy said. "So am I to take it that justice and the law are fine so long as they fit your agenda?"

"You talk like they're the same," I said. "The law and justice may sleep together occasionally, but it's not like they have an ongoing relationship. I'm a much bigger fan of justice than I am the law."

"Don't rely on semantics, Dr. Stone. Sending me to jail for a crime I didn't commit is flouting the law, and it's hardly justice."

"Between your going free for a crime you did commit and going to jail for a crime you didn't commit, I figure the law isn't going to be served either way. And yes, in my opinion, justice *will* be served if you head straight for prison. The bottom line is this, Mr. Willy: I don't pay for no dead horses."

"What's that supposed to mean?" Willy asked.

"It means your whining to me about justice is a little like a cancer cell asking for fair play. Let me put it this way. I am not the sanest human being I know, but I've got enough of my mind intact not to buy what you sell. Actually I just figured out what you sell. You sell the idea that there is no real nastiness in the world.

"The problem is that there is: There is downright evil in the world, and you, sir, are a fair example of it. People who buy dead horses can't really deal with malevolence. But it's there. You meant to hurt me, and you meant to hurt Camille. You get a kick out of other people's pain."

Willy was silent. For some reason, he didn't seem prepared for this. Or maybe there was no good answer to this. Maybe he only had one thing to sell, and you bought it or you didn't.

"I've thought about this. If I interfered with your going to jail in any way, then for the next twenty years, I'd have to wonder if every face I passed on the street was going to be your next victim. I won't do it. I won't help you add more notches to your belt. You're going down for the count, Mr. Willy—and that's who I say I am."

EPILOGUE

I didn't hear from Adam for a while. Hard to blame him, but I found to my annoyance I missed him. Men are habit-forming: They ought to come with warning labels. Carlotta kept telling me to call him, but what was I supposed to say? The truth was, I probably wasn't going to change a whole lot, and if he couldn't live with my craziness, I couldn't blame him. I had, after all, thrown him out of my house for trying to help me. Then I lied to his face, probably several times actually.

But he did call, finally, and he said he wanted to talk. Could he come over? "Not tonight," I heard myself saying. "Tonight is the night I get over my phobia of b-ball courts. I've got to play basketball again, or I'm going to lose my mind."

Adam knew all about the guy who tried to strangle me in a gym—he was the one who rescued me—and he knew, too, I hadn't been able to go to a gym alone since then. I had planned to go to the gym tonight—I wasn't *exactly* lying—but I did hear a little voice inside my head saying, "Well, it doesn't have to be *tonight*, turkey." I ignored it. I had a bad feeling about what Adam wanted to say, and I really didn't want to hear it.

I hung up and looked at the phone. I just wasn't in the mood for an emotional bloodbath. If Adam was gone, he was gone. No point in holding a funeral service. Some people just want to talk things to death, and I'm not one of them.

But when I entered the gym, I found, to my surprise, that Adam was there shooting by himself. I went over and sat down on the bench for a moment just watching him. I should have been pissed off. I sure as hell hadn't asked him to come and keep me company. I was pissed off, sort of, but I had to admit I was mostly just relieved. The silent gym—once upon a time my favorite place in the world—didn't look too good to me these days. Adam waved but didn't speak. Probably he wasn't too sure of his reception.

He looked awfully good. Mostly, playing ball, I don't really notice. When I was a five-seven, one-hundred-pound thirteen-year-old, the gym was absolutely the only place in the universe I didn't feel awkward. People are sexless on a basketball court. They're fast or they're slow. They fake a lot, or they just power their way through. They have the economy in their moves of the well-coached, or they have all the superfluous mannerisms of

FAULT LINES

the self-taught, but whatever it is, they aren't male or female.

So, it was odd, but Adam looked awfully good tonight. He was doing layups, and as he drove, the muscles in his thighs changed definition. I had noticed Adam's thighs before. They never looked bad. He had that kind of basketball long and lean muscle, not that bunchy weight-lifting leg muscle I didn't personally care for. I had had some experience with Adam's thighs up close and personal, and, yes, they were very nice indeed.

But I don't know why I was thinking about it with basketball to play. I finished tying my shoes and walked out onto the court with my ball. "Baby-sitting?" I said. My voice surprised me with its sarcasm. Habit, I guess.

"It's a free country," he replied. "Just working on my shot."

I didn't comment. I just started methodically warming up. Five under the basket on one side, five in front, five on the other side. Me and Bill Bradley. I moved a couple of feet out and started it all over again. There was no sound except the balls bouncing and the net swishing. Thank God Adam knew enough not to ruin the place with useless chatter. I caught my ball and turned to Adam. "I'm sorry I lied to you," I said. In the aftermath of catching Willy, it was the one thing I hadn't been able to say. I tried to tone down the grumpiness in my voice, but I only partly succeeded.

"It's okay," he said. "It goes with the territory."

I turned to shoot, but stopped and turned back to Adam. "What? Now you're saying I'm a chronic liar?"

"You're a predictable liar," he said.

Predictable. I didn't seem to have a comeback to that, so I started shooting again. His voice had this sound in it like he knew me or something. No, more like he knew me, fault lines and all—and he wasn't heading for the nearest exit.

Was that intimacy? I wondered. Not the free fall letting go followed by the I'm-out-of-here-buddy-and-besides-you-have-a-wife-so-don't-try-to-hold-onto-my-shirt kind of thing, which was the closest I had come to intimacy. I was good at the kind of intimacy that came with a safety harness.

I went back to shooting. I was working in a circle from one side to another, foul line distance from the basket. This was easy territory, and I didn't miss much. My range extended to the top of the key, and after that I'd start to get into trouble.

"Horse?" he said.

"In a moment," I replied. Jesus. Does he think he can interrupt my warm-up just like that? He wouldn't have done that to Bill Bradley. Adam seemed full of energy. He was putting more energy into his warm-up than most people put into their games.

Horse was the best idea—it was a straight shooting contest—but personally, I preferred one-on-one. We'd get around to that eventually, although we both knew I didn't stand a chance against Adam one-on-one. He had maybe sixty pounds on me and six inches. I did okay on offense with him, but you just can't defend against that kind of height.

I headed for the limits of my range to finish my warm-up. I started in the corner and to my delight was on. I sank three in a row and moved a couple of feet over and started again. Joy is when the ball just drops for you. It all seems so easy when it works. I was getting my legs under the shot, and the ball was just rolling off my fingertips straight and true. It had a lazy backspin and an arc you could die for. I could feel my mood lift with every shot.

Adam had stopped shooting and was just watching me. I faked and went up again. No sense just shooting without the move before it. You don't get to stand there in a game and just shoot. Adam walked over and stood under the basket. He started catching the ball as it swished through and throwing it back. I dribbled twice and put the ball up again, working carefully around the half-circle. I had caught the wave or something: Everything I threw up was going in. I came in closer and tried a fade-away jumper just for the hell of it.

I saw Adam smiling at me and missed the shot. I turned my back on him and dribbled a couple of times before I wheeled around. What was that smile? He had looked like a male Mona Lisa. The Cheshire cat? Whatever he was thinking, he hadn't said it.

I started to feel self-conscious and missed two more. "One-on-one?" I said, more to stop Adam from looking at me as much as anything. That smile just hadn't been a good-buddies-hit-each-other-on-the-shoulder *basketball* smile. I began to wonder if there was a way of leaving the gym tonight with a far better memory than the one of someone trying to kill me. Would it help with my PTSD—theoretically speaking? Would Adam contribute to a scientific experiment? I laughed out loud.

"What is it?" Adam said.

"Nothing," I said. "I'm losing it."

"One-on-one?" Adam asked. "Not horse?" I should have said horse. Horse was the great equalizer. One person shot, and if it went in, the other person had to make the identical shot or get a letter. If someone got all five letters, he or she was out. You didn't have to be tall or wide; you just had to know how to shoot. I should love horse, and I like it all right, but nothing gets the adrenaline flowing like one-on-one, in-your-face contact ball.

Adam walked up with the ball and handed it to

me. True to the ethics of pick-up ball, he knew better than to just throw it to me: I might take a shot before he had a chance to get into position. Would I do that? Yes, I would.

Adam went into a defensive crouch. He was playing very close to me, which wasn't exactly a surprise. Adam was no dummy, and my outside shot was falling. I'd have to drive on him to back him off or I wouldn't get a single outside shot, but it was hell to drive one-on-one with someone like Adam. Sure, I could fake him and get a step on him, but he'd catch up before I got to the basket.

I faked left and drove right. I got a step on him, and as he accelerated to catch up I stopped, faked in the direction I had been heading, and pivoted back for a left hook. It wasn't a good idea to throw up something I had not tried one single time in warm-up, but because of that, it was the only shot Adam wouldn't be expecting. Yes, and because of that, it was also the only shot I couldn't make. The ball went long and bounced around between the rim and the backboard.

I tried to follow my shot, of course, but Adam had already spun to block me out. He had his hands behind him to keep tabs on me, and I was trapped behind him. I could feel the heat of his body as we stood like two spoons, Adam in front and me behind, waiting for the ball to quit bouncing and come down. Adam was pushing back to keep me out, and I, of course, was trying to push him under the rim so I could get the ball over his head.

It was the usual jostling and pushing under the boards, so I don't know why it bothered me. But I was having trouble concentrating. Adam's hand was on my hip, and I could feel the warmth of it right through my shorts. I was acutely aware of the feeling of his back on my breasts. The ball came down, and I could feel the power in his body surge as he jumped for it.

He dribbled to the top of the key, and I followed. I had barely got in my defensive stance when he headed right back for the basket with the smallest of fakes. Arrogant bastard. I guess he felt he got enough speed he didn't need to bother to fake. I scrambled to keep up and managed to reach in and knock the ball away. Okay, so the NBA might have called it a foul, but in pick-up ball, no blood, no foul.

In any case, Adam didn't call a foul. He just laughed and retrieved the ball. To my surprise, he headed right back in again. He pivoted with his back to the basket and started edging in backward.

It was something Adam rarely did with me. Sure, he could score that way, but proving he had enough height to outscore me under the basket wasn't much of a challenge. If I didn't know better, I'd say Adam was enjoying getting me under the boards. Maybe he hadn't faked before because he wanted me to keep up with him. He kept edging backward, and I, of course, braced against him trying to keep him out. My hips were wedged against his backside, and I don't know who was fouling whom but there was a lot of contact.

Ordinarily this is not a problem. Ordinarily I don't even notice this kind of thing in your average rough-and-tumble game of pick-up ball, but Adam's body was starting to get warm and moist from playing, and his breathing was getting deeper, and I was getting in over my head, which I found very confusing because it was so bizarre. Bizarre to be noticing this kind of thing on a basketball court. He wasn't helping any; he didn't seem to be in any hurry to shoot, but just kept dribbling backward back and forth across the lane.

"Three seconds," I said. In a real game you can't spend more than three seconds in the lane on offense. It's specifically to keep people from parking there, but I had never heard of anyone calling it in a pick-up game.

"Three seconds?" he said. "Now we're calling three seconds? Okay." And he wheeled into a fade-away jumper. 1–0 Adam.

"Losers keepers," I said, meaning if you made your shot, the other person got the ball. I didn't usually play that way, but if I didn't, I could spend all night under the boards with Adam, and I wanted to concentrate on the game. It was sacrilege to be concentrating on anything but basketball in a basketball game.

"Hold it," he said and took off his shirt. Oh, Jesus. Adam did a little weight-lifting, and he didn't have the usual skinny, caved-in chest of the average workaholic middle-aged weekend ballplayer. He had a very nice chest and God-given shoulders. So now he was wearing nothing but a pair of short-shorts. I had a fleeting thought of what it would be like to pull those shorts down, but I banished it. At least I tried to banish it and concentrate on the game. Just kneel down and slowly inch-by-inch pull those shorts down.

I had on a halter top under my T-shirt, and ordinarily, I would have taken the opportunity to take off my T-shirt, but I decided not to. I wasn't feeling any too sure of myself.

Adam caught me looking at him. "You look good," I said lightly. "I see you're keeping up with the exercise." I tried to sound detached. Just a noninvolved observer. I started dribbling as Adam walked up. He went into his defensive stance, and I faked a drive and started to go up for a shot, but Adam grabbed the front of my T-shirt and spoiled the shot.

"Hey," I said, trying to sound annoyed. "What are you doing? We're playing b-ball, for Christ's sakes." But Adam didn't let go. He just stood there holding my shirt. Silence fell in the gym. I didn't know exactly what to do. I didn't even know exactly what I wanted to do. Then Adam started slowly pulling me toward him, gently but insistently. When I was inches from him, he released my shirt and hooked his thumbs in the corners of my waistband.

"It isn't a foul unless you call it," he said. Great minds think alike. He started to slowly pull down my shorts, looking in my eyes all the while. I had a lot of time to call it. I mean, I could have called it, and I knew his fingers would have instantly sprung back. But there was that scientific experiment I'd wanted to do. It's important to support science.

I could feel the shorts slipping down inch by inch.

ANNA SALTER

"Dr. Michael Stone is sure to take her place
beside the major characters in crime fiction."
—Andrew Vachss

SHINY WATER

"A jolting debut."
—*The New York Times Book Review*

FAULT LINES

"An absorbing thriller."
—Amazon.com

Available from Pocket Books

"What is truth?...What is justice?...Terry Kay plunges deeply into the complex and maddening question and emerges with a work whose qualities are those of true art: the capacity to remain in the reader's mind, vexing him, illuminating him, and making him part of a human situation he cannot ignore."
—James Dickey, author of *Deliverance*

"This strikingly poetic novel is a thematic exploration of justice...deeply affecting, tragic in its realism and shocking in the dark truths it reveals."
—*ALA Booklist*

"After reading a Terry Kay novel, you know you have been profoundly touched by a master storyteller. He has scratched at the emotions of love and outrage and opened the door to the darkest region of your soul—that place where evil and good struggle for dominance."
—*Atlanta Journal Constitution*

"This entertaining but violent tale of crime and retribution is not for the faint-hearted....The reader feels Jesse's pain and the community's anger as surely as if the novel were a newspaper account of a real-life friend's ordeal....A WONDERFUL, SATISFYING AND BIZARRE CONCLUSION."
—*United Press International*

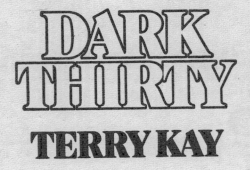

TERRY KAY

PUBLISHED BY POCKET BOOKS NEW YORK

POCKET BOOKS, a division of Simon & Schuster, Inc.
1230 Avenue of the Americas, New York, N.Y. 10020

ISBN: 0-671-60305-1

First Pocket Books mass-market paperback printing September, 1985

10 9 8 7 6 5 4 3 2 1

POCKET and colophon are registered trademarks
of Simon & Schuster, Inc.

Printed in the U.S.A.

For Terri, Scott, Jon, and Heather, my children. The grandest moments I have ever known have been with them.

I wish for them, and for all our children, a less violent world and the understanding that peace is in giving, not taking.

ONE

October 13, 1980

HE COULD SMELL THE MUSCADINES WHICH, WEEKS EAR-
lier, had cracked at the skin and oozed freely and had been
sucked dry in the hulls by bees.

And he could smell the withered October apples still
hanging from trees in the terrace row. And the pollen dust
of autumn leaves sundrying on limbs. And snow that would
not fall until December, but was in the air still—the air
being unexpectedly cold after a warm day.

All these things he breathed into himself and knew them,
distinctively, separately, instantly, and in that surprising moment he was quickly alert to autumn.

The season changed for him in that moment, that precise
clocktick when sweet, thick odors perfumed the air (there
was a steady wind as well) and the falsetto pitch of nightbugs
hurt his hearing, and he could feel his breathing quicken.
He was suddenly very alive, very filled. It was a good time
of the day, though it was not day exactly, nor night. It was
a mutation of time, a soft downcushion of time. Dark Thirty.
That was what the people of the valley called it: Dark
Thirty—the thirty minutes of after-day and before-night. It

3

would be called night by others, because of its thin, dark-liquid color, because it had the feel of night. Yet the day's cooking of earth lingered and the ground was still warm to touch. And the cows and mules and one horse still wandered in the pasture, nibbling at grass along the fence line. That was another thing he could hear: the teeth-snipping of grass. And, far off, a foxhound baying and, close by, a bird, out late, crying for its nest. And in the pillowed sandbed beside the house, the bitch dog sprawled on her grotesquely mis-shapen nipples and lapped the air with her heavy tongue while her puppies yelped and played among the dry stalks of the corn rows.

He stretched and laced his fingers above his head and his body quivered involuntarily. He could feel the muscles of his legs tighten across his thighs and calves. Younger, as a boy, he would have turned from the house and raced across the field until his breathing became fog in the cold air. He pushed his head into his laced fingers and smiled at the thought. He had loved running, leaping imaginary fences, like the pictures of racers caught in an open scissors of their legs over wooden hurdle stands. Jim Thorpe and Jesse Owens. He had wanted to be both. He had never felt as free as he had been as a boy, running. Flying, almost. Almost. Sometimes in his dreams (still, at his age), he began to soar as he ran—effortlessly, his body rising, skimming the trees, and he would become airborne and free. But those were dreams. Now, at his age, he could no longer run. He had smoked too many cigarettes for too many years and the running had been smothered. It was the one thing he re-gretted more than all other mistakes: smoking cigarettes. He could not remember when the smoking had begun to hurt him, but it had. The last game he had played was many years ago. A softball game at an outing for Tickenaley Church. He had played—had tried to play—but he could no longer chase gracefully after high outfield balls, like a hawk in hunt. He had laughed about it, saying he had a slight cold and would soon be well, but he had known even then that it would be the last time he would ever play games. After that, he quit being excited about sports. He smoked and forgot how it had been to swing across the high tension of games. And his children never knew that he had once been spectacular.

He kicked against the side of the doorstep, one shoe, then the other, and he slapped against his shirt and pants with his hands, though there had been little dust from working in the woods. His ritual before entering the house never changed. Never, in all seasons.

The house cat moved lazily across the floor when he entered. It arched its back against a chair and then trotted to him and scrubbed its face on his ankle.

"You worthless, you know that?" he said to the cat, playfully pushing it aside. "Cats ought to be in the barn, chasing rats. You don't even know what a rat looks like, do you? Worthless." The cat returned to his ankle, rubbed and purred.

He moved into the kitchen. His wife sat at the table, reading from a stack of papers. Supper steamed on the stove. He could smell fish frying in a skillet.

"Smells good," he said.

She did not look up.

"Fish supposed to be smoking like that?" he asked.

Her eyes danced quickly to the stove. The fish was not burning.

"Why'd you say that?" she asked. She was annoyed.

"Just said it," he replied. "Thought maybe you'd know I was here." He remembered: she had burned the first meal she had ever cooked for him and they had always laughed about it. "The smoke was good. Tasted a little like meat," he had said.

She folded the papers and stood and went to the stove and began to turn the fish with a long fork. She was tired and he knew it. She had not slept well for months and he knew she often sat numbly, doing nothing, when he was away at work. Her face did not lie; her face had aged sadly.

He washed his hands at the sink and dried them on a towel hanging from a wall ring. Then he sat at the table and watched her at the stove.

"Macy come by the woods this morning," he said quietly.

She opened the stove and removed a pan of cornbread and began to cut it into wedges.

"She said Winston was worked up about his birthday tomorrow," he continued. "Said he was telling everybody about the cake his grandma was making for him."

She dropped the hot pan into the sink and mumbled something he did not understand.

"What?" he asked.

"Nothing," she said. She watched the pan slip into the water, its hot film of grease sizzling in tiny bubbles. "I can't find the candles," she said. "I had some. I don't know where they got to."

"I'll go by tomorrow and pick up some," he said. "Everybody coming?"

"Anna's working at the store," she said. "She'll be by after she closes up."

"Macy seemed happy," he said. "Boy being ten means something, I guess. Especially not having a daddy around."

"Macy expects too much sometimes," she mumbled. "The boy'll be fine, if she'll leave him alone, let him have some room to grow up."

"She will," he replied. "Faron's only been dead a couple of years. She's still trying to do it all."

"You ask me, she makes more out of being widowed than she ought to."

"Maybe so," he said wearily. "She's just now getting used to being on her own."

"What's done is done," she said bluntly. "That's all there is to it."

He nodded and whispered, "I guess." He rubbed his forehead with his hand. The room was warm with the cooking steam and the sizzle of the frying fish. He picked up the papers she had left on the table and looked at the first page. It was from a company in New York. The company's name was Family Finders, Inc.

"What's this?" he asked.

"They look up family names," she replied. "I wrote off for it."

"What for?"

"Tells you about your family. Where they came from. Who they were."

"What'd it say?"

"You can read it good as me," she told him. She poured tea into two glasses of ice and put them on the table.

"Maybe after supper," he said. He put the papers on the shelf of the pie safe near the table.

She filled his plate from the stove and placed it before him and then took a small portion for herself. He no longer said anything to her about not eating. She was easily irritated and would refuse to eat if he questioned her. Her loss of weight in the past three months frightened him. She was pale and thin and weak. Still, she would not eat.

He bowed his head and said, "Lord, for this and all Thy blessings we are truly thankful. Amen."

When he looked up, she was staring at her plate. She picked up a fork and pushed the food across her plate, separated it, pushed it again.

"Looks like we'll be through clearing off the trees in a day or so," he told her. "Carl and Doyle work a little harder than when they was boys."

She continued to stare at her plate. The tip of her fork scraped at the fish.

"Herman Field's boy come by to see about the sawmill work. Said it looked like there'd be enough timber for the house. Maybe the barns."

She drank from her tea and turned her face to look out the window beside the door.

"What's the matter, Jean?" he asked gently. "You hear anything I'm saying?"

"I heard."

"What is it? What's wrong?"

She did not move her eyes from the window. She said, "Maybe won't be no need for the house. Maybe the world's coming to its end, like some thinks it is."

"Jean, the world ain't coming to its end. It ain't, now."

Her eyes jumped on him. "What makes you so God-sure?"

she demanded. "It could be. Lots of people say it's the endtime. People that know more'n me and you."

"Jean, it ain't so," he said firmly. "You got that fixed in your head. It's all from the pamphlets and the Preacher. But it just ain't so. World's just gonna keep on spinning. That's all."

"Not if He don't want it to, it won't."

He bit into his fish and chewed slowly and thought about the grotesque visions locked in his wife's imagination. He could see the tips of her fingers turning the fork nervously in her hand, stabbing at the food.

"Guess so," he said. "Guess He can do what He wants with it."

Her head jerked hard in anger. Her eyes narrowed and her lips trembled.

He took her glare but did not answer it. He pushed his plate away and stood and left the house through the kitchen door. He walked across the yard to the barn. The dog and her puppies followed him, stumbling about his feet, yapping in their sharp voices.

He went into the barn and began to fill the feed bins for the livestock. The barn was his place to think. The history of his father and grandfather and great-grandfather (sometimes, he believed, their presence) was in the barn, carefully stored in the antiques of their farming tools—the plowstocks and wagon pieces, the oxen yoke and mule harnesses, the stalk cutters and steeltooth rakes, the gophers and sweeps and fenders and planters, the hoes and axes, the anvil and the blacksmith firebox and bellows. He could not throw away the tools that his father and grandfather and great-grandfather had used. The handprints of their touch were still on them. The barn was a museum of their history in the valley and it meant, for him, proof that he belonged to something clearly good and noble.

But the barn was not entirely private. The gossip of its treasure had been shared by many, and in recent years there had been people (they arrived always in vans or pickup trucks) asking to see Jesse's collection. And when they had looked and examined and whispered among themselves, they had offered cash or personalized bank checks for the contents of the barn. But Jesse would not sell. He knew the buyers well: arrogant, overly casual, pretending there was little actual value in the collection, but perhaps in Atlanta, in their antique and curio shops, someone might find something amusing and buy it for a conversation piece. A wagon wheel for a frontyard marker (". . . appropriate, don't you think, for the little Negro statues, the ones of shiny clay?"). A plowstock holding a mailbox. Heelbolts for wall decorations. "No," Jesse had said firmly. "No." He knew them well: petty thieves who robbed the mountains of the past, emptying houses like vandals and saying to unsuspecting mountain families, "What a good deal you got out of me."

He thought about his wife's letter as he worked. He should have read it. Maybe he would have known why she had become distant and tense. Something, someone, had frightened her into believing God was readying His Armageddon, His last terrible destruction, and she had become obsessed with that finality. Perhaps that was why she had written away for the history of her family, Jesse thought. To know the names of those long-dead strangers who would leap out of their graves for the great trial and judgment before God Himself. If the world ended in a holocaust of fire, boiling from the hellpits of inner earth, she would be able to fling herself—handholding the ghosts of her people—before God, the Judge, and beg for His goodness. Perhaps it was an illness of incomprehensible fear, the mad, grumbling voices of prophets spellbound by their own oratory, yelling across centuries like a siren of war.

Once, after the birth of Macy, Jean had said to him, "Do you think all those people gone on before us will know about this? About Macy?" And he had answered, "Could be. I never thought of it." She had turned from him and said, very quietly, "I have. All the time I was carrying her, I thought about it."

He did not understand the fear in his wife. He knew only that it was painful to watch her, tortured by something she could not explain. While his wife talked of the endtime and tried to decode God in pamphlets and scripture, his daughter, Macy, had concluded that it was only the woman's change of life, arriving late in her mother, and therefore brutally hard to accept. It would pass, Macy had said. It was not serious. Macy had told him about it triumphantly, as though he did not know of such things, and he had pretended relief. But he knew it was more than change of life. Whatever it was ravaged her, made her mourn over illusions that were spectacularly cruel in their power.

And it had begun so suddenly, so unexpectedly.

One morning she had awakened and dressed and called Macy and Carl and Doyle and ordered them to meet her at the cemetery in Tickenaley. She had made them stay the day with her, at the gravesites of her family, learning (writing on paper) the ancestry of names and dates chiseled into granite headstones—English and Indian together, the blood-mixing of worlds.

"I want the plots redone," she had said to Jesse when she returned home in the evening.

And he had taken Carl and Doyle and remounded the graves with fresh sand, planted new grass and shrubbery, and scrubbed the stones. They had worked patiently at her instruction until the gravesites were remarkably picturesque and for a time she had seemed pleased that people stopped and stood at the gravesites, admiring the sculptured white sand, glittering with mica, rising from perfectly clipped Bermuda grass.

Then she had become angry with the onlookers. They became intruders, gawkers gawking like predators over the obscene rot of death. One afternoon, late, the Preacher's wife had called Macy, and Macy had rushed to the cemetery to find her mother digging furiously at the grass. She had already scattered the sand and toppled (with great strength) one of the headstones. "She was covered up in sand," Macy told her father. "Standing there with a pick in her hands, sweat all over, and the sand—sand was everywhere, like it was a storm. She sparkled, Daddy, like—like she was covered in little glass scales. She looked like she'd been dead herself and rose up through the sand, like she'd uprooted herself."

The people of the valley had heard the story, had wagged their heads sadly, had said among themselves, "It's a pity, ain't it? Such a good woman."

The Preacher began to visit after that day.

More than anyone, the Preacher seemed to calm her. He came wearing his Scottish solemnface, softspeaking his reassurances, saying, "I know, I know." And he leaned forward, close to her, and held her hands and told her to let the demonic unrest fluttering through her pass to him and, from him, to God. "I know, I know," he sighed. "Let it loose. Let it loose." And his conduit hands stroked slowly over her fingers, and his touch made her calm. "I know, I know," he said. "I've had troubles, too. We'll help one another. I know, I know." But the Preacher did not know. He only placated her, like a drug. And she became addicted to him.

Jesse sat at his workbench (his father's workbench, made by his father's hands) in the barn and filed the axe he had used that day for clearing the woods. It may be that Macy was right, he thought. It may be change of life, a withering hormone sac, and maybe that had made her bitter and maybe that was why the Preacher could comfort her, because he had only to listen and sympathize (plugged into God, as he proclaimed) and leave her prescriptions of scripture, like pills from the pharmacy.

He leaned the axe against the door jamb and turned off the barn light and walked across the yard to the house. It was dark and the air spinning from the mountains was cold against his face. It was a night for a wood fire, but he would not have one. He knew she would retire early to bed, as she had done for months. In the night, she would rise from the bed and walk the house. He would listen to her wandering until she sat in the chair by the front window, clutching her Bible, and then the silence around him would become awesome. He was, he thought, more afraid of silence than anything. Sound meant life. It was proportional: the grander the life, the louder the sound. It was the one thing of value that Macy and Carl and Doyle—especially Doyle—had taken from the house: sound.

She was cleaning the table when he entered the kitchen. The oilcloth covering glistened under the globed overhead electric light. He could smell the detergent from the sink.

"Where you been?" she asked.

"Filing my axe," he said. "I dulled it some, cutting out roots."

"Doyle called," she told him. "He's going by Martin Bain's in the morning. Wants to see about getting the bull-dozer."

"That'll help," he said. "Tractor won't pull up some of them stumps."

He sat at the table and watched her stack the dishes in the cabinet. She worked methodically, by the rote of habit. Each dish in its place, precisely.

"It's a good spot, up there," he told her. "You ought to come up and look at it now. Doyle was asking where you thought the house ought to be."

"Put it where he wants," she said. "It's his place, not mine." She was turned from him and he could see the tension in her arms and shoulders.

"You helped Macy and Carl," he said. "Doyle just thought—"

"I told him once," she interrupted. "Sometimes I wonder if that boy ever hears a word anybody says."

He leaned his elbows on the table and pulled his shoulders forward. He said, "Jean, the boy knows what you told him. It's just—well, you was around when we put up Macy's house and Carl's house. There every day, helping out. It's the way we been doing it. Doyle just wants the same, I guess. Seems like it's fair."

She nodded slowly and dropped her head and stared at the drain.

"I'll try," she said quietly. "Maybe in the morning, after the Preacher comes by."

He moved restlessly in his chair. He said, "I thought he was by this morning. Thought I saw his car from the woods, headed this way."

She turned and looked at him. "He was," she told him. "For a few minutes. Said he'd be back this way tomorrow."

"He comes by a lot, Jean."

"We talk," she said. "He helps me. Just talking to somebody helps."

"Talk? What about? Tell me. Maybe if you'd tell me, you wouldn't be needing the Preacher so much."

"You're busy. No need to bother you."

He folded his arms across his chest and raised his head and looked into the hot light above the table.

"It's not you, Jesse," she said weakly. "I—I just can't seem to get anything straight anymore. Talking to somebody outside the family helps sometimes. That's all."

He nodded. "I guess," he said.

"I'm not crazy, Jesse," she said. "I know you and everybody else thinks it, but I'm not. Things change. Sometimes it's not easy, seeing things change."

"It's all right."

She walked to the window and looked outside. She said, "It's cold."

"Want me to make a fire in the fireplace?" he said.

"No," she said. "No need to." She walked past him, out of the kitchen and into the living room.

He sat very still, arms crossed, and listened as she moved through the room. He heard the door to the bedroom open and close. The silence began to close around him. He picked up the letter from the pie safe and unfolded it.

The stationery had a motto stamped across the top in raised lettering: WE PLEDGE TO FIND YOUR FIRST STEP IN AMERICA. A pen-and-ink drawing of a man with a Scandinavian face was in the upper right corner of the page. The pen-and-ink man was holding a shapeless bundle and he appeared awestruck, suspended in a seizure of the future. He had taken his first step in America; his next step would be a child's wailing and then the cry of the child's child. The firm of Family Finders, Inc., specialized in routing bloodlines across centuries of stagnant timepools. It was a zigzagging of places and matings, of names and migrations. There were the lost people, the guesses, the fill-the-blank questions of misplaced records (properly confessed by asterisks), and the courteous underplaying of failure in honor, overwhelmed by the accomplishments of the achievers, recorded like résumés in history books. Phantoms. Names fused in the pumping of lovemaking, with long-dead cries of ecstasy echoing in progeny like prayers of survival.

He read quickly but found nothing important. Births and deaths. Marriages. Children. The people of his wife's history sprouting from the straight lines (limbs?) of the ancestral tree. The records were mostly those that Jean herself had furnished Family Finders, Inc. And somewhere in the New York offices, someone—a part-time worker, a college student, Jesse thought—had pieced together names and dates and made it all sound legitimate. It was believed, the letter said, that Jean's great-grandfather, Asa Daniel Moreland, had served as an aide to Alexander Stephens, the vice-president of the Confederacy. Beyond that, facts were obscure. The first step taken in America may have been that of William Hall Moreland, who arrived from England in the late eighteenth century. But it was only speculation. Family Finders, Inc., had the name of William Hall Moreland because he had been killed in a violent assassination. No one knew where his bones had decayed.

There was no mention of the Indian ancestors. There was no reason. Jean knew they were buried in the mountains around her.

He closed the letter and slipped it back into its envelope and placed it on the pie safe. He thought of the stories of her great-grandfather—her English great-grandfather. He had been the first man buried in the cemetery of Tickenaley Church. He had followed Jesse's great-grandfather to the valley, had married a Cherokee Indian who bore him two sons. In the third winter, before the birth of his second son (Jean's grandfather), he had died. There were stories that he had been fierce.

Jesse picked up the letter again and turned it in his hand.

It did not seem right, omitting the great-grandmother Indian. It was that heritage that had first attracted him to Jean— the high cheekbones and chocolate eyes that marked her like a proud signature.

He lay in bed, away from her, and imagined the great space that separated them. He remembered the nights when she had touched his face before turning to sleep. A touch. Wordless. He remembered how she had fit in sleep, her back curled into the cradle of his body with his arms around her, and how, in sleep, she would pull his hands up and fold them over the delicate flesh of her breasts. But now she moved away, balancing on the edge of the bed, her hands tucked to her own face, her arms covering her breasts.

Outside, it was autumn. He listened to her uneven breathing (she was still awake, staring into the dark off the edge of the bed). He closed his eyes and threw his mind back to the splendor of the quickflashing moment of autumn entering him. Autumn. He trembled. He wanted to touch her, but he did not. The space between them was too great.

TWO

October 14

JESSE WAS AT THE CLEARING BEFORE SUNRISE, BEFORE
Carl and Doyle. It was still cold and he buttoned his coat
tight to his throat as he stood beside his truck, waiting. The
dawnsilver of light fell heavily across the trees from a dark
underbelly of the fluorescent sky. The ground was coated
with the thin crystal skin of frost and it, too, was fluorescent.

As he waited, a stirring began in the woods around him
and the first chattering of day fell from the trees. Squirrels,
he thought. He could hear wings fluttering above him like
soft voices. And the dawnsilver began to lighten and Jesse
saw a spear of sun driving into a single oak high on the
mountain. He heard the barking of a dog far off in the valley.
He lit a cigarette and blew the smoke in a circle from his
lips. The circle of smoke stood for a moment before him
in its swirling blue O, then turned level and fell across the
hood of his truck.

He took his axe from the truckbed and walked across the
cleared land to a large oak that had been left standing. It
would border the house on the southwest, its limbs close
enough to scrape the porch roof.

Jesse knew the house that would be built. Doyle had drawn it out on paper, but the drawing was not necessary. Jesse had seen it in his mind exactly as it would be. Every detail of it was clear to him, and when he and his sons had begun clearing the woods, he had taken only what would be needed for the house and barns. There would be nothing wasted, nothing unnecessarily ripped out. The house and barns would fit neatly among the trees. It would be a good place to live.

The land had been Jesse's and his father's and his grand-father's and his great-grandfather's. Each had tended it well, had extended its boundaries. They had farmed the black soil of the bottomlands and cut timber from the mountains. With each generation, portions had been given for homesites and the buildings had been constructed by the families. It was always assumed that a child would never leave the valley; the heritage was too great.

Jesse's own children had drawn lots for their homesites when Macy married. Though he had never said it to Macy or Carl, Doyle's draw—this land—was the best of the three sites. It was in the palm of a mountain that had split apart into two small peaks jutting above the break. The mountain was ringed in exposed granite that had cracked apart millions of years earlier and had left rooms and tunnels of caves hidden behind purple rhododendrons (the purple-laurel). In the summer, a chilling air blew from the caves. Jesse's great-grandfather had named the mountain Twin Top. The people of the valley called it the Mountain of the Caves.

At the bottom of the mountain, along the road, the site was fringed in white pines that Jesse's father had planted after the virgin timber had been cut. Above the pines, the land leveled like the lap of a chair. A wide, shallow trough collared the land at the base of the peaks and in storms the water swept harmlessly around the lap.

An archeologist had studied the site in the late sixties and reported that it was a man-made plateau. It was too sym-metrical for the evolution of nature, he had said. And he had dug into the earth in criss-crossing ditches and uncov-

17

ered rare pottery and broken seashells used for money by nomadic coastal tribes.

The archeologist declared that Indians had moved the earth onto the plateau in vessels, in thousands of trips, and had carefully scattered and packed it. It was the way burial mounds were prepared, he had explained. But the work was never completed. It had been stopped abruptly, as though something had happened to drive the Indians away. Something fearful.

The people of the valley had listened eagerly to the archeologist. It could be true, they had agreed. Tickenaley—the valley and the town—had been an Indian word Anglicized into obscurity. It meant (as rumored) "place of the gods." And, yes, they agreed among themselves, that, too, could be true. There was a legend about an Indian chief (no one knew his name) who had proclaimed himself a deity and had demanded the worship of human sacrifices. And the gods had gathered at the Mountain of the Caves and begged him to stop the sacrifices, but he would not. The gods had become angry and used their terrible power and the arrogant chief had been consumed in a great, whiteheat flame that scorched the earth.

Yes, the people of the valley agreed, something like that could have happened. At least it was a good Indian story. Much like Moses on the mountain, conversing with God, then coming back down with the Commandments in his hands only to find the children of Israel frolicking in sin. Like that, like Moses. A good Indian story.

But the archeologist had listened to the legend of the chief in awe. The Indians had left the land and never again disturbed it because they were warned by some undeniable presence. And the archeologist began to feel the heat in the ground and began to imagine the dark earth as scorched. He began to have dreams of warning and he, too, left.

But if the Indians had begun constructing the plateau as a burial ground, and if the gods had used it in the firedeath of a chief, it was an ancient, overgrown history. Across the level lap of the plateau, in the wide, shallow trough, and up the ridges of the Mountain of the Caves, the land was thickly covered in massive hardwood—oak and hickory and blackgum and beech and maple and sourwood, trees that were majestic and firmly rooted. The only break in the treeline was the belt of exposed granite, running like a gray scar across both peaks. The caves under the granite shelves had never been explored. The bones of Indians, stored until they could be put into burial mounds, were deep in them, the people of the valley believed. It was not worth investigating. The people of the valley were afraid of being lost in the caves, of falling into a tube of rock and dirt so deep in the bowels of the earth that even their shouts would be swallowed.

It was a good place for a home, Jesse thought. He looked below him, over the pale green rows of the white pines, and above him, to the clusters of hardwoods. The hardwoods had colored for the autumn and the golds and reds and browns blistering on their great chests of limbs waved brilliantly in the first rush of the October sun. Colors so grand they hurt his eyes.

He remembered the night before. He could feel the wonder—the absolute wonder—of the season surging through him. It was like music, and he wanted to stand beneath the pouring of the sound.

He had marked and wedgecut three trees before Carl arrived. Of his children, Carl was the most private. Carl had fought in Vietnam and had been decorated for heroism, though no one knew what Carl had done that was heroic. He would not speak of it. No one had ever seen the medals that had been pinned on his chest in a ceremony thousands of miles away. He had said that he'd lost them, but he had not. They were in the trunk that he kept locked and stored in the attic of his home. Jesse knew there had been horror in his act of heroism. He knew it was deep in his son's memory, like a thick brain tumor that could not be removed. Carl was thirty years old. He had been married for six years to Anna Peeples. Anna was from Tennessee. She was the first wife of any of Jesse's family since 1903 not born in the valley. And that, at first, had been difficult for Jesse to understand or accept. But he liked Anna. His grandmother had been named Anna. Anna was the first word Jesse had said as a baby.

Carl and Anna did not have children. Jean believed that whatever had happened to Carl in Vietnam had made him sterile. If so, Carl hid the secret as carefully as his honors of war.

Jesse watched his son walking from the truck, carrying the power chainsaw that Jesse had reluctantly begun to use. It was faster, but not as clean as the two-man crosscut. The chainsaw smelled of burnt oil and gasoline. It was faster. Only faster. And Jesse had taken his crosscut (his father's crosscut) and mounted it on nails to the wall of his barn. A man had tried to buy it from Jesse, claiming he knew of a doctor in Atlanta who collected such saws. It was after that that Jesse quit showing strangers driving vans and pickup trucks the contents of his barn.

Carl nodded a greeting to his father and switched the heavy saw in his hands. Jesse said, "Good morning, son." He said it softly, as he always spoke when with Carl. Carl's own voice was soft. His eyes were soft (brown, deep, like his mother's eyes). There had always been a gentle look in his face, as though he was preoccupied with something that had not yet happened.

"Cold this morning," Carl said to his father.

"It is," Jesse said. "Feels good."

Carl looked at the clearing below him, at the feathering of frost. He saw a deer in the dark trunks of the trees. "It does," he agreed. "Best time of the year."

"You talk to Doyle this morning?" Jesse asked.

"He called before I left. Said he'd overslept some."

Jesse laughed easily.

"Been that way since he got married," Carl said, smiling.

"Seems that way," Jesse said. "Guess he can't be blamed that much. Young people like being alone." He laughed again and picked up his axe and drove the head of it into a stump. "He'll be on after a while. Called last night to say he was checking on a bulldozer. I guess we can get these trees down and trimmed."

Carl cut the trees with the chainsaw, dropping them exactly as Jesse had planned. The trees fell in a sudden thunder and the airswell from the falls blew up into the limbs of the trees close around, tossing them wildly. And they took their axes (Jesse would not use the power saw for trimming) and began cutting away the limbs, cutting from the bottom upward, pulling the limbs away and piling them for burning. It was slow, monotonous work. The sound of their axes against the tree limbs echoed off the Mountain of the Caves.

It was past nine when Carl saw Doyle's car easing along the logging road leading into the clearing.

"I see he got up," Carl said.

"Looks like he's got somebody with him," Jesse said. "Looks like somebody's in the front seat."

Carl cupped his hand over his forehead and stared at the car. "It's somebody," he replied. "Maybe Florence. Maybe she needed the car to go over and help Mama get ready for Winston's birthday."

"I don't know," Jesse said. "Macy was saying yesterday that she was going by for Florence."

The two men watched the car stop and the doors open.

"Looks like Mama," Carl said.

"It is," Jesse replied. He pulled a cigarette from its package and lit it. He knew why she was there. She could not push Doyle away from her. Not Doyle. Doyle had roared noisily through childhood, always close to her, circling her, celebrating her with his play and with his care. She had become deeply depressed when, three months earlier, Doyle had married Florence Hart and moved into the house of his father-in-law. Was that it? he wondered. Was it Doyle's leaving that had caused her change?

"Doyle," Jesse whispered, saying the name like a discovery.

"What?" Carl asked.

"Nothing."

They watched mother and son walking across the clearing. They could hear Doyle talking excitedly, stopping to gesture over the land with the handle of his axe.

"Knew something was wrong with him," Carl said quietly. "He's been looking off down that road every day, waiting for Mama."

"I guess."

"Mama feeling better?" Carl asked tentatively.

"Has good days and bad days," Jesse answered. "This must be one of the good ones. I left before she got up."

"Guess Winston's birthday gives her something to do."

Jesse drew from his cigarette and spit the smoke into the air. He said, "I guess so."

"Hey, look who I found walking up the road," Doyle called from across the clearing. He pulled at his mother's arm. "Told her she looked like Old Lady Pitts, wandering around the hills like she was lost."

"Mama," Carl said as they approached. He could see the circles, like bruises, under her eyes.

"Morning, Carl," Jean said. She looked away from him.

"You look good, Mama," Carl told her.

"Must not," she said. "Not if Doyle thinks I'm Old Lady Pitts."

Doyle laughed and put his arm around her. "Now, I didn't say that," he teased. "There's a difference in looking like somebody and being somebody. Old Lady Pitts is about ten times prettier. Whole world knows that."

A smile split across Jean's face. She said, "You be quiet before I take a stick to you, boy."

"Why didn't you come up in the car?" Jesse asked.

"Wouldn't start," she said. "Guess the battery's dead. Thought I'd walk up." She looked at him. "Thought it'd help to get out in the air a little bit."

"Don't matter," Doyle said quickly. "You're here. Come on. Let me show you where my house is." He struck his axe into the tree Carl had been trimming. "Why don't you catch a break," he said to his father and Carl. Then to his mother: "Hired hands need a rest every once in a while. Only way you can keep them around." He laughed and pulled his mother away and began to show her his imaginary house, walking her through the groundplot of each room.

"What he needed," Carl said quietly to his father. "Mama."

Jesse did not reply. He watched his wife and son, saw them standing close, saw Doyle speaking and pointing and pacing off the room sizes, saw Jean listening and nodding.

"He's been scared, the way Mama's been," Carl said. "Cried about it one day, when we was talking."

Jesse looked at Carl, surprised. "Doyle?" he said.

Carl nodded. "It was right after Macy found Mama at the cemetery."

Jesse dropped his cigarette and stepped on it. He lifted his axe and ran his thumb along the blade. "Let's finish up," he said.

Jean stayed for an hour and then Jesse walked her across the clearing to Doyle's car.

"I don't need to take the car," she told him. "It's not that far to walk."

"It's more'n you think," he said. "Couple of miles at least. No need to walk. Doyle can come in with Carl. I'm going to town to pick up the candles for the cake."

"I didn't get him a present," she said fretfully.

"It's all right," he replied. "I got him one for us. Got him a rifle put away down at Helton's. I'll pick it up this afternoon."

"A rifle? He's too little—"

"No, Jean. He's old enough. I always told him I'd buy him a rifle when he turned ten. He's old enough."

"I guess," she mumbled.

"I wouldn't do it if I didn't think it was all right," he said. He opened the car door for her and touched her hand and held it for a moment. "I'm glad you came by, Jean," he told her. "It was good for the boy. I can tell."

She looked at him, then quickly turned away, and slipped into the car and closed the door. He leaned with both hands against the car.

"I got to go," she said through the opened window.

"Preacher coming?" he asked.

She looked at him again, then away. She said, "No. No, he's not. I called. Said I'd be busy, doing the birthday."

"Jean, I didn't mean nothing by what I said last night."

"I know it," she replied quietly. She turned her head to stare at his hands.

"Jean."

She lifted her head and looked into his face, her eyes holding him. He remembered her eyes when nothing confused them. Brown, deep, Indian eyes.

"What's the matter?" she asked suddenly.

"Nothing. Why?" he said.

"You just—just shook. Like you had a pain."

"I didn't feel it. Didn't feel nothing."

She looked across the clearing. She could see Carl and Doyle working at the trees.

"Maybe he should of put the house somewhere else," she said. "All those stories about that land."

"It's a good place," Jesse said. "Just a good place. Nothing else."

"Maybe." She continued to watch her sons working. Then: "Tell him I'm glad for him."

"I will. We won't be late. We'll quit early."

He watched her drive away, watched until the car disappeared beyond the white pines. Without turning he knew his sons were also watching. Their axes were silent. He wondered what they were thinking.

In late afternoon, Jesse drove into Tickenaley.

Tickenaley was the town of the valley, and of Jesse's family. His great-grandfather had moved into the unsettled, isolated region in 1869, at age twenty-eight, the same year Jesse's grandfather had been born. Two of his great-grandfather's brothers (bachelors who remained unmarried) had followed in 1870 and, with them, four other families whose lands had been forever lost in the Civil War. One had been a merchant from Madison who decided to become a farmer, failed, and then constructed a log store in 1873. He had called the store Tickenaley. Later, it became a township and the county seat for Onslow County. There were five valleys in Onslow County—the Tickenaley, the Valley of the Two

Forks, the Dobbs Creek, the Cane Bottom, and the Gold Hill. The Tickenaley was the most isolated and the most beautiful.

It was a small town. Its stores and shops were crowded along the narrow highway that stretched like a pencil scratch through the north Georgia mountains. The magazines of Atlanta had published that Tickenaley was the last unspoiled mountain village, the one holdout against the remarkable, triumphant march of progress. The people of Tickenaley had not been impressed by the prose writers from the magazines. To them, there was nothing remarkable or triumphant about the invasion that had crawled over north Georgia like a relentless malignancy. It was not progress; it was destruction. Finely dressed Atlanta land speculators in their chrome and mahogany offices playing at buying and selling and promoting as though it was all merely an amusing game. Summer hamlets and winter homes nestled in the hills, selling daily by the razzle of come-ons and scheming. Guaranteed giveaways—cameras to Cadillacs—to select people on select mailing lists of demographic profiles worthy of the chance-taking. Half-acre lots on special. A-frame/condo/duplex/log cabin blueprints in a mail-order book. Nestled. Nestled. Nestled. A cozy fireplace feeling. Just off the four-lane freeways. Hiking on government-safe woodtrails, clearly marked. Rafting on cold mountain streams. Plenty of handcrafts from quaint old mountain people who had ancient skills and were willing to sell them for pennies. Come on up, for God's sake. Bring picnics and cameras. Find a mountain man (or woman in a sunbonnet) and have your thirty-five millimeter picture taken to show the people back in the office in Atlanta. ("My God, look at them. How do those people live that way, up there in the hills, nestled away like that?" "How? Oh, by the money we take in there on weekends. That's how.")

And all over the mountains, except in the Tickenaley Valley, there were clusters of homes and rich, gleaming city cars in concrete driveways. And on the rivers, it was easy enough to read the trash trails of the rafters. Belligerent.

25

Haughty. Chuting through the spew of whitewater rapids. Kings of the goddamn river. Keeping a watch on the banks for natives that may pop up like the dumbfaced characters out of Snuffy Smith. (Once some mountain boys were swimming in the river and the rafters stopped and one, the leader, berated the mountain boys. Said they were stupid for not having regulation lifejackets and for not swimming in buddy-system pairs. And the mountain boys, saying nothing, threw rocks, driving the rafters cursing downriver. And there followed a solemn story in the Atlanta newspapers about an ambush on innocents. Just like James Dickey's *Deliverance*, the story said. Wild people up there. Can't take good will when it's well meant. Won't be taught. All that in-breeding that causes slobbering and albinos. Progress would never change them. Never.)

And where progress invaded, it did not change the people—it annihilated them. Progress rolled over them like a furious war. Progress reduced them to sideshows, like the summer Indians in the hills of North Carolina.

But in Tickenaley, in the last unspoiled mountain valley discovered by the writers of magazine stories, the only ventures of progress had been the antique scavengers. And when they had bought all that would be sold, they seldom returned. The road was too narrow and crooked. ("Make a snake puke, it's so crooked," one once proclaimed cynically.)

Tickenaley was too far off the four-lane freeways and none of its merchants were wealthy. None seemed to care. It was a quiet and restful place, too small to become embroiled in the uncontrollable anger that seemed to consume the rest of the world in the first year of the decade of the eighties. None of Tickenaley's men fought in World War One (it was lore that the news of the war reached the valley a year after it was over). Only three had been in World War Two. All three had been killed in Germany—ironically on consecutive days. Only four had been to Korea. One had been killed. One had remained in the Navy. Two had returned to Tickenaley. And only two had been to Vietnam.

Carl was one. Guy Finley, a deputy sheriff, was the other. Guy had been wounded. No one knew about Carl. There was no wound that could be seen.

Jesse parked his truck in front of Angus Helton's hardware store. He looked at his watch as he opened the truck door and slipped from beneath the steering wheel. It was ten minutes after five. Angus was sweeping the sidewalk in front of his doorway.

"Well, I'll be damned," Angus said cheerfully, folding his hands over the top of the broomhandle. "What brings you out of the hills, Jesse?"

"Came by for the rifle," Jesse told him. "Today's the boy's birthday."

"Today?" Angus said. "Well, I guess it is. October fourteen. I was talking to Anna earlier about it. She said y'all was having a to-do up at your place tonight."

Jesse smiled and stepped into the store and Angus followed him. Jesse enjoyed talking to Angus. Angus was a descendant of the merchant who had constructed the first log cabin in the town. A sign over the front door of his store read: ESTABLISHED IN 1873. The sign was only partly true. The way Angus explained it, the store had never completely passed out of the family; it had been confused by some confusing marriages.

Angus loved gossip. If he did not know the truth of a matter, he speculated. Angus' speculations were always more interesting than the truth and always listened to and believed. Angus was, by his own declaration, an oracle. His cry was, "Remember, you heard it here first."

"How about it, Jesse?" Angus asked. "You got a to-do going on?"

"We're having a little party," Jesse said. "Boy's growing up. I guess Anna'll be a little late for it."

Angus moved behind the counter. He said, "What she was telling me when I was talking to her about it. Lester won't close that store until six-thirty, come hell or high water. Ask me, he's just wasting time. I close at six, no

matter what the business looks like. Got my bowels trained
for it. Six-thirty, I'm home, sitting on the john. Ain't no
business worth clogged bowels."

Jesse laughed. He lifted a new axe from its stand and
tested its balance. It was heavy and true.

"Well, she likes the job," Jesse said, replacing the axe.
"She and Carl been talking about buying a little more land.
Every dime helps."

"Hell, Jesse, y'all must own half the valley."

"If we do, it's the half nobody wants," Jesse replied
lightly.

"How's the clearing for the house going?" Angus asked.

"Going all right. About ready to put in the foundation."

"Damned if I'd build it up there," Angus said. "Don't
care what you say, Jesse, that place is haunted."

Jesse laughed easily. "Yeah," he said.

"Now, damn it, I mean it," Angus argued. "I been up
there. People tell me they ain't ever saw any animals on
that land. Say they go right up to it but won't go on it."

Jesse shook his head in amazement. "That's a good story,
Angus," he said.

"Story, my ass. You ever see any animals on it?"

He could not remember, Jesse realized. Birds, yes, but
they were in the trees. He could not remember seeing any
animals on the plateau.

"Well, I never stood around and looked," Jesse said.

"I was telling Anna about it," Angus boasted. "She thought
it was funny."

"So do I, Angus. But it's a good story," Jesse said. "Now,
where's the rifle?"

Angus squatted behind the counter and began to pull out
boxes. He talked as he searched for the rifle. "Ask me,
Lester ought to double Anna's pay. Wadn't for her, he
wouldn't be selling doodley-squat. I bet that woman sells
more dresses than anybody in Georgia, including them fancy
stores in Atlanta with them French names. Wish to God she
knew something about the hardware business. I'd turn the
store over to her." He paused and shoved a box behind him.
"Here it is," he said. "Knew it was under there someplace."

He lifted the rifle and placed it on the counter. "Boy'll like that, Jesse. One of the best twenty-twos made. You got some shells?"

Jesse raised the rifle to his shoulder and narrowed his eye over the gunsight. He could smell the woodstain of the stock and the gun oil in the barrel.

"I got some," he said, "but I'd better take along a box. Boy'll be shooting more'n he needs to for a while."

"Well, hell, let him," Angus said. "Not having a daddy around, he needs to do what he can. Good thing he's got you and your boys."

"They watch after him pretty close," Jesse replied quietly. Then: "I need a box of birthday candles, if you got some."

"Birthday candles?" Angus snorted. "Good God, Jesse, this is a hardware store. We ain't got a Hallmark Card section that I know of."

"Thought I saw some the last time I was in here," Jesse said.

"Maybe so. Maybe so," Angus mumbled. He began to walk along the shelves, looking. "I got mule collars and axle grease and baking soda and linament and binder twine and washpots and God only knows what else," he said. "Maybe there's some candles somewhere. Don't ever know what some drummer's pushing off on me. Hell, I got stuff in here my granddaddy bought. Found some medicine for liver spots last week that was so damn old the box itself had caught the spots."

Jesse watched as Angus found the candles and cartridges for the rifle, and he listened to a story about a drummer who specialized in wart remover and how Old Lady Pitts had bought some for a wart on her nose and how the medicine had burned a hole in her nose. "She come after me with a shotgun," Angus swore. "Said she was fixing to blow a wart off my ass if I didn't give her money back. Well, I did, quick enough."

Jesse looked at his watch. It was five-thirty.

"I appreciate you holding the gun for me, Angus," Jesse said. "Guess I'd better be going on. The boy'll be wanting to shoot at some tin cans before it's too dark."

"Well, you and them boys of yours teach him good," Angus advised. "Him not having a daddy around, he'll need it. A gun ain't no toy. Gun'll kill a man in a snap of a finger. Never had one myself. Not at the house. Damn things scare me."

"We'll be careful with him, Angus. He'll be fine."

Jesse took the gun and cartridges and candles from Angus' store and drove north out of Tickenaley. He crossed the bridge at the creek, with its clean, silverflashing water spraying off the shoals of a rockbed. He passed Tickenaley Church, which his great-grandfather had helped organize and build on land that his great-grandfather had donated to the valley. The parsonage was across the road from the church. He could see the Preacher's car in the carport and the Preacher's young, plump wife at the clothesline. She looked at his truck but did not wave. He wondered if the Preacher held her hands and stroked them and whispered, "I know, I know." He felt his body tighten.

He turned right off the highway onto a graveled dirt road and passed the house where Macy lived with Winston. It was a small house, white with navy-blue shutters. The shrubbery grew around it like a blanket tucked to the foundation and along the steps. It was well shaded and cool. The mailbox in front of the house was held by a five-foot Uncle Sam in profile, a quaint holdover from World War Two. Macy's husband, Faron, had kept the wooden Uncle Sam painted in vivid red, white, and blue. Since Faron's death two years earlier, the Uncle Sam had begun to chip and peel (its goatee was also broken) and Jesse had promised Macy he would repair and paint it after clearing the land for Doyle's house.

Jesse thought of his dead son-in-law. Faron had not been a success as a provider, but he had been a good man who had cared for his family. Until the cancer, he had driven a truck. The cancer had killed him slowly and painfully and it had hurt Jesse to see him wasted and ill. But it had also taught Jesse something about his daughter: Macy was strong.

She had continued her teaching at the elementary school and attended her ill husband and her growing son and she had not broken. Macy had a spirit that could not be compromised.

Jesse looked again at his watch. It was twenty minutes before six. It would be late for Winston to shoot his new rifle, he thought. The treeshadows lapped across the hood of his truck like thick splashes of night. The air was cooling quickly. It would soon be Dark Thirty. There would be a fire in the fireplace, sound in the house. He touched the stock of the rifle beside him.

He was a hundred yards from the house when he felt it: the premonition of a sickening silence.

He slowed the truck to a stop and listened to the idling motor. He saw Doyle's car, and Macy's, and his own (the one Jean could not start), but he did not see Carl's. Where is it? he wondered.

He turned the key and the motor of the truck stopped. He opened the door and pulled himself out. He stood behind the door of the truck, holding it open before him like a shield, and looked at the house. He could see lights through the windows. Nothing moved. There was no sound.

He stepped cautiously forward. "Doyle," he called. "Doyle."

There was not an answer.

The dog, he thought. Where is the dog and her puppies? The dog is always around me. Always.

He began to walk slowly toward the house. He could feel the freezing crawl of fear across his shoulders. He said, softly, "Jean? Jean?"

He saw Carl first. Carl had been hurled into the shrubbery beside the front door. His chest was split and caked with blood jelly, as though his heart had exploded. His head was cradled in a branch of the bush, his mouth flung open in a cry that had been blown out through his back.

Jesse's body convulsed. His neck jerked spastically. He reached to touch Carl, but he did not. He tried to speak, but he could not. He turned numbly, breathing in short, shallow swallows, and pushed open the door of the house and stumbled inside.

He found them all. All except Florence.

Doyle in the living room, just inside the door, a butcher knife in his throat, his head almost severed.

Macy on the kitchen table, tied with cord to the table legs.

Jean in the bedroom, also tied with cord to the four posts.

In the backyard, between the house and barn, he found Winston. The cap of his head had been blown away.

He fell to his knees and dragged his grandson to him and cradled him gently. He began to cry and then he vomited, spilling his sickness over the cooling body in his arms.

He lifted his head and screamed like an animal in pain.

He could hear the echo of his voice off the hills. And then he could not hear anything.

THREE

October 15

JESSE COULD NOT HEAR. HE SAT FORWARD IN A CHAIR, with his elbows braced on his knees, his hands hanging limply. He saw the faces—the moving mouths—of the men around him, but he could not hear what they were saying. He knew they were asking questions. Somehow—by the arching of their lips or by intuition—he knew they were asking questions. But he could not hear the sound of their words and he could not answer them. His silence was absolute.

Yet there was a part of his mind that could hear and speak and reason. It was like a separate person, a diminutive, keen-eyed ghost of a person, who was oddly intolerant and restless. And that person wandered effortlessly outside of his body, outside of his seeing, and flew about like a whisper, leashed to him only by an umbilical cord of pity.

There in the Onslow County Courthouse, in the outer office of the jail, in the dustlight of morning, there were two Jesses: one deadened by silence, the other alert and certain and impatient. One could not hear and did not speak; the other knew—all that was happening around him and far away from him, that Jesse understood.

33

The wandering Jesse knew about the slaughter of his family, knew that the silent Jesse had discovered them. He knew the people of the Tickenaley Valley had sat in their homes throughout the night, huddling, afraid of an evil that was somewhere in the darkness around them. He knew the women had hugged their bodies in a mother's pain of loss, swaying in their chairs and weeping. He knew the men had sat with their hunting guns across their laps and guarded against a madness that was invisible and incomprehensible. And through the windows of their homes, in the amber spill of the filling moon, they had seen images of an unloosed hell—shadows disembodying like teasing demons—and what had been familiar and lovely on other nights was now satanic.

The alert Jesse, the ghost Jesse, knew it was the suddenness of the assault that had numbed the people of the valley. He knew they were saying among themselves, "Why didn't we sense it?" There had been nothing to foretell such horror, no preamble or warning. Nothing. Nothing in the sign language that the people of the valley read with prophetic powers. The wind had not spoken in its hisses and sighs like soprano cries from an ether world. The animals had not whimpered or hidden or sniffed the air for a bloodscent. There had been nothing in the trees of autumn—none to die instantly before the eyes (a certain voice). No blights, like soot, on the moon's face. Nothing in the ethereal presence that ran like a shudder of electricity through those with the gift of knowing. There had been nothing.

Nothing? the alert Jesse said cynically to the deadened Jesse. *Nothing?* Jean had sensed warnings. The clearing of a burial ground for a house. Jean had wanted to move the house, had been frightened when she walked the groundplot with Doyle. It had been in her face, in the brown Indian eyes that had a covenant with legend. *Yes,* the alert Jesse wordlessly whispered. *Yes, Jean had sensed it.* The burial grounds and the dreams of the endtime that she had had. *The dreams of the endtime were also warnings,* the wordless voice said argumentatively. *Jean knew. She had seen it. She had seen it. She had seen it.*

And as these cries were being screamed, but not heard, the silent Jesse sat dumbly and stared at the people around him. His eyes knew the faces, but did not know why they knew them. His eyes saw the moving mouths, but he could not hear them. He could hear only the other Jesse—now sweeping like a cosmic light over the Tickenaley Valley—telling him that the wailing of the people was mighty. They were saying, "God, O God, O God."

One of the men, a doctor named Mercer Dole, knelt before Jesse and, holding Jesse's wrists, began to move his mouth slowly, nudging the words out in syllables. He reached up to Jesse's face and turned it to a woman sitting beside him. Jesse's eyes focused on her and a flicker, like a scratch, raced across his mind. It was Anna. Even in his disorientation, he knew Anna. She sat near him in the room of men; her eyes fixed on him. He saw her mouth open and close in a single word. It was his name, but he did not know it. His brain ached from the silence and from a bloodrush of recognition. He did not know how he had come to be in the room, or why the men were familiar, or what had happened from the time he had lifted Winston to him. There was nothing in his mind to tell him those things. There were no images (none that were complete), no sensations. The hours and the happenings of those hours were all in darkness, all in a thick, black, soundless absence. Jesse was in a room with men he knew but could not remember, and with Anna. The man kneeling before him leaned forward, close to his face, and his mouth moved again. The man's eyes blinked sadly in resignation and he released Jesse's wrists and stood and walked across the room and looked out a window. Jesse could feel Anna's hand on his arm, her fingers patting his muscles like a coded language. And then the other Jesse—the alert, ghost Jesse—flew across his face and postured comfortably on the whiteheat of space and said, *She was there*.

Anna sat stiffly erect, as though posed for a portrait. Her eyes wandered to the men who stood around Jesse and questioned him—the doctor; Ellis Spruill, the sheriff; a man named Cale from the Georgia Bureau of Investigation; two other men in State Patrol uniforms, who had not been introduced to her. She wondered why the men did not speak to her, ask her the same questions they were asking Jesse. She, too, had found the bodies. One by one, as Jesse had. Her husband first, hanging in the shrubbery. She had called the sheriff. She had helped the sheriff pull Winston's body away from Jesse. But they had asked her only about the time—the hour and minute—she had arrived at the farm. It was somehow important. They had asked her again and again, "And what time did you get there?"

The doctor and the sheriff had told her they were sorry. They had suggested that she should cry, to let out the hurt. But she had not cried. She could not. Her husband was dead, but she did not yet feel his death. Not permanently. Not eternally. Perhaps in time. But now there was Jesse and Jesse needed her. Jesse had lost so much. Jesse did not need to be alone with these men who asked him questions they would not ask her.

The men in the room could feel Anna's eyes darting over their faces like a curious bird. They did not look at her. It was uncomfortable having her there, like a waiting servant at Jesse's side.

"Looks like he can't tell us nothing right now," the sheriff said wearily.

"It's just shock," the doctor said. "It'll take time."

"Then we'll wait," the sheriff said. He looked at the man named Cale. Cale nodded agreement.

"He's got to get some rest," the doctor said, "or he won't be coherent when he does start talking." He moved closer to Jesse and looked at him. "Christ, he needs to be cleaned up. He's still got the boy's blood on the side of his face."

"It'll help having him tell us what he can," the man named Cale replied. "We're just guessing now. Especially about the other girl."

Ellis Spruill crossed his office and poured another cup of coffee for himself. It did not matter what Cale imagined, he thought. Jesse could tell them nothing. Especially about Florence. Whoever killed Jesse's family had taken Florence with them. Christ, she was pretty. Young and pretty. They would want more of Florence than a single, hammering rape. Cale could speculate his ass off, but it would not change a thing. Goddamn GBI. Standing around, being condescending. Impatient to take over.

"Where do you want to take him, Ellis?" the doctor asked. "The hospital? I don't care myself. We need to get him away from here. You're going to have reporters crawling through the keyhole before long. Way they're peering in the windows, I feel like we're in a freak show as it is."

"My place," the sheriff answered. "Hattie's already told me to bring them home." He paused and swallowed some coffee and thought about his wife. "She grew up with Jean," he added. He looked at Jesse. Poor bastard, he thought. Poor hurt bastard. Then he said, "Hattie wants them there with us. Me, too."

"That's good enough," the doctor told him. "Hattie'll know how to handle it." He knelt before Anna and said softly, "Anna, he needs to rest. You, too. We're going to take you up to Ellis' house, to Hattie. I'm going to give you both something to make you sleep for now. But I'll stay with you for a while."

Anna stared calmly at Mercer Dole. "All right," she said.

"It'll be best, Anna," Ellis told her. He looked at Cale. "I'm going out and move back them reporters. If you'll wait here, I'll take them up to the house and then we can get back to the farm."

"I'll wait," Cale replied. He could read the irritation in Ellis Spruill's face. He did not want to interfere with Ellis.

Ellis ordered the reporters away from the front of the jail, then led Jesse and Anna outside into the morning and put them into his sheriff's car. The only sound from the onlookers was the whir and hiss of cameras and the scraping of footsteps as people pushed closer to see.

The people had arrived early from their homes in the valley. They came to ask questions, to listen, to wonder, to watch the closed door of the courthouse, and to say among themselves that the murder of Jesse Wade's family was more tragic than anything they had ever known. They came to mutter, "Why here?" They came to say (as though one among them could answer), "What can we do?"

And the talking seemed to give them solace.

"He came by for the boy's rifle, the one he had put away for a birthday present," Angus Helton said gravely. "Else Jesse would of been there, too, likely as not. And Anna, working late like that, it saved her life. Sure did."

"Why Jesse's people? Jesse's people settled up here when nobody wouldn't come up. Wadn't a man hold a bad word against Jesse. Nobody. Don't guess they's been a man around here thought of as well as Jesse."

"Whoever done it didn't know whose place it was. Just chanced upon it. They had to be hiding to take Doyle and Carl both."

And as the sheriff's car slipped through the people crowding the sidewalks like watchers of a somber parade, Jesse saw them and the seizure of his shock began to subside and he knew clearly where he was and what had happened. He pulled himself up against the seat of the car and looked out. Faces became names and names became memories. He thought of his sons, of his wife, of his daughter, of his grandson. The faces blurring outside the car window swam in his mind with the faces of his family. He looked at Anna beside him. Anna was alive. The others were dead. All of them. He had found them. All but Florence. He thought of the clearing, of the homesite that belonged to Doyle and Florence. He had never seen an animal on the clearing. Never. Florence was also dead. He knew it.

It was past ten o'clock when Guy Finley left the officers of the Georgia State Patrol at Jesse Wade's home. They had found nothing in their search of the farm—nothing except the dog and her puppies. Each had been killed with a small-caliber gun—a twenty-two—and tossed like rags into a pile. The house cat had been found in the living room under the sofa, alive, crouching.

The men of the State Patrol believed they would also find the body of Florence Wade on the farm, but Guy knew they would not. Florence had been strikingly sensuous, with full, rising breasts. Whoever had been there and had killed so nonchalantly would have taken Florence with them. She would be dead now, but she would have been assaulted many times before she died.

Guy drove east from the farm, slowly, at a crawl, studying both sides of the curving, narrow road that led into the highway of the Tickenaley Valley. He did not know what he would see, if anything. The killer, or killers (there had to be more than one, he thought), had taken Carl's car. They were probably into Tennessee, or beyond. Carl's car would be found on a sidestreet in Chattanooga or Nashville or St. Louis. But they would not have taken Florence out of the valley with them. They would have stopped and raped her, in a pack, like dogs, and then they would have dropped her body, like trash.

Guy unholstered his revolver and placed it on the seat beside him.

The road dropped and passed through a slender branch of water, too shallow for a bridge. The oak and hickory and blackgum and beech were thick beside the rockbed stream and their autumn colors were lush and deep. Guy could smell the water and the trees and the withering ferns that grew in the mossbeds and underbrush. He stopped the car, with its front wheels in the water, and looked up into the trees. The sunlight splattered over the leaves and shattered into crystals of pindots and dropped onto the moving water, glittering off the slicktop stones. He remembered a road in Vietnam, also obscured by trees. He had been wounded on the road, a sniper's bullet gouging into the flesh of his upper leg, and he had crawled along the road and hidden until nightfall.

The water gurgled under the car's wheels. Vietnam, Guy thought. So far away. He absently brushed his hand over the leg that had been wounded. He could feel the depression where the bullet had burned away the muscle. Six inches higher and his guts would have exploded into his chest.

Suddenly he pulled himself up close to the steering wheel. Another image of Vietnam—a paramnesia of a telling inner voice that soldiers learned to hear—drove into his mind and he knew where to find Florence Wade. He closed his eyes and saw the place, completely and in detail.

She was on the side road, no more than two hundred yards from the highway, stuffed into a terracotta culvert that ran under the road.

Guy knelt beside the drain in a deep sandbed that had washed from the fields, and looked at the pale nude body. Her legs were shoved up at the knees and jammed tight against the top of the drain. Her head was bent to her left shoulder. Guy could see gray spiders dancing lightly over her breasts. "Jesus," Guy whispered. He could remember his own cramped hiding, in Vietnam, in an overhang beside the road.

He did not touch the body. He stood and backed away carefully, scanning the ground for footprints. There were none. The sand had been scraped smooth. The murderers of Jesse Wade's family knew Florence would be found; they had only wanted time.

An hour later the body was photographed, removed from the culvert, photographed again, examined, covered, and slipped into the back of an ambulance.

Ellis Spruill stood beside Guy and watched. Ellis' eyes were red and puffed. The hard, gray stubble of his unshaven face made him look older than he was.

"You get a close look at her?" Ellis asked.

"Close enough," Guy said. He knew the bullet that had finally killed Florence was the last fired. He knew the barrel of the gun—a twenty-two—had been pressed against her, above the bridge of the nose. The bullet had left a small red dot, like a deep bruise.

"Jesus God," Ellis said angrily. He spat the bitterness from his mouth. "What son of a bitch on earth could do that?"

Guy looked at the crowd of men who had arrived from Jesse Wade's farm. Most were strangers, outsiders with law badges who had volunteered their help, or had been ordered to Tickenaley by George Busbee, the governor, who had pronounced the crime ". . . horrible, horrible, a violation of mankind. All the missing and dead children in Atlanta, and now this. It has to stop." The governor was enraged, Guy thought. He had sent so many people to the valley. Uniformed state patrolmen, sternfaced and silent. Cale and two other men in suits from the GBI, huddling beside a car, speaking in grave, guarded voices. Men he did not know, standing and watching. Newsmen, perhaps, though there were no cameras. If the newsmen were not there, they were waiting in Tickenaley, vying like collectors for stories of brutal splendor.

Guy saw Aubrey Hart, the father of Florence, sitting in the grassfield beside the road, his body collapsed over his knees, his head down. His hands were laced tightly at the fingers and his body jerked with the sobs that rolled from him. Two men—Dan Alewine and George Thomas—knelt beside him, close. The sound of his crying was like the squeal of a frightened child. Aubrey's wife had died three years earlier. Florence had been their only child. Aubrey was now alone.

"What kind of a son of a bitch could do that?" Ellis said again.

Guy heard the rattling, whirling noise of a helicopter. He looked up. He could see the call letters of the television station on the belly of the helicopter and the gun-aim of a camera trained on the ambulance as it pulled away.

"It's one more thing for Jesse to take," Ellis said, "when he comes around." He paused and spat on the ground. "If he does," he added.

"Jesse, the Preacher's here to see you."

Hattie Spruill stood beside the bed where Jesse rested on his back, his eyes closed. The doctor had forced a sedative into him and the blood of his grandson had been sponged from his hands and face, and he had slept while Anna sat in a chair at the foot of the bed and watched over him. Anna would not sleep. She would not leave Jesse.

"Jesse," Hattie said again. "Can you hear me? Preacher's here."

Jesse heard the voice and recognized it. He opened his eyes and stared beyond Hattie to the Preacher. His head moved slightly on the pillow.

"Can you hear me, Jesse?" Hattie asked.

"Yes," Jesse answered in a whisper.

Hattie smiled happily. "Ellis'll be glad to know that. I know it's been a shock, Jesse. But you're better now." She stepped away from the bed and the Preacher moved close. He took Jesse's hands in his own.

"I know how you're feeling," the Preacher began in a low, soft voice. "Oh, yes, I know. I've been praying God's blessing on you." He looked at Anna. "And you, too, Anna. You, too."

Jesse could feel the Preacher's fingers moving on his hands, over the knuckles, stroking them lightly, nervously. He closed his eyes and heard the hypnotic coaxing: ". . . the only way, Jesse. Jesus said to forgive your enemies, to take pity on those who would defile you. Jesus aches, Jesse. He aches for what happened, but He's taken your wife and your children to Him, and they're resting now, on His shoulder, in His bosom. And He wants us to forgive, to say that none of the forces of Satan can overpower our trust in Him. I pray for that strength, Jesse, for all of us. . . ."

The voice was like a breath on him and Jesse could see Jean sitting, offering her hands to the Preacher, her face begging for promises that seemed real only in the Preacher's mouth. And he could see the Preacher pulling her closer to him, his voice fading to a sigh, his round Scottish face heavy with rehearsed hurt.

". . . when Jesus was on the Cross, being assassinated between the two thieves, He asked God to forgive those who were killing Him. He could do that, Jesse, because He knew God's mercy was boundless. . . ."

The deathfaces of Jean and Macy wandered abstractly

into Jesse's mind, blinking incongruously with the rhythm of the Preacher's voice. There was no forgiveness on their faces, only horror. They had died afraid and screaming, not calling for God. Jesse's vision locked on Macy. Macy. She had been so small, so playful with him. He could feel her sitting on his shoulders, her hands under his chin. He could hear her laughing gleefully. "So tall," she cried again, above the Preacher's hum of words. "I'm so tall!" Jesse could feel her feet in his back, below his shoulders, pushing against him for balance.

". . . wait for God's vengeance, Jesse. That's all we can do. God has ways that none of us understand. But He cares for those who believe and He casts out those who mock Him. The hell we feel today, because of this, is short, Jesse. The hell of those who mock God is eternal. . . ."

The Preacher's voice was stronger. His hands kneaded hard on Jesse's fingers and knuckles. Jesse could see Jean's eyes on the Preacher, her lips moving silently, repeating his words.

". . . how would the Son of God turn from those who need Him?"

Jesse saw his own sons, surprised by death. His sons. Their lean, hard bodies already cooling when he found them. He wondered if Doyle had cried out for his brother. God, Doyle. Doyle. And Carl? Carl sensed things others could not. Had he sensed his death? Did he hear Doyle cry out and rush to die near his brother? Did they know Carl would not die easily? Is that why they had shotgunned him outside the house?

Winston. A wave of sickness struck Jesse, filling his mouth with saliva. He rolled his head on the pillow and a cry, a whimper, rose in his throat. He could feel Winston's body in his arms, then Winston being separated from him. A light sizzled across his memory and he could see Ellis pulling Winston from his arms and he could feel Guy Finley holding him, saying to him, "Let go, let go."

Jesse swallowed the cry and his body stiffened and he jerked his hands away from the Preacher and pulled them in fists across his chest. His mind flew back to his home, to each of the bodies, and to the counting of the bodies as he went to them. He remembered going through the rooms, searching for Florence. But he had not found her.

Hattie stepped to the bed and placed her hand on Jesse's forehead. She said, "Preacher," and motioned with her face toward the door.

"Yes," the Preacher said. He stood with his hands clasped before him, his head bowed. He said, so quietly it was difficult to understand, "Let us pray." He pulled his clasped hands to his chin, massaging his fingers with his fingers, and began to mumble.

Jesse did not hear the prayers. He was again seeing Jean and Doyle at the clearing of the homesite, standing in the grass of imaginary rooms.

In Tickenaley, in late afternoon, the people talked of the finding of Florence Wade's body, and they watched reporters swarming around Ellis Spruill and Guy Finley and Cale and the other men who had been at the culvert.

"Hope them reporters leave Jesse alone," the people said among themselves.

"Looks like they playing it up, all right. Looks that way."

And the people left for their homes in the mountains, tense with the energy of a terrible notoriety.

FOUR

October 15

TOBY CAHILL WAITED IN THE RESTAURANT OF THE VALLEY View Lodge for the waitress to complete her whispered telephone conversation.

Toby did not like using the restaurant telephone, but the twelve concrete-block rooms of the Valley View Lodge were sparsely furnished. None had telephones. His room did not have a dresser, only the shell of a stand-up bookcase where towels and washcloths were folded and stored. It was a room as stark as a prison.

He looked at the large clock hanging on the wall above the entrance to the restaurant, advertising a soft drink. It was twenty minutes after five. Twenty-four hours earlier, the killers of Jesse Wade's family were driving away from the farm. Ten hours ago, in the morning, he had taken the few details available from the Onslow County sheriff's office and had fashioned a story for the first edition of the *Sentinel*.

In Atlanta, he would now be in Charley's drinking beer. Harvey Wills, waiting for his call, would be at home. Harvey was obsessive about being home for dinner. He did not like the late-hour people or traffic of the city. Harvey believed he would die in his car, waiting at a signal light for a color change.

The girl turned from the telephone and looked up at Toby with surprise. She smiled quickly, then dropped her eyes from him.

"Excuse me," Toby said.

"Uh-huh," she mumbled, embarrassed. She stepped away from him and walked through the swinging doors into the kitchen.

He dialed the operator and gave her the number for the collect call. He listened to the Atlanta answer and the clicking of the transfer and then Harvey's voice. "Go ahead," the operator told him.

"Toby? Where the hell you been?" Harvey said impatiently. "It's almost six. Goddamn traffic's stacked up on the sidewalks."

"Almost five-thirty, Harvey," Toby replied. "I told you. There's only one phone here. I've been waiting."

"You got anything?"

"Not much. I talked to a few people. The ones that would say anything. They're scared."

"It's all over the goddamn television," Harvey complained. "Damn bunch of vipers. I hate those frigging deep-voice bastards."

"So I've heard," Toby said.

"You got anything on paper yet?"

"Jesus, Harvey, I just got here. No. I'll call it in in the morning," Toby replied.

"Before seven, so we'll know how to handle it with what we get from AP."

"You want a sidebar from me?" Toby asked. "You taking the AP lead?"

"You give us what you've got," Harvey said. "We'll take some from them, work it around, and give you the lead. But I want the sidebar in the flesh."

"You'll get it, Harvey," Toby told him. "What did the pictures look like?"

Toby could hear Harvey moving paper around on his desk.

"Just came up," Harvey grumbled. He paused. "Jesus," he said. "Nothing. Jesus." Another pause. "Can't use anything but a couple of shots of the house and maybe one of Wade coming out of the jail. Who's the girl with him?"

"It'd have to be his daughter-in-law, Anna," Toby said. "Wife of the oldest boy, Carl. She's the one that was working late. I'll work her into the sidebar. She won't leave Wade, I hear. One of the men in town, the guy that runs the hardware store, said she was from Tennessee. Somebody called her parents and they're supposed to be getting here soon. I'll try to talk to them."

"All right, but watch it, for Christ's sake," Harvey said. "The whole frigging state's up in arms over this. Especially coming on top of all the black kids being killed. We've been getting calls all day, wanting to see what's happening up there. Somebody said Busbee had some of his people over, talking to the brass about not causing a panic."

"The governor?" Toby asked, surprised.

"You got a helluva memory, Toby," Harvey said sarcastically. "We push this and we'll be in shit from tip to toe."

"Yeah," Toby said.

"Christ, I can see it now," Harvey complained. "It's gonna be one of those fry or not-to-fry things. Every frigging freak in the whole frigging world—pro and con—will go after this one like a goddamn horny bass after a whale."

Toby shifted the telephone and turned to look across the restaurant. He saw the waitress behind the counter. She was looking at him curiously.

"I'll be careful," Toby said quietly. "I'll go back up there tonight to see if anything's happened."

"What's it like up there?" Harvey asked. "Nineteenth century, like they say?"

Toby laughed. "I'd say it was just clean and quiet. Nice, that's what. Drive you crazy, Harvey."

"Yeah, well, it won't be that way long, smartass," Harvey said. "Not when the goddamn television whores get through with it. I swear to God, they'll be splattering artificial blood on the sidewalks before it's over."

"Yeah, maybe," Toby said absently.

"They got any idea who did it?" Harvey asked suddenly.

"No one's saying, if they have," Toby told him. "Believe me, they're just scared right now."

Toby could hear Harvey breathing laboriously. "Shit," he mumbled. "They ought to hang whoever did it up by the balls, the bastards. Ought to do the same to whoever's dumping those kids. Christ, I hate such people, Toby."

"Yeah. Me, too," Toby said. "Look, I'll call in about six-thirty. The restaurant opens at six. I'll check with the sheriff's office before I call."

Harvey muttered and cursed the hour and the traffic and hung up. Toby walked to the desk of the restaurant and picked up a copy of the *Atlanta Sentinel*. He had not read the story he had written before leaving for Tickenaley. He wanted to see how the copydesk had amputated it.

"Sit anywhere?" he asked the waitress.

"Anywhere you want to," she replied shyly.

He walked to the corner of the restaurant and sat at a table near the front window. Outside it was darkening. Cars had begun to gather in the graveled parking lot.

He unfolded the paper and read the headline: FARM FAMILY MURDERED. Toby scanned his words. It had been a rushed story, pulled out of his typewriter in takes and translated to word processing. He did not remember it well.

He read the facts of the murdered carefully: Jean Wade, age fifty; Macy Wade Simmons, age thirty-two; Carl Moreland Wade, age thirty; Doyle Franklin Wade, age twenty-four; Florence Hart Wade, age twenty-three; Winston Hall Simmons, age ten—exactly.

Christ, he thought, it was like the destruction of a country. Young. All young. And Jesse, age fifty-three. Still so many years to live. And Anna Peeples Wade, age twenty-eight. Young. All the years of suffering from nothing more than the odds of chance—all those years still to be lived. Toby wondered how long it would take Jesse and Anna to put away the suffering, to realize the dead were dead.

"Need a menu?"

The voice of the waitress was small and thin. He looked

up. She was standing before him, holding a menu and an order pad. She was twenty, maybe older. He could see stress in her face. Her eyes were dull and tired.

"No," he said. "I'll have pork chops if you've got them."

She penciled the order on her pad. "Ice tea?" she asked.

"That's fine."

"You with the newspaper, ain't you?" she asked timidly.

"Yes," he replied. "The *Atlanta Sentinel.*"

"They said you was," she said, gesturing with her head to the desk that served both restaurant and motel. "You writing about them murders?"

"What little there is to know about them," Toby answered.

"I knew Florence," she said quickly. "And Doyle. We was in school together. I couldn't believe it when I heard about it. Them just getting married, and all."

"You knew them?" Toby asked. "Knew them well?"

"I—I used to, when we was in school. But I ain't seen them much in the last few years, since I moved down here." She toyed nervously with the tip of her order pad and looked quickly toward the desk. "I come down here about three years ago. Just up and left. Put all my stuff in a paper sack—I didn't have no suitcase—and I caught me a ride here. I used to work in the sewing plant down the highway, but I been here for six months or so. It's all right. They let me live in one of the rooms—one next to yours, if you got number twelve. Motel don't do much business."

Toby smiled pleasantly. She was embarrassed for talking, for saying too much. He said, "That's good. Sounds like it's working out. You don't mind, maybe we can spend some time talking about Florence and Doyle. I'd like to interview you."

A frown eased onto her forehead. Her eyes widened in curiosity. "You mean, for the newspaper?" she asked.

"That's right."

"I . . . I don't know."

"Well, you think about it. We can talk later."

She nodded and pressed the top of her order book with the heel of her palm. "You want anything else?" she asked.

"No, I don't think so," Toby told her. Then: "Tell me, how far is it to Tickenaley from here?"

"It's a long way," she said emphatically. "Fifteen miles. Maybe longer'n that." She smiled and her eyes brightened. "You want some cobbler for dessert?" she asked. "It's good."

"Maybe," Toby replied agreeably. "By the way, what's your name?"

"Rachel. Rachel Whitfield."

"Well, Rachel, I'm Toby Cahill. I'm glad to know you," Toby said.

It was dark when Toby returned to Tickenaley. He parked across the street from the courthouse and sat, with the car window down, and smoked a cigarette. The street was deserted and Toby knew the people of the town and the valley were still trembling with uncertainty. He had been born in such a town, in the Alabama hills above Huntsville. He knew the people of the Tickenaley Valley well. They were in shock and their herd instinct was great. They would remain that way, together, cowering before an unthinkable threat, until the threat was ended, and then they would become bold and angry.

He knew also there was a great, chilling curiosity among the people. They had been invaded by a sensational horror and then by crowds of strangers with serious, mysterious faces. The strangers were like nameless celebrities and the people whispered among themselves, "Wonder who that is? Wonder what they doing?"

Toby had been attracted to journalism in just such a circumstance. It was in 1955, when he was thirteen, and five men who had escaped from the penitentiary had hidden in his hometown. The men had taken a hostage (the wife of one of the escapees) and there had been a gunbattle. Two of the escapees had been killed. Toby remembered the tension (the quaint thrill) of the townspeople. He remembered the news reporters, writing their stories on borrowed typewriters and rushing them to the telegraph office. He remembered the stories. They wrote only of the men and the gunbattle and the killing. They knew nothing about his town and its people.

He had left his hometown and studied journalism and become a reporter, and often, the older he became, the distance between who he was and who he had been seemed confused, like a familiar land overgrown with trees. He thought of Rachel Whitfield, who had left Tickenaley and by her concept of distance had moved far away—fifteen awesome miles—and had surrendered to compromises that she could not recognize nor control.

She had spoken of Doyle and Florence Wade almost casually, as though the distance from the Valley View Lodge to Tickenaley had depressed her memory. He wondered how she had learned of the killings (a trucker at the counter?) and how she had felt. Did the news frighten her? Or was it only an unexpected shock from the past, benignly out of place? Was the distance of fifteen miles too far for Rachel Whitfield? Was the distance of time—from 1955 to 1980—too far for him?

Toby dropped his cigarette out of the window of the car. In his rearview mirror, he saw the front door of the courthouse open and Guy Finley step outside and stretch in the cool night air. Toby opened the door of his car and got out; he stepped on the tip of the cigarette and crossed the street to Guy.

"You look tired," Toby said.

Guy studied Toby's face, searching for a name.

"Guess I am some," Guy replied.

"What you've been through, I don't blame you," Toby said.

"Yeah," Guy muttered. Then: "Do I know you?"

"Toby Cahill," Toby told him. "I work for the *Sentinel*."

"Sorry," Guy replied. "Never was good at names."

"Don't worry. Anything new happened?"

Guy shook his head.

"Reporters been driving you crazy, I guess," Toby said. "Most of them gone now?"

"I guess," Guy answered. "You the only one I know that's

around. They call the jail every few minutes. I guess most of them went to Gainesville, or back to Atlanta. Ain't many places to stay around here."

Toby laughed easily. "I couldn't exactly recommend the Valley View Lodge."

"If that's where you are, you better keep the door bolted," Guy advised. "It ain't the New York Hilton."

"Not even a good clothes closet, you want to know the truth," Toby said. "Except for the restaurant. Food's good."

"That's where the money is, I hear," Guy said. "All them truckers coming through. Why'd you pick that place?"

"Believe it or not, I like being by myself on these things," Toby confessed. "Always try to land where nobody else is."

"Makes sense," Guy said. He pulled the zipper up on his jacket and looked down the empty street.

"What's the word on Jesse Wade?" Toby asked.

"Sheriff said he'd slept some," Guy answered. "He talked a little, but he didn't say much."

"The girl? Carl's wife?"

"Her folks got here this afternoon. They're from up in Tennessee. Sheriff said they took her to Carl's house."

"Where's that?"

Guy looked suspiciously at Toby. He said, "They don't want to talk to nobody."

Toby nodded agreement. He would not press Guy Finley. He did not believe in pressing anyone for information. Pressing made enemies. Enemies did not talk.

"I can understand that," Toby said. "I won't bother them. There'll be time, when they're ready."

"I appreciate that," Guy said. "Another fellow kept telling us it was his job. Sheriff had to get sharp with him."

"Television?" Toby asked.

"Yeah."

Toby laughed easily. He thought of Harvey. He said, "Tell you the truth, I don't like doing these kinds of stories. No way to say it right. People want it to be like some kind of television detective show, something going on every minute. Hard to make them understand it's not that way."

"Yeah," Guy said quietly.

52

The two men stood on the sidewalk in front of the courthouse and listened to the indistinct voices of the men from the State Patrol talking in the corridor, beyond the door. Toby did not have to ask: the men were plotting a search for the following morning. It was unlikely a search would reveal anything. It would be little more than motion, an expected exercise. He thought of the searches for the missing black children of Atlanta. He had been on one. It had been like a circus.

"Town looks deserted," Toby said.

Guy turned his face to scan the street again. "Guess they're down at the church," he replied. "Somebody said they got up a service late this afternoon. I heard people were calling around about it."

Toby lit another cigarette. The smoke was silver against the purple sky of night.

"I understand it was a religious family," Toby said.

"Wadn't for Jesse, that church up there couldn't open its doors," Guy admitted. "His great-granddaddy started it. Jesse feels strong about keeping it going, I guess. What's needed, he gives, if he's got it. Always been that way. His whole family."

"You liked them?" Toby asked simply.

Guy smiled. It was a kind question, he thought. He said, "Yeah. Yeah, I liked them. Everybody did. I went to Vietnam with Carl. We became pretty good friends when we got back, even though he was quiet-like."

"He talk much about Vietnam?" Toby asked.

"No," Guy replied. "No, he didn't." Then: "Me, neither." Then: "Nobody ever asked us much about it."

A car passed slowly on the street. A man looked suspiciously at Guy. He lifted his fingers from the steering wheel in a hesitant wave.

"Mind if I ask you something?" Toby said.

"What?"

"For myself, not the paper."

Guy looked at him. He did not say anything.

"What would you have done if you had found them putting the girl in the drain?" Toby said.

Guy blinked once at the question. He remembered his revolver on the seat of his car. He said calmly, "I would have blown their heads off."

Toby nodded. He looked evenly into Guy's eyes. "Me, too," he said. "Me, too."

When he left Guy Finley, Toby drove to the church and parked in the churchyard. He walked among the cars and trucks to the door of the church, but he did not enter. He sat on the top step, leaning against the clapboard wall, and listened to the singing of hymns. He had met the Preacher earlier in the day, in Angus Helton's store. He had listened to the Preacher talk about the damnation of men and he had seen the people in Angus Helton's store crowding the Preacher like beggars. "God will watch over us," the Preacher had declared confidently, pontifically. "There is no evil too mighty for God." Toby looked across the parked cars and trucks to the gleaming, waist-high stones of the cemetery, lined in irregular rows like a growing field of death. Monument stones of angels, with their eagle wings silhouetted against the night. Slender stones, like towers in some deserted city. Slick-skinned stones (almost mirrors) with faces and hands and poetry carved into them, as though nothing would be as permanent as the memory of that particular dead one in that particular grave. It/they (the stone and the memory) would last forever and ever and ever. But the memory did not last, Toby thought. Only the stone. And he thought of the six gravesites to be dug and the bodies to be lowered and the stones to be erected above them and the epitaphs to be chiseled deep into the polished granite faces of the stones. So many of them at one time, the field of death would look abundant.

Inside the church, the high, strong voices of the women carried the songwish: "His eye is on the sparrow, and I know He watches me. . . ."

In his room at the Valley View Lodge, Toby worked on his story of the tragedy of the Tickenaley Valley. It was not a story of the living, the people of the valley, of the loss that had struck them like a great weight. It was a story of their fear, their unrest, and how they had appeared at their church—Jesse's church—like pilgrims, bearing their faith before them like alms. It was a story of the grandeur of mourning.

But Toby knew that it was invention as well as truth. He knew that much of it was temporary, a display to invoke the pity of God, to reach His listening ear. He knew also there was a rage in the people that would turn prayer into obscenities and alms into blood-dripping hearts ripped from the chests of men.

And that would be the story that the curious would wish to read. His words about a frightened, praying community (words that were calculated for sentiment) were nothing more than window-dressing for a waiting drama.

Toby finished his story at midnight and opened the door to his room and stepped outside. The night was cold and clean. He could see the clustering of the Milky Way through a stream of high clouds as thin as a spider's silk.

In the room next to his, Rachel Whitfield made love to a man who whispered gently that he cared for her, that if she needed him he would always be there. And Rachel Whitfield believed him.

FIVE

October 17

Ed Meeker was a sensitive man who had been a mortician for twenty-seven years. He believed that when he prepared the dead with the waxface of sleep, he prepared them for an afterlife of glory. He wanted each face to look serene, as though frozen in a smile of recognition—the first happy knowledge that God existed, that God was beckoning to them, that there would be no more suffering. The closed eyes were to be like a blink, caused by the brilliance of God.

When Ed Meeker first heard of the murder of Jesse Wade's family, he had wept uncontrollably.

"I want to do everything I can to make it easier on Jesse," Ed had said to the Preacher. "Tell him not to worry about anything."

And the Preacher had visited with Jesse and said, "We'll make the plans, if you'll let us, Jesse. Ed wants to help out. I do, too. Let me and Ed handle it. You've got your grief. Let us do the rest."

And Jesse had agreed with a nod. He had closed his eyes and thought of the Preacher before a congregation of mourners. The Preacher would pose dramatically in the intense presence of listeners and he would declare that God had filled the sanctuary of the church and His invisible power was forming in the Preacher's mouth. ("Not my word, but His.") Jesse knew the Preacher would exclaim his called-down visit from God like an announcement of royalty.

"I know how you're feeling, Jesse," the Preacher had said. "I know. It'll be all right."

The Preacher had moved boldly into the silence of Jesse and Anna. He had paced authoritatively before them. His voice had lectured: "There'll be a crowd, Jesse. No question about it. I've already had some calls from people. Ed, too. The governor's wife's coming. And the lieutenant governor. And the press. There'll be a lot of reporters. But it'll be all right. It'll be done with dignity."

Yes, Jesse had nodded. He had not been listening. He had been thinking of the church of his great-grandfather and the man who was violating it.

The sanctuary of Tickenaley Church was small. Its walls and flooring and ceiling were made of heartpine that had never been painted, but was colored by many years of being touched and cured by hot days of summer and hot stovefires of winter. It was warm and quiet and intimate.

Jesse knew the Preacher believed Tickenaley Church was smaller than his calling, but he had accepted the appointment without protest. He was a man of God, he had said. He would go where needed. It did not matter that his seminary contemporaries were in large churches in large cities. To the Preacher, they had sold out to arrogance. They were roll-builders, men who lived in burgeoning communities where one or two transfers and/or conversions a week were expected. Their churches were like extended social clubs, the Preacher angrily explained. They built new sanctuaries and classrooms and gymnasiums and advertised their sermon topics like cereal slogans and they became popular with the bishops. The Preacher charged that their status was more a matter of political ambition than the fruits of God's work. He clucked his tongue over their greed for recognition. It would be easy to do as they were doing, if he had so chosen, he said. He clucked his tongue and wagged his head and spoke of humility. He served God in Tickenaley, in this remote place, he said, because it was a test of his sincerity. He could not be enticed to hear the voices of pastoral selection committees of large churches in large cities. (Once, he said proudly, he had turned down an opportunity for a television ministry in Augusta because he did not want people to think of him as God's Johnny Carson.) "I do not care what others do," he preached. "I listen to God's call."

But Jesse knew there had not been any inquiries from pastoral selection committees. Jesse had been told confidentially, by someone who knew, that the Preacher was lazy, a dreamer who had wished to be adored and who had discovered, in his seminary years, that people—especially women—adored men of God. Men of God seemed touched (ordained, plucked out) by the Father's pointing finger—the same finger that had twirled the earth into existence and burned the Commandments into the hard slate of Sinai.

And Jesse had watched the Preacher and knew the report on him was accurate. But he also knew it was impossible to question the acts of the Preacher, as he had tried feebly with Jean. Every utterance of his tongue was profound. Every contortion of his face was holy countenance. Every gesture of his arms and hands was meaningful. Every guess, every speculation, was prophetic. Every opinion was inarguable.

The Preacher also knew these things. He was respected. He was adored. And so he served Tickenaley Church, clucking his tongue, sighing about humility, waiting for the call of God to leave.

"If you want, I'll go over the whole thing with you, Jesse," the Preacher had said. "If not, you can trust me to make sure it's done with dignity."

Jesse had not replied. He had looked at Anna. Anna had said, "You can do it. You and Mr. Meeker."

For the funeral, the Preacher had two rows of pews removed from the sanctuary and the six bronze-tinted coffins—all alike, all simple—were placed before the pulpit, across the width of the church. The coffins were closed (Anna and Aubrey Hart's wish). Each had a small spray of white mums and broadleaf ferns balanced over the chest of the lid.

The seating for the service was planned deliberately and carefully. Front rows for the families. Behind them, the guests—the governor's wife, the lieutenant governor, the senator and representatives from the district, the visiting ministers. The rest of the pews would be for the people of the valley—those who could get inside. The reporters—for there would be many of them, eager to interview the Preacher—would be permitted to stand along the walls. But they could not take pictures inside the church during the service. Only before.

"I will not make a mockery of this," the Preacher said to the reporters. "These were plain, good people. I will not see their families and friends put through a circus."

The television lights were on him and the Preacher stood erect and solemn. His hazel eyes were dull with sadness and responsibility.

"How many people do you expect for the service?" the reporter asked.

The Preacher looked into the flat glass eye of the camera and said, "A lot. I would guess a lot. People want to show they care." He moistened his lips with his tongue and his face became grave with insight. "I know how they feel," he said. "I know."

The funeral was on Friday, October 17, a day of sun, the firecolors of autumn burning in the mountains. More than five hundred people attended the burial service. They came in cars and trucks and vans. They came from Tickenaley and the other valleys of the mountains, from small towns and cities. They came as spectators and stood outside the church, in tight groups, and listened to the Preacher's sermon on Death and Promise broadcast over speakers borrowed for the occasion. It was a sermon about the fiery God of the Old Testament and the gentle Jesus of the New. It was a sermon of evangelism, of shouted warnings about late-waiters, those who thought there was always time to take up with Jesus and God. "You can't be caught waiting," the Preacher intoned. "You put off God and God'll put you off. It's as simple as that. And which of us knows when we'll be called by death? None of these blessed people, closed in these cold coffins, knew death was lurking for them, hiding behind its face of evil. But, thank God Almighty, they were prepared for it. They had surrendered to God and lived godly lives and they knew that man could do nothing to them that mattered. God does not forget those who do not wait to accept Him."

It was a sermon that ordered everyone to live forever with the grotesque knowledge that man was no better than killer beasts without God.

It was a sermon that commanded forgiveness. ("Forgive, but don't forget. Remember, Jesse, Anna, Aubrey, all of you. Remember what has happened, but forgive it. Forgive and be free.")

Toby Cahill watched the unmoving face of Jesse Wade during the sermon. Toby knew that Jesse was not listening. Jesse's mind was locked in memory, or was dulled by the ritual. And it was best that Jesse did not hear, Toby thought. To Toby, the sermon was of wearisome piety by a posturing man who loved centerstage and who knew he would never again have such props for his monologues.

Yet Toby knew the story he would write would not accuse the Preacher. He would write that it was a sensitive message reaffirming the Protestant faith in God's comfort. He would write of the mountful choir music, of the army of pallbearers, of the great blooming of flowers that had arrived in trucks, some from shops as far away as Atlanta. He would write of the hush of the grieving crowd, listening inside and outside the church, of the sobbing that could be heard like hard, hurting breathing. He would write of the short, final earthtrip of the bodies, from the church to the six gravesites, neatly dug. He would write of fragments of comments that said the same thing but sounded somehow different by the authority of those who said them: "They were good people. It's terrible, what happened."

Toby would write that no one present would forget the funeral of Jesse Wade's family. But he knew it was a lie. People would forget. In time, they would forget.

"Who could do this?" a woman cried at the gravesites. "Have we all gone mad?" She wore a black scarf in a band around her forehead. She was young and muscularly lean, like a hiker, but she had been crying and the crying had made her angry. She looked at Toby and said again, "Who could do this?"

Toby shook his head gravely and the young woman turned and stormed away. Maybe we are mad, Toby thought. He remembered (when was it? A week ago?) the discovery of the body of another missing child in Atlanta and the story out of Buffalo, New York, about two black cab drivers who had been murdered, whose hearts had been cut out of their bodies. And this. This in Tickenaley. Six people killed, buried.

Toby thought of Rachel Whitfield. Earlier, at breakfast, she had told him she wanted to attend the funeral, if she could find a relief waitress. He looked around the crowd. He saw a television camera aimed at Mary Beth Busbee, the tall, elegant wife of the governor. A reporter held a microphone to her face. Zell Miller, the lieutenant governor (himself from the mountains, from Young Harris), stood close to Aubrey Hart, whispering to him. Aubrey's head bobbed spastically. He saw the Preacher and Ed Meeker with Jesse and Anna and Anna's parents. The Preacher was introducing them to other men—visiting ministers, Toby reasoned. He saw Jesse's head turn back to the gravesites, saw his face lift and look over the mountains. Anna touched his arm and Jesse turned away and walked with her to Ellis Spruill's waiting car.

Toby again scanned the crowd, but he did not see Rachel Whitfield. He heard a bearded man with thick eyeglasses say to the woman with him, "Pretty up here. Wouldn't mind having a place near by." He could hear the angry young woman asking someone else, "Who? Who?"

Ellis drove from the church to Anna's home. There were cars in the driveway and parked along the roadside and groups of people stood outside the house waiting for the after-funeral custom of acknowledging the grieving family. It would be a quick gathering—mumbled words, brief embraces, awkward looks (or lookaways), and then the people would leave and the house would be empty except for Jesse and Anna and Anna's parents. And the banquet of food that had been delivered out of custom, or sorrow, or helplessness would spoil because no one would be hungry.

"I know you need to go in, Jesse," Ellis said, "but I'd like a minute with you."

"Yes. All right," Jesse said. He looked at Anna. Anna stood beside the car and waited.

"I need to talk to Jesse alone, Anna," Ellis said quietly. "If it's all right."

Anna smiled politely. She said, "Thank you for taking us and bringing us home." She walked away, into the crowd and into the house.

"Let's go down by the barn," Ellis suggested.

The two men crossed the yard to the back of the house, then to a new rail fence that Carl had built beside the barn. Jesse lit a cigarette and watched a cow grazing across the pasture.

"Maybe this is the wrong time to tell you this, Jesse," Ellis began, "just after the funeral. But I want you to know: we found out who did it."

Jesse turned his head to look at Ellis. He breathed deeply and his lips quivered, but he did not say anything.

"A report on the fingerprints came in early this morning," Ellis explained. "From the Army. I told the GBI to wait until after the funeral before we did anything."

Jesse drew on his cigarette. The expression on his face did not change.

"The Vickers boy was one of them," Ellis said. "Him

and two boys from Fort Wayne, Indiana. They were in the Army together."

Jesse trimmed the ash from his cigarette across the rail of the fence. "You know where they are?" he asked.

"No. We're going up to Isom's place. See what we can find out."

Jesse stared at the fence. His face had reddened in the cool October air. His eyes blinked rapidly. "I feel sorry for Isom and Lou," he said at last.

"Yeah," Ellis mumbled. "Thing is, Jesse, it's up to us now. I don't want this to get out before we find them, if it's possible. But I can't take chances. Too many reporters talking to too many people. I wanted to let you know before somebody else said it and you started thinking I'm holding out on you."

Jesse pushed his cigarette into the rail and watched the wind sweep the sparks into the pasture. He said, without looking at Ellis, "You don't need to be worrying about it, Ellis. It's your job. You'll do it."

"I appreciate that, Jesse. Wish you'd keep what I just said to yourself."

"I will."

Ellis reached for Jesse's shoulder and gripped it gently and then walked away.

An hour later a caravan of cars moved inconspicuously out of Tickenaley, through the valley to an untended dirt road that turned abruptly into a thick stand of hardwoods. A mile into the woods, Ellis stopped his car and motioned from the car window for the cars that trailed him to stop and wait.

Guy Finley turned in the seat beside Ellis and looked through the rear window. He saw the cars parking in a line.

"How'd you talk Cale into staying back?" Guy asked.

"I didn't," Ellis replied. "He said he thought it'd be best."

"I'll be damned," Guy said in surprise.

"He's all right. Better'n I thought at first. Knows his work."

Ellis eased the car back into the road and drove up into the mountains, on a road that was like a wrinkle in the land, narrowing with the miles, until it became a wagon trail between trees.

Isom and Lou Vickers lived in the most remote region of the valley. Their home was a cabin shabbily built, leaning at the back. Everything was in one room. A place for cooking, for sleeping, for working. It was old and quaint and dark and it was the only home that Isom and Lou had ever had. They had appeared in the mountains in 1940 in a two-mule wagon, and had built the cabin with few tools and little help, taking its size and shape from the fragmented and confused memory of what a house should be.

Isom and Lou were childlike. Over time (time being the seasons), they had become more isolated, more reclusive. Few people ever saw them, even when Isom went into Tickenaley in his wagon to sell his sourwood honey and to buy the few goods—coffee, tobacco, flour, kerosene—he and Lou required. He was an emaciated man who always arrived late on those town trips—just before the closing of the stores. He attended to his needs (in cash or trade) and left. He was like many of the mountain men of the twenties and thirties, who had lived hidden and made whiskey but had died away. Isom was like them in his secrecy, but he did not make whiskey. He gathered honey.

There was another, peculiar difference between Isom and other mountain men: Isom was always clean. Not merely bathed, but clean. The smell of homemade soap, perfumed by herbs that Lou grubbed from the ground, was always on him. People thought it was because of the bees he worked. The bees did not sting Isom as he robbed them of their cones of honey. They crawled like tranquil friends over his arms and sat languidly in the palms of his hands. People believed the bees thought that Isom smelled like a rich, rare flower.

Isom and Lou were old and they were thought to be harmless, gentle eccentrics. Lou seemed always unpredictable—giddy, then quickly somber. Isom amused people, and baffled them. It was rumored that he sometimes talked of the Civil War as though he had fought in it. Songs of forced, crude poetry played in his mind and when he spoke it was often in verse. ("How do you do? How's your shoe?") Angus Helton was particularly fond of what Isom had once told him after Angus had inquired about the health of Lou. Said Isom: "Her name's Louleen. Caught her tit in a sewing machine. Made her mad and made her mean. Meanest bitch I ever seen." To Angus—and to Isom—it was very funny.

"Ain't nothing wrong with Isom," Angus had declared. "Isom's fox-crazy. That man's got brains on layaway, just in case he needs some for waste."

But Isom and Lou did not live alone.

When Lou was forty-five (by her guess), she had given birth to a son, who was named Zachary Coy Vickers. No one in the valley knew of the birth until a year later, when Isom innocently began to speak of it while in Tickenaley. "God Almighty, Isom," Angus had snorted. "You old coot. You better tie that talleywacker in a knot. How you going to be raising babies up there on the side of that mountain?" Isom had laughed in his old man's cackle and made a motion of tying his penis.

But Angus' question had been more serious than he intended. Isom and Lou did not know how to rear a child, except by instinct. And as Zack grew, he became as mysterious as his environment. By his fifteenth birthday, Zack was uncontrollable. Before he had reached twenty, he was the most feared man in Tickenaley Valley. It was as though he had been sired by animals.

"Them old people can't do nothing with that boy," people said angrily. "Likely as not, somebody'll find them dead up there someday, wild as that boy is. Crazy, too. Crazy as a loon."

"Old people like that, having babies. What happens when they're born late. Somebody ought to put them old people away somewheres."

As they neared the sharp turn leading to the Vickers' home, Ellis slowed the car to a stop beneath a tall hickory that had leaves the color of burnt orange. The two men could see the shingled roofline of the cabin, weathered to a deep mahogany.

"You better get out and wait," Ellis said.

"If they're in there, they'll kill you," Guy replied bluntly. "Let's park and go up from here."

"No," Ellis said. "If they're there, we'll know it soon as I pull up in the yard. If they ain't, I don't want to scare Isom and Lou by sneaking up."

"Jesus, Ellis."

"It's the way I want it done," Ellis said evenly. "Take the rifle and get out. You'll know if I need you."

Guy opened the door of the car and got out, pulling the rifle behind him. "I hope you remember the last time we brought Zack home he said he'd blow our goddamn heads off if we came back," he said to Ellis.

"I remember."

Guy shook his head in disagreement. He curled his lower lip into his mouth and began to gnaw on it. He knew Ellis would not change his mind. He pushed away from the car and stepped behind the hickory. Goddamn it, do it your way, he thought.

Ellis drove slowly into the yard. His right hand was on the revolver beside him on the seat. His eyes scanned the leaning cabin with the single front door and two small cut-outs for windows. The windows were boarded for the cold of autumn and winter. He knew if Zack and the other men were there, it would be easy for them to hide, or to have gunsights on the car. And he knew they could easily kill again if they had killed before.

He stopped the car and opened the door and stood looking at the house. He held his revolver behind the car door.

"Isom," he called. "It's me. Ellis Spruill."

The door of the house opened slightly and Isom's head appeared. He saw the sheriff's car and Ellis beside it and his face cracked into a surprising grin and Ellis could see his gums working, almost in a panting, like a friendly dog.

"Isom here," Isom said, and stepped through the doorway. Ellis could see Lou's face behind him.

"How you doing, Isom?" Ellis asked. "How's the honey been this year?"

"Honey's fine, all the time," Isom crooned, laughing.

"That's good," Ellis said. "Lou, how you feeling?"

"Lou's good," Lou said in a high, breaking voice. "You buying some honey?"

"Maybe so," Ellis replied. He looked again at the door, but could not see anything. "Maybe I will. How's Zack?"

Isom snorted. "Zack? He don't do nothing. Runs off all the time." He laughed suddenly. "That's what he does, runs off."

"Where's he at now?" Ellis asked.

Lou stepped into the frame of the door and leaned against the jamb. "Off somewheres," she said absently. "Took him some food in a sack and went off somewheres. Maybe ain't coming back. Maybe going to do Army again."

Isom looked surprised and confused. "He done Army," he argued.

"Do it again," Lou said defiantly. "He'll do it again."

Ellis listened to the bickering exchange. Isom and Lou were like irritated children. He wondered if they realized that Zack was their son, or if they thought of him as someone who was merely there, a familiar boarder who left and returned at will. The people of the valley believed Isom and Lou were incapable of remembering their histories. Perhaps the people were right, Ellis thought. No one knew where Isom and Lou had lived. They had simply appeared, wandering aimlessly in their two-mule wagon, and had built their home on land that Jesse Wade's grandfather owned, but Jesse's grandfather had said nothing. He had quietly deeded the land to them without telling them. Ellis had never heard anyone speak of any past for Isom and Lou.

"You remember how much food he took, Lou?" Ellis asked easily. "Maybe he's just out in the woods for a few hours, maybe hunting."

"Took it all. Took the sack, he did," Lou said, suddenly angry. "Told him to leave me some, but he took it all. Took the tobacco. Didn't leave none."

"They eat it all anyhow," Isom said bitterly. "Eat everything but the cat." He giggled and his gums worked frantically. "Maybe I'll eat me the cat."

Ellis could see Lou hiding her mouth, laughing into her hands. He remembered the last time he had seen her in Tickenaley, years ago, when Zack was only a child. She had walked the streets, dragging Zack with her, looking in windows, cackling like a hen.

"Cat could be tough, Isom," Ellis replied lightly. "But you said they got everything. Who's they?"

"Zack's boys," Lou answered. "They done Army with him. They eat everything. Like woodhogs. Zack made me cook up everything."

Ellis stepped nearer the house. He held the revolver behind him, hidden. He knew that Isom and Lou did not know of the deaths of Jesse Wade's family.

"Well, that's good," Ellis said earnestly. "Zack having his friends here. They leave with Zack?"

Isom looked at Lou. His face was a question.

"They took off a few days back," Lou said. "Just took off. Never said a word. Just took off and left."

"Zack was with them?"

Isom nodded in agreement. "Zack come back."

"Then Zack left again, with the food?" Ellis asked.

"Took the sack, took the tobacco," Lou said bitterly.

"How long has Zack been gone?"

"Some time now," Lou answered. She looked absently off into the woods. "Maybe yesterday. We ain't had nothing but honey to eat on. Maybe Zack'll bring us a squirrel."

"Damned Army boys eat all they see," Isom said. "Almost eat up the honey."

"How'd the Army boys get here?" Ellis asked.

Isom's face brightened with the memory. "Come up in a car. Big car. Shining on top, so's you could see yourself. Looked like a red mirror. Was, wadn't it, old woman?"

"They left in the car, then?" Ellis said.

Isom nodded. He looked at Lou. He nodded again, more vigorously. Ellis knew that Isom did not remember.

"That what happened, Lou?" Ellis asked. "They left in a red car?"

"They come back," Lou said firmly. "Come back without it." She glared triumphantly at Isom.

"Come back," Isom echoed. He worked his gums proudly and smiled at Ellis.

"What happened to the car?" Ellis asked.

Isom's brow wrinkled in rows of thought. "Lost it," he said emphatically.

"Lost it?"

"They come back without it," Isom snapped.

"How'd they leave later on?" Ellis asked.

"Walked it, I reckon," Isom answered. "Ain't got no car, ain't that far."

Ellis turned in the yard and looked up into the woods above him. A row of sumac, brilliantly red, grew at the edge of the yard. He turned back to Isom and Lou.

"Isom," Ellis said deliberately, "what were the names of the Army boys? One of them named Albert Bailey? One named Eddie Copeland?"

Isom stepped forward, his whole body bobbing in agreement. "Them's it," he said. "Who they was."

"I need to talk to Zack, Isom," Ellis said quietly. "I'm going to be leaving, but I'll be coming back with some more men, and I'll be bringing a bloodhound with me. Just to help find him. I hope you don't mind me doing that."

The smile faded from Isom's face. He stepped back and looked at Lou, then back at Ellis. He dropped his head, bewildered. His mouth worked slowly in a chewing motion. He nodded once.

"Don't let no dogs go biting him," Lou said simply. "Zack's scared of dogs. Always was. Killed ours when he come back from doing Army."

"He won't be bit, Lou," Ellis promised. "I'll make sure of it." He walked to his car and slipped behind the steering wheel and turned the car in the small yard and drove away, easing down the road to where Guy waited.

"It's not good," Guy guessed. "Not the way you look."

"I guess I look the way I feel," Ellis said. "They're in the woods somewhere. We'll need Bobby Truett's dog." He pushed the heel of his hands hard against the steering wheel and stared through the windshield. "Goddamn it," he muttered. "I feel sorry for that old couple."

"Yeah. I know."

"You take the car back down to Cale. Tell him to wait there until you can get the dog, then come on back up. It'll be dark, I guess, but we'll have to go when we can."

"You're staying here?" Guy asked.

"I'll stay. In case they come back."

"You want anything else?"

"It'll be cold up there," Ellis said. "Below freezing. Tell Cale that. Make sure they're dressed for it. And bring back my boots and hunting gear, and tell Hattie I'll be out."

"Anything else?"

"No. Cale's got the warrants." Ellis opened the door to the car and got out and Guy slipped under the steering wheel. "One other thing," Ellis said. "Bring back some food and tobacco for Isom and Lou. Charge it to the jail."

"All right," Guy said. He could feel the afternoon cooling in the treeshadows. He remembered Zack's warning about killing them. "You be careful," he said to Ellis. "That boy knows these woods."

"Yeah," Ellis mumbled. He thought of Isom and Lou and of Jesse Wade and of the pale, slain bodies at Jesse's farm and of the neighbors who had gathered at Jesse's home to scrub away the blood and fleshbits of murder. "Yeah," he said again. "I know it."

SIX

October 17–18

ISOM AND LOU WERE AFRAID OF THE BLOODHOUND, KING, and of the men who arrived in police cars.

The men were strangers with guns. Their faces were set in anger and eagerness. Their silence was terrifying. And Isom and Lou retreated into their house and peeked out of cracks in the window slats.

"It's all right, Isom," Ellis said at the front door. "The dog won't bite. He's just here to help find Zack. I've got some food for you, and tobacco. I want to give it to you. Just me. All you got to do is open the door."

In a few moments the door opened and Ellis stepped inside the house. He returned shortly with clothing that belonged to Zack.

"I want them left alone," Ellis told Cale. "Anybody talks to them, it'll be me."

"Don't worry," Cale said. "Nobody's going to bother them. I'm leaving two men here, but they'll be outside, away from the house."

"Leave four," Ellis remarked bluntly. "There'll be six of us with the dog, counting Bobby. That's enough. The more you have, the slower it'll go. And if Zack and them come back here, it'll take more than two to handle it."

"All right," Cale said. He understood the message in Ellis' command: this was Ellis' hunt; Cale and the patrolmen were along as an act of courtesy.

"What'd you get from the Army report?" Ellis asked.

"Copeland's the leader," Cale replied. "Smart. Bailey's dangerous. Does what Copeland says. You know about the Vickers boy."

Ellis rolled shotgun shells from a box into the pocket of his quilted hunting coat and then he began filling the un-plugged magazine of the twelve-gauge automatic. He looked across the yard to Bobby Truett and King. It had taken three hours to find Bobby. The dog whimpered and pulled hard against its leash as Bobby rubbed Zack's clothing over its face. "Get it, get it," Bobby coaxed. He watched as King's head swept over the cleared yard, his instincts aching for the hunt.

"He ready?" Ellis asked.

"He's got it," Bobby said happily. "We better be going."

Ellis nodded and crossed the yard close to Bobby. "You stay with us," he said. "We got no idea what's out there. Any shooting starts, you get to the ground and stay there."

Bobby laughed. He pulled King to him and rubbed the trembling dog under the neck. "Any shooting starts, you liable to think you got a goddamn mole with you," he said. "I ain't the sheriff; you are."

"You remember that," Ellis warned. He turned to Cale. "Let's go," he said.

"Frank, J.C., come with us," Cale ordered. "Rest of you stay here. Leave those old people alone. We need you, we'll use a flare."

"Yessir," one of the men muttered. He was young and nervous.

Ellis cradled the shotgun in his arm. He looked at the house and thought of Isom and Lou peering out from the boarded windows. He knew they were curious, unable to comprehend why the men were there or why the great dog became restless after sniffing Zack's clothing. He knew they were frightened, but he knew also that he was right about Zack. "Goddamn it," he muttered.

"What?" Cale asked.

"Nothing."

Ellis faced the men in the tight semicircle around him and lowered his voice. "We'll be moving pretty fast. Uphill most of the time, I suspect. You get tired, say it. We can rest some. The dog's trained to Bobby's voice. Only bloodhound I ever saw to do it, but he does. I don't want nobody dead if we can help it. And I don't want no heroes. They'll kill you. It won't mean anything to them."

"We don't want anyone dead, either, Ellis," Cale said. "We'll do it your way."

Ellis looked at his watch. It was eleven-thirty. He could feel the sharp cold of the night. He nodded to Bobby, and Bobby released King.

Cale was amazed by the dog. The dog was magnificent, better than any he had ever seen. Smaller than most bloodhounds, but more sure of himself, moving quietly, gracefully, head down, skimming the groundtop with his nose, obsessed by the prey hidden somewhere in the night, in the hills. And there was great patience in King. When Ellis called for a rest, King stopped abruptly on Bobby Truett's command and stood, as on point, his head lifted in the direction of the scent, his body quivering anxiously.

"Now, he won't be stopping that easy, closer we get to finding Zack," Bobby said proudly. "He likes the run well as the hunt. But that's a penitentiary dog for you. That's what King is. Maybe y'all don't know it, but they's three kinds of bloodhounds. There's them for show, and they ain't worth a shit. There's them for the leash, and they ain't much better. And there's them for turning loose. Them's the ones that are penitentiary dogs. And King is the best that ever was, ain't you, boy?"

King whimpered and looked beggingly at his owner and then back into the woods.

* * *

The footsteps of Zack Vickers, crushed into the leaves and dirt of the mountains like the trail of a phantom, followed a path that Zack had taken out of instinct as much as habit. It had the pattern of an animal—a bear or fox—that roamed by the claw and urine markings of its own making. Zack had moved from place to place, zigzagging over an obscure map that was fixed in his brain like a dim radar. It was a trail that climbed easily, gradually, from ridge to ridge, skirting to the northeast, high above the Vickers house. But to the men in the hunt, it was bewildering; none of them had any idea where it was leading.

"I been up here a lot, Ellis," Bobby said, "but I ain't got the first iota where he's going, or where he might be at. Ain't nothing up here but the North Carolina line. Hell, if he's going up in North Carolina or Tennessee, he ought of been on the highway. Been a helluva lot easier."

"I guess," Ellis agreed. He was breathing hard. His legs ached. The cold was a freezing sting across his face. He was disoriented by the weaving of the trail. "What's that mountain up there?" he asked.

"Mountain of the Caves," Bobby said. "We coming in from due west of it. Looks different from this way."

"Jesse's land," Ellis mumbled. "I'll be damned."

"Maybe Bobby's right," suggested Guy. "Maybe he's going over into North Carolina."

"He is, he's doing it the hardest damn way he can," Bobby said.

It was two hours before sunrise when King led the men into a clearing at the west base of the Mountain of the Caves. The air was thin and bitterly cold. A halfmoon light filtered dully through the trees at the line of the clearing, and below them the men could see fogcaps billowing over streams and, in the fescue fields of the valley, the milky glaze of a thick frost.

"Christ," one of the patrolmen muttered. "How far we come?"

Bobby looked at his watch. "Maybe ten miles," he said. "Maybe more. Hard to tell. But we're close. I know that."

"How?" asked Cale.

"I know King," Bobby explained. "Know it by his whine."

King stood straight, his head lifted high, sniffing the air. His body was tense. A cry trembled inside the folds of skin under his throat.

"Quiet, boy," Bobby said gently, stroking King on his shoulders. "We'll find him. He's close. We'll find him." He looked at Ellis. "You sure there ain't nothing around here?"

"Nothing," Ellis said. "Half a mile or more down the hill is where Jesse and his boys were clearing the woods, but that's all. All I know is, we seem like we been going in a circle." He looked up at the silhouette peaks of the mountain, dark against the blueing dome of night. He could see the moon reflected on veins of ice frozen in streaks down the ring of granite, where topsoil water dripped slowly over the ledges. He wondered how cold it was. Below freezing. It was early to be so cold, he thought. The winter would be harsh.

"What about the caves?" Guy asked. "Maybe they found a place in the caves."

"Where at?" It was Cale. His face was lifted toward the peaks.

"Up there," Guy replied, motioning with his gloved hand. "Under that ring of granite. Supposed to be openings all over the place, if you know where to find them. There's still some old stories left over from the Indians about the caves being used for burying grounds. This whole area's that way. Jesse's land down there was supposed to be for some mounds that never got built."

"Ellis?" Cale said.

"Maybe," Ellis admitted. He thought about the stories he had heard from childhood. Hissing ghosts slithering out of holes no larger than his fist.

"Nobody's ever been in them?" Cale asked in astonishment. "Nobody?"

Bobby laughed lightly. He pulled King close, patting him on the neck. He looked at the mountain, at the ice slivers, like stems of shattered glass, on the face of the granite.

"Nobody we ever heard of," he said. "What the hell for, anyway?"

Cale looked at the two patrolmen. They were smiling at the story of the caves. His eyes narrowed hard on them and their smiles vanished.

"Don't guess it does make much sense to go crawling around under the ground," Cale said. "But if that's where they are, we could have some trouble getting them out."

"Maybe so," Ellis said quietly. "But let's find out if that's where they are first."

They moved silently out of the clearing, back into the woods, walking in a tight, dark line. Ellis had ordered their flashlights turned off. From the mountain, a single match flame could easily be seen.

An hour later, they were hidden behind trees on a ridge parallel with the granite wall. Another clearing was in front of them, a barren wash like a shallow ditch filled with graveled stone. The wash flowed from a wide rockbed that, centuries before, had broken loose from the granite and crumbled into the wedge of the two peaks.

The men had stopped because Bobby had ordered it. Zack Vickers was no more than two hundred yards away, he guessed in a whisper to Ellis. "You have to take my word for it," he said. "Don't ask me how I know, I just do." King pawed at the ground and cried softly, as though wounded, and Bobby held him close in his arms and talked gently to him.

There was an antiseptic graying of light on the granite when Bobby saw the man step from behind a mat of rhododendron growing close to the mountain. The man stretched in the cold morning air and, fumbling for a moment with his pants, urinated. He was tall, slender, with a beard and shortcropped hair.

"Know him?" Cale whispered to Ellis. Ellis shook away the question.

The man zipped his pants and stretched again and looked across the trees below him, then he turned and pushed against the rhododendron, as though opening a door of limbs. He stooped slightly, then disappeared.

"Son of a bitch," Guy said. "Must be a pretty big opening. Don't look like he bent down much."

"Keep the dog here," Ellis told Bobby. "We'll get up there and look it over."

"If I can," Bobby said. "Like I said before, King don't give a shit about what's going on. That's his game up there. That's all he knows."

"You hold him and keep him quiet," Ellis ordered. "He starts barking and they'll be out and gone."

Ellis removed his revolver from its holster and picked up his shotgun. He moved quietly through the woodcover along the clearing, then began easing across the rockbed. The men followed him in file, at intervals, with Cale close behind him and then the two patrolmen and then Guy. Ellis was twenty feet away from the covering of rhododendron when Zack appeared. Zack saw him immediately.

"Shit," Zack screamed. He snatched at the revolver in his belt and fired wildly in the air as he dove back into the cave.

Ellis dropped to one knee, tossing the shotgun to his left. He leveled his revolver and fired three shots. He could hear the bullets singing off the granite wall. He rolled to his left behind a large granite boulder, pulling his shotgun with him. He could hear the firing of guns behind him and Cale barking an order: "Stay down. Stay down."

Then it was quiet. The ringing of gunfire was sharp in Ellis' hearing. He pulled himself up behind two blocks of broken granite and peeked at the covering to the cave. He did not see any movement.

"Zack, this is Ellis Spruill," he called. "I've got a warrant for your arrest and the others with you. Come on out. All of you."

He heard a laugh and the shrill, giddy voice of a stranger: "Fuck you. You want us, come on up here." Again the laugh, then a rain of shots that blew through the rhododendron, shaking it violently.

From behind him, Ellis could hear the baying of the

bloodhound. He turned his head and saw the brown-red body of the dog leaping, bolting across the wash. He saw Bobby running after King, stumbling, then falling over the bed of sharp granite rocks. Bobby was calling, "King, King . . ."

King was halfway up the hill when the shot hit him in midleap. A shotgun. Perhaps two. King flew through the air, his head falling away from his body, his right leg hurled into the rocks.

Ellis fired again at the cave, squeezing the trigger of his revolver rapidly with his finger. Above the explosions, he heard Bobby scream.

"Bobby, get back in the woods, goddamn it. Now." It was Guy. Ellis could tell that Guy was moving toward Bobby. He heard a volley of shots hissing over his head, saw the rhododendron shaking from the strikes. He turned to see Guy leap into the clearing and grab Bobby and roll him away and then lift him and pull him behind a large oak.

"Come on, assholes," the voice cried from the cave. It was a taunting, arrogant voice. "Come on, come on." The laugh was maniacal.

Ellis flipped open the cylinder of his revolver and refilled it. He slipped his face close to the boulder. "Zack, come out of there," he commanded angrily. "Best chance you got is with us. We ain't here to kill nobody, but if we have to, we will, by God. You know that, Zack. Tell your friends. Tell them we'll do it, by God."

There was no reply, only a high, cackling laugh that echoed in the cave. Ellis eased closer to the rock. He looked at the rhododendron, growing in a bed of soil that had washed over the granite ledge. Its trunk was thin and gnarled by years of high winds slamming it snug against the mountain. Ellis placed his revolver on the ground beside him and picked up his shotgun. He put the gunrest against his left shoulder and crawled to the end of the boulder. He could see the base of the rhododendron. He turned to Cale and signaled for gunfire.

As soon as he heard the quick bursts exploding behind him, Ellis rose above the rock and squeezed the trigger of the shotgun three times. He saw the bush break at the base, sag forward, and hang. He heard cursing inside the cave. He pulled the trigger twice more and the bush fell away.

The opening of the cave was perhaps five feet tall and almost as wide as a house door. A sheet of granite lipped over it like an awning. From the woods, Guy could see into the slit. He reached into his hunter's coat and removed a telescope sight and fastened it to the barrel of his rifle. Then he aimed the rifle and focused it on the slit. He could see a pale stream of light on a back wall.

"Ellis, I've got a clean shot straight in," Guy shouted. "They don't want to come out, I can keep them in there for a year."

"Show them you mean it," Ellis growled.

Guy tucked his face against the rifle stock and aimed for the light on the back wall. He touched the trigger lightly. The bullet splattered inside the cave in a dull echo.

"Zack, come out," Ellis shouted. "Now."

There was no sound from the cave.

"Zack, I mean it," Ellis called. "Come out. That gun's a thirty-aught-six and he's the best you ever saw with it. You lift a hair and he's gonna blow it to hell and back."

Still there was no sound from the cave.

Ellis turned his back to the boulder and signaled to Cale with his hands. He wanted Cale and the two patrolmen to move up the rockbed and climb close to the cave opening. He motioned for Guy to fire.

Guy pulled the gun tight against his shoulder and fired three times rhythmically. Through his scope he could see the dust of granite chips in the haze of light. He lifted his eye from the scope and watched Cale and the two patrolmen running carefully over the rockbed, climbing level with the cave.

"Zack, I'm not waiting any longer," Ellis called. "You know me. You know I mean it, by God."

There was a long, tense silence. A crow cawed arrogantly below them, on the land where Doyle Wade's house had been planned.

Ellis raised himself cautiously from behind the boulder.

He had reloaded the shotgun and he held it extended before him. He moved away from the rock, directly below the cave, and walked carefully across the clearing. In the periphery of his vision he saw Cale edge away from the protective corner of the mountain, kneel, and raise his revolver in both hands. Cale was almost in the mouth of the cave. The two patrolmen were behind him, standing. Both had shotguns aimed at the opening.

"Goddamn it, Zack, I'm tired of you," Ellis roared suddenly. He jogged quickly up the short incline, taking the steps agilely, like an animal. Then he was at the cave, standing opposite Cale.

"You see anything?" Ellis asked quietly.

"Nothing. Seems like those last shots echoed a lot. It may be deep."

"Shit," Ellis mumbled. He slipped closer to the opening and yelled, "Zack!" He could hear his voice barreling into the mountain.

"Good God," Cale said in surprise. "It sounds like a well."

Ellis adjusted the shotgun in his hand. He looked back at Guy. He could see the rifle leveled at the cave opening. "One of your men got a flare gun?" he asked Cale.

Cale nodded. He turned to the man behind him. "J.C., hand me the flare."

The patrolman named J.C. pulled the gun from the knapsack he wore on his back, breeched it, slipped a flare into the barrel, and passed the gun to Cale.

"You ready?" Cale asked Ellis.

"I'm ready," Ellis replied. "You fire and I'll go in first." He called across the clearing to Guy, "We're going in. They come out over us, kill them." He turned to the cave. "You hear that, Zack? I promise you he won't miss." He motioned with his shotgun to Cale and Cale raised the flare gun and fired into the cave. A brilliant red light, like the lava pit of a volcano, exploded inside.

"Move," Ellis yelled. He jumped into the cave and fell against a hard dirt flooring. He could hear Cale and the two patrolmen behind him. The light billowed in a blinding, searing flash and then began to dim. Ellis rolled to his right against the wall and covered his eyes and listened to the sizzling of the flare. Then he raised his head and looked into the space around him. It was an incredibly large room, like a bubble in the granite. On the sides of the walls, he saw hanging lanterns and clothes. There were bedrolls on the dirt floor and, in the center of the room, a stone circle for a fire. Jesus, Ellis thought. It's a house.

"They're gone," Cale said. He was across the room from Ellis.

"Where the hell to?" Ellis mumbled.

Cale fanned the beam of his flashlight through the smoke of the flare to the back of the cave. There were two narrow passages cutting into the granite. "One of those, I'd guess," Cale said. "Which one you want?"

"One on the right," Ellis replied. He pulled his flashlight from his jacket and trained it on the tunnel opening. It was small, barely wide enough to crawl through. He began to pull himself across the flooring on his elbows and knees, pushing the shotgun before him. The smoke from the flare burned his eyes and choked him.

"Frank, go with the sheriff," Cale ordered. "J.C., you stay with me." Cale was standing pressed against the wall. He had his revolver cocked and aimed along the beam of his flashlight into the black mouth of the larger opening. J.C. was behind him, also against the wall.

Ellis turned his flashlight into the small tunnel and looked inside. He could see nothing but an irregular tube of rock that seemed to press into a closing in the distance. It was like an underground tomb, and Ellis thought instantly of the burial stories of the Indians. He wondered if the tube was full of bones.

"Anything?" Cale asked anxiously.

Ellis turned away from the opening. "Nothing," he said. He saw Cale step forward. The light trembled slightly in his hand. And then he heard the thundering of the shot. He saw Cale hurl backward into J.C., as though thrown. He saw the flashlight fly from Cale's hand and dance wildly across the wall of the cave.

Ellis rolled to his right into a sitting position, whipping the shotgun up in front of him. He saw Cale and J.C. against the wall. He heard the sputtering echoes of the shot still spitting from the opening in the wall. He knew intuitively that someone was leaping from the opening into the cave.

The stock of the shotgun was against his right hip when Ellis fired. The force of the shell caught the dark figure in the side, under his extended left arm, and blew him across the cave. There was no cry from the man, only the hollow bursting of bones and lungs and heart. And then there was silence.

Ellis could feel the blood pounding in his temples. He could feel the bruise from the shotgun's kick on his hip. His ears were screaming. He could smell the thick smoke of gunpowder.

"All right," a voice called from the passageway. "All right, we're coming out."

"Throw out the guns—all of them," Ellis snapped angrily. "Then crawl, hands on your heads." He wondered if he had killed Zack.

The guns hit the floor of the cave dully. Frank moved away from Ellis and aimed his flashlight on the hole. He held his revolver tight in his right hand. His arm was locked straight at the elbow.

"Don't shoot nobody, boy," Ellis said evenly.

And then the men crawled out of the opening, pulling themselves on their elbows, like spiders. Zack first, then another man.

SEVEN

October 18

JESSE SAT AT THE KITCHEN TABLE IN HIS DEAD SON'S house—now Anna's house—and listened as Ellis Spruill told of the capture of Zack Vickers and Eddie Copeland, and of the death of Albert Bailey. Ellis was tired and Jesse knew it. He could read the aching need for rest in Ellis' eyes and in the way he held—but did not drink—the cup of coffee that Anna had poured.

Ellis had said he wanted personally to tell Jesse about the night and the cave and the expectation of what would happen.

"They may be taken down to Gainesville," Ellis said. "Or Atlanta. A man from the GBI said he'd let me know later. But they'll be here for a while. The State Patrol's helping my men guard them."

The two men sat quietly, facing each other across the table. Anna sat beside Jesse. Through the window behind the table, Ellis could see Anna's parents walking close together in the backyard. Ellis knew they were confused by Anna's devotion to Jesse and her refusal to lose herself in Carl's death. To them, it seemed obsessive. To the people of the valley, it was appropriate. Jesse did not need to return to his farm, though neighbors had cleaned away the coatings of murder. Death, the people of the valley believed, did not easily leave its habitation, and Jesse could not live with the residue of so much slaughter around him.

Anna spoke: "What were their names again? Besides the Vickers boy. Where'd they come from?"

Ellis placed the cup of coffee on the table. He could feel Jesse staring at him. He answered, "Fort Wayne, Indiana. Both of them. One was named Albert Bailey—he's the one that got killed. The other one—the one down at the jail with Zack—is named Eddie Copeland. They knew the Vickers boy in the Army."

Jesse moved in the chair, shifting his shoulders against the slatted back. He coughed quietly, but he did not speak.

"They'll be charged with first-degree murder," Ellis continued. "Maybe assault for shooting the GBI man. Robbery. Rape. Maybe kidnapping. Looks like it's open and shut. That simple."

"Yes," Anna replied absently. She smiled quickly, uncomfortably, and reached to touch Jesse's arm in a motion that was involuntary.

"Why'd they do it?" Jesse asked softly.

Ellis fingered the rim of the cup and shook his head. "I don't know, Jesse," he said. "They ain't said. My guess is they went there to steal a car or something and when people started coming up, they just . . . they just got started. No reason, Jesse. No reason at all."

"No reason," Jesse repeated. He could feel his throat tighten. The muscles around his lips trembled.

"They'll pay for it, Jesse," Ellis said. He looked at Anna.

"You were the one that killed . . . that man?" Anna asked.

"Albert Bailey. Yes. I was. I had to."

Anna drew a sudden breath and lifted her eyes to look evenly at Ellis. She said, "We're glad you weren't hurt."

"I'm all right. Just a little tired. But I wanted to come by here and tell you face to face," Ellis replied. He stood and looked at Jesse. He heard a dog barking outside and the sound of a car stopping in the frontyard. "That'll be the

State Patrol. I asked them to put somebody up here to keep people away."

Jesse listened to the sound of a car door closing. He thought of the uniformed patrolman standing beside his car, near the porch of the house, watching the driveway. He looked at Ellis. Ellis was hurting. Ellis was too old to climb through the mountains, too kind to kill another man. He knew that Ellis needed to sleep away the heaviness of the past three days.

"I appreciate you coming by," Jesse said slowly. "I appreciate all you've done. You and Hattie."

"It's my job, Jesse," Ellis replied. "And me and Hattie wanted both of you with us." He paused and looked at Anna. "There's one other thing," he said.

"What?" Anna asked.

"I don't know how people around here are going to be feeling. They're upset, I know. I saw that down at the jail when we brought those men in. I don't want no trouble. They may come up here asking for some sign of approval from you, Jesse. You give it to them and we could be kneedeep in trouble. You don't, I can handle it."

"I won't do anything," Jesse said. "No matter what I feel, I won't. It's out of my hands."

"I'm sorry I had to say that, Jesse," Ellis told him. His eyes were burning. "I just wanted to let you know."

"It's what you're supposed to do," Jesse said.

Ellis stepped away from the table and pushed his chair beneath it. "I'll go, then," he said. "I told the reporters to leave you alone, but they'll try to get to you anyway."

"There've been some calls already," Anna replied. "We just hang up."

Ellis nodded his approval. "They'll keep trying, I suspect. If you need me, let me know."

"We will," Anna told him. "We'll be all right." She reached for Jesse's arm and stroked it lightly. She smiled pleasantly. "We'll be all right," she repeated.

Ellis lifted his hand to the patrolman and walked to his car and drove south toward Tickenaley. He passed the fields that Carl had farmed, the orchards separating the homesites that had been drawn by Carl and Macy. He slowed at the turnoff to the house that had been built for Macy and Faron Simmons. He saw the Uncle Sam mailbox with its peeling red, white, and blue paint. Someone had fastened a wreath to the bottom of Uncle Sam's outstretched hands and the wreath dangled in the light, cool wind like a somber Christmas ornament. Ellis thought about Faron. He could not remember how long Faron had been dead. Two years? he asked himself. If it was true—what all the preachers promised—then Faron and Macy and Winston were now reunited in some peaceful, cosmic place.

Ellis pushed the accelerator and his car jumped forward, leaving the house and mailbox and wreath. He realized he was hungry. It was early afternoon and he had not eaten in a day, but he did not care to eat. He wanted only to sleep. The killing of Albert Bailey had sickened him. Earlier, in the morning, as he had watched the patrol remove Bailey's body from the cave, Ellis had vomited in the rockbed of the wash and the images around him had become a blur and he had sat on a ledge of the mountain fighting the queasy repulsion of what he had done and what had been done to Jesse's family. He had seen enough death.

He could still hear the airbeating swirl of the helicopter as it lifted Cale off the mountain—Cale wrapped in a blood-sheet, his right arm dangling uselessly from his shoulder. He could hear the urgent babel of voices from reporters at the jail and the slurring of his own words answering their questions (or not answering their questions; there was little he could tell them). The acrid smoke of the burning flare was still caked to his throat and an itching was still in his eyes.

"Damn it," he said aloud. He slapped the steering wheel with the fleshy ball of his fist. "Goddamn it!"

Jesse stood on the porch and watched Ellis' car disappear in a thin sheet of dust along the hard dirt road. He saw the patrolman standing alertly beside his car, his eyes and nose hidden by the wide brim of his hat. The patrolman's body and face were turned to the road, away from Jesse. He does not want to speak, Jesse thought. What could he say if he did speak? I'm sorry? "Look, mister, I didn't know your family, but I hear they were good people, and I'm sorry about it." What else? The patrolman had to feel uncomfortable.

Jesse heard the telephone ring twice, and through the wall of the house he heard Anna's muffled answer. Then he heard her walking across the planked flooring of the hallway, heard her open the front door and cross the porch to him.

"That was William Fred," she told him. "He wants to come out and talk to you. He was down at the jail when those men were brought in."

Jesse looked at her. "William Fred?" he asked.

"Yes. I heard he was pretty upset."

"All right," Jesse said quietly. "Tell him to come out."

EIGHT

October 19

IT WAS SUNDAY, THE FIFTH DAY FOLLOWING THE DISCOVery of the bodies of his family, and Jesse awoke early and dressed and took an axe and drove to the clearing where Doyle had planned his house.

He had told Anna that he could not go to the church services. He knew what the message of the Preacher would be and he knew how the congregation would have stared dumbly at him, waiting for him to say something about the capture of the men who had murdered his family. (It would be talked about earnestly enough by the circle of men smoking beneath the trees before the ringing of the bell; the men would be brave and certain.) And he knew the dying flowers across the six gravesites would give off a light, sweet perfume, like a deceptive, intoxicating poison. If he breathed it, it would never leave him.

On the mountain, the air was cold and the scent was pine and hickory, and he was, at last, alone.

He went to the last trees that he and Carl and Doyle had dropped and left for trimming. They had quit early because the birthday party was more important and because he had known Winston would want to take his new rifle and shoot at tin cans in the pasture.

He remembered suddenly the cold body of his grandson and a wave of nausea filled his mouth and he could feel a film of perspiration across his face. He leaned against his axe and breathed slowly and the nausea began to subside and the image of Winston faded.

He crossed the frostslick clearing to the largest tree and raised his axe and began to cut away limbs. He could hear the crack of the axeblade echoing off the mountain. The men who had killed his family had been found hiding in a cave in the mountain, less than half a mile away. He wondered if they had watched him clearing the land with his sons, if they had seen Jean leave in Doyle's car, had circled through the woods to follow her. He thought of Isom and Lou Vickers and wondered if they knew what their son had done, and if they did, if they were afraid for Zack's life.

He stopped his cutting and looked toward the mountain. He could hear the high wind sweeping like a whisper over the fur-thick needles of the pines growing at the edge of the hardwoods. He heard the sharp, sledgehammer drumming of a woodpecker and the clear-throated jabbering of a bluejay. Then the wind gusted and the pinetops hissed and the birds stopped drumming and jabbering, and Jesse could feel the presence of the caves, running through the granite muscle of the mountain like empty arteries puffed up by air. He remembered the fear in the archeologist's face when he had quit his exploration of the clearing. "There're things to be found there, but I don't want to be the one to find them," he had said. He had left hurriedly. In Jesse's barn, there was a shovel that belonged to the archeologist. Jesse had found it beside a trench the archeologist had been digging. In the trench, half-covered by dirt, Jesse had discovered the head of a clay doll. The doll's face was grotesquely deformed.

One of the men, one of the killers of his family—what was his name? Bailey? Yes, Bailey—had died in the cave, Jesse thought. Ellis had killed him. Or had it been Ellis? Was it something else? Something the archeologist understood? The old stories of the Indians had power. The caves may have been used for burial grounds, the archeologist had suggested. Burial grounds do not like invasion.

Jesse drove his axe into the fallen tree and stood looking at the mountain. The numbness that had been in him was like a dulling anesthesia. He wished to be angry, to grieve, to weep, to hate, to yearn. But he had not felt any of those sensations. He had been conditioned for control, for accepting whatever happened and surviving. It was his heritage, as the work tools in his barn were his heritage. He was Jesse Wade, son of the Wades who came into the valley and struggled their living from the mountains and bottomlands. The Wades had never cowered. Nothing had changed them. Not death. Not nature. Not failure. Not despair. "The Wades bear up," his grandmother had once told him. "The Wades keep going."

But the Wades before him—his father and grandfather and great-grandfather—had never known such needless slaughter. Their people had died of disease or accident, not by violence. Still, Jesse could feel the tug of his ancestors: *Bear up, bear up*. And he had become numb. The memory of holding his grandson—his skin as cool as stone—had washed through him unexpectedly, and he had felt his body respond as though it were awakening from some prolonged sleep of drugs. But it had only been a flash, like an electric pulsebeat leaping through the darkness of amnesia. And then it was gone.

He could see the white heat of his breathing roll over the cold morning air. His body was rigid and tense. And then— somehow, strangely—he was outside his body, separated from it like a vaporous eye. He could sense the lightness of his own suspended consciousness as he watched the body below him in motion, walking steadily toward the Mountain of the Caves, striding easily among the great trees, finding the wheelbed of the patrol Jeeps that had been to the cave.

And then he was at the cave, standing beneath the granite awning that jutted out over the opening. And the gliding, conscious eye sailed gently, silently back into his body.

He stepped cautiously into the cave and stood in the spill

of the aluminum morning light. He could feel the pupils of his eyes opening like a bloom and the dark of the cave began to gray into abstract scratches of rock. He could hear a sound, like a sigh, from far in the cave, more imagined than real. He raised his hands and slapped them together once. The echo of the slap was like a yelp of pain.

He stood, breathing heavily, staring at a rib of granite that ran horizontally across the back of the cave. His eyes began to blur and sting, but they were locked hypnotically on the rib of granite. And then he was again standing above Carl, then stumbling laboriously through his home, from body to body, going to them by instinct but not touching them. Except Winston. He could see himself pulling Winston into his arms, and then he could see Anna and then Ellis Spruill and Guy Finley. He could see the office of the jail and the men around him, and the room where he had been taken and the ceiling above the bed. But he could not hear any sound. There had been no sound at all. Only moving mouths. And he remembered that he feared silence more than all things. There had been no sound after the memory of a scream as he cradled Winston in his arms. He had heard nothing until the Preacher appeared and touched his hands and began his cooing of pity. The Preacher's voice had made him angry, he remembered.

He turned abruptly and walked out of the cave and followed the wheelbed of the Jeeps to the collar of the clearing, and then he crossed back to the trees that he had cut with his sons. He sat wearily on the trunk of the tree he had been trimming and looked below him to the white pines, their even tips blueing and shimmering in the glazed light. He ran his hand over the smooth handle of the axe beside him and pulled feebly against it, but the axeblade held firm in the tree. He thought: Jean saw demons and the Preacher pretended to drive them out—had satisfied himself that what he had done was not unlike the act of some biblical healer. The Preacher had said that Jean wanted to keep secret her premonition of terror heard in the warnings of the hoarse-voiced old man of her dreams. "Jesse will think I'm gone mad," she had said (or so the Preacher had reported). "She told me, 'Preacher, it's the endtime. The endtime's coming. That's what the voice is saying to me.'" Jesse remembered the sudden posturing of the Preacher when he had said all of this—his large Scottish face reddening with authority, his voice punching the air like a fist. And Jesse had wondered if the Preacher was lying, if the Preacher himself had not been the voice of Jean's dreams, if the Preacher had not visited Jean for the warm flesh of her hands. The Preacher had touched her often, milking at her fingers, saying, "I know. I know."

Jesse pushed himself from the trunk of the tree and pried the axe from the wood. He looked at the cleared land, at the place where Doyle had paced out the rooms of his home for his mother. He began to cry, soundlessly, without a muscle moving in his face. He wanted to see his family again. He wanted to hear them. He wanted to touch them. He could feel a great aching burn in his chest and flash into his throat and down the muscles of his arms. He could hear a voice inside his head shouting, "Why are they dead? Why them? Why did they leave me?" The crying spilled into his mouth in a guttural sob, like a swallowed breath.

Far off, dull in the thin air, Jesse could hear the bell of Tickenaley Church. He jerked his axe up, suddenly, angrily, and began to cut viciously across the treetrunk, splitting away thick wedges of wood on each stroke of the church bell.

Inside Tickenaley Church, the Preacher's sermon was a begging, sighing admonition that God in His greatness, God in His wisdom, God in His meticulous planning, would not waste the tragedy of the deaths of Jesse Wade's family and Aubrey Hart's daughter. God would heal the bruises of loss. God would strengthen the frail. God would prove that forgiveness—the same forgiveness found in the teachings of Jesus—would turn the bitterness of the poison of hate into a sweetness that would be like honey on the tongue of those who forgive.

As she listened to the Preacher's sermon, Anna began to feel strangely affected. She could sense a voice inside her saying, "Please, God, please. Help me. Help me. Help me." She could feel the words of the Preacher like a breath on her face, and the breath was cooling and soothing, and as the breath stroked against her she could feel a power swelling inside her. She tried to see the slain body of Carl, but she could not; she could see only his face, at peace, smiling, his eyes saying, "Listen. Listen."

The Preacher cried, "Those of you who know God, who believe that what Jesus taught us about forgiveness is God's way, come forward. Say to God and say to your families and friends that you believe, that you give yourself over to God, trusting in His tender mercies to help you through the tribulations of this earthly life. Come. Kneel and pray and God will hear you."

Anna rose from her seat between her parents and walked forward and knelt at the altar of the church before the Preacher. She did not hear the whispers of awe.

"I forgive," Anna said quietly to the Preacher. "I want God's care."

And the Preacher, trembling with triumph, took her hands and said, "God be with you, Anna. God be with you."

NINE

October 20

THE TRAUMA OF SHOCK THAT HAD TRANQUILIZED JESSE was released in the work of clearing the trees on Doyle's homesite. Each axecut—powerful, deep into the wood— was an act of exorcism. It was an outpouring that Jesse could feel in the ache of his muscles and in the perspiration that ran from his forehead, down the bridge of his nose and off the furrows of his lips. It was in the blisters of his hands from holding the axe too tightly.

He had cut the trees until late on Sunday and then had driven to Anna's house and gathered his belongings and returned to his own farm. Anna and her parents had protested cautiously, but Jesse had not listened to them. "I'll go back," he had said. "I got to sometime."

The first hour had been painful—flashes of memory of the deathscene, rooms whispering with years of voices that had somehow lodged in the walls and fell out easily, tumbling around Jesse as he walked the house. But the work of the day had tired him and he had lain fully dressed across his bed (the bed that neighbors had cleaned and covered) and he had slept surprisingly well. When he awoke, the room was light with early morning and he could smell the odor of coffee and bacon from his kitchen. He knew it was Anna.

"My parents are leaving this morning," she told him as he ate. "They said to tell you goodbye. Said they'd be praying for you."

Jesse nodded. He was relieved. Anna's parents had hovered around him, watching him but not speaking. They had tried to be helpful, but they were strangers. He had not needed the presence of strangers; he had needed to be alone.

"Ellis called early, before I left the house," Anna said. "I think he was surprised you'd come back here. He said he wanted to know if you were going to the hearing this morning."

"No," Jesse said.

"Glad you're not," she told him. She leaned forward with her elbows on the table and watched him eating. She said, "The Preacher came by the house last night, after you'd left. He wanted to spend some time with you, to talk. He told me—"

"No," Jesse said abruptly. "Not now."

"He wants to help, Jesse. He's helped me. All the hurting I've been feeling, it all left me yesterday morning. And it was the Preacher. Last night, I spent a long time just talking. It made me feel better."

Jesse could see the Preacher in Ellis Spruill's bedroom, could hear his voice: "I know, I know. . . ." He could see Jean's face as it drank from the Preacher's words. He could see her fingers holding tight to the Preacher's hands, could see her eyes locked with his eyes, like lovers with some grand, lasting secret.

"The Bible tells about ways to carry on, Jesse," Anna said. "Knowing them helps."

"I guess," he mumbled.

He drank the coffee and gazed at the food still on his plate. What is there about the Preacher? he wondered. What is his power? What makes him unique? Or is he unique? His self-image had grown fat off Jean. And now he was at feast on Anna, bloating on her pain. Jesse could feel his anger at the Preacher deepening.

"What'll you be doing today?" Anna asked.

"Working."

"Where?"

"At the clearing."

Anna studied his face. It had aged. The thick stubs of his beard across his jowls and chin and mouth and under his neck had silver tips and it made his face seem ashen and dry.

"Why, Jesse?" she asked. "Why are you working up there now?"

He looked up from his plate and stared blankly at her. He said, "I want to. It's something that was started. It needs to be finished."

His voice surprised her. "Have I upset you, Jesse?" she asked quietly.

"No," he said. "Guess I'm just a little tired."

"It's all right," she replied. She stood and began to remove the dishes from the table. "Some of the ladies that helped clean up last week wanted to come back today. I don't guess you mind."

"No. Whatever they want to do."

"You sure you want to be staying here now?" Anna asked. "The Preacher was worried that . . ."

"It's my house. It's where I'll stay."

"If you want, I could stay with you," Anna said.

He watched her at the sink, cleaning the dishes. She looked surprisingly like Jean when Jean had been younger.

"I expected you'd be moving back to Tennessee," he said.

She turned at the sink and looked at him. "No," she replied. "I've got my home, too. Here. I'll be staying here."

"Guess I was thinking about your folks being in Tennessee."

"No. That's their home. Carl never wanted to leave here. He said when we moved in our house that that's where he wanted us to stay. That's what I'll do."

Jesse did not reply. He knew she was right. Whatever had bewildered Carl in Vietnam he had controlled by returning to the mountains. Of his children, Jesse had always known that Carl would be the one to live with the land. Macy and Doyle could have left. Macy and Doyle had been too intrigued by the distance of the road leading north and south through Tickenaley.

"I remember when I first came here, Jesse," Anna said. "I knew then this is where I'd live." She smiled and thought of the day when she had first seen Tickenaley—on the highway that curved like the cap of an S high on the mountain above the valley. It was awesomely beautiful, with the greening of trees and plants and grasses so rich they would bleed the dark coloring of the topsoil on touch.

"I'd come to visit Carl, remember?" Anna said. "Wasn't long after we'd met in Knoxville. I told him I was on my way to Florida and just wanted to stop by. I spent the night with Macy. I remember that I wrote my mother a letter that night, telling her I'd found where I wanted to live. And who I wanted to live with."

"I remember," Jesse said.

"I could stay here for a while, Jesse, to help you along," Anna said. She raised her face and her body stiffened. "We have to carry on. Carl always said that. Said no matter what, we had to carry on. Said we had to keep the Wade name alive." She crossed her arms in front of her. "He was proud of being your son, Jesse."

Jesse could feel his hands shaking. "I'll be all right," he said weakly. "It'll take time, but I'll be all right."

"I know that, Jesse. When it's over, we'll make our way. That's what the Preacher was telling me. He was saying if we looked hard enough, we'd find a sign to show us what to do."

It was one o'clock when Ellis arrived at the clearing to tell Jesse of the preliminary hearing of Eddie Copeland and Zack Vickers. He said nothing to Jesse about the cutting of the trees, or about moving back into his home, or about the cave in the mountain above them.

"Just thought you'd like to know, Jesse," Ellis said. "They've been bound over to the Grand Jury. That'll be on

Friday. They'll get a murder indictment and put the trial on the calendar. Not much to it today, if you want to know the truth. Nothing but procedure. Seems like a waste of time, if you want to know how I feel about it. Way it is with the courts, though."

"I guess," Jesse said.

"You know William Fred expects to be appointed the prosecutor," Ellis said.

Jesse nodded and lit a cigarette. "He came by and we talked about it."

"It's all right with you?"

"It's all right. Guess he knows us pretty well."

"Well, everything else aside, he's good, Jesse," Ellis said. "He's damn good. Maybe the best around."

"What I hear, he is," Jesse replied. "I don't know much about it."

"If there's any loopholes, he'll find them," Ellis said. "And you can trust him to work."

Jesse did not reply. He tapped his hand on the handle of the axe and looked beyond Ellis to the limbs he had stacked for burning.

"Nice place up here, Jesse. Real nice," Ellis said easily.

"I appreciate you coming by. You didn't have to."

"I wanted to," Ellis said. "Truth is, I need to be out. I got to go over to see Isom and Lou. We've had a car up there since Saturday, to keep people away from them, but I don't guess anybody can find them. Nobody's been around. Anyhow, I got to thinking that Isom and Lou may not know what's going on. Some fellow from the GBI went in and told them we'd arrested Zack. Don't know if he got through to them, though."

Jesse wiped his brow with the sleeve of his shirt and shook his head sadly. "I been thinking about them," he admitted quietly. "God knows, I hope their boy pays, but I feel for them."

"Yeah, me, too," Ellis said. "Well, I need to be going on." He turned to leave, then turned back to Jesse. "Why don't you come along with me?" he asked. "Maybe it'd help them to know you ain't holding nothing against them."

Jesse thought of Isom and Lou Vickers. He wondered if they understood about the deaths of his family, if they knew how he felt, or why Zack had been hunted and taken away.

"You're looked up to around here, Jesse," Ellis said. "People know you'll keep your head. Maybe going to see Isom and Lou'll help keep order."

"Order?" Jesse asked.

Ellis shrugged uncomfortably. "Nothing I can put my finger on. Just talk. You know how people are. They talk a lot."

"I guess," Jesse said quietly. He lifted his axe and chipped lightly at a small limb on the fallen tree. "Guess I could go up," he added. "If you think it's the right thing."

"Tell you the truth, I don't know what the law says about it, but I don't give a damn," Ellis told him. "That ain't Bonnie and Clyde up there; it's Isom and Lou. I think it'd help, if you feel up to it."

"I'm all right, Ellis."

The only people who had been to Isom and Lou Vickers' isolated home since the capture of Eddie Copeland and Zack were stern, serious-faced investigators who had carried away whatever evidence they thought important. One of the men had bluntly told Isom and Lou that Zack was in jail for murder. Isom and Lou had not asked any questions. They had been too confused.

The deputies of Onslow County had been stationed at the side road leading to the house to stop any reporters from questioning Isom and Lou. The only thing the reporters knew were the stories they had heard from the townspeople of Tickenaley, and those stories had been exaggerated into images of two raving old people as unpredictable as trapped animals. There had been flyovers of news helicopters trying to photograph the small cabin in the tangle of trees, but the helicopter pilots were never certain they had found the cabin. From the air, the cabin was like a lesion on the skin of the mountain, and even the blue cord of smoke from the chimney was lost in the cover of the hardwoods. One pilot was certain. "It's down there," he said to the cameraman, "right below us." And what the news team saw and believed to be the cabin was a rock formation that had a crease like a hat.

It was Lou who answered Ellis' knock at the door. She opened the door two inches and peered out suspiciously.

"Afternoon, Lou," Ellis said pleasantly. "It's me. Ellis Spruill. Me and Jesse Wade. You know Jesse, don't you?"

A smile broke over the leathered wrinkles on Lou's face. "Lives down off the mountains," she said gleefully. "Buys honey sometimes."

"That's right," Jesse said. "How are you, Lou?" He knew she had forgotten about the slaughter of his family—if she had ever understood it.

Lou giggled. "Fine. I'm fine. You come to buy some honey?"

"I could use some," Jesse told her. "I ran out."

"Where's Isom?" Ellis asked. "He around?"

Lou looked over her shoulder, back into the house. Her face hardened into a frown. She turned back to Ellis. "Old fool," she said angrily. "Sitting there by the fire. Ain't doing nothing. Rocking. Ain't doing nothing. Don't do nothing no more. Old fool."

"Mind if we come in and talk to him?" Ellis asked.

"Don't care what you do," Lou snapped. "Old fool pull out the trunk and got in it and he ain't doing nothing but being crazy. Crazy as a bat."

"What trunk?" Ellis asked.

"Trunk he had," Lou answered irritably. "Had it when he come by in the wagon and got me." She jerked her head toward the room. "Got all his old stuff in it."

"All right if we see him?" Jesse asked.

Lou pulled open the door and Ellis and Jesse stepped inside. "You find some place to sit at," she said. She crossed the room and sat in a straightback chair near the fireplace. She began a rhythmic rocking with her body, staring at the fire.

Jesse closed the door and the room darkened. He could

see the outline of Isom sitting in a rocker, in the deepest shadows of the room, his back to the door. An old trunk was beside the rocker, its lid opened and covered with clothing.

"Isom?" Ellis asked.

Isom did not reply. He continued his steady rocking.

"Isom, it's me. Ellis Spruill."

"Crazy old fool," Lou cackled. She leaned toward Isom. "There's people here, old fool," she shouted.

Ellis could smell the sweetness of the soap that Lou made. It was like a flowered day in spring. He looked at the low, planked ceiling above his head. String nets filled with the soap were hanging from nails in the exposed rafters.

"It's all right, Lou," Ellis said. He stepped to the rocker and looked at Isom. "My God," he whispered in astonishment.

"What is it?" Jesse asked.

"Look at this, Jesse."

Isom sat in the chair dressed in the gray, baggy uniform of a Confederate soldier.

"Isom," Ellis said, leaning over to stop the rocker. "Isom, can you hear me?"

Isom's eyes wandered up from the fire. The orange of the flame flickered across his withered face.

"Isom's fine," he said, smiling quickly. "All the time."

"It's me. The sheriff," Ellis said. "I've got Jesse Wade with me. You remember Jesse."

"Jesse," Isom repeated slowly. His head turned to Jesse and his eyes inspected Jesse curiously. Then he smiled. "I know Jesse. Know his daddy. Know his granddaddy."

"Me and Jesse come up to talk to you, Isom," Ellis said.

"Good, good," Isom mumbled. "I like talking."

"You feel up to it, Isom?" Jesse asked. "We can come back."

"Isom's fine," Isom said. "Get some chairs. Somewhere over in the corner." He lifted his hand from his lap and swept it across the air. Ellis could see the barrel of an old pistol shoved between his legs.

"Jesse'll find them," Ellis said. He knelt beside Isom's

rocker. "Where'd you get that old gun, Isom?" he asked easily.

"My gun, by God," Isom said proudly, lifting the pistol. "Used it against the Yankees. Shot their balls off." He pulled the gun to his chest, cradling it, and began to chuckle.

Jesse handed Ellis one of the chairs he had found beside the table and the two men sat facing Isom.

"That old gun's not loaded, is it, Isom?" Ellis asked.

Isom's head snapped up and he glared suspiciously at Ellis. The firelight glimmered off Isom's chin, where he had drooled saliva. He dropped the long barrel of the gun toward Ellis. Ellis pushed slowly back in his chair.

"Is it, Isom? Is it loaded?" Jesse asked uneasily.

"Run out of bullets," Isom said in a hushed voice. "They was a boy stole them. Goddamn his soul to fire in hell. Stole all I had."

"Crazy old fool," Lou said angrily. "Ain't nobody stole nothing."

"Who stole them, Isom?" Ellis asked. "Was it Zack?"

Isom stopped his rocking. He pulled the barrel of the pistol nearer to his face, resting it under his chin. His eyes darted around the room. "They got Zack," he whispered. "Come out with a dog and got him. Dog ate him up."

Lou laughed suddenly, triumphantly. "Ain't no dog ate him up," she said, sneering. "They got him down at the jail. Him and them Army boys took my tobacco. Ain't no dog ate him up."

Isom began to rock again. His eyes blinked rapidly and moistened. His mouth began to move in a chewing motion and the chewing motion matched the woodsqueak of the rocker.

"You know why Zack's in jail, Isom?" Ellis asked quietly. "You understand why?"

Isom continued to rock and chew with his gums. The amber of the fire caught in the dots of moisture around his eyes.

"Zack killed some people," Ellis said. "Jesse's people."

Isom stopped his rocking. He drew in a slow, deep breath and stared at the fire. He nodded once.

Jesse could see a sadness of reality seep into Isom's face. He knew that Isom—part of Isom—understood the crime of his son, and that crime, and his son, burned inside Isom with great shame and hurt. And Jesse understood the sorrow: he and Isom had both lost sons; his were dead, Isom's was condemned.

"I came up to tell you I don't hold nothing against you and Lou," Jesse said evenly. "It wadn't your doing."

"They took Zack," Lou said casually. She opened a tin of snuff and pinched the brown powder in her fingers and thrust it into her toothless mouth. "Guess they'll be keeping him." She spat into the fire and the tobacco sizzled into a brown curl on a log. She nodded affirmatively. "Guess so," she announced.

"Isom? Do you know what's going on?" Ellis asked. "You understand it?"

The fingers of Isom's left hand played over the cylinder of his pistol. He lifted his head and rested it against the chair. He sat very still and his eyes focused on the distance across the room.

"They was coming down the creekbed," he said suddenly in a full, resonant voice, stronger than his normal voice.

"They was coming down the creekbed and we was hiding in the brush, near the mouth, where it dumped into the river. Me and Harley and the Leonard boy. We'd been cut off from our boys for a week, maybe longer'n that, and we was making it back across Tennessee to Chattanooga. But they was Blue Boys everywhere. Goddamn Blue Boys, riding horses, pulling them big guns they was going to use in Chattanooga. We'd hide by day and run by night. Harley's nigger was with us when we started, but he went off one day and Harley said he'd be telling the Yanks where we was, so we waded out in a swamp and stayed a day and a night. They was wads of hair all over that swamp, just floating. Brown hair. When we climbed out, we found some dead horses and mules upstream, rotting in the water. Same water we'd been hiding in."

"Isom," Ellis said gently.

Isom's voice became stronger. "They was coming down

the creekbed, right on top of us. Me and Harley and the Leonard boy. He wadn't sixteen. Couldn't get him a peehard on. They was coming down the creekbed, laughing and singing, not giving a damn about what was around them, and they wadn't no place for us to take off to. Harley says, 'Be goddamn if I'm running another step. Take me some Yankees right here and die myself on good Tennessee dirt.' I says, 'I ain't ready to go dying, Harley. Be still and they'll walk right over us.' And Harley says, 'You see my nigger, he's mine to kill, goddamn him. My daddy paid hard cash for him to follow me.' And the Leonard boy was crying, saying he didn't want to die."

"My God," Ellis whispered to Jesse. "You ever hear him do this?"

"No," Jesse answered. "My daddy said he'd heard it. Said Isom had the Civil War locked in his head, like it was somebody else's brain."

Isom began to laugh. The saliva seeped from the corners of his mouth. He shook his head like an old man remembering suddenly something that was obscure and meaningless, but humorous.

"Leonard boy shit right in his pants, he was shaking so hard," Isom said. "Smelt up the brush. Harley said, 'Boy, wipe your ass on your hat.'" Isom laughed again. He dropped his head forward, then leaned it back. His eyes wandered to the planked ceiling of the room.

"They was almost past us when Harley jumped up out of the weeds and took off running after them. 'Die and be damned to hell,' he was yelling. And them Yankees turned on him and started shooting their guns. And me and the Leonard boy crawled down to the creek bank and slipped in a patch of reeds, but we seen it all. Seen what they done to Harley. They shot him from so damn many sides he couldn't fall down. You'd see them bullets blowing little wads of flesh out of him and he'd start to tumble that way, and then they'd hit him from the other side and stand him back up. You ask the Leonard boy. Me'n him could see the holes all the way through Harley. And then a Yankee on a horse come riding up with his sword and took one swipe and cut Harley's head off, like it was a melon hanging on a vine. Me and the Leonard boy just sunk down in the reeds. Goddamn Harley. He didn't shoot nobody."

Isom laughed quietly to himself and wiped the moisture from his mouth and eyes with the back of his hand. He scratched at the lobe of his right ear with the barrel of the pistol, then dropped it back into his lap and leaned his head against the chair and closed his eyes and immediately fell asleep.

Ellis looked at Jesse and shook his head. "What do you think?" he whispered.

"I don't know," Jesse answered quietly. "I don't know." He looked at Isom's sleeping face. It was calm and restful and the amber of the fire on his cheeks and forehead made his skin appear smooth, like pressed wax. He was not to blame for Zack, Jesse thought. Zack had raged, like Harley. Isom had slipped into hiding and the trickery of his mind (madness?) had left him mercifully confused. It was not Isom's fault that Zack had killed. It was not Lou's fault. They had long stopped being responsible, like helpless animals that lived by habit, not planning. Jesse could only pity them.

"Where'd the trunk come from, Lou?" Ellis asked gently.

Lou's head began to bob in thought. "Told you," she said. "Isom had it on the other side of the mountain. It come with us. Isom hid it out, under the floor planks. What he had in the fighting."

"What fighting, Lou?" Ellis asked.

"The Yankees, that's what," Lou said defiantly. "What Isom said. Said he killed the goddamn Yankees."

"Lou, that was more than a hundred years ago," Ellis said. "A long time before Isom was born."

Lou glared at the two men and then spat a brown stream of tobacco into the fire. "He done it," she said emphatically. "All he talks about."

"Maybe he did, Lou," Ellis replied quietly. "Maybe he did."

"How long's it been since Isom took the trunk out?" Jesse asked.

Lou sat thinking. She turned her head as though listening for a sound, a voice in the distance of memory.

"First time since we come here," she said at last. "He was looking for his Yankee gun."

"Why?" Ellis asked.

"Said he was going to shoot Zack," Lou answered lightly. "Said Zack was meaner'n Yankees."

TEN

October 20

TOBY CAHILL DID NOT SEE THE MAN APPROACHING HIS table in the Valley View Lodge Restaurant and the man's voice startled him.

"Toby Cahill?" the man asked.

"That's right," Toby answered.

"My name's William Fred Autry," the man said, smiling. He shrugged his head toward the counter. "Rachel pointed you out. Think I could have found you, though."

"What can I do for you?" Toby asked.

"Maybe it's the other way around," William Fred Autry said pleasantly. He added in a whisper, "As long as it's off the record."

"Off the record?"

"That's right."

Toby smiled. It always amused him when someone applied for an off-the-record protection. None of them knew how easy it was to skirt such promises.

"Who are you, Mr. Autry?" Toby asked.

"Please. William Fred. Or William. Or Fred." His eyes flashed to the tables around him. "I'm an attorney," he said.

"Nobody knows it yet, but I'm going to be prosecuting in the Wade family case." He smiled again. "Mind if I sit down?"

"Please do," Toby said.

William Fred pulled a chair from the table and turned to sit with a view of the front door. "You're a hell of a writer," he said to Toby. "That series you did last summer—the one on the people in Appalachia—was damn fine. I mean it. What you've done on this story, good work. Making everybody else look a little lost."

"Thank you," Toby said.

"Top it off, I understand you're a gentleman," William Fred added.

"A what?" Toby asked in surprise.

William Fred laughed easily. He knocked an unfiltered cigarette from its package and lit it with a wooden match he pulled from the pocket of his vest. He waved a signal to Rachel.

"Rachel, there," he said casually, "tells me you're a gentleman. Been here—what, almost a week?—and not the first pass at her. God love her soul, that's some kind of record for this place."

"Just say I'm getting old," Toby replied. "Nothing noble about it."

"Don't say that. You can't be much older than me," William Fred said. "Point is, she's worth it, friend. And that's definitely off the record."

Toby watched Rachel crossing the restaurant with a cup balanced in her hand. She was smiling proudly.

"Off the record, as I said," William Fred whispered as Rachel approached. "Lord knows, I've even thought about marrying her someday."

Rachel placed the cup before William Fred. "I see y'all met," she said. "I hope you don't mind me telling him who you was, Mr. Cahill."

"No. It's all right."

"That's good. Y'all talk. I've got some people at the counter." She turned and walked away.

Toby watched William Fred stirring sugar into his coffee.

William Fred Autry was a salesman, Toby sensed, a sleight-of-hand artist who peddled a tonic of good times. There was a rich dramatic aura about him, a kind of clear oilslick that floated on the tides of his personality. Toby knew that William Fred was either very shrewd or very smart. Or both.

"You said you may be able to do something for me: what?" Toby asked.

"Put you at the right place at the right time," William Fred said. "I grew up in Onslow County. Know the people in Tickenaley. My first job was helping keep the records straight at the courthouse, back when I was in high school. I've got a pretty good memory."

"How's that supposed to help me?"

William Fred smiled and pulled a thread of tobacco from his tongue. His eyes swept the dining room lazily and then drifted back to Toby. "Well, I know that Isom and Lou Vickers live on land that Jesse Wade's grandfather deeded to them after they started homesteading," he said. "Isom and Lou don't know even now that they own the land. It's there, they're there. County overlooks the taxes."

"And that's supposed to help me some way?"

"Not that," William Fred replied. "That's just an example, just bait. You wouldn't use that. Some other asshole may, but not you."

"How do you know?"

William Fred laughed confidently. "One, I've read you, like I said. Two, I made a couple of phone calls about you—to your newspaper and your sister, the one that lives in Huntsville. Lied like a snake, to be honest. Told them you were being considered for a special award." He grinned proudly. "They poured it on, Toby. Told me what I suspected from that Appalachian series: you've got integrity. And I do know something about integrity, even if I am a lawyer. You're infected with it." He lifted an eyebrow for exaggeration. "Terminal, I'd say. But, God knows, there's little enough of it around."

"But what you just told me could be a damn good story," Toby argued.

"Would be," William Fred corrected. "Just what people like to know. But it'd make that old couple look like blithering, mindless children, and you wouldn't take that judgment on yourself. You knew people like that in those Alabama hills, unless I'm wrong. Oh, you'd leap to the defense, but you won't start it." William Fred drew from his cigarette and blew the smoke up, toward the ceiling. "Nope. Somebody else will do that one—if they hear about it. Not you. I'd bet on it. I just told you that as a teaser. The things I can help you with will mean more than that."

"You said you were going to prosecute," Toby said. "Are you the district attorney?"

"Me? Good Lord, no," William Fred exclaimed. "I'm just a lawyer"—he mugged a smile—"making sure that justice is done." He jammed the nub of his cigarette into an ashtray and looked directly at Toby. His voice suddenly became serious. "I'll prosecute because I know these people around here, like you knew your people in Alabama. I know Jesse Wade. It's what he wants. And, besides, I think those bastards are guilty as sin and I'm damn good at what I do because I believe in it." He moved his face closer to Toby. "I'll get their asses fried like sausages." He leaned back and lifted his cup in a salute. "Of course, that's off the record," he said.

"And you picked me out to tell me all this?" Toby asked. "Checked up on me—everything—just for the hell of it?"

"No, Toby Cahill."

"Then why?"

"I didn't pick you out. I just suggested you. Eddie Copeland picked you out."

Toby did not reply, but the question furrowed into his face.

"He won't talk unless there's a reporter present," William Fred said. He paused and looked at the suspicion in Toby's face. "No, it's the truth. Damnedest thing I ever heard of, too, but that's the way he wants it. Doesn't even want a lawyer now. The judge called me in and talked to me about it. I went down and talked to Copeland."

"Sorry, Mr. Autry, but I don't believe it," Toby said evenly.

William Fred laughed easily. "Don't blame you. Anyway, this is the deal: the judge agreed to let you be there, on one condition."

"And that is?"

"That nothing can be written about what goes on in that session, or those sessions if there's more than one, until the case is over. Copeland agreed."

Toby absently tapped a cigarette from its package and lit it.

"Well?" William Fred asked lightly.

"Did you really talk to my sister?" Toby asked curiously.

"Marie. Husband's name is Robert. Two—"

"All right," Toby interrupted. "I don't know about this. Why would he want something like that?"

William Fred touched his temple with his index finger. "Smart," he said. "Gambling that whatever you, or anybody else, writes after the trial will get him an appeal. He knows exactly what he's doing."

"You know that and you agreed?"

"Sure. Why not?" William Fred said. He leaned forward again and again lowered his voice. "Look, there's enough evidence for a Boy Scout troop working on a Forgive-and-Forget merit badge to convict the son of a bitch. If I didn't know that, I'd scream my bloody head off. Copeland'll blame it on Vickers and Vickers'll blame it on Copeland. I don't give a damn if Copeland wants to be immortalized in print. All I want is to see his ass burn."

"And what's in it for you?" Toby asked directly. "The district attorney's job? A judgeship? Is that it?"

Toby could see the sting of his question. William Fred's face paled. He bit on his lower lip and played nervously with the handle of his coffee cup.

"I want to do it. That's all," he said at last.

"You're a strange person, William Fred Autry," Toby said. "I guess you're serious, but you make it all sound so . . . so damn casual."

William Fred's voice changed. "It's not," he said bluntly. "Don't ever get confused about that. Never." He turned his body toward the front of the restaurant and waved his hand in a circle in the air and made a pouring motion to Rachel. "Now, let me tell you some things I already know," he added easily.

Toby lay awake in the Valley View Lodge and listened through thin walls to the purring noises of lovemaking in Rachel Whitfield's room, and then the sound of the shower and the door closing and the motor of the car parked outside and the crushing roll of car wheels over the graveled parking lot. William Fred Autry at least had been honest in one thing—off the record.

Toby knew there was another reason that William Fred had consented to have a reporter present during the questioning of Eddie Copeland: William Fred wanted a conduit to the media. The media would be his keen-edged warsword in his courtroom duels. If he did nothing but argue and win his case before television cameras and in the wirespined notepads of newspaper reporters, William Fred could easily sentence Eddie Copeland and Zack Vickers to sizzle in hell with Albert Bailey. It would not be the first such trial by persuasion.

Toby turned under the heavy blankets in the cold room and smiled thoughtfully. It could happen, he thought. William Fred was playing a straight scam as a reinforcement against the brittle uncertainty of the law. He was playing it smoothly, and that was acceptable. Toby did not mind being conned—as long as he knew it was a con. Carl Sandburg had written about that, he remembered. It was in a poem titled "To a Contemporary Bunkshooter"—Sandburg's handslap to the slobbering mouths of maniacal evangelists. William Fred would evangelize, too, Toby realized. He would be a parading instrument of the Lord and Justice, flinging thunderbolts of damnation around like feathered darts.

But what William Fred knew about the murder of Jesse

Wade's family was astonishing—privileged information that he had gathered as easily as ordering lunch from a menu. He had shared it openly with Toby. Off the record. Just being helpful. Friendly.

There were fingerprints on the knife in Doyle's throat that were as distinctive as a Picasso, William Fred had said. And fingerprints in the bedroom and the kitchen. They had already been matched in the crime lab of the Georgia Bureau of Investigation. Albert Bailey had definitely been the one to kill Doyle Wade.

Two cars had been found earlier that day in the Fred Givens rock quarry, three miles from the Vickers home— a red Cadillac and Carl's Ford. It was speculated that the Cadillac had been stolen in Indiana and had been too recognizable and the men had dumped it in the water of the quarry and then had stolen Carl's car after the murders, but had panicked and decided to hide in the mountains until the search had moved away from them.

And there were the records from the Army on the three men. Not a distinguished minute of service among them. "When I finish with that," William Fred had bragged, "it'll read like the diary of Jack the Ripper."

All those truths—inarguable truths—and the gunfire at the arrest. The serious wounding of an agent from the Georgia Bureau of Investigation. The bastards were knee deep in bloodguilt.

Zack Vickers had blithered wildly ("Crazy as they come," William Fred had said) but was too incoherent to believe. Eddie Copeland had said nothing. ("Won't until he knows he's got things his way," William Fred had explained.) But it didn't matter. There would be a Grand Jury indictment (swiftly done) and a trial would be set in Onslow County Superior Court. Defense attorneys would be appointed. ("Poor bastards," William Fred had said bluntly. "I'll have them crawling through their own puke. They won't be able to defend birdshit around here when it's over.")

Even in the embellishments of his own competence, William Fred had not been truly boastful, Toby thought. He had merely spoken freely, as though the trial and conviction of Eddie Copeland and Zack Vickers were preordained. It was only a matter of procedure. And, perhaps, history.

Yet there was something that William Fred was not saying. Toby could sense it in William Fred's sweeping mood—from anger to confidence. It was something hidden behind the blue-colored membrane of his eyes, something urgent and dangerous and determined. And Toby knew it would break and spill out and, if he was not careful, it would blind William Fred.

Toby turned in his bed and reached for his cigarettes and lit one and smoked. William Fred had talked fact—the drama of courtroom theater. A, B, C simple. Evidence summed on a pocket calculator, with its truth of guilt as certain as a digital YES. But Toby knew there were other factors—weapons of emotion that would gather like the arsenal of an invisible army, and that army would move, forcing its weightless power on everyone and everything in its path.

Toby had watched the trembling of the people of the Tickenaley Valley (the same trembling he had recognized in his own hometown, with the escapees and their guns hiding behind their hostage). Now he waited for news of the fury that he knew would fester in the growing bravery of a growing crowd. (That, too, he remembered from the capture of the escapees in his own hometown.) It would be as unsettling as an explosive. *Let us take care of it*, the people of the valley would say. *Let us. Us.* And the more of them that said it, and the more often it was said, the greater the explosion would be. (In his own hometown, men had threatened to burn the jail, and the state troopers had to be called in to quell them.)

And there would be the crusaders against the death penalty, arguing that life was precious, that the death penalty was nothing more than murder begetting murder, like some evil ambisextrous spirit jelling into an unimaginable force. Toby had spent years watching the crusaders at trials for murder. He knew the crusaders would be determined.

And, last, there were the two men: Eddie Copeland and

Zack Vickers. William Fred had counted the evidence against them, but he had not spoken of them—who they were, what they thought, what they would do.

Toby wondered why he thought of them as Eddie and Zack. Why not Zack and Eddie? He could still see them as they were being led from the patrol Jeep to the jail in Tickenaley. Eddie Copeland had walked in a parade gait, his head up, a thin, almost unseen smile pressed into his thin lips. There was an air of arrogance about him that was unmistakable. He was not afraid. Zack Vickers had been different. He had been angry and temperamental. The patrolmen had dragged him from the car with force and Zack had fought with his feet and shoulders and head and had spit obscenities at the quiet crowd of onlookers. Toby knew the two men had nothing in common. Zack was fighting from instinct. Eddie was plotting; he would not die easily.

Toby watched the orange-red tip of his burning cigarette. He could sense Eddie. Eddie was in the Onslow County jail, awake, thinking.

Toby slipped out of the bed and felt the cold air of the room swirling about him. He turned on the light and pushed the heat button on the room heater. The heater fan began to spin noisily.

And, also, there was Jesse Wade, Toby thought as he listened to the heater fan. Jesse Wade, who had been silent. Eerily silent. Not even William Fred Autry knew about Jesse Wade.

ELEVEN

October 21

THE MESSAGE FROM WILLIAM FRED WAS DELIVERED TO Toby on Tuesday morning by Rachel Whitfield. It was seven o'clock when she knocked on his door and pushed quickly inside when he opened it.

"I just got a minute," she said. "I told them I had to run back to my room before it got too busy with breakfast."

"Anything wrong?" Toby asked.

She shook her head. "William Fred called a few minutes ago. He said to tell you to come to the courthouse this morning, at nine o'clock."

"He tell you why?"

"He just said to tell you that," Rachel replied. "Said to tell you to come to the back, at the door in the basement. Said to be there at nine."

Toby looked at her as she leaned uncomfortably against the closed door, her hands behind her back. Her face in the dull light of the room was darkcoated from fresh makeup. A thick odor of perfume seeped from her throat and the sweater she wore under the rabbitskin coat.

"All right," Toby said. "Nine. He say anything else?"

Rachel smiled foolishly and dropped her head. "He said not to tell anybody I'd been here." She looked up at him. The smile deepened. "Said to tell you to be a gentleman."

Toby could feel himself blushing. "Well, you ought to tell him we're running off when this is all over," he said. "Make him worry some."

She laughed easily. "Take more'n that," she said. "You don't know William Fred." She turned at the door. "I—I got to get back now."

"Thank you for letting me know about this morning," Toby said.

"It's all right," Rachel replied. She smiled again. "I just live next door."

She left quickly and Toby sat on the bed and thought of her. The perfume stream from her neck and sweater lingered in the room. She did not require much for happiness, Toby thought. Tenderness, maybe. A few lies. A few inexpensive gifts. Promises. Talk. Christ, so little. Like girls he had known in Alabama. Like girls in too many places. They asked for so little. And maybe that was the way it should be, Toby realized. So little was all they would ever have.

Toby lay against the pillows of his bed and read from the file he had compiled on the Wade family murders. The stories he reread were by Phyllis Warren, who had flown to Fort Wayne on Saturday, two hours after Eddie Copeland and Albert Bailey had been identified, and had filed reports for the Sunday edition of the *Sentinel*.

Phyllis Warren was a respected professional journalist. She did not bother with nonsense, yet her language had surprising power. Once, when drinking, she had confessed to Toby that she had wanted to be a poet, but had never liked the poets she had met. "It's the way they look at you," she had complained. "Like they know something you don't." As a journalist, Phyllis did not have to associate with poets, only people. "There's a difference," she had said wisely.

One of Phyllis' stories had been headlined MOTHER DE-

CLARES SON GUILTY. It was an interview with a woman named Charlene Bailey, the mother of Albert Bailey:

FORT WAYNE, INDIANA: The mother of a man slain in the arrest of three suspects in the murder of a farm family in Tickenaley, Georgia, told reporters Saturday evening that she was certain her son was guilty.

Charlene Bailey, a forty-seven-year-old divorcee and the night manager of a fast-food restaurant in Fort Wayne, admitted openly that her son, Albert Bailey, was capable of murder.

"The police told me Friday night that he was a suspect, and the minute I heard that, I knew he was involved," Mrs. Bailey said tearfully in a twenty-minute interview with members of the media in the living room of her modest home.

Albert Bailey was killed early Saturday morning in the rugged mountains of the Tickenaley Valley of north Georgia. He, with Eddie Copeland and Zack Vickers, was a suspect in the brutal murder of six members of a respected farm family. Those slain included Jean Wade; her sons, Carl and Doyle Wade; her daughter, Macy Simmons; her grandson, Winston Simmons; and her daughter-in-law, Florence Wade.

"I guess I've known something like this would happen," Mrs. Bailey continued. "And no matter what they find out in the trial, I know that Albert had something to do with it.

"He was my son and I loved him, but he got his just reward. Right now, I keep thinking about those poor people who were killed and the families that were left behind to suffer. It's something they'll have to live with as long as they draw breath.

"I know what that is," Mrs. Bailey said. "I've been living with suffering a long time, too."

In response to questions, Mrs. Bailey admitted that her son had been in trouble with the law from his early teenage years.

"I loved him from the time I was carrying him, but then I got divorced and I couldn't do nothing with him when he got older. He seemed to be in trouble all the time. I tried raising him the best I could, being by myself, but I couldn't watch him all the time. He had a mind of his own."

Toby read quickly through the rest of the story. It was a classic profile of a reckless criminal. Albert Bailey had been arrested on suspicion of charges ranging from breaking and entering to trafficking in drugs to rape. He had never been convicted, but a judge had warned him that police would arrest him for nothing more than jaywalking, and Albert had decided to join the Army with Eddie Copeland, a friend and suspected drug dealer.

There was nothing complex about Albert. His mother knew exactly what had happened, and said it openly to the reporters: "He was born bad. That's what he was, a bad seed. Wouldn't matter where he was, or who would have raised him, he would've been the same way."

Toby returned the story to the folder. He knew the arguments for and against the Albert Baileys of the world. Bad seed or bad environment? Toby knew he could never confess it aloud, but he believed Charlene Bailey: nothing would have changed Albert.

Phyllis' story on Reba and George Copeland was different. She had found the parents of Eddie Copeland to be quiet and regretful, frightened by the glare of television cameras and the caustic, exploring questions of reporters. Toby knew by the gentle tone of her story that Phyllis had pitied them. She had written editorially:

They are uncertain people. They are ashamed of what has happened, but they will not say their son is guilty. They say only that he has been accused and they are in prayer that he is innocent. Yet there is a telltale look in their faces: they seem to fear the awful truth that their

119

son may be deeply involved in an alleged crime too
terrible for them to comprehend.

It was unlike Phyllis to assume the editorialist's style,
Toby thought. With Charlene Bailey, she had used direct
quotes (and Toby knew they were not inventions; Phyllis
was too deliberate). The Copelands had affected her, or
disoriented her. She had compensated, Toby thought. He
wondered why.

At nine o'clock, Guy Finley ushered Toby through the
basement door of the Onslow County Courthouse. They
walked along the corridor to a conference room below the
jail. The room was used by the county commissioners for
business meetings. The only furnishings were a large conference table and seven fabric-covered chairs. A map of
Onslow County, with its five valleys color-coded, was
thumbtacked to a corkboard wall.

The others were already in the room: William Fred, Ellis,
a court recorder named Alice Allgood, and Eddie Copeland.

"Eddie," William Fred said, "this is Toby Cahill."

Eddie did not say anything. He sat at the end of the
conference table smoking a cigarette. His hair fell uncombed
over his forehead. His face was unshaven. His eyes, leveled
on Toby, were listless.

"Eddie," Toby said. He saw a flicker of a smile quiver
into the corners of Eddie's mouth.

"You got anything to say before we start, Eddie?" Ellis
asked.

The smile broadened in Eddie's face. He sucked hard on
the cigarette and filled his lungs and let the smoke seep out
of his mouth in a stream.

"Yeah," Eddie said after a pause. He looked at Alice
Allgood. "Before we get started."

William Fred nodded once to Alice and Alice folded her
hands in her lap.

"What you write is what you write," Eddie said to Toby.
"All I want is to make sure that, someday, what I say here'll
be told like it happened, like I said it, and not like some

120

lawyer thinks it ought to be said." Eddie crushed the cigarette hard into the ashtray on the table before him. "They're going to put me on trial and find me guilty and try to put me to death," he said bitterly. "That's what's going to happen." His eyes narrowed on Toby. "And I ain't guilty," he added evenly. "I don't care when you write about it—even if it's after I'm dead. I just want it told. That's what I want."

The room was silent. Alice Allgood moved uncomfortably in her chair and coughed lightly.

"All right, we know the agreement," William Fred said bluntly. "Nothing is to be written about this until the trial is over." He approached Eddie. "You've been advised of your rights and you've been asked if you want a lawyer here and you've said you don't. Is that correct?"

"That's what I said," Eddie replied calmly.

"Is that still your decision? You don't want a lawyer here during this statement?"

"That's right," Eddie answered. "You can put that down."

"We'll ask it again for the record," William Fred told him. "I just want to make sure everybody in here understands that."

Eddie smiled cynically. His eyes turned to Alice.

"This is a statement that you are making of your own free will, knowing your rights," William Fred said. "We're going to ask you to tell us what happened on October fourteen, nineteen hundred and eighty, at the Jesse Wade farm, and what we want is your general description of those events and any events leading up to that date, or after that date, that may be important. Do you understand that?"

"I know why I'm here," Eddie said.

William Fred stood, his hands jammed into the pockets of his suit coat, staring hard at Eddie. He said, "All right, let's get started."

Eddie chainsmoked as he talked. The lighting and crushing of cigarettes were timed to the episodes, like a rhythmic underscoring.

It began, Eddie said, in Fort Wayne, with the stealing of the Cadillac.

"You could say we stole it. Fact is, we took it. Just like we'd done before. Only we didn't take it back that time. You check it out and you'll find out it belonged to a woman named Miriam Broadway and you check her out and you'll find out she's nothing but a rich junkie. Albert was her source, and when her husband—he was a traveling man—was out on the road, she'd call Albert over and he'd get her strung out and then he'd call me sometimes and we'd spend a couple of days partying with her. Albert had a key to the house and the car. We used it all the time. One night we got in the car and Albert decided we'd just keep going. When he called her a couple of days later, she told him she'd reported it stolen. Said there was a lookout for us."

William Fred interrupted Eddie and asked about the stolen car and the drugs that Albert had supplied Miriam Broadway. He wanted to know if Eddie used drugs. Nothing hard, Eddie told him. Grass some. Cocaine once. It was Albert who had the drug connections.

"Go on," William Fred said. "What happened after the phone call to Miriam Broadway?"

"We were up in Kentucky," Eddie said. "We needed some money, so Albert took this twenty-two pistol he had with him and robbed one of those little country stores outside of Lexington. I stayed in the car. When he came out, he said he'd had to shoot the guy that was running the place. I asked him if he'd killed the man and he said he guessed so. Said he looked dead."

"How did he act?" William Fred asked.

Eddie shrugged. "I don't know. Didn't bother him. Maybe he was lying. I never asked again. Albert liked lying about what he'd done."

"Go on," William Fred said.

"Well, that was late at night. We drove on south and Albert remembered that he had a map in his wallet showing how to get to Zack Vickers' place in the mountains. Albert and Zack was friends from the Army. I never liked Zack. He was stupid. But Albert liked him, could talk Zack into doing anything he wanted him to do. Zack helped him burn a car that belonged to this sergeant. And Zack helped him do some dealing off base. Zack was his muscle. Anybody gave Albert any trouble, Zack took care of it.

"But we were up there in Kentucky and Albert said we'd go down to Zack's place and stay a few days and let things calm down and then we'd get rid of the car and go back up to Indiana and Miriam would change her mind about things. Albert had her into him and he knew it. He was her only source. She was scared to try anybody else.

"Well, we went on down to where Zack lived, and I wanted to leave ten minutes after we'd got there. It was like being in a pit. I never saw anything like it. Crazy as Zack was, he couldn't hold a candle to his old man and old woman. They didn't do nothing but sit around and stare and giggle and the old man would tell stories to himself that didn't make a bit of sense, and Zack would listen to him and laugh like he was watching television or something. And the place they lived in, it was like they were moles. After a couple of days I told Albert that I was leaving, and he talked me into helping him and Zack dump the car in this rock quarry Zack knew about.

"Then Albert said he was ready to leave, too, and Zack said he was going with us and he knew where we could get a car. Said he'd been watching these men working on some land down below this mountain a few miles away, and that their farm was close to the highway and there'd be a car down there and we wouldn't have to worry about any men being around. I made Zack show me where the men were working and we watched them for a day—it was on a Monday—to make sure they stayed there.

"And then on Tuesday afternoon we went down to the house, and Zack and Albert had these guns—Albert's twenty-two pistol and a twenty-two rifle and a shotgun—and Albert went up to the house with the shotgun and told the woman that he wanted the car keys and—"

Alice Allgood coughed loudly and rubbed her palms together and pressed a tissue to her lips. She looked anxiously at William Fred.

"So Albert just walked up to the door?" William Fred said. "What happened to the dogs? When were they killed?"

"The dogs?" Eddie replied innocently. "Zack killed them. Right after we first got there, after Albert had gone up to the house. They came running down to the barn, where me and Zack were. A dog and some puppies—I don't know how many. Not many. Zack shot them with Albert's pistol and threw them in a stack behind the barn."

Eddie crushed his cigarette and lit another and looked at the faces staring in disbelief at him.

"Zack didn't like dogs," Eddie said nonchalantly. "Said one bit him one time. Said he'd killed the one at his house."

"All right," William Fred mumbled. "Go on."

"Albert came out with the keys to one of the cars there—there were two of them—and told me to get it started and then he went back to the house. He said he'd tied up the woman and wanted to check on her, but I knew he meant to rape her. Albert had raped a lot of women. Some I knew about in Fort Wayne.

"Anyway, the car wouldn't start and when I went up to the house to get Albert to tell him to find the keys to the other car, I found him in the woman's bedroom. He'd tied her up to the corners of the bed and was raping her and laughing about how he liked old women. Said old women were the best. Zack was behind me in the hallway, laughing, peeking around the corner of the door, watching Albert.

"I told them that we had to get the hell out of there, but they wouldn't listen. Zack said he was going to get him some of the woman. That's when Albert told Zack he'd heard about a man that shot a woman and then had her. Said the body didn't die right away."

"What?" Ellis said sharply.

Eddie drew from his cigarette and spewed the smoke toward Ellis. "That's what Albert told him," he said.

"What did Zack do?" William Fred asked.

Eddie smiled sadly. "It was like turning on a light in Zack," he said at last. "Zack walked over to the bed, put the barrel of the pistol against her head, and pulled the trigger, and then he pulled down his pants and started raping her. I tried to run out of the house, but Albert said he'd kill me if I left. Me and Albert went into the front of the house to look for the keys to the other car, and that's when I looked out of the window and saw the other car coming.

"I thought at first it was the men, but when the car came up in the yard I saw it was two women and a boy. It was about that time that Zack came out of the bedroom, talking crazy."

"Crazy? How?" William Fred asked suddenly.

"Just crazy," Eddie replied. "Some story about Yankees. I don't know. I didn't pay much attention. I was looking out the window and trying to get him to shut up. He was just crazy, that's all."

William Fred nodded and Eddie continued.

"Well, they came in the house and Albert and Zack grabbed the women and the boy ran out of the back door and Zack shoved the woman he was holding to me and he picked up the shotgun and shot the boy in the backyard. And then Albert and Zack started tearing the clothes off the women. They tied one of them up across the kitchen table—she was the older one—and the other one—the pretty one—they made get down on her knees and take turns, you know, licking them, and then they started raping, changing women every few minutes, and Zack kept talking like some fool about the Yankees."

"What were you doing all this time?" William Fred asked.

"Trying to get out," Eddie answered deliberately. "They wouldn't let me. I tried to tell them to stop and get out, but they wouldn't do it. I knew then that it was the end of us. All of us. But I knew they'd kill me if I tried to leave, and they had the guns; I didn't.

"The older woman, the one on the table, started crying out as loud as she could, and Albert took the twenty-two and shot her in the head and pulled the other woman over by the table by the hair of her head and made her watch the woman on the table die. Albert kept telling her, 'You want to live, beg me. Beg me.' And she begged. Fell down on the floor and begged."

Eddie paused and stared at the ashtray. A frown folded

into his forehead. He lowered his head and closed his eyes and then raised his hand to rub across his hairline with his fingers.

"I'd been watching the road from the window because we'd been there a long time," he continued quietly. "That's when I saw the other car coming and I told Albert and Zack I thought it was the men we'd seen at work in the mountains. I recognized the car. And they tied up the woman that was still alive and stuffed her mouth with a dishrag, and waited for the car to come up.

"Albert had a butcher knife he'd taken from the kitchen sink and he killed the first one when he stepped into the house. Zack stepped outside with the shotgun and killed the second one before he could put a foot on the doorstep. Shot him full in the chest.

"We waited around a few minutes to see if the other man would come up. And then they decided to leave and take the other woman with us. Said I hadn't done anything and they wanted to make damn sure I was with them. That's what Albert said, exactly: 'Make damn sure you're with us.' Albert drove and Zack sat up front with him and put me and the girl in the back seat. He had the shotgun aimed at my head and said he'd kill me if I didn't rape her. Zack had her on top of me, with her legs spread out. I didn't have a hard, but Zack didn't know that. And then when we'd gone out a couple of miles, Albert told me to take the girl into a clump of woods and kill her. He gave me the twenty-two. I took her in the woods, away from the car, and I shot the gun, but not at her. I thought we could just leave her like she was, but Albert came over and pushed me aside and raped her again, and then he took the gun— it was the twenty-two, like I said—and shot her between the eyes and then he got Zack to help carry her to this culvert that Zack knew about, which was just up from the clump of trees, and they shoved her body in it, and then we took the car and ran it off in the quarry, like we'd done the Cadillac.

"That's when we went back to Zack's house and then me and Albert went on over to the mountain, to this cave Zack had shown us. He'd been all through them caves, knew them like the back of his hand. Showed us some tunnels where there were stacks of bones. But me and Albert just went to this one cave, where we were when they found us. We stayed there and Zack came over later with some food. We thought we'd hide out there, then slip away a few days later, after they'd stopped looking in the mountains." Eddie paused and looked at Toby. "But they found us, like I knew they would."

Eddie crushed the cigarette he held. He turned his face calmly to William Fred. "And that's what happened," he said. He asked for a glass of water and Guy left the room and returned with water in a Styrofoam cup. Eddie drank in deep swallows and then lit another cigarette.

"That's it?" William Fred asked. "That's your story?"

The expression on Eddie's face did not change. He said, "That's my statement." His voice underlined statement. "That's what happened."

"All of it?" William Fred snapped.

Eddie ran his thumbnail over the Styrofoam cup, cutting an X into the soft material. He said, "When we started, you said just to tell what happened and how it happened, not all the details. That's what you got."

"Uh-huh," William Fred mumbled. He stood and began to pace beside the table, his hands pushed down into the small of his back. "These details," he said. "Some of them must be pretty vivid." He looked at Eddie. "Is that right?"

"I guess," Eddie said.

"Tell me one. Just so we'll know the kind of thing you left out."

Eddie picked up the cup and swallowed again from it. He gazed over the rim of the cup to Toby. "The woman on the kitchen table—"

"Macy," William Fred said sharply. "Her name was Macy."

Eddie's eyes rose to William Fred. He said, "The woman on the table. You know what they found when they found her?"

William Fred did not answer. He turned his back to Eddie.

"After Albert stopped raping her, and after he'd shot her,

he took a fork from the sink and shoved it up—up her. Said it was table-set for the next man."

William Fred's body stiffened. He whirled to face Eddie. "Mr. Autry?"

William Fred turned to Alice Allgood. Her hands were spread before her, frozen. Her face was pale.

"That's enough," William Fred said. He sat heavily in his chair. "I think we've talked enough for today." He looked at Eddie. "Unless there's something else you want to say."

Eddie's eyes blinked lazily, like a man drunk with sleep. He said, "Now I want me a lawyer."

William Fred's body jerked upward in his chair. "Now?" he snapped angrily. "Now? After this? Why not before, when he could be present?"

A smile cracked across Eddie's face. His eyes widened in triumph. "I wanted this writer to know it was me doing the talking, not some lawyer telling me what to say," he replied. He looked at Alice and then at Ellis and William Fred and Guy. "Don't matter, anyway. It'll be the same the next time you ask, and the next, and the next after that. That's what happened. That's how I'll tell it, lawyer or not."

William Fred could feel the heat of anger coloring his face. The son of a bitch, he thought. The lying son of a bitch.

"I'll tell the judge," Ellis said. "You'll get somebody."

TWELVE

October 21

"HUGH, I DO NOT WANT THE JOB. PERIOD."

"Didn't think you would, but that's not the point. You've got it."

"Jesus, Hugh. Jesus H. Christ."

Parker Mewborn bowed forward in the leather armchair and rubbed his temples hard with his fingers. It was mid-afternoon and Parker was still tired. He had returned on Monday from a five-day conference in St. Louis, where he had been something of a celebrity because he lived in Tick-enaley, scene of a mass murder that had received national coverage. He had only been able to say, "I knew them. They were good people, the best in the community." The deaths of Jesse Wade's family had shocked him as it had shocked everyone in the valley. He, too, had been frightened and he, too, had been angry—after he read in the St. Louis newspapers of the capture of the suspects in the Mountain of the Caves. He, too, had been curious about the details.

And he had known immediately what the summons to Hugh Richards' office meant: Hugh Richards, Superior Court Judge of Onslow County, had appointed him to defend Eddie Copeland. It was like being damned without mercy.

"I can't, Hugh. I just can't do it. Good God, I live here."

Hugh Richards cupped the bowl of his pipe in his hands and pushed his body back into his swivel chair. The chair creaked loudly against his bulk. He smiled benevolently at the lawyer sitting across from him.

"Your name is on the list, Parker," he said evenly. "It's your turn in the barrel, and, by God, that's it."

"Shit," Parker said bitterly.

"It's the law, Parker. They got a right. And, just so there's no misunderstanding, I expect you to do it like it was your own life at stake."

Parker looked up quickly and stared unbelieving across the desk at the judge. He said, "You make me do it and it damn well will be my life. At least my working life. My God, Hugh, I won't be able to make out wills in this county if I get involved in this."

"You refuse and it'll be almost as bad," the judge replied. "You'll have me to face."

Parker laughed cynically. He threw his hands in the air in desperation. He leaned his head against the cushioned padding of the chair and closed his eyes and continued laughing quietly.

"You could have given me the Vickers boy," Parker said at last. "Hell, that'll be easy. He's crazy as a goddamn loon. A drunk could get him put away."

"I gave that to Tommy Moss. I don't think Tommy drinks," the judge said dryly.

"You know what I mean."

"I don't know the first damn thing, Parker. In case you missed it, this ain't the courtroom."

"Yeah."

"I expect you and Tommy to work together, after you get through trying to make them rat on one another."

"Zack's not sane enough for any of that," Parker said.

"I don't know. From what I hear, the doctor's got him pretty well tranquilized. Ellis was saying he'd quieted down."

Parker laughed again and opened his eyes. His arms dangled off the armrests of the chair. "Well," he said in a drawl, "I guess Harold's got his case all lined up, anyway." He crossed his arms over his chest and sat thinking. "I had a professor in law school who told us that fighting some cases would be like poking your finger up a boar's ass. I think I can hear the snorting already."

Hugh struck a match to his pipe bowl and sucked on the stem. A blue ring sailed off the bowl and curled in the air.

"Harold Sellers is not the prosecutor," Hugh said calmly. "Harold will be assisting."

"Who is?"

"William Fred."

"Aw, shit," Parker said angrily. "How'd that happen?"

"Officially, it's what Jesse wanted."

"Unofficially?"

Hugh began rocking gently in his chair. He said, "Parker, how much do you think I weigh?"

"Weigh?" Parker snapped. "I don't know. Why'd you ask that?"

"Take a look. How much?"

Parker stared at the judge. Hugh Richards was three hundred pounds or more. The jowls on his face drooped over the collar of his shirt. His shoulders were massive. His thinning gray hair seemed to sprout from a ridge of flesh that padded his skull above his ears. Parker remembered the stories of Hugh Richards as a district attorney, before he became a judge and Harold Sellers became the county's prosecutor. Hugh had intimidated witnesses and juries with his great, trembling size. He had raged his way to success.

"I don't know," Parker said in disgust. "One hundred and twenty pounds. Give or take a ton or two."

Hugh laughed in a roar. The room quivered.

"I was bigger than that when I was born," he said.

"Well, Judge, forgive me for being blunt, but what in hell's name has all that got to do with anything?"

Hugh leaned toward his desk. His chair cried a harsh, metal-voiced scream. He said, as though conveying a secret, "Some things are just naturally too big to be ignored. I expect William Fred's got the same kind of feeling toward this case."

"That same law professor that taught me about a boar's

ass also told me never to become involved in something too personal," Parker said.

"It's his business," Hugh replied.

Parker smiled agreement. "The last time we got tied up in court, he kicked my ass all over hell and half of Georgia."

"He did indeed," Hugh said.

"You know, you could've thrown that case out a half-dozen times."

"But I didn't."

Hugh's voice and look were a warning and a challenge and Parker knew that both were intentional, part of the drama of the law.

"But the preliminary hearing's over," Parker argued. "Why didn't you make the appointments before then?"

"I could say I was waiting for you to get back to town, but that'd be a lie. They didn't want a lawyer. They were asked."

"Both?"

"Both. Zack didn't make up his mind until the Copeland boy made up his. And that was this morning."

"Christ, Hugh, that starts me off at a disadvantage."

"Now, Parker, you know damn well there was nothing to that. You'll get a transcript."

"The Grand Jury's on Friday?" Parker asked.

"That's right."

"Too early for me. I need more time."

"You also know all the Grand Jury's going to do is bind it over for trial," Hugh said in a bored voice. "And this ain't exactly your average case. You or Tommy either one start delaying things and you'll have to have the Secret Service escort you to take a leak."

"I'll ask for a change of venue."

"I expect that."

"But it won't mean a damn thing," Parker mumbled.

"Parker, I'll say it again: this is my office, not the court-room."

Parker nodded. He stood and walked to the window of the judge's office and looked outside through the slats of the blinds. Only a few cars were on the streets. He could see Angus Helton in front of his store, talking to two women bundled in sweaters.

"This is what I'm going to tell everybody," Parker said in a deliberate voice. "I'm going to say I've been appointed to this case by His Honor, the Superior Court Judge, and that it's not one that I've asked for. I'm going to tell them that I became an attorney because I believe people have the right to a fair trial. Then I'm going to tell them that I feel deeply for those dead people, that I am sick that it happened. I'm going to let everybody know that I'm doing this because it's my duty, not because I want to."

"Just don't say anything that'll get you in trouble," Hugh advised.

Parker chuckled over the warning. He continued to stare out of the window. The two women walked away from Angus and Angus stepped quickly back into his store. "There's one other thing, Hugh," he said.

"What's that?"

"I'm going to kick William Fred's ass if I can. I'm going to push him to the goddamn limit. I'm going to fill this county with people who think the death penalty is horseshit."

Hugh turned his chair to face Parker. He put his pipe into his mouth and bit thoughtfully on its stem. "Uh-huh," he muttered. He pulled the pipe from his mouth and aimed it like a pistol toward Parker. "That won't be hard, now, will it?" he said. He added, "Filling the county, I mean."

THIRTEEN

October 21

ON TUESDAY AFTERNOON, WILLIAM FRED CALLED JESSE and told him of Eddie Copeland's statement and of Hugh Richards appointing Tommy Moss and Parker Mewborn to represent Zack and Eddie.

"No matter what Copeland says, he's guilty, Jesse," William Fred said bitterly. "He was lying. I could tell it."

"I guess there's proof enough," Jesse replied quietly.

"There's proof. You're not to worry about it, Jesse."

"Not easy to keep from thinking about it."

"I know it," William Fred admitted. "Just try to put it out of your mind. He won't get off."

"What about the Vickers boy?" Jesse asked.

"Hard to say. I want to try Copeland first. To be honest, Zack may never come to trial. I think there's a good chance he'll be found incompetent—crazy. He is, Jesse. You know that."

Jesse thought again of Isom sitting in the rocker, dressed as a Confederate soldier. "I guess," he mumbled. Then: "You talked to Aubrey?"

"No. I thought I would later. I'm not sure he's ready for it right now. Last time I saw him, he looked bad. Real bad."

"Thought I'd go see him tonight," Jesse said. "Want me to, I'll tell him."

"That's a good idea," William Fred replied. "Maybe it'll help him. Tell him I'll see him in a day or so."

Aubrey Hart lived south of Tickenaley, near the Tickenaley River, in a large house that he had built the year he was married. Once Aubrey had been the strongest man in the valley, a logger with a brawler's reputation. And then he had met and married Judith Miller and Judith had tamed him. Years later, Aubrey's health had failed (a respiratory illness) and he had sold his logging operation and retired to the lakes and rivers to fish. The death of Judith (unexpected, sudden) had left him quiet and reclusive. The murder of Florence had threatened to destroy him.

Aubrey was surprised by the unannounced visit from Jesse. He said, standing in the opened front door, "Good to see you, Jesse. Come on in. I got some heat in the back room."

Jesse followed Aubrey through the house. The rooms leading off the corridor were unlighted and cold and Jesse knew that Aubrey had not entered them since the death of Florence. He did not need the rooms. There was nothing in them except furniture and memories and space. One door was closed. Jesse knew it had been the bedroom of Doyle and Florence. He knew that in the bedroom, Doyle and Florence had begun collecting and storing the goods for their own house. After the funeral, Aubrey had said to Jesse, "You'll be wanting your boy's things. They're all at the house." It was something that Jesse had resisted; he lived with enough reminders in his own home—objects that were like neatly placed souvenirs, always in eyesight, always telling stories.

Aubrey led Jesse to a smaller back room, heated by a propane gas heater that had been placed in front of a closed fireplace. The room was cluttered. A single bed, unmade, was in one corner. A rolltop desk, once used in Aubrey's logging business, was in the opposite corner, beneath two windows. The desk was half open, like a yawning mouth. Papers and magazines covered it. There were only two chairs in the room—a recliner and a rocker. The recliner had a blanket over its back and a slender table beside it. Two glasses, both empty, both stained, and a bowl filled with the hulls of pecans were on the table. There was one picture on the walls of the room: a crude painting of the house. Florence had been the artist. An ancient pie safe was along the wall near the bed. An axe and a shotgun were leaned against the pie safe. The room was dimly lit by a table lamp on the rolltop desk. The room was hot from the row of flames spewing across the face of the propane heater.

"Place needs cleaning up," Aubrey said without apology. "I just ain't got much energy for it, Jesse." He sat in the recliner. Jesse sat in the rocker.

"Looks fine," Jesse told him. "Looks comfortable."

"Just me, it'll do, I guess," Aubrey said. "House gets bigger every day, just me in it."

"I know."

Aubrey looked up at Jesse. He nodded sadly. "You do. I know you do. Sometimes I forget I wadn't the only one."

"Hard to get used to, not having people around," Jesse admitted. "I just try to keep busy."

"It's the thing to do," Aubrey said. "Wish I had the strength for it. Can't hardly get out of this chair sometimes."

"You seen the doctor?"

"I went down there after the funeral. He gave me some medicine."

"You taking it?"

"Trying to. Have to swallow it with milk or Coke, but I do."

"It'll take time," Jesse said. He added: "But you're looking better."

Aubrey pulled the blanket around his shoulders and pushed the recliner back at a slight angle. His body seemed to shrink into the fabric of the chair. He breathed laboriously through his opened mouth and Jesse could hear a coarse gurgling in his chest, like a tearing of the lungs. In the cup of light that fell over his chair from the table lamp, the skin of Aubrey's face was like an ashen shroud over bone.

Aubrey closed his eyes and laughed softly. He said, "That boy of yours, Jesse, he was always on me to go see doctors. He'd read something in some magazine and he'd come in telling me what I ought to do." He laughed again and rolled his head on the headrest of the chair. "He was a good boy, he was. Him and Florence, they made this house seem like something was going on all the time."

"They made some racket, all right," Jesse said. "I always liked hearing it. Almost like they was still kids, like they didn't want to grow up."

Aubrey coughed lightly. He wrapped the corners of the blanket around his waist and abdomen and crossed his hands over his chest, as though feeling for the pulse of his heart. His eyes moistened. His voice became a whisper: "I remember when I quit logging, when Florence was little, and she'd keep on me to take her and Doyle fishing with me. Well, sometimes I'd take them down to the lake and fix up their hooks and just sit back and watch after them. They didn't do nothing but make noise. Great God, they made enough noise to run everything in the lake to the bottom. Couldn't catch nothing, but I liked having them around. They was always into something. I told Judith one time they was bound to get married. Got all their fighting over with when they was little. Guess that's where it got started with them, Jesse. Out there fishing."

Jesse remembered that it was in February—a Sunday— and Doyle had exploded into the house, giddy, shouting (as a boy would brag of a sports feat) that he had asked Florence Hart to marry him and she had accepted. The news had stunned Jean.

"Come on, Mama, what do you think?" Doyle had asked enthusiastically. "You can't just sit there, saying nothing. Your baby boy's getting married."

And Jean had muttered, "I—I don't know." She had looked pleadingly at Jesse.

"Well, I think that's fine, son," Jesse had said. "Florence is a fine girl."

"She's a fine woman, Daddy," Doyle had replied seriously, propping his hands on his hips. "All she's been through, she's a woman now."

"Well, yes, son, she is," Jesse had admitted.

If they had been asked to select a wife for their youngest son, Jesse and Jean gladly would have chosen Florence. She was lovely and energetic and caring and, like Doyle, easily amazed by all that happened around her ("Like the world was a parade and she was in the middle of it," Jean had said of her). Not even the death of her mother had curbed her optimism. She had accepted the responsibility for her father in a matter-of-fact manner. "It's what has to be done," she had said to those who offered their sorrow. "We'll just do it."

The wedding—when was it? June? No, July—ended what Jean had called the summer of parties. It had been a crowded and noisy and colorful wedding, a festival, a celebration of the matching of childhood sweethearts. Jesse remembered the ladies of the valley had declared, "So right. The two of them, they were made for each other. So right."

And Jesse also remembered that Doyle had taken his belongings and moved into the house of Aubrey Hart.

And after Doyle's leaving, Jean had become morose.

"I had a talk with William Fred this afternoon," Jesse said quietly. "He told me the Copeland boy made a statement. Claimed he wadn't part of the killing. Claimed Zack and the other boy did it."

Aubrey did not reply. He stared at the sizzling flame of the heater.

"I asked him about Zack," Jesse continued. "He said Zack may not come to trial. Said Zack could be put away for being crazy."

Aubrey's eyes moistened again. He rubbed them with the knuckles of his hand. He said, "Ellis should of killed them all, when he had the chance."

"Maybe," Jesse said.

"Wish I was younger, Jesse. I'd go do it myself."

"I know how you feel," Jesse admitted.

"Way things are, they'll get off, Jesse." Aubrey paused and licked his lips. His hands fluttered like wings over his chest. "They do and I'll kill them if I can. I swear to God I will, Jesse. Before Jesus, I will."

"William Fred said he had proof," Jesse said. "I guess he has."

"Don't matter," Aubrey replied quickly, angrily. "Proof don't mean nothing. The more proof, the easier it is to get somebody off."

Jesse reached for his cigarettes, remembered Aubrey's illness, and pushed the package back into his pocket. He knew that Aubrey was right: proof meant little in the tangle of law. He could see Aubrey's breathing quicken and quiver across the blanket.

"Aubrey, I want you to do me a favor," Jesse said at last.

"I can, I will, Jesse. You know that."

"I want you to help me build Doyle and Florence's house."

Aubrey looked curiously at Jesse. He stroked his dry lips with his fingers. He said, "What for? Why you wanting to build that house?"

"I want to," Jesse replied simply. "I just want to."

"What'll you do with it?"

"I don't know. Maybe move in it."

"Don't make sense, Jesse."

"I guess not. I just heard them talk about it so much, I guess I just want to see what it'd look like."

Aubrey nodded. He leaned in his chair toward the roll-top desk and pulled papers from it. He handed them to Jesse. "Some of their doodling. All they did around here was talk about that house. Always drawing on a piece of paper, showing me what it'd be. Like a couple of kids playing."

Jesse looked through the papers. There were blocks of rooms, with squares and rectangles of furniture placed along walls. It was like a doll house with doll furnishings.

"Will you help?" Jesse asked. "I talked to Pete Armstrong. He said he'd help out."

"Pete's a good man. Knows his work," Aubrey said. He pulled the chair forward and sat erect, thinking. "I can't do much, Jesse. May be in the way more'n I could help. I reckon you know that. But I'll do what I can."

"That's all I want."

FOURTEEN

October 23

THE TELEPHONE CALL TO ELLIS SPRUILL WAS AT ELEVEN o'clock. It was a woman's voice—whispered, soft—that he did not recognize. She said, "They're coming at midnight. Maybe twenty of them." And then she hung up.

"I've got to go to the jail for a little while," Ellis told his wife. She did not ask him who had called or why he was leaving, and he did not tell her. She watched him dress quickly, heard him dial the telephone and speak to Guy Finley. "I'll be by to pick you up. Ten minutes," he said. Then he left his house.

Ellis drove slowly to the small farm where Guy lived alone. He thought of the call and the woman's voice, tried to place it in his memory, but could not. It did not matter. He knew what she meant. The men of the valley had become brave and restless and encouraged by their boasting gossip; they wanted to pound their chests with their fists of righteousness, to parade in a triumph of a guerrilla strike against coddled killers. Goddamn them.

Guy was waiting outside his house. He looked large in

the heavy coat he wore over his uniform. Ellis could see the frost of his breath in the carbeams.

"What's the matter?" Guy asked as he slipped into the car.

"We're about to have visitors," Ellis answered.

"Aw, shit."

"I want to stop it before it starts. I'd say they'll be at the warehouse."

"Most likely," Guy said. "It'd be like Wyman."

The warehouse was owned by Wyman Stephens. He had opened it in 1968 for the apple growers of the valley and his business had prospered. The Tickenaley Valley apple—the Tickenaley Red—was a hybrid that had been cultivated by the budding knife of Wyman Stephens' father. It was firm and sweet with a deep ruby skin. Over the years the orchards in the valley had spread across pasture lands, and in spring the rich green tongues of apple leaves sprouted in ribbons of rows that ran evenly over the hillsides. Atlanta markets coveted the Tickenaley Red.

The warehouse was south of Tickenaley, at the edge of orchards Wyman Stephens had inherited. A stand of oaks purposely obscured the warehouse from the highway; Wyman Stephens sold only to dealers. He did not care to be bothered by travelers out for a leisurely drive.

It was a large, open building, partitioned only on one end by a plywood wall that divided the storage from the waiting and office areas. An old woodstove was in the office. Ellis knew that Wyman often had card games in the office during the winter off-season. Gambling was Wyman's one obsession and he had a reputation for having remarkable skill. Ellis knew it was a matter of intimidation as well as ability. Wyman was the wealthiest man in Onslow County. And the most determined.

Ellis turned off the headlights of his car as he pulled into the side road leading to the warehouse. He saw the cars parked near the office. Eight of them. There would be more behind the warehouse.

"Goddamn it," Ellis muttered. He stopped the car and got out. "What're you carrying?" he asked Guy.

"My thirty-eight."

"There's a twenty-two under the seat. Get it," Ellis ordered. "I don't plan on using anything, but if we have to, I'd rather it do as little damage as possible."

Guy pulled the pistol from its holster and dropped it onto the seat. He reached for the twenty-two and turned it in his hand, feeling its weight. "I hope you're right," he mumbled.

"Me, too. Let's find out."

The two men crossed the yard of the warehouse to the glass-paneled door. Ellis looked inside. He could see a group of men at a table near the stove. Fifteen, he guessed. He looked again, carefully. Jesse was not among them. That, at least, would make it easier.

"What're they doing?" Guy whispered.

"Damned if I know," Ellis replied. "Looks like they're cutting up some sheets."

"For Christ's sake," Guy said. He laughed sarcastically. "Well, what do you want to do?"

"I'm just walking in there," Ellis told him. "You stay back a little, by the door."

Ellis twisted the knob on the door and shoved hard against it with his shoulder. The men at the table turned in unison to the noise. Ellis stepped into the room with Guy behind him.

"Boys," Ellis said quietly.

"What you doing here, Ellis?" Wyman Stephens snapped.

"I was about to ask the same thing," Ellis replied. He walked across the room. His steps echoed heavily in the empty warehouse.

"You got a goddamn warrant?" Wyman said.

"I need one?" Ellis asked.

"This is private property," Wyman replied sharply, rising from his chair.

"I don't give a shit if it's the halls of hell," Ellis hissed suddenly. He stopped at the table and his eyes swept over the faces of the men. He reached for a patch of the sheet and lifted it and looked at the pattern cut crudely into it. "Jesus," he said. "Eye-holes." He laughed cynically. "Boys, I hope to God this is some kind of Halloween show. If it's not, it's a goddamn joke." He tossed the mask back on the table.

"For Christ's sake, Ellis, go home. This is none of your business," one of the men said desperately.

Ellis whirled to the voice. "None of my business, Boyce?" he snapped. "Then what in hell is my business? What you boys supposed to be, anyhow? The Klan? The Klan ain't never been up here and you know it. Besides, the Klan wouldn't be caught dead wearing those things." He spat on the floor of the office and shook his head sadly. "Y'all would look like shit, boys. I mean it. Like shit."

"You know it's got to be done," the man named Boyce said.

"What's got to be done, Boyce?" Ellis asked quietly. "You got to put on some sheets and go down to the jail and drag those men out and blow their brains out? That it?" He moved around the table, looking at each of the men. "Well, let me tell you, there's four armed state patrolmen down there besides my men and they'll get just about half of y'all before you know what the hell's happened." He kicked hard at Wyman's empty chair and it skimmed noisily across the floor to the wall. His voice rose harshly: "Besides that, goddamn it, this is my job and I don't like nobody but me doing it. When's the last time I meddled in any of your jobs? Frank? Dewey? Wyman? When? You're pissing me off. I already had to kill one man in this and I can tell you it ain't fun."

"Ellis—"

"Shut up, damn it, Wyman," Ellis roared. "I told those men in Atlanta that this place was made out of better men than what you're showing. I want that trial held here, in this town, in this county, where it ought to be. You go down there and they'll yank it in a minute. They even hear about this and they'll pull it."

"Goddamn, Ellis, calm down—"

"You kiss my ass, Wyman," Ellis said, biting the words. "I want all of you out of here, right now, out of my business, and I don't want to hear the first whisper about this going

144

on again. Now, get the hell home, before I start whipping your asses right here, right now."

Ellis stood trembling, his hands curled into fists. The room was still and quiet.

"All right, Ellis," one of the men said meekly. "But them bastards ought to be dead."

"John, I know that," Ellis said. "But that's what the law's supposed to be for, ain't it?"

"The law's weak, Ellis," the man named John replied. "Got too many holes in it."

Too many holes, Ellis thought. Yes, too goddamn many holes. God, John was right. Too many holes. He turned and walked across the office, past Guy, out of the building and to his car.

"I'll drive," Guy said gently. He had never seen Ellis lose his temper before. "Where you want to go?"

"To the jail."

"Why? They're going home."

"The jail," Ellis said sternly.

Guy drove silently to the jail and followed Ellis inside.

"What's going on?" one of the guards asked.

"Nothing," Guy told him. "We just thought we'd come by and check things."

"Nothing going on here," the guard said. "Quiet as a funeral."

"Good," Ellis replied. He opened the door leading to the cells and walked past the two guards sitting in chairs in the corridor. He stood at the cells, staring at Eddie Copeland and Zack Vickers. Too goddamn many holes, he thought again. He saw Eddie Copeland's head move on the pillow and he could feel Eddie's eyes on him. I killed the wrong man, he thought.

William Fred watched from the dark window of his second-floor office as Ellis and Guy drove away from the jail. He looked at his watch. It was one-fifteen. He knew that Ellis had stopped the men before they could make their appearance and he knew no one would ever speak about the night.

He wondered who the men had been—though the guessing would be easy enough. He thought about the man who had called him to tell of the plans of the group: Harley Downs. But Harley would not have been among them. Harley would have been too frightened. He wondered if any of them would become a juror.

William Fred turned from the window and moved across the shadowed office and sat in a chair near Rachel.

"They're not coming?" she asked.

"No," he said. "I don't think so. The sheriff must have gotten to them. He just left the jail. If they were coming, he'd still be around."

"You guess he knows it was me that was calling him?" Rachel asked.

"No. Of course not."

There was a pause. Rachel shifted in her chair and looked around the office. The walls were covered with books, and their odor drifted in the air like a thick musk. The massive oak desk with the massive leather chair behind it seemed foreboding—far too grand, far too imposing.

"I'm scared," Rachel said timidly.

"Why?" William Fred asked. "Of what?"

"I . . . I don't know. I thought there'd be some gunshots, I guess."

William Fred laughed lightly. "No. I knew Ellis could handle that. Nobody out there wanted to kill anybody. They just wanted to make themselves think they could. They wouldn't've done anything even if they'd made it to the jail—except get shot up, if they had tried something stupid. Now, if Jesse had been with them, it would've been a different thing. It would've been personal then. They would have had to do something."

"I guess so." Her voice was small and brittle.

"It's not the men that's bothering you," he said. "It's something else. What?"

"I . . . I don't know," she said. She stood and walked to the desk and touched its slick, oiled top. "I never been here before," she said quickly.

"It's just a place."

"I know that. It just . . . you know . . . feels funny. Standing here in the dark. All them books on the walls. Just feels funny."

William Fred looked at her. She seemed bewildered. Her eyes wandered in awe over the shelves of books. He wondered if she had ever read a book. No, of course not, he thought. Christ, she had never considered books—or anything that was beyond the immediate sweep of her eyes. She had never been taught that it was permissible to be more than she was, more than she had inherited.

"You know why I took this case, Rachel?" he asked.

She smiled foolishly and ran her fingers over the bronze lettering of the nameplate on his desk.

"Do you?"

"Yes," she said simply.

Her answer surprised him. "Why?" he asked.

"You wanted to marry Macy one time," she said casually, looking at his name on the nameplate.

My God, he thought. She knows about Macy. "How do you know?" he asked cautiously.

"My mama told me," Rachel answered easily. "She said you went off to college and Macy married Faron Simmons."

William Fred sat quietly, staring at Rachel. She knew. Yet she was with him, helping him.

"That was a long time ago," he said in a whisper.

"Mama said you'd never get married. She said you never got over Macy."

"That was a long time ago," he said again. "People get over things."

Rachel turned back to him. "I guess," she said. "I don't know."

"That was part of the reason for taking the case, Rachel, but not all of it."

She said nothing. He could see the forehead and cheeks of her face glistening in the nightlight through the window.

"I also took it because I believe those men in jail ought to die for what they've done," he said wearily. "I really believe that, Rachel. They killed. They didn't care. They should be killed in turn. I'm tired of it being easy on people like them. If we don't kill them, it means we somehow condone what they did, that we accept that it's just a matter of chance and circumstance and some goddamn statistic. But it's not. I mean, my God, you don't just murder a body. You murder everything around that body. On my desk, right behind you, there's a phone message from a man named Richard Leamon. You know who he is, Rachel? He's an old friend from law school, living in Atlanta, representing one of the largest real estate developers in the Southeast. You know what he wants? He wants to buy some land on the mountains here. They flew over it today. Took pictures of the whole goddamn spread. They want to put in some kind of vacation resort. Maybe a ski run. They got the idea from watching television reports of the murders. That's what murder does, Rachel. I love this place. That's why I left Atlanta and came back here. I want to see it stay something like it is, because it's best the way it is. But it won't. It won't stay the way it is. They'll come in. I know it. They'll come in with their contracts and money and they'll put up their goddamn ski slope with their snowmakers and they'll murder everything in sight."

He stopped talking and looked at Rachel. He knew he was lecturing and she did not understand him. She understood about Macy.

"Rachel?"

"Yes?"

"Do you know what I'm talking about?"

"I . . . I don't know. I guess."

She did not understand, he thought. But she should. She was from the valley. But perhaps there was a difference between them that was greater than place. Perhaps their only understanding—their only harmony—was in bed when they were naked and locked into each other, frantically pushing in a single rhythm toward a split-second release that was as primitive as the first guttural word out of the first organic mutation that would become man. Dear God, he thought. How could there be such awesome differences?

"Me and Florence used to play together," Rachel said absently. "When we was little. I used to have the seat behind her in school. I guess she was the prettiest girl I ever saw. And the smartest."

Christ in heaven, William Fred thought. He stood and went to Rachel and embraced her. He could feel the body of a young girl against him.

"Come on," he said gently. "I'll take you home."

FIFTEEN

October 24

THE GRAND JURY WOULD CONVENE AT TEN O'CLOCK. AT
eight, Jesse walked into Angus Helton's hardware store and
told Angus that he wanted to order lumber and building
materials.

"What for?" Angus asked in surprise.

"To build a house."

"Whose?"

"Doyle's."

Angus did not ask any more questions. The tone of Jesse's
voice—blunt, hard—warned him against it. It was Jesse's
business. He would not challenge it.

Angus was dazed when Jesse left. He sat on the stool
behind the counter and marked in an order book the list of
materials that Jesse had handed him. Why would Jesse build
the house? he wondered. Was it because he wanted it for
himself, a place to live, away from the slaughterground of
his own farm? Or had Jesse broken under the pressure of
the death of his family? Was he building the house to refute
the death of Doyle? And why now? Why begin it on the

day of the Grand Jury? Jesse had said he wanted to trade
the lumber from his own trees for the lumber in Angus'
supply yard and he had never before done that. The lumber
for Carl's and Macy's homes had been timber from the
clearing of the homesites. Jesse had insisted the same timber
be used. It had been a ritual with him—the cutting and
sawing and building, as though he had not destroyed the
landscape but had only reshaped it. "It keeps me in touch
with what was there," Jesse had once explained to Angus.
"I guess I got it from my daddy and his daddy. They did
the same."

When he finished copying the order, Angus drank a cup
of coffee from the pot that he kept on a shelf beneath his
cash register. Jesse's manner disturbed him. He had mentioned nothing of the men in jail or of the Grand Jury. It
was as though Jesse did not remember that a crime had
occurred. "Damn," Angus said aloud. He called Ellis and
asked him to come to his store. "It's about Jesse," he said
in a low voice. "Just something I think you ought to know."

Ellis was not surprised to learn of Jesse's decision to build
the house. "Just something to keep him busy. That's why
he's been up there clearing away them trees. Keeps his hands
busy. Keeps him from dwelling on things."

"Maybe so," Angus grumbled, "but I wish to hell he
wadn't doing it. People'll start thinking he's crazy. Might
hurt the trial. It could, couldn't it?"

"How?"

"How? I don't know. I ain't a lawyer."

"I don't see how Jesse building a house could have anything to do with it at all," Ellis said. He paused and thought
of Jesse at work on the house. A queasy, uneasy feeling
flowed through him. He thought: Damn Angus. He repeated, "Anything at all."

"But you ain't sure, are you?" Angus said, watching Ellis'
face curiously.

"I just said it, didn't I?"

"You said it twice, matter of fact."

"That's right."

"Ellis, you remember in the Bible when the Lord told Moses to tap once on the rock for water and Moses tapped twice? Moses wadn't sure. Ticked the Lord off."

"Good God, Angus," Ellis said in disgust.

"I always believed a man that had to say something twice wadn't sure about it the first time."

Ellis shook his head in disbelief. "Angus, any man that talks as much as you ought to be scared to death of the Lord, if all that's true."

Angus snorted indignantly. "Maybe so. It just seems funny to me. Him coming down here on the day of the Grand Jury and not saying a word about it. Not saying a word about nothing. You'd think he'd be in town for the Grand Jury."

"William Fred talked to him," Ellis explained. "Those are closed proceedings. No reason for him to just sit around and wait. He'll have enough time in court."

"Just looks funny," Angus muttered. "I know people'll be looking for him. Hope it don't go against him. Jesse's a good man. Hope Parker and Tommy don't use something like that against him."

"Angus, there's nothing illegal about building a house."

"I hear tell Parker's been with that Copeland boy in the jail every day."

"That's his job."

Angus spit a sarcastic laugh from his throat. "Him and that Moss boy, the sons of bitches," he said bitterly. "Don't know why they'd want to take them cases."

"God Almighty, Angus," Ellis said. "They got appointed."

"Yeah." Angus poured another cup of coffee. He offered one to Ellis. Ellis waved it away. "Tell me something, Ellis," Angus said.

"What?"

"I heard Wyman Stephens and some of the boys might be having some plans of their own. You know about it?"

Ellis glared at Angus. He knew that Angus had not heard of his encounter in Wyman's warehouse; it was too early in the morning. He said, quietly, "Yeah. I heard about it. There's nothing to it. Nothing. And anybody starts talking about it, Angus, they're going to get this trial moved down to Gainesville or Atlanta or God knows where. You keep that in mind. Anybody mentions it, you kill it before it spreads."

Angus smiled quickly, then forced his lips into a frown of agreement. "I will," he vowed. "And anybody says anything about Jesse working on that house, I'll let them know it's none of their goddamn business."

"It ain't," Ellis said bluntly.

The Grand Jury of Onslow County returned indictments of murder against Eddie Copeland and Zack Vickers. No one was surprised. "When's the trial?" the people asked eagerly. "Maybe in December," they were told. "The arraignment's next. But that's nothing. December looks like the trial time."

And as the curious talked in huddles about the indictment by the Grand Jury, Jesse and Aubrey and Pete Armstrong began digging along a stretched nylon cord to set the foundation of the house. The cord followed almost precisely the pacing of footsteps that Doyle had made.

By Friday afternoon, the people of the valley and the town had learned of Jesse's plans to build the house, and they wondered aloud, "What's he doing?"

And Angus said to those who asked him, "Ain't nobody's business. I ain't got the slightest idea and I ain't about to ask him. More'n likely it's got something to do with staying at his own place. Must not be easy to do, knowing that's where all your folks were killed. But he's doing it. I saw Anna when she came into town to buy some things. She said Jesse was doing all right out there, but you can't ever tell. She said she went by to cook his breakfast and supper. She said the Preacher didn't like it, Jesse off out there by himself. Preacher told Anna it looked like Jesse was brooding and that brooding could be festering in him like a sore.

"Still, ain't no way to tell what's going on in a man. No way at all. I figure if Jesse wants to build that house, then, by God, that's what he ought to do. Told him I'd help out, if he would take the offer. But he said he could do most of it himself. Said Aubrey would be helping out some and that he'd hired Pete Armstrong. It's what he wants, by God, it's what he ought to do.

"I just know the less said about it, the better it'll be."

Before he left the Valley View Lodge to return to Atlanta on Friday, Toby wrote the story of the Grand Jury indictments. He had ignored a message from William Fred (through Rachel) offering any additional information he might need for his story. William Fred's enlistment of his forces was growing, Toby realized. Guy Finley was one. Guy had spoken privately with Toby after the Grand Jury had adjourned, telling Toby that William Fred was covering the loopholes. "No telling what could happen in this kind of trial," Guy had said solemnly. "Can't overlook anything."

Toby knew that Guy was speaking at William Fred's suggestion. It was one of William Fred's teasing manipulations—making available an obvious contact inside the jail. But William Fred was not a fool. Jesus, not that. He was too thorough to be a fool. William Fred knew exactly what the defense would do. It would wail about the unstable backgrounds of Eddie and Zack, crying in anguished rhetoric about the incivility of capital punishment for unfortunates. The lifestyles of Eddie and Zack would be swept into the courtroom like the stench of a foul incense, and that stench would be as cruel and astonishing as the crime had been. It would be that—that passionate plea—that would be the defense. That and the careful playing of procedure, gambling for a legal mistake, a slipstep reprieve in the ritualistic dance to the gallows. Guy had called it a loophole. But it was more than a single loophole that William Fred had to avoid; it was all of them. The law was a minefield of loopholes, sensitive as hairtriggers, deadly as nuclear missiles. The only way William Fred would be able to counter the melodrama of such gaudy emotional portraits would be the detailing of portraits more gaudy, more emotional—portraits that would be described in the sickening, violent language of assassination.

The story of the Grand Jury indictments was simple: a straight news lead with an obligatory recounting of the events involved in the Wade family murder. It was a story of fact and guarded speculation and mood. Besides the Grand Jury findings (which had been expected) Toby wrote nothing revealing, nothing of substance. It was the journalistic trick of rehash, a rearrangement of sentences and paragraphs he had already written. It was a way to fill the waiting from crime to judgment. But the time of waiting had to be filled. The people demanded it. The people wanted to know, again and again, that the crime had happened and that it was ugly and terrible and that the might of Good was more powerful than the insanity of Evil. The people wanted to read and see and hear and be satisfied that the drama was as great as their imaginations made it.

When he finished the writing, and before he left for Atlanta for the weekend, Toby ate dinner at the counter of the Valley View Lodge Restaurant and watched the six o'clock news report on television. The segment on the Grand Jury indictments of Eddie Copeland and Zack Vickers lasted two minutes. The television report was also rehash, Toby thought. Reused, suggestive videotape, with its blurred rack focusing and sunflares and (in one segment) a slow-motion of Eddie and Zack being led into the courthouse after their arrest on the Mountain of the Caves. Toby knew that viewers would see guilt in the slow-motion faces of the slow-motion men. There were quickcut visuals of the jail and of the cars discovered in the quarry, dangling like slaughtered animals on hoist chains, and, last, a helicopter shot of Jesse Wade's farm, which looked flat, like a postcard photograph.

As he left, Rachel asked, "When you coming back?"

"William Fred want to know?" Toby asked.

"No," she said, embarrassed. "I just asked." Toby could see the hurt in her face.

"I'm sorry," he said. "I don't know. Maybe Monday. At least before the arraignment."

"I guess I'll see you then," Rachel said.

"Sure. Look, I'm sorry about what I said," Toby told her. "I just thought—"

"That's all right," she said. She moved quickly away to a table in the rear of the restaurant.

October 26

PARKER MEWBORN SAT WITH HIS FEET CROSSED—RIGHT over left—and propped on the edge of his desk. In his lap, he held a three-ring binder of notes that he had made in his interviews with Eddie Copeland. Reading them made him ill. His client was a bastard, he thought. His client was guilty and without remorse. His client deserved to die.

He thought about his first visit with Eddie, on Tuesday afternoon, after Hugh Richards had appointed him defense counselor. It had been a playing of moods, of cool-staring messages thrown between the two of them like laser strikes. And if either had won, it would have been Eddie. Parker had taken his anger with him from Hugh's office; Eddie had been calculating.

Parker had rushed the first interview, ending it abruptly. It was meant to be only an encounter, a procedural requirement with little meaning. But Parker had not been able to rub away the portrait of Eddie's face, etched like nail scratches on the tender tissue of his memory. Eddie's face was pale and boyish, marked only by a scar that dripped out of the corner of his left eye and across his cheek like a pink ques-

157

tion mark. His lips were thin. He had the feather trace of a blond mustache matching his straight blond hair. His eyes were deep green, like discolored jade. They were cold and uncaring and Parker could feel them ticking like a bomb.

Parker had asked, directly: "Did you kill those people?"

And Eddie had answered calmly, "No."

"Any of them?"

"No."

"Were you there when it happened?"

Eddie had not answered.

"Who killed them?" Parker had asked.

"The other two."

"Albert Bailey and Zack Vickers?"

Eddie had answered with a slow, lazy blink of his eyes. His eyes had not moved from Parker's face.

"And you want me to believe that?" Parker had snapped.

Eddie's mouth had twisted in an amused smile. "I don't give a damn if you do or don't," he had replied easily. "Prove I did it."

"Well, Eddie, we're off to one helluva start," Parker had said lightly. "You're lying. I can feel it. Jesus, from what I've heard about town, that'll be easy enough to prove, and I haven't seen the first piece of evidence yet."

"Then prove it."

"Eddie," Parker had said deliberately, "they will. You're damn right they will. That's not the point. The point is, how are we going to disprove it? How're we going to keep you from going to the chair? That's the point."

Eddie had not replied. He had not moved. The expression on his face had not changed.

"All right," Parker had continued. "This'll do for now. I just wanted to see you. Hear you say what you've just said. I'll be back. That's when we'll start talking." He had moved close to Eddie, leaning over the table that separated them, and he smiled. "And you'll tell me the truth, goddamn it. You'll tell me everything I want to know, because if you don't, they'll have a parade when they strap you in the chair. And you know what? If you don't tell me what I want to know, I'll be out there with them, riding on a float, throwing stick candy to the crowd."

The smile had stayed on Eddie's mouth. He had licked his lips with his tongue. "What about Zack? You handling him, too?"

"No. No, I don't have that pleasure. A man named Tommy Moss is doing that. I imagine Tommy's already had Zack spilling it out, chapter and verse. He's probably already got you wading up to your asshole in blood."

The smile had vanished from Eddie's face. His eyes had narrowed on Parker, their green coloring changing into dark pits.

Parker uncrossed his feet on the desk, then recrossed them, left over right. He turned a page in the binder and read Zack Vickers' name. Christ, he thought. Tommy Moss had it easy. Defending Zack would be little more than mumbling an incantation of legal procedure. Zack was like an animal maddened by rabies. He was not coherent. The doctor had prescribed tranquilizers for Zack and they had calmed him, but still he babbled insanely about the killing of rabbits and dogs and, when the medicine weakened in his body, he hissed threats against the guards outside his cell. He had even lapsed into stories about the Civil War, like Isom, but they were not complete stories, only fragments of scenes and dialogue. Tommy believed it was because they were the only stories Zack had ever heard, and probably the extent of his education. Zack was certifiably crazy. It would be easy to prove. Tommy would ask for a special plea of insanity and Zack would be shipped off for tests, like the tissue of a tumor, and the doctors who examined him would write to Hugh Richards that Zack was a lunatic. All they would have to do, for God's sake, was ask Zack for his name and then sit back and listen and they would have him fitted for a straitjacket in a split minute. And the people of the Tickenaley Valley would all agree: of course Zack was crazy; everyone knew that.

Eddie was different. Eddie was aloof, caustic, unhurried.

He said nothing to implicate himself in the murders. He had been shrewd, having the reporter present at his statement. It was a bargaining card he had played well, and a mistake that Hugh Richards had made. Eddie knew the reporter was a contact; he knew the reporter would have to write that his statement had been made willingly, before he had requested an attorney. He also knew that Hugh's agreement could be considered a greedy attempt to coerce a confession, and that alone could be worth an appeal.

Eddie admitted only that he had been present when the slaughter occurred, but denied that he had killed or raped anyone. He had been interested only in stealing a car, he said casually. Albert Bailey was guilty. Albert and Zack. But Albert was dead and Zack was crazy. Eddie had his story. He would stick with it. Even the psychiatrist who would examine Eddie would not break him, Parker realized.

On this third visit with Eddie, Parker had said, "Tell me, how do you feel about those people who were killed?"

Eddie's face had furrowed around the question. He had looked up and said, nonchalantly, "Nothing. I feel nothing. I didn't know them. Never saw them. It didn't mean a thing. Just like watching television. Only thing that bothered me was I knew we'd get caught. I knew that from the first minute I saw Albert with the woman in the bedroom."

Parker had raved at the answer. "Goddamn it, you say that in court and they'll come out of the jury box and rip your goddamn guts out. You get in that courtroom, you better be red-eyed with grief. You better fall down on your knees and scream your ass off about how sorry you are."

And Eddie had looked at Parker strangely, with amusement, and he had laughed easily.

Parker closed the binder and tossed it on his desk. He was tired from his reading. He was thirty-eight years old and as athletic as he had been at twenty, but he felt ancient and lifeless. Damn Hugh Richards, he thought. Damn him to hell.

He sat reclining, staring at the binder. He knew it was more than the futility of defending a man who was probably as guilty as Cain; it was also the irritation of his rivalry with William Fred Autry. He knew William Fred too well. Always—*always*—the oddest coincidences seeped into trials involving William Fred. Little surprises, springing out like a magician's props, making everyone gasp with astonishment, and William Fred cuddling them to his case, himself wide-eyed over the "power of fate," as he proclaimed it.

Fate, my ass, Parker thought. It was William Fred's ability to force circumstance, to seize the unexpected and shape it into form before impressionable eyes, that made his "power of fate." Every attorney in north Georgia knew he did it, but none knew how. Trying to counter the bastard was like trying to keep an oyster, slick with its own secretion, lodged in your throat.

And in the trial of Eddie Copeland, William Fred had a personal motive: Macy. Parker remembered the romance, the expectation, the sudden decision by Macy to marry Faron Simmons. It had made William Fred bitter and determined. Those who knew him well believed Macy's rejection had driven William Fred to his success and had brought him back to Tickenaley. He had wanted her to see him, to watch his triumphs, to wonder forever about the mistake she had made. And those who knew him very well believed he had stayed in Tickenaley to see Macy, to watch for her from the window of his office, to yearn for her in each of the women that he conquered in bed. Because of Macy, William Fred would be maniacal in the trial of Eddie Copeland.

Parker closed his eyes and tried to imagine the trial. William Fred would concede all that he could not attack. He would concede Zack's insanity (had already, according to gossip). He would concede the humiliation that the defense could force on Isom and Lou Vickers. He would concede that it was Albert Bailey's fingerprints—not Eddie's or Zack's—on the handle of the knife in Doyle's throat. He would concede that it was Albert's twenty-two that had delivered death to Jean and Macy and Florence. He would concede all those things, and more, but he would not surrender the fact of death by murder. The fact of death by murder would be nailed into the courtroom like spikes.

Maybe that was his secret, Parker thought. Conceding. Ignoring everything but his point. Maybe.

And how would he counter William Fred? Christ, did he even want to? he wondered. He had not slept well since being named to defend Eddie. His family had suffered the indignity of confrontations with those who were angry that Eddie Copeland should have a defense. There had been short, sharp telephone warnings at his home and office. And he did not like Eddie. Eddie was an arrogant bastard. But there was also a nagging thought: maybe Eddie was telling the truth. Maybe he was only a bystander, someone who happened to be involved in the frenzy of a madness too frightening to escape. Nothing that he had said to Eddie had shaken him from his story. That stubbornness was strangely intriguing.

The sudden ring of the telephone jolted Parker like an electric shock. He dropped his feet to the floor and reached for the phone. The caller was his wife.

"What is it?" Parker said sharply.

"Today's Sunday, Parker," his wife said in a whine. "I thought we were taking the children out, to get them away from the house."

"Yeah," Parker replied. "Yeah. What time is it?"

"Three o'clock. Nobody's been over to play with them all day."

Parker looked quickly at his watch. "I'm sorry," he mumbled. "I forgot. Where were we going?"

"You told the boys you'd take them fishing. Did you forget?"

"No. No, of course not. I thought I said next Sunday."

"You said today. They're just sitting here, doing nothing. They don't understand."

"All right. I'm wrapping up here," Parker said. "I'll be there in a few minutes."

"I think I'll take the camera," his wife said happily. "We might find some color left on the trees up by the lake."

"Maybe. I don't know. We'll see. I'll be there soon."

Parker dropped the telephone back into its cradle and stood. He could feel a numbness in his left leg. "Damn it," he mumbled. He began pacing his office, forcing the circulation to sting his steps. He thought about the autumn that had faded quickly into gray. He had always loved the autumn, flaring across the mountains like a majestic fire licking over treeskins, burning freely in the airstreams that flowed through the trough of the valley. Every fall he had taken his sons fishing in the autumn. He had sat on the boat dock of the lake and dropped breadcrumbs into the water and watched tiny fish, almost invisible, feed, leaping like flashes of light to the slick surface of the water. The colors of the autumn were the colors swimming in the water. But the colors had already sizzled and dried into powder and he had missed the heat of their beauty.

"Damn it," he said aloud. William Fred Autry was not worried about a family outing. William Fred Autry did not have a family, only the haunting wish of one. He was probably shacked up with some broad—maybe the waitress at the Valley View, if rumor was correct—telling her how he would handle Parker Mewborn, how he would make Parker Mewborn look like an asshole before Onslow County, the state of Georgia, the United States of America, and the entire goddamn world.

"The son of a bitch," Parker hissed angrily.

SEVENTEEN

October 28

THE REPORTER, TOBY CAHILL, HAD CALLED JESSE TWICE to ask for an interview, but Jesse had refused, even though William Fred had urged him to accept. "Not now," he had said firmly. "Not now."

Jesse had not talked about the death of his family, not openly. Not to Anna. Not to Aubrey. Not to Ellis. Not to Angus. Not to the Preacher. Not to anyone. There was little he could have said. His family was dead. They had been sealed inside caskets and covered with clay and sand and he could not imagine them as they might have been—out from beneath the clay and sand, out of their coffins. He had tried. He had forced the thought of Winston rubbing the stock of his rifle, tucking it tight against his shoulder. And of Doyle, standing under the yellow timbers of his skeleton home, turning in a slow dance to see it all, to feel the wonder of it. And of Carl's silent, watching face. And of Macy. And Jean. And Florence. He had forced each of them into his seeing, each as they had been (or could have been), each in fragments that had seemed whole, but were not.

And even if he talked of those moments, who would believe him? They would want to know things exactly—exactly what and how and why. Jesse knew he could not say, "This is it. Exactly. By its weight and measure, this is what and how and why."

Jesse did not talk about the death of his family because he knew there would be questions that would peel words off his tongue, and those words would be repeated and added to and then added to again, and what he said would soon be exaggerated and bastardized and would become lies. And the lies would come back to him and feed the anger that bloated inside him like a diseased growth.

Jesse had not talked about the death of his family and everyone but the Preacher seemed to understand. The Preacher seemed determined to hear Jesse cry out in anguish, as though the crying would heal him of bitterness and balance his loss with the gain of comfort. The Preacher had called repeatedly, had sent messages by Anna, had talked frankly in Tickenaley about Jesse avoiding the need to face the truth. But Jesse would not see the Preacher. "Maybe later," he said. "Not now." Jesse knew what the Preacher wanted to say. He had heard it from Anna: "Forgive them, Jesse. Leave it up to God, Jesse."

Because of Anna, the Preacher believed he was meant to be an arbiter between the power of God and the jurisdiction of the court. He had been to the jail to see Eddie and Zack, but Ellis would not permit a visit, and the Preacher had left indignant, telling Angus that Ellis was denying Eddie and Zack the right to salvation. "Maybe he's just letting them have some time to think about it," Angus had suggested. And the Preacher had retorted, "The time for salvation is now. Before all hearts are hardened."

Only Anna listened to the Preacher. In the afternoons, the Preacher would visit and sit and hold her hands and stroke them and sigh that he understood her pain. "I know, I know," he would say, and Anna began to sense a serenity, like a dulling sleep. She spoke of her dead husband's desire for children, of his troubled memory of Vietnam, of his fear of finality. "I know, I know," the Preacher said sadly, clucking his tongue, shaking his head slowly. "There are ways, Anna. The Bible's full of ways. Just be patient. Read about Abraham, what God promised him. It took time, but it happened. God gave Abraham everything He said He would. Look to the Bible, Anna. There's an answer there. You'll find it. And you'll know you've found it when you read it. You'll know what to do."

To the people of the Tickenaley Valley, Anna was remarkable. She had strength and composure and understanding. A light globed her face like a pale, pleased blush. "She's found the truth," the Preacher said happily, "and the truth has set her free." And the people who saw her and spoke with her were awed by the peace that seemed to bloom inside her. "She's changed," the people said. "You can see it in her. She's changed."

At night, after she had returned from preparing the evening meal at Jesse's house, Anna would sit for hours with her Bible, reading and searching. She would take her pen and underline passages and say them aloud until they were firm in her memory, and then she would go to bed and dream, and in her dreams she was with Abraham in Ur and Haran and Canaan and Egypt, wandering ancient roadways with nomads who had been blessed by God. She was as Hagar, the handmaid of Sarah, waiting in servitude for God to fill Sarah's womb and make her the mother of nations. And in her dreams, Anna could see clearly the watchful image of God in the blueheat skies above the deserts, nodding His pleasure, waiting patiently for Abraham to become old and tired and uncertain. And Anna wanted to cry out, "God is not lying to you. God is up there, above you, watching. He will give you Isaac. God will give you what He has promised." God's face was that of a smiling, gentle man, who cuddled the embryos of His promise like tiny, bright balloons. And as she watched God watching Abraham, Anna believed God was also whispering to her, "There is a way. There is a way. There is a way." She was a daughter of God. The daughters of God carried the seed that planted the earth.

And Anna would awake in the mornings with her hands crossed over her pubic mound, as in an anointment of praise.

It was raining on Tuesday, October 28, two weeks after Jesse's family had been slaughtered. After his breakfast, Jesse called Aubrey to tell him to stay inside and rest and then he went into his barn and cleared workspace and began to measure and cut the studs and rafters he would need for the house. It was good to be alone, good to be in the barn, good to hear the rain on the tin sheets of the roof. The barn he would build on Doyle's homesite would be small, he thought, but it would be roofed in tin, and there, higher in the mountains, the rain-splattering would echo even into the house and that echoing would bring a hypnotic peace to those who listened.

He worked steadily, laying the two-by-fours across two sawhorses that his father had built and he had repaired. He measured the wood with a retractable tape and then pencil-lined them with a carpenter's square and eased the rip blade of the power saw through each. He coded and stacked each according to the wall frames he had drawn out on paper. When he began the raising of the house, he would only have to keep the walls level and square. He knew Pete Armstrong would watch him carefully. Pete did not like the precutting of the studs. "Need to cut it one by one," Pete had declared argumentatively. "Only way to do it." Aubrey had agreed with Pete. "May work, Jesse," Aubrey had said. "I know that's the way they do things, but Pete's been at it a long time."

"Can't be bad off, cutting them ahead of time," Jesse had said. "If it falls down, it'll be my fault."

"Won't be mine," Pete had said defensively. "I guarantee that."

Pete was an artist as a builder. Once he had left the Tickenaley Valley to work near the town of Helen, building log cabins for an Atlanta investor, but he had returned in a few weeks. He did not like Helen, with its false Alpine storefacings. To Pete, the town of Helen was gaudy and sad, no one cared for anything but money, and the storefacings were like cheap circus billboards. To Pete, the construction of a building was the noblest work a man could do—if the man put something more than nails into it.

As he worked under the drum of rain on the tin sheets of the barnroof, Jesse thought of Isom and Lou Vickers. They were to be pitied. Something they could not control, did not fully understand, had yanked harshly at their already delicate equilibrium. They knew that Zack had been arrested, but they were not certain why. Men they did not know had been to their cabin with papers and they had taken away things belonging to Zack and had left Isom and Lou huddled in a corner of their cabin, wagging their heads at the men they did not know. Zack had done something wrong, they were told. Zack was dangerous. And to Isom, Zack had become an enemy who needed to be killed. To Lou, Zack seemed to be little more than a presence, a visitor who had lived with them, had left and returned and belonged (somehow) to the cabin and the furnishings of the cabin. Jesse believed that Lou had forgotten the child who had been Zack. If the instinct of a mother was still in her, it was vague.

Perhaps they were, in their old age, now completely mad, Jesse thought. As a young man, he had heard of the strange behavior of Isom and Lou Vickers, who lived in a lean-to cabin in the darkest part of the mountains. "Don't go hunting up on that ridge," the other boys had warned in cautious whispers. "Old man Vickers liable to shoot you. He's crazy. My daddy said so." And as the legend of Isom expanded in the imaginative stories of boys, the more fearsome he became. But Isom was not fearsome, and through the years on his trips to Tickenaley to sell or trade his honey, the image of the insane mountain man was tempered to one of a foolish recluse who was harmless and humorous. Sometimes the town boys would go out along the road to walk beside Isom's wagon and ask him questions and listen to his quaint, poetic answers. ("You hear a owl hoot, go poot in your boot.") The town boys said, "Old Isom's better'n television. Somebody ought to put old Isom on a program."

But Jesse could not forget the way he and Ellis had found Isom a week earlier: small, thin Isom dressed in a bulky Confederate Army uniform that made him appear like an emaciated puppet. Holding a pistol used in the Civil War. Telling a rambling, violent story in a voice that was not his, but a mimic of memory. And Lou. Lou sitting beside the fire, idly staring at the flames, oblivious to Isom and the two visitors.

Aubrey had said that it did not matter if Zack was crazy, he should be electrocuted. "You shoot a mad dog," Aubrey had argued. "Ain't no difference. He killed, he ought to get the chair."

And part of Jesse agreed with Aubrey; part of him did not. He could not forget Isom and Lou. His pity for them made him also pity Zack.

Jesse slipped his marking pencil into his carpenter's apron and walked to the door of the barn and opened it. The rain fell steadily from a silver cup of clouds swirling over the mountains out of a black loop that circled in a perfect O along the horizon. He saw Anna's car, and lights in the house. He had not heard her arrive—the noise of the power saw, he realized. She was often at his house, often unexpected. But Jesse had said nothing to her. She had become more talkative, like someone nervous with energy, yet she was more attentive. She talked of things to be done, of plans that seemed to occur to her instantly, in flashes. But, like Jesse (at least to Jesse), she did not speak of death. She had found comfort, she said, in the counsel of the Preacher. "I know I'll find the answer, Jesse," she said. "I can feel it." And Jesse listened and remembered Jean's weak plea about the Preacher: "He just makes me feel better."

He lit a cigarette and stood smoking it in the doorway of the barn and watched the rain pelting over the yard. Across the yard, through the lighted window of the house, Jesse could see the silhouette of Anna. She was standing in the living room, beside Jean's chair. Across the yard, through the rain and the gauze frost of the sheer window curtains, he thought Anna was wearing one of Jean's dresses. Her hair was pulled up, off her neck, as Jean had worn her hair. And for a moment—quickly there, quickly gone—he believed it was Jean.

EIGHTEEN

October 29–30

GUY FINLEY KNEW THEM BEFORE THEY SPOKE. EDDIE Copeland's features had been taken from each, as though surgically structured. Eddie's eyes from their eyes, Eddie's mouth from their mouths, Eddie's chin from their chins. Eddie Copeland looked exactly like his parents and his parents looked exactly like each other. It was as though twins had given birth of themselves, and the child was a spare, a duplicate. Guy could feel himself staring, too startled to speak.

The woman said, "We're Eddie Copeland's parents. We'd like to see him, if we could." She handed Guy their drivers' licenses and Guy glanced at the identification information. Reba and George Copeland. There was a Fort Wayne address.

"Yes ma'am," Guy said politely. He looked at the man's face. It had the same expression as the woman's. "Ah, does Eddie's attorney know you're here?" he asked.

"No," Reba Copeland answered. "We—" She looked at her husband. "We just decided to drive down. We didn't tell anyone."

"I'd like to call the attorney first," Guy told them. "Just to let him know."

"Of course," George Copeland said after a pause. His wife nodded.

Parker Mewborn was surprised at the news. Eddie had insisted that he wanted no contact with his parents, that his parents were not to be involved. Curiously, it had been Eddie's only offer of consideration. "They've had enough from me," he had said. "Leave them alone."

"Tell them to wait until I can get there," Parker said to Guy. "I think they'd better know what they're in for."

"Yeah. I think you're right," Guy agreed. "Parker?"

"What?"

"You're . . . nothing. I'll tell them."

As they waited in the outer room of the jail, Reba and George Copeland sat silently, as though they had lost their power to speak. Speaking was of little value. They had said their words thousands of times—said them in weeping, in shouting fights, in threats, in prayers, in anguish. And now there was no reason to say them. They could not change what had happened. And they could not unleash themselves from the look-alike son who had been drawn in equal portions from each. They were inextricably bound to a child who was a mutant, though his mutation could not be seen. Somewhere in the genetic circuits of their lives—back, perhaps, in the madness of a prehistoric instinct—the first cell of their son was formed as a microscopic puddle of evil. There were no words to undo what had been unstoppable, no incantations, no rituals, no illusions. To his parents, Edward White Copeland had become what he had always been.

Parker, too, was astonished by the physical similarities of the parents and the son. He had arrived ten minutes after the call from Guy and had taken Reba and George Copeland into the sheriff's private office and talked with them about their son's plight.

"I'm going to ask for a change of venue, but I don't think I'll get it," Parker told them. "I did ask the court to gag the press as much as possible, and the judge agreed. I couldn't take the chance on what might happen."

"But we've talked to the press," Reba Copeland said.

"I know. I've got the clips," Parker told her. "Nobody can stop that. It's what Eddie might say that concerns me." He paused and looked away, at a plaque from the Georgia Sheriff's Association hanging at a tilt on a wall of Ellis Spruill's office. Then he said, "I've got to tell you, he's belligerent. Not at all bothered. He's very difficult."

"Did he do the killing?" George Copeland asked.

"That's not for me to say," Parker replied. "The court will answer that. I'll defend him against the charge."

"Was he there when it happened?" Reba Copeland asked.

"Yes."

"Then he did it," she said calmly.

Parker stood and paced the office. He could feel his hands dampen and the heart-rush of nervousness pump through his neck. He loosened his tie and circled his index finger around the collar of his shirt.

"Mrs. Copeland," Parker said, "if you say that to anybody, there's nothing I'll be able to do. Nothing. It doesn't matter if I prove he was asleep under a shade tree, they'll find him guilty."

"But he is," she protested. "We know it. We're his parents. We know it."

Parker looked at the two people seated in front of him. They were hurt and tired and resigned. Their son was guilty. They were ready for it all to end.

"Please," Parker said gently. "Please let me help. Say whatever you want, but not that. Not that at all."

Parker watched them carefully, watched a unison of movement that was like a choreographed dance. Both leaned slowly back into their chairs at precisely the same time, in the same manner, with the same rhythm. Both dropped their heads to stare into the floor before them. Both folded their hands in their laps, right over left. Both drew in a deep breath—together, in the same sighing sound. Parker thought: Jesus God Almighty.

"What do you want us to do?" George Copeland said at last.

Parker continued his pacing, wiping his face with the palms of his hands, forcing the image of what he had seen out of his thinking. "There's only one chance, I think," he said. "The Vickers boy will plead insanity, and, God knows, that'll be accepted. I think everybody expects that. And he'll probably be a witness for the state, but his insanity plea would probably discredit him there. The Bailey boy's dead. Eddie's saying it was Vickers and Bailey that did the killing. We'll get all the reports at the arraignment on Friday, but from what I already know, there could be an argument in his behalf on that claim." He leaned against Ellis' desk and pulled his handkerchief from his pocket and began to rub the perspiration from his palms. "What I'll probably do is suggest that the influence of Albert Bailey was the motivating factor in Eddie even being at the scene of the crime. I'm going to suggest that they all went there to steal a car— Eddie admits that—and that the other two started killing and that Eddie tried to stop them, but feared for his own life. Maybe I can at least get a life sentence out of it."

"But all that's a lie, isn't it?" Reba Copeland said.

Parker looked sadly at her. "Ma'am, I don't know," he said. "That's why I used the word 'suggest.' I don't know if it's a lie. You'd know that better than me. But that's exactly what you suggested—whether you meant to or not— in one of those newspaper stories. You said you'd always worried about his relationship with Bailey."

"And that's true," Reba Copeland said hesitantly, "but I didn't—"

"Ma'am, I can only work with what I've got," Parker said quietly. "That's all I can do. Nothing more."

And Parker watched them turn to face each other, in the same motion, at the same time, with the same expression. He did not know why, but he was afraid for Reba and George Copeland.

* * *

"Eddie."

Eddie Copeland was stretched across his cot on his back. His left arm covered his eyes.

"Eddie," Parker called again.

Eddie moved his arm and lifted his head from the pillow. His eyes flicked lazily from Parker's face to the faces of his mother and father. He had known they would be led to him. From his cell window, he had watched their car arrive. And he had waited, thinking. The lawyer had not called them; he knew that. The lawyer would not challenge him. His parents had arrived because it would be expected, because there was nothing else for them to do.

"Eddie, your parents are here to see you," Parker said.

Eddie dropped his head back on the pillow and covered his eyes with his forearm. "Who gives a shit?" he said casually.

Reba and George Copeland stood helplessly at the door of the cell, looking at their son. They did not say anything. They turned silently, politely, both nodding to the guard in the corridor outside the cells, and walked away. Their son had dismissed them and their trip was over, their resignation complete.

Parker followed them outside the Onslow County Courthouse to their car. He said nothing to them about their son's action in the jail. He stood beside their car and thanked them for talking with him. He pledged to do all he could for Eddie.

"It might help if you could just sit down and write out things you remember about Eddie," Parker suggested. "Just mail it to me, here." He handed them a business card. "Just anything at all." He extended his hand to them. There was a strength in their handclasps, and it surprised Parker. "I can't promise anything," he confessed. "But there's always a chance."

"Thank you," Reba Copeland said. She touched her husband's arm in a signal. Her husband nodded and started the car and backed into the street without looking back at Parker.

"Jesus," Parker said aloud. "Jesus."

* * *

At a Texaco service station on the highway leading north from Tickenaley, George Copeland paid with the exact cash for a filled tank of gasoline and a quart of oil, and asked the attendant, "Where's the house that Jesse Wade lives in?" The attendant drew the directions on a coarse paper towel used for windshields. "Thank you," George said politely.

The directions were easy to follow and George and Reba Copeland drove slowly into the yard fronting Jesse's house. Both got out of the car and walked to the door of the house and both knocked lightly on the door. They waited, but no one answered. They walked around the house into the back-yard. They saw Jesse coming out of the barn, shouldering three lengths of two-by-fours to be loaded onto his truck.

"Mr. Wade?" Reba Copeland called.

Jesse stopped and looked up at the couple. He thought they were twins.

"Yes," Jesse answered.

"We just came by to tell you we're sorry," the woman said.

"Yes," the man said. "We're sorry."

Their voices were strangely lyrical. "Sorry?" Jesse asked. He slipped the two-by-fours from his shoulder and leaned them against his truck. "What do you mean?"

"For what happened," the woman said. Her voice was like a song. "It was wrong. We're sorry for that."

Jesse stepped forward. Their faces were familiar, but he did not know why. He asked, "Who are you?"

There was a deadening silence. The small smile left the woman's face. She and the man turned to look at each other. Both turned back to him.

"Just—just people who care," the man answered hesitantly.

"Do I know you?" Jesse asked.

There was another pause, another look, another turn back.

"No," the woman said. "You don't."

Jesse could feel the muscles in his back quiver, like a warning. He could feel his legs tensing in a backward step. The man and the woman stared at him for a moment, then turned inward to each other, like a dance, and walked in step to the brown car and drove away. Jesse did not move until the car had disappeared and the thin wake of dust from the road had drifted back to the ground.

The following morning, on Thursday, October 30, a jogger found the car on a side road outside the city limits of Chattanooga. A garden hose (new, from a hardware store in a nearby shopping center) had been attached to the exhaust pipe by electrical tape, then run into the back window. Reba and George Copeland were leaning together in the exact middle of the front seat, in positions that were exactly the same, and the investigating police officer was so conscious of their bodies that he ordered pictures made before removing them from the car. "I never saw anything like that," he said to a newspaper reporter from the *Chattanooga Times*. "They looked like—what'd you call them twins that're hooked together? Siamese? That's what they looked like. Strange how some things happen."

Parker insisted on telling Eddie about the death of his parents. "Not you, not Ellis, but me," he said to Guy Finley, spitting the words angrily. "I want to see if the son of a bitch has any feelings at all."

At the cell, Parker ordered the door unlocked and he stepped boldly inside. He stood glaring at Eddie, who sat on his cot, nonchalantly smoking a cigarette.

"You look pissed," Eddie said.

"I am."

"So am I," Eddie replied. "It's boring."

"They're dead, you asshole."

Eddie drew from the cigarette and swallowed the smoke. He looked unblinking at Parker.

"Your parents. They killed themselves," Parker said evenly.

Nothing flickered in Eddie's eyes. Nothing about him changed.

Parker stepped forward. "Did you hear me?" he snapped.

"I heard you," Eddie said calmly.

"It means nothing to you?" Parker asked. "Nothing at all?"

Eddie dropped the cigarette on the floor and covered it with his shoe. "That's none of your goddamn business," he said. "Get out of here."

"What's the matter with you?" Parker demanded. "They were your parents, for God's sake."

"Get out," Eddie commanded in a hard voice.

"Listen to me, damn it," Parker said angrily. He reached for Eddie and caught him on the arm and Eddie ripped away and coiled on the top of the cot.

"You ever touch me again, you bastard, and I'll kill you," Eddie hissed. "I'll cut your fucking guts out and feed them to you."

Parker stepped back. His hands were shaking. Eddie was like an enraged animal that had been trapped unexpectedly. "Okay," Parker said. "All right." He turned and quickly left the cell.

At noon on Thursday, Jesse went into Tickenaley to buy a blade for his power saw and Angus told him about the suicides of Reba and George Copeland. It had just been on television, Angus said. "The twelve o'clock news. I just saw it, but I heard about it earlier." There had been talk at the courthouse that Eddie had refused to see his parents and they had left distressed. It was a sad sight, Angus volunteered, having them stand there at the cell and their son turning his back on them. Just proved what kind of person Eddie was. "That'll be his undoing, Jesse," Angus pontificated. "Don't know what else it takes to show that man's guilty as sin. He just don't give a shit."

Jesse knew instantly that his visitors on Wednesday had been the Copelands. Their faces matched the pictures of Eddie and that was why they had been familiar. They had been to see him as a ritual of their suicides, like travelers readying a trip. It was something they had to do, something on a list of last things.

178

"This the blade you want, Jesse? The one for plywood?" Angus asked, standing on his stockladder.

"Blade?" Jesse said. Then: "Yes. That's it."

"Good Lord, Jesse," Angus said lightly. "You forget what you come in for?"

"I was thinking about what you told me," Jesse said. He would not tell Angus about the visit from the Copelands. Angus would be awed and that awe would grow spectacularly in his mind.

"Word is, the boy don't want to go up to the funeral, so they're going ahead with the arraignment tomorrow," Angus said seriously. "Just shows you what kind he is, Jesse."

"I guess," Jesse said quietly. He paid for the blade and watched Angus wrap it in thick paper.

"How's the house going, Jesse?" Angus asked suddenly.

"All right," Jesse answered. He motioned with his head to the rain falling outside. "Been too wet and cold to do much except cut some of the studs, back in the barn."

"Aubrey holding up?"

"Doing good. Being out seems to help him some."

"Damn good thing you're doing for him, Jesse," Angus said. "Damn good."

NINETEEN

October 31

IT WAS IRONIC, PARKER THOUGHT. THE ARRAIGNMENT FOR
Eddie Copeland and Zack Vickers was scheduled for ten
o'clock in the Onslow County Courthouse, and it was October 31. Halloween.

Now, early in the morning, Parker sat in the noise of his
family at breakfast, and felt greatly relieved. The arraignment would be closed to the press and public, and that would
benefit Parker. The sensational suicides of Reba and George
Copeland would hang over the proceedings like a condemnation. Their deaths had been played boldly across the national news like an anthem of anger, in voices that cried,
"What have we allowed ourselves to become?" There was
a kind of empty pity in the self-ending of Reba and George
Copeland, but there was also an ominous confession: "Our
son is guilty; our shame is too great to bear." That was the
way the national news was saying it and that was what
people who may have attended the arraignment would have
seen in the unfeeling face of Eddie Copeland. When Reba
and George Copeland killed themselves with the acid gas
of carbon monoxide, they also began the killing of their

son—unless Parker could stop it by some magic as ancient as an alchemist's dream. But Parker did not trust himself. His own anger toward Eddie was bitter. He could not understand Eddie's arrogance. Eddie's parents were dead. Because of their son, they were dead. The last words they had heard from their son were, "Who gives a shit?" And if Eddie cared that they were dead, it was an undetectable emotion.

"Look at their costumes, Parker, before they drive me crazy," Parker's wife said.

Parker looked at his two children. They were dressed in black costumes, imprinted with the bones of skeletons. The faces of the skeletons were smiling harmlessly.

"Trick or treat," his sons cried in unison.

The arraignment before Judge Hugh Richards lasted forty-five minutes. There were no surprises. The charges against Eddie and Zack were formally introduced, but the detail reading was waived by consent. The defendants entered pleas of not guilty, Zack by reason of insanity. William Fred presented the documents of the prosecution, including the witness list, crime lab report, and autopsy report. Zack was ordered to Central State Hospital in Milledgeville to begin testing. The trial for Eddie was scheduled to begin on December 8.

The arraignment was almost dull, like a read-through of a script waiting to be performed.

Outside, in the wide corridor of the courthouse, the waiting media surrounded William Fred as though he had summoned them. He stood before them, a concerned wrinkle ironed into his forehead, angrily chewing on his lower lip. Yes, he said, the results of the arraignment were distressing. Yes, he said, he was exceedingly disappointed that Zack Vickers had been referred to Central State Hospital for testing. "By the very act of hiding and resisting arrest, he demonstrated that he was aware of the act of murder," William Fred told reporters in a heavy, serious voice. "We can only hope—and be confident in that hope—that when the examination is completed, he will be returned to stand trial."

"The son of a bitch," Tommy Moss whispered to Parker, as the two men stood behind William Fred and listened. "Goddamn him."

"What about Eddie Copeland?" a reporter asked William Fred.

William Fred crossed his arms dramatically and shook his head slowly. He said, "I don't intend to argue my case here in the hallway, but I can say this: we intend to pursue the conviction of Eddie Copeland as vigorously as possible. Here is a man whose actions probably weighed heavily in the tragic decision of his parents to take their own lives, and those actions will not be ignored."

"Jesus," Tommy hissed to Parker. Parker walked away, pushing past William Fred and through the reporters, shaking away their questions. Fuck him, Parker thought. He'd better be ready. Parker could feel energy flashing through his chest and into his mind. His quarrel with being Eddie's attorney was over. He could hear William Fred's voice behind him, like a taunt. He'd better by God be ready, his mind repeated.

"What was that about?" a startled reporter asked Toby Cahill.

"I don't know," Toby replied, lying. He knew what was happening inside Parker. In one statement, William Fred had aimed the weapon of his assault and cocked it and stood at the hairtrigger. The emotion William Fred would spill in the trial of the murderers of the Jesse Wade family would flow as thick as the bloodletting of the victims, and Parker and Tommy were only bothersome obstacles. William Fred would be more than an attorney; he would be an avenger and he would cause wars of illusion that would destroy anyone or anything opposing him.

"That was Copeland's defense attorney, right?" the reporter asked Toby.

"That's right."

"God, he looked mad."

"I guess he was," Toby said. "I guess he was."

* * *

Jesse was not prepared for the news of the arraignment. It was as though the crime had again been committed, as though the bodies of his family had been exhumed and used as stage props. The old pictures were back, like television reruns—he and Anna leaving the jail, the blood of his grandson smeardried on his face; the helicopter shots of his farm, circled by police cars; the ambulance carrying the body of Florence from the culvert; the sheet-covered body of Albert Bailey; the march of Eddie Copeland and Zack Vickers from the police car to the jail; the family-portrait pictures of Reba and George Copeland and their look-alike son. And there was William Fred before the reporters, his face furrowed, his voice strangely deep and deliberate, speaking of justice and right and determination.

Somewhere in the calm of the day—for William Fred had said it would be nothing more than routine procedure— a madness had escaped, and Jesse could sense the fury of it howling over the mountains like the preamble of a frightening storm. He could smell it in the dust-dry powder of the leaves of autumn. He could hear it in the jabbering of voices that called him to the telephone to ask how he felt about the rulings of Hugh Richards. ("Letting Zack go," they bickered. "Just plain letting him get off.") And when he could no longer bear the madness, he left in his truck and drove to the site cleared for Doyle's house, and he sat in the cab of his truck, in the dark, and listened to the monotonous hum of night-singers. He wanted only to be alone, to stretch and feel the fibers on his muscles weaken into sleep. He thought of a bluejay he had watched in the spring of the year. The bluejay had glided to the ground and nestled into a pile of dead water oak leaves and, fanning its wings and tailfeathers, had eased itself down onto its chest and, turning its head to one side, had slept like a sunbather.

But Jesse could not sleep. The sickness of the deathscene tightened in his stomach and his mind yelped with the high cry of his own voice, rising out of him as he held his grandson. And the face of his grandson floated like a steam cloud through his closed eyes—lifeless, streamed with the blackening fingers of blood, made darker by the haze of the day-night freeze of Dark Thirty. He could hear the echo of his cry and the echo would not stop—voice answering voice answering voice. He threw open the door of his truck and pulled himself out and knelt weakly beside the front fender and vomited in a hard, gagging seizure of pain. And then he rose and stood beside the truck and he could feel anger erupting inside him with each heart stroke, spreading uncontrollably, burning even across his skin.

It was late when Jesse returned to his home. He saw Anna's car and the house lights in the living room and kitchen. He had forgotten about Anna. She, too, must have remembered and ached. I should have called her, he thought. I should have gone to her. She is all that is left.

He parked the truck beside her car and entered the house through the kitchen. Anna was in the living room, in the chair beside the window. A small fire was burning in the fireplace. She sat holding a cup of coffee, a wool shawl that had belonged to Jean over her shoulders. Her hair was pulled up, in the style of Jean's hair.

"Are you all right?" Jesse asked.

She studied his face carefully. "Yes," she said quietly. "There's coffee. William Fred called. I told him you were asleep, to call back tomorrow. And that reporter called. Toby Cahill."

Jesse nodded. He went into the kitchen and poured a cup of coffee and mixed sugar into it and returned to the living room and sat on the sofa. "I went up to the clearing," he confessed. "I suppose I needed to be alone some."

"Me, too," Anna said. "I took a walk. In the pasture. Carl loved to walk back there. Sometimes, at night, the two of us would go walking and Carl would make whippoorwill calls and tell me about nights when he used to camp out in the mountains."

"He liked doing that. I remember."

Anna sipped the coffee and leaned comfortably into the chairback. She looked through the glass of the window to the silhouette of the barn umbrellaed by the fluorescent yard light. She could see her own ghost image in the glass. She smiled and the image smiled. She touched her neck with her hand and the image touched its neck.

"Do you know what happened to Carl in Vietnam?" she asked, without turning from the window.

Jesse looked at her. She seemed older. Jean's shawl fit over her shoulders and around her neck exactly as it had on Jean. "He never said," he told her.

She continued staring through the window. "There was a man—a North Vietnamese—who was hiding in one of those little villages. Carl was out with three other men, trying to find out what was going on near where their unit was located. This North Vietnamese started shooting at them, and ran into a hut. I guess he knew he was trapped. He started killing the family that lived there. One by one, he shot them and threw them outside. Children, mostly, since the men had been taken away to fight the war. He kept killing them and throwing them out, like birds he'd shot. And Carl went through the door by himself and killed the man with his hands." She paused. "Did it with his hands."

Jesse could see Carl again, outside his home, hanging in the shrubbery. He swallowed to hold the sickness that rolled in his stomach.

"I think he was doing that again," Anna said softly. "I think that's what happened when he was killed." She turned to face Jesse. "I know it hurts, Jesse. I know it. But I think Carl was that way. I think he loved so much that he couldn't stand people who would—" She paused and raised her hand to her mouth and cupped her lips lightly, then slipped her hand to her throat. "Who would hurt others like that."

Jesse could not answer. He was numb. He stared into the cup that he held in his hands. The fire in the fireplace spewed as one of the burning logs rolled against the irons.

"He wanted children, too, Jesse," Anna continued gently. "More than anything, Carl wanted children. He believed the Wade family name had to be kept alive and strong. One time, before we married, when I was just visiting, he took me out to your barn and showed me all the things that you'd put up from your family. He knew all about it. Named me everything. Who it'd belonged to. What it was. Said he'd like to have the same kind of thing someday, so he could leave it to his own children." She smiled and pulled the shawl around her bare neck and gazed into the fire. "Once I found a sheet of paper with names on it—boys' on one side, girls' on the other. It was his hope. But he couldn't. At first, the doctors thought it was in his mind—that's how I found out about Vietnam; he told them about it in one of the interviews we had. But it wasn't in his mind. It wasn't. They told us in July, right after Doyle and Florence were married, that he was sterile. That we couldn't have children. That's why he'd seemed so . . . so melancholy. That's why he watched over Doyle so much."

Jesse's mouth began to quiver. He drew a deep breath and held it.

"It's all right, Jesse," Anna said in a voice that was almost a purr. "It's God's way. Carl would have accepted it as that. I do, too. You and I are here. I think Carl knew that. I think that must have been his last thought. That you and I would be left."

Jesse placed the cup on the end table beside the sofa and sat rubbing his face with his hands. He remembered the conversation with Carl at the clearing as they watched Doyle and Jean crossing the land, Doyle ebulliently embracing his homesite with his sweeping arms. "What he needed," Carl had said. "Mama."

"I hope you don't mind me telling you those things," Anna said. "I've wanted to for days. I've been praying about it. I think you needed to know."

"It's all right," Jesse replied. "I think I'm just tired." He looked up at her. "I'm glad you said what you did. I'd wondered about it some. It was Carl's business, but I'd wondered about it." He stood and crossed to her and leaned his face to her forehead and kissed her lightly. He could smell the presence of Jean in the shawl, the light, fading perfume that had rubbed from her skin. "I'm glad you did," he said again. Then he went into his bedroom and lay dressed in the dark across his bed.

There was a sound of weeping, controlling itself, in the living room, and Jesse lay motionless and listened and remembered Jean. She had wandered through the house at night so quietly she had seemed weightless. He had imagined her floating, shimmering like a moth, fluttering on invisible wings. Sometimes he had heard the rocker (thought he had heard it), but he could not remember hearing Jean. Not her steps, not even her breathing. She had been only a room's width from the bed, separated by a single wall, but it had been a space more distant than that between continents. Whatever had driven her to her sleepless nights (sitting beside the window, staring outside), Jean had kept as private as fear.

And now it seemed odd that Jesse could hear Anna's smallest breath. He could hear her move across the room, could count her steps, could hear her brushing her hands across the curtains of the windows, could hear the sound of cloth pulled against cloth. She was controlled now, Jesse thought. He wondered if he had angered her, leaving as he had. She had confessed intimate truths that she had kept sealed inside, and bringing them to him was like the giving of a rare offering. He did not want to offend that offering. Anna was right; there were only the two of them left. Not blood kin, but kin. Related by custom and habit and by a deathscene that both had discovered and could not rub out of their thinking. Anna had proved her devotion. She had not left him to mourn in her own seclusion. She had found the grace of God, she professed. The Preacher had given her assurance; she did not need anything else. Yet Mercer Dole, the doctor, had said to Jesse that Anna was intensely fragile. "Don't be fooled by the way she looks and acts," Mercer had warned. "She could be all right, or she could break. Everybody thinks she's faced the reality of Carl's death. I don't believe it. Be patient with her," he had advised. But Mercer was wrong, Jesse thought. Mercer had not seen her strength. Anna was not fragile. When she talked of Carl, her voice was almost happy.

Jesse heard Anna crossing the room again, heard the faint click of a light switch, heard her movement along the corridor leading from the living room to the bedrooms, heard the opening of the door near him.

"Jesse." Her voice was as thin as a child's.

He raised his head from the pillow and looked at her framed in the doorway, in the graymetal light of the darkened room. She was nude. A bluish film of light swept tight against her body, like a translucent gown. Her breasts were small, round faces. The muscles of her abdomen were in perfect symmetry. The black, feathered mat of her pubic hair triangled off the cradle of her hips. She stood proudly, looking at him. A small, calm smile was on her face. Her upswept hair was soft against her temples.

"I want us to have a son, Jesse," she said evenly.

"Anna—"

"No," she said suddenly. "It's the way. We can keep the name alive. Your seed—the seed of a Wade—in me. Don't you see it?"

"Anna—"

She shook her head gently and the smile broadened happily. "In the Bible, the daughters of Lot went to him at night and conceived children by him, because there were no heirs. It says it in the Bible. 'And we will lie with him, that we may preserve the seed of our father.' It says it, Jesse. And from their children, tribes of people were born, Jesse, tribes that are still alive today. I knew when I read that in the Bible—I knew what I had to do."

"No, Anna, no," Jesse said gently, pulling himself up against the headboard of the bed.

She stepped forward into the room and the light swam over her body, changing colors against her skin. The oil of her hair shimmered. "I will go away and have the child and say that I was pregnant with Carl's child," she said in a whisper. "No one will know, Jesse. It could be. It hasn't been that long. It could be." She stepped forward again. "Please," she said in a begging voice. "I want it to be. I am at my time now. I can feel it."

Jesse eased from the bed and stood looking at her. He could see two strings of tears, like thin silver chains, slipping from her eyes. He stepped to her and embraced her, as if embracing a child, and she turned her face on his chest, beneath his throat, and caught his shirt with her hands and held to him.

"We will not let it die, Jesse," she said softly. "I will take your seed and we will make a nation of people, like it says in the Bible. It's God's way of keeping us alive."

Jesse could feel the pulsebeat of her body and the terror of her handgrip pulling against his shirt. "You're wanting me to do the finest thing a man can do—father a child," he said quietly. "It's—it's like giving me a gift. But I can't, Anna. I can't."

And he held her close and let her cry painfully into his chest.

TWENTY

November 3—14

ANNA HAD SLEPT FROM MERCER DOLE'S INJECTION OF tranquilizing fluids, and the distance of the long ride from Tickenaley to Tennessee had been as dark and vague and restless as a bothersome dream.

And now she was at the hospital in the town of her parents, in a narrow, high bed, and she knew without a mirror that her face was as white and antiseptic and cool as the linens that had been pulled tightly over her and tucked under the sides of the mattress. The room itself was white—walls, ceiling, flooring, furniture, medicine cups, bathing cloths. The room blended into itself and into Anna, and she, with the colorless face of exhaustion, blended into the room. She lay very still, feeling the weight of the bedcovering over her body, and stared at the plastic tubing hanging from the collapsing plastic container. The tubing was attached to a funnel of a needle that had been slipped into a vein in her forearm (a white adhesive strip holding it firm), and a color-less liquid fell from the collapsing container in a slow-dripping so controlled it seemed to Anna to evaporate in the throat of the tubing.

She knew she had been in the room for two days, perhaps three. She had slept heavily from the intoxication of dulling drugs and, when awake, she was drowsy and disoriented. Her mother was always there when she awoke, sitting in one of the white chairs, holding a damp, white face cloth. Sometimes her father was there also. He was always standing near the window, unobtrusive, silent. He always left immediately after she awoke, as though his presence was unsanitary, as though the privacy of a woman in a hospital bed was a darkly secret matter not to be invaded. "I'll be right outside the door," he would say to Anna, nervously. "You need anything, your mother'll get me." And sometimes the doctor was there, an older man with a face like a painting of sadness. Anna liked his voice. It was more mumble than language, a soft growling of deep-chested warnings and irritation. He reminded Anna that he had tended her illnesses for more than twenty years and that he did not enjoy coping with her if she did not want to help in the healing. "Up to you," he said. "You bring yourself about, little lady. I, by God, mean it. I can get you over being tired, but I can't do the first damn thing about facing facts for you. Nobody but you can do that."

She had asked for Jesse during the first confused hours in the hospital, but he was not there. "He's gone back home," her mother told her. "But he's been calling, asking about you." There was a vase of flowers—daisies, the only color in the room—from Jesse. The faces of the flowers were arranged like an umbrella of soft yellow dots, and in her blurred understanding Anna imagined them as a balloon hovering above the windowsill.

She remembered little of what had happened. Stabbing, bright fragments, like a searing, strobing light. Jesse holding her. The uncontrollable sobbing. The doctor, Mercer Dole. The movement of things about her. The car. The droning of a motor sound and then the hospital.

And the Preacher. The presence of the Preacher had been powerful. The face of Abraham of her dreams had been his face, the voice of God of the desert skies had been his voice.

The touch of healing, like a freezing, had been from his hands.

Anna remembered the healing. It had been on the afternoon of the arraignment. The Preacher had sat with her and held her hands and assured her that nothing was too awful for God. She remembered the hammering of her heart muscle, pumping and echoing, its floodtide of blood battering against her tongue. She remembered the healing.

"Can God heal?" she had asked.

"Yes," the Preacher had said.

"By the touch of hands?"

"Yes. If God chooses."

"By the touch of your hands?"

"My hands? Yes. If he chose to."

"Then do it. Touch me."

"God may not choose that way, Anna. He may—"

"Are you afraid?"

"Afraid? No. It's—"

"You've never healed with your hands? Is that it?"

"God has not asked me to do that."

"But you can. I can feel it about you. God's in you. Like God in the stories of Abraham."

"God was different then."

"No. God is the same. You said that. You said God never changes. You said people change."

"Yes. Yes. I believe that."

"Then touch me. Heal me. Heal me with God's might."

She remembered lifting the Preacher's hands and forcibly pressing them against her temples. She remembered the Preacher's tremble as he cried in anguish, "Heal this child, O God. Heal her."

She remembered the cooling sensation, a brittle ice-coating of peace. And she remembered whispering, "I am healed."

The Preacher's face had paled with awe. He had eased away from her, gazing in astonishment at the palms of his hands, as though his hands had become divine weapons. "Thank you, God. Thank you, Jesus," the Preacher had muttered tearfully.

But Anna knew it had not been God. It had been the Preacher playing God, believing in the trickery of the mind. And her mind had broken like a thin, invisible crystal too delicate for dreams.

Anna did not know what liquid chemicals slow-dripped into her body, but its feeding gave her strength and she began to feel the rose of blood return to her face and she became quickly alert. She spoke honestly to her mother and father and the doctor about her illusions. "It happened," she said. "I will not lie about it. It happened. I believed there would be a magic to it, that I could carry my husband's child through my father-in-law's seed. But there isn't any magic. I was hurting and I didn't know it." She paused and added, "I still am hurting, but at least I know why."

Two days later the doctor (still bewildered, mumbling his uncertainty) released her from the hospital and Anna moved into her parents' home.

"For now," Anna told her parents emphatically. "Only for a short time, until I feel stronger. Then I'm going to Tickenaley, where I need to be."

The time was spent quietly (her parents still wondering, still watching). She thought of Carl and she permitted herself to yearn for him, to ache because of his death, to wonder what might have become of their lives.

She spent hours looking at albums of photographs her mother had collected. Her mother had written "Anna and Carl" in the forward sheets of the albums. The backs of the pictures were dated and the places of the poses identified. And she reread the letters that Carl had written to her from Tickenaley and which she had stored in a trunk at her parents' home. The letters were brief, tender, guarded. The letters were as reserved as Carl had been.

She had met Carl in Knoxville. He was a soldier returning home from Vietnam, she a student at the University of Tennessee. She had at first been amused by him and then she had liked his awkwardness and gentleness, and had pursued him with letters and long-distance telephone calls. His reserve had been almost impenetrable and she had been deliberately patient—always light and nonchalant. And then she had lied about the holiday trip to Florida and a chance for a side-trip visit to Tickenaley. She knew immediately she belonged there.

"I think I'll move here," she had said to Carl.

"Only way you can get in is for me to marry you," Carl had replied.

"I like it enough even to put up with that," she had said. "Even that."

Now Carl was dead. In time, Anna knew that the obsession with what she had lost would become bearable. In time, the losses would be replenished.

Each day since returning to her parents' home, Anna had written letters to Jesse—brief, hurried notes, coded with hints of disenchantment. He had written only twice to her. Both of the letters had been short and rambling and, to Anna, humorous. Jesse had never written letters; Jean had. The writing of letters was unnatural for Jesse. It was a skill that artisans had, where thought and eye and muscle moved with agreement and easy grace. In one letter, Jesse had struggled to explain the progress of the building of the house. He had written, "It gets more wood on it every day." Anna had laughed gleefully, startling her parents.

Anna wrote her last letter to Jesse on November 14. It read:

Dear Jesse,

Today the doctor declared that I was well, which I knew anyway. And this will be the last letter from here. I am coming home, probably on Tuesday or Wednesday. I think it's time. I need to face up to things there, not here. Besides, I think my parents need the rest. They keep watching me like I am a baby taking its first steps. It seems like they follow me around with their hands put out, ready to catch me if I fall.

I sometimes feel like a foreigner who can't speak the language of the house where I am staying. We don't really talk very much here, and when we do, my parents come up close to me and make funny faces with their words. (I think they believe I've gone deaf and have to read their lips.)

I know they care and that they're worried about me and it's not easy on them, but I think I'll be better off (and they will, too) when I get back to Tickenaley. That way they won't have to ask me questions and I won't have to try to answer them. I'd like to tell them how easy it is to talk to you, Jesse, but I don't think they'd understand it. I'd like to be able to tell them that you handle things better than anybody I know— especially when those things are surprises. I suppose my own parents know that some things are easy to break, and that makes them afraid of handling those things. And maybe that's the way they feel about me.

But the world goes on. Reagan will soon be President. Voyager I is in the clouds of Saturn. (I do watch the news now. Maybe that's a good sign.)

I want to be back home, Jesse. Where I belong. But it will be a different person who returns. I promise.

After she had mailed the letter, Anna went into town and shopped for a Christmas present for Jesse. She selected a book on cabinet designs and blueprints, then replaced it. Jesse made furniture from his imagination. After an hour, she purchased a new toolbox (knowing Jesse's was old and hard to lock). She then went into a restaurant and sat alone and drank hot tea and thought about returning to Tickenaley and the Christmas of one gift given, one gift received.

She wondered if Jesse had forgiven her. He had said there was nothing to forgive, yet she wondered. She knew she should be ashamed, but she was not. The woman who had appeared nude before Jesse was a woman possessed with grief. But that woman had been put away, exorcised.

There was only one bewilderment: Anna wanted to feel a child growing inside her. She wanted to feel the heat of the saltwarm flooding that would bring a child-to-be leaping into her. She wanted that instant (she would know it by its release) to seize her like a stroke, so that the spark-touch of the child-to-be would be like the sizzling of an exploding star.

And Anna sat in the restaurant and remembered standing nude before Jesse. Even in her disorientation, the feeling of that want had moved inside her, more powerfully than it ever had. But it was not because of Jesse, she argued. It was the obsession. It was the mindgame of her illusion. It was the persuasion of dreams. She looked at her hands. They were trembling.

TWENTY-ONE

November 17

ON THE DAY THAT HE RECEIVED ANNA'S LAST LETTER FROM Tennessee, Jesse went to her house and cleaned it and bought an arrangement of dried flowers and placed it in the middle of the kitchen table. And then he called Mercer Dole and told him that Anna was returning to Tickenaley.

"I know," Mercer said. "I got a call from her doctor. He said she seemed better, but she was still shaky."

"Anything I ought to do?" Jesse asked solemnly.

"Just let her be herself. She may be a little embarrassed around you for a time. Reassure her that everything's all right. If she says anything about me, tell her I said it was a private matter, and that's the way it'll stay."

"You want to see her when she gets in?"

"Not unless she wants to," Mercer said. "Physically, she's fine. And emotionally, she's better. You won't see much difference, Jesse. She'll make sure of that. You just won't hear as much talk about God, I'd guess. And she'll stay to herself more."

"All right," Jesse replied.

"Question is, Jesse, how are you?" Mercer asked bluntly.

"I'm all right."

"You know people are a little worried about you."

"No reason to be."

"Well, maybe not," Mercer mumbled. "You're staying to yourself a lot, that's all."

"I've been working," Jesse said.

"So I hear. If you need me, call."

Mercer Dole did not understand, Jesse thought. The work helped. The work kept him isolated, on the mountain, where he wished to be. From the mountain, from the homesite, he could see the valley below him, and daily when he and Aubrey and Pete worked—when the weather was fair enough for work—he would look out from the plateau the Indians had raised, over the silk tops of the white pines, and remember the timechanges of the valley. The migrations—the wandering farm families—of the thirties, long before the Depression would end. The airplanes of the World War Two forties: whale planes—the C-46s—flying in solemn formation over the mountains, often pulling gliders behind them like banners. The timber cutters of the fifties and the invading bulldozers and tractors that followed the timber cutters, turning the timberland into fields and pastures. The orchards that began in the sixties, when the budwood of the Tickenaley Red became plentiful, filling the fields and pastures where the timber had been cut and the land plowed. The drive-through land speculators of the seventies, stopped (or slowed?) only by the uncertain calculations of small-print numbers on the stock market pages of newspapers, and by the belligerence of sand-desert nations coiling like snakes to strike, hissing loud enough to be heard across the world on color images that were somehow spit invisibly through space and then re-formed whole, but in miniature, on television screens.

All these things Jesse had watched from the mountains of the Tickenaley Valley. And of all that had happened, the most vivid memory was his earliest—the migrations.

He had been only seven or eight, but Jesse remembered the mule-drawn wagons driven by thin, bent men in overalls and straw hats, their women faceless under broad-brimmed sunbonnets, their children shy and hollow-eyed and pale and dumbfaced, trailing after the wagons like leashed animals. Sometimes they stopped at Jesse's father's house for well water, or to sleep in the barn. And Jesse watched the women cook over campfires, stirring flour and water into a gravy and breaking stale bread and rationing it among men and children to dip into the gravy pan. And he remembered how silent they had been. They did not talk. "Leave them alone," his mother cautioned. "They're just God's poor people, wandering around the world like the children of Israel. Don't go poking at them. Don't you do it, now." And his father added—privately, away from his mother—another warning: "You watch out them stealing. Watch out them talking you out of pennies." And Jesse protested, "But they don't even talk, Daddy." His father glared at him wisely. "They talk if they know you got pennies," he said. It was a warning that became a dare for Jesse. One night, with a large family staying in the barn, a family with children near his own age, Jesse appeared outside the barn, shaking pennies in his hand. The jingling drew faces. "What you got?" an older boy asked. "Pennies," Jesse answered. The older boy looked to make sure there were no adults around. "You want to buy something with them pennies?" he asked Jesse. "What?" Jesse said. "Sister. Take her out yonder in the field," the boy replied. "What for?" Jesse asked. "Give you some." "Some what?" "Some pussy, you damn fool, you." The boy's voice turned to a growl. He pulled his sister forward. She was no more than twelve. "Look here," he said to Jesse, yanking up the girl's dress to show her body. "You ever seen that, boy? She's got tits. Look." He flipped his fingers over the girl's small nipples. Then he laughed. "You don't even know what it is, do you boy?" he asked sarcastically.

Jesse remembered the boy's face—tired and angry and desperate and hurting. He remembered the girl's body, with its pale skin and ribbed chest. He remembered his own fear. He remembered putting the pennies—there were twelve of them—on the ground before the girl, and then running into his house.

And when the people of the migrations had left, chasing rumors of mill towns and company-charge stores, the valley itself had become silent. At the end of the summer of the leaving ('35 or '36? Jesse could not remember) a bewildering calm had settled over the mountains. For days, for weeks, there was no rain, no swirling currents of air, no sounds of movement. The people—those who did not leave for the mill towns—stayed close to their homes and watched the skies and waited in the stillness. Jesse remembered his father, sitting on the porch of his home, staring at the limbs of the trees, watching for a single leaf to rise and flutter on a windsigh. Jesse had never forgotten the look in his father's face as he watched the valley die about him. Jesse, too, had watched the valley die—that part of the valley that had been his. It had died abruptly, obscenely, person by person, on a single afternoon of history, leaving the land and the buildings to waste, or to be sold. And that was the bitterness that had settled in Jesse: murder was more than the killing of bodies; it was also the killing of place and time and possibilities.

The house began to take its shape during the weeks that Anna was in Tennessee, yellow ribs of timbers rising in contrast to the gray winter woods bordering the plateau at the base of the Mountain of the Caves. Jesse and Aubrey and Pete had capped its roof rafters with plywood and the house had seemed, at last, permanent.

And each day, as he had worked, Jesse knew the time for the trial of Eddie Copeland was nearing. When he did go into Tickenaley (when he had to go), a gathering was quick to find him, to tell him they were confident that Eddie Copeland would be condemned by any jury—anywhere. The people were indignant, but there was also a disturbing eagerness about them, an expectation that flashed in their eyes. They were like impatient crowds waiting for intense sporting events. And everyone seemed to know far more than Jesse about the pretrial proceedings. Jesse knew that Zack Vickers had been declared incompetent to stand trial, that he was insane; the people knew that Zack had had to be restrained in an examination at Central State Hospital. Jesse knew that Eddie Copeland had been uncooperative with Parker Mewborn; the people knew that Eddie had vowed to say nothing more about the trial, had arrogantly accused Parker of being responsible for his parents' deaths by allowing them to see him. Jesse knew that William Fred had declared that Eddie would die in the electric chair; the people knew that William Fred had traveled to Atlanta numerous times to review his case with his attorney friends.

These were the stories that seeped out of the Onslow County Courthouse and were embellished in tellings that seemed always to begin in Angus Helton's hardware store and then spread by messenger into every place of business in Tickenaley. It was mid-November, cold, and the trial was becoming too personal for the people to bear. "He'll burn," they said to Jesse. "The son of a bitch won't be smirking then. I'd pay to pull the switch, by God, I would. Don't know how you keep from going down there and blowing his goddamn head off, Jesse."

The people said to Jesse, "You're to be admired, Jesse. Keeping calm like you do. Not many men could handle it like you do."

And Jesse's bitterness deepened and he became angry with himself because he could not show what he felt.

Jesse had tried not to think of Eddie Copeland. But there were always reminders. The presence of Eddie was in his house, in the rooms where his family had died. The face of Eddie was on television and in newspapers and magazines. The name of Eddie was in the mouths of the people. The evil of Eddie was pressed on him by William Fred, who would not permit Jesse to forget. William Fred had appeared one night at eleven o'clock and had dropped the collected stories of Eddie on Jesse's kitchen table. "This bastard killed your family, Jesse," William Fred had said bitterly. "You read these stories every day. Every day. I hate the bastard. I want you to hate him also." And he had left without waiting for Jesse to reply.

Jesse had read the stories—from the serious journals that used the word "behavior" like a divining rod to the tabloids that bellowed about circumstance and pressure, anointing Eddie with a kind of suffering celebrity. Jesse read the stories until the biography of Eddie Copeland became part of him. Eddie Copeland: born of quiet, middle-class parents in a quiet, middle-class community, obedient and pleasant as a child, accomplished as a young athlete, admired, promising. And then the radical turnabout, as though he had been infected with a virus of madness. (But wasn't all the world mad in the late sixties and early seventies? the tabloid philosophers asked.) From age fourteen, Eddie had been constantly in trouble. By nineteen, he had been arrested thirteen times. He had always been guilty (or so the stories suggested in the name of professional journalism), but he had never been convicted. In the Army, Eddie had spent as much time in the brig as he had in formation. He had been suspected of a civilian homicide in a nightclub, but the witnesses who had clearly seen the soldier-assailant would not testify against him.

The stories told also of Eddie's parents. Their deaths had made them tragic figures, like characters in stage dramas. Eddie had defeated them, had driven them into an isolation that was as tightening as a noose. After years, there was no one to counsel them, no one to console them but themselves. (Didn't the madness of the world affect everyone? the stories asked. Wasn't the madness contagious? Wasn't it like a plague?) And Jesse could not dismiss the look-alike man and woman who had stood in his yard, telling him they were sorry. They had seemed like tourists (at first, Jesse had thought they had heard of his barn and its antiques). But, also, there had been a sense of dignity about them, as if they were performing a ceremony of honor. The look-alike parents of Eddie Copeland had accepted death as courteously as they would have accepted applause.

Jesse had read all the stories. And then he had realized what was not in the stack of clippings that William Fred had thrown across his kitchen table in anger: there was not a single story about his own family. Nothing. Nothing. Nothing.

Part 2 _____ THE TRIAL

TWENTY-TWO

December 8–9

PARKER MEWBORN'S OFFICE WAS ON THE SECOND FLOOR of the Whitmire Building, directly across the street from the Onslow County Courthouse. From the window of his office, Parker could see into the cell windows of the jail, the dark steel bars blurring like scratches behind the slick facing of the outer glass. Sometimes he could see Eddie Copeland standing languidly at the cell window, smoking a cigarette, staring out. From that distance—behind the glass of the cell window and behind the hard, straight lines of the bars—Eddie was a shadow, a distorted silhouette of a person. There was a man-form, but no features. It was as though the someone, the something, was more imagined than real. And sometimes Parker would see an aura, like a bubble of gray-green light, around the window. Parker wondered if the light came from Eddie, or if the light was a presence, the skin-coloring of an ethereal counselor, that had invaded Eddie.

Before seven o'clock, December 8, Parker was in his office. He closed and locked his door and sat at his desk with the lights off and thought of the trial that would begin at nine o'clock. He held in his hands the letter that he had received on November 1. The envelope had been postmarked in Chattanooga. He had read the letter a dozen times—more, perhaps. He read it again in the window light.

You asked that we write something of our son, but we do not know what to write. We love him. But he is evil.

He was a good baby. We used to watch him sleep. He was peaceful when he was sleeping. He sucked his thumb and we would pull it out of his mouth and listen to the small drawing sound his empty mouth would make. Sometimes he would smile in his sleep. We knew he was dreaming happy dreams. Watching him sleep was something we liked doing.

We did not see the change. I guess we thought of him as a baby sleeping in his bed. We did not see what happened and it happened before us. He changed. We got calls telling us of things he had done, but he said he didn't do them, and we believed him. And then the police came and they warned him and then they came back and took him away and we'd have to go down to the jail and get him out. And he kept saying he hadn't done anything, and we believed him.

We don't know when he changed, or why. I guess we couldn't see those kinds of things in him.

He will say he didn't help kill those people, and you will believe him. But he will be lying. We know.

We wish we did not love him. He is evil. We do not know what to say to you. We do not know what else to do.

The letter was written in a delicate cursive—the woman's hand—but was unsigned. Parker was intrigued by the almost poetic rhythm of the letter's innocent confession, and he knew it was one of the last acts of Reba and George Copeland before they died, as though the words of the letter might calm them and forgive them and save them. But the words were too weak; the words had been too often said, were too worn. Parker wondered again why they had mailed the letter. Habit, perhaps. Methodical people completing a task. He thought of them driving the streets of Chattanooga, searching for a street corner mailbox, patiently searching, while the rubber garden hose lay coiled in the back seat of their car. Mailing the letter could have been nothing more than habit. They had visited Jesse to apologize. And that, too, could have been habit.

There was only one segment in the letter that haunted Parker: "He will say he didn't help kill those people, and you will believe him. But he will be lying. We know."

To Parker, it was more than an observation; it was a warning. He wondered if he would believe Eddie. Or if he did already believe him.

Parker folded the letter back into its envelope and slipped it into his briefcase. No one knew about the letter, not even Eddie, or Donald Bridges, who was assisting Parker in his defense of Eddie. Parker did not know why he had kept it. Someday, after the trial, he would destroy it and all the other references to the existence of Eddie Copeland.

He swiveled in his chair and looked out of the window, across the street to the Onslow County Courthouse and the row of windows that were barred behind the glass. He could not see Eddie's form or Eddie's aura. On Sunday night, Eddie had appeared nervous and timid. He had asked for writing materials and had mumbled to Parker, "You've done as good for me as anybody could."

"Wait until the trial's over before you say that," Parker had replied.

"Don't matter," Eddie had said quietly. "I know what it's going to be."

Parker remembered also leaving the jail and seeing the Preacher sitting in his car, parked along the sidewalk. The Preacher had spoken and Parker had stopped at his car.

"I want you to know I've been praying for your dilemma," the Preacher had said to Parker. "What you're doing's not easy, with everything against you the way it is."

"It's all right," Parker had replied. "It's part of the job."

"People find it hard to forgive, Mr. Mewborn. They set their hearts hard against forgiving. They'll be wanting that boy's life and that's not Jesus' way, taking lives. I've tried to say it in my sermons, but the people don't listen. I can see it in them."

Parker had not replied. He had stood beside the car, looking at the pale, puzzled expression on the Preacher's face.

"I know what I'm talking about," the Preacher had continued seriously. "I've tried to get to Jesse, but he keeps putting off talking to me. Sometimes I think he's mad because I counseled his wife, and then Anna. But that's my calling, Mr. Mewborn. I wish I could get Jesse to see that. I'm afraid his heart's hard against forgiving."

"He lost a lot of people. I imagine that's hard to forget."

The Preacher had clucked his tongue and sighed heavily. "Nobody's asking that he forget it, just forgive it. That boy you're defending, he's got a soul. It needs redeeming."

"Preacher," Parker had said wearily, "I've got my hands full just trying to save him from the electric chair. If there's any redeeming, you'll have to do it."

"God redeems. I shall be praying, Mr. Mewborn."

And the Preacher had rolled up the window and started his car and driven away. And Parker had thought, Yes, you pray, I defend, God redeems, and Hugh Richards judges.

By eight o'clock a crowd—mostly men—had gathered on the sidewalk before the courthouse and stood about in groups and talked with serious expectation about what would happen, or would not happen, at the trial of Eddie Copeland. He was guilty—Christ, yes. Being at the trial was not a matter of doubt but curiosity. "Like watching Perry Mason on the television," one man exclaimed. "Always know Perry's going to win it hands down, but don't never know how." And the men around him laughed.

At eight-thirty, the courthouse doors were opened and the spectators moved inside to stand in the warmth of the corridor. At eight-forty, Hugh Richards summoned Ellis and Guy and a state patrolman named Odell Sidney to his chambers. He told them: "I just want everybody to know this is going to be a peaceful trial. The first man that gets out of line, I'm going to slap in irons and then sell the son of a bitch into slavery. I mean it. There'll be dignity in there or the next session this county's going to be ass-deep in contempt hearings. You all keep watch, for anything. Already been some talk I don't like."

"Like what?" Odell Sidney asked.

"Just talk," Hugh said.

"Hugh," Ellis replied evenly, "I've been hearing talk about this trial for weeks—from everywhere—and I'm going to tell you straight out, if you know something we ought to know, then tell us. Otherwise, just trust that we know what we're doing."

Hugh smiled and the flesh of his jowls rippled across his heavy face. He liked Ellis. Ellis was not afraid of God himself. "Nothing to worry about," he said. "I hear Wyman Stephens has been a little loud, that's all."

"We know about Wyman, Hugh," Ellis said. He added, "And Wyman knows about us. We already spotted him outside. One of my men's got his eye on him."

Hugh nodded. His chair squeaked with each drop of his head. "One thing, keep an eye out for Jack. He's getting older'n creation. He's scared to death of Copeland."

"We'll watch him," Ellis promised.

Jack was Jack Pilgrim, one of the bailiffs. He was a fixture at the courthouse and stubbornly loyal to Hugh.

"One other thing," Hugh said. "We may be here for a while. I don't want any mistakes. I don't care if we have to crawl through it. It'll be right and it'll damn well be fair. Is that understood?"

"That's understood," Ellis mumbled.

"Now, is Jesse going to be here?"

"Not till the jury's picked," Ellis told him.

"That's good," Hugh said. "Be best that way."

At eight-forty-five, the doors to the courthouse were opened and the waiting crowd pushed hurriedly inside, quickly filling the available seats, leaving latecomers in the corridor. "Damn it," the latecomers complained bitterly.

"Wadn't for them reporters, we'd all be able to get in." The reporters had reserved seats—one row on both sides of the center aisle. Hugh had called it "professional courtesy." To Jack Pilgrim, he had confided: "Don't want them on my ass, Jack. They can't have cameras or tape recorders. Might as well make them feel good about something." And Jack had grunted his approval.

At eight-fifty-five, Harold Sellers, the Onslow County district attorney who had surrendered his lead prosecutor's role to become an assistant to William Fred, entered the courtroom with two briefcases. William Fred followed two minutes later. Parker Mewborn and Donald Bridges followed William Fred. Both carried a single briefcase.

At three minutes after nine, Hugh entered the courtroom from his chambers. The trial of Eddie Copeland had begun.

The selection of the jury—the *voir dire* proceedings—lasted almost two days—December 8 and 9—and was made deliberately intense by both William Fred and Parker. Their questions to prospective jurors began innocently, routinely, then became more probing, sometimes caustic. It was as though the two men were shadow-dueling, pricking with needle-pointed words at the thinly shielded underbelly of the legal armor each had chosen to wear. The selection of the jury was only one element of the questioning: the oneupmanship of prosecution versus defense was another issue requiring even more skill. In the procedure, William Fred struck nine candidate-jurors; Parker struck fifteen.

The jury consisted of seven men and five women. All were active church members, though none belonged to denominations that condemned capital punishment. Three were self-employed—a merchant, a cattle farmer, and a greenhouse owner. Two were housewives. The others were employees of small businesses in small villages. Only two had college educations—the merchant and the greenhouse owner (both had once worked in Atlanta, but had returned to the mountains seeking peace). All had been born in Onslow County, but none lived in the Tickenaley Valley, a fact that privately distressed William Fred but pleased Hugh. If a higher court ever questioned this case—and that was an obvious possibility, with the appeals process—Hugh did not want a jury that had been plucked like plums off the Tickenaley ancestral tree.

Jesse and Anna had waited for the phone call from William Fred that would summon them into the courtroom to watch the trial. When William Fred did call, at four o'clock on December 9, he explained that Hugh had recessed after the jury selection. "It'll start tomorrow. I'll be out later tonight to talk to you."

The waiting had affected both Jesse and Anna. As they had neared the trial date, both had begun to feel the razorcut of memory. Both had dreamed of the deathscene. Both had stopped eating. Both were tired. And both knew, without asking, that there was more to William Fred's motive to keep them away from the jury selection than concern for their emotional health: William Fred wanted their absence to cry out with pain.

When William Fred arrived at Jesse's house at six o'clock, he was eager and positive. "I've looked it over a thousand times," he assured Jesse and Anna. "I've put myself in Parker's shoes and tried to figure what he'll do. I can't imagine anything going wrong. The man's guilty. Everybody knows it—especially Parker. I've watched him. His heart's not in it, no matter how much he's argued in the last couple of days. He wants it over with."

Jesse listened quietly. He knew William Fred had never worked as diligently. Everyone—those who had gathered around him in Tickenaley, those who knew more than he about the trial—had lauded William Fred. "Not a stone unturned," they had assured Jesse. "Not one. He's been a worker, all right."

"You're still not planning to use us as witnesses, are you?" Anna asked politely.

"No. No reason. We've got the evidence. No reason to put you through it."

"Parker?" Jesse asked.

William Fred rubbed his mouth with his hand. "No," he

said after a moment. "Parker won't call you. Nothing he could gain by it. Nothing but upsetting the jury by trying to make it look like you were lying about something. No, Parker won't do that."

Jesse and Anna sat silently and waited for William Fred to continue.

"Is there anything I should know from either of you? Anything at all?"

"Not that I know of," Jesse said. Then: "We'll be staying at Anna's house while it's going on. Jeff Carlton said he'd look after the stock here."

"That's good," William Fred said. "It's closer to town. Give you a chance to get away for a few minutes when there's a break in the trial."

"What about the people from the newspapers?" Anna asked. "Do we talk to them, or not?"

William Fred jerked his face toward her. "No," he said emphatically. "I'll do that. I'm glad you brought it up. I'd rather both of you keep pretty much to yourselves. Don't talk to anyone. We don't want anything misunderstood and used against us. Leave all that to me."

Anna nodded hesitantly. She said, "That Mr. Cahill called earlier. He asked me a strange question."

"What?"

"He wanted to know if either one of us had seen that—that man face to face."

"Copeland?"

Anna nodded.

"What did you tell him?" William Fred asked. "You haven't. Did you tell him that?"

"We haven't," Jesse said bluntly.

"Of course not," William Fred mumbled. He wondered why Toby had asked the question.

TWENTY-THREE

December 10

A SHARP, COLD RAIN THAT STRUCK WITH THE BRUTALITY of sleet was falling on Wednesday morning, and still the spectators arrived early at the courthouse and began to huddle under umbrellas, like clusters of dark flowers. It was, Hugh Richards remarked, ". . . a deplorable sight. They got the scent of blood," he said privately to Jack Pilgrim. "Nothing else I could think of, short of starvation or war, could pry the first one of them out on a day like this." Jack Pilgrim, who was suffering a head cold, agreed.

Hugh had read the waiting crowd well. As they stood in the rain, pressing close to the courthouse, talking boldly of a swift trial and a swifter execution, their discomfort and anger increased. Wisely, Ellis Spruill ordered the courthouse opened early, and the crowd poured into the wide corridor separating the courtroom from the jail. Inside, warming, they became more temperate. Yet their opinions were fixed. A newspaper reporter from the *Gainesville Daily Journal* wandered among them and asked the same question: "How do you feel about the trial?"

"Wish I was on the jury," one man said. "I was on it,

it'd last about as long as one cold minute in hell. I'd take care of that boy."

"I'm damn mad," another said frankly. "People like that, always getting by with what they damn well please. Well, it won't happen up here. This ain't Atlanta. Won't happen up here, I'll guarantee."

"What you expect me to feel?" a middle-aged woman said indignantly. "Nothing they can do to him will be enough—if they kill him a hundred times over, it won't be. They won't bring Jesse's family back, now, will they? Seems like you don't never hear nothing about anybody's rights except them that do wrong. That ain't what the law's supposed to be about."

Out of all the people the reporter questioned, only one seemed tolerant. "Jesus taught us to forgive," he said. "I'm willing to do that, if that man on trial would give his life to Jesus. That's what I think." The reporter did not know that the tolerant man was the Preacher.

The courthouse opened, as it had during the selection of the jury, at eight-forty-five. Jesse and Anna and Aubrey Hart were led to their reserved seats by Ellis after the spectators and press had entered the auditorium. The room quieted with their entrance. A few voices murmured, "We're with you, Jesse, Anna. It's all right, Aubrey." Their seats were directly behind William Fred and Harold. William Fred leaned to them and whispered something no one heard. Aubrey Hart sat stiffly alert, his thin face pointed toward the witness chair. His lips were opening and closing slowly, rhythmically, making a faint popping sound, like the dripping of water.

Minutes later, Eddie Copeland was escorted into the courtroom. He was uncuffed and directed to his seat at the defense table. He and Parker acknowledged each other with looks, but they did not speak. Eddie leaned lazily back in his chair and rolled his head to his right, toward Jesse and Anna and Aubrey. His lips curled quickly into a slight smile and his eyes moved slowly to each face like a dull green light. Jesse could feel the blood drain from his face, and his mouth filled with saliva. He swallowed quickly and tried to pull his eyes away from Eddie, but he could not. The Eddie of television, and of newspaper and magazine pictures, had been arrogant but boyish; the Eddie of the courtroom was like a grotesque face of evil—smooth-skinned, blond, the pink question mark scarring his left cheek, eyes of poison. Jesse could see Eddie's face on Jean and Macy and Florence. He could see Eddie's sharp, thin tongue gouging at their bodies.

"Jesse," Anna whispered, leaning to him, taking his wrist in her hand. "Don't. Don't look." She turned her face to Aubrey. His eyes had not moved from the witness chair. "Don't," she said again to Jesse. "It's what he wants." She remembered the question from Toby Cahill. She realized that Toby had tried to caution her.

Jesse could feel his legs trembling and his hands tightening on the edge of the bench where he was sitting. He could feel the heat of his blood in the muscles of his arms. His eyes held Eddie's stare until Eddie lifted his face casually and turned away.

"Jesse?" Anna whispered.

"It's all right," Jesse said coldly.

At nine o'clock, Hugh entered the courtroom and sat in the overlarge leather chair behind a raised desk that had the words "Justice Above All" scriptcarved into its facing. William Fred turned to Jesse and Anna. He nodded once, as if signaling them.

William Fred's first legal pirouette before the jury and the Onslow County Courtroom spectators was a mild surprise to everyone but Parker: William Fred did not deliver the opening statement of the prosecution; Harold Sellers did. The move made Parker smile. Harold was not a match for William Fred in a courtroom, but he knew posturing. Harold had been born in Moncks Corner, South Carolina, had studied engineering, but had been converted to law by what he considered a higher calling to protect the rights of people. He did not want to build bridges of steel but pathways for the pursuit of happiness. To Harold, the law was more evangelistic than the ministry and certainly as noble.

Parker listened to Harold but did not watch him. He shifted his body in his chair and, pretending concentration, watched Jesse and Anna and Aubrey. He knew that William Fred could never prepare them for the shock of hearing, in detail, the story of the deaths.

And Parker was right.

Harold's statement was more than an accounting of facts; it was a telling of horror, wrung from his anguished voice and sweeping hands. He told of the birthday plans for Winston, of the close family traditions, of the expected joy and celebration. And then he told of three men who had appeared, killing and raping, senselessly, gleefully. He told of the men taking Florence and killing her and stuffing her into a culvert. He told of Jesse discovering the bodies, of Anna finding Jesse in the backyard, cradling his slain grandson. He told of the capture of the men, of the gunfight at the Mountain of the Caves. He told of the loss that Jesse and Anna and Aubrey had suffered. And he vowed that the state would prove Eddie Copeland was a murderer.

As they listened to the dramatic telling of murder, Jesse and Anna and Aubrey sat motionless. They did not watch Harold, but stared, with their heads bowed, into the floor at their feet.

Parker knew they were stunned. Harold's statement had been passionate, indignant, demanding, and when he concluded, whispers of shock sighed across the courtroom like a soft wind.

"Mr. Mewborn, are you ready?" Hugh asked.

Parker looked again at Jesse. He could see a muscle twitching in Jesse's face. He had never seen hate in Jesse, but now it was there, screaming.

Parker stood slowly at the defense table. Eddie sat beside him, impassively drawing tornadoes of oblong circles on a scratchpad. Eddie did not look up.

"Judge Richards, members of the jury, when Mr. Sellers began his statement, he told you these remarks are not evidence, and that is true," Parker began in an even voice. "He has said the purpose of the opening statement is to give an outline of what has happened and that, too, is true. And he has proceeded to tell you what you already know—that a crime took place, that that crime was hideous, and that suspects were captured and charged with that crime. And all that is also true.

"The defense concedes these facts. It would be ridiculous to contend otherwise. But you have also heard something else from the prosecution—something deadly and dangerous. It was said not in words but in intonation and suggestion. It was said in looks and in parading before the jury and those here to witness this trial. What you have heard is this: it is the first carnival bark of the prosecution. You will hear it again and again, appealing to your God-given knowledge of right and wrong, guilt or innocence. It will be convincing. It will drain you emotionally, as if somebody had pulled the plug inside you. You will see exhibits that will make you queasy, that will make you wonder why we're here in the first place. Why don't we just take this man out and hang him to some oak tree and leave him there like a side of beef? That's a question the prosecutor would like for you to get fixed in your mind. You will see the prosecution doing heroic acts, such as constantly glaring at Eddie Copeland, as Mr. Sellers just has. And all of these acts are supposed to make you think that Eddie Copeland is the incarnation of the Prince of Hell."

Parker turned to look at William Fred and Harold. He said, "They will draw descriptions out of witnesses, they will stand righteously before you and leave you with the impression that they have irrefutable proof that Eddie Copeland is a madman unlike any in history—a man who makes the Marquis de Sade and Attila the Hun look like Sunday School teachers."

Parker paused and looked at the papers spread before him. He leaned forward on the table, on the knuckles of his hands. "But," he said at last, lifting his face to the judge, "we are here in the name of the law. The law. Just that. The law. The law. The law." He threw the words from his mouth like explosions.

"That means the prosecution must prove, without question, beyond reasonable doubt, that Eddie Copeland is guilty. It does not matter what kind of frenzy the prosecution manages to stage in this courtroom, proof is the only responsibility of this trial. We are not here to pass judgment by popular vote, but by the investigation of evidence. I ask only this of the jury: do not be swayed; be convinced, be certain. Do not start this trial by thinking we are here to say that Eddie Copeland is guilty and we must decide why; begin by accepting the legal fact that Eddie Copeland is innocent and you, the jury, must determine if his accusation of guilt is valid."

Parker swallowed hard and lifted his hands from the table. He looked at Eddie and then William Fred and then the jury. "This man," he said emphatically, gesturing with his head toward Eddie, "is, at this moment, innocent. If, as the jury, you cannot believe that, then the law—*the law*—is a mockery, and by the continued action of this trial—or any trial, anywhere—the law is little more than a cackle of obscene laughter, fit for nothing but the mouths of hyenas.

"I will tell you now that Eddie Copeland has not been a model citizen, but he is not a murderer. I will tell you that his was the only voice of reason throughout the brutal murders you have heard described so vividly by Mr. Sellers. The prosecution knows this. The prosecution knows that Eddie Copeland has been questioned time and again and his replies have always been the same: Yes, he was there. Yes, he saw the crimes committed. But what the prosecution does not tell you is that Eddie Copeland earnestly wanted to stop the slaughter. He was, indeed, fearful for his own life. The prosecution will say they have evidence of fingerprints, that they have the corroborating statements of Zack Vickers, but I will tell you that all of this is pure invention and will not hold up under the testing of facts. And though you may find Eddie Copeland guilty of association—he feels that guilt himself—you will not, by your own conscience as well as the law, find him guilty of murder."

Parker paused again and dropped his head, as though thinking. He said, quietly, without looking up, "I know that what I have said sounds like a desperate claim of 'They did it, not me.' But I believe what I have said. I believe it as earnestly and sincerely as Mr. Sellers and Mr. Autry believe in their case. And I say to them that the defense will not cower. I say to them, let's have at it." He turned his face to William Fred and Harold. "Your Honor, ladies and gentlemen of the jury, thank you." He sat heavily. The courtroom was silent.

Parker's statement fell on Jesse like a chill. He could see Eddie stop the circling with his pen. Eddie's shoulders and head bobbed in a single, silent laugh. William Fred had said the case against Eddie was secure, that it would not get a challenge of substance from Parker, that Parker himself surely detested his assignment. But Parker had answered Harold Sellers forcefully. And Jesse realized, suddenly, that Parker was right: until the jury made him guilty, until they cast their votes and delivered the verdict, Eddie Copeland was innocent. But it was wrong, Jesse thought angrily. Eddie *was* guilty. The evidence bellowed his guilt. He had not been a frightened bystander; he had killed with the others like it was an amusement, a casual afternoon game. It did not matter that his plea was not guilty. His plea was a lie, as Aubrey had insisted (building his courage to assassinate Eddie, as he dreamed of doing). Eddie's plea was a lie and his statements were lies—excuses to rinse the flood of blood from his hands. Still, the law that would try him, that would test his lying, began by declaring that Eddie Copeland was innocent.

The law was wrong, Jesse thought.

It was all wrong. All of it.

The stories had made Eddie Copeland famous, his face and name familiar.

But there were no stories of his family, only the listing of their names, like afterthoughts.

TWENTY-FOUR

December 10

THE FIRST WITNESS CALLED BY WILLIAM FRED WAS ELLIS
Spruill. Guy Finley and the GBI agent Cale (Quinton Cale)
followed. William Fred asked only general questions, using
the lawmen for mood setting. Quinton Cale's appearance
was startling. He was gauntly thin and wore a suit that was
overlarge. The sleeve of the right arm was empty and pinned
discreetly to the side of the coat. He wore a black patch
over his right eye. A graying beard, trimmed high on the
cheek, covered his face. When he spoke his voice trembled.
William Fred posed him like an exhibit, asked two minor
questions, and dismissed him. The impression was unfor-
gettable: Quinton Cale was the only survivor of the killers.

Parker waved away cross-examining the witnesses. He
sat calmly, watching William Fred's histrionics. William
Fred was eager, he thought. Perhaps too eager. The eagerness meant rushing, being too sure. It was dangerous, being
too sure.

But William Fred was not concerned with Parker. He had

planned carefully. His witnesses were overpowering. His evidence was conclusive. Parker could stand on his head and cry tears upstream, he could fart the preamble to the Constitution, and none of it would matter. William Fred would see the goddamn smile burned off Eddie Copeland's face and if Parker was in the way, he would get scorched.

"Your Honor, I call Henry Upchurch," William Fred said triumphantly.

Henry Upchurch was the chief of the crime laboratory of the Georgia Bureau of Investigation. He was forty-eight years old and a man obsessed with being precise. He was short, trimly built, with a prominent mustache and goatee. He wore bow ties. The *Atlanta Sentinel* had once profiled Henry Upchurch in a series on the GBI. In the article, he had been described as ". . . an expert with little tolerance for the trickery of defense attorneys who attempt to discredit him." Translated, the description meant that Henry Upchurch could become an angry, unyielding opponent, a man who would take tissue samples from Satan to prove a point. He was smart, well-trained, cocky, and almost always right. And he had personally handled the details of the murder of the Jesse Wade family on orders from the governor, George Busbee.

William Fred immediately offered for exhibit a collection of photographs taken at the murder scene. Parker objected on grounds that the defense was not arguing that the crimes had occurred. The photographs, Parker protested, would do nothing but prejudice the case by overdramatizing the incident. Hugh overruled his objection. Parker knew that he would.

"I am not presenting these photographs—exhibits six through sixteen—as a means of impressing or inflaming the jury," William Fred said innocently, "but as a graphic fact that what Mr. Upchurch will be questioned about is a true representation of the facts. It is the belief of the prosecution that the jury will be greatly aided by having such material as reference. It is not, as Mr. Mewborn has suggested, an effort to promote lurid and biased images. It is an effort to do exactly what he has called for in his opening remarks—to ascertain, establish, and follow fact."

Parker slapped his pencil across the desk and pushed angrily away from the table and shook his head. Hugh glared at him and a rumble of expectation rippled through the audience.

The photographs were tendered into evidence, one by one, with Henry Upchurch's examination and explanation. As the pictures were passed to Hugh for viewing, he glanced quickly over each. He had seen hundreds of pictures like them, had used them himself in cases. Not lurid? he thought. Christ. They would make a maggot puke. As an attorney, he had spent hours looking at such photographs, deadening himself to them. But jurors did not have such an advantage. Jurors saw the photographs while sitting in the jury box, before a judge and lawyers and curious spectators. Christ, he thought again as he looked at the pictures and passed them back to William Fred. Blood puddled in dried pools, flesh folded over flesh like closing mouths. At one picture— exhibit thirteen—he could feel his eyes widen. It was a close shot of the knife in Doyle's throat, like a slender guillotine. Hugh's chest trembled. God Almighty, he thought. He looked at the jury. They were watching him apprehensively.

"The court has accepted these exhibits—what numbers?" Hugh asked.

"Six through sixteen," William Fred answered. "That's State, or S-six through S-sixteen."

"Yes. Six through sixteen. But I want to caution the jury that they should be viewed simply as evidence."

The courtroom spectators sat quietly as the photographs were passed among the jurors. At first there was no sound except the lash of rain against the windows. Everyone knew what the photographs must be—more awesome than even the gossip of their guessing. They waited and watched the jury. Then one of the women jurors gasped audibly at the picture of the knife in Doyle's throat. She jerked her head and the muscles in her neck tightened like cords as she fought to control her sudden nausea. The spectators stirred restlessly in their seats. Parker looked at William Fred. William Fred lifted his head piously and sighed. Parker wanted to laugh.

Hugh did not want to recess the trial, but was forced: the woman juror had become ill. It was ten-forty-seven. He peered down at Jesse and Anna and Aubrey, seated close. Jesse's head was bowed. Hugh knew the appearance of the photographs in the courtroom had affected Jesse, that Jesse was seeing mind-pictures more vivid than anything a camera could produce. He moved his eyes over the benches where the reporters were sitting. They all had stoic, aloof faces, he thought. Trying to pretend they were immune to terror. An artist for a television station was glancing at him, making quick strokes over a pad in her lap. Hugh suddenly felt conspicuous. Probably making me look like Porky-damn-Pig, he thought. "Court will recess until one o'clock," he declared in a loud voice.

Jesse and Anna left the courtroom immediately and drove through the rain to Anna's house. They said nothing during the drive. At the house, Anna made coffee and sandwiches, which she knew that neither would eat.

"It's worse than I thought," Anna said at last, pouring coffee at the kitchen table.

"It'll take getting used to," Jesse told her. He was watching the rain from the kitchen window. The rain whipped in gales across the yard.

"He was laughing at us," Anna said bitterly, sitting. "It was just like he was laughing."

Jesse lit a cigarette, his second since arriving at the house. "Looked that way," he said.

"You guess that man from the newspaper knew it'd be that way? You guess that's why he asked if we'd seen him?"

"Maybe."

They sat in silence, listening to the rain and the wind. The lights of the house flickered, dimmed, flickered again.

"Going to be colder tonight," Anna said absently.

"Probably so."

"Eat, Jesse."

Jesse gazed at the sandwich on the plate before him. He felt numb, as though his body had been anesthetized. He could see the face of Eddie Copeland, the half-shut eyes, the curling, quick smile, the teasing cock of his head. Anna was right: the face was laughing. Laughing. The son of a bitch was laughing.

The lights snapped suddenly off and they sat in the shadowed room with the howl of the storm about them.

"Jesse?" Anna said quietly.

He looked up at her.

"I—I haven't said anything straight out to you about it, but I want to," Anna said.

"What?"

"That night, that night I came to you in your bedroom, the way you helped me out. I'm grateful for that. I don't know what made me do it. I don't know. Maybe hurting so much because of Carl. Not just because he was dead, but because of what he wanted. I don't know——"

"It's all right," Jesse said.

"No. I want to say it. I've thought about it, thought I'd be ashamed and not able to even be around you again. But I haven't been. I ought to be ashamed, but I haven't been. And that's because of you, the way you handled it. It helped me a lot."

Jesse pushed his cigarette into the ashtray. "There's nothing to be ashamed of," he said.

"After I was out of the hospital, when I went shopping for Christmas, I thought everybody knew. I remember walking into a store and seeing a group of people sitting around a counter, talking, laughing. Laughing. I thought they knew. And all the Christmas colors were there—all the reds and greens and sparkling things, lots of color, just being put up. And all of a sudden, I couldn't see the color, just black and white. Everything black and white, like the color had been drained out. And I couldn't hear the people laughing. I could see them, but I couldn't really hear them. And I felt this weakness in my knees, like my knees had begun to melt and the muscles around them were turning loose, and I wanted to fall. I tried to stand up, but I couldn't. My knees were melting, and I could feel myself falling. I sat down and looked at the people and they never stopped laughing. And I sat there and thought about it. They couldn't know. I knew they couldn't know. It was something that only you could know. And I began to feel better about it."

"It's all right," Jesse said again.

"The Preacher made me have dreams, Jesse," Anna said. "I think he made Jean have dreams, too."

Jesse could hear Jean: "He helps me. Just talking to somebody helps."

Anna touched her sandwich, but pushed it away. "What happens when it's over with, Jesse? What do we do?"

"We keep living," he said after a moment. "Only thing we can do."

"What if they let him go?"

Jesse watched the ash of the crushed cigarette close over a pinspot of burning tobacco like a shutting eye. He shook his head.

By one o'clock the storm had subsided, though the cold lingered, and the courtroom was again crowded. The ill juror had recovered, though she privately begged a bailiff not to be shown more of the photographs. Henry Upchurch was returned to the witness stand. Guided by William Fred's questions, he described the deaths of the Jesse Wade family.

The three women, Henry Upchurch said (he named them: ". . . Jean Wade, Macy Wade Simmons, Florence Hart Wade"), had been slain by a twenty-two-caliber pistol. Carl Wade and Winston Simmons had been killed by a twelve-gauge shotgun, and Doyle Wade had died of a blow to the throat by a butcher knife. William Fred introduced the weapons into evidence by holding them triumphantly, like trophies. Henry Upchurch testified that the weapons were those used in the crime.

"Now, Mr. Upchurch," William Fred said, "would you

describe for us the findings of your investigation regarding the condition of each of the bodies of the victims?"

"Objection," Parker snapped, rising at his chair. "The defense is on record conceding the event of those tragic slayings. There is no doubt that death occurred by acts of violent murder. The purpose of this trial is not to haggle over points already conceded, but to determine if the defendant was responsible for the act of murder."

William Fred moaned aloud in pained disbelief. He said, "Your Honor, the prosecution is indeed grateful to defense for such a magnanimous concession, particularly since the fact of murder has been inarguable from the very beginning. The purpose of defining any aspect of this crime is to resolve that 'guilt without question, guilt beyond reasonable doubt' possibility that defense so eloquently addressed in opening remarks. Again, we cannot here debate the essentials of issues without hearing those essentials that make up the issues. The defense would have us omit any and all reference to the horror of this crime, because it may impact the image of the defendant's alleged participation. But if we are not permitted to show evidence, in whatever detail and description necessary, then we have nothing but rhetoric."

Hugh looked at both attorneys. He tapped the eraser of his pencil monotonously on the pad before him. He knew both attorneys were simply playing Ping-Pong with procedure. Parker would object like a broken record; William Fred would deliver a state-of-the-union address to answer each objection.

"I'm going to overrule, Mr. Mewborn," Hugh said. "Evidence is the basis of any trial, even if it does seem obscure at times. And as for you, Mr. Autry, the court recognizes rhetoric only impedes the process, which I will impress upon you to remember in your responses."

"Yes, Your Honor," William Fred replied. He could feel his face redden. He turned to the witness chair. "Now, Mr. Upchurch, would you describe for us the death of—ah, Jean Wade?"

The courtroom was silent. A man in the balcony killed

a cough in his hands. The spew of steam from four radiators hissed heat into the courtroom. Anna reached for Jesse's hand and held it tightly. Jesse could feel his heart racing. The muscles at the corners of his mouth began to tremble. What he had not wanted to hear was being said. He looked at Eddie Copeland. Eddie was folding a piece of paper into a tight square, carefully, lazily.

TWENTY-FIVE

December 10

THE TELEVISION NEWS REPORT OF THE FIRST DAY OF TES-
timony in the trial of Eddie Copeland praised Henry Upchurch's detailed descriptions of death. ("Exacting answers,"
the reporter said somberly. "The terrifying story of murder
seemingly without reason.") And the pen-and-ink face of
Henry Upchurch, with shades of penciled color streaked
across him like spotlights, appeared on the screen. In the
pen-and-ink sketch by the courtroom artist, he was sitting
erect, jabbing the air with waving, explaining hands.

The reporter said, "Upchurch replied to the questioning
of special prosecutor William Fred Autry in terms that left
courtroom listeners stunned by the brutality of the crime."

As the reporter spoke, the artist's sketches of the setting
blinked on the screen—the amazed look of jurors and the
glaring thoughtfulness of Hugh Richards, postured above
the scene of Henry Upchurch's testimony like a robed Bud-
dha. And William Fred, pointing to evidence. And Parker,
listening intently. And the one study of Eddie, his eyes
down, his hand holding a pen idly above a pad. There was
no emotion in his face, only the look of patient boredom.

There were no sketches of Jesse or Anna or Aubrey Hart.

The three had been videotaped leaving the courthouse, escorted by deputies of Onslow County.

The reporter said, "For these survivors, the testimony of Henry Upchurch had to be particularly painful."

Anna moved from the sofa and turned the television off. "I'll make dinner," she said quietly.

"Don't go to much trouble," Jesse told her. "I'm not hungry."

"I thought some soup," Anna said. "It's cold out."

"That's good. That's enough," Jesse replied.

He pushed the reclining chair back and closed his eyes and thought of the artist's rendering of the courtroom. The face clearest in Jesse's mind was William Fred's. It had been exultant. In the courtroom, on the first day of testimony, William Fred had achieved exactly what he had promised Jesse and Anna: persuasion. He had used Ellis and Guy and Quinton Cale—Quinton Cale especially—like trumpets in an overture. He had used Henry Upchurch's expertise in death as a ventriloquist would have used a hand puppet (ironically, Henry Upchurch had a voice much like William Fred's, Jesse realized). William Fred had fanned the steam-heat air with ghost wings of mutilations too terrible to bear, and then he had closed his interrogation of Henry Upchurch with a single question that fed the collective awe of the listeners like the elements of a communion: "None of them had a chance, did they?"

It was a quick question, hotly protested by Parker, swept out of the proceedings by Hugh Richards, unanswered by Henry Upchurch, but the objection meant nothing. The question was in the room, shouting itself like the mob chant of a slogan which said exactly what people wished to hear. The people repeated it among themselves as they left the courtroom, whispered it to one another, first for confirmation, then for righteous support. "That's the nub of it," they said. "None of them had a chance. Not a chance." And Jesse had felt them turn their faces to him with anger and pity.

William Fred had assessed himself well, Jesse thought.

He had said he was good at his job, and he was. He had won the first day in court. Henry Upchurch's description of the bodies had soured in the air of the courtroom like a bitter and lethal gas released in the spurts of questions and answers. It had been an inventory of bodies, categorized by name and age and exact spot of death—facts audited in forensic detachment, leaving the listeners stunned (yes, the television reporter was right). Jesse had sickened of the story, but he knew it was what the listeners had come to hear—the word of the expert. But the telling (the detail, the fact) was more vivid than their imaginations and their gossip had been.

And Parker had sat and let it happen. He had allowed William Fred to lead each witness freely, like a tyrannical conductor of an orchestra. And William Fred, sensing surrender in Parker (he had said as much to Jesse), coaxed from Henry Upchurch testimony that was abusively excessive.

"I told you he won't put up much of a fight," William Fred had said to Jesse during a recess. "He knows how much of a chance he's got."

Jesse pushed his weight forward in the reclining chair and sat straight. He could hear Anna working in the kitchen. Anna had said of Parker, "He looks lost, sitting there. Like he doesn't know what he's doing."

Parker had seemed defeated, Jesse thought. He had asked only one question of Henry Upchurch, and it had sounded weak: "You have offered meticulous description, Mr. Upchurch," Parker had said. "More meticulous than I have ever heard in a trial. You're to be complimented for your investigation and your knowledge. Now, can you tell me if the man here on trial for first-degree murder—if Eddie Copeland—committed those crimes?"

Henry Upchurch had arched his eyebrows, looked once at William Fred, sniffed the air contemptuously, and replied, "That's not my duty, Mr. Mewborn. He was at the scene. We know that."

And Parker had stood staring at Henry Upchurch, as though waiting for words to fill his mouth.

"Is there anything else of this witness?" Hugh had asked at last.

"No," Parker had replied bluntly. He had added, cynically, "I think we've heard enough. To add to such detailed, Technicolor proof of a crime already acknowledged would seem to do nothing but make it more sensational than it already is. The defense has no appetite for such feasts of gore." Parker had turned to look directly at Jesse. "And, frankly, I don't care to see people suffer from facts they already know all too well."

Jesse remembered the silence in the courtroom. He remembered watching Hugh's eyes slide from Parker to William Fred and then back to Parker, his heavy head bobbing irritably.

"The court is pleased that this line of questioning is complete," Hugh had said. "It's unfortunate that the survivors and friends of the victims have had to listen to such detail, but we all know the law is not as precise as we may want it to be. To disallow testimony that may be pertinent, on any grounds, is a risk that the court just can't take, plain and simple." He had paused, pulled himself up in his chair, and rested his elbows on the table before him. "I will ask, however, that everybody in this courtroom understand that what they've heard are only the findings of an investigation. I'm going to take up Mr. Mewborn's argument for a moment and remind everybody in here that this investigation tells us what happened, but not necessarily who did what. Those findings may or may not be important in the final deliberations. None of us know that now. Now, this is not a warning to either counsel, or a charge to the jury. It is merely an exercise of privilege on the part of the bench to caution against undue emotional reaction. This will be a trial of fact, not imagery."

And the court had been recessed for the day. And William Fred had won, Jesse thought. He had won on one question: "None of them had a chance, did they?"

Not a chance. None of them. They were helpless.

The picture of Carl's body thrown back into the bushes rushed into Jesse's mind. And Doyle. Doyle had not even raised his hands against the blade of the knife. Henry Up-church had described it. Doyle had been almost jogging as he shoved open the door of the house. The knife had caught him in midstep. And that would have been true, Jesse realized: Doyle had always entered the house running. He did not stand a chance against the swinging blade of the knife.

None of them had a chance. None.

Jesse could see himself, holding a knife. He could see the surprised flash of horror on Eddie's face as the knife split his throat.

"Jesse," Anna called from the kitchen. "Supper's ready."

Harvey Wills had taught Toby a valuable lesson about the reporting of murder trials: never drink with other reporters. "Coffee, maybe," Harvey had lectured, "but no whiskey." He had explained: "Put a bunch of them neo-Hemingways in a bar and they're like a goddamn circus. Give 'em thirty minutes at happy hour and they'll have the whole goddamn thing settled—one way or the other—and then they'll start writing that way just to prove their point, no matter what's going on in the frigging courtroom. No way around it, Toby. Everybody likes knowing the frigging answer, but they ain't worth a pinch of owl shit once they make up their minds."

It was not eloquently stated, but it was advice that Toby understood and followed. He did not drink with other reporters. He always left the courtroom immediately, always to a private place, and on a sheet of paper made coded notes about the proceedings, the questions and arguments and absurdities, and then he made an outline of what his story should be. It was his exercise in remaining objective, of avoiding the distraction of making judgments.

But the exercise failed him with the trial of Eddie Copeland. He had been with Eddie twice—once when Eddie's statement was given to William Fred and again when the statement was repeated to Parker. He had listened to a confession (a claim?) told as casually as a tired complaint about the weather. He had watched Eddie's eyes in their dull flickering of stubbornness. And he had believed that

Eddie's statement was nothing but a skillful improvisation, rehearsed to perfection in Cell Four of the Onslow County jail. Eddie Copeland had lied. Intuitively, Toby believed it was a lie. It was a lie as great as his crime had been.

Toby sat in the back corner of the Valley View Lodge Restaurant—empty except for three truckers sitting at the counter—and he scribbled words of nonsense on paper. Even the notes he had made during the trial seemed incoherent. He could not erase the faces of Jesse and Anna and Aubrey Hart from his mind. He had sat behind them, had watched as Henry Upchurch's precise, vivid language slashed them with a force that left no bleeding, no wounds. The only sign that they had even heard Henry Upchurch was the occasional quiver of a stone muscle on their stone faces.

It was still cold when Toby left the restaurant. The wind swirled rainmist in his face as he crossed the graveled parking lot leading to his room. It was a prelude to snow, he thought. He could feel snow in the air, the air coming from the northwest, from the Tennessee and Alabama mountains. He remembered the snow warnings of his own childhood, when the rainmist tasted of snow before it became snow.

He saw the note on the floor when he opened the door. It was from Rachel. The note read, "Knock on my door when you come in." He mumbled, "Damn," and stepped outside and knocked lightly at her door. She opened it quickly and motioned for him to enter. William Fred was sitting in a padded chair, his feet crossed lazily on the edge of the bed. His shirt was open down his chest, the sleeves rolled high on his arms. He held a half-filled glass. Toby knew immediately that he had been drinking heavily.

"It's about damn time," William Fred said. "Where've you been?"

"Trying to eat," Toby replied. "What're you doing here?"

William Fred laughed and swallowed from his glass and refilled it from a bottle of scotch beside the chair.

"Tell you the truth, I'm hiding," he said. He looked at Toby and smiled. "You know how it is with reporters. Hound your tail like it was rabbit. Some television woman was doing everything but putting a hammerlock on me." He laughed. "May regret that," he added. "Damn pretty, that one." He winked at Rachel.

"I—I was waiting for him," Rachel said proudly. "That's why I wadn't in the restaurant tonight. I swapped off my time."

"Want a drink?" William Fred asked.

"A short one," Toby replied. He removed his coat and folded it over a chair and sat. He wondered what Harvey Wills would say about drinking with lawyers.

William Fred poured the drink without moving from the chair. He handed the glass to Rachel, who handed it to Toby.

"Well, here's to justice," William Fred said in a toast. He drank in a large swallow.

"I thought you'd be working," Toby said.

"Working? I've been working," William Fred replied easily. "It's over now. Now it's nothing more than putting it all together. Can't do that without the judge and jury."

"I guess." Toby sipped the scotch. It was bitter.

"Well, what'd you think?" William Fred asked.

"About?"

"Today."

"The man's descriptive," Toby said.

"The man's a goddamn genius at his work," William Fred corrected.

"I wonder if Jesse Wade, or his daughter-in-law, or Aubrey Hart thinks so," Toby said.

William Fred shook his head slowly and sighed and his face furrowed sadly. He said, "Yeah, I know. I didn't like that part of it, either. I told them it'd be bad, but I don't think they knew what I meant."

"You talk to them?" Toby asked.

William Fred nodded, sipped from his drink. "Jesse," he answered. "He said he understood, but he was quiet. Said he wished Aubrey didn't have to hear it. Aubrey's heart's been bad, he said. I didn't know that. Rachel said she'd heard it, too."

"I sure hope he don't have a heart attack," Rachel said

earnestly. She was sitting at the foot of the bed, looking at William Fred like someone watching scenery.

"Hush, baby," William Fred whispered. "Don't go thinking things like that. Aubrey'll be all right. Fix yourself another drink."

"I don't want another one, William Fred."

William Fred lit a cigarette and dropped more ice from the Styrofoam container beside his chair into his glass. He said, casually, "You see them up at the restaurant?"

"Who?" Toby asked. He did not remember seeing anyone he knew.

"The bleeding hearts," William Fred answered in an exaggerated British accent. "Saw them when I came in. Three cars from Atlanta. Got little tags on their bumpers—'Ban the Death Penalty.' I recognized the van with them. Go anywhere they can to campaign."

"Why're they here now?" Toby asked.

William Fred flicked the ash of his cigarette toward an ashtray. "Parker's bringing them in, I'd guess. This group won't say much. They'll just stand around, parade a little. They'll bring the heavyweights in later, if they're needed."

"You don't seem worried," Toby said.

William Fred shrugged. "Why?" he replied. "You know damn well I've got him, good as strapped in. They can bring in Ringling Brothers if they want to."

Toby did not want to talk about the trial, but he could not resist William Fred's arrogance.

"You think today did it?" Toby asked.

"Lord, no," William Fred said. He smiled smugly. "Only thing we did today was state some facts and make people mad." He winked at Toby. "Don't go worrying about it."

Toby could feel his face flushing with anger. "I'm not," he said coolly.

"I did something today I think you ought to know about," William Fred told him. "Hope you don't mind too much."

Toby said nothing. He sipped the scotch and waited for William Fred to continue. Rachel's eyes darted expectantly to each of the men.

"Judge called me and Parker in after the session today," William Fred said at last. "Told us he'd gotten word from the sheriff that Copeland wanted to talk to you again. I stopped it."

Toby did not reply.

"The deal was for before the trial," William Fred continued argumentatively. "Couldn't allow it now. That sly son of a bitch could have anything up his sleeve."

"Who?" Toby asked.

"Copeland," William Fred answered with a snort. "You don't think I meant Parker, do you? Jesus. Parker's got his hands full as it is. He's not about to start an end run."

Toby finished the scotch and stood and picked up his coat. He said, "You don't think Parker's got a case at all, do you?"

"None," William Fred said flatly. "I feel sorry for him. He surprised me with his opening statement. Good. I mean it. Then he looked like he was lost the rest of the day. Couldn't believe what he let me get away with. Problem is, he's got nothing. Nothing. He'll put Copeland up. He has to. But I don't know if he'll put up anybody else. Maybe the shrink that's talked to Copeland a few times. I don't even know about that. He'll hang it all on us not proving Eddie did the killing. That's why he's not bargaining for manslaughter. He's going for broke—as in neck."

Toby walked to the door. He pulled his coat over his shoulders and stood, thinking. Then he asked, "Can you do it? Prove it?"

William Fred laughed easily. He rubbed his face with his hand. He was tired and the scotch had puffed his face and aged him. "Toby," he said, "the jury's got to believe it. That's all. And they do. Or will. I watched them today. You did, too. They'll believe it."

"Yeah," Toby said quietly. "I watched them. Thanks for the drink."

"Before you go, I've got something for you," William Fred told him. He reached for an envelope that was on the night table.

"What is it?" Toby asked.

"Well, it looks like a letter," William Fred replied, turning the envelope in his hand. He flipped it to Toby. "Just because I put the stops on seeing Copeland in person didn't mean I could stop him from writing. I told Parker I'd deliver it since I was coming down here." He winked at Rachel. "For dinner," he added.

Toby looked at the envelope. His name was written in a clean print on the front. He asked, "You know what's in it?"

"My God," William Fred mumbled. "I don't care. What kind of person do you think I am, anyway?"

"Sorry," Toby said. "Thought Parker might have told you."

"I don't guess Parker knows," William Fred said. He added, "But Parker trusts me, even if he is trying to cut my guts out, and vice the versa. Do you?"

Toby blushed at the accusation. He had insulted William Fred. He deserved the rebuff. "I trust you," he said.

"Goodnight, Toby Cahill. I'll see you in the morning."

"Better get some rest," Toby advised. "And go light on the scotch."

"I'm blessed," William Fred said. "There's a clock in me. No matter what I drink, I'm sober at six. That's six in the morning."

"Yeah, well, sleep a little while before then," Toby said. He nodded a message to Rachel. She understood. Her eyes blinked a yes.

In his room, Toby read the letter. It was laboriously penned in an awkward cursive, like the writing of an old man.

Dear Mr. Cahill,

I hope you could see they stacked the odds against me today. The way that man talked, there is no way for that jury, or any jury, to give me a fighting chance. I would hate to have him tell how to clean chickens or kill cows. I don't guess I could ever eat chicken or cow again.

If something is not done to show that it was Albert and Zack who did all that, I will be burned to death in the chair and nobody will ever know that I was the one trying to stop it from happening. Zack won't tell the truth. Him and Albert was close buddies. That's why he was so crazy when they got us at the cave. It was because Albert was killed and Zack had always been the one to do Albert's fighting for him. To tell it like it is, Zack never did like me too much and I never did like him at all. It didn't surprise me one bit when they said he was insane. He always has been. Someday he'll kill somebody else in the crazy house or wherever it is they put him at, and then maybe people will say I was right. But by then it could be too late for me. I could be buried by then.

I've been thinking a lot about it and I know I did wrong by just standing around there watching Albert and Zack. I could have tried to stop what they did, but I was afraid. I was thinking more about my own life than I was them people, who I had never seen.

There's one more thing I want to say. I know I give off the "tough boy" look most of the time. I guess I always have. When I got in some trouble in high school, they took me to a doctor and he said it was because I was trying to hide the fact that I was afraid. I tried to say that to the doctor I been seeing since all this took place, but he don't seem to care. He just sits there and listens and looks. I swear he's in the right line of work. If a man's not crazy, he'll drive you there.

I wanted to say all this and some more things in person, so you'd know how I was feeling about things, but they wouldn't let me. So I guess I'll just have to write them down on paper, which is a poor second but will have to do.

Yours truly,
Eddie Copeland

Toby read the letter three times. There was a meekness in it, and fear. It was as though Eddie had hired someone to write it. Or maybe he had been wrong, Toby thought as he smoked to check the tension he felt. Maybe there was another Eddie, one not easily seen or heard.

TWENTY-SIX

December 1

THE MORNING OF THURSDAY, DECEMBER 11, WAS CLOUD-
less and cold in the Tickenaley Valley. The sun, in the
awkward tilt of its winter arc, labored to reach and hold the
southeastern ridge of the mountains, and its light skimmed
the valley and burned into the fogcap of night like a searing
torch. The air was crisp and clean and sweet to breathe.
Sounds carried easily. The wingbeat of birds split the air
like fluttering banners. Yard dogs barked without reason and
cows in milking lots lifted their heads to moan complaints
and stabled horses snorted restlessly against locked barn
doors. And the morning of Thursday, December 11, began
noisily, in cold air, sound by sound.

The people of the valley also had awakened sound by
sound—by the stretch and yawn in warm nests of bedcovering, by the dragging of footsteps, by the rattle of breakfast
dishes, by the steamhiss of coffee pots and the spray and
gurgle of bathwater. And then by the opening and closing
of house doors and by the lungsigh of the first surprised
swallow of air, like a stunning, remarkable drug leaping
into their bloodstreams.

And the people arrived early in town, at Asa Hill's café, to wait for the courthouse to open and to talk of bringing Zack Vickers to the stand to testify against Eddie Copeland. "Ought to be something," the people said eagerly. "Crazy bastard ought to be something, just like old Isom."

Kentley Whiteside, the psychiatrist at Central State Hospital, had agreed reluctantly with Tommy Moss that Isom and Lou could visit with Zack before Zack's testimony in the trial. "On two conditions: first, you have to have some guards around; second, you'll be solely responsible, Mr. Moss."

"I understand," Tommy had said into the telephone.

"I'll put it straight, Mr. Moss. He's classic. You ought to see his graphs. He could snap like a toothpick."

It had been a cold comment from a man too familiar with insanity. Kentley Whiteside's patients were numbers and case studies, like caged mice bred for experimentation. He interviewed them in protected cells and then he dissected the interviews as he would dissect bugs jabbed to cardboard with straight pins. He looked for patterns, for behavioral profiles that followed zigzag lines on impressively colored graphs. The graphs explained sickness, like the tissue examination of a malfunctioning organ. To Kentley Whiteside, it was simple: match the mind with the graph. The zigzag lines told everything. To Tommy, Kentley Whiteside was diseased with indifference.

The meeting of Isom and Lou with Zack was early, before the stores and shops of Tickenaley opened. Zack had arrived from Milledgeville the night before, and had been retained in the women's cell of the Onslow County jail (the only isolation available). He had rested comfortably in a deep, drug-induced sleep.

Isom and Lou were confused about the early morning trip into Tickenaley with Tommy and Guy Finley. They were to see Zack, Tommy explained, but still they did not understand. Lou believed that Zack had joined the Army again and was away somewhere, wearing the same green-brown uniform he had worn before. Isom did not talk. He looked at Lou and nodded absently, habitually. He sat in the car and stared out the window like an amazed child.

"It'll be all right," Tommy told them. "Zack's fine. And you'll see Angus, too. I asked him to come over. You remember Angus, Lou?"

"Man at the store," Lou answered. "I seen him."

Isom nodded and smiled.

Angus waited alone in the commission conference room in the basement of the Onslow County Courthouse. He knew that Tommy had asked him to be present because Isom would feel comfortable. He liked Isom, but he was afraid of Lou and Zack. Lou and Zack were crazy. They had the look of rabid animals, or drunks. Their faces had the slack jaw of a retarded mind. Angus did not want to be around them. But Tommy had said it was important. It might be the last time Zack would ever see them. And Tommy was right, Angus reasoned. Isom and Lou were old. They'd have to be dying in a few years and Zack would be locked away in a mental institution. It was a good thing to do, helping bring child and parents together for a last time. Tommy Moss was damn decent. Especially for a lawyer.

Angus walked to the window of the room and looked outside. Good day, he thought. Town'll be full of people, with the trial. Didn't matter if it was a little cold. Make people frisky, standing around in the cold. There'd be a run on coffee at the café. Nothing better than coffee on a cold day.

Angus saw the car pull into the parking space near the back door. He saw Tommy and Guy get out and help Isom and Lou from the car. They're old, he thought. It was a wonder they were still alive, being so old.

Isom looked suspiciously around the large room with the long conference table in the middle. He saw Angus and smiled.

"How you doing, Isom?" Angus said. Then: "Hello, Lou."

"Isom's fine," Isom said. His eyes widened. "Lou's mean."

Lou glared at Isom and then at Angus.

"Now, Isom, that ain't so," Angus said easily. "Lou's the best woman you ever saw. Where'd you find such a good woman anyhow?"

"Stole me," Lou snapped. "That's what he done. Stole me right out of the house."

Isom cackled. He wiped his eyes with the back of his hand.

"Well, it's good to see you again, Lou," Angus said. "It's been a long time."

Lou sniffed the air arrogantly and turned from Angus and saw the color-coded map of Onslow County on the wall. She walked to it and began looking curiously at the colors. She touched the map gently with her fingertips.

"That's the map of the county, Lou," Tommy told her. "Got every valley in it colored a different color."

"I like colors," Lou mumbled. She touched the orange of the Valley of the Two Forks.

"Want me to show you where you live?" Tommy asked.

Lou looked at him. She trusted Tommy. "Where?" she said.

"There," Tommy replied, pointing with his finger to the yellow of the Tickenaley Valley. "See, that line's the road leading out of town. It cuts off here and that's the road going up to your house."

Lou watched Tommy's finger moving along the lines of the map. She did not understand him. "Where's the house?" she asked irritably.

"About here," Tommy said, pointing on the map.

Lou shook her head sadly. She could not see the house.

Isom laughed. "Old woman can't see nothing," he said. "Nothing."

"Now, that's not true, Isom, and you know it," Tommy said gently. He nodded to Guy and Guy left the room. "Come on, sit down here, Lou. Zack'll be down in a minute." He helped Lou into her chair. "Angus, Lou's looking good, don't you think?" he said.

Lou was as ugly as a pig's ass, Angus thought. He said

cynically, "Just like Farrah Fawcett. Good thing she's already married to this old coot, or I'd be up there with flowers and candy."

Isom giggled. Lou stared contemptuously at Angus.

"I swear it, Isom. Lou looks like a movie star," Angus said.

Isom laughed harder. His body rocked in the chair. He sang, "Uh-huh, uh-huh, uh-huh. Does, does, does."

"Don't let them bother you, Lou," Tommy said. "You look fine to me." His eyes narrowed in a warning to Angus. Angus looked away.

"Listen," Tommy said. "It won't be but a minute until Zack gets down here. Now, like I told you, he's been in a hospital and they've been giving him some medicine. He may seem like he's a little different, but he's all right. You understand that?"

"Army boys with him?" Lou asked seriously.

"No, Lou," Tommy answered patiently. "Remember, I told you Zack's not in the Army now. He's in a hospital. They're taking care of him."

"Got him in jail," Isom said suddenly, lifting his face angrily.

Tommy looked at Angus. He said, "That's right, Isom, but that's just while he's here, in Tickenaley. He'll go back to the hospital."

"Killed them people," Isom said. "What the man said. Killed Jesse Wade."

"No, Isom. Not Jesse," Tommy whispered. "Jesse's family. But that's done. Now they're trying to get Zack well."

Isom sank in his chair. He pushed his hands under the beltline of his pants and stared into the floor. His breathing relaxed. He mumbled, "Old woman can't see nothing."

"It'll be all right, Lou," Tommy said quietly. "Zack'll be here in a minute." He sat near Lou. The waiting became uncomfortable. Tommy said again, "Won't be but a minute."

Isom and Lou had never seen Zack as he appeared in the room with Guy. He was clean, his hair neatly combed. He was subdued, like a shy child. His eyes were like dull candlelight. A strange, expectant smile was on his face. (Guy would later tell Tommy that Zack had repeatedly asked if his mother was mad at him.)

"Zack, how are you?" Tommy asked.

Zack looked at Tommy and then Angus.

"You remember Mr. Helton, Zack?" Tommy asked.

"Zack, how you doing?" Angus asked nervously.

"Fine," Zack said softly. He looked at Isom and then Lou. "Mama," he said. Then: "Daddy."

Lou's eyes moved up and down Zack curiously. She said suddenly, "Where you been? You got my tobacco."

"I told you, Lou. Remember?" Tommy said easily. "You know. The hospital."

"You coming home?" Isom asked. His small eyes were moist.

"Maybe so," Zack answered.

"Come on, Zack, sit down over here," Tommy urged. He led Zack to a chair between Isom and Lou. "Tell you what we're going to do. We're going to step outside here for a few minutes and let you visit some. We'll be right outside if you need anything."

"Tommy—" Guy said.

"It's all right," Tommy told him. "I'll be responsible."

"The doctor said—"

"I know what the doctor said," Tommy replied. "The doctor's not here."

"All right," Guy said in resignation. "It's up to you."

"I know. Come on."

Tommy and Guy and Angus left the room and closed the door and stood in the hallway, listening. They could not hear anything.

"Goddamn it, Tommy, that boy could be killing them two old people right now," Angus complained.

"I think we'd hear it if he was," Tommy whispered irritably. "Let's leave them alone. Dear God, they deserve to be treated like people sometime in their lives."

"How long you want to give them?" Guy asked.

"Fifteen minutes. Twenty. I don't know," Tommy said.

"What's long enough for the last time? Let's just keep listening for anything."

They stood in the corridor near the door and listened and smoked cigarettes and waited. The corridor was cool and dark. Footsteps clicked off its walls like sharp slaps. The sweep-second wall clock over the door leading into the tax office hummed monotonously and the slender red needle moved in its crawling circle of seconds.

Tommy leaned against the wall near the door and thought of the brittle minds of Isom and Lou. They thought, understood, spoke in fragments, like the strobing of a dimming light. It was as though the nerve endings of their brain cells—the microscopic wet wiring between pinspots of message centers—had frayed and broken. And in their brains there were pockmarks of scar tissue where the electricity of their thinking sizzled and burned, leaving a dance of visions and a babel of voices, meaning nothing.

But they had always been that way, Tommy realized. The kindest remark ever made of Isom and Lou was that they were eccentric. Tommy's father had once said, "Listen close to crazies. Sometimes they say the truth too clear to understand." Did they? Tommy wondered. Did Isom and Lou tell about themselves too openly, too honestly? Did Isom steal Lou, as Lou had claimed? Did he walk into a house somewhere and take Lou by the arm and drag her outside and drive away with her in his wagon? And if Isom had stolen her, why didn't she run away? Why had she stayed?

Zack was insane, Tommy thought as he paced the corridor. And maybe it wasn't his fault. Maybe it was nothing more than diseased genes locked in a single fishtailed sperm, slipping through the hot, slick walls of a womb, wiggling its way blindly to a waiting egg. But Zack at least had chemicals to quiet him and to contain him. Zack would be fed and clothed and attended. There was no one to care for Isom and Lou.

The basement employees of the Onslow County Courthouse began to arrive. They were surprised to find Tommy and Guy and Angus in the corridor, standing apart, not speaking. But none of the employees spoke. They ducked their heads in nods and hurried into their offices and closed the doors.

"Curious, ain't they?" Angus said sarcastically.

"Yeah," Guy muttered. He lit another cigarette.

"What time is it?" Angus asked.

"A little after eight," Tommy said.

"Damn it, Tommy," Angus snapped. "Maybe it ain't bothering you—which don't surprise me none in the least, since I never saw a lawyer bothered by the first damn thing—but I'm getting restless as a whore in church about this standing around. I got to open the store. Either you go in there or I'm going to."

Tommy looked again at his watch and then at the clock over the doorway to the tax office. "All right," he agreed. "It's been a little over twenty minutes. Let's see what's happened."

Isom and Zack were sitting exactly as they had been, in the exact postures, with the exact expressions on their faces. Lou was standing by the map, looking at the place where Tommy said she lived. Tommy knew they had not spoken a single word.

"Well," Tommy said pleasantly. "I guess it's time we got you back up to your house and let Zack get some rest."

Isom stood. "Time to go," he said heavily, seriously.

"Say goodbye to Zack," Tommy said. "Zack, say goodbye to your folks."

Zack stood and stepped toward his father. He extended his hand and Isom accepted it and their hands rose and fell once.

"I come home, you can tell me some more stories," Zack said.

"Tell you about them Yankees," Isom said. He turned his head as though looking over his shoulder. His body stiffened. A strange smile crowded onto his small mouth.

"Say goodbye to your mother," Tommy urged.

Zack turned to Lou. He walked to her and awkwardly embraced her. Lou was confused. She stood unmoving and then her arms folded slowly around him and her hands opened on his back and she patted him gently.

"Goodbye," Zack said in a loud voice.

"Goodbye," Lou whispered. She drew a quick, deep breath. "Goodbye, son."

Zack stepped back and looked at Guy and offered his wrists.

"It's all right, Zack," Guy told him. "We won't need to do that." He opened the door and Zack stepped out into the corridor and Guy followed him.

Angus swallowed hard. He said, "Well, Isom, you come down to see me soon. Bring me some honey. I'm needing some."

Isom smiled foolishly. "You got money, I got honey," he said.

"Yeah," Angus mumbled softly. "I got money, you got honey." He looked at Lou. "Sure wish you'd make me some soap for sale one of these days, Lou. I guess it'd make us all rich."

Lou did not reply. She stared at the closed door. Her face was empty. Her mind could not tell her that she would never again see Zack, but she knew it. Something had said it. Some forgotten instinct, as distant as the pain of her splitting body and the memory of the warm, wet baby flesh that she had pulled from the split and rubbed against her face.

TWENTY-SEVEN

December 11

BECAUSE SHE HAD NOT SLEPT WELL AND BECAUSE SHE knew that Jesse had not slept well, Anna had prepared breakfast before sunrise and the two had eaten in silence.

"Think I'll drive up and look at the house," Jesse said after breakfast. "See what needs to be done. If the weather's right, Pete'll be up there."

"You'll be back in time to go to the courthouse?" Anna asked.

"I'll be back."

"Want us to pick up Aubrey and have him go in with us?"

"All right."

"Almost wish I didn't have to go," Anna said. "I don't want to hear Zack."

"Guess I feel the same," Jesse replied.

Jesse had missed the work on the house, missed being on the mountain with Pete and Aubrey. The house preoccupied him, made his hands busy with timbers and tools, filled time, quieted him. And when he needed it, the house could blot out (like an eclipse) the torture of memory. He knew that it was a trick of the mind, an induced hypnotic state, yet it worked. He could call up the house on command by seeing the last act of work—the last driven nail, the last pencil mark for the saw—and then he could take the house apart, board by board, until there was nothing left but fallen trees and earth and, near the house, the criss-cross ditches of the frightened archeologist.

The house (or his mind) had failed him only once: in the testimony of Henry Upchurch. He had not been able to blot out Henry Upchurch, or Eddie Copeland.

Jesse was not surprised to find Pete Armstrong at the house. Pete was old and the habit of early work was old with him. His face was gray in the cold, his eyes watered. A dribble of snuff was frozen in the cracks of his lips.

"Aubrey ain't with you?" Pete asked.

"Didn't go by for him," Jesse said.

"Just as well. Too cold up here for Aubrey, him having his trouble."

"I guess," Jesse said. "He wants to do more than he can, anyway. Worries me some."

"Knows his lumber. Sure does," Pete said admiringly. "I knew his daddy. His daddy was a logger, too. His daddy couldn't add one and one, but he'd walk a tract of trees and tell you how many two-by-fours you'd get from it. Down to the shavings. He was good at it."

"I remember," Jesse replied.

"Weather holds, I'll get more siding up," Pete said. He nodded rapidly at his own decision. "Air's clean, Jesse. Clean as I ever saw it. Get this kind of day two, maybe three, times a year."

"It is. You feeling all right, Pete?"

"Fine, fine," Pete replied. "You ain't planning on working up here today, are you?" he asked, fumbling with his snuff tin.

"No," Jesse told him. "Just came up to look around. The trial's still going on. I'll go back down for it."

"Yeah, yeah," Pete said, smacking his lips. "Went by Angus' store yesterday, about night. He was saying they's lots of folks in there at the courthouse. Said they ought to hang the bastard."

Jesse lit a cigarette and watched Pete playing nervously with his snuff tin. Pete was embarrassed about the trial, uncomfortable because he had said what he did. Jesse remembered suddenly the day that his father had died and Pete's late-night visit at Ed Meeker's funeral home. Pete had dressed in a faded gabardine suit that was heavily odored by mothballs. His face had been nicked by a razor and the nicks were covered with small shreds of tissue. His hair had glistened with a perfumed oil. He had held a small felt hat discolored by sweat stains. He did not know what to do, or what to say, but he was there, standing bravely before the coffin, looking at the serene face of an old friend. "Fairest man I ever seen," Pete had said. "Make you work, but give you the wage, and let you know he'd appreciated what you'd been doing." He had tried to laugh at some small incident he'd remembered, but the tears had clouded his small eyes and he had had to wipe them away with the knuckles of his fingers. And as he stood before the coffin, someone had entered and said aloud, "What's that I smell? Mothballs?" And Pete had left quickly, ashamed. He had not attended the funeral.

"Can't ever tell what's going to happen in a thing like that," Jesse said slowly. "Hard for me to think about it."

"Would be, would be," Pete said. "Uh-huh, uh-huh." He sucked on the snuff and rolled the tobacco tin in his hand. "Angus was saying Isom's boy was going to show up today."

"What they say," Jesse said.

"Makes a man wonder," Pete mumbled. "Boy's crazy. Always was. Been knowing his daddy since he showed up, forty years ago."

Jesse was surprised. "That long?" he asked.

Pete nodded and slipped the tobacco tin into his pocket. "Helped him out putting the roof on that shack of his. I just come up on him up there in the woods. Didn't know nothing about what he was doing. I done some work there, sure did. Always liked Isom. Lou, too. They's strange enough, but I liked them."

"I never saw too much of them," Jesse said.

"Nobody did that I know of. Nobody. Way they like it, I guess." Pete wiped his eyes again and looked proudly at the house. He said, "Weather may be all right for putting up some sideboards."

"We had some covered, didn't we?" Jesse asked.

"Some. Enough to work on."

"You be the judge, Pete. You know it better'n me," Jesse said.

"Uh-huh," Pete mumbled absently. "Well, I wouldn't do it if I didn't think it was all right. Sure wouldn't."

Jesse dropped his cigarette. He said, "I'll try to get back up before the day's over. If it don't take too long."

"Don't matter," Pete said quickly. "I'm fine. Do all right with it. Long as them holes don't start talking to me."

"What holes, Pete?"

"Them that fellow made when he was digging up here, over by where we gone put up the barn."

"Didn't know they was talking," Jesse said gently.

Pete nodded vigorously and looked suspiciously toward the ditches. He spat a brown stream over his shoulder. "They was doing something a few days ago," he said gravely.

"Probably the wind," Jesse replied. "It swirls around up here."

"Wadn't no wind blowing," Pete said firmly, shaking his head.

"Maybe it was a bird got down in there, or a squirrel," Jesse replied. He thought of the story Angus had told him, that animals would not go on the land.

"Wadn't no bird. Wadn't nothing else. I looked."

Jesse knew Pete was not arguing. Pete believed he had heard something. But Pete was old. The old heard voices. His own father had heard voices, Jesse remembered. Before he died, his father had conducted bold conversations with apparitions that appeared outside the window above his bed. There was nothing mystic about it, his father had declared angrily. The people were there, asking him questions. It was his duty to answer them.

"Well, there's lots of Indian stories about this place,"

Jesse said slowly. "Gets in a man's mind sometimes." He looked at Pete. Pete was staring at him, puzzled. "I've had some thoughts about it myself," Jesse lied. "Working up here by myself. One day, late in the summer, I thought I could hear the air coming out of the caves up on the mountain."

Pete laughed softly. He rubbed at his eyes with his fingers and sucked on the snuff with his tongue. "Well, if it's haints, I might ought to get to knowing them. Be one myself soon enough."

"Pete, you been saying that for twenty years," Jesse told him.

Pete cackled loudly.

The courtroom was again filled and the corridor crowded. The people talked expectantly of Zack Vickers being called as a witness by William Fred. The story had been started in Angus Helton's hardware store, by Angus. He knew that Zack would be in Tickenaley, he had said. Never mind how he knew, he did. It was personal. Something he was involved in that was nobody's damned business. And no one had doubted Angus. Surely he knew. He had known about Quinton Cale and Henry Upchurch. He had known about the photographs. And he knew about Zack.

"They got him fixed up so he can testify," Angus had said. "I don't know how. Drugs, I guess. Somebody was saying they'd been giving him electric shock treatments. Maybe that's it."

Angus had made it seem vague—whispering the news, as he did when he really knew the truth. And Angus knew. He knew also that Isom and Lou would not attend the trial.

"Don't push me on how I know that, but I'll guarantee it," Angus had whispered. "No need for them to be there. Told Ellis myself that it wouldn't do nothing but make them look like freaks. Guess I know Isom as good as anybody does. Better'n most."

And as they talked of the day's spectacle inside the courtroom and in the corridor leading to the courtroom, the people of the valley did not recognize the strangers mingling quietly among them, their faces solemn, their eyes angry. They were the crusaders that William Fred had accused Parker of importing, and they were feeding their energy from the brave gossip of an executioner's justice. The placards of their belief were locked in the trunks of their cars and in the van, like the weaponry of small, fierce bands of liberation fighters.

The courtroom exchange that began at nine o'clock had been prearranged in Hugh Richards' chambers. William Fred called Zack Vickers as a witness for the state and Parker objected, requesting a mistrial. Hugh cited Georgia law and permitted the witness. Parker smiled pleasantly. His argument in chambers had been purposely weak; he wanted Zack on the witness stand more than William Fred did. Zack was a greater risk for William Fred than for Parker. William Fred had to make the jury believe that Zack was telling the truth; Parker knew that he only had to discredit what Zack said.

Zack was dressed in a tan suit with a white, open-neck shirt. Clean-shaven, his hair groomed, Zack looked boyish and uneasy. His eyes danced anxiously over the silent, watching crowd. He saw Eddie Copeland and a quick, involuntary smile flickered over his mouth and then disappeared. Eddie sat rigid, his eyes alert, his lips in a thin, hard bite. Zack was led to the witness stand and sworn. His voice was barely audible.

"Now, Zack, I don't want you to be afraid of this courtroom or any of the people here," William Fred said gently. "I'm going to ask you some questions and I want you to answer them to the best of your ability. Do the best you can, I mean. Just tell me what you think. If the question confuses you—if you don't understand what I mean by it—just let me know, and I'll try to ask it in a way that will make it clear. It may be that Mr. Mewborn, sitting over there—" he gestured to Parker "—will want to stop the questions, and the judge will make a decision on that. But that's the way the court works. It's not meant to scare you. Do you understand all of that?"

Zack looked at Hugh Richards and mumbled, "Yessir."

"Tell Mr. Autry," Hugh said.

"Yessir," Zack repeated, turning to William Fred.

"Do you know the man sitting over there—" William Fred pointed toward Eddie "—who is named Eddie Copeland?"

Quietly: "Yessir."

"You've known Eddie Copeland for a long time?"

Zack nodded. He said, "Uh-huh."

"How long?"

"We was in the Army."

William Fred shuffled papers on his desk. He said, "Let's see, that was from 1977 to 1979." He looked at Parker. Parker sat placidly. "Is that right?"

Zack's face brightened. It was a question he remembered from the rehearsal. He said, "That's right."

"That's good, Zack," William Fred said. "That's good. Answer out loud and clear." He began a slow pacing in front of the witness stand. "Now, Eddie Copeland came to visit you in October, with another friend, Albert Bailey. Is that right?"

"That's right," Zack said quickly.

"And you know that during that visit you and Eddie and Albert went to the home of Jesse Wade on October fourteen, which was a Tuesday, and there were several people killed at that house. Do you remember that?"

"That's right."

"That's right?" William Fred asked. "You mean, yes?"

"Yes," Zack corrected timidly.

"Now, Zack, I want you to think very carefully. Did you kill any of those people?" William Fred asked.

"No sir," Zack answered emphatically. He looked at Eddie. The smile flickered again across his face.

"Who did kill those people?" William Fred asked. He turned to face the objection from Parker, but Parker did not object.

"Albert did it," Zack said. "Albert and Eddie."

"Jesus," Eddie hissed in a harsh laugh. Hugh slapped the palm of his hand sharply on his desk. A rumble rolled through the courtroom. Parker caught Eddie by the arm and clamped it in a visegrip. He leaned to Eddie. "You shut up," he whispered angrily. "That man may be your only way out of this."

"He's lying," Eddie snapped.

"I mean it. Shut up," Parker ordered.

Zack's story, told in rehearsed yes-and-no answers to the narrative of William Fred's questions, was a story of the chronology of death and accusation. By Zack's accounting, Albert had murdered Jean, Macy, and Doyle; Eddie had killed Winston, Carl, and Florence.

Zack admitted that he had killed the dog and her puppies. "Dogs scare me," he volunteered. "They was barking and jumping around and I shot them." He also admitted that he had watched the raping, but denied that he had participated. Albert had raped. And Eddie. Albert had raped all three women. Eddie had raped Macy and Florence and maybe Jean; Zack was not certain about Jean.

"How is it you remember about two of the women and not the other one?" William Fred asked.

"She was in the bedroom," Zack said haltingly. "I didn't go in there but one time, when Albert was on her."

"You saw the other rapes?"

"Yessir. They was in the kitchen," Zack said. "I was watching them."

"Did the younger girl—Florence Wade—beg for her life?"

"Yessir," Zack mumbled. "She didn't fight back."

"Who did she beg for her life?"

"Eddie. She begged Eddie."

Hugh stirred restlessly in his chair. He rubbed his neck with his hand and looked curiously to Parker. He said, "Mr. Mewborn, you must recognize that the direction of these questions leads the witness."

"I do, Your Honor," Parker replied calmly.

"Well, if you don't care to object, I think I have to," Hugh said. "Mr. Autry, please refrain from leading the witness."

William Fred bowed his head to hide the smile. He mumbled, "Yes, Your Honor."

The questioning of Zack lasted for an hour and a half. Whatever had been used by doctors to calm Zack caused him to slur words and his answers were often repeated. It was a tedious process and, when William Fred yielded his witness to Parker, Hugh called for a recess.

Parker used the thirty minutes in the holding room to warn Eddie against any further outbursts in the courtroom.

"Every time you open your mouth, you lose a juror," Parker lectured, "and I'll guarantee you you don't have that many you can lose—if any at all."

Donald Bridges agreed. "Believe it, Eddie," he said. "That's the way it works, and that's minimum."

Parker paced the floor, stretching the muscles of his back. He said, "You've got one chance in all of this and that's to leave some doubt—just enough. Right now, Zack's ripping you apart."

"I say he's lying," Eddie said calmly.

"He's a witness that could serve you up well done, goddamn it," Parker snapped. "Now, it's time you left that chip on your shoulder in here and gave me a little bit of help." He lit a cigarette and smoked and paced and thought. He could feel Eddie's eyes following him. They were eyes that belonged in the body of a reptile, not a human, he thought. "Did he say anything we didn't cover?" Parker asked at last.

"He didn't say nothing, period. He told lies," Eddie said.

"The stuff about Albert?"

Eddie shrugged. "I told you that myself."

Parker whirled to face Eddie. He hissed, "Listen, damn it, don't get smart with me. You know goddamn well what I'm talking about."

"There's nothing else about Albert," Eddie said sullenly.

"What'd he leave out?" Donald asked thoughtfully.

"He left out the goddamn truth," Eddie said desperately. "He left out humping that old woman. He left out holding the shotgun on me."

"What about the Civil War stuff?" Parker asked.

"What stuff?"

"The Civil War. All that raving you talked about in your statement."

"It was crazy. Just crazy," Eddie said. "It was nothing."

"How'd he sound?"

Eddie looked at Parker in disbelief. "Crazy, like I said. He sounded crazy, like his old man sounded sometimes in the cabin."

Parker pushed the cigarette into the ashtray and pulled his papers from his briefcase and began reading. Donald Bridges looked over his shoulder.

"You going to do what I think?" Donald asked.

"I'm going to do what I have to," Parker replied.

Parker asked his first question as he walked toward Zack in the witness chair: "Who wanted to go to Jesse Wade's farm?"

The sudden, unexpected question and Parker's bitter tone confused Zack. He licked his lips with his tongue and looked at William Fred.

"Who wanted to go to Jesse Wade's farm?" Parker said again, standing in front of Zack.

Zack's eyes blinked rapidly. He did not answer.

"It's a simple question, Mr. Vickers," Parker said. "You answered Mr. Autry's questions, now you have to answer mine. Was it you that wanted to go to Jesse Wade's farm? Or Albert? Or Eddie?"

"Albert wanted a car," Zack mumbled.

"So it was Albert?"

"Yes—yessir."

"Did you know Jesse Wade?"

Zack nodded and whispered, "Yessir. Some."

"Did you know Carl and Doyle Wade?"

"Yessir."

"And you knew they were working on the land below the Mountain of the Caves. Is that right?"

Zack breathed deeply. He dropped his head. He mumbled, "They was cutting down some trees."

"Did you know Jean Wade, the wife of Jesse?" Parker asked.

Zack's head stayed bowed. "She lived at the house," he said, his voice quivering.

"Had you ever been to the house before you went there with Albert and Eddie?" Parker asked.

Zack shook his head once.

"Let the record show the witness indicated a no," Parker said. He began to walk back toward the defense table, then stopped and turned. "Zack," he said softly, "did you kill any of those people?"

Zack shook his head rapidly. He rubbed his hands together in a washing motion. "Albert did. Albert and Eddie."

"But you were there? Is that right? You watched it happen?"

Zack nodded. "Yessir," he said in a whisper.

"And what you're telling us is the truth? You know it has to be the truth, don't you?"

"Yes—yessir."

Parker began to move back toward the witness stand, close to Zack. He could see Zack's pulsebeat jumping in the temple of his forehead.

"Zack, tell me what you know about the Civil War," Parker said. "Do you know any stories about the Civil War?"

"Objection," William Fred snapped, springing from his chair. "That is an immaterial and deliberately baiting question, and counselor knows it."

"Immaterial? Baiting?" Parker growled. "It happens to be a significant issue in the statement that the prosecutor himself took from my client. It was said repeatedly that the witness told a story about the Civil War while the crime was being committed. Defense has listened, without objection, to probably the most detailed description ever given in a murder trial in this state. It would seem that the prosecution should exercise the same kind of tolerance."

"What point are you driving at?" Hugh asked.

"Just this, Your Honor," Parker said wearily. "If the witness was not in a coherent state during the commission of the crime, how can we expect his testimony to be unbiased and valid beyond reasonable doubt? I think the defense needs to establish this point, but it cannot if it is handcuffed by objections over what the prosecutor considers immaterial."

Hugh laced his fingers and propped them against his lower lip. He looked at William Fred and then at Parker. If he denied the questioning, an appeals court would kill him, he thought. He admired Parker. Parker had been patient. He looked at Harold Sellers, sitting beside William Fred. Harold was writing frantically.

"I'm going to allow the question, Mr. Autry," Hugh said at last. "It would seem that this issue is not one that Mr. Mewborn has made up out of the blue, but has taken from official documents of the trial. However obscure it may seem, the court must consider relevant the question of competence during the commission of the crime. I'm going to permit this line of questioning, but I want to caution Mr. Mewborn that I will not allow him to draw conclusions. This is a matter for experts in the field."

"Thank you, Your Honor," Parker said. He stared triumphantly at William Fred, waiting for him to sit. He had never before seen bewilderment on William Fred's face; it had the look of a timid child.

"Now, Zack," Parker began easily, "tell me, do you remember telling Eddie and Albert a story about the Civil War when you were at Mr. Wade's house?"

Zack's lips were parted. A vague expression was on his face. He stared beyond Parker, looking at nothing.

"Do you remember, Zack?" Parker asked. "You remember telling a story about the War Between the States?"

Zack did not reply. His expression did not change. A sudden fear tightened in Parker's throat. Did Zack understand him? he wondered. Did he know what the Civil War was? Or did he only know stories? He could hear Donald Bridges coughing signals at the defense table.

"Did you talk about it, Zack?" Parker pressured gently. "Did you talk about the Yankees?"

It was as though Parker had waved his hand through the beam of some hidden electric eye that began a machinery deep in Zack's memory. A smile, like a coveted knowledge, leaped into Zack's face. His body raised in the chair. He leaned forward comfortably, his elbows resting on his knees. His eyes brightened. His head began bobbing.

"Daddy knows about the Yankees," he said proudly.

Parker stepped closer to Zack. He said, "He does? Did he tell you stories about the Yankees, Zack?"

Zack's head stopped bobbing. He leaned slowly back into the chair. His mouth opened and closed in a chewing motion. His eyes rose toward the balcony of the courtroom. He seemed to be staring into another place, in another time. He cleared his throat and the voice that rose from him was the mimicked voice of an old man, a deep bass softened by years and by phlegm.

"Me and Ross found them when we was going home," the voice in Zack said.

Parker stepped back suddenly and looked at William Fred.

"Your Honor—" William Fred began.

Hugh raised his hands to both attorneys. His eyes widened in astonishment. He instinctively leaned toward Zack.

"The Yankees done all the killing they could up on the ridge and everybody was scattering," Zack continued, smacking his lips.

"Your Honor, please—" William Fred said.

"Let him talk," Hugh hissed.

Ellis stood near the door leading to the holding room. He looked at Jesse. Jesse's eyes were fixed on Zack.

Zack wagged his head and laughed strangely. He lifted his head and wet his lips. He said, "Goddamn Yankees. Killing like it was hog-killing time. Couldn't walk on the ground in some of them places, bodies was so thick. Blood like it was mud puddles after a rain. Slick as all. Man and boy and horse and mule, sliding in blood. Couldn't nothing stand up. Goddamn Yankees. Didn't matter. It was alive, the Yankees killed it. You could smell blood like it was flowers blooming in a pasture.

"But they was Yankees that was dead, too. Me and Ross counted up to a hundred and quit. Wadn't worth it, Ross said. If you couldn't count a million they wadn't worth counting at all. Ross said he'd killed twenty Yankees in one day down there below Chattanooga. Said he'd killed Yankees until his gun barrel got hot enough to cook meat on. Said he'd killed one with his knife, cut him gut to neck. But Ross was lying. Maybe Ross killed one man in all the time he was out there. Maybe killed a mule. But Ross was good to have around. Wouldn't sleep. Keep watch all the time and left me to rest some. Had eyes on him like a cat, but after a while they was bags drooping down under them like they was sacks. But old Ross wouldn't sleep. Said he'd wadn't sleeping except on his own bed.

"We was going round by Stanley, where the Yankees was, down there below Knoxville. That's when me'n Ross saw the house, from up in the woods. They was some horses out front and me'n Ross settled down and watched out. Wadn't long to three Yankees come out and rode off, fast-like, pulling a packhorse with them. Ross said to wait and see if they come back, and we stayed up there in the woods but nothing happened and Ross said the Yankees was gone, said Yankees couldn't keep still long enough to shit. Yankees had to be moving south or they wadn't happy. Ross said, 'Well, by God, let 'em keep going, goddamn 'em. Go on off down there in the ocean. I'm tired of fighting the bastards.'"

Zack laughed quietly and smacked his lips and pulled on his chin with his fingers. He said, "Yeah, that's what Ross said. Ross, all he wanted was to go home. He was tired of fighting. Said he wanted to wash off and climb on his woman and stay there a week. What he said.

"We stood off and looked at that house for two, three hours, me'n Ross. Then we just walked up, like we owned it. Walked right up on the porch and opened the door, like it was ours.

"Didn't take no time to find 'em. The man was in the hallway. Had his face shot off. Old man. Too old to fight the Yankees. The two women was in the front room. One of them was dead. Had her throat cut. Other was beat bad. They was both naked. The Yankees had took them both, done their way with them.

"Me'n Ross, we got the one that was beat bathed up some and put her in the bed and went out and buried the two that was dead. We stayed around there a few hours and when the woman could talk she said it was drunk Yankees that done it. Said they come roaring in and killed her daddy and then took her and her older sister—that was the dead woman—and did their jobs on them, over and over, taking turns. Said her sister started fighting back and one of them Yankees just took his knife and slit her throat like he was killing a rabbit. Didn't mean nothing to him. Nothing.

"Woman said they was neighbors up the road and they'd come to get her if we'd stop off and tell them. Said to leave her a gun to have if the Yankees come back. Ross said we'd tell the neighbors. He left her his pistol. Showed her how to use it and we took off. We wadn't a half-mile off when we heard the gun go off. Ross just shook his head. 'Knowed she'd do it,' Ross said. 'Goddamn Yankees,' he said. 'Ain't no girl of the South stand a Yankee's goober in her,' he said. Ross said he bet they wadn't no neighbors living where she'd said. They wadn't."

Zack shook his head sadly and smiled absently and lifted his face and looked around the courtroom. He began nodding as though greeting the onlookers.

"Ellis," Hugh said quietly, waving his hand toward Zack.

Ellis crossed the courtroom and touched Zack on the arm and said, "Come on, Zack. Let's go get some rest."

Zack obeyed the pull of Ellis' hand. He eased from the witness chair and walked limply beside Ellis out of the courtroom. Eddie looked down at the floor as Zack passed him.

TWENTY-EIGHT

December 11

JESSE LEFT THE COURTHOUSE WITH ANNA AND AUBREY and drove away hurriedly, turning the car south toward Aubrey's house. Zack's story and Zack's voice—a mimic of the voice that Isom had used, though more strained—had stunned him. It was as though a ghost had been bred into both Isom and Zack and they had become unwilling mediums of a powerful, heckling spirit too loud to die.

And the story itself—the same as the slayings of his own family. The same. Murder and rape and arrogance. And Zack in the middle of it, confusing what he had heard and memorized with the killings happening randomly around him. It was mockery, Jesse thought angrily. It was not enough that his family had died savagely; they had to be slain again in the fantasy of an unexpected story. The people in the courtroom would make it part of the lore of the trial. The people would say, "Just like what Zack said, that's the way Jesse's people died. Same thing."

"I ain't going back, Jesse," Aubrey said abruptly from the back seat of the car. "I'm going up to help Pete on the house."

"Don't much blame you," Jesse replied bitterly. "Having to listen to what we just heard."

"Boy's crazy, like I said," Aubrey complained. "Could of guessed it."

"Do you think he did any—any of it?" Anna asked.

"I don't know," Jesse answered. He turned the car into the driveway of Aubrey's house. "Maybe not."

"The other'n did," Aubrey said emphatically. "You can tell it by looking at him. Tell it by his eyes." He slapped his hand against the seat. "I ain't going back, Jesse. I ain't sitting through any more of it. I do, I think I'll kill that boy right there."

"I know the feeling," Jesse said quietly. "I'll tell William Fred."

"You tell him. You tell him the next time I see that boy he'd better be strapped in the chair, or I'm gone kill him myself."

At Anna's house, Jesse tried to rest, but he could not. He could hear Zack's story, told proudly. The way Zack sat in the witness chair, the wagging of his head and the wandering of his hands, had been exactly like Isom. And though the story (the suddenness of it, the violence of it) had angered Jesse, he felt only pity for Zack and Isom. Their condemnation was greater than any punishment; their condemnation would not be over until they died.

At twelve-forty-five, Ellis called to speak to Jesse.

"Are you all right?" Ellis asked.

"I guess."

"Judge should of stopped it. Wadn't no need to make you hear all that."

"I guess he did what he thought was best," Jesse said.

"There may be somebody asking you if you've ever heard Isom do the same thing. I think it's best if we don't talk about when we went up there."

"I don't plan to," Jesse said.

"I heard some reporters talking," Ellis told him. "Sounded like they was more interested in whether there'd be a mistrial. Maybe Parker said something to them."

"Could that happen?" Jesse asked.

"Jesse, that's a court of law," Ellis said bluntly. "Any goddamn thing could happen. They could feed Copeland to the lions or give him the Congressional Medal of Honor. Nobody knows." He paused and Jesse could hear a confused sigh. "Tell you the truth, Jesse, it's got me worried. They get a mistrial and he's liable to walk out sooner or later. William Fred's got the best case he'll ever have, but I ain't sure. He never should of put Zack up. Damn fool. Got too eager. Thought he had Parker whipped. All Parker needs is a thread to grab hold of. He could unravel the whole thing."

Jesse held the phone in silence. He remembered the bright, expectant look on Eddie's face as Hugh Richards lectured the courtroom after Zack had been led away.

"What'd they do with Zack?" Jesse asked.

"Took him down to the hospital. They'll take him back to Milledgeville this afternoon," Ellis answered. Then: "Poor, crazy bastard. Sounded just like Isom. Wonder where all that comes from."

"No telling."

"You heard about Isom and Lou coming down to see Zack this morning?" Ellis asked.

"No."

"Tommy Moss set it up. Guy was there. Said it was so damn sad it almost made him cry. Said they were like strangers."

"Guess none of them know what's going on."

"Yeah," Ellis agreed. "I just wanted to check with you. I'm going to walk down and see if Hugh's finished his meeting with William Fred and Parker. I'll see you this afternoon."

"Aubrey's not coming back," Jesse said. "Said he couldn't hear any more. Said he was afraid he'd kill the Copeland boy if he saw him again."

Ellis laughed cynically. He said, "You know, Jesse, if that's so, maybe I ought to go bring him in myself. Way I feel right now, Aubrey makes sense."

* * *

267

Hugh's meeting in chambers with William Fred and Parker was deliberately informal and brief. Hugh poured each man a single shot of straight bourbon without asking if he wanted it. He lifted his glass in a toast and said, "To sanity." And the three men swallowed the bourbon quickly and Hugh put away the evidence of the glasses.

"Gentlemen," Hugh said in an exaggerated drawl, "that was damn well something else. First for me, I'll tell you."

"I didn't know he'd do that. It wasn't what I was after," Parker said.

Hugh laughed. "Ain't none of us that good. Clarence Darrow wadn't that good."

"Surprised me," William Fred admitted. "I've interviewed him a half-dozen times, maybe more, and there's never been a hint of it. I even asked him about it once. He said he didn't know what Eddie was talking about. He's got no idea what the Civil War was. If I'd known he was going to do what he did, I damn well wouldn't have put him up."

Hugh paced slowly beside his desk, exercising the tightness in his shoulders and back. He mumbled, "Got to change that chair out there. Gets smaller every year."

William Fred and Parker smiled in unison.

Hugh continued: "Y'all get a look at old Jack when Zack was in that tale? Poor old bastard. Turned white as a sheet. Thought he was going to bolt and run. Think he would have if Ellis hadn't been standing in his way."

"Couldn't much blame him," William Fred said. "I didn't feel too good about it myself."

"Damn good story, though," Hugh said. "Damn good. Reminded me of one I heard one time. Almost the same thing. Southern girl raped by a Yankee. Fellow from Georgia found her. Fellow looked a little like Clark Gable, or me. Girl spread her legs out and said, 'Give it to me. If I'm pregnant, I want to think it's got a chance of being Southern.'"

Hugh chuckled at himself. William Fred and Parker smiled pleasantly. At least it was a new story.

"What Zack said sounded a lot like what we've got here," Parker said.

Hugh continued pacing. His entire body shook in agreement. "It does," he said. "Rape, murder, three men." He looked at Parker and smiled. "Even Yankees," he added. "Well, what'd y'all think about this fix we're all in?"

Parker spoke first: "I kind of thought you'd tell us."

Hugh laughed. "Parker," he said, "I have to run for this office. Which just means I wear the robe and sit in the chair" —he looked at both men—"and get to kick ass once in a while. Fact is, there's some times I'd just like to be lawyering, so I could talk things over."

"I think it's Parker's play," William Fred said earnestly. "If I get a witness flipping out, all I want to do is get him off the stand. And that's my position. Far as I'm concerned, Zack's testimony is over."

"Ummmmmmh," Hugh rumbled, standing beside his desk, lighting his pipe. "Parker, what'd you think about that?"

"Well, I know there's some options," Parker said cautiously. "I'll have to think them out."

"Uh-huh," Hugh said, sucking on his pipe. "Options." He said the word like it was an object he was studying. "That's true. Options." He blew a circle of smoke and looked thoughtfully at Parker. "Mistrial?" he asked. "Is that one?"

"Could be," Parker answered.

"Drawing a parallel to Zack's story?" Hugh asked.

"Good God, don't give him any ideas," William Fred exclaimed.

Hugh laughed again and drew on his pipe. "You ought to know by now that Parker ain't dumb," he said. He sat on the edge of his desk. The desk moved slightly under his weight. "Well, Parker, I sure as hell hope you don't ask for a mistrial. Fact is, the behavior of a witness, unless he just out-and-out confesses to everything and brings in some Polaroids to prove it, is shallow grounds for a mistrial." He pulled hard on his pipe and wads of balled smoke rose in the room. "At least in my court," he added. Then: "Let me say this to you, gentlemen: I ain't going to let you make much of it. Copeland's on trial, not Zack. If they find Copeland guilty, it'll be on evidence, not some ghost story."

"I'll go along with that," William Fred said eagerly.

Parker did not say anything. William Fred had been right: it was his play. He would at least make William Fred and Hugh wonder.

"All right," Hugh said. "Y'all go get some lunch or do your plotting or pull your pud or whatever it is you do out of my sight." He sat at his desk. "If you see Jack cowering around out there, tell him to go get me a whole ham and a pound of potato salad. I'm hungry." He smiled cynically at the two men.

William Fred did exactly as Parker had predicted: he announced at one-thirty that the state had concluded its case. He would not call any more witnesses. Donald Bridges wrote on a pad: "Didn't have any that was worth it." Parker smiled. Donald was right. There was the Army drill sergeant with proof of Eddie's expert marksmanship, but how could anyone miss from an inch away? There was a parole officer from Fort Wayne, the minister who had buried Eddie's parents, a psychiatrist who had examined Eddie at age sixteen—all willing to say that Eddie was cunning and unfeeling. But William Fred believed he had his evidence with the fingerprints and weapons and Henry Upchurch's testimony (which had been highly praised by the press). William Fred wanted the jurors to receive the case as quickly as possible, with those early impressions clear in their minds.

Parker did not ask for a mistrial. He knew his chances were better with Zack's outburst. He was not trying for a decision of guilt or innocence—only doubt. He believed that Zack had discredited his accusation of Eddie with his strange, sad story.

"Is counsel for the defense ready?" Hugh asked.

"Yes, Your Honor," Parker said.

Parker's first witness was a mild surprise—even to Donald Bridges. It was an impulse that Parker obeyed: he called Ellis Spruill.

"One thing, Mr. Spruill," Parker said. "I don't think this was covered specifically in your earlier testimony. Do you know for certain that the defendant participated in the gunfire at the cave during the arrest of the suspects?"

"I do not," Ellis said stiffly. "They were hidden. We couldn't tell who was firing. There was a lot of it."

"I see," Parker replied. "One other thing: from your description, the defendant emerged from a kind of tunnel at the back of the cave after you had been forced to kill one of the suspects—one Albert Bailey—and had ordered the surrender of the other two. Is that correct?"

"Yes."

"He was the last one that crawled out? The one at the very back of the tunnel?"

"Yes."

"And did the defendant resist arrest at that point?"

Ellis looked curiously at Parker. "No, he did not," he said.

"Was he relatively cooperative? I mean, did he say or indicate anything that would make you think he was a dangerous suspect?"

"We consider all suspects dangerous," Ellis answered. "It's best that way."

Parker smiled. "I can understand that, Mr. Spruill. I sure can. But the defendant didn't offer any resistance, or fight, did he?"

"No."

"That's all, Mr. Spruill. I thank you," Parker said. He looked at William Fred. William Fred was amused.

Parker had considered offering no witnesses, relying only on cross-examination and summation and the repeated, hammering reminder that guilt required proof beyond reasonable doubt. He had changed his mind before the trial began. Eddie had been unwavering in his statement. Not even David Buring, the psychiatrist who had interviewed and tested Eddie, could persuade him to change his statement. "That's the way it happened," Eddie said again and again. "That's the way I'll tell it." The only risk with Eddie was the chameleon moods of his personality. It was a risk Parker knew he must take: Eddie would have to be called as a witness.

And to prepare for Eddie's appearance, Parker called Dr. David Buring.

David Buring was from the Buring Clinic in Atlanta. He was fifty-five years old, a slender man with small, close-set eyes and thick auburn hair that he fingered constantly. His credentials were impressive, his reputation inarguably sound. During the month and a half that he had examined Eddie, he had become certain that his patient was a complex, disturbed man, but he doubted if Eddie had murdered anyone; Eddie was too methodical for an impulsive act that could potentially trap him. ("He's intelligent," Dr. Buring had explained to Parker. "But he's not easy to motivate. You'd call it laziness. It is, and it isn't. There's a lot of deliberation in him. He's calculating. He'd have to know what he's doing before he'd commit to it.")

Dr. David Buring wanted to be an important witness in the trial of Eddie Copeland. He was not. He was a preliminary act, a crowd baiter. Parker asked a series of questions that Donald Bridges had prepared. The answers sounded profound when said, but were too often qualified with the caution that human behavior was not an exact science.

"In your expert opinion, Dr. Buring, is Eddie Copeland psychotic?" Parker asked routinely.

"That's not easy to answer," the doctor replied. "Given varying moods and behaviors, as well as environmental influences, everyone in this room could be called psychotic to some degree. The real question is one of control. Eddie Copeland, in my opinion, has control. Perhaps even fear of not being in control."

"Your witness," Parker said to William Fred.

William Fred could sense the end of arguments. He rushed through a meaningless cross-examination challenging the validity of the tests that David Buring had administered to Eddie. The challenges were indignantly answered, citing research and data. And when he had become impatient with the exchange, William Fred said caustically, "I've heard enough from this witness from Atlanta, Your Honor. I have no more questions."

It was three o'clock and Hugh called for a fifteen-minute recess. He had become sleepy during David Buring's testimony; he needed to walk, to have his afternoon coffee.

He needed to clear his mind before Parker called Eddie Copeland to the witness stand.

"Are you afraid of what's going to happen out there?" Parker asked Eddie in the holding room.

Eddie's eyes blinked lazily. "I'm not," he said. "Are you?"

"Autry's not a fool," Parker warned quietly. "He'll rip you apart if he can."

Eddie stretched against the chair. He pushed his fingers together and his knuckles cracked.

"I mean it," Parker warned. "He can smell a lie like a bloodhound."

"I ain't worried about it," Eddie said easily. "You are."

Parker laughed incredulously. He stood and began pacing the room. He looked at his watch.

"I'll make you proud," Eddie said. "You'll see. I'll make you proud."

Parker's questioning of Eddie lasted forty-eight minutes. William Fred objected five times, accusing Parker of leading the witness. Hugh sustained each objection. Parker re-phrased each question. Eddie told the same story he had given in his statement.

It was Eddie's voice that angered Jesse. He had not heard Eddie speak before the testimony and Eddie's voice—listless (casual, brief) in the answers to Parker's questions—was irritating. The voice and the face were alike—belligerent without expression. Jesse knew it was a voice that reporters would write about and judge as weak, defenseless, timid. The reporters would be astonished that Eddie Copeland's voice was that of a murderer, Jesse thought. By their words (or by the implications of their words), the reporters would declare, "It seems unlikely that this man could kill." And Jesse knew that readers would try to hear Eddie's voice from the pages of newspapers and they would think of the voices around them and would agree that people were, in fact, very much as they sounded.

But none of the reporters would wonder how Jean

had sounded. Or Macy or Carl or Doyle or Florence. Or Winston.

As Jesse listened, Eddie's voice became a dull hum, like a bored reader of boring words, and Jesse could hear over it Winston's shrill, eager questions about his birthday and the gift of the rifle promised by Jesse. He remembered suddenly that Winston had stuttered slightly when excited. "C-c-can we shoot it?" Winston had begged. "Wh-when I get it?" And Jesse remembered (how had he forgotten?) that Macy had joked playfully with Winston, calling him Mr. Fastmouth. "Mr. Fastmouth, slow it down. One word at a time."

But the reporters would not judge Winston. They had never heard him speak.

Jesse saw Parker moving deliberately along the railing of the jury box. He was nodding thoughtfully. Then he stopped and faced Eddie and asked, "Did you kill any of the victims named in this case?"

"No," Eddie replied quietly. "I did not."

"Your witness, Mr. Autry," Parker said.

William Fred stood at the prosecutor's table. He stared at Eddie. He crossed his arms and began to sway slightly at the waist. He lifted his face to the ceiling. He sighed deeply, wearily. He said, "Do you really expect us to believe all of this, Mr. Copeland?"

"Objection, Your Honor," Parker snapped.

"Sustained," Hugh said. He pushed his face toward William Fred. "Do you have any questions of this witness, Mr. Autry?" he asked bluntly.

"Questions, Your Honor?" William Fred said. "Questions? Yes. I have the same questions of this witness that everyone in this courtroom has." He paused and glared at Eddie. Eddie's eyes narrowed. His mouth parted, then closed.

"Then ask them," Hugh ordered.

"I don't think I need to, Your Honor," William Fred whispered. "I think we all already know the answers." He sat heavily in his chair.

A voice murmured in the balcony.

Hugh dismissed Eddie from the witness stand and then

turned in his swivel chair to face the jury. He thought of William Fred. The son of a bitch. Not a single question. Putting it all on the crowd. "I know we've just had a recess," he said, "but I'm going to declare another one before Mr. Mewborn calls his other witnesses."

"I have no other witnesses, Your Honor," Parker said. "The defense rests."

"Then we'll recess before we begin summation. Thirty minutes," Hugh replied. He looked at Jack Pilgrim. "Mr. Bailiff, please see to the needs of the jurors."

Hugh stood and walked out of the courtroom and into his chambers. Jack stared at him quizzically.

TWENTY-NINE

December 11

DURING THE RECESS, WILLIAM FRED WASHED HIS FACE and brushed his teeth and dabbed his neck with aftershave lotion. It was his ritual before addressing a jury. It made him use his hands and gave him an opportunity to be alone, to think, to plan.

He did not feel comfortable. His handling of Eddie had not worked as he had wished. He had wanted a rush of voices behind him, agreeing. He had wanted the jury to feel an electric shock of voices, a mumbling of anger and power and warning. It had not happened. And there was Zack. A mistake. Zack's unexpected, rambling tale about a senseless killing during the Civil War had affected the jurors. He could see it in their faces. They had listened, transfixed, to the strange voice (more commanding than Zack's own voice) and they had forgotten the story of the killings by Eddie Copeland. Or, if they did remember, Parker would make Zack's testimony seem absurd in his summation. William Fred looked at himself in the mirror of the restroom. His eyes were red, his face sickly pale. I would, he thought to himself. I damn well would ride Zack's craziness like it was a goddamn parade horse.

He was left with one thing: the facts—the forensic facts. Henry Upchurch had been magnificent. He had made a strand of hair found on Jean Wade sound like a discovery of the cure for cancer. It was a hair from the head of Albert Bailey. He had explained fingerprints found in the house like a curator leading visitors on a tour of an art museum. The only thing he had not identified about the weapons used in the murders was the name and Social Security number of the craftsmen who made them.

William Fred had the facts. He had more facts than he had ever had in a case. But he did not have the one thing he needed: he did not have disagreement from Parker Mewborn. Parker had been like a parrot repeating a single line for the amusement of its master: Prove that Eddie Copeland did the killing. Prove it beyond a reasonable doubt.

Parker, by consent, gave the first summation. He had written three words on a three-by-five index card. The words had a curious rhyme scheme: "Fact, Zack, Attack." He held the card in the palm of his hand as he stood before the jurors.

"This will be a brief statement," Parker began. "First, I want to thank the jury for this service it is giving to the judicial process. Believe me, Judge Richards and Mr. Autry feel the same way. It is not an easy job. Mr. Autry and I represent the same system, but from two different points of view. Our job is to prosecute and defend to the best of our experience and ability. The juror's job is to listen and discern, to deliberate and decide. Your job is far more difficult than ours, but it is the cornerstone of our process of law. I sincerely thank you for what you are doing."

Parker let his eyes meet the face of each juror, searching for the unseen flicker of agreement. There was one man, stern-faced, leaning forward who seemed to be listening intently. Perhaps, Parker thought.

"I want to say this," Parker continued calmly. "Mr. Autry has presented one of the cleanest cases of pure fact that anyone could want. I am impressed by it. I agree with everything that Mr. Autry and Mr. Upchurch offered into evidence. I think I have related that during testimony. I believe Mr. Autry went overboard when he slipped in that question about the victims not standing a chance. It's the kind of thing that inflames the mind and insults the spirit.

"The fact is, the victim did stand a chance. My client, Eddie Copeland, who is on trial for their murder, was their chance, but he was afraid to do anything about it. He stood by and watched the murder of six innocent people. And, God knows, that fear, that failure to act, is a crime in itself. My client is aware of that. But that kind of fear is a difficult thing. What would any of us have done? I would like to think that we could give up our own life for our neighbor, as we are taught, but how many of us are ever truly faced with that option?

"So Mr. Autry has presented a case of fact. The only thing—the *only* thing—that he has not been able to prove is Eddie Copeland's guilt as one of those who committed the act of murder. And that is what this trial is about. Not that murder took place, but did Eddie Copeland murder.

"There has been so much sensationalism about this trial that it has been difficult to keep a clear head. Eddie Copeland's parents killed themselves, probably because they were distressed over it. There are those who say that Eddie killed them. But none of those people have asked how Eddie felt about it. He was hurt and ashamed. He elected to not go to the funeral, not because he didn't care but because he felt he had caused his parents great grief and did not want to insult their memory.

"But is the death of Eddie Copeland's parents a fact of his guilt in the murder of Jesse Wade's family? No. It is a tragedy. It is an awful, aching tragedy. It is a memory that Eddie Copeland will have to live with. And I will tell you truthfully, it is a memory that I will live with, because I was with them. I talked to them. I tried to counsel with them. In some strange way, I think their act was firmly in their mind even then."

Parker paused. He had not moved away from the jurors

since beginning his summation. He could see the stern-faced man's eyes blinking rapidly. Parker turned and began pacing. The click of his heels cracked off the walls of the courtroom. He could hear the deep breathing of the audience.

"At no time in the testimony of these witnesses did anyone say that Eddie Copeland definitely took part in anything," Parker said in a strong voice. "The sheriff admits that Eddie Copeland did not resist arrest. He says he does not know if Eddie participated in the gunfire at the arrest site. No one has lodged a complaint about Eddie Copeland threatening their lives since he has been incarcerated. He may have been a silent and sullen prisoner, but he has not attempted to escape and he has not refused to cooperate with authorities who have questioned him. All that is part of the record.

"Dr. Buring has said that Eddie is smart, not the kind of person to do a senseless, impulsive act. Now, I know that clever, shrewd people can fool even the most professional psychiatrists. But that is not an easy accomplishment. You, as jurors, must make that decision among yourselves. Did Eddie Copeland fool Dr. David Buring? That is an important decision for you to make."

Parker continued pacing. His heel click was sharp. He rolled the index card into a tube in his hand. He could feel the eyes of the courtroom on him.

"The only direct testimony accusing Eddie Copeland of murder came from Zack Vickers, who has been found mentally incompetent to stand trial for his own participation in the crime—whatever that participation may be." Parker cleared his throat. His voice softened. "I will not dwell on this," he said. "State law permits Zack to testify in this trial. I believe that Zack's answers cannot be responsible answers. His behavior on the stand is proof enough of his incompetence. My client even related a similar incident during his original statement, and all the statements he has given since. It was an incident of Zack telling a kind of disjointed Civil War story. My client has stated to me since Zack's testimony that this was the same story Zack was telling while on the witness stand."

William Fred interrupted. "Your Honor, I object to counselor's remarks," he said irritably. "They're immaterial and suggestive."

"The court sustains," Hugh said. "Mr. Mewborn, please refrain from developing testimony."

"I apologize," Parker said quietly. He continued: "I could rave and shout and spew forth a volcano of objections to Zack Vickers' testimony. But there is no need. The jury saw. The jury heard. The jury will decide."

William Fred's right leg was braced against the table. His hands were tight on the chairarms. He waited for Parker to compare the murder of Zack's story to the murder of Jesse Wade's family. Parker would do it dramatically, as an afterthought, a kind of "Isn't it strange how the two crimes seem to fit? Three men. Murder and rape."

But Parker did not speak of the comparison. He stood before the jurors and looked across the room to William Fred. It was a long, challenging look, one of contempt and anger.

"What bothers me most about all of this," Parker said in a low, growling voice, "is the attitude of the prosecution in its disregard for showing—definitely, beyond reasonable doubt—that Eddie Copeland murdered. If Mr. Autry could show that, could make me believe it, then I would gladly relinquish my responsibility to my client and stand with Mr. Autry and ask that you find Eddie Copeland guilty.

"The state has made much of what it does know, and nothing of what it is supposed to prove," Parker snapped. He whirled to the jury. His eyes shot to the stern-faced man. "Ladies and gentlemen, the law—*the law*—requires that you find, beyond reasonable doubt, that the charge against the defendant is true before you can convict him. It is not the responsibility of the defense to prove Eddie Copeland is innocent beyond reasonable doubt. It is the responsibility of the prosecution to prove him guilty beyond reasonable doubt. I will tell you that my entire case is there, in that one right-or-wrong, innocent-or-guilty element of the law. This is an emotional case. God knows it is. But it is more than Eddie Copeland that is on trial; it is also the law—*the law.* It is not a matter of how you feel but how you think, how you reason. I could stand here—Mr. Autry could stand here—and both of us could pick at the evidence like men trying to pull fleas off a dog. But that would be nothing more than flea-picking, and ultimately we would have to turn this case over to you. And you do not have the choice of recognizing the effect of reasonable doubt on this case. You *must* recognize it. If you ignore that and condemn Eddie Copeland, his conviction, his punishment—whatever it may be—will be nothing compared to the conviction and punishment you administer to the law itself."

Parker paused and drew a deep breath. He closed his fist over the index card in his hand and slipped the wadded paper into his coatpocket. He had covered Fact, Zack, Attack.

"I apologize for becoming passionate," he said calmly. "Once you've been with a thing, as Mr. Autry and I have been with this case, you tend to feel the strain of it. Again, thank you for your service. I am certain that your judgment will be the result of serious deliberation, with great respect for the system of law that has kept us a civilized, free people."

Parker looked once at the stern-faced man, then turned and walked to his seat. Donald Bridges patted him on the arm. Eddie kept his eyes on the sheet of paper before him. Parker saw that the paper was clean, the pen for doodling wedged between Eddie's fingers.

The only sound in the courtroom was the sound of bodies shifting in seats, of legs being uncrossed and crossed, of shoes scraping the floor, of muffled coughs and hard breathing, of the steamhiss of the radiators.

"Mr. Autry, is the state ready?" Hugh said.

"Yes, Your Honor," William Fred said.

"Before you proceed, I would like to ask the bailiffs to arrange dinner to be brought in for the jurors," Hugh said. "Because of the time, I'm going to go ahead and charge the jury this afternoon and permit them to begin deliberation. Now, if you would, Mr. Autry."

William Fred rose from his seat and approached the jurors. He had the palms of his hands pressed together under his chin, as if in deep thought.

"Ladies and gentlemen of the jury," he began, "I, too, want to thank you for your service to this serious trial. Mr. Mewborn is correct: yours is the hard job. Mr. Mewborn and I present, you decide. And in cases such as this one, you are not obscure people. You will be known as the jury that heard the Eddie Copeland case. That carries with it a certain degree of recognition, of notoriety. That makes the decisions you must consider even more perplexing. You are to be commended for being willing citizens.

"I have listened with interest to Mr. Mewborn's summation. He has hit hard at the state for not having irrefutable proof that Eddie Copeland killed anybody. Hearing Mr. Mewborn, it would seem that what he really wants is a videotape replay of the crime, like one of those slow-motion reruns on Sunday afternoon football games. He wants us to show Eddie Copeland in the act of the crime. Well, we can't do that. Plain and simple, we can't. If we could find a way to do that, the need for a trial of any kind would not exist. We would simply put on the tape, push a button, and say, 'Yep, that's him, all right. The man in the red shirt and the black wingtips did it.' But we can't do that—except maybe in some bank robberies, where the robber is videotaped at the scene of the crime. Few crimes of murder are that precise, however. People are elusive. People cover up. People lie. And those people who murder and rape and steal and kidnap and torture can, indeed, fool anybody. You know that. We all know that.

"Mr. Mewborn said you would have to decide if Eddie Copeland fooled Dr. David Buring. Well, I'm sure Dr. Buring would admit that that was possible. That's the nature of people who have practice in deceit. It's second nature with them. It comes as naturally to them as it would be for any decent person in here to help up a person who's tripped and fallen on the sidewalk.

"Mr. Mewborn has praised the state's evidence. He is kind. It took hard work, long hours, determination. The

state went to this detail because it wanted to make certain—
beyond reasonable doubt—that it had a substantial case
against Eddie Copeland and Zack Vickers."

William Fred balled his fist and drummed out his words
on the railing of the jury box: *"We have that case."*

He put his hands behind his back, under his coattail, and
began a slow pacing before the jury box.

"Yes," he said wearily, "Mr. Mewborn would have you
think that we have looked at a few pictures, compared a
few fingerprints, peeked into a few microscopes, and said,
'Boy, oh boy, oh boy, we've got them nailed.' No, ladies
and gentlemen of the jury. That is not our way of doing
things. We did not find three men in a cave and decide to
pin a crime on them. That's called target law. We found a
crime and rooted the three men who did that crime out of
a hole in the ground. They resisted arrest. One man was
killed. Another was found mentally incompetent to stand
trial at this time. The third is here. Not because of a witch
hunt with experts, but because we have the evidence. The
hard, cold evidence. The facts.

"Dear God," William Fred said in a desperate, pleading
voice, "you have heard the defense admit that the evidence
is correct. You have heard the counselor for the defendant
say that his client was there. You have heard Eddie Copeland
say he was there, on the scene. Well, if he was so afraid,
so timid about trying to stop this slaughter of helpless people, why didn't he run off when he had a chance later on?
Why didn't he find somebody and say, 'Look, the men that
killed those poor people in that farmhouse are hiding up
there in a cave in the mountains'?

"And Mr. Mewborn wants more proof? More proof than
fingerprints, weapons, bodies? What would he have us do?
Exhume the dead and interview them?"

"Your Honor," Parker snapped, "counselor has gone beyond the limits of courtroom behavior and, more seriously,
human decency."

"I agree, counselor," Hugh said in a hard voice. "Mr.
Autry, you will not make such references again."

William Fred was embarrassed. He knew he had offended

the court and the people who were listening intently to him. He turned his head to the audience. He saw the faces of Jesse and Anna looking at him in disbelief. His eyes jumped to find Aubrey Hart, but Aubrey was not in the courtroom. Dear Jesus, William Fred thought. Why did I say that?

"Your Honor, Mr. Mewborn," William Fred mumbled, "I deeply apologize. Mr. Mewborn is right to enter his strong objection. I violated the dignity of the court with an unnecessary statement. I would also like to apologize to the jury, to those hearing these proceedings, and especially to the families of the victims. As Mr. Mewborn said earlier, the strain of such cases often leads to passionate, and sometimes ill-advised, remarks. I did not mean to offend anyone."

"Please continue, Mr. Autry," Hugh said coolly.

William Fred was numb and confused. He stared at the floor, at the tips of his shoes. He thought: Where am I? What should I say? He remembered being in a play in college and forgetting his lines and standing stupidly until a chorus of giggles jarred him to move and think and improvise. He walked slowly, heavily, to the prosecutor's table and fingered through some stacked papers.

He turned at last to the jury and said, as if he were making a confession, "I cannot do more than I have done in this case. I know the evidence is here for a conviction. I know that the death of Albert Bailey is not sufficient for the crime committed—one criminal in exchange for six of the finest people in this valley. I know that—I know that Eddie Copeland has lied to all of us. I know he is guilty."

The words were running over his tongue and he could not stop them. "But it's a curious trial," he said. "We are here worried about proving, beyond reasonable doubt, that the defendant took part in the slaying of six people. We have peeled back layer after layer of fact and testimony and supposition, and have gotten to the core of the matter. Yes, counselor for the defense is correct: it is the law that we must adhere to. Yet that element of the law is, in the end, a matter of personal conviction. It cannot be measured or weighed. It does not have color or texture. It is not a hammer or a pillow. It cannot be lifted and held up and examined for flaws, like a jeweler would look at a diamond. It is the sum of things, like the quality of thoughts. It is a matter of decision. For the ladies and gentlemen of the jury, it is also the realization that they must live with their decision. It is like a lovely woman I remember seeing many years ago. She was one of those commanding, sophisticated people—the kind that makes you look twice because she has a presence that cannot be ignored. The only thing wrong with her was a scar that was at the base of her throat—a scar from an operation she had had as a child. It was there for everybody to see, and everybody looked at it. The jury here has that same kind of worry. If they find Eddie Copeland innocent of the charges, they must forever wonder if they made the right collective decision. They must wear that scar."

The words flooded in William Fred. Images snapped in his mind. His voice became a singsong of intensity. He began to pace rapidly in a circle. "But, ladies and gentlemen of the jury, there are so many other sides to this, or any, trial. Besides the open, terrible murder of people, there is also the ravaging of the community fabric. Wildfire gossip, emotion against emotion, theory against theory. Things going on that most of us never know about.

"How many of you know that some land speculators in Atlanta are making plans to buy up farms in the Tickenaley Valley and turn those farms into resorts or vacation homes? It's true. I've had some of them call me, asking me about landowners and property values and asking me if I would represent them. I've told them, 'No, I won't help you. I don't want this valley to be like all the other places in the mountains.' But that's not going to stop them. Pretty soon you'll see helicopters flying around, circling around out there like buzzards over some dead animal on the side of the highway. And if they start buying the land up here, it'll be like that. But it's not some dead animal they'll be flying over. It'll be us. All of us."

Hugh looked quickly to Parker for an objection. Parker sat silently, watching William Fred with pity.

"That's a byproduct of this trial," William Fred continued, beating the fist of his right hand into the open palm of his left. "And that's something this jury can't answer, or deal with. This jury must deal with the question before it."

William Fred turned to face the jurors. He was tired and bewildered. He did not know why he had begun to talk about the land speculators. It made him feel uncontrolled and defeated. He wanted to stop talking, to return to his table and sit and rest and think.

"Forgive me for those aside comments," he said, forcing his voice. "I made them because I want to emphasize the impact of this case and this trial. The state has presented its case. We believe that what we have presented is more than sufficient to find Eddie Copeland guilty of the charge of first-degree murder—guilty beyond reasonable doubt. We believe that Zack Vickers did tell the truth, regardless of the later behavior he exhibited on the stand. We were with Zack for too many hours not to know fact from fiction. When you begin your deliberations, I ask that you remember that the defense has not disputed that evidence.

"Thank you for your attentiveness and I hope my remarks haven't offended you. I am confident that your verdict will satisfy the legal and human need for justice. For if we cannot have justice in the courts, we will have justice in the streets. If we cannot have the assurance of due process to protect us, we will soon exercise the right to protect ourselves. And in today's world, where criminals roam free, wearing their prizes of legal technicalities like medals, we must be more responsible than ever for seeing that justice—in the court—prevails."

William Fred could feel the trickle of perspiration rolling from his temple as he walked to his chair. He did not see the startled look of confusion from Harold Sellers.

THIRTY

December 11

JESSE HAD NOT ANSWERED ANY QUESTIONS ASKED HIM BY reporters. He had resisted William Fred's urging to permit Toby Cahill to interview him. He had not talked of the stories that had been written, or of the radio and television reports. And to the reporters, Jesse was as his neighbors and friends and relatives had described him: an independent man with uncompromising integrity and conviction. "Jesse will bear up under it," the reporters had been told. "He's strong. Won't say much, but what he does say people listen to. If Jesse didn't do nothing but nod his head toward the jail, everybody in this valley would burn it, with them boys in it. But he won't do that. Not Jesse."

The reporters had written (and said) that Jesse was remarkable during courtroom testimony in the trial of Eddie Copeland. He was "granitelike," "dignified," "extraordinary," "a model of courage." The writers had described his face (its worklines and firm muscles) as a face of pride and power, a hillman's face that knows more than it reveals. Jesse Wade was a distinguished man, the writers and announcers had declared. Other men would have broken under the pressure; Jesse Wade had not. In his silence and in the erect, military carriage of his body, the reporters had determined that Jesse was majestic in his control.

The reporters had not expected Jesse to break his silence. When he did—in the afternoon of December 11, after the jury had received its charge from Judge Richards and had retired to begin deliberation—the reporters were startled.

It was a routine question, routinely asked in the corridor outside the courtroom: "Mr. Wade, are you satisfied with the case against Eddie Copeland?"

"I won't know that until the jury makes its decision," Jesse said.

The crowd, moving around Jesse, stopped abruptly.

The reporter cautiously asked a second question: "You've listened to a lot of detail this week about the murders. Hearing that detail, reliving it, how have you felt about it?"

"How have I felt?" Jesse said bitterly. He could feel Anna close to him, holding his arm. "It hurts, hearing it. Guess it would anybody." He swallowed hard.

"Anger?" the reporter asked.

"Yes," Jesse admitted. "A lot of it."

Another reporter pushed close to Jesse. "If Copeland's found guilty, do you think he'll get the death penalty?"

"I don't know what else he could get and be fair," Jesse said.

The reporters began to talk at once in a babel of questions.

"Are you expecting a quick verdict by the jury?"

"I don't know."

"The defense claims there's reasonable doubt that Eddie did any of the killing. Have you got any doubt about it?"

"I don't. But I'm not on the jury."

"Have you had any word from Eddie Copeland, any messages from him?"

"No. I don't want any."

"There's a story that his parents came to see you before they committed suicide. Is that true?"

"Yes. They didn't tell me who they were, but they came to my farm."

"What did they want?"

"I don't know. To say they were sorry, I guess. That's what they told me. That they were sorry. But I didn't know who they were. They left without telling me."

"You're building a house on the land where your son was going to build his home. Will you move there?"

"I'm just building my boy's home."

"Do you know the parents of Zack Vickers?"

"I know them. They're good people. I feel sorry for them. They didn't have anything to do with what happened."

"Do you think Zack is insane?"

"I can't answer that. I think he's sick. I don't know about insane."

"Mr. Wade, you haven't said anything at all during this trial. Why are you doing it now?"

"The trial's over. The jury's got it. I didn't think it was right before now."

"What happens if the jury finds Eddie Copeland innocent?"

Jesse looked at the reporter who had asked the question. He shook his head. He could feel Anna's hand tighten on his arm and then he could hear William Fred's voice: "All right, that's enough. No more questions." He could feel William Fred beside him, pushing against his back. He began to move through the crowd of faces leaning eagerly toward him. He could hear a wave of questions lapping against the walls of the corridor behind him.

And still the reporter's voice was clear in Jesse's mind: "What happens if the jury finds Eddie Copeland innocent?"

At eight o'clock, the jury was called to the courtroom by Hugh Richards. The foreperson was Tate Yarborough, the nurseryman. He glumly admitted that the jurors had not reached a decision.

"Then I'm going to recess until eight-thirty in the morning," Hugh announced. "The jury will reconvene at that time and continue its deliberation. Please remember that you are not to discuss this case with anyone, or to allow anyone to discuss it with you. If you need anything, please ask a bailiff for assistance."

Outside, under the streetlights, the strangers denouncing the death penalty paraded in short defiant steps before the courthouse. They held hand-lettered placards in gloved hands. Their faces were tucked into hats and coathoods, and they did not look at the passersby who stared curiously and then hurried away, cursing. The strangers were like workers striking against an unseen force, saying nothing, holding their placards face high.

Hugh stood at the window of the empty, darkened courtroom and watched the protesters. Jack Pilgrim was with him. Hugh said, "Goddamn them, Jack. Not even a verdict and they're making a play for the sentencing. Goddamn them. Makes a man sick enough to puke."

And Jack said, "Ought to be a law, Hugh. Ought to be a law."

At ten minutes after eight, William Fred called Jesse from his office. He said, "I don't think it's a sign one way or the other, Jesse. One jury may rush through a thing like this, while another takes hours, maybe a day or so. Let's don't go reading anything into it. I'm confident, Jesse. Absolutely. Could be that they don't want it to look like they're too hasty. This is a big trial. Sometimes it happens that way in a big trial. Don't let it worry you, Jesse. You or Anna either one. They'll come in tomorrow. You'll see."

"Maybe," Jesse replied. "Let me know if you hear something. We'll be here."

"I will. Get some sleep. Tell Anna not to worry."

"All right."

"Jesse?"

"Yes?"

"I ran into some of those reporters back at the courthouse tonight," William Fred said. "Talking to them this afternoon helped us. I'm glad you did it. In case anything at all goes wrong, I think they'll side with us." William Fred paused, then added quickly, "But nothing's going wrong. I can feel it. We'll get the verdict."

William Fred's lie was weak, Jesse thought. William Fred was not confident. He had expected the jury to return a verdict before seven. Delay meant doubt. Doubt meant surprise. Surprise meant anything.

"What did he say?" Anna asked.

"Nothing happened," Jesse told her. "They'll start again tomorrow."

"I thought William Fred—"

"They're just waiting, so it won't look like they decided too fast," Jesse said, also lying. "There's some pickets at the courthouse. Maybe the jury saw them."

"Want some coffee? I just made some."

"No," Jesse said. "Not now. I think I'll walk around outside for a while."

The cold of the day was still in the air, very near freezing, but the night was clear and the stars brilliant, like scattered dots of heat. Jesse looked at the stars as he walked, picked out the two dippers and Orion the Hunter. Or was it Orion? Would Orion and the two dippers be visible in December?

In the fifties—the late fifties—he and Jean had been in Atlanta and had stopped one night in a coffee house near Emory University. Jean had been surprised by the people in the coffee house. "Beatniks," she had whispered in horror. "So what?" Jesse had said. "Let's get a look at them." And they had stayed to drink thick coffee and listen to a thin woman singing of inhumanity. The young woman had leaned dramatically against a wall under a pool of theater light that fell over her like an amber veil, her face lifted up, her eyes closed, her voice carrying over the dull clatter of dishes and mumbled talk. There was one song—startlingly lovely— about the stars, the dot-to-dot faces of the constellations. Later, outside, walking to their car, Jean had begun to hum the tune to the song and she had looked up and said, "I see Orion. He was really one of ours." And Jesse had asked, "Ours?" She had laughed playfully. "One of the Indians.

There's even a headdress of stardust if you look hard enough. We just didn't claim him in time," she had replied.

Jesse had looked for Orion often after that night.

The cold pressed hard against his face. His steps crushed over the dry grass lawn of the backyard. He could hear an owl off in the pasture below the barns.

He could hear the reporter's voice: "What happens if the jury finds Eddie Copeland innocent?"

"He's going to get off," he said aloud, softly, stopping in the middle of the yard. He said it again: "He's going to get off."

He could feel a rage rising in him. "He's going to get off," he said a third time. The rage flashed through his body and he began to walk rapidly toward the barn. William Fred had lost the case, he thought. He had stammered before the jury, wandering aimlessly and listlessly, like a man in argument with himself. The jury had watched William Fred closely, Jesse realized. The jury knew. William Fred had not cracked Parker Mewborn, and that was what he had wanted to do—make Parker surrender. But Parker had surprised him by not debating, by saying, "You're right. Everything happened just like you said. Except for one thing: Eddie Copeland did not do the killing." Parker had said it over and over. He had not stopped saying it throughout the trial.

Jesse stopped at the fence near the barn. He shoved his hands deep into the pockets of his coat. There was proof, but the proof did not matter, he thought. The proof was unimportant. Eddie was guilty. Eddie had raped and killed. He could not be freed.

Jesse lit a cigarette and smoked nervously, drawing the smoke hard into his lungs. He thought of the editorial on the six o'clock television news out of Atlanta. The commentator announced that Jesse Wade had broken his silence about the Eddie Copeland trial. "After weeks of refusing to make any comment, he has spoken, at the proper time. But Jesse Wade's conduct has been a testament to his faith in the judicial process. Jesse Wade has suffered loss that most of us would find unbearable, yet he has chosen to let the law work. He has not criticized or complained or cried for street justice. He has waited, as he now waits, for the due process of law."

The commentator was wrong, Jesse thought. The commentator had lauded Jesse's tolerance, but it was not tolerance: it was fury. Jesse remembered that Ellis had told him of Wyman Stephens' plans for assassinating Eddie and Zack. "Just to warn you," Ellis had said. "Just to let you know there's a bomb ticking away out there. You're the fuse. You even look like you're in favor of what Wyman wants, it'll blow this case sky high." And Jesse had remained silent. He had avoided looking at Wyman Stephens and other men who had reputations for being short-tempered and irrational. But he had known they were there—in the courtroom, in the corridor, on the sidewalk—watching him closely, anxiously wishing him to signal them.

Jesse spit the cigarette from his mouth and crushed it with his heel. Maybe Wyman was right. The law was uncertain. The law was arguable. The law too often faltered. But if Wyman had succeeded, it would not have been called justice. Not by the Preacher. Not by the strangers outside the courthouse, holding up their signs of protest. Not by the television news commentator. The Preacher, the protesters, the commentator would call it vengeance, and their indignation would become a wailing that would shake the earth with the power of its righteous scream.

But what could they know? Jesse thought angrily. What? They foamed at the mouth in the name of a cause that had the sound of dignity and civility. They had never held the stiffening body of a grandson and looked into the sponge of his brain.

Jesse looked across the pasture behind the barn—Carl's pasture, Carl's barn. Carl had been much like him, he thought. Carl had loved the land and the history of the land. He had been quiet and reserved. But Carl had killed. In Vietnam, in war, he had killed. He had killed because it was the only thing he could do. He had killed because it was right, because nothing else could stop the insanity.

Jesse walked slowly away from the fence toward the

house. He looked again at the stars. He saw Orion the Hunter. And near Orion the Hunter he saw (imagined he saw) the face of Isom. I need to see Isom, he thought. It was strange: Isom also had been willing to kill out of anger. Isom. Ready to take his Civil War pistol and aim it at the chest of his own son and squeeze the trigger. In his murky world of reason, Isom had known what was right.

Jesse stared curiously at the imagined face of Isom. Deep within himself, he sensed that Isom somehow knew answers he did not know. He thought again, I need to see Isom.

William Fred had insisted that Toby drink with him in Rachel's room and Toby had reluctantly agreed.

It was eleven o'clock. Toby sat in the one cushioned chair in the room and held the glass that William Fred had forced into his hand. William Fred was sitting crosslegged in the middle of the bed, balancing his drink between his feet. Rachel was behind him, massaging his shoulders. Her hair dropped in a curl off her right shoulder. The heavy makeup on her face seemed dry and caked. She wore a tight cashmere sweater, with a deep V scoop, that William Fred had given her. She had said, giddily, "William Fred don't want me wearing a bra with it." Her nipples were erect and hard against the soft scrubbing of the material.

William Fred did not talk about the trial, only his surprise over Jesse's answering questions. "Had no idea he was going to do that," William Fred said. "I thought he was right behind me, going up the hall, and when I turned around he was talking. Still want to get him to let you do an interview, Toby. Maybe when it's all over."

Toby did not stay late. At eleven-thirty, he left for his room. He could hear William Fred's laughter and then the quiet of lovemaking. At six-thirty the following morning, he heard William Fred's car leaving the parking lot. He wondered if William Fred's boast about always being sober at six was true. Rachel had sworn it was.

At seven-thirty, Rachel tapped lightly at his door and stepped inside when Toby opened it. She wore a robe. The makeup had been washed from her face. Her lips looked bruised.

"He's scared," she told Toby. "Watch out for him."

"Why's he afraid?" Toby asked.

"He thinks he's losing."

"He's lost cases before."

"I don't know," she said. "I don't know nothing about what he does. I just never saw him scared before."

She was very much a small girl, Toby thought. Without makeup, her hair brushed straight, she had the face of a curious child.

"I know he's worried," Toby said. "I'll watch him."

"He said it wouldn't be right, letting that man go. He don't want that to happen. He said if that happens, something's wrong with the law."

"Maybe," Toby mumbled. Then he asked, "Why's he so caught up in all of this?"

Rachel lifted her face quizzically to him. "You don't know?"

"No."

"One time he almost married Macy," she answered. She opened the door and stepped outside.

THIRTY-ONE

December 12—13

THE JURY DELIBERATED THROUGHOUT FRIDAY WITHOUT reaching a verdict. Hugh Richards recessed the deliberations until Saturday morning at eight-thirty.

At seven-thirty on Friday, Angus called the jail and asked Ellis, "What happened in there? They do anything at all?"

"I wadn't in there, Angus," Ellis replied curtly. "Only thing I know is that Hugh read the charge to the jury again this afternoon."

"Damn," Angus exclaimed in disgust. "They taking too long, Ellis. It's them people marching around in front of the courthouse. You ought to throw them in jail."

"Now, why didn't I think of that?" Ellis said cynically. "What's the matter with you, Angus? I start doing that for no good reason and the press'll make a field day out of this."

Angus snorted indignantly. "Well, they the ones that's making the jury stay out. Ain't no two ways about it."

"I wish that was it," Ellis said wearily. "I wish to God it was."

* * *

William Fred did not call Jesse on Friday night. He went from the courthouse to the Valley View Lodge and drank himself into an early sleep, with Rachel holding his head in her lap.

In his next-door room, Toby reread the letter that Parker Mewborn had handed him earlier in the day. The letter was from Eddie.

Dear Mr. Cahill,

I don't know what's going to happen to me. I know I'm going to be kept in jail—to maybe die or just spend my years there. I guess the lawyer has done his best. I don't know about such things. I guess he tried hard enough. He told me it would be a gamble, but I didn't know what he was talking about. I do now. Me in the chair or me in the jail. I don't want neither one, but if it comes to a choice I'll take the jail.

Maybe you will never write about this and what it has been like for me. If you want to, I will see you when you can after this is over with. A man I used to know (he went to jail for killing his wife) got somebody to write a book about it all and a lot of people must have read it. Last I heard, somebody said it was made in a television show. Maybe we could do something like that. Tell the story like it happened.

I remember one time my daddy got mad enough at me to say he wished I had never been born. He said I was nothing but a rotten limb on the family tree. Said I wouldn't amount to nothing. I guess he was right. I don't guess I've done much good in this world. I've done things that I could be put in jail for and have the key thrown away. But that don't mean I killed anybody. They are dead wrong about that little story.

I sure told the truth about Zack, didn't I? He was crazy as a loon. You heard what he said up there on the stand. That's the way he was at the house, except he was running around and shouting it to the top of his voice.

One of the things I didn't tell, because I just forgot about it, was when Zack made us turn over the girl in the kitchen— the one him and Albert took with us—and he started doing it to her from the back. He started slobbering all over her back. I took a dishrag and wiped her off. You know what she said? Thank you. That's what she said.

I guess she thought I could save her. I wish I had tried. She was pretty and I thought she must be pretty nice.

If you ever want to talk about maybe writing my story like it really is, let me know. The sooner the better. I don't guess I'll be going off anywhere.

Your friend,
Eddie Copeland

The letter was perplexing. The handwriting was evenly spaced and clean, not as forced as the first letter had been. The letter had the rhythm of a voice. Yet there was a crudeness to it, an awkward accent of illiteracy. It was as though Eddie Copeland was baiting him, Toby thought. And laughing about it.

Early on Saturday morning, December 13, Jesse drove to Isom and Lou's cabin. He had not been able to dismiss the vision of Isom dressed in a Confederate soldier's uniform, holding a pistol, with the opened trunk beside him. He had dreamed of it on Thursday night. He had thought of it on Friday as he worked with Pete and Aubrey on the house. He had dreamed of it again on Friday night. The dream was the same both nights: Isom beside the trunk, Lou across the room, absently rocking and staring into the fire.

No one answered the door at his knock and Jesse opened it cautiously and stepped inside. He could see a small fire in the fireplace and smell the perfumed soap hanging from string nets. He saw the outline of Lou sitting beside the fire in the rocker. She was not moving. He saw Isom across from her, in the chair beside the trunk. The trunk was closed.

"Isom," he called. "It's me. Jesse Wade. All right if I come in?"

Isom turned his head slowly toward Jesse. Jesse could see a feeble smile crack across his face. "Ain't got no honey," Isom said hoarsely.

Jesse stepped toward him. "Just came by to visit, Isom. How's Lou?"

"Maybe she's dead. Won't say nothing."

Jesse crossed the room quickly to Lou and knelt and touched her. Her head jerked up and her eyes opened weakly. She was holding a pillow cradled in her arms. Jesse could see that her dress was open and one corner of the pillow was pushed against her sagging breast. She pulled the pillow close to her.

"Lou, it's me, Jesse Wade. You all right, Lou?"

Lou's eyes wandered over Jesse's face, then back to the fire. She leaned her head down against the pillow.

"Ain't said nothing since we come back," Isom said bitterly. "I been feeding her honey, but we run out."

"Since you came back from where?" Jesse asked.

"Seeing Zack," Isom answered proudly. "Zack looked good. Got him dressed up good."

"Lou needs a doctor, Isom," Jesse said. "I'll send him up when I go back home. I'll get you some food, too."

"She won't say nothing," Isom complained. "Old bitch. Just sits there, holding that pillow, rocking it, like it was Zack." He laughed sarcastically. "Ain't Zack. Ain't nothing but a pillow."

Jesse could feel a sickness of pity caking in his throat. Lou's mind had shattered. In the fragility of her memory, she was holding her baby, and the pillow baby was warm against her empty, withered breast.

"Want me to put Lou in the bed, Isom?" Jesse asked gently.

"Don't matter none to me," Isom answered nonchalantly. Then he said, "Fire needs some wood."

"I'll put some on," Jesse said.

Jesse turned back the covers of the bed and carefully lifted Lou from her chair (she was almost weightless) and put her in the bed, still holding the pillow to her breast. He covered her and then added wood to the fire and stood in front of the fireplace, watching the flame glow.

"Lots of wood, makes it good," Isom crooned gleefully.

"Yes, it does," Jesse said. He took a straightback chair and sat close to Isom. "Isom, can you tell me something?" he asked.

"Try to."

"Those stories you tell about the Civil War, like you told the last time I was up here with the sheriff, when the Yankees came to the South—"

"Goddamn Yankees," Isom snapped. His small eyes gleamed angrily.

"Isom, where'd you learn those stories?"

Isom's face furrowed and then lifted in a knowing smile. He leaned forward toward Jesse, then reached for the trunk and tapped the top of it with his finger.

"In the trunk?" Jesse asked. "They're in the trunk?"

"Where they are," Isom said in a whisper. "Just like I wrote them down."

"You wrote them?"

"Said I did, didn't I? I said it, I did it." Isom was irritated.

"You care if I look at them, Isom?"

"Look all you want," Isom said. "Don't matter none to me. Ain't worth nothing."

Jesse opened the trunk and removed the Confederate uniform, which had been neatly folded with the pistol wrapped in the pants. He removed each item carefully, stacking them on the floor beside Isom's chair. Suits, shirts, old garments from another time, all too large for Isom. Near the bottom of the trunk there was a framed photograph of an elderly man with a majestic white beard, posing proudly. His eyes were the same as Isom's. At the bottom of the trunk there were three thick packets wrapped in cloth and tied with a string. Jesse lifted them out and put them on the floor before him.

"This it, Isom?" Jesse asked. "These the stories?"

Isom nodded rapidly. "They tied," he said. "Did it myself."

"I'll tie them back," Jesse said. He pulled at the string on one of the packets and it broke easily. He unfolded the cloth and read from a handwritten sheet: "The History of the Civil War in Tennessee." At the bottom of the page, in fading ink: "By Zachary Coy Vickers, as Written by His Grandson, Isom Coy Vickers."

My God, Jesse thought. It was true. Isom had written the stories. He snapped the string on the other two packets and pulled away the cloth. The pages were written in a clean, smooth cursive. Jesse glanced through the words. They were in the first person, written as Isom and Zack had told the stories, in bold, harsh language.

"Isom, you did this?" Jesse asked quietly. "You did all of this?"

"Did. Sure did," Isom said simply. "Uh-huh. Wrote it all down, just like he said it."

"Your grandfather?"

"He said it, I wrote it."

Jesse pulled a yellowed news clipping from one of the packets. The headline read: ISOM VICKERS WRITES HISTORY. Beneath the headline there was a short story:

Isom Vickers, whose verse is widely admired in Farbis and other towns of Tennessee, is said to be writing a history of the Civil War in collaboration with his grandfather, Zachary Coy Vickers, the only local survivor of the War Between the States.

If what is reported is true, readers can look forward to a colorful telling of that now famous war. Mr. Coy Vickers is well known for his flamboyant stories and his sharp mind, even at his advanced age.

The story was dated October 11, 1937.

Jesse read hurriedly through the stories, scanning them. He found the stories that he had heard from both Isom and Zack. Incredibly, the stories had been repeated exactly as written, memorized from many tellings.

Jesse's eyes darted quickly through the pages, stopping for sentences and expressions. He knew that he held in his hands the history of Isom, just as his own history was locked in his barn, in the antique tools that buyers had wanted for resale in Atlanta. Isom's history was remarkable, he thought. Far grander than anyone would believe.

Suddenly, Jesse's eyes stopped. He read the sentence: "We took the Yankee to the barn and made the killing son of a bitch pay for what he'd done."

He read the story slowly. It was like a whisper from his subconscious, telling him what to do. And he knew the reason he had been led to Isom.

Before he left the cabin, Jesse replaced the papers and articles in the trunk and cut firewood and stacked it beside the fireplace. He found cubes of beef bouillon (from the grocery supply ordered by Ellis) and made a hot soup for Isom, and he forced Lou to drink some. Lou lay in the coma of her dreams, nursing the pillow baby.

"I'll be back," Jesse promised Isom. "But I'll send the doctor up today, and some food."

"Need me some tobacco," Isom told him. "Army boys took it all."

"All right," Jesse said. Then: "Isom, don't tell anybody else about the trunk. Don't ever tell anybody else. They'll want to take it off."

And Isom whispered, "It's mine. Ain't nobody taking it. Nobody."

THIRTY-TWO

December 14

ANNA MADE THE DECISION IN THE SLEEPLESS HOURS OF
Sunday morning.

It would be simple, she thought. Only Jesse and Mercer
Dole knew what had happened to her, and they had not
spoken of it. To the people of the valley, she had been away
visiting her parents. Her parents (worried as they were)
needed proof that she had conquered the horror of her husband's death, the people told her admiringly. She was right
to visit them; they deserved to see the miracle of their strong,
forgiving daughter.

Since her return to Tickenaley, Anna had appeared in
public only with Jesse to attend the trial of Eddie Copeland.
To those who had called, Anna politely explained that she
wanted to be with Jesse during the trial. The callers had
warmly praised her for her devotion. "That's good," the
callers had said. "He needs you. If we can help out in any
way, let us know."

(And the callers had marveled among themselves: "She's a saint, that's what. I couldn't be that way. Not me. Not with all that's going on in the trial. But she holds her head high, she does.")

Even the Preacher—one of the callers—had been impressed. "I'm just trying to help Jesse," Anna had said, and the Preacher had believed that Anna was using the power of his teaching, of the healing in his hands. Anna was a disciple, the Preacher believed, an extension of himself. And that was another unexpected triumph for the Preacher— the multiplying of his own gifts through someone else; rich seed in rich soil. "I'm proud of you," the Preacher had said earnestly. "God's working in you. God'll help you help Jesse."

In her bed, in the sleepless hours of Sunday morning, Anna thought of the Preacher and the curious, hypnotic effect he had had on her (and on Jean; it had to have been the same). His hands had stroked her and his voice had begged her to believe in him. He had fed from her hysteria like a plump leech, and he had delighted in the taste of her anxiety. The Preacher had put his face close to her face and whispered, "God, God, God," until the name became a codeword to enter her mind and control her. And she had willingly submitted to his stroking hands and to his whispering voice, and she had believed in him.

Anna said nothing to Jesse of her decision. There was no reason and no time. On Sunday, Jesse left early to return to his own home. Anna knew he wanted to be alone. It was a mood—the hard line of the jaw, the restlessness of the hands, the absent, hollow look of the eyes. She knew the mood well. She had seen it often in Carl. Carl and Jesse were much alike.

"Maybe I'll go back up to see Isom and Lou," Jesse told her before he left. "The doctor said Lou may have to be committed somewhere if she doesn't come around. He said she's weak as much as anything."

"I'll go up and help with her, if you want me to," Anna said.

"Not now. Mercer's had a nurse up there. Pete went up to stay with Isom," Jesse said. "We'll wait and see what happens."

"Is anything else wrong, Jesse?" Anna asked.

"No," Jesse replied. "Just thinking about Lou and Isom."

At eleven o'clock, when she knew the churches were in service, Anna drove into Tickenaley and parked in front of the courthouse and went inside to the jail. Ellis was in his office.

"Anything wrong?" Ellis asked her.

"I want to see him," Anna said calmly.

"I'm sorry, Anna, I can't let you do that."

"Why?"

"Why do you want to?"

"To give him this," Anna answered. She pulled a small Bible from her purse and handed it to him.

Ellis turned the Bible in his hand. It was bound in white leather, stamped in gold leaf. He opened it and thumbed the pages. The red-lettered voice of Jesus blurred under his fingers.

"Anna, that man probably killed your husband," Ellis said softly. "Why do you want to do this?"

"I think he needs it," Anna said uncomfortably.

"What'll people think, you doing this now?"

"It doesn't matter."

"All right," Ellis said. "I'll give it to him. Tell him it came from you."

"I want to go with you."

Ellis hesitated. He looked through the glass partition separating his office from the outer office. A state patrolman was sitting near the front door, drinking coffee. Ellis was bewildered by Anna. He had been told of her testimony in church, of her willingness to forgive Eddie Copeland and Zack Vickers. He had listened to the Preacher's passionate sermons of Anna's example. He had watched the people of the valley stare at her in awe during the trial. He did not understand her.

"Just for a minute," he said at last. "With me."

"That's all I want," Anna replied.

A guard, one of the deputies, was inside the corridor leading to the cells. He was sitting, leaning against the wall, reading the sports section of the Sunday newspaper. He looked up in surprise as Ellis and Anna entered.

"Give us a couple of minutes," Ellis said. The deputy nodded and left the corridor. Ellis motioned with his head and Anna followed him.

Eddie was sitting on the cot in Cell Four. He had a writing pad in his lap. He stood as Ellis and Anna approached.

"You know who this is, Eddie?" Ellis asked.

Eddie bobbed his head once. His eyes covered Anna suspiciously.

"She wanted to give you this," Ellis told him. He pushed the Bible through the bars.

"It belonged to me and my husband," Anna said quietly. She stepped closer to the bars and stared into Eddie's face. "It was used at our wedding." She could see Eddie's eyes narrowing, the blackdot pupils closing. His eyelids shuttered slowly. His thin mouth tightened. "I don't know who did what," she continued evenly. "Maybe it doesn't matter any more. I just wanted you to have this. Read it. It's helped me. Maybe it'll help you."

Eddie did not reply. His eyes wandered across Anna's face to Ellis.

"Maybe you don't know it," Ellis said bluntly, "but this woman believes in forgiving. She's said it. To everybody. That may not mean anything to you, but it does to people around here."

Anna could see Eddie's eyes brighten. She could see the flare of surprise in his mind. She thought of the Preacher. She could feel his hands and hear his voice. She said suddenly, "The Preacher helped me." She could taste the bitterness of her words.

"You want to say anything?" Ellis said to Eddie.

Eddie's hand curled around the Bible. He looked at it, then back to Anna. "I thank you," he mumbled.

"I hope it helps, like I was helped," Anna said. "Maybe you should talk to the Preacher," she added.

Eddie lifted his eyes to her. He smiled slightly. "Maybe," he said.

Ellis followed Anna outside to her car. He asked, "Did Jesse know about this?"

"No."

"You going to tell him?"

"I don't know."

"Why did you do it, Anna?" Ellis asked. "The truth."

Anna looked down the empty street. Christmas streamers glittered like ropes of splintered glass on storefronts. A gusting wind blew a loose sheet of newspaper across the sidewalk. "I just wanted to bring an end to some things that's been bothering me," she said. "That's all."

"The truth, Anna," Ellis said again.

Her eyes flashed to him, then away. "I've . . . I've been through some things," she replied quietly.

"I know. You're not in church this morning. Why?"

"I haven't been since I've been back. I've been with Jesse."

"You're not with Jesse now."

"I know."

"There's more to it than that," Ellis said. "The Preacher?"

Anna nodded hesitantly. She wanted to tell Ellis, but she knew she could not.

"I don't mean to talk ill of a person," Ellis said softly. "But he's not much of a man, the way he's acting. People around here'll only take so much being preached at."

"I suppose so," Anna replied uncomfortably.

"He's used you some." Anna looked away. "I know," she mumbled.

"But you wanted to come down here for another reason, Anna. What was it?"

Anna thought of the question. Ellis was right. She said, "I wanted to look at him. Straight in the eyes, to see if he's been lying."

"And?" Ellis asked. "Has he?"
"Yes."

At two o'clock on Sunday afternoon the jurors began their fourth session of deliberation. At six o'clock, they asked to be heard by the judge. A verdict appeared impossible, reported Tate Yarborough. The jurors were deadlocked.

William Fred slumped in his chair. He had known what would be said, but still it was incomprehensible. He shook his head sadly. Parker sat erect, his eyes on Hugh Richards.

Hugh leaned far back in his chair and studied the jury. They were tense and irritated. All but one man. Hugh knew the holdout. He turned his eyes to William Fred and then to Parker. Both attorneys knew he was about to deliver the Dynamite Charge, so-called because it was intended to blow apart the obstacles of indecision. It would be a stern lecture about the worthiness of the jurors, the nobility of the jury process, the need to exhaust every possibility in resolving disagreement.

"Well, ladies and gentlemen of the jury, I am not going to dismiss you," Hugh began in a direct, accusing voice. "Not at this time. But I've got something to say."

He delivered the charge like an assault, with the power of his bulk and voice and black-robed authority, and the jury returned meekly to the jury room. "That, by God, ought to get some action," Hugh said in his chambers to Jack Pilgrim. "Tell you what, Jack. Let's me and you have a dose of medicine and watch some television. Some wrestling. I like wrestling. Thought about taking it up myself one time. Come out in my robe and have them saying, 'Here come de judge, here come de judge.' Beat hell out of people with my gavel."

Jack dutifully locked the doors leading into the corridor and courtroom and poured the bourbon. "Sure helps this old hacking," Jack said, rubbing his throat with his fingers. "Sure does." He swallowed deep from his glass.

At seven-fifteen, Ellis called Hugh. Eddie had asked to

see the Preacher, Ellis explained. Hugh laughed into the telephone.

"Wondered when he'd get around to that," Hugh said.

"Yeah," Ellis replied. "Me, too."

"That ought to be a sight. Call him up. Tell him to come on down."

Ellis mumbled agreement.

"Blessed are they that mourn, for they shall be comforted," Hugh said flippantly. He hung up the telephone and turned back to the television screen.

At eight o'clock, the jury was again summoned into the courtroom by Hugh. Nothing had happened, Tate Yarborough told him.

"No progress, Mr. Foreman?" Hugh asked.

"None, Your Honor."

"Then you will continue at eight o'clock in the morning," Hugh ordered.

"Eight o'clock?" Tate Yarborough said with surprise.

"Eight o'clock, Mr. Foreman," Hugh replied bluntly.

William Fred left the courtroom at ten minutes after eight without speaking to anyone. He walked past Ellis and Guy and two state patrolmen standing near the front of the courthouse. He walked past Toby and four other reporters who were talking to the protesters of the death penalty. He crossed the street and went into his office and called Jesse and told him of the deadlocked jury.

"I've got to be honest, Jesse," William Fred said. "I wouldn't bet on anything now. I think there's one holdout. I don't know why, but I think there's only one. Maybe I missed something when we picked the jury. I don't know."

Jesse ignored the self-pity in William Fred's voice. "What'll happen?" he asked.

"There's still a chance that it could change tomorrow," William Fred replied quickly. "It could happen. With pressure. If not, it'll be a mistrial. Hugh won't keep them after tomorrow, I don't think. We'll just do it all over again."

"Will he get out?"

"I guess Parker'll ask for bond," William Fred said. "But it won't do any good. Be nothing to it but talk."

"Let me know what happens," Jesse said.

"Soon as I know something," William Fred muttered.

William Fred sat at his desk and reviewed his notes on the jurors. He knew the holdout was a man. The five women would be incensed over the brutality of the deaths. He had watched them biting their lips to keep from screaming. The holdout was a man, but which man? There was nothing in his notes, or in his memory, that made him suspect anyone. He closed his eyes and forced the faces of the jurors, in their seating arrangement, through his mind. Nothing. Nothing. He checked each face. He could see nothing.

He looked at his watch. It was nine o'clock. He had promised Rachel that he would call, but he wanted to be alone.

He walked to his office window and looked across the street to the courthouse. The protesters had retired for the night. They had become increasingly confident, William Fred realized. One had boasted to a reporter: "Looks like they won't even find Copeland guilty. But we want everybody up here to know how we feel."

Harold Sellers had called the protesters Parker's Pickets. "It's like a circus," Harold had said bitterly. "Hard to believe Wyman and some of the others are letting them get by with it."

Wyman had better sense, William Fred thought. The sheriff's deputies and the State Patrol guarded the protesters like visiting dignitaries. Besides, Ellis had already intimidated Wyman. Wyman would do nothing but boast and preen and snarl. Wyman was afraid of Ellis.

"Dear God," William Fred murmured sadly. He thought of the telephone call that had warned him of Wyman's plans to storm the jail wearing hoods and carrying guns. If he had left it alone—if he had not had Rachel call Ellis—maybe it would be over. Maybe it would be forgotten. And, God knows, that was one way of doing it. Maybe a more civilized way than the Ping-Pong questions and answers of the court.

He sat in the leather chair in front of his desk and stared at the row of law books on the wallshelves. He wondered if he would ever be in one of the books, his arguments heralded by some fierce attorney in another court in another state.

The telephone rang sharply in the quiet room, startling William Fred. He thought: Rachel. Damn it.

"Hello," he said.

"William Fred?"

"Yes."

"It's Jesse. I want to see you."

THIRTY-THREE

December 15

SNOW HAD BEEN PREDICTED IN THE TICKENALEY VALLEY for Monday, December 15, but it did not snow. The morning sky was pale—a white-and-blue smoke that silvered the sun. The only clouds (shreds of clouds, like the contrails of jet motors) were over the mountains of the northwest, where the Appalachian range rose up from the valleys to shoulders of darkstained granite, like breaching whales in a sea of feathered winter trees. The snow that had been predicted was gathering in clouds beyond the Appalachians, swirling in their ceremony of wind dances before leaping the rim lines of the range and crystallizing in chilling updrafts.

A necklace of Christmas lights had been strung store to store along the main street of Tickenaley, and the beads of light blinked red-blue-green and glittered off the slick mirrors of store windows. Wreaths of velvet-and-silk ribbons, buttoned into flowering loops by pins of plastic holly, hung from the doorfacings. A wide banner—MERRY CHRISTMAS! —was stretched across the street between the utility pole in front of Angus Helton's hardware store and the utility pole in front of Pierce's Drugs. The music of Christmas played sprightly from hidden speakers in the stores.

In Berry's Five and Ten, an electric train rolled on a circle of tracks in the center of a special display table near the section for toys. The train made a monotonous, three-blast whistling sound, a toy warning of a toy danger. The sound could be heard throughout the store. It irritated Ed Berry.

"Before it's over I'm going to get me a tank from that War Raiders set and blow that thing to kingdom come," Ed complained to Martha Luther, one of his salespeople.

"I don't know," Martha said. "Sounds kind of nice to me. Sounds like Christmas. Kids love it."

"I guess," Ed mumbled.

"You remember last year?" Martha asked. "Jesse Wade bought a train just like it for his grandson. I think about that sometimes, when I hear it."

"I remember."

"Puts a damper on Christmas for me," Martha said. "With the trial going on. I wish they'd waited."

"Yeah," Ed agreed. "I saw Jesse and Anna the other day, when they came out of the courthouse. Don't guess they've been thinking about Christmas."

In his chambers at the courthouse, Hugh Richards read the morning newspapers and drank coffee. Jack Pilgrim was stationed outside his door to guard against intrusion. Hugh knew that Jack could not stop a gnat if challenged, but he was fiercely loyal and his old-man squealing would at least be an alert. "Don't let anybody in, Jack," Hugh had instructed. "Especially them goddamn lawyers."

"Ain't nobody getting in," Jack had vowed, patting the handle of the pistol holstered like a weight around his brittle hips. "I'll shoot their balls off."

"That's good, Jack. That's good."

The stories in the newspapers had been the same for two days: the jury in the Eddie Copeland trial was still in deliberation, though the jurors had declared irresolvable differences. Soon the judge would have to make up his mind,

the stories suggested. He would have to accept the indecision.

Hugh clipped the stories and slipped them into his briefcase. The reporters had been fair enough, he thought. None
had pestered him. They had been patient and, in an odd
way, respectful. The stories were worth keeping, worth re-
reading. Maybe he would make a scrapbook of them.

Hugh poured more coffee and thickened it with three
teaspoons of sugar. He thought of the frenzied telephone
conversation with the Preacher late on Sunday evening. The
Preacher had visited with Eddie and had washed his soul
clean and Eddie was praising God in Cell Four like an
inspired television evangelist. Eddie wanted people to know
of his sorrow and of his love. Eddie was ready to repent
and do good works.

Hugh smiled. It was amusing. Eddie knew what he was
doing, by God. Eddie had timing, if nothing else. First there
was Toby Cahill, the reporter, listening to Eddie's statement
under a strange agreement of silence until the trial was over.
And then the Preacher. Eddie had timed it well, all right.
And he had the people he needed: a reporter to write of his
plight, a preacher to verify it. Toby Cahill would not be
bothersome; the Preacher would.

The Preacher had consoled Jean Wade (the visits were
widely known, even whispered about) and had bragged
openly about the calming effect of God's presence in the
life of Anna. And now the Preacher had prayed behind
prison bars for the soul of Eddie Copeland. Now his importance was even greater and more select—the arbiter
between good and evil, heaven and hell, victim and accused.
Eddie Copeland had said he was sorry, said he wanted Jesus,
said he knew God would forgive him. And the Preacher
had embraced him like a wandering son and promised the
inheritance of God's mercy. The Preacher had said to Hugh,
"No matter what happens, that boy's been reborn. He accepted Christ as his savior. And it wasn't an act. I could
tell. I could see it in his eyes."

Hugh laughed quietly and tapped the dead tobacco from
his pipe. Sure he has, Hugh thought. Sure. Eddie and Jesus

were best friends now. And if anybody doubted it, all they had to do was ask the Preacher.

Hugh looked at his watch. It was eight-fifty. He lit his pipe and sucked the smoke into his mouth and thought of Jesse. He had never known a more gentle man than Jesse. It was not surprising that Jesse had coaxed Aubrey out of his house or that Jesse had visited Isom and Lou and sent the doctor to their cabin. Jesse was a kind man. But William Fred had said that Jesse was angry, that he would not let the deaths of his family go unanswered. "Why do you think he's building that house?" William Fred had asked. "To work off his feeling. That's it. Nothing more than that. He's just waiting for us to try the case."

Maybe William Fred was right, Hugh thought. If so, Jesse's waiting would soon be over. All their waiting would soon be over.

At ten o'clock, Ellis called Hugh and asked when he planned to summon the jury.

"In a few minutes," Hugh told him. "Why?"

"There's been some people in the courtroom since about nine. They're getting a little restless."

"Jesse here?"

"In my office," Ellis said. "Him and Anna."

"All right," Hugh replied. "It won't be long."

Hugh stood and pulled his black robe over his shoulders. He called Jack into his office and gave him a cup of coffee.

"Jack, what'd you think about this case?" Hugh asked.

"Guilty," Jack said bluntly. "Guilty as sin. Ought to burn. Ain't no doubt about it."

Hugh tapped the tobacco from his pipe. A palm of smoke cupped the ashtray. "You think we beat around the bush out there, don't you, Jack?" he said.

"More'n they used to," Jack replied solemnly. "That's the truth. Law ain't what it used to be. People gets off too easy."

Hugh looked at Jack and smiled. To Jack, the law was meant to punish the guilty, to protect the innocent. The law was that simple. Damn the fancy talk of fancy lawyers.

Damn the microscopes and chemicals and other nonsense of evidence. There was a stench about guilt. And Jack had been around long enough to smell the odor.

"I guess you're right, Jack," Hugh said. "Come on. Let's get this over with."

Hugh sat in his chair behind the elevated desk and watched the jurors. Their faces were anger-masks of frustration. Hugh knew what Tate Yarborough would say. He turned in his chair and looked at William Fred and Harold Sellers and then at Parker and Donald Bridges and Eddie. Eddie was staring at him calmly. Hugh lifted his eyes. Tommy Moss was seated in the first row behind Eddie. Angus Helton was beside him. Damn nice boy, Hugh thought of Tommy. Damn nice. What he did with Isom and Lou and Zack was good. Maybe it'd help Angus, being with Tommy. Or maybe Angus would corrupt Tommy.

Jesse and Anna sat directly behind William Fred. Hugh could see the hard face of resignation on Jesse. Anna's eyes were on Eddie, watching him curiously.

The reporters seemed tense, ready to bolt from the court-room and bellow with voices and fingers the news of the Eddie Copeland trial. The reporters knew what would happen, Hugh thought. They had guessed it for two days. He looked for Toby Cahill, found him, studied him. He wondered if Toby had already written the story of Eddie's statement. No, he decided. Not yet. Toby would not be premature.

The courtroom was half-filled with men whose wives were shopping to Christmas music in the decorated stores of Tickenaley. The men looked anxious. Hugh knew that most of them had followed Angus into the courtroom. The men believed that Angus had a special gift for knowing privileged information, and Angus would have said to them, "Bound to happen this morning. Bound to." Angus always seemed to know.

Sitting alone in the balcony, the Preacher leaned near the railing, his Scottish face raised godlike over the people below him. Hugh could feel the Preacher struggling to call down God's intervention in the trial of Eddie Copeland, the born-again Christian.

It was ten-twenty. Hugh asked, "Mr. Foreman, has the jury reached a verdict?"

"No, Your Honor, we haven't," Tate Yarborough said meekly.

It happened swiftly. Hugh declared a mistrial and dismissed the jury curtly. A new trial would be set for February 1981, he announced.

At the defense table, Eddie stabbed a checkmark on a piece of paper. He wrote beneath it: *"Get me out."* He shoved the pad to Parker. He looked over his shoulder to Toby and lifted his eyebrows in a signal of relief. A smile played across his mouth.

Parker stood. "Your Honor, if it please the court, I would like to petition for bond on behalf of my client," he said routinely. He turned to William Fred. William Fred was sitting calmly, turning a pencil in his hand as though preoccupied.

"Obviously, the state did not tender sufficient evidence to convict my client," Parker continued. "But due to the nature of the charges and the time allowed to prepare for a new trial, defense feels it is imperative to have the defendant free from jail to assist in preparing for his defense. Under these circumstances, I think that it's proper for the court to set a reasonable bond." He paused and looked again at William Fred. William Fred had turned his body and was facing the jury box. "Defense, of course, accepts the court's decision in qualifying such a bond," Parker said hurriedly. He sat at the table and turned to look at Jesse and Anna. Anna's head was bowed. There was no expression in Jesse's face. Except for his eyes. His eyes seemed almost gleeful.

Hugh leaned forward, resting his elbows on the table before him. "Mr. Autry?" he said.

William Fred looked up casually. He stood. "Your Honor, the state has no objection to bond," he said easily.

Parker jerked his head to Donald Bridges. My God, he thought.

"Are you sure, Mr. Autry?" Hugh asked.

"I am, Your Honor."

"In that case, the court will concur with the defense," Hugh said. "The court will accept petition for bond and set same in an appropriate amount on, let's see, December 17. That's the day after tomorrow."

"Thank you, Your Honor," Parker mumbled.

"Until that time, the defendant will be held in the Onslow County jail," Hugh added.

The questions from the reporters were meaningless and Parker answered them meaninglessly. But he did not care. He wanted to be away from the reporters and from Eddie Copeland and from the angry sputtering of the men in the courtroom—men he knew well, men who had expected a quick verdict of guilty and who had become impatient waiting as the jurors argued among themselves over the innocence of Eddie Copeland. Parker wanted to see William Fred and Hugh. He wanted to know why William Fred had not objected to bond, why he had been so damned nonchalant. He wanted to know why Jesse had not reacted. Except for the eyes. Or had he only imagined that?

He wanted to know what in the name of God was happening, and why.

"Hope to hell you're happy, boy," Angus snapped as Parker passed him. "Hope you sleep good." Parker could see the thin white lines of anger around Angus' lips.

Parker did not reply. He rushed through the courtroom, past the staring eyes of men who had been his friends. He could feel their hate. He thought, My God, I don't believe this. They could kill me. Here. Now. And it's Christmas. Christmas. What the hell's happening?

He thought he could hear music from the street.

Part 3 THE JUDGMENT

THIRTY-FOUR

December 15–16

TOBY WAS LEAVING THE COURTHOUSE WHEN GUY CALLED him.

"Got something for you," Guy said, handing Toby the letter.

"What is it?" Toby asked.

"From Copeland. Sheriff gave it to me a little earlier."

"Yeah. Thanks."

"Guess I'll see you around," Guy said.

"Looks that way."

In his car, before driving to the Valley View Lodge, Toby opened the letter from Eddie and read it.

Dear Mr. Cahill,

I don't know where I'll be when you get this. They'll be taking me away to wait for the electric chair or I'll be waiting for another trial. Right now, it don't matter very much. I'm just tired of it all.

I've been thinking about what I wrote you last time. I keep thinking that maybe my story would make a good one for people to read about and maybe make into a movie. What do you think? I guess you know just about everything about this case. Enough has sure been said about it. But what you don't know about is me. I could tell you things that nobody knows. The kind of things that people like to hear about. (To tell you the truth, I watch some of them television shows and want to laugh, or throw up. Nobody I know of is like some of them people.)

Let me know what you think. I believe we could make us some money. Of course, I may never be able to spend mine, except to pay some lawyer, but you could spend yours and enjoy it.

> Your friend,
> Eddie Copeland

It had begun to rain in the afternoon. Toby sat in the restaurant of the Valley View Lodge and nibbled at a sandwich and talked with Rachel about the mistrial. Rachel was worried about William Fred. "He called to tell me about what happened," she said. "But he didn't seem too upset. I guess that means he'll go off by himself for a while. He gets that way sometimes."

"I didn't get a chance to talk to him," Toby told her.

"He asked if you was still here," Rachel said. "I told him you hadn't checked out yet, but I hadn't seen you."

Toby did not try to console Rachel. She understood that William Fred was using her, but the trade-off was acceptable. To Rachel, William Fred was smart and influential and heroic and occasionally he cared for her. That was enough. She would not presume to make demands. If she could open her body to him and take the spillings of his anxieties, she was doing all that she could, all that she knew how to do. And maybe that was what she wanted, Toby thought. Her gift of subservience was almost lovely, and more generous than most men deserved.

In midafternoon Toby returned to his room and stretched across his bed with the letters from Eddie and reread them. There was a pattern to the letters, he realized, a subtle begging for publicity. The last letter—the one written earlier in the day—was almost blatant: make me a deal; let's get rich. Curiously, though, Eddie had not written of his conversion to God.

It was nearing five when William Fred knocked at Toby's door.

"You're still here, I see," William Fred said pleasantly. He stepped, uninvited, into Toby's room and closed the door.

"Sometimes I wonder what you'd do without Rachel," Toby said. "She tell you I was here?"

"I called. She said she'd seen you in the restaurant," William Fred confessed. "If the damn place had phones in the rooms, I wouldn't have to go to so much trouble. Why'd you stay?"

"Thought I'd do a follow-up tomorrow. Talk to some of the people."

"They're pissed," William Fred said.

"I can imagine."

William Fred picked up Toby's coat and handed it to him. "Well, come on," he said.

"Where're we going?"

"To see somebody."

Toby followed William Fred to his car and William Fred drove north toward Tickenaley.

"If I didn't know better, I'd think I was in the middle of an Edward G. Robinson movie," Toby said idly. "Come to think of it, you look a little like Edward G."

William Fred laughed. "I'd say Robert Redford."

"We going to see Jesse Wade?" Toby asked.

"We are."

"He looked like he took things pretty well," Toby said. "So did you."

William Fred shrugged. "Sometimes you lose," he replied. He repeated, "Sometimes."

"You'll get another chance."

"I know."

William Fred's mood changed. He twisted his hands on

323

the steering wheel. The muscles in his face hardened. He glanced quickly at Toby. "He's guilty," he said. "We know that." He paused and looked again at Toby. "So do you."

"Do I?"

"Yes."

William Fred drove in silence. A thin mist, almost ice, struck the car, and the wipers slapped rhythmically against the rubber strip of the windshield. Toby leaned against the door of the car and watched the rain begin to splatter in thickening drops. It would soon turn to snow. He knew that William Fred was still using him, but the game—the reason—was different. It was no longer merely for posturing.

Anna was alone in Jesse's house when William Fred and Toby arrived. She was surprised to see Toby.

"Jesse's out in the barn," she said to William Fred. "He's been out there working this afternoon. He's got a little heater, but it's still cold."

"We'll find him," William Fred said.

"I'll put on some coffee," Anna said. "Tell him I'm cooking. He'll need to eat soon. Maybe you and Mr. Cahill—"

"No," William Fred replied. "That's all right. We've eaten. Maybe some of that coffee later."

Jesse was stacking endcuts of timber when William Fred and Toby entered the barn. The smell of sawdust was heavy. A row of three electric lights burned down the center of the room.

"Still working, I see," William Fred said.

"Just cleaning up some," Jesse replied. He extended his hand to Toby. "Mr. Cahill."

"Mr. Wade," Toby said. He could feel the strength of Jesse in the grip. A powder of sawdust covered Jesse's face.

"Appreciate you coming up," Jesse said.

"Glad to be here," Toby said. He looked down the center of the barn and along the walls. "I heard you had something of a museum up here. Now I believe it. Haven't seen some of these things since I left home."

"I'll show you around," Jesse told him. "Some of these things go back more than a hundred years. Belonged to my great-grandfather." He began walking through the barn, pointing to the displays he had assembled in categories of tools and implements, beginning with the yokes ("Some that men wore, some used by cattle") and ending with a collection of mallets and axes. He spoke softly of his father and grandfather and great-grandfather and Toby knew that they had been men who conquered the mountains slowly and stubbornly.

At the last display—the mallets and axes—William Fred said, "Looks like you've added some axes, Jesse."

"I did," Jesse said. "They belonged to Carl and Doyle." He turned and walked away.

Toby and William Fred followed Jesse back to the heater. They sat on sawhorses and watched Jesse wrap the electric cord of the ripsaw around its handle. When he finished, Jesse lit a cigarette and stood near the heater.

"William Fred said you'd grown up in the mountains," Jesse said to Toby.

"I did," Toby replied. "In Alabama."

"Said you know people like us."

"I think so. My father used to have a lot of tools in his barn. Not like this, but a lot. What you've got here reminds me of him. I don't think he ever left the mountains more than five or six times in his life. To Florida once, to the beach at Daytona. Depressed him for a month."

"I think I would have liked him," Jesse said.

"I think so, too," Toby replied. Then: "Why did you want to see me, Mr. Wade?"

"We want to ask you something, Toby," William Fred said quickly.

"What?"

"We want you to talk to Eddie."

"Why?"

"It's like I told you in the car," William Fred said. "Eddie's guilty. We know it and so do you."

"What can I do about it?"

William Fred looked at Jesse, then back to Toby. He said, softly, "He'll tell you."

Toby laughed easily. He shook his head and pushed his

hands into his coatpockets. "Why would he tell me any-thing?"

"He needs you," William Fred said. "He knows it. He wants you to make him famous."

"What makes you say that?" Toby asked.

"I read the last letter," William Fred answered. "Forgive me."

Toby smiled. He had wondered how private Eddie's letters were.

"Only the last one, and I mean it," William Fred added.

Toby looked at Jesse. Jesse was watching him patiently. "And you think he's going to be after me to make him some kind of national figure?"

"I do," William Fred replied confidently. "And, frankly, we don't give a damn about that, Toby. This trial was a fluke. Parker pulled off a miracle without even knowing what he'd done. He had one shot—reasonable doubt. It worked. There was one man who held out—too scared to make a mistake. Next time that won't happen."

"Then what are you worried about?" Toby asked.

William Fred bowed his head and smiled wearily. He looked up at Jesse. He stood and rubbed the back of his legs where he had been sitting on the sawhorse. He said, "Peace of mind."

"I don't understand," Toby said.

"Just that. Peace of mind," William Fred replied. "The next trial will be the same. Eddie'll tell the same story. He'll do that forever. We just want to hear him say that he did it, even if it's to somebody else. Just for the peace of mind of it, Toby. Goddamn it, that's important now."

"He won't tell me anything," Toby argued.

"Yes, he will," William Fred said harshly. "He'll tell you the truth. Sooner or later, he'll tell you."

"And?"

"It's what I know about you, Toby," William Fred replied. "What Jesse knows. You were born in the mountains. You're a lot like us. Same background, same influences."

"I'm sorry, that's not an answer," Toby said bluntly.

Jesse spoke quietly: "Yes, it is, Mr. Cahill. You'll know what to do. You'll know."

"Tell me something," Toby said, looking at William Fred. "You know damn well this is unorthodox at best, not to mention a violation of every legal right a defendant has. Why are you taking this chance?"

William Fred laughed. "We're not fools, Toby. We know it's a chance. But I told you—and you know it: Eddie's guilty. He helped slaughter Jesse's family, like it was a hog killing. He did it. And you're the only person he's going to tell, and he'll do that because he'll want you to be awed by him. I know that man, Toby. Goddamn it, I've lived with him for more than two months. Every hour, every day. I know him inside out." William Fred began to walk away angrily, toward the door. He whirled and pushed his outstretched hand toward Jesse. "I knew that man's family, too. And they're dead. Dead, goddamn it," he snapped. "And there's a lying, evil, sneering son of a bitch living off the luxury of a law that says he has to be given chance after chance after chance." He began to walk toward Toby. His voice lowered. "I can convict him. I know that. And I'll be doing it for years, or somebody will. But he'll never say it. He'll never say, 'Yes, I did it. I killed those people.'"

"And if he does tell me, you expect me to tell you?" Toby asked quietly.

"Jesus, Toby," William Fred said desperately, "how can you ask that? Of course I want you to tell me. Don't you understand it? We want to hear those words."

"I'm a reporter," Toby said evenly. "My whole profession is—"

"You're a human, goddamn it," William Fred said. "That's what you are. And you're from the mountains and you know us."

The barn was suddenly quiet. Toby could hear the rasping breathing of William Fred and the dull striking of the rain on the tin roof. He looked at Jesse. He could see Jesse's heartbeat fluttering in the ribbon of muscles in his throat.

"You'll know what to do, Mr. Cahill," Jesse said. He

nodded absently. Toby could see the flash of moisture in his eyes. "You'll know what to do," Jesse repeated.

The meeting with Jesse and William Fred ended without either asking Toby to keep their discussion private. It was unnecessary, Toby realized. William Fred had been right: he was much like them; he understood privacy.

William Fred drove Toby back to the Valley View Lodge without speaking. He did not invite Toby into Rachel's room for a drink. "Tomorrow morning, at ten," he told Toby. "You can see Eddie then. It's been arranged. They'll be expecting you." And Toby went into his room and drank from his own bottle of scotch and thought of the meeting with Jesse and William Fred. He knew they had talked for many hours about involving him. Jesse would have argued against it, but he had lost the argument to William Fred. It was not just a confession that Jesse wanted. A confession would not satisfy him; it would enrage him. But the confession by Eddie was necessary. It would give Jesse cause. But cause for what? Toby wondered. Jesse Wade was known as an honorable man, a civil man. If anything, his nobility had increased since the murder of his family. Everyone who knew him had said, "Shows you what kind of man Jesse is. It's a wonder he ain't cracked up, but he ain't." But did they really know him? Toby thought. They saw only the physical presence, the outside Jesse. To Toby, the Jesse in the barn was another man. Toby had watched him staring at the displayed axes of his dead sons—a bitter, unfinished history of their lives. The Jesse in the barn had reached his conclusion. He was waiting only for the certainty of Eddie Copeland saying, "I did it."

Toby knew also that William Fred agreed with Jesse. It was in his anger and in the storm of his voice. He knew that William Fred had not been afraid to involve him. It was not trust. It was simply the power of William Fred's will, and Toby realized that he had been affected by that power.

And Toby thought of one other thing: his own father. His

own father had reduced the complexities of the world to a firm observation (often repeated, always in the same voice): "Sometimes there ain't no answer but the right one, no matter what anybody says." Toby's father had lived by his statement. He did what he believed to be right.

My father and Jesse would have been friends, Toby thought. Good friends.

Toby was at the Onslow County Courthouse at nine-fifty on Tuesday morning, December 16. He was led into the basement conference room by Guy, and at ten o'clock Eddie was escorted into the room by both Ellis and Guy.

"We're leaving you alone," Ellis said. "As long as you want. There'll be a guard outside, in the hall. When you get ready to leave, just knock on the door."

Eddie was more relaxed than Toby had ever seen him. His voice was spirited, his eyes flashed with expectation.

"You think they can hear us?" Eddie asked as Ellis closed the door.

"I wouldn't think so," Toby said. "But we can move to the far corner of the room if you're worried."

"Yeah. Let's do that."

They sat close in chairs. Eddie leaned forward, his elbows on his knees, and said quietly, "What'd you think about yesterday?"

"I think you were lucky," Toby told him.

Eddie smiled quickly. "Yeah. Mewborn was better than I thought he'd be. But there's the next time."

"May not come out the same," Toby said.

"Won't be so easy for them, either," Eddie replied.

"I guess not."

"Did you hear?" Eddie asked. "The Preacher's asking me to stay with him when they let me out."

"Are you?"

Eddie looked at Toby with surprise. "Wouldn't you?"

"I guess."

"You get my letter?" Eddie asked eagerly.

"Yeah, I got it," Toby answered. He could feel himself

forcing his words. He could hear William Fred's warning: "He needs you."

"What do you think? Can we sell it?"

"I don't know," Toby said. "Yeah, there's a good chance we can. The trial's had a lot of publicity. Depends on the story."

"I've been writing down some stuff, just for ideas," Eddie said. He laughed easily. "Not much else to do." He pulled a cigarette from the package in his shirtpocket and lit it. He took an ashtray from the conference table and balanced it on his right knee.

"What kind of stuff?" Toby asked.

Eddie shrugged comfortably. "Maybe you won't think it's much. I got to wondering how it'd be told on television. I just wrote down some short scenes. Some stuff about Albert and Zack. Nothing much."

William Fred was right, Toby thought. Eddie wanted to be famous. Eddie lived in a dream of himself. His ego was his blind spot.

"Look, Eddie, before we start talking there's two things you have to understand," Toby said.

"What two things?"

"First, what you say to me and what I say to you is private. It's like a doctor and a patient. Private. You talk to anybody else and I walk and you get nothing out of me."

"Don't worry about that," Eddie said. "You're it." He smiled. "If you want to make some money."

"I do," Toby replied.

"What else?"

"Second, you have to tell me the truth," Toby said. "No matter what you've said to anybody else, I have to know the truth, regardless of what it is. It may be that the real story of Eddie Copeland has very little to do with the trial."

Eddie cocked his head and looked at Toby with an amused smile, as though he had expected the lecture. He twirled the burning tip of his cigarette around the rim of the ashtray.

"You got it," he said. "What do you want to know?"

Toby could hear William Fred: "He'll tell you. Sooner or later, he'll tell you."

"First of all, did you kill any of those people?" Toby asked.

Eddie looked up. He licked his lips with his tongue. "Yeah," he replied easily.

Toby could feel the surprise of Eddie's answer shocking him. He could not stop it from flaming on his face.

"You asked me," Eddie said. His eyes were hard on Toby. He drew from the cigarette and let the smoke seep from his lips. "You can say I said it and it won't matter," he added casually. "I'll just deny it." He smiled again. "You can't win on that one. You'll never beat me at that. Nobody ever has."

"Sooner or later," William Fred's voice whispered in Toby's mind. Toby had believed it was possible, but not so quickly, not so blatantly.

"Didn't expect me to say that, did you?" Eddie asked.

"No. No, I didn't. Why did you?"

"There's a lot about me that's going to surprise you," Eddie said. "I'm the best story you'll ever write."

"Maybe," Toby said quietly.

"You ain't going to like me worth a damn, but that won't matter. I'll make you rich."

"All right," Toby said nervously. "I asked you. You told me. It's private. If you get off in the next trial, it's usable. If not, we'll go with another angle. Now, tell me about it."

Toby made the telephone call to William Fred at three o'clock.

"You were right," Toby said. "He told me."

There was a pause, then: "Are you willing to help us?" William Fred asked.

"I don't know."

"You know he'll never do anything but serve time. You know that."

"Yes."

"He can't beat us like that."

"What would you want me to do?" Toby asked.

"Just bring him to us. You can do that."

"Then?"

"Then go. Go home."

"I'll call you later," Toby said.

Toby went to his room at the Valley View Lodge and pulled down the shades and lay across his bed in the dark. He thought of Eddie Copeland's rambling, gleeful narrative about the murder of Jesse Wade's family. To Eddie, it was something that had happened. Only that.

Toby could feel his queasiness at suspecting what William Fred and Jesse would do. William Fred knew him well, he thought. Too well. He was from the mountains, a hillman. He belonged to a race of people—not Irish or Scotch or English or German or any other strain—that survived by its own silent wars. Obligations had been born in him. He was Jesse Wade with another name. He thought of Jesse's barn and the displays separated by items, like mausoleums containing skeletons. He thought of Jesse's telling of the displays. The telling was a litany, a chanting of a past that Toby could not forget.

THIRTY-FIVE

December 17

ON WEDNESDAY MORNING, DECEMBER 17, BEFORE HE WAS
scheduled to be released on bond, Eddie met for an hour
with Toby in the basement conference room of the Onslow
County Courthouse.

Toby explained that he had talked with a publisher in
Atlanta and the publisher was eager to sign a contract for
an immediate book on Eddie and the trial.

"We can do that book first," Toby said, "and another one
later, if it works out."

"Two books?" Eddie asked.

"If it works out."

"What about movies or television?"

"I'd guess so," Toby said. "But that'd come later."

"What do you need to do?"

"First thing, I want some pictures of you for my meeting
with the publisher," Toby said.

"What kind of pictures?"

"Some we don't have. At the quarry. At the culvert.
Maybe at the cave."

"We can do it today, after I'm out," Eddie said enthusiastically.

Toby shook his head. "It's not that easy. If we're seen riding around together, somebody could figure it out. I don't want anybody to know about this."

"All right," Eddie said. "What do you want to do?"

"I think I know a way," Toby replied. "I want you to take a walk this afternoon. By yourself."

Eddie listened closely to Toby. It would be easy, he agreed. The Preacher would understand his need to be alone, a free man.

"And you know where to meet me?" Toby asked.

"I'll find it."

At ten o'clock, Eddie was released on bond and driven to the Preacher's house by Parker. The Preacher accepted Eddie warmly. "It's God's will," he announced as he introduced Eddie to his wife. The Preacher's wife was quiet. She was afraid of Eddie and afraid of the telephone callers who had warned the Preacher against taking Eddie into his house. The callers had said there would be trouble. "God's will does not buckle under to fear," the Preacher had boasted boldly. "Whatever crimes this boy's committed, he'll pay for. But he has accepted Jesus and there's no punishment he can't take. This boy's under God's protection until he goes on trial again." The Preacher was proud of his bravery.

After lunch, Eddie went into the guest bedroom and slept. At four o'clock, he told the Preacher that he wanted to take a walk alone. "To think about things," he said.

"It could be dangerous," the Preacher cautioned.

"I'll be out in the woods, not on the road," Eddie said. "It's been a long time. I'd just like to walk around outside."

"All right," the Preacher reluctantly agreed. "But be careful. Stay in the woods."

"I will."

Thirty minutes later, Eddie met Toby in the backyard of the closed house of Faron and Macy Simmons.

"Any trouble?" Toby asked.

"None," Eddie said. "You're right about that mailbox. Goddamn thing's like a sore thumb." He got into Toby's car. "Where to?"

"I'll drive," Toby told him. "You just stay down, out of sight."

Toby drove first to the quarry and posed Eddie and took ten pictures of him near the ledge, where the cars had been rolled into the water. He then drove to the culvert where Florence's body had been stuffed. Eddie stood beside the road, looking into the culvert. His face was calm, almost amused. He said nothing to Toby at either location.

"Let's go up to the cave before it gets too dark," Toby said. "You don't get back soon, the Preacher'll be out looking for you."

"I'm just along for the ride," Eddie replied cheerfully, "even if I am seeing the scenery from the floorboard. Whatever you say, I do." His voice was energetic. Toby knew he enjoyed the posing.

The clouds over the valley were rolling like a dark smoke from the northwest, and a thin, cold mist fell against the car as Toby drove carefully over the workroad leading to the house that Jesse and Pete and Aubrey were building on the cleared plateau.

"How do you know this is the way?" Eddie asked curiously.

"To the cave? I went there," Toby told him. "Remember, I'm a reporter. I went to all these places."

"You take a look in the cave?" Eddie asked.

"Yeah, I looked in it."

"Hell of a place," Eddie said, laughing. "Goddamn crazy Zack knew them caves like the back of his hand."

Toby parked the car in the clearing near the house, and took his camera equipment and began to walk hurriedly through the woods above the house. Eddie followed.

"Day we watched them working, they were cutting trees," Eddie said. "Now they got a house there. Who's it for?"

Toby stopped and turned and looked through the trees.

The house was below them, a rich yellow against the winter gray. He said, "I don't know. Guess he just felt like building it."

It was after five o'clock. The woodshadows were deepening when the two men reached the logging road and began following it. Ten minutes later they were at the base of the cave. Eddie stood staring up at it. His face had reddened in the cold. His eyes watered.

"I'll tell you one thing," Eddie said. "The guy that was shooting into the cave from the trees was pretty damn good. Hadn't been for him, we could have stayed there a week."

"Who killed the dog?" Toby asked casually.

Eddie smiled arrogantly. "Me," he said. "Blew his head off in midair."

Toby did not reply. The light was fading quickly. The granite breaks in the mountain were becoming grotesque faces of shadows. He remembered what Angus Helton had said while talking with reporters: "Jesse found them at Dark Thirty. Worse time of the day for finding something like that." It had been the first time that Toby had heard the expression since his childhood. He unsnapped his camera cover. It would soon be Dark Thirty, he thought.

"Why don't you climb up there, near the opening of the cave," Toby said. "I'll get a couple of shots from down here."

"Yeah. All right," Eddie said. "Let's get them fast, though. I'm freezing my balls off." He began to climb agilely up the granite slope to the cave.

"Near the opening, but out far enough so I can see you," Toby called. The heat of his blood rushed through his skin. His hands began to shake.

"You got a flash?" Eddie called back.

"Don't need one. Not with this film," Toby said. He saw Eddie positioning himself at the ledge. Behind Eddie, the mouth of the cave was black.

"How's this?" Eddie called.

"It's fine. Hold it there. Let me get the angle."

Toby stepped back and slowly began to walk away. It was over for him. At a large oak he turned and watched.

The men came out of the cave behind Eddie. In the dulling light, they were like moving rocks. Their arms wrapped Eddie. Toby could see Eddie struggle hopelessly. He could hear Eddie's cry, like an angry animal. He could hear the echo of the cry in the throat of the cave. He turned and began to walk rapidly and then he began to run and he did not stop running until he had reached the house and his car. He dropped the camera into the back seat of the car and drove away. On the road below the plateau, the road leading to Jesse Wade's house, he stopped and got out of his car and lit a cigarette and stood, looking back into the hills. The night was pouring like liquid over the Mountain of the Caves.

He had asked William Fred what would happen to Eddie.

"He'll have more of a chance than he gave," William Fred had said.

"What does that mean? What're you going to do?"

"What Jesse wants."

"What does that mean?"

"Something he found out from Isom," William Fred had admitted. "No need to tell you about it. Believe me, it fits the crime."

Jesse stood deep in the cave, in a spill of yellow lantern light, and watched as William Fred and Guy dragged Eddie inside. He breathed deeply and held the air in his lungs. If there would be regret—if he would want to walk away—he would know it immediately. It would rise in him like a sickness. He would taste it in his mouth, feel it in his chest and throat. He stood very still, watching the angry, quick struggling of the three men in the shadows of the cavemouth. And he waited for the signals of his senses. He felt nothing.

Aubrey Hart stood rigidly beside Jesse, watching intently as William Fred and Guy forced Eddie to his knees by bending his arms behind his back. A leather belt was looped around his neck and tightened and a thin hood was slipped over his head and tied under his chin. "Now," William Fred said, and Jesse lifted the carrying yoke of his great-grand-father and placed it across Eddie's neck. He watched as

Guy pulled up Eddie's arms and tied his wrists securely to the arms of the yoke. "His ankle," William Fred said, and Guy looped another cord around Eddie's left ankle, like a leash. Guy tugged hard on the cord, forcing Eddie's legs awkwardly apart.

Eddie was on his knees on the floor of the cave, his head bent forward, his arms stretched like wings to the yoke. His body rose and fell with his deep, hard breathing. The thin hood billowed in and out against his mouth.

"Let's go," William Fred said quietly. He pulled on the belt and Eddie struggled to his feet.

Jesse and Aubrey followed the men from the cave. Outside, in the dimming light, Jesse lifted the glass shield of the lantern and blew out the flame. He could smell the musk of the woodsground, still damp from rain and snow, and he could feel the ice of the air on his face.

Jesse walked slowly behind the single file of men leading Eddie out of the cave and into the woods. The men were silent and unhurried. If they had worried over what they were doing (and Jesse believed they had), they had settled their concerns. There was no longer a question of right and wrong. All of them had agreed, all understood: what they were doing must be done.

Jesse had trusted William Fred's judgment in selecting the men. Aubrey he had understood, but not Guy. "For Carl," William Fred had said. "They were closer than you knew. Vietnam, I guess." Still, Jesse knew the men would leave the night and never again speak of it, not even among themselves. Speaking of it would violate the night, make it common, like some robed fraternity of terrorists. And the men were not terrorists. Not William Fred or Guy or Aubrey. Or himself. Not the reporter, Toby Cahill, who had led Eddie to them. None of them were terrorists. They were men exorcising a madness.

Jesse could see the house from the woods. It was silhouetted against the clouds rolling and silvering in the mountains. He remembered Jean's fear of building the house on the plateau. The plateau was the place of gods, where ancient voices whispered an ancient language from dead mouths. Jesse believed that Jean had heard the voices and, to her, the stories that were told in the valley were not quaint legends of ghosts. The stories were true. The gods had been there. The great fire had been real and the plateau belonged to no one.

The men stopped before the house and stood, waiting. Jesse walked past them and stepped onto the porch and walked to the doorway. He could hear the wind seeping through the plastic coverings over the openings of the windows and doors.

"You're sure?" William Fred asked.

"Yes," Jesse answered. He pulled the plastic sheet away from the opening for the front door. "Take him in."

William Fred and Guy pushed Eddie forward and lifted him onto the porch and guided him into the house. Jesse could hear the dull echoes of their steps as they moved through the house.

"Which window?" Aubrey asked.

"The one on the side, in the bedroom," Jesse said. He stepped from the porch and walked to the side of the house. Aubrey followed him.

"Where'd Isom learn about this?" Aubrey asked.

"I don't know," Jesse lied. "I just remember him telling it."

"Wish old Isom was here. It was them boys that messed up his boy."

Jesse thought of the story in Isom's papers. The story had been written with brutal directness and the voice of Isom's grandfather had been a triumphant yell of celebration.

Inside the house, in the bedroom, Guy tore away the plastic sheet covering the opening to the window. He stood looking at the men below him.

"Take off the hood," Jesse said.

Guy stepped back and pulled the hood from Eddie's face and pushed him to the window. Eddie dropped his head and lifted it cautiously. The deep aluminum of the day was fading quickly in low clouds. Eddie's eyes blinked rapidly. He saw Jesse and Aubrey.

"What're you doing?" Eddie whispered hoarsely.

"What we have to," Jesse said evenly.

Eddie's eyes narrowed. He pulled his shoulders straight. The yoke across his neck struck against the walls at the window opening. A bitter smile curled into his face. He said, "Fuck you."

Jesse stepped near the window. He could feel his face burning with anger.

Eddie glared at him. "You ain't gonna kill me," he said arrogantly. "I know what you're trying to do, but it ain't gonna work." He spat angrily through the window opening at Jesse. "You assholes think you're scaring me. You ain't."

Jesse could feel himself becoming calm. He said, softly, "My wife, my daughter, my sons, my grandson, my daughter-in-law."

"Fuck you," Eddie snapped.

"My wife, my daughter, my sons, my grandson—"

"I ain't saying nothing," Eddie shouted, his voice quivering.

"My wife, my daughter—"

"Kill him, Jesse," Aubrey growled. "Kill the son of a bitch."

Eddie's eyes widened. He looked at the thin face of Aubrey. He could see saliva foaming on Aubrey's lips. "It was Albert and Zack," Eddie said weakly. "I didn't do it. It was Albert and Zack." He jerked against the hands of William Fred and Guy. Guy pushed him hard against the window opening.

"My sons, my grandson, my daughter-in-law," Jesse said evenly.

Eddie stopped struggling. His body became limp. He shook his head slowly. "I didn't do it," he whined. "I didn't."

"Yes," Jesse said. "Yes, it was you." He stepped closer to the window and looked up at Guy. "Now," he said.

William Fred pulled Guy back from the window. He nodded to Guy and Guy stepped in front of Eddie and yanked Eddie's pants and underwear down to his knees. Eddie kicked awkwardly at Guy and William Fred pushed him back to the window.

"Fuck you," Eddie snarled.

"You want one of us to do it, Jesse?" Guy asked.

"No," Jesse said.

Jesse opened his coat and pulled a hammer from his belt. He reached into his pocket and removed a nail.

"What're you doing?" Eddie asked weakly.

"Let me help, Jesse," Aubrey said. "Goddamn him."

"Just hold him," Jesse whispered. "Just for a second."

Aubrey reached for Eddie's penis and pulled it hard and placed it on the windowsill.

Eddie fought with his legs against the wall, but Guy held him.

"Do it, Jesse," Aubrey urged angrily. "Nail it."

"No, no. God Almighty," Eddie begged.

Jesse placed the nail on Eddie's penis and pressed it down with his thumb, breaking the skin. A single drop of blood bubbled at the nailpoint. He raised the hammer quickly and struck the nail hard, driving it through the flesh and into the windowsill. Eddie screamed. His body jerked spastically. Jesse hit the nail again and again, driving it deep into the wood. The hammering exploded through the empty house.

And then Jesse said, "Let him go."

William Fred and Guy released Eddie.

"You son of a bitch," Aubrey said in sobs. "That's for my baby, you son of a bitch." He was crying openly.

"Cut him loose," Jesse said.

Guy pulled a hunter's knife from its sheath and cut the cords holding Eddie's wrists to the yoke. William Fred took the yoke and handed it through the window to Jesse. Eddie threw his arms against the walls of the house to keep from falling. Streams of saliva poured from his mouth. He licked the air with his tongue. His eyes were closed against the pain.

"Look at me," Jesse commanded harshly. "Look at me."

Eddie opened his eyes. He could see Jesse standing before him, holding Guy's knife.

"This is our place," Jesse said. "We won't let it be killed." He raised the knife and stabbed it into the windowsill in front of Eddie. "You have a choice," he whispered bitterly. "That's more'n you gave."

"Ple—please," Eddie begged. "I—I'll tell you." He began to sob and slap at the walls with his hands.

Jesse watched him impassively. He thought of Jean. He bit his lip and tasted the blood. Jean.

"Jesse," William Fred said. He had left the house with Guy and was standing beside Jesse. "You sure, now? You sure this is what you want to do?"

Jesse did not move his eyes from Eddie. "I'm sure," he said.

"All right."

Jesse stared at Eddie. The anger surged in him, pumping in his body. He thought of the Preacher. He could feel the Preacher's hands on his hands, squeezing them. He could hear the Preacher's voice mumbling of God and forgiveness and love. He could see the Preacher's puffed face, indignant in the spotlight of his own righteousness. Strangely, he wanted to laugh. He could sense the shiver of a giddiness in his body.

"Guy lit the torches, Jesse," William Fred said. "We're ready."

Jesse looked at William Fred and Guy holding the torches. He looked once at the house. He could hear Doyle's noisy, bragging chatter.

"Burn it," Jesse said.

On the valley road, Toby watched the leap of flames above him. A shower of sparks billowed up from the white heat of the fire, caught in the wind and spewed like exploding candlebombs. He reached into his car for his camera. He pulled the roll of film and stripped it and dropped it in the road and lit it with his cigarette lighter. He watched the film curl. Then he got into his car and drove away, toward Tickenaley. He passed the church and the Preacher's house. He saw the Preacher standing in his backyard, looking toward the woods. The Preacher would see God's warning in the unexplained burning of Jesse Wade's strange house, he thought. He looked at his watch. It was after six. Dark Thirty.

About the Author

TERRY KAY grew up in Royston, Georgia, in a family
of twelve children. He is the author of two previous novels,
The Year the Lights Came On and *After Eli*. He now lives
in Lilburn, Georgia, with his four children.